Stolen Beginnings

Susan Lewis is the bestselling author of twenty novels. She is also the author of *Just One More Day*, a moving memoir of her childhood in Bristol. She lives in France. Her website address is www.susanlewis.com

Acclaim for Susan Lewis

'One of the best around' *Independent on Sunday*

'Spellbinding! … you just keep turning the pages, with the atmosphere growing more and more intense as the story leads to its dramatic climax' *Daily Mail*

'Mystery and romance *par excellence*' *Sun*

'The tale of conspiracy and steamy passion will keep you intrigued until the final page' *Bella*

'A multi-faceted tearjerker' *heat*

'Erotic and exciting' *Sunday Times*

'We use the phrase honest truth too lightly: it should be reserved for books – deeply moving books – like this'
Alan Coren

'Susan Lewis strikes gold again … gripping' *Options*

Also by Susan Lewis

A Class Apart
Dance While You Can
Darkest Longings
Obsession
Vengeance
Summer Madness
Last Resort
Wildfire
Taking Chances
Cruel Venus
Strange Allure
Silent Truths
Wicked Beauty
Intimate Strangers
The Hornbeam Tree
The Mill House
A French Affair
Missing

Just One More Day, A Memoir

SUSAN LEWIS

Stolen Beginnings

arrow books

Published by Arrow Books 2007

2 4 6 8 10 9 7 5 3

First published in Great Britain in 1990 by William Heinemann
First published in paperback in 1991 by Mandarin Paperbacks
Arrow Books
Random House, 20 Vauxhall Bridge Road,
London SW1V 2SA

www.rbooks.co.uk

Addresses for companies within The Random House Group Limited can be
found at: www.randomhouse.co.uk/offices.htm

The Random House Group Limited Reg. No. 954009

A CIP catalogue record for this book
is available from the British Library

ISBN 9780099514688

Printed and bound in Great Britain by
CPI Cox & Wyman, Reading, RG1 8EX

For Linda Margaret Smith . . .

– Acknowledgements –

I should like to express my gratitude to all who have helped me during the writing of and research for this book. Karen Ford of Models 1; Francisca Blackburne and Lesley Morgan; the CID at Chelsea Police Station; Richie Horowitz who drove me round New York; Max Eilenberg and Piers Russell-Cobb, for their support at the time the first *Stolen Beginnings* was wiped – and never recovered – on the computer; and the man, who must remain anonymous, who gave me the character I love most in the book – and much more besides . . .

But most of all I should like to thank Sandra Brett for the 'dry run' which has now become an on-going series . . .

His face was more exquisite than that of any man alive: the bone-structure was perfect and the Italian ochre eyes seductive, mesmerising; the nose was long and straight, and the mouth wide but not too full. He was their leader.

As Sergio Rambaldi raised his magnificent head, his hand moved like a bird through the air. The silver blade glinted. The cave was dark, lit by just one candle and the light that seeped through the branches covering the entrance, shielding those inside from the brilliant sun. Laid out before them was the girl's body – naked and very still. Arsenio lifted his eyes and stole a look at the others; two women and five men, including him. This was their *bottega* – their workshop. They were grouped silently round the marble slab that he, Arsenio Tarallo, had brought to the mountain three days ago. He had known it was to bear her body, but he had not loved her then.

The leader turned from the candle and moved slowly to the marble slab. Briefly his eyes met Arsenio's and Arsenio lowered his head. He knew there had been much debate over him. He knew he did not yet have their trust. But Arsenio Tarallo understood that only time would prove the extent of his dedication to and belief in the *bottega*. He was honoured to be there – and terrified.

He closed his eyes and tried to concentrate on the dank smell of earth, widening his nostrils and inhaling deeply but quietly. The leader murmured to the woman beside him and she took a step back. Arsenio guessed what had been said, and his eyes flew to the face of the girl lying before him.

Nooo! Every nerve-end screeched. His muscles were

tensed, poising his body to spring. But he knew he wouldn't. Nor would he cry out.

She had come to him two nights ago. He had been expecting her, but the look of her had taken his breath away. He had touched the blonde silk of her hair as she removed her coat, and then moaned softly at the beauty of her naked skin. She turned, and her face was beneath his, her lips pale and her eyes blue and serene as the Madonna's. It was her duty to give herself to one of the *bottega* and she had chosen him. Their love-making was exquisite, spiked as it was by the knowledge that this would be the only time.

The fine hair on her arms lifted as a swift breeze blew through the cave. The candle flickered. Arsenio's skin prickled. The blade cut through the air and Arsenio dropped to his knees, echoing the words of the leader: *'Lunga vita alla donna! Lunga vita al nuovo rinascimento!'* Long live woman. Long live the new renaissance.

There was a deathly gasp. Arsenio's head snapped up. His mouth opened but the screams only gurgled in his throat as he rolled to the floor, his eyes blinded by blood.

Madeleine dashed up the narrow staircase, giggling and spilling bread rolls, party-poppers and vol-au-vents from the shopping bag she clutched in her arms. Behind her Marian was trying to grab her ankles and trip her up.

'I've never been so embarrassed,' Marian cried, 'just wait until I get hold of you!'

Madeleine shrieked as Marian's hand closed around her ankle and she staggered against the wall. The shopping scattered and Marian snatched up a can as it rolled down the stairs.

Madeleine screamed, 'No!' But Marian's finger was pressed firmly on the nozzle and a shower of Christmas snow covered Madeleine's blonde hair. 'Right! That's it!' Madeleine declared, and scooping up a vol-au-vent, she crushed it in her hand and rubbed the gooey pastry in Marian's face.

Marian spluttered and gasped, all the while spraying snow over her cousin, the stairs, the shopping and herself.

A door opened on the landing below and Pamela Robbins – an assistant film producer – came out of her flat. There was a moment's truce in the mayhem while Marian and Madeleine, looking like nothing on earth, turned to watch their neighbour as she locked her door, threw a bag over her shoulder and trotted off down the stairs without so much as a glance in their direction.

When they heard the front door slam, four flights below, they exploded into laughter. 'Snooty old bag!' Madeleine shouted. Then lowering her voice and rolling her eyes, she said: 'I expect she's gone to make a movie!'

'I don't suppose you thought to invite her tonight?' Marian said, starting to clear up the debris.

'Not on your life.'

'And yet you'll stop complete strangers in the street,' Marian said, giving her a shove, 'and invite them.'

'Well, they were gorgeous, at least the short one was. Just the right height for you.'

Marian shot her a look. 'You're asking for more trouble!'

Madeleine's snowy face looked even more comical as she pulled down the corners of her mouth and widened her beautiful eyes. 'I was doing you a favour,' she protested. 'I mean, what's the point in us having a party if there's not going to be anyone there you fancy?'

'That,' Marian said, as she took out her keys and opened the door at the top of the dingy staircase, 'is assuming that someone *you* fancy will be?'

'Do you think he'll come?' Madeleine said, as she hauled herself to her feet and followed Marian into the darkened flat.

Marian turned to look at her with an expression of exasperated irony. 'When has a man ever been able to refuse you anything?' she said.

Madeleine hugged herself as she savoured the prospect of Paul O'Connell coming to their New Year's Eve party that night. She had been trying to get off with him for weeks, but so far he was proving the most elusive man she'd ever come across. 'I wonder what he'll come as?' she mused. 'Come to that, what are you wearing? No! No! I'm not having any of that boring old rubbish you were talking about yesterday. It's a fancy dress, Marian' – she crept along the hall towards her cousin – 'the chance to make yourself wild and exciting – and naughty!'

Marian yelped as Madeleine dug her fingers into her sides. 'Naughty is your department,' she chuckled, 'I shall just stand by and watch while you captivate every man in sight, and worry about how we're going to pay for it all.'

Madeleine threw back her head and gave a howl of frustration. 'I want a New Year's resolution from you, madam,' she said. 'To give up being sensible.'

Marian tossed her coat onto the solitary, battered armchair. 'I gave that up three years ago when I agreed to let you come up to Bristol and live with me.'

'And just look at all the fun we've had since.' Madeleine swivelled in the doorway and went into the kitchen to unload the shopping.

'Yes, just look,' Marian muttered to herself as she glanced around the shabby room, then turned on the gas fire.

They'd moved into this garret at the top of a grand house in Clifton's West Mall three months ago, after Celia, Marian's mother, had sent enough money to fly them back from Rhodes. They hadn't intended the Greek islands to be their final destination on their tour of Europe, but shopping sprees in Paris and Rome, coupled with visits to nightclubs in Amsterdam, Nice and Hamburg, had swallowed up every penny of the profit they'd made on the flat in Stokes Croft – something else Celia had financed. Marian still felt guilty about spending her mother's meagre capital, especially when it chiefly consisted of the insurance money Celia had received after Marian's father had died in a fire at the paper factory where he'd worked, just outside Totnes in Devon. It was the year Marian won her place at Bristol University. Madeleine had taken her uncle's death so badly that Marian almost turned down her place, but Celia – who was as 'proud as punch' of her daughter's achievements – stepped in and said that providing Madeleine got herself a job in Bristol, then she could move up there too. Marian had been delighted. Madeleine had lived with them ever since she was eight and Marian was ten, so they were more like sisters than cousins, and secretly Marian had been dreading life without her.

When she joined Marian in Bristol, Madeleine was

sixteen and already blossoming into an exceptionally beautiful young woman; and once out from under Celia's protective eye, with the prospect of a big city like Bristol to conquer, her escapades and her reputation soon became legendary. Marian's student friends were disapproving to the point of contempt – especially when Madeleine took a job as a stripper in a nightclub just off Blackboy Hill. She'd worked there for almost a year, hoping that someone would recognise her talent and whisk her off to London; but no one did so she left and became a strip-o-gram girl.

She loved stripping. There was nothing that gave her a greater thrill than to have her honey-coloured skin, long legs and abundant breasts admired. It excited her in a way that the act of sex never did – though she had sex regularly, sometimes with men she met and fancied in the local wine bars, but mostly with men who told her they could help her become a model or an actress. She was easily taken in because of her obsessive craving for fame, and it was left to Marian to mop up the tears when nothing came of the promises. If Madeleine had been bright enough to get to know the right people, to behave in a way that at least came close to being socially acceptable – if she hadn't so firmly believed that her sexuality had to be demonstrated rather than suggested – then her route to the top might have been assured. As it was, her skirts were too short and her tops too low, she wore too much make-up, her voice was coarse and her behaviour brazen. Yet even these shortcomings could not detract from the effect of her remarkable violet eyes, luscious wide mouth and incomparable figure. She had the lazy, sensuous look of Bardot and the voluptuous body of Monroe – a breathtaking combination which, in the right hands, might rocket her to fame and fortune. By anyone's standards her beauty was extraordinary, and she knew it.

Marian was used to Madeleine's shameless exhibitionism; ever since she'd had breasts, she'd shown them to any boy who was willing to pay; but being used to it did not mean that she approved. However, her disapproval was something she only ever voiced to Madeleine in private, and she took great exception if anyone else uttered a word of criticism. So when, one night in the Coronation Tap, she overheard one of her friends describing Madeleine as a common little tart, she had so violently torn into the girl that she fully expected her friends to drop her as a result. But if anything, after that, they treated her with a greater respect; as if someone they had until then regarded as retiring – almost dull – might at any time burst into flames of rage or passion. Marian found their baffled esteem amusing, secretly knowing that the likelihood of her firing up like that again was remote; Madeleine was the only subject she ever got heated about.

Despite the endless ebb and flow of men through their Stokes Croft flat, and the outrageous parties that vibrated on into the early hours of most Sunday mornings, Marian managed to get her philosophy degree. And to celebrate Madeleine had suggested they sell the flat and go on a tour of Europe. Still heady with her success, Marian had thrown her inherent caution to the winds, and agreed. They'd returned to Bristol four months later, with a hundred pounds – which they'd used as a deposit for this one-bedroomed attic – and enough anecdotes to make them – or at least, Madeleine – the centre of attention for weeks.

Now Madeleine was back working for the strip-o-gram agency and she, Marian, was a struggling temporary secretary with the Sue Sheppard Agency in Park Street. One day, she told herself, she'd think about what she really wanted to do, but for now the only thing that mattered was that they should earn enough money to pay the bills . . .

At eight o'clock they were still decorating the flat with the tinsel and trimmings they hadn't bothered with for

Christmas – they'd spent Christmas in Devon with Celia – when some of Madeleine's crowd from the Chateau Wine Bar showed up, bearing crates of wine, trumpets and streamers. Music blared from the cassette player Marian had bought Madeleine for Christmas, and squealing with delight at the men's preposterous costumes, Madeleine made them all dance while she rocked and gyrated between them, all the time watching her reflection in the cracked mirror over the fireplace. 'You'll have to go back to the Chateau,' she told them ten minutes later, 'the party doesn't start until nine, and besides, Marian and I aren't ready yet.' She handed one of them a cheque for the wine; knowing it would bounce, Marian winced.

'What you wearing, Maddy?' one of the men asked.

Marian watched as Madeleine pouted her lips and studied him through narrowed eyes. Then, running a hand through her blonde mane, she slowly broke into a grin. 'Nothing!' she declared, then pushed them out of the door.

When she turned back Marian was waiting for her. 'I told you, not Eve!' she cried. 'If you're going to prance around here with no clothes on, I'm calling the whole thing off.'

'Nag, nag, nag.' Madeleine tripped lightly past her and disappeared into the bedroom. Marian followed.

'You won't mind sleeping on the sofa, will you, if I manage to get off with Paul O'Connell?' Madeleine said, flopping down on her bed.

'What, or who, are you going as tonight?' Marian demanded.

'You'll have to wait and see. No, it's not Eve,' she said, as Marian began to protest. 'And what about you, where's your costume?'

'You'll have to wait and see,' Marian said, and went to pour some wine.

'I got you a wig in Dingles,' Madeleine told her when

– 8 –

she came back with two glasses. 'Cover up that horrible old hair of yours.'

'You're so charming,' Marian answered. 'I won't ask how you paid for it, but you know where you can stick your wig. Now, who's first in the bath?'

'You were yesterday, so it's my turn today.'

'Well, don't let the water go cold like you usually do,' Marian called after her.

Two hours later the flat was jammed with oddly-attired people. Music shook the walls, and dancing feet scuffled over the dull brown carpet. A fog of smoke was beginning to gather around the dimmed lights, and red and white wine flowed into glasses, over fingers and down the furniture. Marian stood in a corner beside the meagre buffet, watching the heaving mass, her eyes darting from one squealing, grotesquely laughing face to another. Tinsel was dragged from the walls and draped round necks, champagne corks popped and glasses smashed. Marian bit her lips and wondered how they were going to pay the off-licence for the damages.

Most of their guests were Madeleine's friends, girls from the strip-o-gram agency, old and current boyfriends, and the regulars from the Chateau Wine Bar. Marian had kept in touch with a few of her university chums, like Rob and Mary, the bookworm and the bluestocking, and they had deigned to attend this decadent party before flying off to some obscure part of the world the following week. They had brought along a couple of friends from America who were staying over the Christmas period, and the discussion in the kitchen, on the merits of Buddhism, couldn't have been more at odds with the writhings and shenanigans in the sitting-room.

'Where's that Madeleine?' someone yelled to no one in particular. 'Get her in here, shaking that body about!'

'What's the matter, mine not good enough for you?' a

brassy-looking blonde answered, pressing herself against the man who was done up as Madonna.

There were whoops and cheers as the girl fondled his false breasts, and picking up a bottle of wine, Marian wandered through the crowd, smiling shyly and offering refills. She could have been invisible for all the attention she was receiving, but she didn't mind, she was used to it. The music changed, and Whitney Houston's 'I Want to Dance With Somebody' rocked the room. 'Excuse me,' Marian said to Anthony and Cleopatra, squeezing past them and slipping out into the hall. As she started to open the bedroom door it was slammed back in her face. 'Madeleine!' she shouted. 'Let me in!'

The door opened a fraction and Madeleine popped her head round. 'Is he here yet?' Then her expression changed as she saw Marian's costume. 'Who the bloody hell are *you* supposed to be? What's that on your head?'

'I'm the cook,' Marian answered, adjusting the chef's hat she had bought in a secondhand shop.

'Jesus! And you're supposed to be the one with all the imagination. Anyway, is he here yet?'

Marian rolled her eyes. 'Not yet. Look, what if he doesn't come? You can't stay in there all night. Everyone's asking where you are.'

'I'll give it another ten minutes,' Madeleine said, 'then I'll make my entrance whether he's here or not.'

'You'd better have some clothes on,' Marian said meaningfully.

'Oh, go and get drunk,' Madeleine snapped, and snatching the bottle of wine, she closed the door before Marian could say any more. Marian pressed a path down the hall, grabbed another bottle of wine and took it into the kitchen.

'The Labour party's nothing more than a turd that the Thatcherites can't quite flush away,' Rob was saying. 'There's no hope for us here, man. The great canker capitalism is raping this land of conscience and morality.

I doubt if Mary and I will ever come back from Tibet. Ah, Marian, any more of that revolting Leibfraumilch going?'

He held his thin, serious face on one side as Marian poured. 'Why don't you come to Tibet with us?' he said. 'You're not cut out for the superficialities of life. You should write, I've told you that a hundred times. In the mountains of Tibet you could do some serious thinking, make a serious analysis of the soul, an exploration of Why?'

'I could also seriously vegetate,' Marian said, and winked at one of the Americans. When his face remained impassive she blushed. 'Sorry,' she said, smiling at Rob. 'An exploration of why what?'

He gave her one of his pained looks. 'Why anything, Marian? Why the sun, why the moon, why the stars, why life?'

'For fun?' she suggested.

The mute Americans shuffled their Roman-sandal-clad feet and glanced sympathetically at Rob.

'But what is fun?' Mary interjected. 'You could write a whole tome on what really makes fun. I mean, to begin with, what's fun for one man could be gross tedium for another . . .'

'I'd go along with that,' Marian said, not without irony.

'Exactly!' Rob proclaimed. 'Just take the people here tonight, Marian. They could be the very subject of your study. Push it to its limits, find out why the empty-headed pursuit of cheap wine, easy sex and new clothes fulfils them. Dig right to the root, Marian, find out what has lured them into the Penelope's web of our time. Put the rot of their lives under a microscope . . .'

'Ah, poppycock!'

The voice simmered with delight, and in one movement the five of them turned to the door. A strange sensation coasted across Marian's heart, and the corners of her mouth twitched with laughter. Paul O'Connell's frame filled the doorway. His thick blond hair, falling windswept and damp across his forehead, contrasted strikingly with his black eyebrows; his eyes were alive with humour.

'If you look round a party long enough,' he said, 'you'll always find it.' He held his hand out towards Marian. 'Paul O'Connell,' he said.

She mumbled, 'Yes, I recognise you. I'm glad you could make it. Shall I take your coat?'

He took it off, but just as he was about to hand it to her, he jerked it away again, saying, 'No, don't go. I'll hang it here on the back of the door. Now, what was all this about the rot of life being put under a microscope?'

Mary answered. 'Rob was trying to persuade Marian to get to the bottom of society's deterioration. The time-wasting, the irrelevance of the fun those people out there would claim to be having.' It was evident, from the slight catch in her voice, that Paul O'Connell's presence was affecting her every bit as much as Marian.

Paul nodded. 'Undergraduate rhetoric.'

'On the contrary,' Rob rebutted, looking and feeling absurd in his Spiderman costume. 'A philosophical debate among graduates.'

'Bristol?' Paul enquired. 'I'm a Cambridge man myself. Several years ago now, though.'

'What do you do now?' Rob asked.

'I write. You?'

'He's conducting an exploration of motive,' Mary chirped, then almost giggled at the look that came over Paul's face.

'What do you write?' one of the Americans asked, startling Marian who was beginning to wonder if they'd taken a vow of silence.

'Literature,' Paul answered. Then, as a sudden whoop of hysteria sounded from the next room, he treated them to a sardonic look and left.

Marian glanced over Rob's reedy frame in its Spider-man suit and couldn't stop the grin as she said, 'Why don't you try walking up the walls?' and then she followed Paul into the sitting-room.

In the centre of the room Madeleine was lapping up the attention her costume had provoked. Marian stopped in the doorway, shaking her head and smiling; at least she had something on!

'I am Marlene Deitrich,' Madeleine purred in what she hoped was a German accent. In her black high-heels she towered above most of the people in the room. Running her hands slinkily over her corseted hips, she threw back her head and lifted a long, slender leg onto the arm of the sofa. 'Who will light my cigarette?' she said, placing a tapering black holder between her lips and scanning those closest to her with dreamy, close-lidded eyes. There was a rush of lighters, but 'Dame Edna' got there first, and slipped his hand under a black suspender as Madeleine blew a cloud of smoke into his face.

'Quite a performance.'

Marian looked up at Paul, but his eyes, like everyone else's, were riveted on Madeleine. Even Madeleine was watching herself as she sauntered slowly towards the mirror. Her body had only one flaw in its otherwise classical perfection, but it was a flaw that Madeleine felt to be her greatest asset. Her breasts spilled over the 38D cup, the soft flesh rippling gently as she moved. With no resentment, Marian felt herself blending into the wall-paper. With her long mouse hair, small eyes and narrow lips, she was as plain as Madeleine was beautiful. And – except with people she knew well – she was as shy as Madeleine was confident. But it didn't matter to her that she was never noticed when Maddy was around; in fact, to be centre-stage herself would make her extremely uncomfortable. Thank God for Madeleine, she thought to herself now, because without her, her life would be as empty as the proverbial sack. She chuckled quietly as she considered what Rob would have to say to that, and as the music started up again she went back to the kitchen.

Madeleine was dancing with one of her bosses from the gramming agency, throwing back her head, flinging out her arms and wiggling her hips in the sensational routine she practised most evenings. It was only when her boss offered her a rise in salary for a night between the sheets, and in answer she looked at him to give him what she called her Marilyn Monroe lick of the lips, that she noticed Paul O'Connell standing by the Christmas tree, talking to her colleague and arch-rival, Felicity. Her heart gave a giant leap and her boss was abandoned on the instant. Just looking at Paul O'Connell did things to her no man had ever done before, and as she cut a path through the clustered, jiving bodies she could feel her senses starting to tingle with anticipation. Bluntly she informed Felicity that she really ought to check out the red stain on the back of her Miss Piggy costume, then grinned as Felicity hissed that it was 'the Pink Panther, actually', and swept off to the bathroom.

Madeleine watched her go, then turned her sultry eyes to Paul. 'I was beginning to think you weren't coming,' she said, looking him over hungrily. 'You know you have to pay a forfeit for not wearing fancy dress?'

His eyebrows rose and his smile was lazy and knowing. Then he caught her as a cavorting couple jolted into them, and his smile widened as she made no move to break away. 'Tell me what it is,' he said, 'and I'll tell you if I can pay.'

Her eyes roamed his face before answering. 'I'm sure I'll think of something to take off you before the night's out,' she purred.

'I'm sure you will,' he said. 'Now, if you'll excuse me, there's someone over there I'd like to say hello to.'

He didn't miss her sour look as he gently pushed her

back on her feet, but he was bored by women who threw themselves at him.

She didn't see him again until the countdown to midnight, when she found him in the kitchen with Marian and the eggheads. 'God, you could get high on the air in here,' she remarked, scowling at Rob, who was sucking at a joint. 'Come on,' she said to Marian, 'it's almost midnight.' Her voice was high, trying to inject some excitement into the soporific atmosphere, and grabbing both Paul and Marian by the hand, she dragged them into the sitting-room as the countdown finished and the New Year was given a roar of welcome. Immediately she threw her arms around Paul and pushed her tongue into his mouth. He did nothing to resist, but neither did he respond. When she'd finished, she let him go and kissed Marian. Then everyone joined hands and jostled and cheered through a chorus of 'Auld Lang Syne'.

'OK, Gerry!' Madeleine called as the circle broke up. Gerry pushed a button on the cassette player and Marian buried her face in her hands as the music started. It was 'The Stripper'.

A space was quickly cleared for Madeleine and everyone clapped their hands in time to the music as she peeled off the few items of clothing she wore. For a fleeting moment Marian thought she was going to stop at the microscopic scrap of lace she wore round her hips, but with the final beats of the music that too was removed, and stepping back into her high-heels, Madeleine threw out her arms and let the applause wash over her naked body.

The music changed to a soft Christmas-time melody and she turned to find Paul, her face flushed with excitement. But only Marian stood behind her, and as her eyes darted about, searching, Marian shook her head.

'He's gone,' she whispered.

'Gone? What do you mean, gone?'

Marian shrugged. 'He just said he was leaving, and went.'

'Didn't you try and stop him?'

'How could I? What was I supposed to say?' She sensed a tantrum coming on, and for once watched in relief as two large hands reached around Madeleine and squeezed her breasts. It was her boss.

'My dance, I think,' he said, and pulled Madeleine into the middle of the room . . .

The party broke up around two, by which time the atmosphere had been soured by Madeleine's disappointment, and by Marian's marked disapproval of her nudity. In fact Madeleine would have got dressed again if it hadn't been for Marian; irrational though it was, she blamed her cousin for Paul's early departure and wanted to make her suffer.

It was past midday when Madeleine finally dragged herself out of bed. She found Marian in the sitting-room, trying to sponge red wine stains out of the sofa. 'You're wasting your time,' she said, flopping into the chair. 'It won't come out, red wine never does. And what are you bothered for anyway, it doesn't belong to us.'

Marian stood up and planted a hand on either side of her ample hips. 'Did you have to go to bed with that horrible man?' she asked.

Madeleine tutted and sighed. 'Here we go.'

'Well?'

'No! I didn't have to, but it was a good thing I did. You're the one who's worried about how we're going to pay for everything – well, I've just fucked my way to a pay increase. Satisfied?'

'Don't be ridiculous! Of course I'm not satisfied.'

'No, neither was I as it happens, but then that wasn't the point, was it?'

'God, I hate it when you're crude. Do you know what I heard someone say about you last night? "Just tell her you

– 16 –

know a photographer and the legs open like the door to Ali Baba's cave." Everyone's laughing at you, you know.'

'So what? You don't really expect me to care about a town full of turnip-heads, do you? And as for *me* being a laughing stock, what about you? *You* should be in a bloody side-show. Twenty-two and still a virgin. So cut the preaching and remember that I'm not the only one who's been out spending on those credit cards. And they're in your name, so think yourself lucky I'm doing something about it. What have you done? Bought another raffle ticket, I suppose. Or have you filled in the football pools this time?'

'You can mock, but at least I'm not going around behaving like a slut.'

'No, you're just running around getting deeper and deeper into debt, and expecting me to bail you out. Well, I'm telling you one of these days I'm going to walk out of here, and then we'll see how far you get without the slut!' She jerked herself to her feet and stormed off to the bedroom.

Marian went after her. 'Look, I'm sorry,' she said. 'I shouldn't have called you that. But . . .'

'There are no buts about it! Get away from me! I loathe your bloody self-rightness.'

Marian didn't correct the malapropism, the way she normally did. She just looked on helplessly as Madeleine worked herself into a lather.

'You're supposed to be the one with all the education,' she said, snapping out the words nastily. 'So what the hell are you doing with it? Not a lot as far as I can see. Just as well you learned to type, otherwise you'd have nothing. And without me you'd *be* nothing. Stuck with those boring prats you call friends.'

'Rob's offered me a ticket to Tibet,' Marian told her.

'Then go! Go on, fuck off with them, see if I care. I

don't need you.' She snatched up a brush and started dragging it violently through her hair.

Marian watched her, her heart turning over at her cousin's confusion. 'No, I know you don't,' she said, quietly. 'But I need you.'

At that Madeleine dropped onto the stool behind her and burst into tears. 'I'm sorry,' she sobbed. 'I'm such a cow, and it's not your fault he didn't stay. Why didn't he, Marian? Why didn't he fancy me? Why doesn't anyone want me?'

Marian walked over to her and put her arms around her. 'I want you, Maddy. I know it's not the same, but you mustn't think no one cares about you because it's not true. You're the most popular person in your crowd.' She smiled. 'If anyone, it's me that no one wants, and I'm not crying, am I? As long as I've got you then I'm happy.'

'Oh, Marian, I love you more than anyone in the world. It's just that I want a boyfriend. A real one, not all those idiots who just use me. If I had someone as clever and good looking as Paul O'Connell, I know I'd make it.'

'You'll make it anyway,' Marian assured her. 'You wait and see. You'll be more famous than you've even dreamed about.'

Madeleine smiled through her tears. 'Do you think so?'

'I know so.'

'You're not going to go to Tibet, are you?'

Marian shook her head solemnly. 'I don't think I could take all that fun.'

Madeleine grinned, then ran her hand over Marian's face. 'Five hundred thousand pounds,' she said.

Taking her cue for their favourite game, Marian said: 'A yacht in the south of France, with big beefy waiters to service all your needs.'

'And a skinny little brainbox to service yours?'

Marian turned her nose up at that. 'Lots of photographers and TV cameras waiting on the harbour, because the famous Madeleine Deacon might come ashore any second.'

'An apartment in Cannes?'

Marian shook her head. 'A villa in Monaco. And another in Tuscany. A chauffeur, a cook and a butler. And Paul O'Connell begging at the door for you to let him in.'

'Should I?'

'I don't know yet. But what I do know is that we've seen off more than five hundred thousand in a few short sentences. So how about seeing off the remaining ten pounds in the kitty and going to the wine bar?'

As they dressed, and Madeleine chattered on about the party the night before, Marian was only half listening. Rob's offer of Tibet didn't appeal to her in the least, but it had highlighted the probability that, one day, she and Madeleine would go their separate ways. Madeleine was set for stardom, she was certain of it. She would appear on page three of *The Sun* – her current ambition – and she'd win Paul O'Connell eventually, too, because there wasn't a man born yet who could resist Madeleine. So when the time came, Marian knew that she would have to let her go. It terrified her. Madeleine might be two years younger, but ever since she could remember Marian had lived in her shadow. And now she knew only too well that without Madeleine she would be consumed by the bitter truth of what she was really like: ugly, dull, and worst of all, a coward.

The first week of the New Year was a busy one for Madeleine because of all the late Christmas parties in offices and restaurants around Bristol. She enjoyed her job even more at this time of year, when passions ran high and tips were generous. But tonight she was particularly excited because straight after doing a policewoman strip in the Spaghetti Tree, where the CID from Bridewell were having their Christmas bash, she was off to the HTV studios to deliver a French-o-gram for someone's birthday.

She was in and out of the Spaghetti Tree in less than half an hour. Stuart, her driver, was waiting outside, and while he drove around the city centre, then headed out towards the Bath Road, Madeleine deftly slipped into a black pencil skirt, skimpy underwired bra, hooped T-shirt and spotted neckerchief. The black stockings and suspenders she was already wearing from the policewoman strip.

A man called Jimmy was waiting for Madeleine at the studio complex and took her to the club bar, a small but crowded L-shaped room where the birthday boy was sitting over by the windows, surrounded by a particularly rowdy group. Madeleine handed Jimmy her coat, and as she carried her cassette player over to the bar she searched the room to see if she could spot anyone famous. Not that it was actors she was after – it was producers and directors she was really on the look out for.

Jimmy clapped his hands, and silence fell. As everyone turned to look at Madeleine, the smoky air became charged with expectancy. As usual, the tension stimulated her, and she was already sorry that the rules forbade her to remove anything beyond her bra. Her cheeks were flushed from the wine she'd drunk at the Spaghetti Tree, and as she slipped on her beret she ran her tongue around her full, wide lips while letting her eyes roam lazily from one face to the next. Her Svengali was here, somewhere in this room, she just knew it.

'She's a stunner,' she heard someone behind her whisper, and she raised her chin and jiggled her shoulders as though he had caressed her back.

Before she started the music, she read the ditty her boss had composed, pausing when everyone laughed and responding shamelessly to the hungry looks of Steve, her subject. Then handing him the poem, she pressed a button on her cassette player, and the seductive strains of 'Je t'aime' filled the bar.

The whole room was spellbound as she gyrated her hips, ran her elegant long fingers over her breasts and slowly unzipped her skirt. Hands tightened around glasses as she stepped out of it, revealing the stockings, suspenders and tiny briefs underneath. Hooking her fingers either side of the elastic, she pulled it up over her hips and turned around to show her almost naked buttocks. She danced some more, waiting for the music to build; then taking her beret, she spun it across the room, before lifting her T shirt over her head and throwing that too. When she turned to Steve, placing her hands on the table in front of him and rotating her hips, his face turned crimson – her breasts were spilling from the bra, and she ran her index finger deep into her cleavage before putting it in her mouth and sucking. Then, as the air began to fill with the heavy breathing of the song, she sat down in a chair, lifted a slender leg onto the table, and let her head roll back while her chest heaved with her own deep breaths. Her hands explored her body, her back arched, and as the song chanted to its sexual climax she unfastened her bra and let it fall away. The general gasp was almost a moan, and feeling the thrill of power that male arousal always gave her, she took a copious breast in each hand and sauntered slowly towards Steve. She stood over him, circling her hips and holding her breasts towards him. There was nothing in her mind beyond the pure ecstasy of what she was doing. She wanted the music to go on forever, but finally it petered out and she sank into his lap.

'Holy shit!' she heard someone mutter into the quiet, then the room was suddenly alive with applause. She laughed, intoxicated by her own performance. Her nipples throbbed, and she almost melted as Steve's fingers closed around them and everyone cheered.

The barman brought her a drink, and Steve moved

along to make room for her to sit between him and another man. A crowd quickly gathered around the table, and she lapped up the attention, flicking her hair over her shoulders and fixing the men with her luminous violet eyes.

'So which one of you is a director?' she said, when she was halfway through her second glass of wine. 'Come on, who's going to give me my big break?'

'Steve there's a producer,' one of them answered, 'how would that suit you?'

Madeleine's eyes widened as she turned to Steve. 'Are you really?' she asked.

He nodded, his small green eyes moving between her breasts and her face. His auburn hair was brushed into a side parting, his ruddy cheeks were pock-marked and unshaven. 'It's been a long day,' he explained, running a hand over his beard as he noticed her dubious look.

Somebody refilled her glass and she took a sip before saying, 'I've always wanted to be an actress, you know. Or a model. Do you think I've got the talent?'

Steve spluttered in his beer. 'Oh, sure, you've got the talent all right,' he answered. 'You've got just . . .'

'You've got great potential,' a man on the other side of him interrupted. 'As a matter of fact, we're casting next week for a new drama, and there might just be a part in it for you?'

'Really?' Madeleine gasped. 'Are you serious? Do you think I could do it? What's the part?'

'Actually,' Steve said, catching his mate's drift, 'it just so happens we're looking for a stripper. Can you act?'

'Come on, Maddy, time to go.' Madeleine looked up to see Stuart standing over her.

'Oh, not yet,' she groaned. 'Sit down, have a drink. We haven't got any more stops tonight, so relax.'

'We'll take her home, mate,' Steve chipped in.

Immediately Stuart shook his head. 'No, she comes with

me.' He knew there would be hell to pay with the boss if he didn't get her out, but he also knew how determined Madeleine could be, and he groaned inwardly as she stood up and whispered in his ear.

'I won't tell,' she said, giggling as someone groped her bottom. 'As far as anyone will know, you took me straight home after HTV. Now don't spoil this for me – that guy with the ginger hair's a producer!'

Stuart rolled his eyes. 'You haven't fallen for that one, have you?' he said, but Madeleine wasn't listening.

'Of course I'm staying,' she was assuring Steve and his friends. She turned back to Stuart. 'Go on, go,' she hissed. 'If it'll make you feel any better, I'll ring you when I get in, let you know I'm home safe and sound.'

'Do that,' he said, and casting an ominous glance around the circle of men, he left.

Madeleine drank her wine and listened with rapt attention as Steve told her about television – the long hours, the hard work, the actresses who cracked under pressure. 'It's a rough, tough world,' he said, 'you've got to have what it takes.'

'Do you think I have?' she asked.

'Most definitely. In fact I'm surprised no one's snapped you up before now. What a find, eh, John?' he said to his mate, who agreed wholeheartedly.

'John's going to be directing this drama,' Steve informed her, 'so I'd be especially nice to him if I were you.'

Madeleine shifted in her seat and gave John the benefit of her most beguiling smile. Then suddenly she gasped as her skirt, T-shirt, bra and beret were flung in her face.

She looked up to see a woman standing in front of her. Despite the fury that blazed from her green eyes, Madeleine couldn't help noticing how striking she was. She was tall and slim and had a careless elegance Madeleine would have killed for. And her auburn hair, smattering of freckles and subtle pink lips all added to her impeccable chic. 'Yours, I believe,' the woman spat. And when Madeleine only continued to look at her, she said through gritted teeth, 'It's sluts like you that give women a bad name.' Her eyes darted to the men on either side of Madeleine. 'Where the hell's your self-respect?' she said. Then turning on her heel, she walked out of the bar.

'Who the hell's she?' Madeleine asked, turning to Steve, whose expression seemed to have sobered a little.

'Stephanie Ryder,' he answered. 'Some hot-shot producer from London.'

Madeleine looked at the door in dismay. She'd never given any thought to the fact that producers could be women, and to have one speak to you like that . . . She turned back to Steve, who straightaway realised that Stephanie Ryder's attack was in danger of spoiling the evening's sport.

'Take no notice,' he said. 'She's only jealous.'

Madeleine perked up a bit at that. 'Silly old cow,' she said, but it was forced, and though she took a large mouthful of wine to restore her confidence, somehow the mood was broken.

'You're sure you're not having me on about being a producer and director?' she said on the way home, as John drove round the Clifton triangle and up towards the Victoria Rooms.

'Just give us a call at the studios tomorrow,' Steve answered, turning round to look at her. 'We'll arrange for an audition.'

Madeleine still wasn't convinced, but whoever they were they worked in television, so they might be able to do something for her.

'Of course,' John put in, 'there are quite a lot of others we have to see, so we can't promise anything.'

Madeleine's face fell.

'However, there are ways of getting over that,' Steve

said. 'Certain things you can do to make sure of getting the part.'

'Like what?' Madeleine asked.

Steve and John exchanged a look, then John said, 'Have you ever heard of the casting couch?'

Madeleine shook her head. 'No. What is it?'

Steve's eyes magnified with amazement. 'Tell you what, seeing as you've perked up my birthday I think you deserve some special privileges. What do you say, John?'

John nodded. 'Definitely.'

'So you invite us in for coffee and we'll explain the casting couch. It'll put you streets ahead of the other girls.'

Madeleine had the flat to herself that night as Marian had gone to Devon to ask her mother for money. Which was just as well, she thought, when she woke with a raging hangover the following morning; two men in one night would have sent Marian into a blinding fury.

But, when Marian returned two days later with enough money to pay the rent, Madeleine was so miserable about the way things had turned out at HTV that it wasn't difficult to get out of her what had happened. Madeleine knew now that Steve and John were props men. She also knew that they would be doing nothing to help her career, as they had gone away filming for the next three months.

Marian hid her anger well, though she did deliver a bit of a lecture, but since Madeleine had heard it all before, she didn't take much notice. In fact, now that she'd unburdened herself she felt distinctly better, and Stephanie Ryder, the real cause of her misery, was given the status of a frustrated old spinster and forgotten . . .

'I'm finishing early tonight,' Madeleine said on Friday. She was trying out a new pale pink lipstick, and wondering what she might look like with freckles. 'Why don't you meet me at the Chateau, Marian? Everyone else will be there.'

'I don't think so,' Marian answered. She was sitting at

the dilapidated dining-table, a pile of bills in front of her and a pay packet that contained fifty-five pounds for one day's work – all she'd managed to get that week.

'Oh, come on,' Madeleine insisted. 'Leave all that, it'll only get you depressed. Let's go and get pissed, and to hell with bills – and men.'

That decided Marian. If Madeleine was intending to get drunk then she wanted to be around to make sure she came to no harm.

At nine o'clock she was waiting outside the wine bar. Several of Madeleine's friends passed her as they went inside, but none of them spoke – they didn't even notice her. Finally at nine fifteen Madeleine turned up, wearing her jeans and a fancy lace top Marian hadn't seen before.

'Before you say anything, I borrowed it from Jackie,' Madeleine lied. 'And what are you doing out here? Why didn't you go in and wait, everyone's there,' she said, peering through the window.

Marian didn't answer, but followed Madeleine glumly through the door. Not looking where she was going, she bumped into Madeleine's back, then glancing up, she saw why Madeleine had stopped. Paul O'Connell was standing in front of them. To Marian's dismay, Madeleine stuck her nose in the air and walked on. Marian gave him an apologetic look and he grinned. His white, even teeth and intense eyes turned her heart over.

'How are you?' he said. 'How did the party go on after I'd left?'

Marian shrugged, her cheeks were on fire. 'Oh, not bad,' she mumbled. 'It broke up around two.'

'And have your friends gone off to Tibet yet?'

'They went yesterday.'

He nodded. 'So you decided life with the lamas wasn't for you?'

She smiled at his wry look, and he laughed. Then,

giving another self-conscious shrug, she started after Madeleine.

'What did he say?' Madeleine wanted to know.

'He asked about the party.'

'Bloody cheek.' Madeleine threw him another nasty look. 'Did he say anything about me?'

Marian shook her head. 'Why did you ignore him like that?'

'Because he deserved it. And besides, now he knows I'm not interested I'll bet he comes running. Just you watch.'

Marian bit her tongue. Madeleine's judgement of character had never been her strongest point. But to Marian's complete astonishment, when the phone rang the following Monday afternoon it was Paul.

'There's a lecture on the Italian Renaissance at the museum tomorrow night,' he told her, 'I wondered if you'd like to come.'

Marian froze, and looked at the receiver as if it were playing her some kind of trick. Then, with a pang of disappointment, she realised he had mistaken her for Madeleine.

'It's Marian here,' she said, almost laughing now at the idea of Madeleine going to such a lecture – though for Paul O'Connell she would probably suffer it. 'I think you've got us confused. Madeleine's the tall one with blonde hair. She'll be back any minute. She's just popped . . .'

'I know who I'm speaking to,' he interrupted, 'and I'm asking you if you'd like to come to the lecture.'

Again Marian looked at the receiver. 'Yes. Well, yes, that would be very nice,' she said, hardly able to speak her insides were in such a commotion.

'Good. It starts at seven. Would you like me to pick you up?'

'No! No, that's all right. I'll meet you outside.'

'OK. See you then,' and he rang off.

When Madeleine came in ten minutes later, Marian was still in a state of high agitation. Fortunately Madeleine was engrossed in a magazine article and munching on a chocolate bar, which she held out for Marian to take a bite. Marian shook her head and went into the bedroom.

For half an hour she sat in front of the mirror, too stunned to move. Of course, he didn't mean anything by the invitation, she told herself, he was just being friendly. And after all, it was only to a lecture. But the question had to be asked, why her? There wasn't a woman in Bristol who wouldn't have sold her soul for an evening out with Paul O'Connell. She could just see the reeling shock on everyone's faces if they were to find out that Marian Deacon, Madeleine Deacon's boring, fat little cousin, had a date with Paul O'Connell. Suddenly she found herself laughing. Why should she care what Madeleine's friends thought? Besides, boring and fat she might be, but they'd soon look at her in a different light if she actually started going out with Paul O'Connell.

Slowly her eyes came into focus again and she looked at her face. The dreamy expression gave her the look of a constipated ferret, she thought, and she grimaced. Paul O'Connell's girlfriend indeed! The idea was about as credible as a fairy tale. Still, there was no harm in giving a free rein to her imagination once in a while – after all, reality would soon sort it out. She bunched her lank, mousey hair on top of her head and pouted, the way Madeleine did. The result was so absurd that she burst out laughing. Her face was too thin, her hips too wide, and her breasts too meagre to mention. Nevertheless, she was the one he'd asked, and now all she had to do was find something to wear. There was certainly nothing in her tired old wardrobe, so she'd have to buy something new. She was over the limit on her Barclaycard, but there was fifty pounds left on Access, so she'd use that.

Over the next twenty-four hours she tried several times

to tell Madeleine, but the words wouldn't come. When she got ready she dressed in the bathroom, taking her coat in with her so she could hide the new skirt and blouse she had bought in the C & A January sale. When it was time for her to leave, she glanced down the hall and saw that Madeleine was painting her nails in the sitting-room while watching the local news on TV. But when Marian called out that she'd be back later, Madeleine got up and wandered into the hall.

'Where are you going?' she asked, eyeing Marian's lipstick.

'Only to a lecture at the museum,' Marian answered breezily.

Madeleine pulled a face. 'I thought we could go to see a film,' she said. '*White Mischief*'s on at the Whiteladies. Charles Dance is in it. You like him, don't you?'

Marian nodded.

'Forget the lecture. I'd have thought you'd had enough of them to last you a lifetime, anyway.'

'Actually, I'm meeting someone.'

Suddenly she had Madeleine's full attention. 'Oh? Who?' she asked.

Marian looked at her helplessly, then blushed as Madeleine started to laugh.

'It's a man, isn't it?' she said. 'That's why you're all dolled up.' She gave a little leap of excitement. 'Marian! You've got a date! You crafty old thing, you. Why didn't you tell me? Well, come on, who is he?'

Marian knew there was nothing she could do but come straight out with it. 'Paul O'Connell,' she said flatly, and watched with mounting dismay as the laughter died in Madeleine's eyes and her face twisted into a scowl of distaste.

'That's not very funny,' Madeleine said. 'If you don't want to tell me who he is, then just tell me to mind my own business.' She spun round and stomped back into the sitting-room.

Marian waited for her to sit down, then went to stand in front of her. 'Maddy,' she said quietly, 'it's only a lecture, and I wouldn't poke fun at you that way, you know I wouldn't. Somebody let him down so he asked me if I'd like to fill the place.' It was what she had told herself. 'But, if it's upsetting you, I'll stand him up.'

Madeleine looked up at her, her eyes glassy and her mouth pinched. 'When did you arrange it?'

Marian tensed. 'He rang yesterday afternoon, while you were at the shops.'

Madeleine's top lip curled. 'He rang yesterday, and you've only told me now? Did he realise he was talking to you? I mean, if he's got our names mixed up and you turn up there tonight, then he's going to have a pretty horrible shock, isn't he?'

Marian turned away and walked to the door. 'I don't know what time I'll be back,' she said, 'but don't wait up.'

As she closed the door her heart was thudding violently and her nerves were drawing sickeningly at the base of her stomach. She got as far as the Victoria Rooms, then almost turned back, but somehow she made herself keep going.

When she arrived at the museum he was already there, sheltering in the archway from the rain that had just started. She hurried up to him. 'Hello,' she said shyly. 'I'm not late, am I?'

'No.' He smiled, and her heart gave an acrobatic lurch. 'I just got here earlier than I expected,' he said. 'Shall we go in? I've reserved us a couple of good seats near the front.'

The two-hour lecture passed Marian by in a haze of Raphaels, Titians and da Vincis, and no matter how deeply the lecturer analysed colour, to her everything seemed rosy. Several times she grimaced at her own mawkishness, straightening her back and tried to pay attention, but to no avail.

'There's a tapas bar along the road,' Paul said, when the lecture was over and they were being jostled into the street by the rest of the small crowd. 'If you're not in a hurry we could have a coffee, and you can give me your own thoughts on the Renaissance – and old Judd's lecture.'

Marian's heart sank. She doubted if she could remember a word, and even if she could, it would be impossible to express any of her thoughts to a man like this. She was so much out of her depth she could feel herself drowning in her own temerity. She should never have come.

Reading the situation perfectly, Paul took her arm and leading her off up the street, he made jokes about the lecture, told her stories about Michelangelo and Botticelli, and astonished her with his knowledge of the Medicis. He was careful not to put her in a position where she would have to respond with anything more than a laugh or a question, sensing that for the moment she was too shy to assert an opinion. On the few occasions he'd seen her, usually at the Chateau with her cousin and her friends, she had always been on the periphery, trying very hard not to look left out, but never quite succeeding. Her bright, intelligent eyes were what had first drawn his attention, though he'd given her no more than a cursory glance at the time. Had Madeleine but known it, it was her interest in him that had provoked his in Marian. Girls like Madeleine were two-a-penny – maybe not quite so beautiful, nor quite so vain, but they were all predictable, empty-headed, and on the whole, coarse. But if Madeleine hadn't made such an obvious play for him, he might not have given Marian a second thought. As it was, he hadn't been able to help noticing her sinking embarrassment on the occasions when Madeleine engaged him in what she considered a flirtatious exchange, nor had he missed Marian's many but fruitless attempts at joining in the inane conversations and raucous laughter that circled her cousin.

It was because of Marian that he'd turned up at the New Year's Eve party – he had sensed something different about her, something unusual. He'd never been involved with anyone quite so plain before, but looks meant little to him. It was her mind he found intriguing, and that impish sense of humour he'd caught a glimpse of on New Year's Eve. He admired her humility, though it was a touch extreme; and her obvious love for Madeleine, and the way she so subtly tried to protect her, fascinated him. She would make for an engaging character study, he felt – probably worthy of a novel if she was as pliable as he suspected. If not, then she would be an entertaining diversion for a while.

An hour later, sitting in the tapas bar, he said, 'It's your turn now. You know all about me, what's there to tell about you – and don't say not much.'

Marian laughed, because that was exactly what she'd been about to say. 'Well,' she began, 'I didn't go to Harrow like some.' She threw him a look and he winked. 'Neither do I come from the north. I've never flown in Concorde, written a book or danced barefoot with the Prince of Wales.'

'Who said anything about the Prince of Wales?'

'Me.'

He laughed. 'So what have you done?'

'I got my degree in philosophy, which I don't know what the heck I'm going to do with. I learned to type, and can barely get a job with that either. I accumulate bills the way a teenager gathers spots, and apart from the thrills and spills of the occasional museum lecture my life is so ordinary that one day I'm sure I shall disappear inside one gigantic yawn.'

She'd hoped to make him laugh again, but he was serious as he said, 'It's not really that bad, is it? I mean to say, having a cousin like Madeleine must make life – well, interesting at the very least.'

'Oh it does,' Marian agreed. 'But I'm a bit like an outsider looking in; I expect you've noticed. Sometimes I think it's a bit spineless of me to live through Madeleine, but I'm not one of the world's great extroverts, I'm afraid. People don't exactly beat a path to my door begging for the stimulus of my conversation, or insist that a party wouldn't be complete without me, like they do with Madeleine. So yes, she does make life more exciting – in fact, I couldn't imagine it without her. But it'll change one day, and I'll be forced into making some decisions about myself. I dread that, to be honest, because I haven't got the first idea what I want to do, but I'll think about it when it happens. Until then, Madeleine and her career must come first.' She stopped, feeling suddenly dizzy and hardly able to believe she'd said so much.

'Why must she?' he asked. When Marian only looked at him he went on. 'It seems to me that your cousin is more than capable of looking after herself.'

'That's just where you're wrong. But she will be.'

'And you? Are you capable of looking after yourself?'

Marian laughed. 'I doubt it. But until Madeleine achieves her dream I suppose I won't really know. The trouble is, I'm weak and cowardly, and I wouldn't have any friends at all if it weren't for her. Not now Rob and Mary have gone to Tibet.'

'Why do you say you're weak and cowardly?'

'Oh, that's easy,' she smiled. 'Because I am. I'm not proud of it, but knowing your limitations, your faults, is part way to beating them, don't you think?'

He nodded thoughtfully. During the pause Marian felt embarrassment take a nauseating grip on her stomach. She couldn't understand why she was saying all this. She'd never spoken to anyone about her inmost feelings before, she'd hardly even admitted them to herself. He must be appalled by what she had told him, disgusted even. Her hand trembled as she pushed her cup away, then she jumped as he took it between his.

'I think you're right about knowing your faults,' he said, his black eyes seeming to reach right into hers. 'It *can* help to overcome them. But you're wrong in thinking you know what yours are. You're not a coward, Marian, and neither are you weak. You're simply afraid of being alone, and guilty of needing someone to love. If that's a fault, then it's one common to the entire human race. Tell me about your boyfriends.'

Marian tensed and quickly drew her hand away. She was looking past him when she answered, staring sightlessly at the people passing outside. 'I've never had one,' she said candidly. And then she gave a slight toss of her head. 'Please don't pretend surprise, I'm quite aware of my shortcomings in the looks department.'

'You really don't like yourself too much, do you?' he laughed. 'Well, I'm going to let you into a secret. I do.'

Marian's grey eyes rounded, and as she stared at his handsome face it was as if the room had started to spin, and she felt suddenly faint.

'Why do you really make such a fuss of Madeleine?' he asked. 'The truth.'

She swallowed hard, trying to get a grip on herself. 'The truth is all that I've just told you,' she answered.

'Uh-uh,' he shook his head. 'There's more. Something in the past.'

'What makes you say that?'

'Because you're so protective. You know her failings better than anyone else, you know she doesn't match up to you intellectually and you secretly despise her exhibitionism, yet you tolerate it all. Why?'

Marian's face was stiff. 'Because her parents, my uncle and aunt, as good as abandoned her when she was only eight years old. They went off to America, promising they would come back, and they never did. Then when Maddy was ten they were killed in a plane crash. She's never shown any signs of grief, and that's why my mother and I make such a fuss, as you call it. So did my father when he was alive. You shouldn't look down on Madeleine, you know. She might seem flighty and capricious to you, but she has feelings like anyone else, and she's the most generous person I know.'

'And probably the most selfish, too. No, don't look at me like that. It's true. She's sapping every ounce of self-esteem from you, and you can't see it.'

'That's not true,' Marian replied hotly. 'She includes me in everything she does. I'd be nothing without her. And really you shouldn't pass judgement on people you don't know and situations you have no understanding of.'

Paul's face was comically contrite, and after a moment or two Marian gave a grudging smile.

'You think it's you who needs her,' he said, 'but it's the other way round. She's a very lucky girl to have a cousin who cares about her as much as you do. But one of these days it'll be you who's swept off her feet with love, not Madeleine. I wonder what she'll do then?'

Marian couldn't help being flattered that he should think that even remotely possible, so she didn't answer.

He rested his chin on his hand and looked at her. 'How old are you?' he said.

'Twenty-two. Madeleine's twenty.'

'Is she? Well, I'm thirty. And if you don't think I'm too old for you, I'd like to court you, Marian. Now, what do you say to such an old-fashioned proposal?'

She blinked, as if trying to wake herself up. The corners of his eyes were creased in a smile. Then, suddenly aware that her mouth was gaping, she snapped it shut.

He signalled to the waiter for the bill, then reaching into his raincoat, he took out his wallet. 'I can do it with flowers and chocolates,' he said. 'Or with walks across the

Downs. We can go to the theatre, more lectures, the cinema. We could even drink at the Chateau if that's what you'd like. In fact, we could do it all.' He took a pen from his inside pocket and scribbled something onto a card. 'I can see you're not going to give me an answer now, so here's my number. Give me a call when you're ready. Now, can I walk you home?'

Dazedly, Marian got to her feet. A damburst of joy, of incredulity, of sheer amazement was threatening to engulf her, but she struggled to suppress it. She was afraid. If she gave in to it now, then her life would never be the same again. The safe obscurity she had always known would be smashed, the door would close on her mundane, everyday life and she would step into a world of recognition and excitement that until now she had only ever known when she stood beside Madeleine. Paul O'Connell would be her boyfriend, his time would be spent with her, his secrets would be hers, his desires, his ambitions. She would know him in a way no one else would. She gasped as pictures of their life together unfolded in a crazy, euphoric pattern. At last she was going to be somebody. Marian Deacon had a boyfriend, and it was Paul O'Connell. How could she go through with it? But how could she not? Suddenly she burst out laughing. He had asked to court her and shock had jolted her mind into a ludicrous turmoil of melodrama and trepidation.

He didn't ask what had amused her but pulled her arm through his, and they walked off down the road. She had no idea, that night, of how accurate her instincts were, how right she was to think of melodrama, because she had no way of knowing, then, the earthshattering effect that Paul O'Connell was going to have on her life and on Madeleine's.

— 2 —

Madeleine's hand cracked like a whip across Marian's cheek. 'You sly, conniving little bitch!' she screamed. 'I don't know how you've got the nerve to stand there and say that to me.' She made a cruel mimic of Marian's voice: ' "Paul O'Connell wants to court me!" *Court*. What kind of word's that when it's at home? And you know I've been trying to get off with him for weeks, so just what the hell are you playing at? What have you told him about me? What did you say to poison his mind?'

Marian was rubbing her cheek and blinking back the tears of pain. 'I'm going to bed,' she said, and turned to walk from the room. But Madeleine grabbed her and yanked her back again.

'What did you say!'

'I didn't say anything about you,' Marian answered calmly. 'At least, nothing horrible.'

'You liar! Well, I'll tell you this for nothing, it won't last. He's only using you to make me jealous.'

'Maybe,' Marian said.

Madeleine gave a scream of rage. 'You surely don't think he fancies you, do you? A man like that with someone like you – it's too ridiculous for words.'

'I know.'

Madeleine sneered. 'You know! You're out of your league, Marian. And you only want him because I do, which is just typical of you. You want everything I've got, you always have.'

Marian took a deep breath. 'Maddy, I'm going to bed. Maybe we can talk about this more sensibly in the morning when you've calmed down.'

'Don't act stuck up with me!'

'I'm sorry. But you don't mean the things you're saying so there's no point in dragging this out.'

To her surprise Madeleine let her go, but Marian knew that wasn't the end of it.

The following morning, as she dressed for a day's work at the Bristol and West Building Society, she knew Madeleine was awake, but judging it better to leave her, she went off to work, intending to phone her later. But when she did, Madeleine hung up, and when she returned home at six o'clock Madeleine had already gone to work and there was no note waiting for her. Her heart sank. Obviously Madeleine was still angry and she shuddered at the thought of another scene like the night before's.

She wandered into the kitchen and lit the gas under the kettle before setting about the pile of washing-up Madeleine had left. It would be foolish to let him come between them, she told herself, after all he was little more than a stranger. And Madeleine was probably right, it wouldn't last, so what was the point in creating all these problems? But in her heart she knew she wanted to see him again, and her eyes filled with tears as indecision racked her. Paul had denied that she was weak, but he'd change his mind if he could see her now. She didn't have the courage to tell Madeleine she would carry on seeing Paul, and neither did she have the courage to ring Paul and tell him she wouldn't see him again. If only Maddy could understand how wonderful it would be for her to have someone she could really talk to. She knew already that she could discuss anything in the world with Paul, including her own feelings and insecurities. But Madeleine wouldn't understand. She would ask what was the matter with discussing things with her, after all she was family, wasn't she? To explain to Madeleine would mean hurting her, and Marian wasn't prepared to do that, no matter how much she wanted to see Paul.

When Madeleine came in just after midnight, Marian

was in bed. Neither of them spoke as Madeleine flicked on the bedroom light and hummed tunelessly while she undressed, as if there were no one else in the room.

'Good night?' Marian asked.

Ignoring her, Madeleine continued with her nightly beauty routine. A few minutes later she picked up a magazine and got into bed.

'It's rather lonely in Coventry,' Marian quipped. 'Can we talk?'

Madeleine sighed and flicked over a page.

'If I told you I'd decided not to see him again, would you stop behaving so childishly?'

'What you have or haven't decided is beside the point now,' Madeleine answered loftily. 'You've obviously turned him against me, so it's too late to start crawling round me now.'

'I'm not crawling round you,' Marian snapped. 'I'm trying to discuss this in an adult manner. But it's difficult when you insist on acting like a selfish, spoiled little brat.'

'Just fuck off,' Madeleine said.

'Does that have to be your answer to everything?'

'As far as you're concerned, yes.'

'All right. If you're going to take that attitude then I might as well see him again. It doesn't seem I've got much to lose.'

'You do that. And don't come crying to me when he dumps you.'

The next day was even more difficult; they were both at home, but Madeleine carried on as if Marian wasn't there. A couple of her friends came round and they drank a bottle of wine without offering her any. If she attempted to join in the conversation there was a hostile silence, and then they continued as if she hadn't spoken. Madeleine answered the phone to the Sue Sheppard Agency and told them she'd never heard of a Marian Deacon; and when Marian called the agency back, Madeleine turned the stereo up so loud she couldn't hear a thing. So she put on her coat and went out to a call-box. After she'd got her typing assignment for the following day she wandered around for an hour, and only went back to the flat when she was sure Madeleine had gone to work.

And here, she thought to herself as she started to clear the mess Madeleine had left, is proof of my cowardice.

'I shouldn't let her get away it,' she told Paul when he came round later, 'but I simply don't know what to do about it.'

'Yes, you do,' he said. 'In fact, you've already done it.'

Marian frowned. 'Have I?'

He smiled. 'You called me. Which, I take it, was what you wanted to do.'

Marian gave him a shy look and offered him another cup of tea. He wrinkled his nose, and going out to the hall, produced a bottle of red wine from his raincoat pocket.

'I shouldn't have told you all that,' she said, when they were in the kitchen hunting for the corkscrew. 'She accused me of turning you off her, and she's not exactly wrong now, is she?'

'Marian,' he said, 'I was never "on" Madeleine in the first place, as you know full well. So stop this self-chastisement and give me that corkscrew.'

Marian watched his hands as he poured the wine, then had to swallow hard as he handed her a glass. 'Madeleine will be furious if you're still here when she comes in,' she said.

'I'll be long gone, if that's what you want. But if she asks, you're not to deny having seen me. Unless you're ashamed, of course.'

She smiled at that, and led the way back into the sitting-room. He sat on the sofa again, but when she headed towards the chair he caught her hand and pulled her down next to him. 'And if she hits you again then I *will* have something to say on the matter, whether you like it or not. Now, shall we change the subject?'

Despite the peculiarly hot vortex that was whirling about in her chest, Marian couldn't resist a tease. 'Are you by any chance trying to tell me you've found my conversation boring so far?'

'*Trying* to tell you? You mean I've failed?'

Marian laughed. 'In that case, maybe you'd like to bore me by telling me what your book's about.'

'Ah! Now we're talking deeply dull. Male adolescence.'

Marian yawned. 'Mm, *deeply* dull. In fact . . .' She giggled as he put a hand over her mouth and gave her a warning look. Then tucking her feet under her, she sat back to listen.

Several times her mind wandered, but it had nothing to do with being bored. It was because she simply couldn't get to grips with the fact that he was really there, and she was responding to him in such a natural and relaxed way. She even started to challenge some of the things he said, and he listened, considered her suggestions and often admitted she might have a point. His feet were resting on the wooden box they used as a coffee table, and Marian was finding it difficult to keep her eyes from wandering the length of his muscular legs. She liked the way his hand swept through his hair from time to time, and the droll look that came into his eyes when he compared the boy in his book with himself as a teenager.

At nine o'clock they went out for a Chinese takeaway, and as they ate she told him about her mother, her father, her schooldays, and the little terraced house they'd lived in in Totnes.

'And you?' she said. 'Where are your parents?'

'They died when I was in my teens. My aunt took over from there, but I'm afraid she's dead now too.'

'Oh.' Marian's face was filled with concern. 'Don't you have any family at all?'

He shook his head. 'No family, no roots. And indeed, no job to speak of. Unless you call writing a job.'

'But what do you do for money?'

As he answered his eyes were full of humour. 'I sign on, like plenty of others.' He laughed at her evident shock. 'It was a deliberate choice,' he continued. 'I wanted to write, and it was no good trying to do it on a part-time basis.'

She looked at his clothes, recognising the expensive cut. 'What did you do before?' she asked.

'I ran several businesses, made a great deal of money and spent it all.'

'Really?'

'That's what money's for, isn't it?'

'What did you spend it on?'

'Women, mainly.'

Marian looked away, but he reached out and pulled her face back to look at him. 'And now I've met you, I'm a pauper. But in certain situations, with certain people, money is irrelevant, wouldn't you agree? And I think you know that what I can give you, if you will allow it, no amount of money in the world could buy.'

Marian's small grey eyes looked at him. Her tongue was knotted somewhere in the back of her throat, but the wonderful latency of his words had started a rush through her veins that made her skin glow.

He smiled, and she looked at his white teeth, then at the dark shadow on his chin. His eyes were watching her from beneath the black arches of his brows. She wanted to say something but didn't know what. Then he glanced at his watch and got to his feet. 'Now, if you want me out of here before Madeleine returns,' he said, 'I guess I'd better be on my way.'

She followed him into the hall, still unable to speak. In a way she was glad he was going, she wanted to savour that moment alone and unobserved.

As he opened the door he turned to look at her. 'Can I call you tomorrow?'

She nodded.

'Around seven?'

Again she nodded, and with a smile that was so intimate it seemed to touch her, he left.

She rushed into the bedroom and went to look at herself in the mirror. She was amazed at what she saw, and pinched herself, sure it was all a dream. She tried to stop smiling but found it was impossible. Her eyes had never sparkled like that before, and her skin was flushed and tingling. She felt as if she was floating, as if she could fly even. How could just a few words have had such an effect?

Madeleine didn't come home that night, and secretly Marian was glad. She'd never have been able to hide her feelings and she didn't want Madeleine to say anything to spoil her happiness.

After that she saw him every day, usually in the evenings, but if she wasn't working they wrapped up warmly and strolled across the Downs, or toured the zoo, or window-shopped for things they couldn't afford. Her heart was like a volcano, erupting with such happiness and love that it gave her a radiance even Madeleine couldn't fail to notice. But even Madeleine's peevish resentment did nothing to destroy her euphoria.

'It's classic, isn't it?' he said one day, when they were standing outside a jeweller's in Broadmead. 'Now I've met someone I really want to spend money on, I don't have it.'

She wanted to put her arms round him and tell him it didn't matter, but they hadn't got as far as an embrace yet, and she was too shy to make the first move. Sometimes he held her hand as they walked, or even put an arm round her shoulders, but he never seemed inclined to kiss her. She told herself it didn't matter, but despite feeling gay and carefree when she was with him – and sometimes even reckless when she made him laugh – there was nothing she could do to stall the flood of panic that sometimes overcame her when she was alone. In the middle of the night she would stare into the darkness and convince herself that any day now he would meet someone else. Someone he would want to kiss, someone he would want to make love to – and she, Marian, would be forgotten. But in the morning, when he called to tell her he would meet her from work, or take her to Bath or Weston-Super-Mare for the day, all her fears disappeared.

Then one afternoon, while they were giggling at being ticked off for making a noise in the library, he told her he wouldn't be able to see her for a week.

Her heart started to pound and she knew that the day she'd been dreading had arrived. 'I see,' she breathed. Then she forced a smile before looking down at the book in front of her.

'Aren't you going to ask me why?' he said.

Keeping her eyes lowered, she shook her head.

'I think I'll tell you anyway. I'm taking my manuscript to a publisher. I've spoken to him on the phone and he's interested enough to want to see me, and I can use the opportunity to sort out other business in London while I'm there.'

Since she assumed that the other business meant a woman, this did nothing to cheer her, and when she saw him off on the train the next day, though she smiled bravely, her volcano was spent and her heart was a dull, leaden weight.

When Madeleine came in early from work that night she found Marian crying on her bed.

'Dumped you, has he?' she said acidly.

Marian looked up. Her face was ravaged. 'I think so,' she whispered.

Madeleine tossed her bag on her own bed and went to sit on Marian's. 'Well, don't say I didn't warn you. If you must play out of your league, you must expect to lose.'

'Don't be nasty, Maddy,' Marian said.

Madeleine looked at her cousin's face, and seeing how heartbroken she was, she felt herself start to soften. 'Well you've always got me,' she said. 'That is, if I'm good enough for you now.'

Marian sat up and put her arms round Madeleine. 'You say the most ridiculous and the most monstrous things sometimes,' she said, 'but you're more important to me than anyone else in the world.'

Madeleine swallowed the lump in her throat. 'I'm sorry about the past few weeks,' she said. 'But it's over now, so shall we put it behind us, forget it ever happened?'

Marian nodded, wishing she could.

'If you like you can tell me about him,' Madeleine said, as she was getting into bed. 'I mean, what was he like? Did he make you come? I'll bet he's got a fantastic body, you lucky old cow. Fancy having someone like him for your first time!' She sighed and gave a little shiver of lust. 'You did do it, didn't you?' she said, when she realised Marian hadn't answered.

Marian was sitting up in bed, drinking the cocoa Madeleine had made. 'No,' she said quietly. 'If you want to know the truth, he never even kissed me.'

'What! Then what the hell *did* you do?'

'We talked.'

'Talked! What about?'

'Everything.'

'Bloody hell,' Madeleine muttered. Then she shrugged, feeling rather pleased that her cousin hadn't succeeded where she'd failed after all. 'Where does he live?' she asked.

Marian looked down at her cup. 'I don't know,' she answered. 'He never told me.'

'Didn't you ask?'

'Yes, but he always managed to avoid the question somehow.'

'Oh,' Madeleine said knowingly. 'Well, it's obvious, isn't it? He's married.'

Marian felt crushed at having her own suspicions voiced. She put her cup down, and turning off her bedside lamp she said: 'If you don't mind, I don't want to talk about him any more.'

At seven o'clock the next morning he rang. And again at seven in the evening. His calls continued in that pattern until the following Monday, when he asked Marian to meet him at the station on Tuesday morning. She was so relieved that she didn't sleep a wink all night and simply poked her tongue out at Madeleine when she said: 'Haven't you got any pride? He snaps his fingers and you go running like a faithful old dog. He doesn't want you,' she yelled as Marian put her coat on, 'let's face it, he can't even get it up where you're concerned.'

The train arrived early and he was already waiting outside Temple Meads when she got there. She longed to run into his arms and have him spin her round the way they did in films, but she made do with his beaming smile and his arm draped loosely round her shoulders as they walked to the bus stop.

'Madeleine thinks you're married,' she said as they rode through the city centre.

He gave a shout of laughter. 'Well Madeleine would, wouldn't she? And what do you think?'

'I think, I hope, you're not.'

'Well it's my aim to make all your hopes and dreams come true.'

'Does that mean you're not?'

He shook his head, his face still alight with amusement. 'No, I'm not married,' he said. Then looking into her eyes, he added, 'At least, not yet.'

Her heart erupted in a storm of incredulous happiness and she closed her eyes.

'You haven't asked me how I got on in London,' he said.

She turned to look at him. 'Well?'

'I don't know yet. The editor I saw is going to give me a call sometime next week, when he's read the script. Which reminds me, I gave him your telephone number, I hope you don't mind.'

'No, not in the least. But natural curiosity is going to make me ask why?'

'Because, my darling, I am homeless. I called my landlady yesterday and she's terminating my tenancy as of this Friday.'

'Oh no!' Marian gasped. 'What will you do?'

He shrugged. 'At the moment I don't know. But I'm sure I'll come up with something.' As the bus was approaching their stop he stood up and rang the bell. Marian noticed that the two girls sitting behind her were looking at him in awed admiration, and she felt herself go almost dizzy with pride.

When they got to her flat, Madeleine was there with her friends Jackie and Sharon. They all looked at Paul as he followed Marian through the door; their lascivious appraisal of him, and their open coquetry, made her stomach churn. She went to make some coffee while Madeleine took Paul's arm and sat him down. She couldn't quite hear what they were asking him, but from their frequent shrieks of laughter she guessed that he was exercising his charm.

When she joined them she felt even more awkward because there was nowhere for her to sit, so excusing herself, she went into the bedroom. A few minutes later there was a knock on the door and he came in.

'You're not jealous, are you?' he teased when he saw her glum face.

With a wry smile she said, 'Yet again you've seen through me.' She was sitting at the dressing-table and he went to stand behind her, looking at her reflection in the mirror. She turned away, uncomfortable at the striking contrast between his beauty and her ordinariness.

As she stood up he watched her walk past him, and when she reached the door he said, 'Are you afraid of me?'

She turned, her face showing only mild surprise at the question. 'Sometimes,' she answered frankly.

He held out his hand, and when she took it he led her to the bed and sat her down. 'Why?' he asked, as he sat down next to her.

'Truthfully?'

'Of course.'

'For the same reason I'm afraid of everyone else.'

'And that is?'

'I don't think you're going to like the answer much,' she smiled, and seeing the sadness in her eyes, he squeezed her hand and ran the back of his fingers over her face. 'It's because people can be exceptionally cruel to people who look like me. It's as if we don't count. Because we aren't beautiful, or attractive, we aren't credited with feelings. You'd be amazed at some of the things I've had said to me – though most of the time I'm just ignored. No matter how often it happens I still can't get used to it, and though I'm always half expecting it, it still comes as a shock. So I'm afraid of you – of people – because I'm ugly, and because I don't like being hurt.'

She was looking down at their entwined hands and tensed as a tear splashed onto his wrist. As he lifted her face she tried to turn away, but he wouldn't let her, and when she looked up she found he was gazing straight into her eyes. As he moved slowly towards her, her mouth trembled. His lips were soft and tender and slightly parted. She closed her eyes as her own lips parted, and she felt his arm move round her shoulders as he pulled her closer. He kissed her again, caressing her mouth with his and tracing her jaw with his thumb as his fingers splayed through her hair.

'Marian,' he whispered, still holding her close, 'you really don't know how beautiful you are, do you? It shines from your eyes when you speak. It's in your honesty and humility. It lives inside you like a light that will only be extinguished on the day you die.'

They heard a giggle outside, and Marian sprang to her feet as the door opened.

'Sorry if I'm interrupting something,' Madeleine said, 'but I need to get changed for work.'

Paul took Marian's hand, and turning so the others couldn't see, he winked. 'Nearly caught in the act,' he said. 'I told you to wait.' He turned back to the others. 'She can't keep her hands off me for more than two minutes at a time,' he said. 'But then I can't keep mine off her either.' And before Marian could do a thing to stop him, he tumbled her onto the bed and covered her with his body.

Within seconds they heard the door close, and lifting himself onto his elbows he looked down into Marian's face. Her expression made him burst out laughing; she hit him, then pushed him off the bed.

'Can't keep my hands off you indeed!' she cried, her voice bubbling with mirth. 'What's everyone going to say?'

'Do you care?' he asked, looking up at her from the floor.

'Not a jot!'

'Keep up that sort of defiance and I'll kiss you again,' he warned, then laughed as she blushed. 'Your cousin sure knows how to pick her moments,' he said as he got up. 'And there was me trying my damnedest to be romantic.' He pulled her to her feet. 'But I meant what I said. And you must stop under-rating yourself, and very definitely stop feeling sorry for yourself.'

'Sorry for myself!' she cried indignantly.

'Yes, and you know it. In fact I think you only did it to make me kiss you.'

Her mouth was opening and closing as sparks of affront and delight flashed from her eyes.

'Yes, go on,' he said, 'what are you trying to say?' and she collapsed against him, laughing.

'I was thinking,' she said later, while she dished a spoonful of beans onto a piece of toast, 'how would you feel about moving in here with Madeleine and me? I mean, until you find somewhere else,' she added hastily, in case he should think her forward. 'You'd have to sleep on the sofa, but it's better than the streets.'

She turned to look at him. He was spooning tea into the pot and her heart gave a flutter at the pleasure of their domesticity.

'And what would Madeleine have to say to this very improper suggestion?' he said. And when he looked up, their eyes locked for a moment before they burst out laughing.

'What, shack up with you two!' Madeleine stormed when Marian asked her. 'Are you serious? Because if you are, you'd better get your brain fixed.'

'It wouldn't be for long,' Marian pleaded. 'And it'll help with the rent. We've fallen behind again, and I've had a nasty letter from Barclaycard. That's not to mention the other bills we can't pay. We could do with the money, Maddy, and it would mean a lot to me if you said yes.'

'I'll bet it would. Well, I'm not going to, so don't bother asking again.'

Marian didn't then, but she wasn't going to give in that easily. In fact, she was determined to win. And when Madeleine came home at half-past one in the morning, she was waiting up. 'I want to talk to you again about Paul moving in,' she said, as Madeleine flopped into a chair.

'Oh good,' Madeleine answered. She was smiling cheerfully and Marian's hopes lifted. 'I've been thinking about it too,' Madeleine went on, 'and you're right. We could do with the money, so tell him it's all right by me.'

'Are you sure?' Marian said, hardly able to believe her ears.

'Of course I am,' Madeleine answered. 'In fact I've come to the conclusion I've been behaving very childishly over all this, and I want you to know that really, deep down, I'm happy for you. Anyone can see he's head over heels in love with you, so who am I to stand in your way?'

Marian was amazed. 'You mean, you really don't mind about us any more?'

Madeleine shook her head, and Marian fell back into the sofa. 'Thank God,' she breathed. 'Oh, thank God. I've been longing to talk to you about him, tell you all the things he says. I've missed you, Maddy, even though you've been here. Does this mean we can be friends again?'

'I certainly hope so, because I've missed you too.'

'Shall we have some cocoa to celebrate?' Marian grinned.

'No, we'll have some wine. And then we'll sit up half the night while you talk about him to your heart's content.'

While she waited for Marian to fetch some glasses from the kitchen, Madeleine was mulling over what her friend Jackie had said earlier. 'You're mad for saying no,' she'd told Madeleine. 'If he's there, under the same roof, then you'll have no problem pulling him. And what's more, if you get Marian to tell you everything he likes and doesn't like, and all that sort of thing, then you can make use of it yourself, and he'll be eating out of your hand inside a month. In fact, if he isn't laying her, two weeks in your company and he'll be begging you for it.'

'Do you think so?' Madeleine said.

'I know so. But just in case, be nice to Marian. That'll show him what a wonderful person you can be, and hey presto, he'll be in your knickers before you can say fuck me.'

Jackie was right, of course; in fact thinking about it now, Madeleine couldn't believe that she hadn't seen it for herself.

— 3 —

Paul glanced up from his typewriter and looked across the table at Marian. She was staring at the diamond-patterned wallpaper and tapping a pen against her teeth, obviously engrossed in thought. 'What on earth are you doing?' he asked after a minute or two.

'Trying to think of a ten word slogan for this competition,' she answered cheerfully.

He shook his head, and leaning his elbows on the keyboard said, 'What might you win?'

'A car. Which I can then sell and pay off all our debts.'

'I see.' Then after a pause, 'How about a cup of coffee?'

Immediately Marian put down her pen.

'No, no, no,' he protested, as she started to get up. 'I meant, I'll make you one. After all, it's pretty serious business you're up to there, so far be it from me to interrupt.'

She grabbed her pen and threw it at him as he disappeared into the kitchen. 'Can I read what you've written this morning?' she called after him.

'Go ahead.'

She leaned across the table and wound the sheet of paper out of his typewriter, and by the time he came in with the coffee she'd read the four paragraphs at least half a dozen times.

'Thanks,' she said as he put a cup down in front of her.

Then with her head on one side she watched him as he sank into the armchair and picked up the newspaper.

He'd been living with them for almost two weeks now, but the more she got to know him, the more of a mystery he became. She was as jealous of his past as she had been of the time he spent at his typewriter – until he'd sensed how she was feeling. Now he shared his work, asking her opinion, arguing through her ideas, and even asking her to write down her thoughts and feelings so he could use them. The main characters in his latest story were based on her and Madeleine, and there was a great deal of hilarity and cushion-throwing when she read his deliberate misinterpretations of something one of them had said or done. There were uncomfortable moments, too, when he wanted to explore the depth of her feelings for him. On that she always held back, and though he didn't push her, he generally wrote what he thought, then asked if he'd guessed right. He usually had, but her answer was always the same: 'That's for me to know and you to find out.' Of course she was in love with him, and it wasn't that she minded him knowing, she just wanted him to be the first to say it.

Now she shifted in her chair, disturbed by the line her thoughts had taken. Despite the fact that on one level they were closer than she'd ever dreamed possible, on another – on the matter of love – there was a distance between them which was only made worse by his casual dismissal of the questions she couldn't stop herself asking.

'Does it really matter how many girlfriends I've had?' he would say. 'Or who they were, what they looked like, or where they are now?'

'Yes,' she answered once, 'it does matter. I don't know why, but it does.'

'It doesn't. And you're falling into the typical female trap: of convincing yourself I'm hiding something, when all I'm doing is protecting you from things that you don't need to know. Of course there have been other women, but I'm with you now, and not one of them ever meant half as much to me as you do.'

She knew it was the kind of answer that should satisfy her – but perhaps if he showed some inclination to do more than kiss her, the torturous images of him with other women might disappear. Perhaps if she didn't have a cousin like Madeleine, their lack of sex-life might not seem so odd or so important – but a hungry worm of doubt wriggled away inside her, demanding the food of reassurance.

'A very pensive face,' he said, looking up from the paper. 'What are you thinking about?'

'You,' she admitted.

'What about me?'

'I'd like you to tell me about Florence.'

'Haven't you just read that bit?'

'Yes, but that's in a novel. You mentioned once that you used to go there every spring. Tell me about that.'

'There's not much to tell, really,' he answered. 'Except that I hated it. Being dragged from church to art gallery to palazzo wasn't much fun for a little boy, but my mother was a fiend for Italian culture so my father took her to Florence every year; they even spent their honeymoon there, I believe.' His eyes were laughing; he knew she'd pictured him there much more recently, and with another woman, and hadn't missed the look of relief that she'd tried to hide. 'But I have to confess I did love the ice-cream,' he went on. 'My mother had hundreds of photographs of me with the stuff plastered all over my face. Have you ever had real Italian ice-cream?'

'I don't know.'

'It's beyond description. And one of these days, when a publishing house wises up and accepts my first book, I'll take you there, sit you down in the Piazza Signoria and feed it to you on the end of a long spoon.'

As usual her heart leapt at any suggestion of a shared future.

'Actually,' he went on, 'I'd rather take you to Rome than Florence. The food's better, the culture is quite different, and I think you'd enjoy it more. Florence was a sluggish sort of place, I always felt, as if it's snored its way through time since the quattrocento, whereas Rome is vibrant with its past. Much more exciting, and as alive to the twentieth century as it is to Caesar, Michelangelo and Puccini.'

'I know what you mean,' she said dreamily, her mind conjuring up a wondrously romantic image of them strolling through the cobbled streets together. 'Madeleine and I were there last summer. We only stayed a few days but I loved it, though I didn't get to see much beyond the Via Condotti. I would have stayed longer, but Madeleine wanted to go to the Greek islands and soak up the sun.'

'I can imagine,' he said in a dry tone. 'Still, some day we'll explore the city together.'

As if they were tangible things she held onto his words wanting more than anything that they should come true. It was a while before she let the fantasy go and asked, 'Did you call the publisher again this morning?'

He nodded and sighed. 'He's now given the manuscript to someone else to read and says he'll be back to me as soon as he has some news.'

'At least it's not a no,' Marian said. Then seeing how despondent he looked, she went to sit in his lap. 'I wish there was something I could do to cheer you up,' she sighed.

'Just having you here is enough,' he smiled, and pushing her head back against his shoulder he kissed her.

'You two love-birds at it again?' Madeleine complained as she came in from the bedroom. She yawned and stretched as Paul and Marian looked up, then checking herself in the mirror, she dropped down onto the sofa. As she crossed her legs Marian winced at the glimpse of pubic hair. 'God, what a night last night,' Madeleine groaned, 'I didn't get in until gone three.'

'Fancy some breakfast?' Marian offered.

'Do I? I could eat a horse, but I'll settle for toast and coffee.'

'No butter, I'm afraid,' Paul said.

'Not to worry, I'll pop out for some,' Marian said, getting to her feet.

When she'd gone Madeleine lifted her legs onto the sofa and lay down. 'You comfortable enough sleeping on here?' she asked Paul.

'It's fine,' he answered, watching her with mild amusement.

Her mind was working fast. Her previous attempts at seducing him, by leaving the door open while she was in the bath, or coming home from work with very little on under her coat which she took off in the sitting-room – while Marian was safely tucked up in bed – had so far failed. She'd taken her problem to Jackie and Sharon, who had told her that the first thing she must do was get Marian out of the way. Perhaps a trip to the shops wasn't quite what they'd had in mind, but Madeleine was ready to seize any opportunity. To steal Paul O'Connell from her cousin had now become more than a resolution, it was an obsession. He was the only man she'd ever come across who had been able to resist her, and that she just couldn't accept. She gave no thought to the consequences of what she was trying to do; all that mattered was that she should get him into bed. Jackie's advice was that she must somehow get him to admit he didn't have sex with Marian, then once they were on the subject of sex and the fact that he wasn't getting it, she could really go to work.

'If you like,' Madeleine said now, 'Marian and I could push our beds together and you two could sleep in there. I wouldn't mind the sofa.'

'That's very generous of you,' he smiled. 'Maybe you should ask Marian.'

'OK, I will,' she said, not liking his answer much. 'But what about you? I mean, don't you want to sleep with her?'

'When she's ready.'

'You could be waiting a long time,' Madeleine scoffed. 'I take it you know she's a virgin?'

He nodded.

'Ludicrous, isn't it, at her age? Still, she's never had much luck in finding a boyfriend. Until now, that is.'

'I imagine she's been rather overshadowed by her beautiful cousin,' he ventured.

Madeleine allowed herself a few moments to bask in the compliment. This was much more like it. She pouted her lips and gave a little flutter of her eyelashes. 'Oh, I don't know,' she said coyly. 'Well, I have to admit I've had a lot of boyfriends, but Marian's pretty brainy, you know, some men go for that. The only trouble is, she's not very street-wise. She doesn't really know what's what when it comes to men.'

'Which you do, of course.'

Madeleine stretched her long limbs, then feigned modest surprise that her dressing-gown had fallen open. 'I've got a fair idea,' she answered, taking her time about pulling it together again.

'I'm sure you have.' He got to his feet and went back to his typewriter.

For a moment Madeleine was stymied. Their little chat had been shaping up nicely, so what was he winding paper into his bloody typewriter for? 'It must be pretty frustrating for you,' she said.

'What must?'

'Marian's chastity.'

When he didn't answer, she sat up. She looked at his profile, the long straight nose, the dark lashes and brows, the irresistible beauty of his mouth. His hands were bunched together under his chin, and her insides lurched at the imaginary sensation of those tapering fingers exploring her body. No man had ever turned her on like this before. Having sex was just something that came after someone had admired her body, a gift she could bestow should she feel so inclined. With Paul O'Connell it was different. She wanted him – on top of her, beneath her, inside her, all over her. Not in a million years would she admit to never having had an orgasm, but she wanted one as much as she wanted him, and a sixth sense told her that he could give it to her.

'If you like,' she said, wandering over to him, then running her fingers across his shoulders, 'I could help you to . . .'

'No thanks, Madeleine.'

'No thanks! You don't even know what I was going to say.'

'I think I do.'

She pulled her hand away. 'As a matter of fact, I was going to offer to let you make love to me.'

'And I was trying to spare us both the embarrassment.'

For a moment Madeleine was rigid with shock. An ugly colour swept across her face and he smiled as, from the corner of his eye, he saw her fingers twitch. If she slapped him he'd slap her back, and then what might she do? But she didn't, and he felt vaguely disappointed when she swept out of the room and slammed into the bedroom.

Turning back to his typewriter, he dismissed her from his mind. It wasn't that he was unaffected by her offer. Quite the contrary; she had perhaps the most sensuous body he'd ever seen. But Marian, with her shy smile, quirky humour and obvious devotion to them both, had come to mean a lot to him, and he wasn't prepared to jeopardise their relationship for a quick roll in the hay with Madeleine.

Madeleine flung herself down on her bed, beside herself with rage and humiliation. Seeing Marian's bedside lamp – the one her mother had bought her for Christmas – she grabbed it, and was about to hurl it at the wall when she stopped herself. She wouldn't give him the satisfaction, the bastard! He wanted it as much as she did, and he was just stringing her along so that she would go crawling to him on bended knee. Well, he could forget that, she didn't beg anyone. If anything, they begged her. And as for his farce of a relationship with Marian, she'd soon put the mockers on that. She'd make damned sure they shared a bedroom now, then they'd see just how long it took him to get fed up with the pious little bitch.

Half an hour later she heard him moving about in the hall. When he knocked on the door she snapped for him to come in, then nonchalantly carried on with her make up.

She was sitting at the dressing table. Her sleek hair gleamed as she shook her head, and her tanned skin glistened in the wintry sunlight. She was wearing a pair of jeans and a tight polo neck sweater. She didn't turn round, but she didn't have to – he could see her face in the mirror. His own was inscrutable as he took a moment to wonder at the incredible beauty that was so at odds with the coarse, self-adulating person who inhabited it.

'Changed your mind, have you?' she said tartly.

A smile flickered across his mouth before he answered. 'Actually,' he said, 'I'm worried about Marian. She's been gone over half an hour.'

Madeleine's face tightened. 'So?'

'I think I'll go and look for her.'

She turned round, her top lip arching into a sneer. 'Well, what are you waiting for, my permission?'

He shrugged. 'I was wondering if you might have some idea of where she'd be.'

'Why should I? She said she was going to the shops, so I presume that's where she is.'

He turned back into the hall and took his coat from the rack. 'If she comes back, tell her I've gone looking,' he said.

'I will – if I'm here.'

He didn't bother to remind her that Marian had gone out to get butter for *her* toast, he knew only too well that the girl had no conscience.

He'd been gone no more than five minutes when the front door opened again and Marian came in. Her face was flushed with excitement as she tore off her coat, then snatched up the carrier bag she'd dropped on the floor.

'Maddy,' she said in a whisper as Madeleine came into the hall, 'I've got to talk to you.'

Madeleine gave her a peculiarly acrimonious look – Marian really did look so much better these days, even that dull, long hair of hers seemed to shine. 'If it's something you don't want Paul to hear,' she said, 'then don't worry, he's gone out.'

Marian stopped, her eyes losing some of their sparkle. 'Oh? Did he say where?'

Madeleine sighed. 'As a matter of fact, he's gone looking for you. Where have you been?'

'Looking for me?' Marian's rapt smile irritated Madeleine and she tossed her head impatiently. 'I just can't believe the way he fusses over me,' Marian laughed. 'Oh Maddy, I love him so much. I feel like a different person since I've known him.'

'I'd never have noticed,' Madeleine replied. 'Anyway, I've got a surprise for you.'

'Me first!' Marian declared. 'I've got some news and a surprise. The news first.' She pushed Madeleine back into the bedroom and closed the door. 'I've been downstairs with Pamela Robbins,' she said. 'She's going away filming next week for twelve weeks and she's letting her flat to a director who's going to be in Bristol shooting a film for

Channel Four.' Just as she'd known it would, this immediately sparked Madeleine's interest. 'And you'll never guess who it is,' Marian went on. 'Matthew Cornwall!'

Madeleine's face was blank. 'Who's he?'

'Oh Maddy! He's just about the best known director in the country, and he's absolutely gorgeous. You were only reading about him the other day in one of your magazines.'

'Was I?' Madeleine said. 'I can't remember. When's he moving in?'

'Next Monday apparently. Oh Maddy, just imagine, Matthew Cornwall right here in our house. This could be just the break you've been looking for.'

'It could indeed,' Madeleine answered, but carefully hid what she was really thinking – that another man on the scene, and one like Matthew What's-His-Name, could be just what she was looking for to make Paul as jealous as hell. 'We'll have to invite him up for a drink,' she said.

'Whatever you like. Now, what's your surprise?'

'You'll have to wait and see. And yours?'

'You're going to have to wait for that too,' Marian chuckled, 'but if I can pull it off it's absolutely fantastic.' She took a packet of butter from her carrier and handed it to Madeleine. 'Now go and put the kettle on and make us both some tea and toast.' She waited until Madeleine had gone, then opened the wardrobe door and pushed the carrier bag to the back.

When Paul returned he found them sitting on the floor munching toast and flicking through old magazines, trying to find the article about Matthew Cornwall. When she saw him, Marian jumped to her feet and put her arms round him.

'I was worried about you,' he smiled as she kissed him. 'Where have you been?'

'Planning a surprise,' she said, 'and talking to our neighbour downstairs.'

'What kind of surprise?'

She gave a sigh of exasperation. 'It wouldn't be a surprise if I told you, would it?'

'She's being very mysterious,' Madeleine yawned.

'Speak for yourself,' Marian retorted. 'Anyway, want some toast?'

Paul nodded, and once Marian had left the room he caught Madeleine's eye and held it until she looked away. He might not be prepared to do anything about it, but he got quite a kick out of teasing her. She was sitting cross-legged on the floor and looked daggers at him, before turning round to switch on the TV, stabbing the button hard and leaving him in no doubt that she'd have taken great pleasure in doing the same to him.

'What's the telly on for?' Marian said when she came in with a tray of more toast and coffee. No one answered, so she put the tray on the table and turned Paul's wrist to see the time. 'The lunchtime news should be on the other side, shall we watch that?' she said, looking at Madeleine. When Madeleine only shrugged she started playing around with the tuner button, trying to get a decent reception for BBC 1.

'Stop!' Madeleine suddenly shouted. 'Go back! Go back!'

Marian fiddled with the knob until she found the hazy picture she'd just passed. 'This?' she said.

Madeleine was staring at the screen, and surprised by the intent, almost angry expression on her face, Marian turned to watch too.

'I'm not sure that coup is quite the right word,' Stephanie Ryder was telling her interviewer, 'but naturally my partner and I are delighted to have the rights.'

'Olivia Hastings has been missing for some five years now,' the interviewer said. 'Just about everything that is known about her disappearance has been

– 62 –

published in the press, heard on TV, indeed written about in Deborah Foreman's book. Will you be introducing anything new? New evidence, new theories about what happened in Italy?'

Stephanie smiled. 'You'll have to wait for the film to come out for the answer to that, I'm afraid.'

'Olivia Hastings,' Marian said, thoughtfully. 'Isn't she the girl . . ?'

'Sssh!' Madeleine slapped her hand.

'And will the film be released here first, or in America?' the interviewer wanted to know.

'America. I hope to make it with an English crew, but the finance, of course, is totally American. As indeed, is Olivia.'

Madeleine snorted. 'God, she's a stuck-up old cow, isn't she?'

Astonished by this sudden outburst, Marian turned to look at her. 'Who?' she asked.

Madeleine sprang to her feet. 'Her there! That stupid bitch of a producer, Stephanie whatever-her-name-is. God, she thinks she's it just because she's being interviewed on the telly. Someone should tell her, she looks like a constipated pig!'

'But she's stunning,' Marian objected, as Madeleine stormed from the room. 'What on earth was all that about?' she said, turning to Paul.

'Search me.'

Concerned that someone she had never met before had so upset Madeleine, Marian followed her into the bedroom. She was sitting at the mirror, dragging a brush furiously through her hair. 'What's wrong?' Marian asked.

'What do you mean, what's wrong?'

'Well, isn't it a bit strange to . . .'

'Oh shut up, Marian!'

'No, I won't. I want to know why you flew off the handle like that.'

Madeleine jerked herself round to face her cousin. 'Because, if you must know, she was the old bag who threw my clothes at me in the HTV club bar. Satisfied? And if you tell Paul, I'll kill you.'

Feeling her mouth start to twitch, Marian thought it wise to leave the room before Madeleine noticed. As she walked back into the sitting-room she looked at Stephanie Ryder, whose interview was coming to an end. No wonder Madeleine had been so upset, Stephanie Ryder wasn't only a producer, she was beautiful too. Madeleine had never told her that. With Stephanie's air of cool self-confidence and sophistication, it was no wonder Madeleine felt so wretched and humiliated.

That evening Madeleine wasn't working, so after she'd been for her sun-bed session the three of them pooled their resources and went to the Chateau Wine Bar. Neither Marian nor Madeleine was in a particularly good mood because they'd had a row about the way Madeleine squandered money on beauty treatments when it could have been used to pay off some of the bills. Madeleine's defence was that she had to look her best if Matthew Cornwall was arriving the following week, and ungraciously, Marian had given in.

Madeleine's set, as usual, were grouped round the back bar, and after a few drinks Madeleine became increasingly animated. It was all an attempt to demonstrate to Paul how popular she was, but he was sitting at a table with Marian, engrossed in an amusing discussion of existentialism and completely oblivious to the way Madeleine was flirting with any man who came her way.

By eleven o'clock Madeleine was at screaming-point. Jackie and Sharon had now witnessed how close Marian and Paul were, and both had grudgingly admitted that they didn't think Madeleine was going to win after all.

'I mean, look at the way he looks at her,' Sharon said. 'He hasn't got eyes for anyone else.'

'In a way you can hardly blame him,' Jackie chipped in. 'I'd hardly have recognised her. Of course, she'll never be a raving beauty,' she added hurriedly, 'but you know what being in love does to a woman, and I'm telling you, I've never seen such a transformation. Has she lost weight?'

'God knows,' Madeleine answered through gritted teeth.

'I think you're going to have to bow out graciously this time,' Sharon said.

'Not on your life,' Madeleine hissed, now more determined than ever. 'I've got another card up my sleeve, and this one's bound to work.'

'What was all that about?' Marian asked when they were leaving. Madeleine was still laughing because Jackie had shouted out something about a three-card trick.

'Oh, nothing,' Madeleine answered. 'Now come on, let's hurry up and get home, I've got a surprise, if you remember.'

'Well?' Marian said, when they got in the front door. 'What is it?'

Paul watched Madeleine throw her coat on a chair and rush to the mirror to check how much damage the sudden downpour had caused. He hadn't been as oblivious to her during the evening as she'd thought, but if she'd known what he was thinking she'd have wished he had been. He was repelled by the way she prowled shamelessly about the wine bar on the hunt for a man, and her loud laughter and suggestive eyes were cringe-making – though he was intrigued to see what lengths she would go to in pursuit of her goal.

'Madeleine!' Marian half shouted with frustration.

Madeleine looked at Paul, but he was turning on the

gas fire. 'I,' Madeleine declared, dragging her eyes from him and turning to Marian, 'have decided that from now on I am going to sleep on the sofa. So you two can have the bedroom to yourselves.'

Paul turned round, his eyebrows raised and the corners of his mouth tight. He should have been prepared for her to pull a stunt like this and he was angry, as much with himself for not having foreseen it as with Madeleine for putting Marian in this position.

'Madeleine,' Marian gulped. Her insides were in an uproar and her voice did nothing to hide her mortification. 'Do you think we could talk about this? In the bedroom?'

Paul caught Madeleine's arm as she started to leave, and pulled her back. 'No, Marian,' he said, 'you and *I* will talk about this.' Then letting Madeleine go, he took Marian's hand and led her down the hall. 'Sit down,' he said, as he closed the bedroom door.

She did, but before he could speak she immediately started to gabble an apology for Madeleine's lack of tact. 'I promise you I didn't put her up to it,' she was saying. 'I had no idea. It was as much of a shock to me as it . . .' She stopped as he put a finger over her lips. Then he sat down and took her hands in his.

'I'd like to take Madeleine up on her offer,' he said.

Marian's eyes and mouth formed three circles as she stared at him. Then a rush of colour stained her white face.

'If you're completely averse to the idea,' he continued, 'then of course we can forget it. Or, if you like, we can keep the beds separate and I will promise not to molest you.' Slowly her eyes started to reflect the humour in his. 'I think you would be wise to say yes,' he went on. 'If nothing else, it will stop Madeleine from embarrassing you in this way again. Which, given the opportunity, she will, I'm quite sure.'

'She doesn't mean anything by it, you know,' Marian

said, aware that she was veering away from the point. 'It's just her sense of humour.'

'I'm not sure whether humour's the right word,' he muttered, 'but I'm not interested in Madeleine. What I want to know is your answer.'

Marian bowed her head. Her heart was thumping violently and she was sure he must be aware of the way her hands shook. Eventually she nodded, and he pulled her into his arms.

'I take it that's a yes,' he whispered. 'But it shouldn't have happened like this. We'll push the beds together, but I'll keep to my side until you tell me yourself that you're ready for more. Until then I think it might be better if you let Madeleine think that we are making love. Now stay here and I'll go and tell her to come and fetch her things. And would madam like a nightcap?'

'Madam would.' The words tripped out so lightly that she was amazed they had been spoken by her own voice, but she was smiling when Madeleine came flying into the room, closed the door and threw her arms round her.

'Oh Marian, I'm really glad you said yes,' she cried, almost choking on her rage. 'Let me help you push the beds together, and I'll give you a few hints.' Letting Marian go, she dived between the beds and picked up the small cabinet that separated them. Marian watched her, still too dazed by the events of the last few minutes for anything approaching coherent thought.

'We'll suppose you're already in the nude,' Madeleine said, carrying the cabinet over to the window. She stole a quick glance at her cousin, and satisfied with Marian's dismayed expression, she carried on: 'You should keep the light on, men always prefer that, and when he kisses you – has he used his tongue yet?'

Marian shook her head.

Madeleine hid her amazement and continued. 'Well, when you're building up to it,' she said, 'he'll put his tongue in your mouth. It's sort of the first part of foreplay. You should put yours in his too, by the way. Then he'll probably kiss your neck, then your boobs. Now when his hand touches you down below . . .'

'Oh, stop it, Madeleine.'

'Why? What's the matter?'

Marian shrugged. 'It's personal, isn't it?'

'I thought you wanted some advice?'

'I do – did, but . . .'

'Look, if you're going to be this bashful with me, how the hell are you going to be with him? Anyway, it's all perfectly natural, everyone does it – well, everyone except you. And he'll have done it hundreds of times before, he'll know exactly what he's doing, so you're going to look pretty stupid lying there like a dummy, aren't you?'

'I won't lie there like a dummy!'

'Then what are you going to do? Come on, tell me! See, you don't know, do you? What if asks you to put his thing in your mouth?'

Marian looked at her, aghast. 'He wouldn't . . . would he?'

'Oh, for heaven's sake, of course he would. And you'll gag, everyone does, especially if he asks you to swallow his sperm, but you'd better get used to the idea because men just love oral sex. And get him to do it to you too, it's *fantastic*!'

'I'm not listening to you any more,' Marian cried. 'You're insane if you think I'm going to ask him to do that to me.'

'Do what? You don't even know what a man does when he's got his head down there, do you?'

'Not really, and I don't want, to either.'

'All right! All right! Forget that. But whatever you do, you've got to play with his balls.'

Despite herself, Marian giggled. 'Honestly, Madeleine!'

'Hold them in your hand for a while, and make sure his

thing's absolutely rock hard, then squeeze. I'm telling you, it'll blow his mind.'

Marian looked dubious. 'But I thought men found that painful.'

Madeleine rolled her eyes. 'God, you've got a lot to learn. That's why I told you to make sure it's really hard, it doesn't hurt then.'

Marian flopped down on the bed. 'I'm going to make a real hash of this, I just know it,' she groaned, forgetting for a moment that it wasn't going to happen that night.

'You won't,' Madeleine assured her. 'Just do as I've told you and have plenty of tissues at hand, the blood makes a real mess.'

'Blood? Oh yes, the blood.'

Marian could feel herself sinking into despondency and was more relieved than she should have been when she remembered that Paul had said they'd do nothing until she was ready.

She undressed in the bathroom, wishing she had something a little more fetching to put on than a flannelette nightgown. When she studied herself in the mirror she was amazed to find her own face looking back at her with such calm, when inside a tempest of conflicting emotions raged. Her chest heaved with nervous breath, yet she felt light-headed with exhilaration. She longed for him to touch her in the intimate places that were tingling so warmly, yet the thought frightened and embarrassed her.

He was already in bed when she went into the bedroom, and she almost gasped at the sight of his naked chest. It wasn't that she hadn't seen it before, but for some reason it looked different tonight. She felt a thrill run through her veins and quickly turned away.

He looked up from the book he was reading. 'Ah, my turn in the bathroom,' he said, throwing back the sheets. 'Your nightcap's on the dressing-table.'

'Thank you.' Her voice was hoarse, and her legs wobbled as she walked. In case he was naked she kept her eyes averted, but caught his reflection in the mirror as he went out of the door, and seeing that he wore his shorts she didn't know whether she was disappointed or glad. But the dark hair on his thighs affected her so severely that it took the rigidity from her knees and she sat down, clutching the brandy and shivering.

When he reappeared, smelling of toothpaste, he got back into bed. Then, reaching across and throwing open the sheets on her bed, he said, 'Come along, you'll freeze sitting there. And as I said, I'm not going to molest you.'

She walked to the bed and climbed in. In all her life she'd never felt quite so strange.

He picked up her hand and kissed it. 'Are you all right?' he asked.

She nodded. Then a few seconds later she whispered his name.

When she didn't continue, he took her chin and turned her to face him. 'What is it?'

For a long time she looked at him, not really knowing what she wanted to say, except to let him know that she was glad he was there. But it seemed so trite, and in the end she lowered her eyes and shook her head.

He leaned over and touched her mouth with his. Then pulling back the sheets on his bed he said, 'Come here. Get in beside me and let me hold you.'

When all she did was stare at him with confused, wide eyes, he smiled. 'I'm not going to do anything you don't want me to,' he said. 'I only want you to feel safe in my arms.'

She moved awkwardly, then her foot caught in the hem of her nightgown and she tumbled against him. She wanted to cry with humiliation. But he laughed, and turning her round, settled her head on his shoulder. 'Just think,' he said, kissing the tip of her nose, 'now we can tell everyone that you literally fell into bed with me.'

A bubble of laughter collided with a sob, and suddenly she was so happy that she put an arm round his neck and lifted her face to kiss him.

'Don't push your luck,' he said, unwinding himself, 'I'm only flesh and blood after all. And you're becoming more desirable by the minute.'

He turned off the light and she lay back in his arms, sighing contentedly as the tension ebbed from her body. For now it was enough just to be with him like this, and to know that when she found the courage to tell him she was ready, he would be too.

In the sitting-room Madeleine lay staring up at the ceiling, her breathing quickened by fury. Her only consolation was that any minute now, if Marian adhered to her instructions, she would hear Paul O'Connell howl with pain.

But it didn't happen; in fact, once the sliver of light from under the bedroom door had disappeared she heard nothing at all. This reassured her a little, but it was still a long time before she fell asleep.

The next morning she found Marian in the kitchen making breakfast, humming along to the radio and practically skipping between the toaster and the kettle. One look at her face was enough to tell Madeleine that despite the silence, something *had* happened between Marian and Paul the night before, and she swept out of the kitchen, mumbling that she didn't want any breakfast. She headed straight into the bedroom, remembering too late that Paul was in there.

He was standing beside the wardrobe, but turned round as she came in, doing nothing to conceal his nudity. His face registered only mild surprise when he saw it was her, and then he laughed quietly as her eyes flew to his penis, at the same time taking in the firmness of his thighs, the clutch of black pubic hair, and the hard muscles of his abdomen.

'I'm sorry,' she murmured, experiencing a rare embarrassment, but when she made to close the door he said:

'What's the matter, Madeleine? You've seen a naked man before, so why are you running away?'

'I'm not running away,' she hissed. 'For all I care, you can walk around naked all day long.'

He grinned. 'I expect you'd like that, wouldn't you?'

'It makes no difference to me what you do.'

'What's the matter, have you lost your nerve now Marian's around? If you care to look again, you'll see you're having something of an effect on me.'

Unable to stop herself, she looked at his hardening penis. Under her scrutiny it grew further still, until slowly she started to smile. Then looking back at his face, she said, 'Well, you know who you can stick that up, don't you,' and she flounced out of the room.

His explosion of laughter annoyed her, but the fact that she'd given him an erection was what really mattered. And the very morning after he'd first slept with Marian, too! So her little plan of forcing them into bed together had worked after all. Obviously Marian hadn't satisfied him – he'd made that more than plain. Well, if he thought she was going to drop her knickers now that it suited him, he could think again. She'd get him on the run a bit before she gave in, she might even try and get him to beg.

Over the following weekend Madeleine's mood fluctuated between depression and elation. The problem was that since their short encounter in the bedroom, Paul had behaved as though nothing had happened, almost as if she didn't exist. In her better moments she managed to convince herself that it was because Marian was always around, and he was just biding his time. But in her worst moments she hated her cousin with such bitterness that she could barely be civil to her.

Then on Monday Matthew Cornwall arrived. They knew he was there because a package arrived for him, by hand, which Marian carried up the stairs. The man who answered the door told her that Matthew was on the phone, so he had taken the package. Then Marian dashed up the stairs to tell Madeleine.

In her excitement and eagerness to cheer her cousin up, she didn't notice how pinched Madeleine's face was. Paul was at his typewriter where she'd left him, and dropping a kiss on his head, she spun round and grasped Madeleine's hands. 'He's here!' she cried. 'He's downstairs now.'

'Who?' Paul asked, looking up.

'Matthew Cornwall, of course.' She turned back to Madeleine. 'I brought a parcel up for him,' she explained. 'I'd have invited him up for a drink there and then, but he was on the phone when I knocked. I caught a glimpse of him, though. He's really good-looking, Maddy! Anyway, what do you think? Shall we write him a note?'

Madeleine looked at Paul, but he was laughing at Marian's enthusiasm. 'Give the man a chance,' he said. 'If he's only just got here, then . . .'

'Oh, don't go all cautious on me,' Marian cried. 'We've got to do this for Madeleine. I know, you go down and invite him . . . Oh Paul!' she groaned, when he held up his hands and started to shake his head.

'I'm having nothing to do with this conspiracy,' he said, and circling Marian's waist, he pulled her onto his lap. 'Now, how about a proper kiss when you come in the door?' he demanded.

Marian shot a look at Madeleine. She hadn't missed her cousin's looks of desolation, even malice, when Paul kissed her lately. But Madeleine had turned away and was already walking out of the door. Only then did Marian realise that Madeleine hadn't spoken a word since she'd returned. She turned to Paul. 'What's wrong? Did you two have a row while I was out?'

'No,' he answered. And before she could ask any more he tore a piece of paper from his typewriter and told her to read it.

He found Madeleine in the kitchen. 'Well,' he said, filling the kettle, 'the man's arrived, so what are you going to do now?'

'That's my business.'

'Not more than ten minutes ago you were threatening to have sex with him to make me jealous.'

'Would it?'

He turned to look at her, surprised by the note of uncertainty in her voice when only moments before Marian walked in she had sneeringly informed him that he could drive himself mad thinking about what she was going to do with Matthew Cornwall. Now her lovely violet eyes looked sad, and realising that perhaps he'd gone too far in teasing her, he swallowed the sarcastic remark he'd been about to make and said, 'It might.' It was a lie, but he knew it was important to Madeleine to have her sexuality confirmed.

A contemptuous smile suddenly warped her mouth. 'Well, I hope you fucking rot with it,' she said, and pulling herself upright, she stalked out of the kitchen.

Not knowing what to do next, she decided to consult Jackie and Sharon. They met at Sharon's flat in Henleaze.

'If I were you I'd go for it,' Jackie said. 'I mean, what have you got to lose? A bit of rumpy-pumpy with Matthew Cornwall and all your problems could be solved.'

'How?'

'In the first place he might give you a part in the film he's doing, or at the very least put you in touch with some influential people; and in the second, Paul's admitted it would make him jealous. That's what you wanted, isn't it?'

'Yes,' Madeleine answered slowly. 'But making him jealous doesn't necessarily mean he'll dump Marian.'

'If you can get some decent contacts out of Matthew Cornwall,' Sharon said, 'or even better, get him to cast you in his film, then Paul O'Connell will be eating out of your hand.'

'How do you work that out?'

'What's the most important thing to Paul? His writing. If you were to become famous you could open all sorts of doors for him, and he'll see that in less time than it'll take you to get Matthew Cornwall in the sack.'

Madeleine wasn't too sure about that, in fact her self-confidence had waned to an all-time low over the past few weeks. That men were still calling her up all the time, that heads turned whenever she walked into a room, even that she'd managed to give Paul an erection, didn't matter; she still hadn't been able to get him away from Marian. And if Paul was managing to resist her, what was to say that Matthew Cornwall couldn't too?

She didn't voice her reservations, but went home to mull them over in her own time. But as she walked upstairs to the flat, Marian came rushing in behind her, waving an envelope and shouting, 'I've got it! I've got it! I've got it!'

'Got what?' Madeleine asked, watching Marian's face and feeling her heart turn over with a painful combination of envy, love and incredulity. Sure, Marian did look a whole lot better these days, but what did a man like Paul see in her?

'The surprise I told you about,' Marian answered, and she ran on ahead, telling Madeleine to hurry up if she wanted to find out what it was.

'OK, are you ready?' Marian asked five minutes later. The three of them were in the sitting-room, Paul at his typewriter, Madeleine perched on the arm of the sofa and

Marian beside the table. Her eyes were glittering, and as she looked at Paul he laughed and pulled her into his lap.

'What are you up to?' he murmured, giving her a squeeze and brushing his lips against her hair.

Madeleine coughed loudly, then said, 'If you don't mind, there are other people in the room. And I've been waiting almost a week to find out what this surprise is, so shall we get on with it?' In fact, she'd forgotten all about it, but now she was intrigued enough to have pushed her problems to the back of her mind – at least until she knew what Marian was up to.

'Sorry,' Marian said, turning to look at her. Then remembering that she wanted to see Paul's face when she told them, she moved across the room and stood in front of the fire.

Both Madeleine and Paul watched as she tore open the envelope she was holding and, with a theatrical flourish of her arm, produced three air tickets. 'We are going to Rome!' she announced.

Madeleine and Paul stared at her, dumbfounded, and she burst out laughing. Madeleine was the first to recover her senses and pounced on the obvious question. 'Where the hell did you get the money?'

There was a flash of discomfort in Marian's eyes before she answered. 'I cashed in an insurance policy,' she lied. She didn't want to tell them how, after being turned down for a loan at the bank – who had asked her to hand over her cheque card while she was there – she had gone to a finance company in Horfield and managed to wheedle the money out of them. 'I got fifteen hundred pounds,' she said, 'and I thought, to hell with the bills, we could all do with a holiday. So, my loves, we are going for a long weekend in Rome.'

Paul was shaking his head, knowing she had done it for him. He walked over to her and took her face between his hands. His eyes looked searchingly into hers, and then he whispered, 'I love you, Marian Deacon.'

'I love you too,' she breathed, and suddenly she was crying.

'Oh God!' Madeleine muttered, but managed to restrain herself from going any further. But as she watched his fingers run through Marian's hair, his lips cover Marian's, her heart started to pound, and before she could stop herself she screamed and ran from the room.

Tearing herself away, Marian rushed after her. 'Maddy! Maddy! What is it?' she cried, but Madeleine slammed the bathroom door in her face. 'For God's sake, let me in!' Marian shouted, rattling the handle and banging on the door. But Madeleine couldn't answer. Her voice was engulfed by sobs and tears of desperation coursed down her face. 'Why?' her heart was crying. 'Why doesn't he love me?'

Marian knocked again and again until in the end Paul came to get her. 'Leave her,' he said. 'She'll come out when she's ready.'

Marian looked bewildered, but at the same time, as they went into the kitchen she'd already guessed what was wrong. 'We shouldn't flaunt things in her face like this,' she said quietly. 'More than anything else in the world she wants a boyfriend, someone who really loves her. She'd never admit it, but it means even more to her than being famous. She's lonely, and the way she carries on with men is all an act to cover it up. She's always been terrified of being ignored. It's why I got her a ticket to come to Rome with us. I couldn't leave her behind. You don't mind, do you?'

'Of course not.'

'You're so wonderful to me,' Marian whispered. 'I wish she could find someone too.'

Paul shrugged. 'Who knows, maybe this Matthew Cornwall could be the answer to all her prayers. Now, about Rome.'

Marian held up her hands. 'No, I know what you're going to say. That it's very generous of me, you'll be grateful 'til the end of your days, but you can't accept.'

He nodded.

'Which is why I bought non-refundable tickets, so now you have to go whether you like it or not.'

He threw back his head, then laughing, he scooped her into his arms, lifting her right off the floor. 'I like it,' he said. As he put her down again he noticed that her cheeks had turned pink and she wasn't able to look at him. 'What's on your mind?' he asked. And when her face turned an even deeper red and she started to wipe down the draining board, he smiled, quickly understanding what she wanted to say but couldn't quite find the courage for. 'A kind of honeymoon?' he suggested, and she turned her head to one side, pursing her lips with shy laughter.

Using his fingers to bring her face round to his, he leaned forward and touched his lips against hers. At first the kiss was so gentle she could barely feel more than his breath, then slowly his arms encircled her and he pushed his tongue deep into her mouth.

When he pulled away she clung to him, knowing that her legs were too weak to support her. 'Something tells me you rather liked that,' he whispered. His eyes were soft and teasing, and a gurgle of laughter escaped her reddened mouth.

'I wish I could buy you a trousseau,' he said, still holding her against him and pushing the hair back from her face. 'But then, that flannelette nightie just drives me wild!'

He yelped as she kicked him, and spinning out of his arms, she said, 'For that you can have the single room and Madeleine and I will share the double.'

'We'll see about that,' he said. 'And now I'm off to the library to give you and Madeleine a chance to talk.'

'You're too bloody perfect for words,' Marian quipped,

and as she helped him on with his coat she wanted to tell him she loved him again, but was too afraid she might be overdoing it. She walked downstairs with him, on the pretext of seeing if there was any afternoon mail, but really in the hope he would kiss her like that again. But he gave her no more than a fleeting peck on the lips, and left her clutching a red telephone bill.

She was surprised to find Madeleine in the kitchen when she went back upstairs, and unsure what to say, she hovered in the doorway, watching as Madeleine poured wine into two glasses, then turned and handed her one. 'I'm sorry, Marian,' she said. 'I don't know what came over me. I suppose it's the thought of losing you.'

'You're not going to lose me,' Marian answered, taking the glass and following Madeleine into the sitting room. 'Nothing's going to change. The three of us will stay together, and then when you meet someone, well, there'll be four of us.'

Madeleine fell back on the sofa. 'I can't come to Rome, Marian. I . . .'

'I'm sorry, but you have to,' Marian interrupted. 'As I told Paul, the tickets are non-refundable, and besides, I want you to be there. Now, I've hidden the brochure in the bedroom so let's have a look at the hotel. And I've had another idea, too. Why don't we open an account at Debenham's or John Lewis and buy ourselves some clothes to take with us?'

Madeleine's face was an amusing combination of exasperation and misery. 'There's no stopping you, is there?' she said as Marian laughed. Then her eyes lit up. 'Ten thousand pounds!' she challenged.

'*Ten*?' Marian scoffed. 'Two hundred thousand pounds!'

She shrieked as Madeleine pinched her, and cried, 'A Mercedes sports car for me and a Reliant Robin for you!'

'A mansion for me with a shed at the end of the garden for you,' Madeleine countered.

'A tropical island for me and one acre of the Pacific for you.'

'What am I supposed to do with that?' Madeleine cried.

'I don't know. A nice intimate cruise for you and Matthew Cornwall?'

Madeleine thought about that, then said, 'Yes, why not? Now go and get that brochure, and tomorrow we'll go to Debenham's and spend, spend, spend.'

By the time Paul came back Madeleine had been out for another bottle of wine, and while Marian was tipsy Madeleine was 'pissed out of her skull', as she informed him.

'And now,' she said, staggering to her feet, 'I'm going downstairs to introduce myself to Matthew Cornwall.'

'Oh God, no, Maddy!' Marian cried. 'Not like that. You'll ruin everything.'

'Rubbish!' Madeleine declared. 'And I'll tell you what, if he plays his cards right he can do whatever he likes to me, just so long as he gives me a part in his film and makes me rich and famous.' She looked at Paul but her eyes were too blurry to read his expression.

Marian giggled. 'Paul, stop her,' she said, but Paul merely stood aside and watched as Madeleine teetered down the hall and somehow managed to wrest her bra from under her sweater. Turning back, she laughed and threw it at him.

'I'll have to go after her,' Marian said.

As she passed him, Paul caught her arm. 'Let her go,' he said. 'She'll only turn nasty if you get in her way while she's in that state.'

'I suppose so,' Marian sighed. 'And with any luck he won't be in.'

Madeleine was picking her way carefully down the stairs. When she reached the landing below, she rapped hard on the door. She didn't have long to wait before he answered, and when she saw him she blinked several times. They'd never found that picture of him, but Marian had said he was gorgeous. Well, he wasn't bad, but she'd been expecting someone taller and not quite so thin. Still, he had a nice enough face, despite the glasses, and until Paul came along she'd always quite liked dark men.

'Hello,' she slurred. 'I'm Madeleine. I live upstairs.'

He smiled. 'Hello.'

'I was wondering whether you'd like a drink.'

'Well this isn't . . .'

'I'd invite you up to my flat, but my cousin's there with her boyfriend. But we could always have a drink in yours.'

'As I was saying, this isn't my flat, exactly.'

'I know. It's Pamela's, but she won't mind. We're having drinks together all the time down here.' She brushed past him. 'Come on, I'll show you where everything is.'

He stood aside and watched Madeleine walk down the hall. Then taking a deep breath, he closed the door and followed her into the bedroom.

'Oops! Silly me!' she giggled. 'Took the wrong turning.' She backed out and weaved her way into the kitchen. 'Now, where does she keep the wine?' she said, looking round.

'I've got some already open,' he told her.

'Wonderful. Lead me to it.'

He took her into the sitting room and gently eased her into a chair. 'So you live upstairs?' he said, his lean face alive with amusement.

'With my cousin,' she answered. 'Who I hate. Well, I don't exactly hate her, but I can't stand her.'

'Oh,' he said. Then after a pause: 'And what do you do, Madeleine?'

'Do?' She looked perplexed. 'Oh, do! I'm a shtrip-o-gram girl. You know what that is?'

'I think so,' he smiled.

'Can I have a drink?'

'Certainly.' He walked over to the sideboard and poured her a glass of wine.

'Actually,' she said, trying out her best voice, 'that's why I came down here. You see, I want to be a model and I thought you might be able to . . . I mean, I want to be an actress and I hoped you might give me a part in your film.' She took a gulp of wine, then fumbled the glass onto the small table beside her.

'I see,' he said. 'Well, it's not that . . .'

'I know all about the casting couch,' she interrupted, 'but I'd rather do a proper audition. You know, prove what I can do.'

He covered his smile with his hand. 'I think it might . . .'

'But if you want to do it first, that's all right because it'll make Paul jealous, but only if you promise to give me an audition.'

His eyebrows shot towards his receding hairline and this time he actually laughed. 'And who's Paul?' he asked.

'My cousin's boyfriend.'

'I see.' He was thoughtful for a moment, then said, 'So what you're saying is, if I promise to give you an audition you'll . . .' he hesitated, not quite sure how to finish the sentence.

'Let you fuck me,' she supplied, sitting back and crossing her legs.

He couldn't help being shocked, but laughed all the same. 'That's very generous of you, Madeleine,' he said, 'but I think you should . . .' He stopped as she suddenly yanked her sweater over her head.

During all the years he'd worked in films, he'd come across dozens of women who were only too keen to make themselves available, drunk or sober. In that respect Madeleine was no exception. But what did set her apart from the rest was not only the size of her breasts – he'd always found it difficult to resist large breasts – but the look in her eyes as she waited for his reaction to them. He'd never seen anything quite so erotic.

She stood up and walked towards him. 'Do you like my tits?' she said.

'Very much,' he murmured, watching them as they swayed gently against her ribcage.

'Everyone likes my tits,' she said, scooping them into her hands. She rolled her nipples between her fingers until they were rich and red and succulent. 'If you want to touch them, you've got to promise to give me a chance,' she told him.

'OK.'

'But I don't want an audition, I want a part.'

He shrugged. 'Sure.'

She brushed her hand across the front of his trousers and feeling the erection, she suddenly moaned. It was weeks since she'd had sex, and in all that time her body had been on fire for Paul. Now, at the touch of a man lust charged through her veins, and she closed her eyes, whimpering as she told herself it was Paul's mouth that had closed around her nipples; it was Paul's hand pressing into her crotch, it was Paul's trousers she was undoing.

And it was Paul who removed her jeans, pushed her urgently to the floor and opened her legs. And when he jerked himself inside her it was still Paul. She wrapped her legs around him, returned his kisses with fury, pulled at his hair and shouted for him to go faster and harder. Then suddenly she could feel it starting to happen; the heat rushing to her loins, the muscles tensing around his penis, control fleeing, and her fingers dug into his buttocks, urging him to push her over the edge.

But then his hips slowed and he ground them into her as he shouted, 'JEE-SUS!' before gasping and spluttering at the burning flood of semen that spurted from his body.

He was lying over her, sweat pouring from his skin and the breath still shuddering from his lungs. She turned to look at him and blinked. For a moment she wondered who he was, then remembering, the corner of her mouth dropped in a wry smile. If it could be that good just pretending it was Paul, then God only knew what it would be like if it was him. But right now Matthew Cornwall was more important, and because of the way he had succumbed so easily, then yelled with such desperation for his maker when he came, she felt an intoxicating swell of pure victory enfold her.

'Would you like to come and meet Paul and Marian?' she said, as they were getting dressed.

He glanced at his watch. 'I've got to go out. Perhaps some other time.'

'But you'll keep your promise?'

He nodded. 'Sure.'

'What's the part?'

He looked at her blankly.

'You said I had a part in your film.'

'Oh, yes, sure. We're always looking for support cast, lucky I met you, really.'

Her face broke into a beaming smile. 'You mean, you really have got a part for me?'

He turned to the table and scribbled down a number. 'Here,' he said, handing it to her, 'call this number tomorrow morning. Ask for Dorothy and she'll tell you when to turn up.'

Madeleine snatched the piece of paper, threw her arms around him, pushed her tongue deeply and sensuously into his mouth, then rushed out of the flat.

Marian and Paul were sitting on the sofa watching TV when they heard the front door slam and Madeleine come running down the hall. 'I've cracked it!' she squealed, waving her piece of paper and dancing round the room. 'I've got a part.'

Paul and Marian exchanged looks. 'Well done you,'

Marian said, not even bothering to hide her surprise. 'What is it?'

'I don't know yet. I have to call this number tomorrow morning and "Dorothy" will tell me where I have to turn up.'

'So it's an audition?'

'No. I told you, he's cast me in a part.' She pulled Marian off the sofa and spun her round. 'I'm going to be in a film!' she cried.

After what had happened with the props men at HTV, Marian couldn't help being sceptical. But she said nothing, and the following morning when Madeleine called Dorothy, Dorothy asked her to report to the Holiday Inn the following Tuesday at seven in the morning, when there would be transport waiting to take her to location. Marian heaved a sigh of relief and went off to the Bristol Hippodrome to do a half day's typing.

'And what did you have to do to get the part?' Paul asked when he came back upstairs after seeing Marian off.

Madeleine was reading her horoscope and didn't bother to look up as she answered, 'What do you think?'

Paul sat down at the table, leaned back in his chair and grinned. 'So you actually screwed him.'

'Don't sound so surprised. Believe it or not, there are men around who behave like men – not like some I could mention.'

'Meaning me?'

She looked up with an arrogant smile on her lips. 'Well, let's face it, apart from flashing it at me, you've done nothing with yours in months.'

His shout of laughter nettled her, and she threw him a filthy look and started to get up.

'A word of advice before you go,' he said. 'You don't make people jealous by sleeping around these days. All you make them is afraid of what they might catch.'

He caught her hand before it struck his face, and twisted it behind her back.

'You bastard!' she hissed.

He nodded. 'You can call me anything you like, Madeleine, but I can't help wondering – if she knew what you were really up to – what Marian would call you?' He let her go, and whistling tunelessly he walked into the hall, picked up his coat and went out.

– 4 –

The trip to Rome was marred by only one thing: totally unused as she was to planning for these eventualities, Marian started her period on the very morning they left. Paul laughed, but Marian was mortified, and it took every ounce of cajolery he could muster to persuade her that it didn't matter, and he really didn't mind. Hoping that the untimely occurrence would spoil the weekend, Madeleine could barely restrain her glee. However, it irked her to see Paul feeding ice-cream to Marian on the Piazza Navona, just as if they were lovers barely an hour from intimacy; and the way they threw coins in the Trevi fountain and spent hours strolling around St Peter's Basilica and the Sistine Chapel, getting a crick in their necks from looking at all that boring stuff on the walls and ceilings, was enough to make someone puke.

All she wanted was to get home and prepare herself for Tuesday morning. She'd made up her mind now that Matthew Cornwall's film was going to be the turning point for her. Though she'd never acted before in her life, she'd been to the cinema enough times, and watched enough films on television, to know it couldn't be that difficult. In secret she'd already been practising in front of the mirror, making up the dialogue as she went along, and she was pretty impressed with the results. She'd show Matthew Cornwall that she wasn't just an easy – though good – lay; she'd work really hard; then once she'd done that film, and before he left Bristol, she'd let him screw her again, this time for the promise of another job, or at least a decent contact, in London. Then somehow, no matter what it took, she'd get onto Page Three. And by keeping in with Matthew Cornwall she might well stand a good chance of becoming both a model and an actress. She was vaguely aware that her plan had flaws, but it didn't matter, she'd survive somehow and then, when she was rich and famous, and Paul O'Connell and her holier-than-thou cousin came begging at her door, she'd tell them to go to hell.

She was standing at the altar of some church she couldn't remember the name of, and thinking of the word hell made her feel a touch uncomfortable, so she closed her eyes quickly, apologised to God, then thanked Him for sending Matthew Cornwall to Bristol.

On Saturday night they dined at Alfredo's, where Marian had her fettucini served with a gold spoon and Paul bought her half a dozen red roses from a peasant woman who came round with them in a basket. Madeleine was serenaded by the guitarist, and she too had roses bought for her, but when the waiter told her they were from the old man sitting at a table in the corner, who was uglier than sin, it was left to Marian to thank him and Paul to carry them out of the restaurant.

It was their last night at the Hotel Giulio Cesare on the Via degli Scipioni, and despite her preoccupation with herself, even Madeleine couldn't help noticing how happy Marian was. People were even smiling at her in the streets, and Madeleine half-suspected that she and Paul must be doing it anyway, because no one glowed like that unless they were. In fact, after she had plucked up the courage to ask him, Paul had shown Marian how she could satisfy him – at the same time warning her not to do what he'd overheard Madeleine telling her to. It had been a momentous experience for Marian to witness a man in the throes of ecstasy and to know that she could give such pleasure to someone she loved made her want to do it again and again. Though highly amused by her fascination with his body, Paul was astonished at how willing a pupil she was, and there were increasing occasions, now, when it took more willpower than he ever knew he had to stop himself turning her on her back and making love to her there and then.

'Why don't you get in with me?' he'd asked her earlier as she sat on the edge of the bath, soaping him. 'Let me do the same to you.'

She shook her head and tried to explain that just looking at him was enough for her.

'You won't be saying that this time next week,' he grinned, then yelped as she splashed him and went off to get dressed for dinner.

It was seven thirty on Sunday evening when they arrived back in Bristol, and trudged from the bus stop to the West Mall in the drizzling rain. Paul opened the door and Marian groaned as she picked up her bank statement, a letter from Barclaycard and the red gas bill. Madeleine walked slowly on up the stairs, stopping just before the first-floor landing to let someone past. He brushed by without so much as a glance in her direction, but Madeleine turned to watch him run down the stairs. As he reached the bottom, Marian said hello, and though he answered politely enough, he showed no sign of recognising her. She could see from the dark look on his face that he was angry, and she flinched as he slammed the door behind him. Then turning back, she looked up the stairs at Madeleine.

Madeleine's eyes were wide and she was staring at the door. 'Who was *that*?' she breathed.

Marian looked confused. 'It was Matthew Cornwall,' she said haltingly.

Madeleine's eyes flew to Marian's as her mouth fell open. 'What?'

'Oh God,' Marian muttered, and thrusting the mail at Paul, she ran up to her cousin.

Madeleine slumped onto the stairs. Then looking up at Marian she screamed, 'I don't believe it! You're lying!' But when Marian only blinked at her, she buried her face in her hands and burst into tears. 'Oh Marian,' she wailed, 'why is this happening to me?'

Marian shot a look down the stairs at Paul, but he only shrugged. Turning back to Madeleine, she said, 'So I take it that the man who's just gone out of the door was not the man you . . . you saw in Pamela's flat.'

'No,' Madeleine sobbed.

'Are you sure?'

'Do you think I'd forget someone like that?' Madeleine spat, waving her hand towards the front door. 'Oh Marian, I thought everything was going to work out this time. I had everything planned, I was going to work really hard in that film. I was going to prove to everyone that I could do it, that I really could make it. And now . . .'

'You will,' Marian said, quickly sitting down next to her and hugging her. 'I mean, you've got a part, haven't you? You've even been told where to turn up and what time, so whoever he was, he must have been something to do with the film or else . . .'

'How do I know that?' Madeleine snapped. 'He could have been the fucking plumber for all I know.'

'It must have been the man I gave the parcel to,' Marian said. 'But you've spoken to this Dorothy,' she added encouragingly.

'And who's she when she's at home? I've never met her, have I?'

'I'd hazard a guess,' Paul said, wandering up the stairs,

'that Dorothy is a booking clerk. The man you screwed, Madeleine, was Matthew Cornwall's first assistant director. His name's Philip Forrester, otherwise known as Woody.'

Madeleine's face was drained of all colour as she looked up. 'How do you know?' she whispered.

'I met him on the stairs the morning after you did your – audition.'

'You bastard!' she spat. 'You knew all this time and you never said a word.' She lunged towards him, but Marian caught her and Paul stepped back. 'I hate you!' Madeleine screamed. 'You're a sly, conniving . . .'

'Madeleine, stop it!' Marian shouted. 'Paul, help me get her up the stairs.'

As they passed Pamela's flat Madeleine screeched, 'You wanker!' But whether it was directed at Woody or at Paul no one knew.

'Now,' Marian said, once they were inside the flat. She pushed Madeleine onto the sofa and turned to Paul. 'What's going on? You say you met this Woody character. What did he say?'

Paul shrugged. 'That it was quite some girl I shared a flat with and he couldn't wait to see what the other cousin was like. And by the way, if you want to be in the support cast there's a part for you too.'

Marian's frown deepened. 'But there is a part for Maddy?'

'Sure. As an extra.'

'A what?'

'An extra,' he repeated. 'You know, background action, passers by, supermarket shoppers, could be anything. They walk about but don't speak. They're what's called the support cast.'

Madeleine let out a howl. 'No! He's lying. He's doing this on purpose, Marian. He's trying to make a fool of me.'

Marian went to her, and looking at Paul she mouthed, 'Make some tea.'

It was some time before she could persuade Madeleine to accept that Paul was very likely telling the truth. 'I mean, no one's sent you a script, have they?' she pointed out. 'You've not actually met the director, and I would think he must be the one who decides who's actually in the film.'

'So what you're saying,' Madeleine sniffed, 'is that this Woody is lying, even about me being an extra?'

'No.' Paul was standing in the doorway. 'A first assistant director usually casts the extras, so Matthew Cornwall probably knows nothing about you.' When Marian gave him a look, he answered it by saying, 'I'm only trying to point out that if Cornwall doesn't know who she is, then the field's still clear for her to try again. And if she's on the set, even as an extra, he can hardly not notice someone like her, can he?' He shrugged. 'The rest is up to Madeleine. Plenty of extras, if they're good enough and impress the director in some way, get made up to main cast.'

Marian turned to Madeleine. 'What do you think, Maddy?'

Madeleine looked from Marian to Paul and back to Marian.

'I say, go on Tuesday,' Paul said, turning back to the kitchen. 'You've got nothing to lose. Unless, of course, Woody's told Matthew Cornwall what happened, but even then . . .'

Madeleine closed her eyes and let her head fall back. 'I can't do it, Marian,' she said. 'I can't go.'

'But why? Paul's right, you've . . .'

'Think about it. If that Woody bloke as good as told Paul, someone he's never even met before, then he's bound to have told Matthew, isn't he? I'll bet he's told everyone, and they'll all be laughing and pointing their fingers at me from the minute I turn up.'

Marian had to admit that this was a possibility, and in the end she agreed to call Dorothy and tell her that Madeleine was not available after all. Which she would have done first thing on Monday morning, had she not lifted the phone to discover they had been cut off.

On her way back from the telephone box Marian stopped at the newsagent's to pick up Paul's paper, as it hadn't been delivered that morning. 'Hello there, Mr Biggs,' she said cheerfully, as she walked in. 'I see I didn't win on the pools again this weekend. How about you?'

'Not a brass farthing,' he answered, as he handed a customer his change.

'Never mind,' Marian sympathised, 'got to keep trying, haven't we? I'll be in again on Thursday with my coupons. Now, I'll take the *Independent* if I may.'

Biggs nodded to his assistant, then walking round the counter, he beckoned Marian to come out of earshot of the steady flow of customers. 'Were you wanting your paper on account?' he asked quietly.

Inside Marian froze, but somehow she managed a smile and said, 'Only if that's all right. I can pay for it now if you prefer.'

'I think it would be better,' he said, his kind old eyes shifting with embarrassment.

Digging into her purse, Marian took out a fifty-pence piece and handed it to him.

He took it, then said, 'When do you think you might be paying off your bill, dear? You see, it's gone over forty-five pounds and we don't usually . . .'

'What!' Marian gasped. 'How much did you say?'

He looked at her with a helpless expression. 'It's the magazines young Madeleine has, they cost a lot nowadays,' he said.

Marian quickly lowered her eyes, not wanting him to see her anger. 'Of course,' she mumbled. 'Well, would it be all right to pay at the end of the week?'

'That'll be just fine,' he answered. 'Now, you pick up your paper and I'll get you your change.'

When she walked out of the shop the cool air was like a balm on her burning face. She knew already that she couldn't say anything to Madeleine. After the shock she had received over Woody and Matthew Cornwall, she was upset enough, and Marian didn't want to add to it by shouting at her over a few magazines. But the question was, how on earth were they going to pay Mr Biggs at the end of the week?

One thing's for sure, she told herself as she headed for home, the telephone will have to stay cut off for the time being. She thought of Paul then, and knowing that in his heart of hearts he still hadn't given up hope of hearing from the publisher, she started to consider what it might be like to live without electricity instead. But Madeleine would never stand for that. No TV, no hairdryer, no proper lighting to put her make-up on. Well, that was one area where they could definitely cut down. No more beauty treatments, and no more nights out for a while, either. Then she remembered the red gas bill, the TV licence demand and her bank statement. Her heart plummeted and a horrible buzzing started up in her ears. She had to get back and sort out just how much of a mess they really were in. But as she ran up to the front door, she suddenly stopped dead as she remembered the loan she had taken from the finance company. The repayments on that were over a hundred pounds a month. How could she ever have thought that she'd be able to pay it back?

She walked slowly up the stairs, a nauseating dismay churning in her stomach. She'd wanted to go to Rome to make Paul happy, and Madeleine too, but now she couldn't believe how irresponsible she'd been. She couldn't even ask them to help with the repayments because she'd told them she'd got the money from an insurance policy. Dear God, how could she have been so stupid? How could she have let things get so out of hand?

When she reached the fourth-floor landing, she stopped outside Pamela's door. She looked at it for a moment or two, then, hardly thinking about what she was doing, she knocked. She had some vague notion of trying to explain to Matthew Cornwall about Madeleine, though exactly what she would say she had no idea. But there might just be a chance that Woody hadn't said anything, and if he hadn't, or even if he had, there still wasn't any reason why Matthew Cornwall shouldn't at least meet Madeleine.

As she waited she could hear voices inside, and as if she were waking from a dream, she suddenly realised that she was about to make an unspeakable fool of herself. She turned to make a hasty escape up the stairs, but it was too late.

'Can I help you?'

Marian turned back, surprised at the female voice. The woman was about thirty, dressed in jeans and an anorak, with a large paisley shawl draped round her shoulders. She was smiling, but Marian could tell from her manner that she was in a hurry.

'No, not really,' Marian stumbled. 'Actually, I was hoping to speak to Mr Cornwall.'

'I'm sorry,' the woman answered, 'we're having a production meeting at the moment so he's a bit tied up. Can I tell him who called?'

Marian's face suddenly flooded with colour. 'Well, my name's Marian Deacon, I live upstairs.'

'OK,' she smiled. 'I'll tell him.' She leaned out of the door and looked towards the landing window. 'Bloody rain,' she grumbled. 'Our whole schedule's gone to pot because of it, so this meeting'll probably drag on most of the day, and if we can get it together we'll be on a night shoot tonight and tomorrow, so unless you want to see Matthew urgently you'd better leave it until the end of the week.'

'OK,' Marian answered. 'Thank you.'

She was about to leave when the woman said, 'Did you say Marian Deacon?'

The way she enunciated her name made Marian's heart sink. So they did all know about Madeleine. 'Yes,' she mumbled.

'And you live upstairs?'

Marian nodded miserably.

The woman gave her a peculiar look, then casting a quick glance over her shoulder, she said in a low voice, 'Between you and me you were lucky you happened upon Woody the other night. Of course, there's no excuse for the way he took advantage and allowed you to think he was Matthew, but from the way he tells it, you were a bit pissed and wouldn't let him get a word in. Anyway, if Matthew had been in and you'd tried to pull a stunt like that on him . . .' She shuddered. 'Matthew's got a real thing about women who . . . Still, that's beside the point. The point is, we seriously are looking for extras, so if you're still interested . . .'

'Actually,' Marian said, 'you've got the wrong person. It wasn't me, it was my cousin, Mad . . .' Feeling shamefully disloyal, she broke off.

'Madeleine! That's right. I thought . . .'

'Does Matthew know about what happened?'

The woman nodded.

'Then would you mind not telling him I called? I think it's better if we forget the whole thing.'

The woman shrugged. 'If that's what you want.'

When Marian let herself into the flat, Madeleine was in the bath and Paul was still in bed, asleep. For the last few days he'd had all the symptoms of a heavy cold, which Marian was convinced was turning into flu. She tiptoed into the bedroom and put a hand on his forehead. He stirred. 'How are you feeling?' she asked.

He blinked and tried to sit up, but the effort was too great and he closed his eyes again. 'Terrible,' he croaked.

'I think you've got a temperature,' Marian told him. 'Would you like me to call the doctor?'

He shook his head, and kissing him gently on the cheek, Marian went to take off her coat.

'How did you get on with Dorothy?' Madeleine called from the bathroom.

Marian pushed open the door and went to perch on the edge of the lavatory. 'She was OK about it. Apparently the schedule's changed anyway, so nothing's happening today. How are you feeling now?'

Madeleine shrugged. 'How do you think? Like nothing in the world's ever going to go right for me. And now, having seen Matthew Cornwall . . .' She sighed. 'It wouldn't be so bad if he wasn't so fucking handsome. God, I really missed out there. I mean, next to him even Paul . . . Do you think I've really blown my chances?'

'I think so,' Marian had to admit. 'Besides, looks aren't everything, he might be a real bastard for all we know. Or happily married.'

Madeleine lifted a long leg from the soapy water and inspected it closely. 'Don't think I'm putting on weight, do you?' she asked.

'No,' Marian answered. Then as Madeleine checked out the other leg, she said, 'Maddy, we've got to talk about money.'

'Ugh,' Madeleine groaned, and disappeared under the water.

Marian waited for her to resurface. 'Do you think you might be able to go in to work a few more nights a week?' she asked. 'It's only that I think we're in a worse mess than I realised.'

'And if we are, whose fault is that?'

'Mine. And yours.'

'So what about you? What are you going to do?'

'I'll have to sign on with a couple more agencies, I suppose, and maybe see if I can get a part-time job in one of the department stores. The bank have taken my cheque card and asked me not to write any more cheques until the overdraft's clear.'

There was a swish of water as Madeleine sat up. 'You're not serious. When did that happen?'

'Last week some time,' Marian answered dismissively. 'How much money have you got?'

'None in the bank. All I've got is in my purse.'

'Well, when you've finished in here we'd better sit down and go through everything and find out just how we stand.'

'What about Paul?'

'I think he's got flu. Besides, *I've* got his money.'

'How wifely! Hand me the towel, and if we can afford it I wouldn't mind a cup of tea.'

Their predicament was even worse than Marian had feared. Their combined resources amounted to little more than a hundred pounds which, not counting her loan, was eleven hundred pounds short of what they needed to pay off their bills.

'We don't have to pay the credit cards all in one go,' Madeleine said. 'We can pay them monthly.'

'Yes, but what about the gas and electricity? We've had the red notice for both, so we'll have to pay now, and I've promised Mr Biggs we'll pay him at the end of the week. Then there's food, what do we do about that? And the rent's due next week.'

'Oh God,' Madeleine groaned, 'we're going to end up on the streets at this rate. There's only one answer.' She looked at Marian, but seeing the look in her eye, Marian shook her head.

'No. I can't ask Mum again. It's not fair. We've spent practically all she's got already.'

'Well what else can we do?'

'I don't know.'

The next three weeks were a nightmare. Marian went to the South Western Electricity Board and arranged to pay their bill in instalments. Madeleine did the same at the Gas Board. They ignored the rent demand, avoided Mr Biggs, and sent off ten pounds to each of the credit card companies. Though she didn't tell the others, Marian continued to fill in the football pools, sending off her money by postal order in the now almost vain hope that a miracle might occur.

It was over a week before Paul recovered from his flu, then Marian went down with it. By the time she was better Madeleine had caught it, so what little income they had was greatly reduced by their inability to work. Marian was unable to sleep at night, and knowing that she had already failed to meet her first repayment on the loan turned her cold with terror.

In the end she knew she had to tell someone about it. For a whole day she agonised over whether it should be Madeleine or Paul, but the decision was made for her when Paul came back from the post office and found her crying.

'There's nothing else for it,' he said when she told him, 'I'll have to get a job.'

'But what about your writing?'

'It'll have to wait. No,' he said, when she started to protest, 'you took the loan for me, and therefore it should be me who pays it back. Besides, I've been living off you long enough.'

'That's not true!' she cried. 'You give me your dole money every week, which is usually twice what I earn.'

'Nevertheless, I'll get a job.' He wrapped her in his arms and hugged her tightly. 'You are an idiot,' he said, 'getting yourself into this mess for me. But I love you. And as soon as we get that Madeleine out of the bedroom and back on her feet, I'm going to prove it.'

'One hundred thousand pounds,' Marian repeated, trying her hardest to inject some cheer into her voice.

Madeleine raised two fringes of heavily mascaraed lashes and treated Marian to all the scorn her violet eyes could muster. 'Shut up!' she seethed, then turned away and started to rub a circle into the steamy café window. Outside in Broadmead, shoppers hurried past, stooping under wind-blown umbrellas and heaving heavy bags from one arm to the other.

Marian watched anxiously as Madeleine's face, still pale from her bout of flu, stiffened with contempt. It was clear that this time their childhood game wasn't going to work.

She gazed about the damp, overcrowded café. Several men were glancing in Madeleine's direction, but Madeleine was too depressed to notice.

She turned back as Madeleine started to tap her spoon against the sugar bowl. 'Money, money, money!' she cried, pushing her face towards Marian's. 'It's no wonder we're sitting here like fucking down and outs when we've got nothing. Oh, don't look at me like that, those silly little eyes of yours get on my nerves.'

'Anything else?'

Madeleine looked up to see the waiter with his pen poised over a notepad, but as she started to shake her head, Marian interrupted.

'I'd like another coffee, please.'

Before he went away, the waiter cleared their used cups and ran a wet towel over the plastic tablecloth. Madeleine waited, glaring at Marian, but Marian was looking out of the window.

'What the bloody hell's the matter with you?' Madeleine

exploded, once the waiter had gone. 'You know damned well we haven't got the money to pay for it.'

'But we can't sit here with nothing or they'll throw us out, and it's raining outside. And Paul's not back yet.'

'Marian,' she raged, 'we counted this up to the penny. One meal between us and a coffee each. It comes to five pounds exactly, which is all we've got. Where do you suppose we're going to get the other eighty pence from?' When Marian didn't answer, Madeleine snatched up her bag and stood up. 'I'm leaving,' she snapped. 'Sort it out yourself.'

'Maddy, sit down.'

'Then cancel the coffee.'

Marian looked down at her hands, cupped round the plastic salt and pepper pots. 'There's no point,' she said quietly. 'We can't afford to pay for the meal anyway, so one more coffee won't make a lot of difference.'

Madeleine moved slowly back into her chair. 'You bought it, didn't you?' she hissed. 'You fucking well bought it!'

Dumbly, Marian nodded.

'You stupid cow!' Marian winced, but Madeleine went on. 'Our phone's been cut off, we can't pay the rent, we've got bills up to our eyes, we can't even afford to eat, and you go and blow our last five pounds on a fucking lottery ticket!'

Marian looked up. 'I might win,' she said with a ridiculously optimistic smile.

Madeleine shot forward, but Marian jerked herself away and Madeleine's hand grabbed at thin air. 'Win!' she sneered. 'When have you ever won? All your life you've been a loser, so what the hell makes you think you're going to win now?'

Marian's eyes filled with tears. Their predicament was now so bad that she no longer knew which way to turn. Buying the lottery ticket had been a gesture of defiance that had given her only a moment's pleasure, and now she regretted it bitterly.

Madeleine expelled her irritation in a loud sigh. 'I'm sorry. Come on, don't cry. We're in this together. And besides, you know I didn't mean it.'

'Didn't mean what?'

Neither of them had seen Paul come in. He was standing over them, his blond hair dripping rain onto the collar of his jacket and his black brows drawn together in a frown. Madeleine's heart turned over as he smiled and tucked Marian's mousey hair behind her ear. Then noticing the tears, he sat down quickly.

'How did it go?' Marian asked, before he could ask why she was crying.

He shrugged and used a paper napkin to wipe the rain from his face. 'The secretary couldn't find the script, and my money ran out before she came back to the phone.' His voice was light, but Marian knew how disappointed he was. It had been over two months since he'd taken his manuscript to London, and still there was no word. She started to speak but he put his finger on her lips and shook his head. 'So now my last pennies have gone on a fruitless telephone call,' he sighed, 'I'm what you might call brassic. How about you two? Any chance of a coffee?'

'Marian has spent our money on a lottery ticket,' Madeleine spat.

Marian tensed, praying Paul wouldn't be angry with her too. But he smiled and held his hand out for hers. 'What am I going to do with you?' he chuckled, and her face glowed her adoration as he leaned over to whisper in her ear.

Madeleine wanted to scream, and as Marian's face turned as red as the tablecloth she sprang to her feet, hugging her bag to her chest. 'Well, while you two sit there behaving as if you haven't got a care in the world, *I'm* going to sort out this bill. And *you*, Marian Deacon, are off to Devon tomorrow to beg some money from your mother.'

Instantly Marian's glow was swallowed into the greedy throat of misery. 'But what about the rail fare?' she protested feebly.

'Write a cheque and say you've lost your card. And don't come back until . . .'

Marian had turned back to Paul. 'I can use the phone there!' she cried. 'I'll call the publisher, try and sort out what's happened.'

On a snort of disgust, Madeleine stalked off across the café. From the corner of his eye Paul watched her go, knowing exactly how she was going to get out of paying the bill. He wondered if the owner would be content with just looking at those magnificent breasts.

– 5 –

Marian watched her mother with a heart-rending mixture of pity and love. Her small, creased face was smiling happily as she poured tea from her best china pot, while chattering on about the little cleaning job she'd managed to get herself over at the school.

'You remember your old teacher, Mrs Webb, don't you?' she said, putting the cosy back on the pot, then cutting off two slices of home-made angel cake. 'She asks after you and our Madeleine, regular like.'

As Marian took the slice of cake she felt a lump rise in her throat. She knew her mother rarely baked these days – there was no one at home to bake for now. 'How is Mrs Webb?' she asked.

'Still having trouble with her leg.' Celia's grey eyes twinkled. 'And her back, and her stomach, and her neck.'

Marian laughed awkwardly, then sat down in the corner

of the sofa that was closest to her father's armchair, where she'd always sat as a child. The guilt she felt at having neglected her mother since she'd met Paul was gnawing at her heart, making it difficult for her to speak. And knowing that it had taken Madeleine over two weeks to persuade her to make the trip to Devon, only intensified the feeling.

The room they sat in hadn't changed in all the years they'd lived there – small and cluttered, with rose-patterned wallpaper, display cabinets of ornaments, souvenirs and photographs from over the years. Dad's old armchair was still beside the hearth, cushions plumped out and crocheted arm-covers neatly in place – it was as if it were waiting for him to come home, Marian thought sadly. She watched as, out of habit, her mother took a duster from her apron pocket and ran it over the grate. She was approaching sixty now, and though she looked it, she still kept herself smart, visiting the hairdresser's every Friday for a wash and set, and always putting on a tidy dress for her twice-weekly game of bingo down at the British Legion. She felt such a surge of love for her mother that she had to look away in case she cried. She was the kindest, gentlest woman, who would put herself out for anyone and never expect anything in return. She wasn't particularly well-educated, neither of Marian's parents were – 'There wasn't the money nor the opportunities in them days', was what her father had always said.

After tea Marian and Celia walked arm-in-arm down to the church so Marian could put flowers on her father's grave. On the way back Mrs Cooper was out by her gate, so they stopped to chat. She wanted to know all about what Mrs Deacon's two girls were up to in Bristol, and did Marian have a lovely job now she'd finished at the university? Marian had to admit she didn't, and no, neither did Madeleine. Mrs Cooper didn't show any surprise about Madeleine. 'After all, she didn't go to the university, did she?' Mrs Cooper had never been too fond of Madeleine, ever since Madeleine had called her a nosey, interfering old bag. Madeleine had been thirteen then, and she'd said it because Mrs Cooper had rushed up the road to tell Mrs Deacon she'd just seen her niece going off over the Bluebell Field with one of the boys from Dundridge Farm.

People had always been complaining about Madeleine then, but neither Marian nor her mother and father would believe anything bad of her. Oh yes, she was a bit of a tearaway, Celia was ready to admit that, but she was young, and hadn't it been hard enough for the girl being abandoned by her parents like that when she was only eight?

But no one could ever say Madeleine had been starved of love. Since the day she had come to live with them in their little two-bedroomed terraced house just outside Totnes, she had been the apple of everyone's eye, particularly her uncle's. Marian was sure that was why Madeleine was the way she was now. She rarely talked about him, but Marian knew that Madeleine missed her uncle terribly, and longed for someone to make her feel secure and loved in the same way. Suddenly Marian found herself thinking about the first time Paul had told her he loved her, and her heart turned over painfully. She was missing him already.

'You thinking about that young man of yours, are you?' her mother asked.

Marian looked up as her mother came in from the kitchen, wiping her hands on a teatowel.

'When am I going to meet him, then?' Celia asked.

'I've got some photos here,' Marian said, opening her bag. 'We took them in Rome.'

'Oh yes, I'd forgotten you'd been to Rome, the three of you. Let's have a look, then.' She leafed slowly through the first few, then lifted her head. With a faint colour staining her powdered cheeks and a sheepish smile that made her look more huggable than ever, she asked: "Tis in Italy, Rome, isn't it?'

Marian smiled. 'Yes.'

Her mother's eyes widened. 'Italy. There's nice. Looks a bit rough, though, all that damp on the walls and tiles falling off roofs. Oooh, Marian, is this your young man?'

Marian looked over her mother's shoulder. 'Yes, that's him,' she answered, her voice faltering on a wave of pride.

'Well, what would our Dad say if he could see him? Real good looking he is. How old is he?'

'Thirty.'

Celia frowned. 'Bit old for you, isn't it?'

Marian laughed. 'I'll be twenty-three this summer, Mum.'

'Ah, I suppose so. So it's serious between you, is it?'

'Well . . .'

'No wedding bells yet?'

Marian's mouth was pursed in a smile as she shrugged. 'We'll see,' she answered.

Celia looked at the picture again. 'Why didn't you bring him home with you?'

Marian's eyes shot to her mother's, then slowly she broke into a grin. 'I could always give him a ring now,' she said. 'He can get the first train tomorrow.'

Celia's eyes were sparkling too. 'Go on, then. Give Mrs Cooper something to gossip about, won't it, you bringing your boyfriend home. I'll go and put the chops on while you use the phone.'

Marian was already in the hall before she remembered. Their phone had been cut off. Paul couldn't pay the rail fare, and she had yet to tell her mother the real reason for her visit. She sat down on the bottom stair and dropped her head in her hands. What a God-awful mess this was. She hadn't been able to get any work, Madeleine was still recovering from another bout of flu, and these past two weeks only Paul's dole money had kept them from going hungry.

Celia Deacon's hands were folded inside her apron pockets and her kind, innocent grey eyes were gazing up at the mantlepiece when Marian finally went back into the room. Her heart leapt at the eagerness in her mother's eyes as she looked at her expectantly.

'I can't make the call, Mum. Our phone's been cut off.'

Celia looked blank. 'Cut off?'

'We haven't paid – couldn't pay – the bill.'

'Oh.' A moment later Celia smiled and stood up. As she walked over to the sideboard she patted Marian's arm. 'You're a silly girl, you should have told me before. I 'spect that's why you're here, isn't it? So we'd better see what's best to be done.' She opened a drawer and took out her purse.

'No, Mum.' Marian covered her mother's hands with her own. 'It's worse than the phone. A lot worse.'

Celia was nonplussed, and then became agitated as her daughter started telling her about limits on Barclaycards and Access cards, loans from finance companies, unpaid gas and electricity bills and threatening letters from the bank.

'We haven't paid any rent for seven weeks and we don't have a penny between us,' Marian finished.

Celia was shaking her head. 'There's a fine old mess to go and get yourselves in,' she said. 'And you with your education now. Still, there's nothing else for it, we'll have to go down the post office first thing tomorrow and draw out some money. Oh dear, what would your poor old dad say?'

Marian knew only too well what her father would say. What are you doing sponging off your mother at your age? You've had the best part of her insurance money as it is, the rest belongs to her, not you. Oh yes, she could hear her father's voice all right, and she agreed with every word he was saying.

'But what else has she got to spend it on?' That was what Madeleine had said when Marian had made the very same point a week ago. 'She enjoys giving it to us, you know she does. It makes her feel needed.'

When they came out of the post office the following morning, Celia handed her daughter an envelope. 'I left ten pound in there,' she said in a whisper, 'didn't want to close the account right up. But that's all that's left, Marian, so you girls are going to have to learn to stand on your own feet from now on.'

Marian's guilt swelled like a miserable, loathsome creature, and as she gazed down at the envelope she knew she couldn't do it. She just couldn't take the last of her mother's nest-egg and leave her with nothing. She pushed the envelope back into Celia's hand. 'I can't,' she said. 'I can't take it, Mum.'

'Don't you be so daft now. You're in a state, the two of you, that's obvious. You use that to sort it out. What about jobs? Does Madeleine still deliver those birthday messages?' Avoiding her mother's eyes, Marian nodded. 'And you? You still temping with the agency, are you?' Again Marian nodded. 'Then you're going to have to learn to live within your means, the two of you. You tell that Madeleine to get down the phone box and ring me when you get home, I'll talk to her myself. She doesn't ring me enough as it is. Nor you, madam. Now, let's go home and have a nice cup of tea before you go, eh?'

Marian eyes were awash with tears. 'You're the best Mum in the whole world, do you know that?'

'Oh, go on with you, you soppy old thing.'

'I'll stay another night if I may,' Marian said as they walked in the front door.

''Course you can. You don't have to ask, this is your home. Now, I'll go and peel some potatoes for dinner and you go on upstairs and put that money away safe in your suitcase. And you mind, if there's any left over you're to share it with our Madeleine.'

'Of course,' Marian answered. Then, as she started to walk up the stairs, she turned back. Her mother was watching her, and suddenly her guard dropped and she threw her arms round her and burst into tears. 'I love you, Mum,' she sobbed.

'I know you do, dear,' Celia said, patting her head.

Madeleine's eyes moved in an incredulous sweep across the mirror to find Paul's reflection. He was sitting up in bed, a sheet barely covering his nudity. 'You mean, steal it?' she whispered.

His only answer was to smile benignly as he settled his hands behind his head.

Rotating herself on the dressing-table stool, the pressing need for new highlights forgotten, she looked at him, and for the first time since he had seen Marian off at the station, it wasn't with an eye for sex. His teeth were clamped over his bottom lip, but his eyes were narrowed in the semi-caressing smile he normally reserved for Marian. Madeleine shivered, but whether because the look was so seductive or his suggestion so shameless, she couldn't have said.

She giggled. 'You're not serious – are you?'

He glanced down at the cheque lying beside him on the bed, and read aloud: 'Pay Miss M. Deacon the sum of seven hundred and fifty thousand pounds.' He looked up.

Madeleine stared at him. Was he really thinking exactly what she had been thinking ever since the two men from the lottery paid their visit the day before?

'Miss Deacon?' one of them had asked. And of course she had said she was, because she was. It wasn't until she invited them in and they explained why they were there that she realised it was Marian they were looking for. Of course, she should have come clean right away, but she'd let them go on talking, telling her how her request for no publicity was to be respected and that a financial adviser would come round to see her sometime in the next few days. Madeleine had listened to it all, too stunned to speak. Her only thought was that if she hadn't made Marian go to Devon . . . But she got no further than that.

Coming back to the present, she saw that Paul was still watching her. She heard Matthew Cornwall close a window downstairs, but didn't give him a second thought. If she was reading Paul right, she no longer needed the Matthew Cornwalls of this world. But Paul couldn't mean it. It was too . . . It was just too extreme. They couldn't seriously pick up that cheque and walk out without saying a word to Marian. Could they? But how was Marian to know?

Paul yawned, though he was amused by her evident struggle of conscience.

'She'd share it, you know,' Madeleine said.

'Yes, she would.'

Her eyes moved to the cheque, then slowly back to Paul. As she watched him, and remembered all that he had done to her in the past forty-eight hours, she felt such an overpowering surge of lust and triumph that she couldn't stop it bubbling from her lips in a harsh, brittle laugh. She would have him, she would have the money, she would have everything!

Seeing the way her nipples were standing out, Paul flipped back the sheet, crooked his finger and beckoned her over to the bed. She stood up, but before she went to him she had to be sure.

'What will you tell her?' she asked.

He shrugged. 'What's there to tell?'

'She thinks you love her.'

'I know.'

'Do you?'

He studied her, his intense eyes making a slow journey from the tips of her toes to the very top of her head. It was debatable who was the more beautiful of the two, herself or Paul, but in case he should be at all forgetful of the completeness of her beauty, Madeleine undid her robe and let it fall. 'Do you want me to tell you I'm in love with you?' he said.

'Aren't you?'

'No.'

'You are, you know. I'm Miss M. Deacon.'

His eyes narrowed, just for a fraction of a second, and then he laughed. 'Sit here,' he said, pointing to his erection.

Obediently she walked across the room and climbed onto the bed. As she positioned herself over him he took her breasts in his hands and leaned forward to bury his tongue in her mouth. She kissed him back, sucking his lips and his tongue while lifting his penis from his belly. Slowly she lowered herself onto him, then moaned into his mouth as the length of him filled her. He pushed her back to look at her; her hair tumbled over her face and her lips were moist and parted.

'Move,' he told her. Then jerking himself hard into her he growled, 'Come on, fuck me.'

Her eyes clouded and he laughed. 'Fuck me,' he said again, and gently slapped her breasts. 'Then I'll tell you just how much I love you.'

'And adore me?' she murmured, as she put a hand on either side of the pillow.

'I worship you.' He pushed his face into her breasts and squeezed her nipples.

'Oh yes, yes,' she groaned, rotating her hips. As she moved faster and faster her breasts swung heavily and he lay back to watch them, his hands circling her waist, his own hips jerking to meet hers. Then, as she started to lose control, her head dropped back and she cried, 'Do it to me! Do it!' He ran his hands over her thighs, but his fingers stopped before they reached the join in her legs. 'Do it!' she screamed. He snatched the hair from her face and pulled her forward. Her eyes flew open and suddenly, in one almighty surge, he felt the seed being sucked from his body. He had never seen anything like it – the power, the hunger, the sheer concupiscence of that look slashed his control so that his whole body was rocketed to the point of explosion.

'Fuck me!' he yelled, hammering into her and pushing his fingers between her legs.

'Oh God!' she seethed. 'Oh yes, yes, yes.' Her eyes burned into his and a white heat seared through his loins. 'Now!' he shouted. 'Come now! Now! Now!' With every word his seed was bursting into her, and his fingers rubbed harder until he could feel her muscles tightening around him and her screams resounded round the room in a deafening echo.

It was another two hours before they finally uttered words unstressed with urgency. Madeleine was dressed by that time, and waiting for him in the sitting-room where only half an hour before he'd taken her over the chair. She leaned forward and took another peep at the cheque that was lying on their coffee-table box. As she did so, her heart was seized with a frenzied greed that fired through her body again and again until, unable to bear the assault any longer, she leapt up and went to stand at the window. She had him. He was hers now, and so was the seven hundred and fifty thousand smackeroos!

Her decision was made. She'd thought it over carefully, waiting for her sense of decency to prevail and smash her dream to smithereens. It hadn't happened. In her mind the future had not yet taken on any definite shape – though geographically she moved with ease and splendour from continent to continent. It was only when she tried to sort out her exit from Bristol and her entry into this proposed new life that she became confused and agitated, and resentful. But beyond that she felt an exalted anticipation like nothing she'd ever experienced before. Because from now on it would be just the three of them. Paul and Madeleine, and Miss M. Deacon's – Miss *Marian* Deacon's – lottery win.

Paul was looking thoughtful as he came into the room. He walked over to his typewriter and wound in a sheet of paper. Then stepping back, he said: 'It's all yours. I take it you are going to leave her a note?' he added, when all she did was look at him.

'You're the writer.'

'You're family.'

'And you're the one she's in love with.'

He looked troubled, then sat down, covering his face with his hands.

'What's the matter?' Madeleine asked nervously, when he'd remained like that for several minutes.

He looked up and she could see he was angry, but more than that, he was in pain. 'For once, Madeleine, look beyond yourself,' he cried. 'Look at *me!* Can't you see what this is doing to me? God, you're so beautiful it's tearing me apart. But don't you understand how much I hate my weakness for you? How much I hate being unable to stop myself from wanting you? I don't know what happened the moment I stepped into bed with you, but you've got me now, Madeleine. That is what you wanted, isn't it?'

His words filled the air around her. She inhaled deeply, then held her breath as though absorbing them into herself. Expressing her beauty, his pain at her presence, his declaration that he was hers. 'Yes, it's what I wanted.' She tried to disguise her triumph, but her voice shook with it. 'And I want a whole lot more.'

'I'm back,' Marian called out. She closed the door behind her, put her bag on the floor and took off her coat. Then noticing that there weren't any others on the rack, she felt a pang of disappointment that there was no one in to greet her.

She picked up her bag, took it into the bedroom, then walked into the sitting-room. She shivered. They must have been out all morning, because the chill in the room meant that the fire couldn't have been on for some time. Then it occurred to her that the gas might have been cut off, and she crossed the room quickly to find out. At the turn of the switch the fire burst into life, and she smiled as her momentary panic subsided.

Turning back to the kitchen, she was just wondering what treats she could buy at the supermarket to surprise them when her eyes were drawn to the table. She frowned. There was something different about it. Then she realised what it was. It was empty. She pulled back the chair to see if Paul had packed his typewriter away somewhere. But why would he do that? she was asking herself as her eyes scanned the room.

Her heartbeat quickened and her hands started to shake as she realised that the pages of his new manuscript were missing too. Immediately, she turned to the shelf above the TV, and her heart almost stopped when she saw that his books were gone too. Despite the horrible dread that was drawing her back, she ran into the bedroom and pulled open the wardrobe door. The empty hangers clattered against one another in the draught.

She stepped back, her eyes wide with disbelief. Then a terrible buzzing started in her ears and her throat began to close in a dry, constricting knot. She stumbled into the bathroom; where he'd kept his razor and toothbrush there was nothing.

'Paul,' she breathed. She spun round, and as if she still couldn't take it in, she went back to the sitting-room. She stood staring at the table, as if she could will the typewriter to return. Then she closed her eyes and covered them with her hands, and in the black depths she saw his face.

'Paul,' she whispered. '*PAUL!*' Her scream unleashed the panic that was erupting inside her, and she fell to her knees, cradling her head in her arms as if to protect herself from the terrible pain. 'No!' she sobbed. 'Please God, no!'

Her shoulders slumped against the sofa, and when she looked up her face was ashen and her eyes were wide, dry circles. She gazed at the cushions, at the carpet, at the fire, at the blank TV screen. Then she heard him laughing, and quickly turned to look down the hall. In the dim light there was a line of sunshine that broke from the bedroom door. Nothing moved. Then her chest started to heave, and a searing pain engulfed her. She clasped her hands to her head as the buzzing started again. 'No, no, it can't be true. It can't be true,' she cried. 'Maddy! Oh Maddy, where are you?'

Hour after hour passed, and still she sat on the floor, waiting. From time to time a tear trickled down her face, but it hurt too much to cry. It was past midnight by the time she dragged herself to her feet. She walked to the window. The night sky was black and empty. She stood looking into it, willing herself to move, but she was afraid. Afraid to think, afraid to feel, afraid to know.

In the end she made herself do it. As if in a trance, she walked into the bedroom. She turned on the light and blinked as the glare stung her eyes. Then carefully she moved to the wardrobe and opened the other door. And then she knew the whole, terrible truth.

For two whole days and nights she neither ate nor slept. She simply sat on the edge of her bed, hardly able to move. Whenever she did, the pain gripped her with such pure, stark intensity that she wanted only to die. Any movement outside took her eyes to the door, but no one came. She searched the flat for a note but found nothing. No letter arrived either.

On the third day she washed and dressed and went to pay the telephone bill. Again she waited, but nobody rang. She went to the library, called the strip-o-gram agency, even went to the Chateau Wine Bar. No one had seen them, no one could help.

As she walked back to Clifton she passed the museum. She stood outside for over an hour, closing her eyes as she willed time to turn back. But when she opened them again she recoiled from the life that continued around her, and her heart was like an organ of torture pumping loneliness through her veins.

She went to the bank and paid off the debts. She went to the supermarket and bought a can of beans and some bread. She went to the newsagent's, picked up her football coupons and the *Independent*.

Some days she went to work, and afterwards she walked round for hours, afraid to go back to the cold and the emptiness of the flat. Eventually the money her mother had given her started to run out and she knew she had to pull herself together.

She met Janey in the Chateau. Jackie and Sharon introduced her – Janey was desperate for somewhere to live.

'It might help to have someone around,' Jackie said kindly. 'Why not let her stay for a while?'

'Are you sure you don't know where Maddy is?' Marian asked.

Jackie shook her head, then found she had to swallow a lump in her throat. She had never seen such torment in a person's eyes.

As Marian walked out of the wine bar with Janey, Sharon turned to Jackie. 'Do you think she'll ever get over it?'

'I don't know. But what I do know is, we should keep an eye on her.'

'Why?'

'Because I think she might do something you and I would bitterly regret.'

'What do you mean?'

As she answered, Jackie looked Sharon straight in the eye. 'They were her whole life, Sharon, and if they don't come back, I think she'll kill herself.'

Marian led Janey into the sitting-room as Janey dug into her voluminous canvas bag and pulled out a purse. 'Two hundred pounds for the deposit? Is that right?'

Marian nodded. 'Would you like some coffee?' she offered.

'Sure, why not? I'll make it if you like. Got to keep in with my new flat mate, eh?'

Marian stared at her. For a fleeting second she thought she saw Madeleine's face, but then it was Janey again. 'I'll do it,' she mumbled. And as she walked into the kitchen and put on the kettle, tears swelled in her eyes. She could hear Janey moving about in the next room, and suddenly she had to grip the edge of the sink as her shoulders started to heave and her breath shortened. It was as if a great hand was pushing her heart into her throat. 'Please God, don't let me break down,' she whispered.

'Did you say something?' Janey said, fiddling with her portable stereo as she came into the kitchen.

Marian turned away quickly, shaking her head. 'Do you like sugar?' she sniffed.

'No. But I like music. What about you, Marian? Do you like music?' And suddenly the whole flat was alive with it.

6

It was seven fifteen in the morning. Matthew Cornwall flung back the bedclothes, kicked his shoes out of the way and slammed the window shut. Being a man of newly acquired privacy, which in turn had brought newly acquired habits, he was even angrier than he might have been. These days, when he wasn't filming, he liked to ease himself into the day at a leisurely pace. What he liked even more was to have his bedroom window open – a luxury that had been denied him throughout the years of his marriage. As it was he had been kept awake for hour after hour by what seemed to be a recurring nightmare in his life – music throbbing through the walls of his room, thudding into his brain until he was drum-beaten to a state of near-catatonia. The only difference now was that the noise was coming from the flat upstairs instead of the bedroom next door. Hadn't he lived with din for the best part of twenty years? Hadn't he had life's share of other people's obtrusiveness? He hated people, really hated them. At least, this morning he did, so it wasn't any wonder that, unrested as he was, and with a temper simmering just below exploding point, he should slam the window as hard as he could in the hope that it would release some of his fury.

The panes of glass trembled in their frames and he waited to see if any would break. Then, half-grinning at the futility of his gesture, he turned back into the room. He winced. It was like an ice-cream parlour – everything covered in a froth of pink and white lace. The curtains were tied back with huge satin bows, and everything was done in the reverse-match style created by Laura Ashley. The duvet matched the curtains, so did the wallpaper, so did the panels in the wardrobe doors, the lampshade and the picture frames. On the dressing table his watch and loose change looked decidedly uncomfortable amongst the perfume bottles and cottonwool puffs; even more out of place in this sea of femininity was his own naked male body. Still, he shouldn't grumble. It was good of whatever-her-name-was to lend him her flat while she was in Hungary filming.

He'd been there for just over two months now, but still he couldn't get used to being alone. Not that he didn't like it. In fact, if it wasn't for the inconsideration of his neighbours upstairs, he would have taken great delight in imagining he was the only person alive on the planet – for a few hours in the day, anyway.

The need for solitude was the result of a marriage that had been loud, obstructive, and eventually an almost constant irritant. 'That's what it's like, being married,' his brother had informed him laughingly, and Matthew could picture now the rippling splendour of his brother's belly filled out over the years by his own raucous wife.

He still wasn't sure exactly when Kathleen had turned into the insufferable person she now was, or indeed whether it was he who had made her like that. All he knew was that one day he had realised that he couldn't stand her any longer. Her strident cockney voice seemed to scratch at the very fibres of his brain. He didn't recall it being like that when they got married – but he didn't recall much of those days. He did remember that he had wanted to be a musician, and that at nineteen he had been on the brink of signing a big record deal that would take him to Germany for a year. Then Kathleen had become pregnant, and before he knew what was happening the wedding was arranged, he was at the altar, and away on a honeymoon in Spain. Goodbye to Germany and goodbye to the record deal. At least that was one thing he didn't regret; if he'd become a musician he might never have become a director.

That was almost twenty years ago. He'd only stayed with her as long as he had because of the children, and because, for a man as busy and ambitious as he was, it was easier to give in to Kathleen than to fight her. He'd had affairs along the way, but Kathleen's method of dealing with them – the ones she'd found out about – was too excruciating to think about now. And then the day dawned when he realised that the children he'd always adored had become raving monsters. No one in the house spoke any more; everyone yelled and screamed, laughed and sang and cried at full volume. Tuneless pop records, TV sets, motorbikes and exhaust-free cars – all introduced by the screeching imbeciles that his children and his children's friends had become, and indulged by his shrill, maternal, Hoover-brandishing wife – had forced him to admit to a rabid dislike of his own family.

He'd left six months ago, just before his thirty-ninth birthday. He had been shooting a film in London at the time, not far from the marital home. Kathleen paid no heed to the fact that he'd gone, and continued to turn up on set – with her mother – bringing flasks of hot soup and the latest family tittle-tattle. They were an embarrassment that made his toes curl. What he never understood was the way the other people on the set, cast and crew alike, had done everything they could to make them feel welcome.

Stupid of him, of course, not to have understood. He was the director, and though a director's lot could be an enviable one at times, it did have its drawbacks – like being surrounded, imprisoned even, by sycophancy.

Cynical, cynical.

He laughed, and rubbing his hand over a dark face that was becoming even more handsome with age, he walked into the bathroom. He wasn't really cynical, he was just tired. And today he was going to have one of the trickiest meetings he'd had in a long time.

Another of the drawbacks in being a director – it was the producer who held the real power, not to mention the purse-strings. And this producer, the one who was coming to Bristol especially to see him while he was down here shooting a feature film for Channel Four, was someone who was very definitely going to make him sing for his supper. However, for this particular supper he'd do a lot more than sing. Just as well, because there was no doubt in his mind that Stephanie Ryder – the producer who owned the rights to *Disappearance* – would have every intention of making him sing, dance, cartwheel or anything else that took her fancy. He wondered idly if one of her conditions would be that he take her to bed again. But no, that wasn't Stephanie's style.

The phone brought him dripping out of the shower.

'Matthew? Are you there?'

'No Woody, I'm in Wazoo Wazoo land.'

'Great! When will you be getting back? I'll get someone to meet the balloon.'

'This repartee can't even begin to be described as witty, so get on with it, Woody.'

'It's a problem. One that only you can sort, guvnor. It's . . .'

'Sandy. Yes, what is it now?'

'You mean, you can't guess?'

'I mean, I can guess, I just have this vague hope it might not be motivation for once.'

'Sorry to disappoint you, but you're right. Can you come over?'

Matthew turned his wrist to look at the watch he wasn't wearing.

'It's seven forty-five,' Woody supplied, 'and you've just got out of the shower to answer this call, and you're wondering if you can get here before you go to your meet at the Hilton?'

'Well, smart ass, can I?'

'No.'

'Then why are you asking?'

''Cos I said I would, and I'd be failing in my duties if I didn't report to the director every whim of our star.'

'Which means, if I don't get there she's threatening to hit the bottle? Shit, why are they all the same?'

'You got it.'

'Tell her I said Cheers.'

There was a chuckle at the other end of the line. 'You mean that?'

'I mean that. It's her ugly mug we're putting up there on the screen, and if she can't take responsibility for it I don't see why we damned well should.'

'And Stephanie Ryder's got you into a lick.'

'And you're a pain in the ass. Tell Sandy I'll be there in time to take her to lunch. Get Jan to book a table at Harvey's, and Christ, aren't we all enjoying our day off?'

'Richard Collins flies into Lulsgate at midday, will he be joining you for lunch too?'

'If you were as smart as you like to think you are, you wouldn't have to ask that question. Book us a private room at the Holiday Inn for three o'clock. Until then, keep him out of my way. Fix an air traffic controllers' strike, or something.'

'The air traffic controllers I can handle, the room may take a little more time.'

At that moment the music upstairs started to blare again. Matthew yelled, 'Just keep him away from me 'til three, that's all I ask. Jesus! Two producers in one day I could do without.'

'Should I call your wife to come and soothe the angst?'

'Any more suggestions like that and you can call the nearest employment agency.'

'On my way.'

'No, don't go. Put Sandy into the hands of that wimpy dresser of hers and come and collect me. You can drive me to the Hilton.'

'On my way.'

At eight thirty sharp, during a fortuitous break in the music, a car horn sounded outside. Matthew was dressed. Jeans, trainers, navy sweat-shirt over white shirt, and black leather jacket. His dark hair was still damp, and needed cutting, and his razor had all but let him down. Well, Stephanie had seen him in far worse states than this, and he was damned if he was going to let her think he'd made an effort specially for her.

He opened the door and checked his pockets for keys before closing it. Woody blasted the horn again, and Matthew swung round to dash down the stairs. How he managed to save himself from going head-first he didn't know, but he had given whoever was in the way a sharp crack on the skull with his knee cap.

'What the hell . . .! What are you doing sitting there, for Christ's sake! I could have broken my neck.'

Marian was holding the back of her head, but didn't turn round. 'I'm sorry,' she said, reaching out for the stair rail to pull herself to her feet.

'Are you all right?' Matthew snapped, already edging past her to get down the stairs.

'Yes. Yes, I'm fine. No damage.' As she lowered her hand, her lank, mousey hair parted to reveal a pair of swollen red eyes, white cheeks – if one politely ignored the blotches – and bitten lips that were trembling with the onset of another tear-storm.

Matthew sighed, and trying very hard not to roll his eyes, took a step towards her. 'Aren't you the girl who lives upstairs?'

Marian nodded. 'I know, you're going to complain

about the noise. Complain away. If you can get her to stop, there'll be no one more grateful than me.'

Woody tooted again. Matthew glanced over his shoulder and thought hurriedly. He didn't want to leave the girl in such obvious distress, but on the other hand he was in no mood to play Sir Galahad. 'Look, I can't stop now,' he said, 'but this music business . . . we've got to get something sorted. I'll be back later, around six. Perhaps you'd like to come down and we can talk about it?'

Through their puffed lids Marian's eyes looked at him with such gratitude that he already regretted the offer. 'Are you sure?' she said. 'I mean . . .'

'Around six,' Matthew interrupted, and fled.

Woody, Matthew's ever capable, ever loyal first assistant director, roared his Porsche to a standstill on the cobbles outside Bristol's Hilton Hotel. Matthew got out, gave Woody a few more suggestions as to how to fill his day off, then laughing at Woody's response, walked up the steps into the hotel.

His arrival caused quite a stir amongst the starchly-uniformed receptionists. Over the past year, in fact ever since his film *Monsieur et Mademoiselle* cleaned up at BAFTA, the press had taken it upon themselves to turn him into some kind of sex symbol. The whole thing made Matthew cringe, but his embarrassment at finding himself a celebrity – and even his rudeness to the journalists who pounced on him in the street – only seemed to increase his appeal. Their prime interest was his sex life which, being an extremely private man, he kept under tight wraps. However, the press were not to be done out of their stories, so they made them up. If he had even half the stamina they credited him with, he'd be in a circus, as he told Kathleen when she called him to complain – loudly, of course.

The senior receptionist, exercising the privilege of rank,

led him across the foyer, leaving a stifling waft of perfume in her wake. She chattered away to him, her flat 'a's and over-pronounced 'r's typical of the Bristol accent – an accent he enjoyed. When they reached a door that gave no introduction to the room beyond, Miss Carter – he'd read it on her badge – stood aside to let him pass, then smiled so suggestively when he thanked her that he actually blushed.

The room was empty, but that didn't surprise him. It was a fairly typical producer ploy – to make sure he arrived first so that she wasn't the one to be kept waiting. What was surprising was the size of the room. It was a full-scale conference room, complete with table, chairs, blotting-pads, jugs of water and glasses. He looked round for the video screen, certain there would be one, and there was. The cabinet beneath, containing the playback machine, was open, and several cassettes were stacked up beside it. He picked one up but it was labelled in some sort of code.

Several minutes ticked soundlessly by while, with his hands stuffed into the pockets of his jacket, he paced the room.

He couldn't help wondering, why a conference room? It was to be only the two of them, as far as he knew. Suddenly he had an image of himself performing on the table before a kangaroo court of investors, executive producers, screen-writers and associate producers, showing them how he would shoot the film, before falling on his knees to beg them to let him do it. And the video. What if there'd been a hidden camera the last time he and Stephanie were together? Was she going to play it back for him, frame by atrocious frame, while she sat there, impassively observing the destruction of his dignity? Jesus, he hadn't thought about that final night in years. He shuddered, then laughed – his imagination was into double time.

At last there were footsteps outside. He turned as the door opened, and she was there. Stephanie Ryder. The first production assistant he'd ever worked with, and had continued to work with until . . .

She smiled. 'Hello, Matthew.' She closed the door behind her and walked towards him. Her titian hair swung gently in a sleek bob, a style that was new and suited her better than the curls she'd had when he knew her. Her make-up was light, no longer trying to disguise the smattering of freckles, but the slanting green eyes and generous mouth were still as enticing as ever. She put her briefcase on the table and slipped off her raincoat. She was wearing a navy pin-stripe trouser-suit, with a white shirt pinned at the throat by a cluster of fake diamonds. This style and composure were also new.

As she turned he started to extend his hand, but she was already on tip-toe, kissing his cheek. 'It's good to see you,' she said, then laughed. 'Not what you expected me to say? It's true, it *is* good to see you. You're looking very . . . what's the word? Rakish. How have you been?'

'Surviving. You?' His eyes were holding hers, and she didn't look away.

'The same.'

The sub-text was unmistakable, and it was only with superhuman effort that he stopped himself reaching out for her. Christ, he hadn't expected that. He hadn't really known what to expect, but suddenly to find that after all this time she could still . . .

'Shall we sit down?'

He shrugged. 'Sure. Who else are we expecting?'

'Expecting? Oh, the room. All there was available. We have to be out of here by eleven, eleven thirty at the latest. That'll be enough time, won't it?'

Again he shrugged. 'You're the boss.'

She turned away and started to unpack her briefcase. Watching her – almost feeling her, she was so close – he couldn't stop himself remembering. Remembering the pale smoothness of her skin, the generosity of her mouth, the life and the energy of her that had once been his to take, to use and to love – until he walked away.

'You're staring, Matthew.'

He looked away, rubbing his hand over his chin and wishing he'd bothered to try a little harder with the razor. 'So how are you?' he said. 'You've done well. I keep hearing about you. Seen most of what you've done, at least, I think I have. It's good. The series of plays on the BBC . . . Didn't you write one of them?'

She nodded. 'With my partner, Bronwen.' She looked older, but unlike most women, it suited her. How old would she be now? Thirty-eight? No, probably thirty-nine. Her birthday was ten days after his. She'd sent him a card just after it all broke up. He'd returned the compliment by ignoring her birthday, believing that the cleaner the break, the easier it would be for her – and for him. But none of it had been easy. They'd had to work together for three more weeks after that last night, and then after that – when she'd gone, emptied her office, taking everything with her – that was when the real loss had begun.

But perhaps he had done her a favour by getting out of her life. She had loved him so much then, she'd have done anything, sacrificed anything for him; and had it not been for Kathleen, he'd have let her.

'Shall we talk about it, or would you prefer we forgot that anything ever happened?'

That was just like her. First she would read his mind, then whatever he wanted, whichever way he wanted to play it, she would follow. No man on God's earth was worthy of a woman like this. That was a strange thing to think. He'd never considered her such a paragon before. 'How about you?' he said. 'Do you want to talk about it?'

'Not really. I don't think it'll serve any purpose. Not now, anyway.'

He lowered his head, and it was a while before he spoke again. Stephanie waited. She had plenty of time. After all, she'd waited six years for this.

'How did you get the rights?' he asked.

The abrupt change of subject startled her, but she didn't let it show. 'From Deborah Foreman, you mean?'

He nodded. 'How did you get her to sell? I thought she'd vowed she never would.'

'Not her decision. She may have written the book, but the rights belong to the Hastings – so I went to see them.'

A slow smile spread over Matthew's face. 'I've got to hand it to you, Stephanie.'

She inclined her head and sat down.

'Well,' he said, pulling up a chair, 'you can't just leave it at that. How did you get to them? As far as I knew, they'd always refused to talk about the girl's disappearance publicly.'

'I got to them through Debby.' She paused. 'Look, this is strictly between you and me, Matthew, and I mean that – but the Hastings are hiding something about Olivia.'

'Why should they do that? Besides, there was an investigation second only to Watergate when she went missing. If there was anything shady, which is what I assume you're suggesting, surely it would have come out then.'

'Or would it? The Americans are pretty good at cover-ups.'

'Then why should the Hastings agree to the film?'

She shrugged. 'I don't know. But two years ago, just after Deborah's book was published, new evidence was found – or I should say, received.'

'Do you know what it is?'

She nodded.

'Are you going to tell me?' he asked, when she didn't continue.

'No. At least, not yet.'

The implication was clear. She would only tell him if she decided that he was to direct the film.

'But whatever it is, I take it it's the reason for the film.'

Stephanie sighed. 'Again, I'm not sure. They're playing everything pretty close to their chests. Frank Hastings is financing the entire project.'

Matthew looked impressed. 'Nice to be so rich. And why you?'

'They like me.' She grinned. 'Or so Deborah tells me. But I think the real reason is that they didn't want the film Hollywood-ised, or glitzed in the American way, so they've decided to go British.'

There was a lengthening silence. In the end he decided to come right out with it. 'Who told you I wanted to make this film?'

'Word gets round.'

'Did you go after it for that reason? So that we'd be in the position we're in now? You the boss?'

Stephanie laughed. She laughed for quite some time. 'I don't remember you being so arrogant, Matthew. But yes, I went after it because I knew you would want it. *And*, because like most other people, I'm fascinated by it. The daughter of one of the wealthiest men in America, who at the age of twenty-one becomes an overnight success as an artist, who has every eligible man in the world vying for her hand, and a social diary that would make Princess Diana's look like a teddy-bear's picnic – who in other words has everything to live for – disappears from the New York scene, resurfaces in Italy, then disappears altogether: who wouldn't be interested? It'll make a bloody good film once it's in shape. So shall we get down to it? Tell me what you have in mind.'

'Before I start, can I be sure you're not on some kind of revenge trip?'

'No.'

His left eyebrow flicked a reaction, then, grinning, he

stretched his long legs out in front of him and settled himself more comfortably in his chair.

'Approach and interpretation,' she said.

He reached inside his jacket and took out a battered copy of the first draft screenplay her secretary had sent a couple of weeks before. 'This is going nowhere,' he said, throwing it onto the table.

'I know. Go on.'

There followed a quick-fire exchange of ideas; disagreement, enthusiasm, laughter at his literal interpretation of stage directions; then rudeness, threats, and the old familiar feeling of grudging but mutual admiration.

The meeting went on until ten past eleven, by which time there seemed nothing more to be said for the moment. Stephanie collected her things and placed them neatly in her briefcase. 'Thanks for coming,' she said. 'Your ideas are interesting. And it was good to see you.' She was standing as she spoke, her coat already over her arm.

'Is that all?'

'I think we've discussed everything, yes.'

'Except one vital piece of the plot.'

'I'll be thinking it over after I've seen a couple more directors. I'll be in touch by the end of next week.'

He got slowly to his feet. 'I see.' His expression was inscrutable but she knew he was angry. 'Are you sure you want to play it this way, Stephanie?'

'I'm not *playing* it any way, Matthew. But I think you should know that I've worked with a lot of other directors since you. Good directors, who could make this film work too. And their contracts wouldn't come loaded with conditions, the way yours would. Are you prepared to meet my conditions?'

His eyebrows arched. So she *was* going to make him pay for that night. 'It would depend what they were,' he said.

'I think you know, Matthew. And let me tell you something while you're making up your mind. I'm a different person now. I'm a producer, with responsibilities to executives, investors, script-writers and cast. I won't put up with unprofessionalism on my sets. The family burden you carry with you from one film to the next is fast becoming the laughing stock of the industry. You're only surviving it because you're good. But I won't have one of my films, or anyone connected with it, mocked in that way. And I don't think I want to speak any plainer than that.'

'You don't have to.' She noticed that a dangerous gleam had leapt into his eye. 'And if you were half as well informed as you claim to be, you'd know that I've left her. Six months ago – which is six years later than I should have done. Does that suit you? Is that what you wanted to hear?'

Her harsh expression dissolved as the blood drained from her face. All the years of carefully considered strategy were suddenly blown to pieces. But she couldn't think about it now. She needed to be alone, because if what he said was true, it changed everything. 'I didn't know,' was all she managed to utter.

'Well, you do now. So is that condition number one fulfilled? I've left my wife. Condition number two?'

The sarcasm in his voice brought her sharply to her senses. 'You flatter yourself, Matthew Cornwall. And condition number two will be spelt out as and when I am ready. As for the first condition, I'll think about it and let you know if it's enough. It just might not be. Now, if you'll excuse me, my secretary will call you.'

He waited until she was at the door. 'Bitter and twisted were never words I'd thought to use to describe you, Stephanie. Make sure you don't try for more than the pound of flesh.'

The door slammed on his last word.

*

By the time Stephanie reached her car, parked at the back of the hotel, she was still trying to simmer down. Just thank God she had managed to keep her cool during the moments it had mattered most. But what a disaster at the end. If only she hadn't let herself get out of control. But when had she ever had control where Matthew Cornwall was concerned?

She thumped her hand against the steering wheel. How could she have forgotten what it did to her just to look at him? And to know that without him she wouldn't be where she was today only incensed her further.

He had believed in her, had given her the confidence she needed to take the breaks when they came. If he'd been around to witness her success then things might have been very different – as it was she'd fought her way to the top for the sole reason that they should find themselves in the position they'd been in that morning. He'd seen straight through it, of course, and now her revenge seemed petty and trivial. And what was the point in it anyway, when it wasn't what she wanted? It was him that she wanted, it always had been, and all these years she'd blamed him for the way she'd humiliated herself.

Six years ago he'd promised her the earth. That was in the days when she'd been his production assistant and his lover. He was setting up his own production company and she would be the producer. Together they would take the world by storm. They'd leave mainstream television and take on pop videos, commercials and eventually feature films. They'd be partners. Partners in everything, because together they had what it took. That was until that night – the night that still haunted her every time she thought about him, the night when everything had fallen apart.

They'd been to dinner, celebrating the fact that the new company had now been registered. Nothing was mentioned then about him leaving Kathleen, but it was implicit in all they talked about. He was about to hit the big time and couldn't afford to have his wife walking onto set ordering people about, telling them they weren't giving him enough time, that the scripts were dreadful, that the costume designer had got it all wrong. But what he could afford even less was that hideously embarrassing bag she brought with her, filled with hot soup in winter or iced lemonade in summer, and sandwiches, sausage rolls and cakes, together with the latest creation from the mother-in-law's oven.

When they'd left the restaurant they'd strolled back along Park Walk in Chelsea, ducking under branches that were weighed down with blossom – yes, it really was as romantic as that – and stopping every now and then to kiss. Their love-making that night was urgent, possessive and almost insatiable.

They were still wrapped in each other's arms, whispering and laughing quietly in the wake of such intensity, when a voice suddenly screeched: '*You bastard!*' And Kathleen, all five feet nine inches of her, was standing in the room.

Matthew shot out of bed, grabbing for his clothes, but Kathleen was on him, beating her fists on his back and knocking him to the floor. Then, before Stephanie could move, Kathleen had torn the sheet from the bed.

'You slut!' she screamed. 'Can't get a man of your own so you steal someone else's. Well this is one man you won't get!' And she launched herself across the bed. Stephanie only just managed to roll out of the way, and fled to the other side of the room.

Still naked, Matthew leapt to his feet and tried to pin his wife to the bed. 'Stop it!' he yelled. 'Kathleen! Stop!' But she threw him off and scrambled over the bed towards Stephanie.

'I'm going to kill you, you whore!'

Stephanie was backed into a corner and grabbed the nearest thing to hand – a china pig filled with coins.

'No!' Matthew vaulted over the bed. The china pig crashed to the floor and Kathleen grabbed Stephanie by the hair.

Stephanie screamed and Kathleen went on shouting obscenities as she slapped and scratched at her naked body. The struggle seemed to go on for ever as Matthew fought to get a hold on his wife. When eventually he did he yelled for Stephanie to get out of the room.

'I'm not leaving you in here with her, she's mad!' Stephanie yelled back. And again Kathleen lunged at her. But this time Matthew had a strong enough grip and spun her round, throwing her onto the bed.

'How could you?' Kathleen spat, looking up at them. 'How could you do this, you bastard? You've got a sick daughter at home crying for her Daddy, and you're out fucking around with that little scrubber! I always knew you were no good, you bitch! I told him . . .'

'Shut up!' Matthew roared. 'What do you mean Samantha's sick? What's the matter with her?'

'How the hell do I know? Even the doctor doesn't know. And what do you care?' She turned her face into the pillow and sobbed.

He looked at Stephanie. 'I'll have to go,' he said, quietly.

'No!' Kathleen howled. 'You stay here. Stay with her.'

'If Samantha's ill then I'm coming home,' Matthew said.

'The only way you're ever coming back into that house is if you swear to me now you're never going to see that tart again.' She drew herself up from the bed. 'Go on, swear it! Because if you don't, Matthew Cornwall, you can forget about that precious company of yours, you can forget about everything, because I'll take you for every penny you've got. And you can say goodbye to your children at the same time.'

Matthew's face was pale and strained as he looked at Stephanie.

'Swear it!' Kathleen screamed. 'Let her hear you. Let her know that she's just another screw. Because, darling, that's all you are. So go on, tell her!'

'Did you bring the car?' Matthew snapped.

'Swear it!' Kathleen was almost hysterical. 'Tell her she's just another tart.'

'I said, did you bring the car?' he shouted.

'Make the choice, Matthew. Your daughter, your company, or *her!*'

'There is no choice,' he hissed, 'and you know it!'

Kathleen's eyes gleamed with triumph. 'Did you hear that?' she spat at Stephanie. 'There is no choice. So you can kiss goodbye to that cosy little future you've been planning. It's none of it going to happen. I'll wait five minutes,' she told Matthew.

She left then – the same way she'd come in, through the window Matthew had left open.

As he dressed, Stephanie stood in the corner watching him. Neither of them spoke until he was ready to leave. And then she did something she had never, not even in her worst nightmares, dreamt she would be capable of; something that even if she lived to be a hundred, she would never forgive herself for. She threw herself to the floor, clutched her arms about his legs, and begged him to stay. 'Don't go,' she sobbed. 'Please, Matthew, don't leave me.'

He tried to pull her to her feet, but she wouldn't let him.

'She's making you choose between me and Samantha. It's not fair, Matthew. It's just not fair.'

'Stephanie, please, stop this,' he groaned. 'Please stand up.'

'I can't! I can't until you tell me that I'm more important than Samantha. That what we have means more to you than your family.' She waited, her cheek pressed against his knees, while tears streamed down her face. 'Please!' she screamed, as he prised her hands apart.

'Please, Matthew, tell me! Say you're coming back. Say you love me!' She looked up into his face, but he couldn't meet her eyes. 'Matthew! Matthew, please!' she begged, as slowly he turned and walked out the door. 'She's lying, Matthew! Can't you see that? Samantha's not ill – there's nothing wrong with her. She's just a spoiled girl crying for her own way. Matthew, please don't leave me.'

His telephone call had come the following night, telling her Samantha was in hospital with suspected meningitis.

Neither of them said anything then, until she whispered: 'I'm sorry. I'm sorry for everything I said, Matthew. Do you think you can forgive me?'

'Of course.'

She braced herself then, not wanting to ask, but knowing she had to. 'And what about us?'

She waited, and finally he said the words that tore her heart to shreds. 'I'm sorry, Stephanie. There can't be any us.'

Remembering those words now the great, hollow ache she'd carried with her since that night began to churn. She'd loved him so much that for a long time she hadn't wanted to go on living. But she had, and it was only by making herself believe that one day he would come back to her that she had made it through. And now he'd left Kathleen. Six years later than he should have done. That's what he'd said, and as she sank into a swamp of exhaustion she closed her eyes. The road she had travelled for so long had suddenly changed and she no longer knew where she was heading, or why.

'. . . and when I got back, they were gone. Both of them. There wasn't even a note.' Realising that she was gabbling, Marian took a deep breath and cast a look at Matthew. 'Anyway, you don't want to hear about that,' she said. 'It's just that, being on my own, money started to get low again, and when Janey offered me two hundred pounds as a deposit I had to take it.' She dabbed at her eyes and waited. It was the first time since Madeleine and Paul had left that she had actually talked to someone about it. But why him, she was asking herself, when he so obviously isn't interested? She felt a sudden longing for Paul, and was again overwhelmed by the bleakness of her situation. 'How could they have walked out on me like that?' she whispered. Then realising she had spoken aloud, she turned her head away, embarrassed.

Matthew watched her, ashamed of what he was thinking. She looked so awful that he could easily have walked out on her himself. Besides, he'd had a nightmare of a week, which was why he hadn't got to see her until tonight. Even then he would have avoided it but for the fact that the music was driving him crazy.

'Can't you ask her to turn it down?' he said lamely.

'Don't you think I've tried that? She just laughs.'

'Then kick her out.'

'She won't go.'

He sighed, and got up to answer the phone. He wouldn't be having to bother with this at all if the film wasn't overrunning. But now, thanks to a massive continuity error which had involved the recall of three frigates to the Bristol Channel, coupled with an alcoholic stupor which had seen his star in bed, in the bar, in the river even –

anywhere except in front of the camera – he was stuck here for at least another week.

It was Woody on the phone. Matthew waited until he'd finished, then said: 'Woody, I don't give a . . .' He winced as Marian blew her nose, then started again. 'Woody, you sort it out. It's what you're paid for. I know, I know. But I'm not coming down there again tonight. Just make sure she's on that set at eight o'clock tomorrow morning.' He listened, then groaned. 'Why, Woody, did no one check the tide times before? Then you'd better be the one to explain to Richard Collins why we've lost yet another half day shoot.' With that, he slammed down the receiver.

Marian dragged herself to her feet. 'I'm sorry. You're busy . . . I'd better be going . . . At least you know now why . . .'

'Sit down!' Matthew barked. As he turned round, he almost burst out laughing at the look of horror on Marian's face. 'I'm sorry,' he said. 'It's just that things aren't going too well at the moment. Now, you were saying.'

'I'd finished, actually.'

'Oh.'

There was an awkward silence.

Marian sniffed. 'About Paul. I don't suppose you saw him before he left, by any chance?'

'No.'

'Or Madeleine?'

Matthew shook his head. 'Don't you have any idea where they might have gone?'

Her eyes followed him as he sat down. 'You're assuming they've gone somewhere together, and I honestly don't think . . . Well, I can't imagine they'd have . . . They did go off together, didn't they? You saw them. You can tell me, I won't cause a scene, I promise.'

'No, I didn't see them. But I'd say it's pretty obvious they've gone together. I mean, it's a bit too much of a coincidence otherwise.'

Marian's mouth started to tremble. 'Oh God, this is so awful. I'm sorry, but I don't seem to be able to stop crying these days.'

Saved by the doorbell, Matthew shot from his seat and closed the door behind him.

'Hello, Matthew.' It was Stephanie. His eyes widened, then after glancing over his shoulder, he looked at her again. 'Are you just going to stand there gawping, or can I come in?' she said.

It was rare for Matthew to find himself at a loss, but for the moment he very definitely was. Since he'd last seen Stephanie he had thought about her a great deal, and what he'd been thinking had unsettled him more than he liked to admit. The truth was, he wanted to see her again as much as he wanted to do the film – but with a love-torn teenager sitting in his flat, and knowing Stephanie as he did, this was hardly the moment.

'If it's inconvenient I can always go away and come back again,' Stephanie said in a tight voice.

'No, no. Come in,' he said, and throwing the door wide and himself into the lap of the gods, he stood back to let her pass.

As they walked into the room Marian looked up. Her face was like a battlefield. Stephanie stopped in her tracks, then turned to Matthew; his eyes closed.

'Obviously, I'm interrupting,' she said, her voice coated with sarcasm. 'So if you don't mind . . .'

'Stephanie, will you . . .' He stopped himself in the nick of time. He was going to say *look at her*. 'Will you just listen?'

'No, thank you. I don't know what goes on in your life these days, Matthew, but if you ask me, you get a kick out of screwing up women's lives.'

'Hold it right there!' He grabbed her arm and spun her back to face Marian. 'Stephanie, this is Marian. Marian, this is Stephanie. Now Marian, perhaps you would like to explain to Stephanie exactly why you are here, and I'll go make us all a large drink.' He pushed Stephanie into a chair and escaped into the kitchen.

He gave them a full ten minutes, by which time he'd managed to run through every conceivable reason why Stephanie should have arrived unannounced like that. In the end he gave up. She would have to tell him herself, once he'd managed to get rid of the girl from upstairs.

'I just wish they hadn't gone off without saying a word,' Marian was saying when he walked back into the room. 'What do you think I should do? How can I find them?'

'I shouldn't think they want to be found,' Matthew answered. 'If they did, they'd have called you by now.'

'Matthew!' Stephanie was glaring at him. He rolled his eyes and handed her a drink. 'For God's sake, have some heart,' she hissed as she took it. 'Can't you see how distressed the girl is?'

His mouth twitched with amusement as Stephanie turned her attention back to Marian. 'I think we'd better deal with the most immediate problem first,' she said. 'That is, how to get this Janey out of your flat.'

Matthew looked at her with unrestrained enthusiasm. 'Absolutely,' he agreed.

'You can deal with that, Matthew.'

'I can?'

'Well, you're a man. The girl might listen to you. If she doesn't, just pick up her things and dump them outside.'

'And what about the landlord? Why can't he do it?'

'Because it'll take far too long. No, you deal with the noisy tenant. Give her her two hundred pounds back – don't look at me like that, you can afford it; give her the money and send her on her way. I'll deal with the rest.'

'Oh.' He folded his arms. 'I can't wait to see how much this little rescue mission is going to cost *you*.'

Stephanie shot him a look and turned back to Marian.

'You say you haven't got a job. Well, as it happens I'm in need of a secretary.'

'You've got one!'

Ignoring Matthew, Stephanie continued, 'Can you type?' Marian was stunned. 'Well, can you?' Marian nodded. 'Shorthand?' Again Marian nodded. 'Good, that's that settled. The salary's fifteen thousand plus overtime and expenses. You can pay Matthew back as soon as you're on your feet. I'll give you a trial run of six weeks. If you're not up to it, or you decide you don't like me or the film world, then we'll call it quits. How does that sound?'

'Film world?' Marian gasped, and then it dawned on her where she had seen Stephanie before. 'You're – you're Stephanie Ryder, aren't you?' she said, suddenly overwhelmed by the company she was in.

'She most certainly is,' Matthew grinned.

Again Stephanie threw him a look before continuing. 'It'll mean moving to London, of course,' she said. 'How would you feel about that?'

Marian looked from one to the other of them, aghast that she should be sitting here, pouring her heart out to people like this. But then Stephanie smiled, and she felt a peculiar sensation stir in her heart.

'Excuse me,' she said, choking, and before she could disgrace herself any further, she ran from the room.

As she sat on the edge of the bath, her arms clasped tightly about her body, she tried to sort her thoughts into a coherent pattern, but on a shelf above the basin Matthew's razor seemed to mock her with a cruel reminder of all she had lost, and the tears she tried to force back scalded her eyes. Five weeks they'd been gone, and as each day passed she felt herself shrinking back into the person she'd thought never to be again. But now it was worse. She had never felt so alone, and never so afraid. Their treachery tore at her with talons so vicious that she cried out with the pain. Her sense of worth was gone; she loathed herself with all the passion that had once fuelled her love for Paul. They'd never come back, in her heart she knew it, but still she couldn't reconcile herself to leaving the flat where she had once been so happy.

After a while there was a knock on the door and Stephanie came in. 'How are you feeling now?' she asked.

Marian had to swallow hard before she could answer, but even then her voice was hoarse. 'Better, thank you. I'm sorry, I'm making such a fool of myself.'

Stephanie sat down next to her and put an arm round her shoulders. 'We've all been there,' she said, 'but there's only one way out of it, and that's to try to get on with your life.'

Marian nodded. 'I'm trying,' she smiled, 'it's just that sometimes . . .'

'I know,' Stephanie said, hugging her. 'But if you'll come to London it'll help, I promise you. Here, you're surrounded by all sorts of reminders of the past, and it'll be almost impossible to forget. And you must put it behind you. It hurts to hear that, I know, but believe me, it's the only way. And you're young, you'll fall in love again.' When Marian turned to look at her, she laughed. 'I know, you don't want to. Neither did I.'

'But did you?' Marian asked.

Stephanie breathed in deeply. 'When I was your age, yes. I still remember when the first man I ever slept with dumped me; I thought the end of the world had come. I take it Paul was your first boyfriend?'

Marian nodded. 'But we never actually . . .' She looked down at her hands and whispered, 'I'm still a virgin.'

'Oh, my darling,' Stephanie said, 'you don't know how glad you'll be of that one day. I know you love him now, but try to see him for what he really is. I mean, if he could do what he did to you, just think what he might do to Madeleine.'

'Yes. But I don't want Maddy to suffer like this. I wouldn't wish it on my worst enemy.'

'Then she's a very lucky girl to have someone who loves her so much. Now, how about putting on a brave face and coming out for dinner with Matthew and me?'

'Oh no! I mean, it's very kind of you but I couldn't.'

'Oh yes, you could. After all, if you decide to take the job I've offered you, the three of us are going to be working on *Disappearance* together, so it'll give us a chance to get to know one another a little.' She stood up, and pulled Marian to her feet. 'Pop upstairs and clean up if you like, we'll leave in fifteen minutes. And Marian,' she said as Marian was walking through the door, 'things have a habit of working out in the end, you know. It just takes time.'

'You're an amazing woman, do you know that?' Matthew said, as he and Stephanie waited to hear Marian's door close upstairs. Stephanie gave him a smug grin and followed him into the flat. 'Nightcap?' he offered.

'Just coffee.'

She leaned against the kitchen door, patiently listening as he objected to Marian's over-indulgence of grief in – of all places! – a restaurant. The expression of distaste was punctuated by the clattering of crockery and three trips to the fridge, where he opened and closed the door without taking anything out.

'Milk,' Stephanie said eventually. 'I'd hazard a guess you're looking for the milk.'

'Thank you,' he muttered, not without irony. 'Anyway, as I was saying, she's a nice enough kid, reminds me of my daughter in a way. Not so pretty as Samantha, of course, but then Samantha takes after her father.' He grinned, waiting for her reaction, but she only lifted her eyebrows. 'But you didn't have to offer the girl a job. *Or* my money!'

'Don't be stingy. And I offered her the job because I really do need a secretary. Tanya's leaving at the end of the month, and quite frankly I don't fancy taking on one of those bright young things that parade about Soho – they frighten me with their widow's weeds and ghoulish make-up. Marian could be just what I'm looking for – and her lack of sophistication will be a refreshing change for us all.'

'Lack of sophistication?' he laughed. 'I didn't know it was possible to be so green in this day and age. If you ask me . . .'

'Which no one did . . .'

'. . . the girl adds a whole new dimension to the meaning of gullibility.' He picked up the tray and she followed him into the sitting-room. As he poured the coffee Stephanie kicked off her shoes and curled up in a corner of the sofa.

Until then they'd spent the best part of the evening concentrating on Marian and her predicament; Stephanie had found it rather endearing, the way Marian livened up when she'd considered what Madeleine would say if she knew she was going to be moving to London. Matthew had swallowed his irritation and tried several times to manoeuvre the conversation round to *Disappearance*. He hadn't had much success, except to talk about what Marian's role would be. Then came the question of where she would live. For one alarming moment he thought Stephanie was going to suggest Marian moved in with him. His glass had hit the table and he'd already drawn breath to protest before he realised that Stephanie was quite expertly sending him up. Now it seemed that for the time being Marian was going to take up residence in Stephanie's spare room. At that point Matthew had thrown up his hands – what wasn't Stephanie prepared to do for this girl?

'A degree in philosophy, who'd have thought it of her?' Stephanie mused.

'Me, for one. It's just the sort of useless thing kids go for these days. Well, it hasn't got her very far, has it?' he added in response to Stephanie's look.

'I wonder what did happen to that boyfriend and cousin of hers?' she said. 'Still, not our problem. If you ask me, she's better off without them. They sound a very dubious pair, don't you think?' She looked up. He was standing over her and her heart kicked against her ribs when she saw the lambency in his eyes. 'Are you going to stand there all night, holding that cup of coffee?' she said awkwardly.

The corner of his mouth dropped in a grin as he relaxed onto the sofa beside her and put his cup on the table.

'Now tell me how pleased you are to be doing *Disappearance,*' she said.

'How would a bit of obeisance do you?'

'Oh yes. I could go for that.'

He made a noise that said 'fat chance', and she laughed.

'What made up your mind?' he asked. 'I mean, about me. And how come the visit? Not that I'm not honoured, of course.'

'I wanted to tell you in person,' she answered, avoiding the first question, 'so we could celebrate together. And I thought it would give us a chance to catch up, bury the hatchet, or whatever it is we need to do.'

'So you invite Marian Doolittle to join us?'

'Don't be unkind. She was unhappy and frightened, surely even you could see that. And in case you'd forgotten, I've been there myself.'

His eyes shot to hers, held them for a moment, and then he shook his head, laughing. 'God, I'm slow. It's the broken hearts club, isn't it? That's why you're doing all this for her. And I suppose that I, as a distinguished member of the offending sex, have to be grateful I'm home in one piece.'

'What do you mean, Matthew?'

'Oh, nothing,' he answered lazily. 'But perhaps we should change the subject before I start choking on my own foot.'

Stephanie sipped her coffee. She still felt trapped, even though he'd given her a way out. But the lid of their own Pandora's box was open now, and despite the fear of going on, there was nothing she could do to stop the words that were clamouring for escape. 'I've done a lot of thinking since we last met,' she said finally. She hoped he might help by asking what her thoughts had been about, but he didn't. 'I did and said a lot of things on that last night – things I'm so ashamed of now that I don't know where to begin to . . .'

'Don't,' he said. And when she turned to look at him, 'It's in the past, Steph.'

'But we have to talk about it. If we're going to work together we can't pretend that nothing happened. And I want to tell you how awful I felt about everything I said, the way I behaved. I knew, even as I was saying it, that I shouldn't be talking about Samantha like that. But God, Matthew, I was so desperate I hardly knew *what* I was saying.'

'I know that. And I'm the one to blame, Stephanie, not you.'

She gave a dry laugh. 'Oh, I blamed you all right. You'd promised me so much, I'd built my whole life round it – so that when you went, you took everything. *Everything*. And then, after you'd told me there couldn't be any future for us, you never called again, you didn't even write, not even to answer my letters. God, I hated you then.'

He leaned forward and rested his elbows on his knees, looking down at the floor. 'I had to do it that way, Steph. I didn't know any other. It was touch and go whether Samantha would live, and Kathleen was on my back with threats every minute of the day. I won't go into all the guilt I suffered, but it was as much because of what I'd done to you as it was because of them.' He turned to face her. 'The letter you sent, the one you put in my birthday card?' She nodded. 'I don't think I realised quite how much I loved you until then. Leaving you was the most difficult thing I've ever done.'

She sighed and half laughed. 'I wish I'd known, it might have made things easer – does that sound dreadful? But I needed a reaction from you, something that told me I *had* mattered, even if I didn't any more. That was the worst part of it, really – not knowing how you were feeling.'

He took her hand and locked his fingers through hers. 'I'm sorry.'

She looked at their hands and felt the stirrings of an almost forgotten warmth. It was a long time since she had allowed herself to remember that dreadful sense of meaninglessness and confusion she'd felt when he had gone. Eventually she'd managed to fill the void – or thought she had, until the other day. Abruptly she drew her hand away. 'Listen to us,' she laughed. 'And you accused Marian of over-indulging.'

'Oh no, not her again,' he groaned, then ducked as she made to hit him.

They were both sorry the moment was broken, knowing there was still a great deal to be said, but Stephanie changed the subject to *Disappearance* and he followed her lead. They discussed who might be suitable for the role of Olivia Hastings; how long they would need to shoot in New York; when would be the best time to go to Italy; and, inevitably they speculated on what had really happened to Olivia. All the time they talked, the old wounds and long-stifled feelings were unfurling, snatching their smiles, tugging at their hearts, until emotions were running amok inside them like dormant imps given a new lease on life.

'Are you going to tell me,' he asked, swallowing what

he really wanted to say, 'what the new evidence is concerning Olivia?'

'I wondered when you were going to ask,' she answered, looking at her watch. 'You can read the note when you come to London. It was sent about a year ago, to Frank Hastings.'

His mind was racing. He knew she was on the point of leaving, but he didn't want her to go yet. 'When do I get to meet him?'

'We'll go over to New York in a couple of months. Probably when this film you're doing now is at the dub stage.' She wanted to ask him more about the film, anything to prolong her stay, but at the same time she needed to be alone – to think.

'At the dub stage?' he repeated. 'Could be tricky.'

'We'll work something out.' She looked at him, and he didn't look away.

'And what about us, Steph?' he asked eventually. 'Will we work something out for us?'

She tensed, and when she spoke her voice was hoarse. 'You said once that there couldn't be any us.'

'I was wrong.'

'Were you?'

'Stephanie, you're the only woman I've ever . . .'

'No, don't.'

He pulled her round to face him. 'You can't run away from it, Stephanie.'

'No! What I can't do is go through it all again,' she said angrily. 'No, please don't touch me. It's too soon, Matthew. No Matthew, please . . .' She sobbed as his mouth closed over hers.

When he let her go she was shaking, and he smiled at the confusion in her eyes.

'Please don't smile at me like that,' she said.

'I'm sorry. I don't know any other way.'

She turned her head away. 'Oh God, Matthew, if only

you knew how often I've dreamt about that smile, about this, about the way you . . .'

'The way I what?' he chuckled.

She pushed him away. 'I'm not ready for this, Matthew. I'm . . . it's come as a shock, seeing you after all this time and finding out that . . .'

'A shock? But you admitted yourself that you'd bought the rights to the book because you knew I'd want to do it. Surely you must have known then . . .'

'No! You're wrong! I didn't know anything then. Except that maybe I could hold it in your face and then snatch it away.'

'Revenge?'

She nodded.

'Why didn't you do it?' He waited. 'Because . . .?'

'Because my feelings for you haven't changed!' she shouted. 'Is that what you want to hear? Well, it's true, they haven't. Seeing you again has been just about the worst thing I could have done. For Christ's sake, why do you always have this effect on me? I don't even know what I'm saying!'

'Why are you getting so angry?'

She leapt to her feet, kicking around for her shoes. 'Oh, it's all so easy for you, isn't it? You haven't suffered the way I have these past six years. And now you tell me you've left your wife and expect me to come running. Well, I'm not going to, Matthew. I'm telling you, I'm not!'

'OK, OK.' He was laughing and holding up his hands in defence.

'Please don't laugh at me, I feel undignified enough as it is.' She picked up her handbag. 'Now, if we are to work together, I think it's better that we never refer to our past again. This is to be a purely professional relationship, and I'd like you to respect me as a producer, as I shall obviously respect you as a director. Are we agreed?' By this time she was at the door, but turned back when he didn't answer. 'I said, are we agreed?'

He tugged a forelock of his black hair. 'If that's what you want, Stephanie, then agreed. Purely professional.'

'Good. Please call me when you're back in London; by that time Bronwen, my partner, will be anxious to see you. I take it you'll want Woody as a first and Bob Fairley lighting?'

He nodded.

'Goodnight, then. I hope you can sleep through that terrible din,' she said, referring to the music that had just set the ceiling shaking. Then she left, hating him for agreeing to her conditions, but hating herself even more for behaving in the way she had.

As she sat at the upstairs window, watching Stephanie drive away, Marian could feel fate creeping up on her, and she wrapped her arms more tightly round her body, as if resisting it. Now that the initial excitement of meeting Stephanie and having her life taken in charge had worn off, she was again being sucked into a vacuum of loneliness. Everything she'd done in her life had been done with Madeleine, and it panicked her to think that in a few weeks she was going to embark on a new life without her.

But she would do it, if for no other reason than that she could no longer bear to look in the mirror and see herself shrivelling inside a cowardly shell of defeat. Because she missed them so much, because without them there seemed no purpose to her life, she had become ugly again, her hair was lank and the very pores of her skin seemed to close in the misery. But for a while, for a few short months, she had been alive, vibrant and happy – there had been no cowardice, no weakness, because Paul had loved her and . . .

Her breath caught in her throat, and as she turned from the window and walked slowly towards the bed, tears ran silently down her face. 'Where are you?' she whispered into the darkness. 'Paul, Maddy, where are you?'

— 8 —

The long, low whistle came from a hole in the ground. Looking down, Madeleine saw two workmen peering up from under their helmets and surveying her legs appreciatively. She laughed and waved, then crossed through the busy Knightsbridge traffic to the row of shops opposite. Glancing at the piece of paper she clutched in her hand, she checked the address, then inspected herself in a shop window before carrying on down the Brompton Road. Finally she arrived at a set of glass doors with two rows of intercom bells on a side panel. The Crabb Agency was on the third floor. She announced her name, and the door was released. Though she strolled nonchalantly up the stairs, her stomach was a tight knot of nervous excitement.

She reached the third floor and pushed open the swing doors. A receptionist looked up – but before either of them could speak, a dour-looking woman emerged from an office and introduced herself as Deidre Crabb's secretary.

'If you'd like to come this way,' she said, standing back for Madeleine to walk ahead. Madeleine smiled her thanks, but the woman's face remained lifeless as she ushered her into a small office. At the far side of the office was another door, which the secretary opened without knocking. 'Madeleine Deacon,' she announced, and turned to look up at Madeleine, whose silver and gold tin bracelets jangled at her wrists as she raised a hand to sweep the mass of dishevelled hair from her eyes.

Deidre Crabb turned from her computer screen and stood up. Her dark auburn hair frizzed round her head and fell in jagged points far below her shoulders. There was so much of it that it made her body appear more willowy than it actually was, and her handsome face softer. 'Ah, Madeleine,' she smiled, holding out both her hands and walking across the room. 'Come in, do come in.' Even taller than Madeleine, she was able to put an arm round her shoulders as she guided her to a pair of black leather sofas in the corner. Glancing back, she nodded to Anne, who went out, closing the door behind her. 'This is splendid,' Deidre intoned. 'I've been so looking forward to meeting you since our little chat on the phone.' Her voice was low and melodic, and when she smiled Madeleine felt herself responding to the warmth she exuded.

'Me too,' she said chirpily, as Deidre pushed her gently onto a sofa. 'I feel really honoured to be here. I mean, everyone's heard of you, and everyone told me that you were really difficult to get to see.'

Deidre's feline eyes narrowed as she looked down at the frank, upturned face. So this was the girl who was waving ten grand in the face of anyone prepared to give her a chance. She chuckled. 'It's true that I don't see every girl who gets in touch, where would I find the time? There are other people in the agency who deal with the day to day enquiries; it would have been more usual for you to see one of them first.'

Madeleine watched Deidre as she moved round the coffee table and relaxed onto the opposite sofa. She crossed her slim legs and tugged at the cuffs of her mustard suit. Then resting her head on a loosely clenched fist, she said, 'So you want to be a model, Madeleine?' She laughed. 'But of course, why else would you be here?'

Madeleine giggled; but then, as a gentle glow of admiration suffused Deidre's eyes, she experienced a swell of confidence that turned her smile to one of languid self-satisfaction.

Deidre inclined her head, quietly impressed by such a

rapid, yet nonetheless remarkable transformation in the girl's poise. 'How much modelling work have you done?' she enquired.

Up to now, in all the other interviews she'd had, Madeleine had lied, but there was something about Deidre that told her it wasn't necessary. 'None,' she answered.

Deidre nodded. 'I don't think that should prove too much of a problem, I suspect you're a remarkably beautiful young woman beneath all that make-up. Turn your face to the light a little, would you?'

Shrugging off the comment about her make-up, Madeleine raised her face so that it was bathed in the yellowy glow of the lamp beside her. So far she'd been to see four other agents, and though they'd all seemed interested at first, they'd all of them turned her down in the end. Of course, she had no idea that Deidre Crabb was behind the rejections, because she had no idea how much power Deidre Crabb wielded in this exclusive world. But there was something about Deidre that made Madeleine want to impress her, and somehow she knew that if she succeeded, this woman would change her life. Her pulses started to race as the prospect sent a quick, electrifying thrill through her body. It aroused her in a way that stained her cheeks with colour and made her lips tremble as she circled them with her tongue. She thought of Paul, and suddenly she was hot, burning, and as a dark fire seeped from the violet depths of her eyes, Deidre leaned forward, mesmerised. The look was charged with such powerful yet indolent eroticism that she felt a jolt of excitement flash through her veins – an excitement so vivid that it seemed to seize a beat from her heart. She had never, in all her years as an agent, seen such a look.

'Oh my God,' she murmured.

Smiling, Madeleine lowered her head. Her face was flushed and her skin still tingling, but she was apparently unaware of the extraordinary effect she had had on Deidre.

But though Deidre's mind was still in excited confusion, her manner was composed as she said, 'You have exquisite bone structure, Madeleine. Do you suffer with spots at all?'

'No, I don't!' Madeleine retorted testily.

Deidre raised a hand. 'Plenty do,' she explained, 'though you'd never know it. And how about the skin on the rest of your body? Any blemishes, birthmarks, warts . . .'

'Warts! You must be joking. Only old people get them . . . don't they?'

Deidre's face was alive with amusement as she slowly shook her head. The girl was proving to be the most fascinating paradox she'd ever encountered – one moment steeped in the erotic sensuousness of her beauty, the next, gauchely naive.

'Well, I haven't got any,' Madeleine said sulkily. 'I'll take my clothes off if you like, and prove it.'

'No, that really won't be necessary,' Deidre laughed. 'Unless you want to do nude modelling, of course.'

Madeleine's face lit up. 'As a matter of fact, I do,' she enthused. 'I want to be on Page Three, and in the men's magazines and all that.'

'You do?' Deidre's surprise was genuine. That was one little snippet of information that hadn't reached her about Madeleine Deacon. 'Well, there's no reason why you shouldn't. But what about fashion? Does that interest you?'

Madeleine shrugged. 'Yes, I suppose so.' Then, more definitely. 'Yes, it does. You mean like catwalks and all that?'

'Catwalks, and magazine spreads, cosmetics maybe, perfume, sun tan lotion, cars, soft drinks – the list is endless. It's just a matter of introducing you to the right photographers, the right directors, the right clients . . .

We're getting a little ahead of ourselves. How old are you, Madeleine?'

'Twenty.' Madeleine's voice was vague, she was still struggling to take in everything Deidre had just said.

'Mm, a little old to be . . .'

'Old!'

'. . . starting out, but again, I don't anticipate that being a problem. Some girls have already reached the top by the time they're your age. I take it it's to the top you're hoping to go?'

'Oh yes,' Madeleine confirmed. 'I've always wanted to be famous.'

Deidre couldn't help being touched by such guileless honesty. 'Then we'll have to see what we can do, won't we?' she smiled.

Madeleine blinked several times, and Deidre stood up and walked over to the coffee percolator. 'I'm a little concerned about your desire to be on Page Three,' she said. 'Have you given any thought to the way that kind of exposure might affect your credibility? Milk or sugar?'

Madeleine shook her head. 'Neither, thank you. What do you mean, my credibility?'

Deidre let out a deep breath, then walking back with two cups of coffee, she smiled as she handed one to Madeleine. 'Well, the centrefold of, say, *Penthouse* or *Playboy* carries a great deal more prestige than page three of *The Sun*, wouldn't you agree?'

Madeleine shrugged. As far as she could see there wasn't any difference, except that you showed everything in one and only the top half in the other. She said so. 'And,' she added, 'a lot more people buy *The Sun*.'

'Well I can't argue with that,' Deidre laughed.

Madeleine put down her cup and leaned forward in a conspiratorial manner. 'I've always wanted to be on Page Three,' she said gravely. 'Always, ever since I've known there was one.'

Again Deidre sighed. 'If your heart's set on it . . .' She walked over to her desk and picked up a foolscap pad and pen. She wrote for several minutes, and though she was aware from the jangling bracelets that Madeleine was moving around behind her, she didn't turn round until she'd finished. When she did, her eyes flew open, and for a moment she was unable to find the breath to speak.

'See, no warts,' Madeleine declared.

'Good God,' Deidre muttered, then had to turn away before she burst out laughing. 'Well,' she said, once she had herself sufficiently under control, 'now I can see why you're so keen to do nude modelling. Your body is flawless, my dear. Walk to the window, turn slowly, then walk back again, will you?'

'Of course,' Madeleine said happily.

As she sauntered across the wide office she glanced around at the framed posters of magazine front covers. To her, the vacant eyes seemed to ooze envy, and her mouth curved in a superior smile. She was quite oblivious of the fact that the look she had shown Deidre earlier had been more than enough to seal her destiny; as far as Madeleine was concerned, it was her body that was her magic. And now that it was uncovered, she was impervious to everything beyond the supreme glory of her most intimate charms. She looked down at her breasts, and touched her fingers lightly against the smooth skin of her buttocks. There was only one thing in the world that could exceed the pleasure she gained from looking at her body, and that was Paul making love to it. As she thought about him now, a dull, pulsating ache spread through her loins, and she wanted him with a hunger so acute that for a moment she forgot where she was and her fingers began to caress the ache from her nipples. Then she looked up and saw that she had reached the window. As she looked down into the street, she suddenly wanted this meeting to be over. She wanted to go to him, to lie beneath him and feel his thighs against hers, to hold him in her hand and feel the hardness of him, to have him deep inside her, pounding against her until he wrenched the orgasm from her body in the way no other man had ever been able to do. Nothing mattered except him.

A brisk knock on the door brought her back to her senses, but as she turned round the light in her eyes suddenly flared again.

'Ah, Roy,' Deidre said, her voice brimming with laughter at the look on his face. 'Come and meet Madeleine Deacon. Madeleine, this is one of my partners, Roy Welland. He handles all the press and publicity for the agency. Madeleine was just displaying her talents,' she informed Roy.

Roy's eyes remained fixed to Madeleine as he closed the door. Aware that Deidre was watching him, he tried to look away, but there was an aura about the girl that was so compelling it seemed to draw him right into her. In all his forty-four years he had never felt such urgency, nor such helplessness. And then the feverish light in her eyes receded and it was as though a spell had been broken. He flicked a glance at Deidre, then at last he managed a smile and extended his hand as if he were introduced to naked women every day of his life. 'How do you do?' he croaked. Then clearing his throat, he tried again.

Deidre choked, and knowing she was going to howl with laughter any second, started to forage in her desk in an effort to control herself. Roy and Madeleine turned to watch her, waiting for her to say something, but though she tried several times, it was impossible. In the end Roy's lean, pock-marked face broke into a grin, and lifting one of Madeleine's arms he cried, 'What can I say? Except that if you can switch that look on and off at random, then the world's your oyster.' He glanced over his shoulder at Deidre. 'What do you say?'

'Oh yes, absolutely,' Deidre agreed, her self-control still teetering very close to the edge.

Madeleine looked from one to the other, not entirely sure what they were talking about. Then, shrugging, she laughed and said, 'So you'll take me on?'

'Without a doubt,' Roy answered.

Madeleine turned to Deidre. 'All we have to do now,' Deidre said, 'is convince the photographers.'

Roy sucked in his breath and started to shake his head. 'Yes, well, that is something else altogether. I wonder . . .'

'I've got some money,' Madeleine interrupted. 'I don't know if it'll do any good, but I've got ten thousand pounds to get me started.'

Deidre's tongue formed a lump in her cheek as she pondered this for a moment. She'd been wondering when Madeleine would make the offer, though now she'd met her, she knew she'd have taken her on whether she made it or not. She jerked herself abruptly to her feet and said, 'Get dressed, my dear. You must be getting cold.'

Avoiding Roy's eyes, she waited until Madeleine was pushing her arms into her jacket, then walked to the door. 'Leave your cheque with my secretary,' she said. 'I'll call you in a few days.'

Madeleine was winding her scarf round her neck, but at that her arms froze. 'I'm not that stupid,' she declared.

Deidre's smile was one of offended astonishment. 'What on earth do you mean, Madeleine?'

Madeleine's face had turned pink. 'Well . . .'

'Oh, I see,' Deidre laughed. 'You think we're going to steal the money.'

'No,' Madeleine answered hastily. 'I just meant that . . .'

Deidre glanced at Roy as she put an arm round Madeleine's shoulders. 'Let me tell you something, Madeleine,' she chuckled. 'From just this first meeting I already know that you have qualities that are extremely rare. Roy and I have another partner, Dario – he's a photographer – and together we are going to tap your qualities, and take you to the very top. You have my word on that. Now, I'll be in touch as soon as I have something for you.'

'When do you think that will be?' Madeleine ventured.

'Soon enough.' Deidre opened the door and stood aside to let Madeleine pass. 'Oh, and Madeleine . . .' Madeleine stopped. 'The newspaper nudes. Shall we set ourselves a deadline? Say, one month?'

'One month!' Madeleine gasped, and it was only with a supreme effort that she managed not to screech with joy.

Deidre nodded, then watched while Madeleine handed a cheque to her secretary. She smiled as Madeleine turned back to say goodbye, then closed the door.

Her green eyes were brimming with mirth as she turned to look at Roy. 'I wish you could have seen your face!' she laughed.

Roy's mouth twisted in a wry smile, and he shook his head. 'It's been a lot of years since the sight of a naked woman took my breath away like that,' he admitted, 'but did you see that look?'

'Oh yes, I saw it,' Deidre answered as she walked over to the window and looked down at the Brompton Road. 'So what do you think?'

He dropped onto the sofa and lifted his feet onto the coffee table. 'That it's very obliging of her to finance herself.'

Deidre threw back her head and laughed. Then casting her arms wide, as if ready for an embrace, she said, 'And how easy that's going to make it. Tell me, how famous shall we make her?'

'If she keeps coming up with that sort of money, then as famous as you like.'

Deidre looked down into the street again and smiled as,

three floors below, Madeleine sauntered out of the building. When she turned back, her eyes held that catlike quality he'd come to know so well.

They both looked round as the door opened and Anne, Deidre's secretary, walked in.

'Did you get everything?' Deidre asked.

Her secretary nodded, then flicking open her notepad, she said, 'She's staying at Blake's Hotel with her boyfriend. His name's Paul O'Connell – a writer, by all accounts. Unpublished.'

Deidre looked at Roy, a question in her eyes, and he nodded.

'They moved up from the West Country five weeks ago,' Anne went on. 'When she was in Bristol she worked for a strip-o-gram agency and shared a flat with a cousin. Her aunt brought her up from the age of eight – her parents were killed in a plane crash when she was ten.'

Deidre frowned. 'Poor Madeleine,' she murmured.

'And the money?' Roy asked.

Anne shook her head. 'It might belong to the boyfriend, we're still checking him out.' She turned back to Deidre. 'Shall I give her details to the bookers?'

'Yes,' Deidre nodded. 'And I think we should inform Dario. Is he at the studio?'

'As far as I know,' Anne replied. 'Would you like me to get him for you?'

'No. I'll do it myself.'

When Anne had gone, Deidre sat at her desk and picked up the direct dial phone. Roy was watching her closely, and as she returned his gaze, her shrewd green eyes mirrored the smile in his.

Blake's Hotel, in Roland Gardens, South Kensington, was where the very rich and very famous stayed – Madeleine had read that in *Elle* magazine. So, five weeks ago, when they had arrived at Paddington Station, that was where she and Paul had headed.

For forty-eight hours they'd made love in the Manhattan Suite and fantasised about what they would do with the money. First stop, when they resurfaced on the third day, had been Coutts Bank in the Strand, because Madeleine had heard somewhere that the Queen banked there. Paul let her handle everything, though he'd made sure the account was opened in joint names. It wasn't that he intended to steal any of the money, it was just that he, like the stunned cashiers and account manager, knew that three quarters of a million pounds couldn't possibly live in a current account. So, for the past month, while Madeleine had been out shopping and trying to find herself an agent, Paul, together with his accountants, had been paying regular visits to Coutts. Madeleine would probably never know about her wise investments, because it had been arranged that if the current account ever looked like falling below the stipulated minimum of two thousand pounds, stocks and shares would be sold and the account replenished. And so on, until she had spent it all – which Paul had no doubt she would.

To begin with, the mews house in Holland Park was going to set her back three hundred and fifty thousand, probably more by the time she'd finished dishing out bribes to estate agents and potential gazumpers. He was amused at the way she used her money to cut through red tape, and fascinated by how little persuasion was needed to make people take it. There was no use telling her that half the time it wasn't necessary, she had it fixed in her head that everything *had* to be bought. He'd have given a great deal to see Deidre Crabb's face when Madeleine made the offer she couldn't refuse, because, unlike Madeleine, he had heard of Deidre Crabb and knew she handled only the cream of the crop. His guess was that Deidre would show her the door and Madeleine would debase herself even further by shrieking a few obscenities. He spent some time considering exactly what she might say, then, bored by it, he went back to his perusal of the *Writer's Handbook*.

Paul O'Connell was the only son of Hammond O'Connell, financier, hotelier and patron of the arts. He had been what one might term an over-privileged child. His parents, already in their forties when he was born, had indulged his every whim, and after their death his aunt had continued in the same fashion. Now she was dead too, and the combined income from his inherited estates would do him very well indeed, should he care to avail himself of it. But for the past two years he hadn't touched it; being rich was something he'd always known – he wanted to try something different. He was twenty-eight when he moved to Bristol with a sports bag and fifty pounds.

He'd lived off several women before Marian Deacon saved him from being kicked onto the street – at least, that's what she thought. In fact he had been lodging with a woman in St. George whose husband was working in the Middle East. The arrangement had been quite satisfactory until the woman started to become too involved, and when he'd called her from London and she had told him she'd asked her husband for a divorce, he had known it was time for him to get out. That was when he'd rather cleverly manipulated Marian into inviting him to live with her and Madeleine.

From the start he had set out to make Marian love him, believing that her gratitude and adoration, and his response to it, would make a good study. It had, for a while. What was more, he had grown reasonably fond of her, had even found himself stimulated by her, until Madeleine, and the arrival of the cheque, had provided material for an exceptional exploitation of human nature that he simply couldn't resist. Nothing excited his writer's mind more than making people behave out of character.

He excelled at it, throwing himself and those around him into unexpected and unnatural situations until, with the detachment of a stranger, he sat back to observe individual responses to shock, or grief, or pleasure. His detachment, even from his own feelings, was something he exulted in, as was his ability to manipulate people; occasionally he wondered just how far he was prepared to go for the sake of his craft.

Suddenly he threw his book across the room. He'd always had everything he wanted, *everything*, but getting published was proving difficult – and tiresome.

The phone rang. He and Madeleine had agreed that she should be the only one to take phone calls, and since she wasn't there, he didn't answer. This was a precaution Madeleine had come up with, just in case Marian should find out where they were. When it stopped ringing, he wished he'd picked it up. If it had been Marian he'd have liked to talk to her. And what would Madeleine say to that?

He laughed aloud. Simple Madeleine. So pliable, so vain. Getting her to steal that money – *and* her cousin's boyfriend, he mustn't forget that – had been so easy it was almost disappointing. If he thought about it long enough, he guessed he might feel sorry for Marian, but it was all part of life's tapestry and one day, when the time was right, he might even go back to her.

Several minutes later, Madeleine walked in. 'I,' she said, dropping her handbag on the bed and spinning round, 'have an agent. And it is none other than Deidre Crabb herself.'

Knowing it would please her, he didn't hide his surprise.

'What did I tell you?' she went on. 'Everyone has her price, even Deidre Crabb. So how about that?' He got up from the sofa and strolled over to the bed. Madeleine turned as he passed her. 'Aren't you going to say something?' she asked, as he lay down.

He settled his hands behind his head and stared up at the ceiling. 'When you rang from the lobby just now, I take it you were testing me?'

A quick temper flared in her eyes. 'Is that it? Is that all you can say?'

He nodded, then turned to look at her. 'Now I've passed the test, maybe you'd like to tell me why it took you so long to come up in the lift.'

Catching the gleam in his eye, Madeleine's temper abated and she chuckled. Then, slowly, she sauntered over to the dressing table and perched on the edge. Paul watched her, knowing she was taking time to think. During the past five weeks he'd observed her closely, analysing everything she did in an effort to find out just what it was that made her tick. The answers had remained elusive, until suddenly it had hit him in one blinding flash – there were no answers where Madeleine was concerned, because Madeleine was nothing. She put him in mind of a beautiful Russian doll – as each shell was removed, underneath there were only more of the same, except smaller and smaller until there was nothing. Without that face and body Madeleine would cease to exist. And now the Russian doll was his to do with as he pleased, because he knew the effect he had on her and the power he wielded over her whether she was with him or not. Only he could bring that look to her eyes, the look that had almost blown his mind when he'd first seen it – and still did, no matter how many times they made love.

Now she was slowly opening the front of her shirt, while moistening her lips with her tongue. 'Do you see these buttons here?' she murmured. 'I undid them all, like this.' She shrugged her shirt and jacket down over her shoulders and just as he'd expected, she wore nothing underneath.

'And who was in the lift with you?' he asked, vaguely fascinated by the effect her magnificent breasts never failed to have on him.

'Just the operator.'

'Was he looking at you?'

She nodded. 'Oh yes.'

'What did you do then?'

She walked over to the bed and picked up his hand. 'I did this,' she said, putting it over her breast.

'Did he like it?'

'He seemed to.'

'And was he as excited as this?' He opened his bathrobe to reveal his semi-erect penis.

'More,' she breathed, then moaned as his long fingers toyed lazily with her nipples.

'Go on.'

She moved away, and turning to the mirror she watched herself remove what remained of her clothes. 'I stood in front of him, like this,' she said.

As she turned to face him, Paul sat up and shrugged off his robe.

'Here,' she whispered. 'Do it here, in front of the mirror.'

He walked across the room, and putting his hand on her shoulder to turn her away from him, he pushed her down to her hands and knees. Then kneeling over her, he said: 'Did this happen next?'

'Oh yes,' she whimpered, as he eased himself into her and began to move his hips slowly back and forth. Then, watching their reflections, she elaborated even further until he gripped her round the waist and slammed himself against her, so that she was gasping for breath and he was no longer listening.

Afterwards, as they lay on the floor, Paul thought about the lift operator, knowing not a word of it was true. But it excited him to hear her talk out her fantasies. Not that she wouldn't exhibit herself in that way – it was just that, as they both knew, the lift in Blake's Hotel was fully automatic.

'What about you?' she asked later, as she was taking a

bath. 'You haven't told me what you did today. Any luck on the agent front?'

He moved the razor away from his face and shook his head. 'But I'm working on it. So what's your first assignment?'

'No idea yet,' Madeleine answered, lifting a leg out of the water and watching the soft white bubbles trickle over her bronze skin. 'She's going to call me in a few days.'

'So you haven't parted with the ten grand?'

'I trust her, Paul. She'll deliver. She says I've got special qualities and that I'll go right to the very top.'

'Sure she did. For ten grand she'd say anything. What kind of modelling is it?'

'All kinds, I think. And a one month deadline on the newspaper.'

For a fleeting moment his face was grim. Then he said: 'Just remember, when you're out there being looked at by all those men, that you belong to me.'

She closed her eyes and let her head fall back. He caught her hands as she lifted them out of the water. 'Do you hear me?' he growled.

'I hear you,' she purred. 'But say it again.'

He smothered her hands with his lips. 'You've got to me, Madeleine Deacon. I've never known what it was like to feel this way about a woman. I adore you.'

She lay still, feeling his words thrill her body like caresses. 'And together,' she breathed, 'we're going to be the great love, the great beauty and the great writer. We'll be on every television, in every newspaper, every bookshop the world over.' *And that silly bitch, Marian, can eat her heart out*, she thought. Abruptly he let her hands go and she opened her eyes. 'What's the matter?' she asked, suddenly afraid that she might have spoken aloud.

He smiled down at her. 'Your beauty is undeniable, Maddy, but what if I can't make it? What if I don't get a publishing deal . . .'

She pulled herself out of the water and put her arms round him. 'You will, I know it. These things just take time.'

'And sometimes they never happen. No, don't say anything, I want you to think about it. I can't tell you what it does to me to know that you want so much for us. It's what I want too, to be with you every step of the way, but there's always the chance that it might not happen. And you've got to ask yourself, will a failed writer be enough for you?' He kissed the tip of her nose and unwound himself from her embrace. He would have walked away, but seeing the way she was looking at him, he found himself kissing her tenderly on the mouth.

But no matter what she did to his heart, he was determined to see this game through to the end. The first moves had been made and now the stage was set for . . . His imagination suddenly soared, like a bird broken free of a cage – the stage was set for anything. She was the instrument, he was the player, and he would use her, strum her, beat and cherish her. She would be a slave to his tune until the music ran out.

– 9 –

When Deidre Crabb got off the train at Stazione Centrale in Florence there was no one waiting to meet her. The May sun was still hot but not uncomfortable, so she decided to walk to her destination, stopping on the way to reacquaint herself with the city she loved above all others.

At Giacosa's on the Via Tornabuoni she drank negroni and flirted with Gennaro. The old man was pleased to see her and listened as she spoke, understanding the pleasure she gained from rolling her tongue round his language. From Giacosa's she took a circuitous route, wandering down cobbled alleys that snaked between cracked and crumbling buildings whose façades were a patchwork of russet and sand-coloured stone, until she reached the Duomo and then the Piazza della Republica. There she paused again, listening to the happy sound of waiters in pavement cafés calling to one another while they balanced trays of *cappuccino* and *birra* for the tourists. One of them beckoned her to a seat, but she had lingered long enough – he might be waiting for her.

When she arrived at his apartment building on the left bank of the Arno, the shutters were closed – like eyes, she thought, looking up at the wrought-iron balconies where geraniums bloomed in their pots. Using her key, she let herself in and walked up the dusty stone stairway to the third floor. The apartment was airless and dark, so she opened the window that overlooked the Palazzo Torrigiani and the river beyond. Immediately the noise of Florence crescendoed and the sun streamed in, throwing light into a room that was strewn with the paraphernalia of an artist. As she looked around, the smile that curved her mouth was one of indulgence – and pride. The paintings were mostly new to her, though every one she recognised. They were startling and accomplished details taken from the works of Bellini, Giorgione, Carpaccio and countless other Italian Renaissance painters. There were drawings too, done in charcoal or lead pencil, and from the smell she guessed he had recently mixed his own tempera.

The bedroom was empty, the bed unmade. She sighed. Perhaps, after all, she might be in for a long wait.

It wasn't until noon the following day that he returned. Deidre was in the bathroom, washing his clothes and hanging them out of the window to dry.

He sighed when he saw her. 'Ah, *cara*. You do all this for me and I forget you come.'

'Where were you?' she asked, after he had kissed her.

He was unshaven and his black Armani suit was crumpled and stained with marble dust.

'At the *bottega*. There was much to do.' His finger was under her chin and he looked searchingly into her eyes. 'You understand?'

Yes, she understood. 'You must be hungry,' she said. 'I'll makea di pasta, sì?'

He laughed, but as she moved away he pulled her back into his arms. 'I have missed you, *mia donna*, maybe first we makea di love, no?'

Later, as Sergio slept, Deidre gazed down at him, feasting her eyes on every muscle of his body. At forty his beauty was darker and more heart-breaking than ever. Loving him had always been painful for her, but she knew that it was nothing to what she would suffer if she were to lose him. It was seven years since Roy and Dario had first brought her to Florence to meet him, but it was hard now for her to remember a time when her life hadn't been filled with loving him. If he'd allowed it she would have given up everything to come and live with him here, but he had refused, and it was Roy who had explained that Sergio was unlike other men and that if she wanted him, she must accept him on his own terms. His terms were that they should never marry, never stay together for more than three weeks at a time, and never have children. He would remain faithful to her, but she must never demand his love, else she would destroy it.

'But he does love me?' she had begged Roy.

Roy looked past her and she had turned to see Sergio standing in the doorway. He held his arms out to her and she went to him, melting into his embrace. 'Yes, I love you, *cara*,' he had whispered. 'But you must understand that I cannot permit you to come between me and my work.'

She had always known that love exacted its own price;

for her it was a high one. But she loved him so much that she was prepared to pay, no matter what the cost.

She left him sleeping and went to prepare his pasta. When it was ready she woke him and served it to him on a tray, then she sat beside him on the pillows while he ate, dabbing his lips with a napkin and laughing as he frowned at her.

'You seem happy, *cara*,' he said.

'I am.'

'Because of Madeleine?'

'You know about Madeleine?'

'Dario told me.'

She stretched out on the bed, and cupping her chin in her hands, she gazed up at him. 'I'm happy because of you, Sergio. Because I love you, because I'm with you.'

'How long will you stay?'

'Forever, if you'd let me.'

A dark look eclipsed the humour in his eyes, and she immediately regretted the mistake. 'But I have to return in a few days,' she said quickly.

Putting his plate to one side, he leaned forward and combed his fingers through her rambling mass of hair. 'Why don't you tell me about Madeleine?' he said, smiling, and his black, turbulent eyes reached for hers in a way that seemed to draw her into his very soul.

Her breath shuddered and she rolled onto her back, unable to bear the intensity of him. But, like him, she could pretend, so she kept her eyes from his sinewy shoulders and buttocks as he walked from the room, and waited until he returned. Then while he sketched, she told him about Madeleine.

'She is a delight,' she sighed, warming to the sound of his laughter as she told him how Madeleine had removed all her clothes. 'If you met her in the street you would think her just another pretty girl.' She corrected herself. 'No, you would look twice, because there is something about her that demands it. She has a lazy, almost pompous air that smiles in the face of admiration . . . You know, it's as though she is astonished that you have only just woken up to the fact that she's beautiful. In fact, I've seldom seen a girl so satisfied with the way she looks.' Knowing that he was only half listening, she stopped for a moment and ran a finger down the length of his leg. There was no response, he was engrossed in what he was doing.

'But she's as special as she thinks she is, probably more so. It's hard to say why – except that there are moments when sexuality seems to ooze from her every pore. There's a look . . . It starts in her eyes. And I don't mind admitting that when I first saw it, it even turned me on.' She cupped the hard flesh at the back of his calf and started to massage it gently. 'If it weren't for that look, she'd be brassy; she is brassy, actually, but we're working on that. I can't make up my mind whether to try and train the voice; I suppose I'll have to a little, she sounds like a country bumpkin. Of course that wouldn't matter if she had even a modicum of intelligence, but sadly for her, and luckily for me, she hasn't.'

'Why lucky for you, *cara*?'

'She's paying us to get her to the top. She could get there anyway, but the money will speed things up. It'll be quite a challenge, getting the girlies to change their centrefolds at the last minute, and the glossies to change their front covers – but Madeleine's money will make it worth their while. Roy reckons that if we plan it carefully she could be an international name by the summer, or by the end of the year at least.'

Sergio's hand stopped and he held his head back to survey his work. 'That would be a great accomplishment, no?'

'Yes, it would.'

His pencil started to move over the page again, and Deidre yawned contentedly. 'You know, someone I can't quite get to the bottom of is her boyfriend. We investigated him, mainly because we wanted to know where Madeleine's money was coming from, and it turns out that I know him. Well, that's a slight exaggeration – my family knew his once, about fifteen or twenty years ago. If I remember rightly there was a bit of a scandal when his parents died, but it all got hushed up and I can't even remember what it was now. Anyway, he inherited a fortune when he was still quite young, and when his aunt died, she left him everything too. He's worth millions. And that's the funny thing. He doesn't use his money – except for the running of his estate, of course – but he has almost nothing to do with it, and neither does he draw a penny of income from it. So he's not the one who's financing Madeleine; if anything, she's financing him. He's a writer.'

'This would be good for her image, no?'

'Absolutely, if he were a published writer. However, Roy's working on that. We've managed to get them both in a couple of the gossip columns, and I have to say I think he's going to cause almost as much of a stir as she is. If I were ten years younger and not so madly in love with you, Paul O'Connell wouldn't have too much trouble making my pulses race.'

Sergio's fingers tensed, leaving a dull smudge across the face of the Madonna. 'What did you say is his name?'

Deidre rolled onto her front and kicked her legs in the air, laughing. 'Paul O'Connell. Why? Don't tell me you're jealous because I won't believe it!'

He was looking down at his drawing, his eyes shielded by their lids, but she noticed that his hand was shaking.

'Sergio?' she whispered. When at last he looked up it was as though a mask had dropped over his exquisite face, leaving it remote and expressionless. Then, as she looked again his eyes began to dull, as if something inside him was trying to extinguish his life. 'Sergio,' she breathed, and when he didn't answer she felt an icy shiver run down her spine.

As he moved from the bed she could sense the tension in his body; it was as if he were in the grip of a deathly trance. 'I will take a shower,' he said, 'then we shall walk in the sunshine.'

Her eyes followed him across the room. 'Sergio,' she said again.

He turned, and seeing her bewilderment, his face softened and the strange, ungodly aura left him. 'You are unhappy, *cara*, that I am jealous? I am, you know, but I have no right to be.' He smiled and walked back to the bed. 'You look so desirable with your hair spread about you – like the Rosetti Pandora. I think of you like this when you are not here.'

She lifted her arms towards him, and it was as though the movement had freed the breath from her lungs. He was as much of a mystery to her now as he had been seven years ago, but never before had she seen him like this. A sixth sense told her not to question him, and as he embraced her she relaxed into his arms.

She stayed three more days, and in that time they made no mention of Madeleine or Paul again until he took her to the station. 'Sergio,' she said, as they walked away from the ticket desk, 'do you know Paul O'Connell?'

'Do I know who?' he asked.

'Paul, Madeleine's boyfriend.'

'But how can I, *cara*?'

She shrugged. 'I don't know. It's just that your reaction, when I mentioned his name the other day, was . . . Well, it was odd.'

'It was? I do not remember. But you know how we artists are, we are all odd, no?'

'*Yes*,' she said, laughing as he kissed her. It wasn't until she boarded the train for Pisa airport that she realised he had neither confirmed nor denied knowing Paul.

*

'But why should it matter?' Roy asked when she told him.

'I don't know,' she answered, flicking through the photographs of Madeleine that Dario had left on her desk. 'It just bothered me that he reacted in that way.'

'In what way?'

'I don't know,' she said again. 'But I have to tell you that for an instant, just a split second, it frightened me.'

'Frightened you? In heaven's name, Deidre, aren't you being a touch theatrical?'

'I expect so,' she said, holding a photograph up to the light. After she'd studied it for a moment or two, she put it back on the pile and turned her eyes to Roy. 'But when he looked at me it was so eerie. I mean, it was as though there was no one inside his body. He looked . . . He looked dead.'

'Dead?' Roy burst out laughing, and pursing her lips Deidre carried on through the photographs.

'I've got the answer,' he said, once his hilarity had passed. 'Paul O'Connell is Sergio Rambaldi's *doppelgänger*. How does that sound?'

'Don't be ridiculous,' Deidre said, laughing despite herself. 'Still, you've met Paul, what's he like?'

'Decent enough chap, I quite like him. Bit of an intellectual when Madeleine's not around, but you can't dislike a fellow for that. What you could dislike him for, though, is those looks.'

'Oh Dario,' she muttered. 'These shots are great as test shots go, but you haven't captured the look.'

'Oh yes he has,' Roy said. 'Take a gander at the ones in the other envelope.'

She did, and immediately her spirits soared. 'Shit! How did he do it? How does *she* do it?' She put them down quickly. 'If I look at them any longer I'll be begging you to fling me down and have your wicked way with me on the sofa,' she grinned.

'Always happy to oblige. But back to Paul. I got in

touch with that friend of yours, Philip Hoves. He's going to set up a meeting with Paul and Madeleine, just do it casually, and see what he thinks.'

'*See what he thinks?* Didn't you offer him . . .'

'I did. And he's taken it, so Paul's as good as got an agent. What are you doing now?'

'Calling Madeleine to tell her she's being photographed for the *Sun* next Thursday.'

'One of the bookers has already done it.'

'Then I'll call to tell her I'm back.'

'While you're at it, why don't you speak to Paul, ask him if he knows Sergio?'

'What for?'

'You're the one who was so concerned about it only five minutes ago.'

'Was I?' She shrugged. 'Well I'm not any more. Besides, what difference does it make if they do know one another?'

Roy stared at her, open-mouthed; then shaking his head, he muttered something about women and left the room.

Since Madeleine had been taken in under the Crabb umbrella, she and Paul were out almost every night. They dined at all the well-known restaurants, danced at exclusive night clubs and gambled into the early hours. Everywhere they went, photographers were at hand, and Madeleine's pleated mini and over-the-knee socks caused a sensation when one photographer caught her whirling round a dance floor and revealing the microscopic G-string she wore underneath. As she was dancing with a distant relative of the royal family at the time, the picture was all over the tabloid press the following day, and thanks to Roy's and Dario's friends her name was already starting to appear in gossip columns.

'It's me! It's me!' she would shriek whenever she opened a paper. 'What do you think, Paul? Do I look good there? No, I prefer the picture in yesterday's paper, my hair looked better. Look! You're here too. Where were we? We must have been coming out of that restaurant. What was it called? Who's that we're with? Can you remember their names? Oh, isn't it the couple who invited us . . . Where did they invite us? Paul!' And Paul would drag himself from his typewriter, study the picture for a moment or two, tell her she looked wonderful, remind her where they'd been invited, then kiss her before ambling back to his machine.

Madeleine was ecstatic about her new life. She hardly ever thought about Marian or Bristol or her aunt, they belonged to a past so dim and distant that it might have been a dream. And on the rare occasions when they did manage to break through to her conscience, she merely shrugged them to the back of her mind and returned to the mirror. While she watched her reflection she practised laughing, frowning, pouting, eating, and once – after Paul had dragged her out of a nightclub and slapped her face for letting one of Roy's rock star friends fondle her while they danced – even crying. After the incident Paul had taken her home, and she'd been so aroused by his violent display of jealousy that they'd all but made love in the back of the taxi. It was only when they reached the hotel that she discovered he was still angry.

'You behave like a common little slut!' he had snarled as he slammed the door behind him. 'And the reason you behave like a slut is because you are one. Marian would never dream of making a public spectacle of herself the way you do.'

Madeleine was so shocked by the attack that she could only stare at him; she had thought that the moment they were in the privacy of their room, they would carry on where they'd left off in the taxi. Then he flung the door key onto the dressing-table and told her to get out of his sight before he hit her again. She fled to the bathroom – and that was when she practised crying.

She had remained in the bathroom for over half an hour, determined not to speak to him and planning how to make him suffer. But her anger turned to unease when he made no move to come and get her. After a while she unlocked the door, but still he didn't come. In the end, her heart pounding with dread that he might have gone, she crept back into the room. He was sitting on the bed with his head in his hands.

'Paul?' she said tentatively.

He didn't look up but reached a hand out towards her. She grabbed it and fell to her knees in front of him. 'I'm sorry!' she cried, smothering his hand with kisses. 'I shouldn't have done it. I just didn't think. I'm sorry.'

He snatched his hand away and pulled her into his arms. 'It's I who should be sorry,' he groaned. 'But I was so jealous, I couldn't help myself.' He cupped her face between his hands and kissed her roughly on the mouth. 'They can look at you, Madeleine, but for God's sake don't let them touch you.'

'No, no,' she sobbed, 'I won't. Not ever again.'

'If there'd been a photographer there it would have been all over the papers, him with his hand up your skirt. Can't you see what a fool that would have made of me?'

She nodded, sniffing back the tears.

His hands tightened their grip. 'There's no one in the world I'd have left Marian for, except you. Don't drive me back to her.'

Her eyes widened with terror and she threw herself against him. 'No! No! Don't say that. I love you, Paul. I won't ever do it again, I promise.'

'It's all right,' he said, holding her close and smoothing her hair. 'It's all right. I love you, and I'm here. I shouldn't have hit you, I'm sorry, my darling, but I'll make it up to you. Tomorrow night I'll take you to dinner, just the two of us.' He laughed. 'We can celebrate surviving our first row.'

She giggled, and wiping away the tears with her fingers, she watched his hands as they unzipped his trousers.

'Now you can make it up to me,' he murmured, and pulling her towards him, he guided his erection into her mouth.

On the morning of their move to Holland Park his hangover was ferocious. He was aware that they couldn't go on celebrating every little thing they did like this – otherwise he'd never finish his second book. However, the pleasure he was getting from Madeleine had far exceeded his expectations, and she was providing the most satisfactory raw material for his writing. At this very moment she was ordering delivery men about and getting MFI wardrobes constructed in the bedroom. Three hundred and fifty thousand pounds she'd paid for this mews house, and she was doing it up from MFI! Still, at least she was keeping her body covered, which made a change. Last night she'd had the idea that he could screw her in the bathroom with the door unlocked while all this was going on, and if anyone walked in, all the better.

Thankfully she seemed to have forgotten that now, and was leaving him alone to loll about on a sofa that would deeply offend his eyes even if he weren't hung-over. Decent of her, though, to have considered him when she'd been house-hunting; it was quite a study he was going to have – but he would furnish it himself.

Madeleine popped her head round the door. Even with her hair screwed up, no make-up and the sloppy T-shirt that fell off one shoulder, she managed to look desirable. 'Just nipping out for some food. Keep an eye on the men, will you?'

Paul closed his eyes, lifted a hand to wave her off and waited to hear the car pull away. It was on hire until the cars she'd bought the week before could be delivered. Thank God he'd gone with her on that particular spending spree, otherwise he'd have ended up with a Porsche or, even worse, a Rolls Royce. As it was, she had blown a hundred grand on a Range Rover for him and a Maserati for herself. The cars had been to celebrate the fact that she had her first modelling assignment and he now had an agent. He couldn't recall now how many days it had been since Madeleine had invited Philip Hoves round to Blake's Hotel and introduced him as a friend of Deidre's. Friend of Deidre's he might be, but Paul knew full well that the man was the biggest independent literary agent in the country. Well, however long ago it was, the chap hadn't elicited any response from a publisher yet.

Paul fell asleep then, and didn't stir again until six that evening. Madeleine was sitting in front of a newly installed gas log-ette fire, leafing through photographs of herself and muttering replies to an imaginary interviewer – something she'd been doing ever since Deidre had mentioned coaching her for television appearances. He looked round the room, winced, and closed his eyes again. This time it wasn't the weight of his hangover that hurt, but the sight of all those ornaments. Horse brasses hanging by the fire, china ladies in hooped skirts decorating the tops of fake wood sideboards, glass vases filled with plastic flowers, and paintings of children with tears in their eyes.

He struggled to his feet, making for his cigarettes on the mantlepiece. He howled as he trod on something, and looking down, saw that he had ended the life of a nodding dog.

'You idiot!' Madeleine cried, picking it up.

'Well, what the hell was it doing there?'

'I put it there to remind me to take it out to the car – when I get it,' she added sulkily.

This was too much. He lit a cigarette. 'Later, Madeleine, you and I are going to have a talk about credibility – and taste. Where are the delivery men?'

'Been and gone. Do you want to look round?'

'I'm not sure I'm up to it, not if this room's anything to go by.'

'What's the matter with it?'

'Everything. Did you get to the bank?'

She shook her head. 'I got lost, then when I got to the Strand I couldn't find anywhere to park.'

He didn't even bother to ask why she hadn't taken a cab as he had instructed her. 'So how did you tip the men?'

A light shot to her eyes, and inwardly he cringed. She'd let them fondle her tits, or that's what she was going to tell him. Knowing her though, he was pretty sure she'd shown them and the fondling bit would be added on to spice up the foreplay. He didn't feel like sex right now. 'I'm going to take a shower,' he said.

He stepped into the bathroom – and then immediately stepped out again. The gold taps and accessories he could just about live with, even the pink-spotted plastic shower curtain, but the picture of the Queen, never!

'Get out here!' he yelled.

'Don't speak to me like that,' she grumbled as she sauntered into the hall.

'Make your choice, Madeleine. That photograph, or me. And that goes for every other piece of tack you've got scattered round this house.'

'How can you call the Queen tack?'

'It's where she's hanging that's tacky. The throne room. That's what you were thinking, wasn't it?'

'I thought it was witty.'

He groaned. 'You're not out in the sticks now, where they write letters on lined paper' – he was referring to the note of apology she had written after walking out on some minor photographic session – 'and spray air freshener round the rooms. Shape up!'

'I happen to like air freshener,' she snapped. 'And I like the Queen too. She stays.'

He cast her a glance — and nearly laughed at her mutinous face. A battle of wills. He might not be quite up to it, but he was going to do his best to enjoy it anyway. Lowering the lid of the lavatory seat, he sat down. She waited while he looked round. 'Even Marian had more style,' he sneered, knowing it was a remark guaranteed to bring out her claws.

'Don't you mention her name to me! You keep doing that. You did it last night, going on with all that crap about ancient egg-heads and the rubbish they talked.'

He grinned. 'Metempsychosis. Transmigration of the soul. Marian would have known what I was talking about.'

'She would, wouldn't she? She's just as boring.'

Paul watched her agitation increase as she tried to think of something else to say. He knew it was cruel to taunt her with her intellectual inadequacies, but she was so easy to provoke and sometimes her responses were a sheer delight.

'Anyway, she wouldn't know what style was if it hit her in the face,' Madeleine went on. 'Going about in those baggy Laura Ashley frocks, trying to cover up her fat bum. Christ, it doesn't even bother her that she's ugly . . .'

'I think it does. Besides . . .'

'Oh yeah? When did you ever see her pluck her eyebrows or paint her nails? There's something wrong with her. All she can ever talk about is those boring philosophy things, and you encouraged her. If she'd been a bit more like me she wouldn't be the one wallowing in misery now, would she? Stuck up little bitch! Always had to tell people she'd been to university, just because I hadn't. Had to let everyone know what a wonderful mother and father she had, always using long words when no one knew what the hell they meant, anything to try and belittle me. Well, she's no one, and she's ended up with no one, which is just what she deserves. So why the hell should I feel sorry for her?'

Paul's eyebrows were raised. 'So your conscience *is* troubling you, Madeleine. What a surprise.'

'What are you talking about?' she snapped.

He smiled. 'She's worth a lot more than you think, your cousin Marian. Beauty isn't everything, you know.'

'No, money's the rest, so just you remember who's paying the bills around here. And shut your mouth about Marian.'

She slammed the door and ran upstairs to the bedroom. If he didn't keep flinging Marian in her face, she wouldn't feel guilty at all. For God's sake, Marian was a loser, even he knew that. She'd never been able to do anything. It was she, Madeleine, who'd had to go round those pubs, stripping to earn them some money, because Marian had got herself a degree that was no bloody use to anyone. So what if she was on her own now, it would do her good to stand on her own feet for once. And if she wasn't surviving, what was that to do with her? She couldn't go on looking after Marian for the rest of her life, she had other fish to fry. And everything was working out fantastically. All the newspapers were calling her gorgeous and glamorous and things like that, and she had Paul, which was even more important, so what did she want with Marian?

An hour later, bathed and shaved, Paul came into the bedroom and found her watching herself crying. He sat on the bed and pulled her onto his lap. 'I'm sorry,' he whispered. 'I didn't mean to hurt you.'

'Then why did you have to start on about Marian again? I thought you said you didn't care about her any more.'

'I don't. Now come on, stop crying. It's your big day tomorrow and you won't want a puffy face, will you?'

That he minded what she looked like on her big day was more than enough to pacify her. She gave him a look of pure worship and he kissed her gently on the mouth.

'Now,' he said, 'how about showing me some of the poses you think you'll be striking?'

She shook her head. 'I want you to explain to me the trans . . . the emigration . . . you know, of the soul.'

He laughed. 'OK, but only after you tell me exactly how you tipped the delivery men.'

The next morning Madeleine was up early. She didn't have to be at the studios until three, so there was time for one last sun bed session, and Paul wanted to take her for an early lunch. She loved their togetherness, and the tremors of excitement she felt when he told her how very special their relationship was, reminded her that at last she had someone she could call her very own. Someone who loved her for herself, and not out of pity like her aunt and Marian. She never allowed herself to dwell too long on the fear that he might leave her – as her parents once had; besides, she was doing everything she could to learn things, and prove to him that his career meant as much to her as it had to Marian – more, even.

When she returned from the beauty salon he had left a message for her to meet him at Julie's Wine Bar. She was disappointed because she had wanted him to check her tan before she went off to Wembley, but when she read the rest of his note she actually jumped up and down with joy. He had gone to see his agent; Freemantle's, the publishers, were interested in his book.

She was early getting to Julie's, so she sat down to wait with a newspaper someone had left behind. She didn't pay much attention to what she was reading, but kept glancing round to see if anyone was looking at her.

The instant Paul walked through the door she could tell he was in a foul mood. He didn't even bother to kiss her, but flung himself into a chair and started ranting on about characterisation, belief in motive, and structure – none of which Madeleine understood.

'Anyway,' he growled, 'if I make Jim Penn a rich adolescent so that the female readers can fantasise about him – Jesus, anyone would think I was writing for Mills and Boon – then they'll publish.'

'That's fantastic!' She threw her arms round him. 'You see, I told you you'd find a publisher once we got in the papers.'

He unwound himself. 'You're not listening. The jerk of an editor wants changes.'

'Tell him you won't do them.'

'Then he won't publish.'

'Oh.'

'Philip Hoves will be here in a minute. I'm going to tell him just where this Harry Freemantle gets off.'

'You can't do that.'

'Like hell I can't! It's my book. I thought about it in the cab on the way over, I've made up my mind. For God's sake, will you stop reading that paper!'

'No, don't screw it up, Paul.' She tried to snatch it back. 'I haven't read my horoscope yet.'

'For Christ's sake!' he exploded.

'Don't you want to know what yours is?' she offered, hoping it might calm him down. 'They might say something about . . .'

He shot to his feet and in a flash she was beside him, grabbing his arm to pull him back. He shrugged her off, and then she saw that Philip Hoves had arrived. The two men shook hands, and Madeleine stooped awkwardly to give the agent a quick peck on the cheek before they all went upstairs to the restaurant.

Madeleine struggled to keep up with the conversation. Knowing how important all this was to Paul, she tried to voice some support, but her efforts were ignored. Then, just after the table had been cleared and coffee was being poured, Paul suddenly slammed his hand down on the table and declared that she was the answer to the problem.

Philip looked uncomfortable and shook his head, but Paul was behaving as though he had lighted upon a solution to Catch 22. Madeleine didn't have the faintest idea what they were talking about, and since it was approaching two o'clock she got up to leave. Paul got up too and walked her down to the car.

'Knock 'em dead,' he said, as he closed the door behind her. She wound down the window and he leaned in to kiss her. 'Tell me you love me,' he murmured.

She did, and added: 'After this session everyone will see my body, but it belongs to you, Paul. Everything of mine belongs to you.'

'Just you remember that,' he said, brushing his hand lightly over her breasts. 'I'll be waiting when you get home.'

When she arrived at the Marmoth Studios Madeleine was led through a maze of corridors by a pimply young boy who prefaced everything he said with a giggle. She asked what the red lights were above the doors, and when he told her that they signified the studios were in operation, she asked if they could take a peep.

'You can't do that,' he tittered. 'The photographers don't like just any old person looking in.'

'What, not even the models?' she said huffily.

He wrinkled his nose and looked her up and down. 'You a model?'

'What do you think?'

Scratching his head, he looked down at the clipboard he was carrying. 'Aren't you Sandra Turnham from St. Ivel?'

Madeleine stopped dead. 'No, I am not!'

He looked at his list again. 'Then who are you?'

Her nostrils flared. 'My name is Madeleine Deacon.'

His mouth dropped open, then slapping a hand against his head, he giggled, 'Of course. You're the one for Page Three, aren't you?' He tucked his clipboard under his arm and turned round. 'We're going the wrong way. Herbie Prosser's doing *The Sun* today. He's in Studio 6. He's doing Faye Broad's shots at the moment, so I'll take you straight to the make-up rooms if that's all right.'

Madeleine followed him back down the corridor, then up some stairs and through a door marked 'Authorised Personnel Only'.

The room beyond was stark white – white tiles, white chairs, white lights, white windows. Even the towels that had been tossed casually aside were white. There were three girls already in the room, two sitting at mirrors tissuing off make-up, and one massaging fake tan into her body. They were all naked, and not one of them turned so much as a hair when the pimply boy yelled, 'Chrissie!'

One of the girls got up from the mirror and padded across to a washbasin. As she passed, she gave Madeleine the once-over. Madeleine smiled, but the girl's face remained stony.

'Chrissie!' the boy yelled again.

'She's gone to get some coffee,' the girl with the fake tan answered.

'Oh,' he giggled. He glanced up at Madeleine, then shrugging, he said, 'I'll leave you to it, then. I'll give you a shout when Herbie's ready.' He looked at his watch. 'About half an hour I expect, maybe a bit longer. You ready, Dawn?'

Dawn put down the fake tan and unhooked a robe from the door that led into what Madeleine presumed to be Chrissie's office. As she followed the boy out of the make-up room, she didn't even glance in Madeleine's direction.

The last thing Madeleine had expected to feel was nervous, but her stomach gave a horrible lurch as the door closed and she turned back into the room. What should she do now?

The girl who was still sitting at the mirror came to her

rescue. 'Hi,' she said, looking at Madeleine's reflection. 'You new?'

Madeleine nodded.

The girl, who was Indian and had the most glorious mane of black hair Madeleine had ever seen, turned round. 'Thought so. My name's Shamir. There are lockers in Chrissie's office to hang your clothes in. Might just as well get undressed now, be ready for her when she gets back. What's your name, by the way?'

'Madeleine.'

'What are you doing?'

'Actually,' Madeleine answered, trying to sound modest, 'I'm doing Page Three.'

Shamir nodded. 'What of?'

'*Exchange and Mart.*' The girl by the washbasins shrieked with laughter as she said it.

Madeleine swung round. 'For *The Sun*, actually,' she drawled, emphasising the last word.

'Oooh! Are we supposed to be impressed?'

'Take no notice of her,' Shamir whispered, 'she's like that with everyone. Anyway, if you're doing *The Sun* that means you'll be with Herbie, so you'll be safe. He's a queen. Lucky girl, getting him your first time out. I take it it is your first time?'

Madeleine shrugged. 'More or less. I did some shots a couple of weeks ago, but they were done in my agent's studio by one of her partners. They weren't for anything particular.' She wanted to say how excited Deidre had been when she'd seen the results, but decided it might sound a bit big-headed.

'Who's your agent?'

'Deidre Crabb.'

Shamir seemed perplexed for a minute, then her beautiful face brightened. 'She's my agent too. I didn't know she represented girls like . . .' She stopped quickly, realising she was about to be rude. 'Hear that, Vera?' she called out. 'Madeleine's agent's Deidre Crabb.' Then in a lower voice, 'Her name's Lynn so we call her Vera, she hates it.'

The other girl didn't bother to answer, and seeing that Shamir was laughing, Madeleine grinned, and walked into the office to get undressed.

When she went back into the make-up room, Shamir was at the washbasin shampooing her hair, and Vera had gone.

Madeleine wandered over to a chair and sat down. 'What are you doing?' she asked Shamir.

'Already done it,' Shamir called back. 'Dubonnet on a tropical beach in sunny Wembley with Randy Roger, just thank God the client was there.' She rinsed off her hair, then just as she was wrapping a towel round it, the door opened and a round, jolly figure backed into the room, carrying a tray of coffee.

As she turned round and saw Madeleine, she started, sloshing the coffee over the sides of the cups. 'Oh my goodness, you must be Madeleine,' she cried. 'Sorry I've been so long, couldn't find any milk. You've got yourself undressed, good girl. I'm Chrissie, by the way. I'll just buzz down to Mervyn and tell him you're here. Like a coffee while you're waiting?'

'Mervyn?' Madeleine asked.

'Costume. They're dressing you up a bit. Here.' She passed Madeleine a polystyrene cup. 'Sugar?'

Madeleine shook her head, and watched Chrissie as she tore the wrapper off a Kit-Kat and bit into it.

'That's better,' she sighed, her mouth still half-full. 'I was absolutely starving.' She jumped. 'Oh, Shamir, I didn't see you over there. Dawn gone down, has she?'

'Ten minutes ago,' Shamir answered. Then looking at Madeleine, she gave a long, low whistle. 'Well, well,' she said. 'Stand up, let's look at you.'

Madeleine put down her cup, straightened her back and rose gracefully from the chair.

'Turn round,' Shamir demanded. Madeleine did. 'Chrissie, will you just take a look at those legs. And those tits. Jesus, I hate you, Madeleine.' She turned to Chrissie who was devouring the remains of her chocolate bar. 'Is she perfect, or is she just perfect?'

'Fabulous,' Chrissie confirmed. 'Now let's get Mervyn up here.'

Twenty minutes later Madeleine's eyes were laden with make-up and she was dressed in an assortment of black leather and rubber. Girls swarmed in and out of the make-up rooms, either ignoring her totally or hissing barbed comments about all the attention she was receiving. Madeleine stuck her nose in the air and paraded up and down the room for Mervyn to inspect his work. He was a short man with frizzy grey hair and a neat beard. As he watched Madeleine, his right hand hung limply from his wrist and his left rested on his hip.

'OK,' he said, 'take it all off, one item at a time, let's see what happens. Are you watching this, Chrissie?'

'I'm watching!' she cried from the office, and then she appeared at the door.

'Right, Maureen . . .'

'Madeleine!' Madeleine interrupted.

'Sorry, hen. Right, Madeleine, unzip the skirt to just above the pubes and stick out your ass.'

Madeleine did.

Mervyn nodded. 'OK so far. Now, take hold of the cups of the bra – no, no, at the edges, just under your arms, that's it. Now pull . . . Harder!'

Madeleine yanked at the flimsy material – there was the sickening sound of ripping fabric and to her dismay she looked down to find the cups of the bra in her hands and the frame around her body.

'It works!' Mervyn squealed. 'I'm a genius! It'll be up to Herbie how he wants it, all I needed to know was that they would come off. Tell him there are peepholes in the cups, they're held together with velcro too, he might prefer them. Now, let's see if we can get these cups back on again. Take the bra off, darling, it'll be easier.'

Madeleine unhooked the bra and passed it over. She was about to complain that the boots were too small when Chrissie said, 'I think you'd better have a haircut.'

Madeleine's head snapped up, and she was already backing away. 'Oh no,' she said, shaking her head vigorously, 'you're not touching my hair.'

'Not on your head, ducky, down there. We'll just give it a trim.'

At that point the pimply-faced youth came into the room. 'Ready for you, Madeleine.'

'Two minutes, Derek,' Chrissie answered, and taking the hem of Madeleine's leather skirt in both hands, she heaved it up over her bottom. 'Legs slightly apart,' she said, turning her round and reaching into her pocket for a pair of scissors. 'Just a quick snip, that's it. Much better. Now let's look at the face again before we go.'

After her final check Madeleine put the bra back on, did up the skirt and followed Derek and Mervyn out of the room. Chrissie came after her with a robe, and draping it round her shoulders, she said, 'As it's your first time I'll come down with you. Normally one of my assistants supervises in the studio, but I'm not expecting anyone else until five.'

The studio was dark when they walked in, with just a small pool of light around a platform near the back. Once her eyes had adjusted, Madeleine realised there were several people moving quietly about the room. Then a man stepped out from behind a screen and walked towards them.

'Madeleine?' he said, looking at her.

Madeleine nodded.

'This is Herbie Prosser,' Derek whinnied. 'He's the photographer.' He looked up at Herbie with saucer-like eyes, but Herbie ignored him and held his hand out to Madeleine.

'Pleased to meet you,' he said. 'This shouldn't take too long. We'll just keep it straightforward, nothing fancy. Let's see what Mervyn's come up with.'

Chrissie whisked the robe from Madeleine's shoulders, and Herbie stood back to survey her costume. It took him all of three seconds before he turned abruptly and snapped, 'Get it off!'

Madeleine looked at Mervyn, Mervyn looked at Madeleine, then they both looked at Herbie. He was walking back across the studio.

'Herbie! Herbie!' Mervyn cried, mincing after him, 'I've gone to a lot of trouble to make up that . . .'

'Get it off!' Herbie repeated. 'Straight tits and ass, that's all they want.'

Looking like a kicked puppy, Mervyn turned back and nodded sadly at Madeleine. He and Chrissie helped her remove the skirt and bra, and with relief she kicked off the boots.

'Put the boots back on,' Herbie called. 'They're great.'

Madeleine pulled a face, heaved a sigh, and pushed her feet back into them.

'OK, let's get the show on the road,' someone shouted, and Chrissie took Madeleine by the arm and led her over to the lights.

After one or two test polaroids which were handed round the room, Herbie waited for his assistant to load the camera, then stepped up to the tripod and pressed his eye to the viewfinder. 'Hands on hips,' he barked, 'head back, left leg up. That's it. And another. Head further back, look up at the ceiling, bring your left shoulder round to the camera. That's it. And another. Spread your fingers, baby oil on the nipples, someone; that's it, lift that leg higher, that's it.' It went on like that for several minutes, then Herbie moved away from the camera while it was reloaded. 'Relax,' he told Madeleine. Then at the top of his voice, 'Who the hell keeps walking in and out back there?'

No one answered, and scowling, he turned back to Madeleine. She was perched on the edge of the stage, the towelling robe round her shoulders again and Chrissie standing over her, flicking at her hair. Herbie walked over to them, sat down next to Madeleine and told Chrissie to scarper.

'Actually,' he whispered in Madeleine's ear, 'I'm just a cuddly old teddy bear who's squeak has turned into a squawk. No one's in the least bit frightened of me, they just humour me by pretending.'

Madeleine's relief was evident in the way she laughed.

'Now,' he said, 'that was just for starters. What I'm after really is the face. The look. I've heard all about it from Dario, so do you think you can turn it on for me?'

'I expect so,' Madeleine answered, still not entirely sure what her 'look' was. She'd heard enough people talk about it – Deidre, Roy, Dario and now Herbie – but as far as she was concerned, she just looked into the camera and thought about what Dario had told her to think about.

'Imagine that man of yours, heaving away on top of you,' he'd said. 'What's his name? Paul, isn't it?'

'Yes.'

'Does he make you come? I mean *really* come?'

'Yes, he does,' Madeleine had giggled shyly.

'Then think of him, think of what he's doing to you when you come, imagine he's right here with you, then look straight into the lens.'

And when Herbie was ready and waiting, that was exactly what she did. And it wasn't until half an hour later, as he called the session to an end, that Madeleine realised no one had spoken a word during the entire shoot. She gazed round the room, slightly startled by the sea of faces she was sure hadn't been there before. They were all watching her, as though they were in some kind of trance. Her eyes darted uncertainly to Herbie, who expelled a prolonged breath and laughed.

'Wow!' he said, walking over to her and draping an arm round her shoulders. 'Now I know what all the fuss is about. You've even given me a hard-on, and that's something no woman's been able to do in years. That man of yours must be sensational.'

'You know about . . .'

'Dario told me. Now put something round you before one of these guys loses his grip.'

When she got back to the make-up room it was teeming with naked bodies. Chrissie started to lead her through the crowd, but then a voice hissed, 'It's her!' and as though someone had grabbed a tuning fork, the hum of conversation stopped dead.

Madeleine's eyes moved from one face to the next, at first baffled, then suspicious, then, as realisation dawned, supremely and unashamedly disdainful. They had all been there, watching her, and they were all, every last one of them, creeping sick with jealousy.

– 10 –

The small suite of offices, just off Dean Street in Soho, was normally buzzing with activity. Messengers came and went, together with editors, make-up artists, costume designers and actors. Marian met them all, since they had to come to her office first, where she sat at her desk sorting the mail, operating the fax machines and the photocopier, and attempting to master a word processor Stephanie had had installed just after her arrival. Every telephone call came through Marian, too, and she fielded them out to Stephanie, who was in the office upstairs, and Matthew if he was there. Stephanie's partner, Bronwen Evans, was in America at present so Marian hadn't met her yet, but she had spoken to her on the phone. Bronwen's was one of the very few friendly voices she'd heard in the four weeks since Stephanie had driven to Bristol to collect her and her worldly possessions – which hadn't amounted to much – and brought her up to London.

She couldn't get used to the way people had so little time for one another, and avoided each other's eyes in the street as they rushed about their business. The Underground was nothing short of a nightmare to her, so she took the number fourteen bus to work, passing Harrods, the Ritz and Piccadilly Circus – that, and the bright theatre lights of Shaftesbury Avenue, was all she'd seen of London so far. She travelled alone and spent her evenings alone. Stephanie's flat in Chelsea was small, but as Stephanie was so rarely there it didn't matter – however, Marian longed for company. She missed Madeleine more as time went on, and any thought of Paul inflamed the hurt so badly that all she wanted was to hide from the world in an effort to shield herself from any more pain. Her self-confidence was now even lower than it had been before she met him, and though she tried hard to fight her feelings of inadequacy, each time she looked in the mirror the same pallid, stricken expression seemed to haunt her face, mocking her with the evidence of her rejection. That he could have effected such a transformation in her, first with his love and then with his treachery, made her heart cry out for a reason why he should have done it. She called her mother on the pretence of telling her about the actors she'd met, but really to find out if Madeleine had been in touch. But every time her mother said the same thing: 'Our Madeleine still hasn't rung me, dear. What's she up to? Has she got a job yet?' Marian's replies were always vague. Her mother thought they had gone to London together.

As she thought about her mother now, Marian's eyes dropped sightlessly to her sandwiches. Then suddenly her throat was so choked with misery that she knew she couldn't eat. She threw her lunch in the bin and turned again to the newspaper. Thank God her mother didn't get *The Sun*, it would break her heart to see Madeleine displaying herself like that; but Marian knew it was only a matter of time before some obliging neighbour pointed it out. It was the second time Madeleine's picture had appeared; she'd been in last Tuesday's edition as well.

'Isn't that your cousin?' Woody had said, laying the paper out on her desk. He'd been passing the office on his way to the bank and had popped in for a coffee.

Even before she looked at the paper Marian froze with apprehension. Of course it would be Madeleine, hadn't this always been her ambition? But when she saw the face smiling up at her, she frowned. 'No. Well, yes. I mean, it looks like her. But . . .'

'Madeleine? That is her name, isn't it?' Woody's finger was pointing at the square-inch of print attached to the picture.

'You should know.'

They both looked up as Matthew wandered into the office, and Marian's cheeks turned crimson. He was wearing a black leather jacket and jeans, and Marian couldn't make out whether it was because he hadn't shaved that his face looked so dark, or because he was in a bad humour. His brown eyes surveyed the two of them lazily and he rested an elbow on the corner of the filing cabinet beside him. It was always the same when he came into the office – his presence was so overwhelming that her tongue seemed to twist itself into a knot, her blood either left her face completely or rushed to it with unprecedented vigour, and the palms of her hands became embarrassingly damp. If he spoke to her, which was rare, her lungs flatly refused to take breath and her brain simply upped and died. She wondered if it was his looks that made her react as she did, yet Paul had been handsome and she'd never, not even in the early days, been so overawed by him. But then Paul wasn't as fierce as Matthew.

'Afternoon, guvnor,' Woody said wryly.

Marian watched as Matthew's face broke slowly into a grin, and though she vehemently disliked him she was forced to admit that the journalist who'd written about him in *Screen International* the week before might have had a point when she'd described him as devastating. Even Paul's smile wasn't as attractive as Matthew's. 'Have you still got my script for the Bristol film?' he asked Woody. 'Or have you thrown it away?'

'Thrown it away!' Woody repeated, aghast. 'Guvnor, would I do such a thing?'

Matthew's ironic expression made Marian giggle. 'Then perhaps you wouldn't mind sending it over to De Lane Lea where Trevor's struggling with the rough cut.'

'Will do.'

Matthew was already half out of the door when he suddenly turned back. 'By the way, I'm shooting a BMW commercial in Scotland next week, have the production company been on to you yet?'

Woody shook his head. 'But I can't do it, guvnor, I'm going on holiday next Friday.'

'Go on Saturday.'

'Yes, sir!' Woody saluted, when he'd gone. Then turning to Marian he grumbled, 'If he'd only say please.'

'Does he ever?' Marian asked, dolefully aware that, as usual, Matthew hadn't uttered a single word to her.

'No, he's usually too busy. Now, where were we? Ah yes, your delectable cousin. I'm telling you that is her.'

Marian nodded. 'It's just that she looks sort of different. Maybe it's the make-up.'

Woody pushed his glasses back onto the bridge of his nose and looked down at the page. It was on the tip of his tongue to say that he wouldn't mind having another little session with Madeleine Deacon, when he realised that it probably wasn't quite the right thing to say to Marian. 'Anyway,' he said instead, 'at least you've got some idea where she is now. Give the paper a ring, see if they can help.'

But when she'd phoned, the man at the other end had explained that he couldn't give out details about the models – though he had agreed to pass on a message. Marian had left both her home and office phone numbers, but a week had gone by and Madeleine still hadn't called.

Now her picture was back in the paper, and having hit a lull in the day, Marian toyed with the idea of calling the man at the newspaper again. She was halfway through dialling when she suddenly hung up. She was afraid of annoying the man and simply couldn't face someone else being unkind. *But no one's being unkind*, a little voice told her. *It's you, you're a coward*. She tried to ignore it, but the voice persisted. *Do something brave for once, pick up the phone*. No. I won't do it because I know Madeleine doesn't want to see me. *Maybe not, but you're still a coward – just look at the way Matthew treats you and you never stand up to him*. How can I stand up to someone like him? He's a director, for heaven's sake. Besides, Matthew Cornwall's the least of my problems. *Is he?* Yes. *Then why do you mind so much that he ignores you?* I don't. *Oh yes, you do, so why don't you pull yourself together and show him just what you're made of?* Which is? *Mettle*. I've never had mettle in my life. *You've always had mettle, now use it*. How? *You could start by being honest with yourself*. What about? No, don't answer that, this argument was supposed to be about Madeleine. *There you go, running away again. Life moves on, Marian, stop fighting it*.

'I wish I could,' she said aloud, pressing her fists onto the desk. But her life had changed so dramatically and so bewilderingly over the past few weeks that taking refuge inside herself had seemed the safest and most natural thing to do. Lately, however, her subconscious had been troubling her a lot, urging her to face things she was afraid of, questioning her excuses for weakness, and ultimately demanding an existence for a person she hardly recognised as herself. Take the other day, for instance, when she'd made Stephanie howl with laughter at her impersonation of Woody. Afterwards she could hardly believe she'd done it; she'd had no idea she had such a talent for mimicry, and displaying it in public like that had astonished her even more than it had Stephanie. But she couldn't deny the thrill she had got out of seeing Stephanie laugh. She adored Stephanie, not only because of what she'd done for her, but because when Stephanie was around she didn't worry about what other people thought of her.

A light flashed on the panel in front of her, and she lifted the receiver to take an incoming call.

'Marian? It's Bronwen. How you doing, *cariad*?'

'Bronwen!' Marian was suddenly animated. 'I'm fine. How are you? Are you back in New York?'

'No, I'm still at Bennington College, up in Vermont. I shall be flying back to Manhattan tonight.'

'I've got lots of messages for you.'

'Fire away. And then I've got some news for you.'

It took several minutes for Marian to read all the messages out, which she did slowly, in order that Bronwen could write down the telephone numbers she passed on. As she came to the end of her list she laughed at Bronwen's weary groan. 'Nearly there,' she said. 'Your husband called late yesterday, he said to tell you he's at your house in Wales . . . Oh, you've spoken to him. OK. I've been round to your flat and picked up the mail . . . Stephanie's got it, and she wants to speak to you urgently.'

'OK, *cariad*, put me through. I'll come back to you after.'

'She's not here at the moment, but I can . . .'

'Any idea what it's about?'

'Matthew wants a full rewrite of the *Disappearance* screenplay.'

'Don't we all. Has he spoken to Deborah Foreman? She's the writer, not me.'

'I don't think so. I think the general idea is that you should speak to her because you're in New York.'

'Well, lucky old me,' Bronwen said dryly. 'Will I be doing this by telepathy, or is Matthew going to call me?'

'He's shooting a commercial this week, so he'll be flying to Scotland tomorrow. But he's at home this afternoon. The only thing is, Stephanie says she wants to talk to you before he does.'

'Does she now? That can only mean that Matthew's being every bit as demanding as his reputation says he is. I think it's going to prove rather interesting working with Mr Cornwall, don't you? Anyway, instead of me spending hours on transatlantic telephone calls, get them to dictate whatever wit and perspicacity they've come up with to you, and then you can bring it over when you come.'

Marian blinked. 'Come?' she repeated.

'Yes. That's what I wanted to talk to you about. I need some help out here with the research. There's no point in me asking Deborah Foreman, she's in cahoots with the Hastings – and like Stephanie I'm convinced they're all hiding something about Olivia and I'm determined to find out what it is. Of course, whether we can use it in the film is a different matter, seeing that Frank Hastings is providing all the money. He and his wife are in Florida now, so you won't get to meet them, but you'll fall in love with them when you do. Everyone does. Anyway, remind that Stephanie that you're my secretary as well as hers, and right now my need is greater. Can you fly out tomorrow? No, perhaps that's too soon for you. Come the next day. Ring me with your flight times and I'll meet you at JFK And bring some warm clothes, it's freezing in New York.

I'll have to rush now to get my flight. See you on Thursday *cariad*.'

Once Bronwen had rung off, Marian gazed round the office and was slightly startled to find that it looked the same: rain on the windows, a filing drawer half-open, her sandwiches in the bin where she'd thrown them a year ago – at least, that was what it felt like. She gulped as a sudden shout of excitement threatened to burst from her lips. New York! Tomorrow! She was going to take a plane to the United States of America and when she got there . . . It was all too much to take in, so she picked up the phone and called Stephanie.

Stephanie replaced the receiver and shouted: 'That was Marian. Bronwen's telephoned.' When there was no response she opened the bathroom door. 'I said . . .'

'I heard.' Matthew was towelling his hair.

Stephanie leaned against the door and watched him. 'She wants Marian to fly out to New York.'

'Does she?' He dropped the towel and picked up a comb from the washbasin. Then catching her reflection in the mirror, he grinned. 'What are you looking at, Stephanie Ryder?'

'Your legs, actually.'

He turned round and pulled her into his arms. The hard masculinity of his body never failed to trigger a response in her, and with a somewhat crooked smile she relaxed against him and lifted her mouth for a kiss. They were at his flat in Chiswick where she had all but lived for the past six weeks. Since the day after she'd walked out on him in Bristol she had known it was pointless to continue deluding herself, so she had waited until he returned to London and then set about seducing him – as he put it. In fact she had driven round to his flat, knocked on his door, and when he answered she had told him she loved him.

'Then you'd better come in,' he'd said.

She would never forget that night and the tenderness with which he made love to her. It was as if he had been trying to soothe away all the pain he had caused her. Nor would she forget the roses he had sent the following day, nor the way his door was already open when she arrived in the evening. She had walked in and found him sitting on the sofa reading the paper, a bottle of champagne and two glasses on the coffee table, a toothbrush on the seat beside him. He had looked at his watch and with that hateful, adorable irony of his he had told her she was late – then carried on reading the paper.

Her happiness was so visible that whenever she looked in the mirror she felt like an old painting that had been lovingly restored. Sometimes she felt so filled with love that no matter where they were or what they were doing, she had to tell him, and he'd laugh and fold her into his arms. Now that there was no longer any pretence between them, it was as if the pain and separation of the past six years had never happened.

At last he released her from his embrace, and looking down into her face he murmured, 'I love you, Steph.'

Her heart skipped a beat, and she knew that as long as she lived she would never tire of hearing him say that. 'I love you too,' she said. 'But if we carry on like this we'll be back in the bedroom, and we've got a lot to get through this afternoon.'

By the time he joined her in the sitting-room she had made some coffee and was jotting notes onto the second draft of the script. This was the part of their relationship she was proudest of – the way they could be making love one minute, then debating the script the next. On the agenda that day was casting, and though they weren't making much headway, the most important, and therefore the most difficult hurdle had been eliminated. The signing-up of Eleanora Braey to play Olivia had been quite a coup: the Oscar she had won for her last movie had come after two successive years of nominations for best supporting actress.

As they ploughed through *Spotlight*, making lists they would eventually hand over to the casting director, Stephanie sensed that Matthew's concentration was waning.

'I'm thinking about the overall interpretation,' he answered, when she challenged him. 'OK, so Eleanora Braey knew Olivia; it helps, obviously. But I didn't – don't. God, I don't even know whether to refer to her in the past or present tense. All we know is that for a year or so she was a celebrity in New York. Why? I mean, Jewish American princesses are two a penny in that town, so what was so special about Olivia? She didn't act or sing or model or write, in fact, as far as I can make out she didn't work at all.'

'She was an artist. A successful artist.'

Matthew looked at her from the corner of his eye. 'Did Daddy orchestrate the success?'

Stephanie shrugged. 'Who knows?'

'Somebody must.'

'Is it relevant?'

'Stephanie.'

'All right, all right, I know. Everything's relevant. And something's being hidden. But what? I wonder how Bronwen's getting on. She'll be back at the Dorset tomorrow, I'll . . .' She stopped as the phone rang and Matthew got up to answer it.

For several minutes he said nothing, only listened, and Stephanie turned to a photograph of Olivia. She'd studied the picture over a hundred times, yet still it chilled her. The delicate oval face was beautiful beyond description, but there was a callousness about it that had made Stephanie's blood run cold the first time she'd seen it. Olivia had been only twenty-two when the photograph was taken, but there was an air of worldliness about her that belonged to a woman twice her age. Sometimes, looking at it, Stephanie got the impression that the girl was mocking her, or tantalising her, or sneering at her. She'd never admitted this to anyone, but she knew Bronwen felt the same. 'I hate her,' Bronwen had said once. 'I hate her because she hates me.'

Why? Stephanie asked herself. Why should a girl so young, with so much going for her, seem so filled with malevolence? And where was she now? What had happened to her?

She looked up as Matthew started to speak. 'OK, I'll look into it,' he said. 'No, don't do that . . . Tell her . . . Will you listen for a moment? Now look here . . .' The line went dead, but he held the receiver for several seconds before replacing it. When he turned round his face was strained, and Stephanie could see he was angry.

He expelled a deep sigh and combed his fingers through his hair. 'My daughter,' he said. 'Apparently the maintenance money hasn't arrived this month and Kath . . . her mother's having a blue fit.' He walked over to the sofa and sat down. 'Now, where were we?'

Stephanie gave him a long look before answering. Then deciding that he really did want to change the subject, she said, 'Hypothesising. Theorising. Whatever you want to call it. Perhaps we should call a halt for now, at least until I've spoken to Bronwen. By the way, she wants us to dictate our "wit and perspicacity" to Marian so Marian can take it over to the States with her.'

'Where's that note Hastings received?' He foraged around on the table, then picking up a crumpled scrap of paper he read aloud: '"Mr Hastings, your daughter was not dead, I know. Please find her. A."' He looked up. '*Was* not dead. Does that mean she is now? And who is "A"? I suppose Hastings is convinced it's not a hoax?'

'No. How can he be?'

Matthew shook his head, then buried his face in his

hands. 'Shit! I can't even begin to imagine what the man's going through. His only daughter. His only *child*. I'd be out of my mind if it were Samantha.'

Stephanie sat forward and began gently to massage his shoulders. 'You miss her, don't you. When did you last see her?'

'Over a month ago.' He slammed his fist on the table. 'She's as bitter as Kathleen, godammit! And Kathleen's doing everything she can to make it worse.'

'What about your son?'

'He's at university, isn't he? Well out of it. Still, at least he keeps in touch. God, what a mess.' There was a long, simmering silence before he finally turned to face her. He took her hands in his, and seeing the grave expression in his eyes, her heart faltered. 'Steph, there's something I have to tell you,' he said quietly, and it was as if the blood in her veins had turned to powder. 'Kathleen knows I'm back with you. Don't ask me how she found out, but she has. I hope to God there won't be another scene like the last one, but . . . Well, you know Kathleen. But whatever she does or says, I want you to know that it's over between her and me. It was over six years ago, when I met you.'

Stephanie closed her eyes as relief washed over her, calming her heart to a steady rhythm. She had thought he was about to tell her that he was going back to his wife. Dear God, was she always going to live in such terror of losing him again?

'Do you think you can handle it?' he asked. 'I mean, if she does try one of her stunts?'

Stephanie laughed. 'For you, Matthew, I could handle anything – even Kathleen.'

He grinned. 'How about this script?'

'Ah, well, that's another matter altogether. When I speak to Bronwen I'll get her to bring Deborah Foreman back to London with her when she comes.'

Matthew pulled a face.

'I'm sorry, Matthew,' she chuckled. 'Frank wants Deborah on the film, and that's that!'

'It must be good to be Frank, calling all the shots,' he snapped. 'But what does he know about making a film? Give him the credit as an executive producer, why not, but can't he leave the rest to the experts?'

Stephanie didn't answer. They'd gone over this a hundred times before.

'The woman can't write,' Matthew went on, 'at least, not screenplays.'

'Bronwen will see to it. Between us we'll make it work.'

'I hope you're right, because we sure as hell can't shoot a line of what's there right now. There's no structure, no depth, not even any imagination.' He looked at his watch. 'I've got to go, Trevor's expecting me at four, he wants to show me a rough cut of the Bristol film.'

She started to gather up the *Spotlights* and script. 'Back for dinner?'

He shook his head. 'I've got an executive meeting about the title of the Bristol film. It'll take half the night if I know Richard Collins. Producers, they're the bane of my life.'

'I thought it was writers,' she said wryly.

'Don't remind me,' he grinned. 'Anyway, I should be back around midnight. Will you be here?'

'No. I'd better dictate our "wit and perspicacity" to Marian, and then I think I'll take her out somewhere.'

'Marian?'

'You know who she is.'

'Oh, you mean my rival for your attentions. Well, have a good time. Pick me up at six in the morning?'

'What time's your flight?'

'Eight.'

'I'll pick you up at half-past six.'

After he'd gone, Stephanie called Marian. She sounded so pleased at the prospect of spending an evening with

Stephanie, even if they would be working for the best part of it, that Stephanie immediately felt guilty. From her point of view, bringing Marian to London had been one of her better ideas – she was a good secretary, the best she'd ever had. But it was obvious to anyone who knew her that Marian was lonely. Still, loneliness happened to most people when they first arrived in London, and Marian would find her feet soon enough.

She was still thinking about Marian as she crawled through the traffic on her way to the West End. Marian had been the cause of the one row she and Matthew had had since their reunion. He'd walked out of the office when Marian had shown him a picture of her cousin in the newspaper, and Stephanie, watching Marian's uncertainty turn to hurt and embarrassment, was angry with Matthew that he could be so dismissive of someone who meant so much to Marian. When she confronted him about it later he was furious.

'You're surely not expecting me to drool over some pornographic picture of one of her family? No, don't lay it all on me again, I already know: her heart's been broken. But that doesn't mean everyone's got to treat her as if she's got a terminal illness, or that you have to keep leaping to her defence. Jesus, don't you think I get enough of this from Kathleen and Samantha?'

'But Marian's tried everything to be friends with you, and all you do is ignore her. And yes, I do always leap to her defence and I always will, because you're unreasonable where that girl is concerned, Matthew, unreasonable and cruel. I just hope you don't treat your daughter in the same way.'

'I'm absolutely hopeless with gadgets,' Bronwen was saying in her husky, melodic Welsh voice, 'and people don't always take too kindly to you writing things down as they talk, especially not under these sort of circumstances;

that's the main reason I wanted you here. You know, two heads and all that. Between us we should remember everything – well, the salient points, anyway.'

It was just after four o'clock in the afternoon. The rain was beating down and the dank, dull mist Marian had seen from the plane as it circled New York was thickening to a fog. She shivered. Three times they had asked the driver of the yellow taxi to wind up his window, but to no avail – the man hardly spoke a word of English.

Bronwen had met her at the airport, recognising her from the photograph Stephanie had faxed over; Marian knew she'd have recognised Bronwen, no matter what, because Bronwen, with her long, jet-black bob, unruly fringe, and slim, animated hands, was exactly as Marian had imagined her. Apart from the rosy stain on each of her high cheek-bones, her skin was pale, and she wore no make-up on either her lips or her eyes. She was as tall as Stephanie, and just as glamorous, but there the resemblance ended. Whereas Stephanie's manner – at least outwardly – was relaxed, dignified, almost aloof, Bronwen's warmth, zest and garrulous friendliness gave her the air of a mischievous, fun-loving scatterbrain.

'God, this traffic's terrible,' she complained as they crawled along the Van Wycke Expressway on their way into Manhattan. 'Now, you haven't told me, how was your flight? Is this the first time you've flown alone? You're from the West Country, aren't you? Beautiful part of the world. How are you finding London? As miserable as this, I'll bet. God, I loathe London when it's cold.'

Marian laughed. 'Yes, it's cold,' and experiencing a surge of spontaneous affection, she added, 'And yes to everything else.'

'Oh, very rash,' Bronwen teased. 'Have you got Stephanie's notes?'

'Yes. And Matthew's. But he dictated them into a tape

recorder while Stephanie was driving him to the airport, and I can hardly hear a thing.'

'I'm sure we'll manage between us, if not we'll make it up. You know, you're much prettier than your photograph let on, it suits you with your hair in a pony tail.'

Marian blushed. 'That's what Stephanie said.'

'Me, I look like a clown if my hair's not covering my face. Especially with the way my ears stick out. My husband calls me jug, you know.'

Marian burst out laughing, and had to check a sudden impulse to let her euphoria boil over into an embarrassing and unnecessary compliment.

Giggling, Bronwen opened her diary. 'This is what I've arranged so far for the weekend. You don't mind working the weekend, do you?'

'Not a bit.'

'Good girl. We'll put you to bed early tonight, get you over your jet lag, then tomorrow we'll sort out the mess Matthew's given us. It must be wonderful being a director, don't you think? Speak, and we minions shall obey. Now tomorrow night I've booked us into one of my favourite restaurants, down in the Village. We'll have a drop of wine and a long chat about you. I want to hear all about that bastard who walked out on you. It sounds to me like . . . Oh, *cariad*, I'm sorry, I didn't realise it still hurt,' she gasped, as Marian's face paled. 'Oh, me and my mouth, running on like that. Are you all right?'

'I'm fine,' Marian chuckled. 'It was just a bit unexpected, that's all. I didn't know Stephanie had told you. Not that I mind, but I try not to think about him, you see.'

'Very wise too. So we won't talk about him, we'll talk about that Matthew and Stephanie. Is the honeymoon still going on?'

'Oh yes,' Marian answered, shocked as well as flattered by Bronwen's frankness.

'It's great, isn't it? While we're over here working our butts off, they moon about making eyes at one another. But tell me about Steph, does she seem happy? She's been in love with that man ever since I've known her, you know. Never been anyone else, at least, not that I know of. Trouble is, being a career woman you tend to neglect your love life. Good job I got married first, I always say, or I'd be a spinster, I'm sure of it. And there's me, forty next month. No kids, though, didn't have the time.'

'Do you mind?' Marian asked.

'Yes, I do a bit.'

'But surely it's not too late.'

'No, not yet. Maybe when this film's over.' She laughed mirthlessly. 'That's what I always say, but then the next film comes up and before I know it another year's gone by.'

'What about your husband? Does he mind you working so much?'

'Oh, heavens no. He's a writer, and you know what they're like. Want to be left alone. Suits him perfectly, me not being around too often. To be honest, I think I drive him nuts. Now, where were we? That's right, going for dinner tomorrow night. Then on Sunday I thought I'd take you for brunch at Tavern on the Green. You'll see all the rich Americans there, oh, are some of them ghastly! Jewels and limousines like you've never seen before in your life. And caked make-up you could plant trees in. Deborah Foreman will be coming too, so you can meet her. Crabby old cow, she is, but don't tell her I said so. Then on Monday I've managed to get us an appointment with Rubin Meyer. He's the guy who runs the art gallery where Olivia's paintings were exhibited. He's been refusing to see me, but Frank Hastings called him from Florida and told him it would be all right. Now what do you make of that? Ah, here we are at last. This is Fifth Avenue we're crossing now, you know, where all the smart shops are.

See there, there's Gucci, and if you turn back, look down there on the left, there's Tiffany. Oh, you missed it, never mind, it won't go away.'

As the taxi came to a halt outside the hotel, a man in green livery shot forward with an umbrella and opened the door.

'Hi, Tony,' Bronwen said as she clambered from the car. 'This is Marian. It's her first time in New York so I want you to look after her.'

'Sure thing,' the man grinned. He waited while Bronwen paid the fare and refused to give a tip.

'For someone who can't speak English, that's the best Anglo-Saxon I've heard in a long time,' she chuckled, as the driver pulled away. 'Now come along, Marian, let me introduce you to the Dorset Hotel. They've turfed some poor unsuspecting bugger out of his room so that you can be next to me, isn't that obliging?'

Marian nodded, laughing as she tried to imagine anyone not obliging Bronwen.

Her near silence in the taxi had not only been because it was difficult to get a word in with Bronwen, but because she was still too dazzled by being actually in *New York*! Having hardly had time to get used to London, she was now slap bang in the middle of a city exploding with life – the people, the traffic, the sky-scrapers were faster, louder and higher than she could ever have imagined. It was almost surreal; she felt as though she was being swept along on a current of almost unbearable excitement, and she was about to ask if they might go out despite the rain, when Bronwen suggested it herself.

'We'll just pop up and look at your room, make sure there's nothing lurking in the bath, then you can have a quick freshen up and we'll wander up to the Plaza and have some tea in the Palm Court, or whatever they call it. You can stuff yourself silly with wonderful gooey cakes, drink orange tea and listen to the string quartet. It's just like being at the Ritz, just as American.'

Half an hour later they were being shown to a table, and Marian was trying very hard not to be overwhelmed by her exotic surroundings. She even pinched herself to check she wasn't dreaming, because although she had seen places like this on TV and at the cinema, she had never imagined that one day she would actually be there herself. What on earth would Madeleine say if she could see her? The sudden, unbidden thought fell like a cloud over her exuberance and she glanced about her, horribly aware of how shabby she must seem amongst such splendour.

Stop it, that little voice inside told her. *You weren't supposed to bring your old self with you, and it's only thinking of Madeleine that's making you feel like this. This is your life now, and though you might not be as rich or as chic as some of the people here, you've got nothing to be ashamed of.*

'Now, what are we going to have?' Bronwen said, perusing the menu. Suddenly she reached across the table and squeezed Marian's hand. 'Oh, you don't know how good it is to have some company, *cariad*.' Then she laughed as Marian's face turned pink with pleasure.

Marian was too excited to eat more than a cucumber sandwich, but Bronwen was nowhere near so reticent. She had a generous helping of chocolate gateau, and a bowl of trifle to follow.

'Don't you ever put on weight?' Marian asked, hardly able to believe anyone could eat so much.

'You're kidding. I've always been this thin. High metabolism, I suppose. My mother always used to say . . . oh, speaking of mothers, I can't wait for you to meet Grace Hastings – Olivia's mother. She's a dream. It won't be on this trip, though, I'm afraid, because they're in Florida; I think I told you. But next time.'

A few minutes later Marian asked, 'If the Hastings are

hiding something about Olivia, why do you think they want to have a film made about her?'

Bronwen shrugged. 'Baffling, isn't it? But I promise you there's something very peculiar going on. Nobody will talk unless Frank Hastings tells them it's all right – not even the police. He's a really powerful man, Frank, you only have to meet him once to know it – it sort of oozes out of him.'

'What does he do?'

'What doesn't he do would be easier to answer. Banking mainly. Actually, he's not bad looking for someone his age; nor is his wife, come to that. Olivia's inherited the best of both of them. Have you seen the photographs of her?'

Marian nodded.

'Beautiful, isn't she?'

'Well, yes,' Marian answered hesitantly.

'Oh, you too. They give Stephanie the willies, but she won't admit it. They do me, too.'

'I thought maybe they were just bad shots.'

Bronwen shook her head. 'No, they're all like that. It doesn't matter whether she's smiling or serious. Grace didn't want to hand them over at first, I think she only did in the end because she knew I'd dig them up from newspapers anyway. And that was a funny thing, because when I did go through the papers I found that all the pictures used during the time she disappeared were at least two years old, despite the fact that the papers themselves must have had a whole collection of shots taken when she was at the height of her fame. She was probably *the* most celebrated heiress and artist in New York up until the time she disappeared. Her photo was on the covers of all the magazines, she was always in the society pages, she was courted by every eligible bachelor in town and women all over the country were copying her look. There haven't been so many blondes in America since the days of

Marilyn Monroe.' Bronwen paused for a moment, then, as if something had just occurred to her, she went on, 'It was uncanny, you know, the influence she seemed to have on people – especially since she was so young. She wore a certain pair of sunglasses that she'd designed herself, and some entrepreneur made a fortune out of copying them. Everyone had a T-shirt with OH! on the front, which is how she signs her paintings. Of course, all the papers exercised their usual eloquence with headlines like, *OH! She's a genius* or *OH! What a girl* or *OH! What a surprise*. It was a kind of trade mark. And when she went missing there were the inevitable *OH! Where is she?*'s or *OH! Who's got her?*'s or in the case of one paper, *OH! What a con!*'

'Con?' Marian asked.

'That's what it said. Saw it myself in the library. In fact it was an editorial, and would it surprise you to hear that the editor was sacked shortly afterwards?'

Marian's eyes widened and several seconds passed before she asked, 'What did the accompanying article say?'

'Most of it was a bit disappointing, really. Just that her paintings weren't brilliant at all, that it was all just a load of hype and the great American public had fallen for it. But at the end it said something about making connections and coming up with answers people in high places might not like. I've got a copy of it back at the hotel, you can read it yourself if you like.'

'Yes,' Marian answered thoughtfully. Then, 'Isn't this editor someone we should try to get to see?'

'Easier said than done.'

'He won't speak without Frank's permission?'

Bronwen shook her head. '*Can't*.' And when Marian looked puzzled, she leaned across the table and in a low, meaningful voice said, 'He's dead.'

A waiter came between them with the check and Marian

waited while Bronwen paid, then followed her out into the street. The rain had stopped but the wind was biting cold.

'Very convenient, don't you think?' Bronwen said, as she linked Marian's arm and they started to walk the few blocks back to the hotel.

'How did he die, do you know?'

'Road accident, somewhere in the Bronx.'

'But you don't think it was an accident?'

'As I said, it was very convenient, wasn't it? Can't ask a dead man questions, can you?'

Later, when Marian was lying in bed, too tired to sleep, she thought back over all Bronwen had said. Something about it bothered her, but she couldn't seem to put a finger on exactly what it was. It was only when her eyelids finally started to droop that the answer came, but by then she had already drifted too far down the road towards sleep to consider it.

The phone woke her in the morning, startling her from a vivid nightmare in which someone in an OH! T-shirt silently chased her through Bristol. The streets were deserted, except for her and her pursuer. At first it was Paul, but when she looked back it was Matthew, and Madeleine was with him. She didn't know why she was running away from them, but her terror was like a living thing. Her ears droned a dreadful, whining tattoo, her lungs were on fire, her eyes bulged from their sockets, and as her pursuers drew closer her legs seemed to dissolve with pain. She rolled to the ground and a car sped towards her, Olivia was driving . . . she was going to die. Her mouth swelled with huge, empty screams – and then the phone rang.

She snatched at the receiver, still too shaken to know whether it was a part of the dream, but when Stephanie's voice came across the line, laughing and demanding to know if the jet-setter had arrived in one piece, she relaxed.

Ten minutes later Bronwen was knocking at the door.

She whisked Marian off to breakfast, left her in the dining-room while she went off to make a few phone calls, then spent the rest of the day in Marian's room trying to decipher Matthew's instructions, and wondering how on earth she was going to come up with something that would even remotely satisfy him.

'And what the hell's *this* supposed to mean?' she grumbled, as Marian passed her the final sheet of dictation. '"To get the right depth you must achieve it by degrees, always considering changing ambience, i.e., sound, colour, temperature. A patchwork portrait of a sybaritic society is not good enough. Sinister undertones would be welcome, if you think there are any. Get complete! unexpurgated! character studies of friends and colleagues."' Bronwen looked up. 'Are the exclamation marks yours?'

Marian grinned. 'It's how he said it.'

Bronwen laughed. 'I'd love to know what was going through Stephanie's mind while he was dictating all this.'

'Read on,' Marian told her.

Bronwen did for several minutes, until she reached the bottom of the page and burst out laughing. '"If I didn't love him, I'd hate him. Anyway, hope you enjoyed your lesson on how to research a story, you have my full permission to tell him to f . . . off, however I wouldn't advise it, he bites." Stephanie's voice, I take it?'

Marian nodded.

Bronwen sighed. 'Well, *cariad*, we've certainly got our work cut out trying to impress Matthew Cornwall. Still, I guess being a pedantic perfectionist is what's got him to the top, and we lowly individuals should be grateful to be working with him.' She pulled a sardonic face and got to her feet. 'You know, it's true, most people would give their eye teeth to be in our position – but I need mine, I'm famished. Let's go and get some dinner.'

While she was in the shower Marian's mind was over-flowing with thoughts of Olivia. Though they had spent the entire day discussing her, analysing everything they knew of her, she still remained maddeningly elusive. In her notes Stephanie had said, 'Of course, we will never come up with complete answers to this mystery, but the intention is to get as near to the truth as possible – or should I say, permissible?' Marian took rather a dim view of such defeatism, and was certain that if they worked hard enough and delved deep enough they would inevitably find a solution to what was proving such an irresistible enigma. And now that she understood why the business of the editor had played on her mind, there was at least one part of the puzzle she might be able to solve.

She wasn't too sure yet how to go about it, but once she'd spent some time with Bronwen and listened to what Olivia's friends had to say, she was sure that something would occur to her. She intended to make her investigation alone, not in order to take credit from Bronwen, but – if she pulled it off – in order to try and change Matthew's attitude toward her. Loathing him as she did, it irked her to think that she was even bothering to try and impress him – but she couldn't bear the way he dismissed her as somebody unworthy of even so much as a civil hello. She was determined to prove that there was a great deal more to her than either of them realised. And if she didn't get anywhere with her investigation, no one would be any the wiser and she wouldn't have risked making a fool of herself.

As it turned out, she didn't get an opportunity to do anything for over a week. She was with Bronwen every minute of the day, very often in the company of the sons and daughters of New York's wealthiest and most influential families. They travelled all over Manhattan, and Marian would never forget the police car that sped past their taxi in Washington Square when they were on their way to see Rubin Meyer. It squealed to a halt almost in front of them. Then, with the siren still wailing and lights flashing, four policemen leapt out, guns clenched in their fists, and ran into a building. She would never forget it for the simple reason that she hadn't even been alarmed by it. For her, driving round New York was like touring a movie set. Nothing seemed real, because she'd seen it so often in films. Like the steam that swirled from drains, the criss-cross of rusty fire escapes on tenement buildings, and most of all the intimidating, soaring, skyscrapers. The city both exhilarated and daunted her, but not once did it frighten her.

In the evenings she and Bronwen had dinner sent up while they sat in her room typing all they could remember of the interviews they'd done that day. Rubin Meyer had told them nothing they didn't already know. Yes, he had put on Olivia's exhibitions. Yes, she had lived in the apartment above his gallery. No, he knew nothing about her private life except what he'd read in the press – and that you had to take with a pinch of salt. Her ex-boyfriends either refused to talk at all, saying they'd told the police all they knew at the time, or theorised wildly about what might have happened. Her friends described her variously as reckless, exciting, exotically erotic, selfish, often cruel, never vulnerable, and in one case, evil. It was that particular friend Marian went back to see, alone, the morning Matthew arrived.

They had known he was coming because he'd left a message for Bronwen the day before.

'Oh, that's all we need,' she groaned when she picked it up. 'Still, at least some sort of pattern's beginning to emerge. But I can hear him now: "It's a patchwork portrait of New York's sybaritic society – it's not good enough." Well, it's all we could get so he'll just have to lump it. In any case, I think it's all rather visual, don't you? I mean, the locations are seedy as well as smart, the people are weird and wonderful, and those druggy-type parties she used to have in that wasteground of an apartment should make for a few good scenes.' She sighed. 'Not very substantial, though, is it?'

'It would help, I suppose,' Marian said, 'if we had found a boyfriend, or even a girlfriend, whom she'd been more than superficially involved with.'

'Wouldn't it just. Of course, a lot of them know more than they're letting on, that's obvious, but even if we succeeded in getting anything out of them, Frank Hastings probably wouldn't allow us to use it.'

'How much do you think he actually knows about what went on during the two years before she disappeared?'

'A lot more than he's telling us. But one thing I'm pretty certain about, he doesn't know where his daughter is now. To be honest, I don't think any of them do.'

'Well, couldn't that be the story? I mean, if Deborah Foreman were to write the script in such a way that each scene ends on a kind of question mark – you know, the way our interviews have – surely it would get people thinking, if nothing else.'

'Thinking about what?'

'About what Olivia was really like as a person. About what *might* have happened during those two years. People will come up with their own conclusions, but it'll get her talked about, and if someone does know where she is, they might be more inclined to speak up in the glare of publicity. I mean, nobody's going to bump them off when the whole world is watching them – assuming that being bumped off is what they're afraid of.' She shrugged, suddenly embarrassed at exposing her ideas, though not for one minute attaching any credibility to what she was saying. To her it was all fiction, so the casual suggestion that people were afraid of being killed held no plausibility whatsoever in the real world – the real world being England.

Bronwen's head was on one side and she was staring at Marian intently. 'You know, you might have a point, *cariad*. If we make the film one huge question mark, that's like an umbrella for all sorts of allusions . . .' Slowly her face started to light up. 'He hasn't exactly said so, but I'm sure that's Frank's motive for making the film. To get people talking, to encourage whoever has the answers to come forward. Because someone must know where she is. By George, Marian, I think you've got it. All we have to come up with are the allusions.'

'Murder. Kidnap. Love affair. Artistic commitment. Satanism. Drug-induced memory loss . . .'

'Perfect. I like the satanism, it might well account for the way she changed over those two years. I'll have to check this out with Frank, of course, see how much artistic licence he'll allow us, and we'll have to change all the names to avoid libel suits, but damn me, Marian, I'm feeling quite excited all of a sudden. I'd better get Deborah Foreman over here tomorrow, so we can put it to her and Matthew together.'

'Will you be needing me?' Marian asked, and when Bronwen looked surprised she added, 'I thought I'd do a bit of shopping. Climb the Empire State – you know, all the touristy things. But only if it's all right.'

'Of course it is, *cariad*. You could do with a day off. But these are your ideas, I thought you would want . . .'

'No. You'll be able to articulate them much better than me. And I don't much fancy the idea of trying to convince Matthew. He's not too keen on me.'

Bronwen laughed. 'Is Matthew keen on anyone, I ask myself? All right, you go and enjoy yourself, leave his nibs to me.'

The next morning Marian was hoping to get out of the hotel before Matthew arrived, but as the lift doors opened and she walked into reception her eyes were immediately drawn to the tall figure standing at the check in desk. Immediately a discomfiting heat mushroomed through her body and her heart jerked with an unnatural thump. She glanced quickly over her shoulder and would have stepped back into the lift, but the doors had closed. In panic her eyes hunted about for somewhere to hide, but there was nowhere. *What are you so afraid of?* Her other self asked. Shut up! she snapped back, and as a porter passed with a rack of hanging luggage, she slipped in behind him.

'And where might you be off to?'

His voice was smooth and deep, and when she looked up at his face her heart seemed to grind to a halt.

'Oh, just going to do a bit of . . . ' The word escaped her, and two crimson patches flared across her cheeks.

'Sight-seeing?' he suggested, concealing his amusement at the way she'd tried to slide past him.

Dumbly, she nodded. 'Bronwen said it would be all right.'

'Then take that damned camera from round your neck and put it in your bag.'

She looked at him with wide, blinking eyes.

He sighed. 'A girl your age – or any age, come to that – doesn't walk round New York alone advertising the fact that she's a tourist. Not unless she's completely stupid, that is.'

'Oh,' Marian mumbled, and reached round the back of her neck to unhook the strap of her camera. It had somehow got tangled in the loop of her coat, and though she would willingly have torn either to get them apart, neither would budge.

Taking her by the shoulders, Matthew turned her round, undid the knot, slipped the strap over her head and handed her the camera. 'What's Bronwen's room number?' he asked, his face unyieldingly impassive.

Marian told him, then was about to make good her escape when he said, 'Marian?'

She turned back, dreading what he might say now.

'Enjoy yourself,' he smiled, and picking up his key he followed the bell captain across the lobby.

For several seconds Marian was too stunned to move. That was the first time he'd ever smiled at her. The first time he'd ever called her by name, even. She watched as the lift doors opened and he walked in. For one wild moment she thought her feet were going to rush her across the room so she could return the smile, but then the doors closed, and realising she was causing a jam in the busy traffic of early morning hotel life, she spun round and walked jauntily towards the door.

Tony, Bronwen's friend, was outside, so she asked him to hail her a taxi, and less than half an hour later she was delivered to an imposing apartment building on the Upper East Side.

The doorman called up to Jodi Rosenberg's apartment to announce her arrival, then showed her to the lifts. In less than five seconds she was on the thirty-third floor, the doors opened, and to her astonishment she was in Jodi's vast apartment.

Jodi was on the telephone, but as she saw Marian she beckoned her to come in.

Marian walked uneasily across the room, wondering how many times Stephanie's flat would fit into this one. It must be bigger than the entire Bristol ice rink, she thought as she looked around at the vibrant abstract paintings. At the opposite end of the room, on a podium, was a king-size bed with a majestic carved headboard and yards upon yards of rose- and oyster-coloured silk, satin and lace. The walls were a muted wash of pink and orange, and the thick, luxuriant carpet was a silvery blue. It was a bit like walking into a tropical sunset, she decided, and the sumptuous white furniture was the surf.

There was a copy of the *New York Times* on a glass dining-table so she opened it and made a pretence of reading. In fact her courage was beginning to fail her. Calling up Jodi and asking to speak to her again had seemed no more than an adventurous thing to do when it was just an idea, but now she was here it felt different. To begin with, what did she intend to ask this woman? Why was Olivia evil? Well, yes, that was what she was here for, but it seemed so trite now. And she could hardly come straight out with it. Besides, it might just have been one of those flip remarks that Jodi had made without thinking. Even if it wasn't, what right did she have to go round questioning people like this? She didn't even have Bronwen's permission. She looked across the room at Jodi Rosenberg, and felt herself shrink by inches. Even in her jogging suit, sneakers and sweat-bands Jodi managed to look imperious.

Eventually, just as Marian was wishing the ground would open up and swallow her, Jodi put down the phone and spun round.

'Hi,' she cried, 'come over here and sit down. Can I get you some coffee? Tea? Juice?'

'Juice would be very nice,' Marian answered.

'Let me get your coat,' Jodi said, and she whisked it off Marian's shoulders before Marian had a chance to lament its shabbiness.

'I hope you didn't mind me calling you,' Marian said, as Jodi handed her a glass of freshly squeezed orange juice. 'It was just that . . .'

'I was expecting your call,' Jodi interrupted.

'You were?' Marian asked, surprised.

'Sure I was. Your associate's pretty smart, feigning that kind of absent-mindedness, it catches people off their guard. I knew after I said what I did that it wouldn't rest there.' The genial smile suddenly dropped from her face. 'I've thought a lot about what I would say when you did come, and I'm still not too sure.' For a long moment Jodi regarded her with wide, unfathomable blue eyes, then at last she said, 'I told you she was evil, didn't I?'

Marian nodded.

'She wasn't always that way. She fell in with a bad set,

here in Manhattan; drugs, you know. It's easy in this town, there's crack or heroin sold on just about every street corner. We all dabble, for fun, you know, at parties and places, but Olivia took it too far. She got hooked and that's what changed her. We all tried to help, but she wouldn't let us, it had a hold on her and there was nothing we could do. She was a regular junkie. In the end her father got to find out and that was when the real trouble started. Frank didn't mean for it to blow up the way it did, but . . .' she shrugged '. . . well, it did, and now Olivia should be made to pay for what she's done. They all should.'

Remembering how Bronwen kept silent when a revelation was about to break, and hardly able to believe that it had happened so quickly, Marian returned Jodi's stare and waited. But she wasn't experienced enough to carry it off, and in the end she said, 'But what did she do?'

'If I told you that . . .' Jodi stopped, looked round the room, then suddenly seemed agitated. 'Look, I don't know any more. I've told you too much already.'

'You haven't told me anything,' Marian protested.

'And that's the way it's gotta stay. I told you nothing. You haven't been here today. I never said Olivia was evil, I said nothing.'

'Why did you agree to see me if you're not going to tell me anything?'

'I agreed because I had some fancy notion of morality. I fooled myself into believing there was something you people could do. But I was wrong. I've gotta keep my mouth shut, like everyone else.'

'Can't you tell the police what you know?'

Jodi laughed. 'Are you kidding? The cops know more than I do. And it just kills me to think she's walked away like she had nothing to do with it. Frank Hastings was trying to protect her, he still is, but it'll all come out in the end, it has to.'

'Are you saying that Frank Hastings knows where Olivia is?'

'No, he doesn't know. None of us do. Like it said in the papers, Frank arranged for her to go to Italy to study art under Sergio Rambaldi – at the Accademia. She finished her course, she said goodbye and no one's seen her since.'

'But people don't just vanish into thin air.'

'Well, Olivia managed it, didn't she?'

'Do you think she's still alive?'

As she answered, Jodi's face was bitter. 'I'm telling you, Marian, I hope that bitch is rotting in hell. I hated her. We all did once we found out. She might have been a drug addict, but she knew what she was doing all right, and she didn't care so long as she got her fix.'

'Look,' Marian said, affecting a conspiratorial tone, 'if you're worried about trusting me, I swear to you I won't reveal your name, no matter what you say. Only you and I will know. I'd go to prison rather than betray you,' she added dramatically. She'd heard about journalists and researchers going to prison rather than revealing sources.

Jodi's mouth curved in a slow, patronising smile. 'If I told you all I know, Marian, you wouldn't go to jail, you'd probably die. We both would.'

Marian suddenly wanted to laugh. Not only was New York like a movie set, but its people were like movie stars. Nobody would ever say anything like that in real life, and mean it. 'Die?' she repeated, unable to stop herself grinning.

Jodi's face was frighteningly solemn as she nodded. 'Oh, sure. A lot did, Marian. A lot did, and Olivia . . .'

'Olivia what?' And when Jodi didn't answer, 'Was the newspaper editor one of the dead?'

Jodi showed no surprise. 'So you know about him. Sure, he was one.'

'I was thinking,' Marian said, after a pause. 'That he –

the editor, I mean – well, I think he probably told someone else on the paper what he knew.'

Jodi's head snapped up. 'Why do you say that?'

Startled by the response, Marian went on carefully, 'They usually do, don't they? Tell a colleague they trust? Especially if it's something . . .'

'Well, you're wrong this time.'

'But how do you know?'

'I just do.' Suddenly Jodi was on her feet. 'Look, I know I said I was free this morning, but something came up at the last minute. I'm sorry, but I gotta go out.'

Marian stood up, her eagerness deflated by the abrupt dismissal. But then she remembered that she was now able to confirm that there was a cover-up, though of what she still had no idea. More importantly, she was now convinced that the editor *had* told someone else. The question was, how on earth could she find out who?

She smiled as Jodi handed her her coat. 'Thank you for seeing me,' she said.

Jodi waited while Marian buttoned her coat, then walked her to the lift. When Marian was inside Jodi pressed her finger on a button and held the doors open. 'I'll call you at your hotel tonight,' she said. 'There's someone you should talk to. The guy's gone to ground, he's running scared. I don't even know if he'll talk to you. But if he will, before I give you his name I want you to think long and hard about whether you want to go through with this. You could be putting yourself in a lot of danger, Marian.'

The use of her name sent a cold chill down Marian's spine. 'But what about you?' she asked. 'Won't it be the same for you?'

'Sure. But like everyone else in this town, I love Frank and Grace. They don't deserve what's happened to them and I wanna help.' She smiled. 'Do yourself a favour, Marian, and don't tell anyone you've been here today, it'll be safer that way for both of us. And if I'm asked, I'll deny it.' She let the button go, and as the doors started to slide quietly together she said, 'I'll call you, but my advice is, take the easy way out. Go back to England and forget you ever heard the name Olivia Hastings.'

As Marian stepped outside into the cool, dank air of Park Avenue she glanced up at the apartment building, half expecting it to have disappeared. For days she had felt as though she was drifting through a preposterous illusion. Nothing seemed to surprise her, confound her or even alarm her because she was unable to attach any credibility to anything she was told. In fact, since Jodi had suggested her life might be in danger, she'd given up trying to make any sense out of it. It was all just too absurd.

Shrugging, she walked off down the street and hailed a cab to take her to the New York City Library. Once there, she buried herself in the newspapers of five years ago. Yet still, when hours later she finally resurfaced and wandered out into the dismal, cloudy evening, she was no closer to accepting that people like those she'd been reading about could possibly be bothered with someone as lowly as her. She felt as though she had been reading a kind of detective novel in which she had to come up with the solution herself. So she saw no harm in having written down the name of the editor who had died, the telephone number of the paper, and a list of the journalists who had worked on it at that time.

By the time she reached the hotel, it was night. That did surprise her, mainly because she must have been walking in the dark without realising, and also because it seemed only an hour ago that Tony had hailed her a cab to take her to see Jodi. She glanced at her watch, and almost simultaneously her stomach started to rumble. It was just after seven o'clock. She'd look in on Bronwen to see how the meeting had gone with Matthew and Deborah Foreman, then she'd get a sandwich sent up to her room.

When she reached Bronwen's room she was on the point of knocking when the door suddenly swung open and Matthew, thrusting his arms into the sleeves of his coat, careered into her.

Quickly she bit her tongue to stop herself crying out at the pain of his foot on hers, and was about to apologise for being in the way when he suddenly grabbed her shoulders.

'Where in God's name have you been?' he cried. 'Bronwen's been half out her mind with worry. I was just about to go out looking for you.'

'Me?' Marian asked stupidly.

He rolled his eyes, then letting her go, he stood back and motioned her into the room.

'Where's Bronwen?' she asked, when she saw the room was empty.

'Where do you think? Out combing the streets in a taxi. Where the hell have you been all day?'

'I'm sorry, I didn't mean to make anyone worry. It's just . . .'

'Where have you been?' he demanded.

'All over, really.'

'All over where?'

'New York.'

He sighed. 'I know New York, but where? The doorman said you took a cab to the Upper East Side.'

She shrugged, then cowering away from his forbidding black eyes, she turned to stare at the window.

'Marian, I think you'd better tell me exactly what you've been up to today.'

'What do you mean? I haven't been up to anything.'

'Then why did you go to Jodi Rosenberg's apartment?'

She flinched, but stayed mutinously silent.

'Marian,' he said, 'look at me.' When she didn't, he put

a finger under her chin and lifted her face. Then pronouncing each word with harsh deliberation, he said, 'What did you think you were doing going to Jodi Rosenberg's apartment?'

To her horror, her mouth started to tremble and tears pricked at her eyes. Then suddenly she was shouting. 'I hate you! You're always nasty to me just because I'm ugly. Well, it doesn't mean that I haven't got feelings.' She gasped, hardly able to believe what she'd said.

For a moment he looked startled, then he threw back his head and roared with laughter. 'So the mouse squeaks.'

'Don't call me that!'

He held up his hands. 'I'm sorry. No, you're right, I shouldn't call you that. But I meant timid, not ugly. And where in heaven's name did you get the notion I was nasty to you because you were ugly? Which, incidently, you're not.'

She looked at him blankly, and again he laughed.

'You're patronising me now,' she snapped. 'I'm not a child, and I resent being treated like one.'

'Then stop damned well behaving like one. Why did you go to Jodi Rosenberg's apartment?'

'If you must know, I did it for you. I did it to try and prove to you that I wasn't a miserable little nobody. I thought if I could find something out that would work for your film, you might be a bit nicer to me.'

He shook his head, as if trying to clear it, then before he could answer she said, 'Now if you don't mind, I'm tired and hungry, so I'm going to my room.'

She moved swiftly past him, but he was even quicker. 'Oh no you don't,' he said, grabbing her arm. 'You're going to give me a proper answer.'

'Stop treating me like a child,' she seethed.

'*Then answer me!*'

'I went to Jodi's apartment to find out why she said that Olivia was evil,' she spat.

'And did it ever occur to you to wonder why Bronwen didn't pursue that herself?'

She'd already taken a breath to answer, but as that had never occurred to her, her mouth fell silently closed. She shook her head.

'Was she in? Did you speak to her?'

'No and no.'

'Are you telling me the truth?'

'*Yes!*'

'Then it's lucky for you that she wasn't. You can't go around dabbling in this sort of thing, Marian. It's not a game, it's serious, and dangerous.'

'Why?'

'You know the answer to that. There's been a massive cover-up in this town to conceal what really went on before Olivia disappeared. Now Bronwen's told me about the ideas you came up with earlier, they're excellent, and as far as we are concerned, we leave it at that. OK? We're film-makers, not detectives.'

'But don't you want to know what happened to Olivia?'

'Of course. Everyone does, Frank Hastings most of all. But leave the spade-work to him, Marian, and don't attempt anything like that again – especially not for me.'

Suddenly she was so choked with misery that she couldn't speak, and terrified she might break down in front of him, she shot to her feet and ran out of the room.

'It's OK, *cariad*,' Bronwen said later, 'it was my fault. I got you all worked up with curiosity and it was only natural you should do what you did. But I thought Stephanie had told you ... I should have told you. I didn't take what Jodi said any further because, you see, it was enough. To have pursued it might have meant putting not only us in danger, but Jodi too. Frank explained all this to us right at the start – don't dig too deep, he said. Of course, just like you, my own curiosity made me want to, but my sense of self-preservation stopped me. Something very nasty's been going on in this town, but there are a lot of very influential people involved, that much we know, so that's where we must leave it.'

Marian looked at her, wanting to tell her that she had seen Jodi, but she couldn't. She'd promised Jodi, and after all, Jodi hadn't actually told her anything. And when Jodi called later she would simply tell her that she had decided to take her advice to leave things alone.

'Now, are you coming down to dinner?' Bronwen said. 'Matthew wants to buy you a drink to say he's sorry for upsetting you.'

Marian smiled. 'Is that what he said? Well, please thank him for me, but tell him I've already ordered some dinner to be brought up to my room and then I'm going to bed.'

'As you like. I'll tell him the lady has pride and can't be bought off that easily, shall I?'

Marian giggled. 'Yes, you tell him that.'

By the time the phone rang at half-past nine Marian was asleep, but the moment she heard Jodi's voice she was alert. She started to tell her that she'd decided to take her advice and didn't want to know any more about Olivia, but Jodi interrupted.

'It's no good,' she said hurriedly. 'He won't speak to you.'

'That's OK,' Marian answered, aware of the tension seeping from her body.

'So can we forget today ever happened?'

'It's already forgotten.' And when the line went dead, Marian got out of bed, fumbled in her coat pocket for the notes she'd taken at the library, and tore them to shreds.

It was some time before she fell asleep again, but when she did, it was with a smile at the memory of Matthew telling her she wasn't ugly.

– 11 –

'My feet are killing me,' Madeleine groaned. 'Why don't we go and get a coffee somewhere?'

'What a wonderful idea,' Shamir sighed. 'I think we've successfully managed to buy up Bond Street, so I'd say we deserve one.'

They looked around at the expensive shops, and when nowhere seemed to offer itself, Shamir hooked her arm through Madeleine's and started to walk her towards Grafton Street. 'We'll go to Brown's Hotel,' she said, 'they do a terrific afternoon tea there and I'm starving.'

'It's not far, is it?' Madeleine wailed.

'No, just round the corner in Dover Street.'

'Bastard!' Madeleine screeched as a taxi swerved into a puddle and soaked them up to the knees.

'I swear he did it on purpose,' Shamir snapped crossly, kicking off her shoes and emptying out the grimy water.

They had met several times since the day Madeleine had gone to the Marmoth Studios to do her shots for *The Sun*, and since at first the two of them were doing quite different kinds of modelling, they had become friends rather than rivals. Then Madeleine's success had started to blossom and she began taking on the same kind of work as Shamir – the occasional fashion show, a TV commercial for a soft drink and another for a shampoo, a series of advertisements for underwear – but their closeness had unexpectedly continued. The world they moved in was not only highly competitive, but bitchy, devious and down-right cut-throat at times, so that Madeleine was extremely proud of their friendship, particularly since Shamir had a reputation for being not simply aloof, but thoroughly supercilious. But though she was dubbed by some the

Queen Bitch, Madeleine felt that she had come to know the other side of her that was occasionally shy, always self-critical, and often inordinately generous – as she was with her compliments on Madeleine's glamour work.

Madeleine had appeared in *Men Only* and *Playboy* so far, but there were features to come in other magazines that had not yet gone to press. Since she had appeared as the centrefold in *Men Only* letters had poured in by the sack-load, and she, Deidre and Shamir spent hours giggling, and very often blushing, at what her fans proposed to do to her should they be lucky enough to get their hands on her. At night she would recite some of the letters to Paul in a way that made it sound as though the readers' fantasies were a reality, and the savagery with which he made love to her as a result would leave her reeling from such violently sated lust. But she would never, no matter who the man or what the situation, be truly unfaithful to Paul. He was the focal point of her life, nothing was as important to her, not even her steady rise to fame. She was as devoted to him as any one person could be to another, and despite his unpredictable temper – which meant that he could be savagely cruel as well as wonder-fully kind – she believed him when he told her that he loved her just as much as she did him.

'OK, here we are,' Shamir declared a few minutes later. 'And I'm going to stuff myself rotten.'

'All right for those who can,' Madeleine griped, as she followed her into the hotel.

'Well, some of us aren't blessed with deliciously volup-tuous figures,' Shamir pointed out. 'Instead we carry the curse of the great god bean-pole, whose only blessing is that we can eat cakes. Now, where shall we sit?'

As a waiter showed them to a sofa in the corner, every eye in the room followed their progress. It would have been difficult to say which of them was the more striking. They both wore loose, trench-style raincoats, jeans and white polo-neck sweaters – a coincidence that had made them laugh when Madeleine picked Shamir up from her Kensington apartment earlier – but while Shamir had her mass of thick black hair curled into a knot at the back of her head, Madeleine's was loose and straight and fell around her shoulders like a shimmering fountain of white gold.

They dumped their bags on the floor, and Madeleine would have kept her coat on but for the trio of businessmen who were sitting at a table in the opposite corner, watching them. She shrugged off the coat and gave her shoulders a quick jiggle before sitting down, which elicited an extremely satisfactory response from the three men.

Shamir sighed. 'You really should wear a bra sometimes, Maddy. Your boobs are too big, and they'll start to droop if you aren't careful.'

'I know,' Madeleine answered, 'but Paul doesn't like me wearing a bra. He says when he wants me, he wants me now, and not after he's fumbled about with hooks-and-eyes, and straps and whalebones.'

'But you're out shopping, you could have worn one today.'

'If I had one! He threw them all away when we moved to London.'

Shamir smiled fleetingly. 'You'll need one if you're going to buy that dress you were trying on in *Chanel*.' she said.

Madeleine picked up the menu. 'I'm not too sure about that dress, actually – but I need something to wear for this charity ball at the Grosvenor. Are you going, by the way?'

'Can't. I'm off to Turkey to do a video for a holiday company the day after tomorrow. They're paying a fortune, you know. You ought to get Deidre to organise one for you.'

'She's asked me to pop in later, I'll ask her then.' But Madeleine doubted if she would, she knew that Deidre was handling her career in her own way and didn't much relish interference. But Madeleine couldn't admit to Shamir that she was paying Deidre rather than the other way round. Of course, she received the occasional fee for her work, but Deidre kept the money to use as an incentive to magazines to change their front covers at the last minute, or to encourage newspapers to include her and Paul in their gossip columns.

After Shamir had ordered she turned in her seat to face Madeleine. 'Now tell me all about this cosmetic range,' she said. 'It sounds fascinating. No – first tell me when your commercials are going out.'

'Apparently the shampoo one starts next Wednesday. I'm still not sure about the other.'

Shamir nodded. 'Sometimes it takes ages before they reach the screen. Still, as long as they do . . . Have you seen the edited versions yet?'

'Of the shampoo, yes. It's fantastic. We shot it at Holmes Place, you know, the health club in the Fulham Road. I got a free membership out of it.'

'Oh, I did something there, ages ago now. Can't even remember what it was, but they gave me a membership too. They've got a swimming pool, haven't they?'

'That's where we shot the commercial, in the pool. Did I tell you, there was this bloke in it too, all he had to do was put his arms round me at the end – outside on the street. Could he get it right? He was fantastic to look at, but queerer than a nine-bob note. I was obviously such a turn-off he couldn't bear to touch me. And I can tell you, the feeling was mutual. Ugh! I don't like queers, do you?'

'Oh, they're all right. God knows, we meet enough in this job. Anyway, tell me about the cosmetic range.'

'Well, apparently it's going to be ozone-friendly. Deidre wanted us to be thoroughly up-to-date, you know what she's like. *L'Oréal* or is it *Lancôme*, are manufacturing the stuff and they're calling it . . .'

'Don't tell me, The Look.'

'You got it! But it's not all fixed yet, I expect that's what Deidre wants to see me about. If it comes off I'll be even more famous than that silly cow who does *Estée Lauder*. What's her name?'

'Lillie Toppit. Ever heard such a ridiculous name? Actually, I've got a wonderful story about her. I don't know if it's true, but if it is I have to say she goes up in my estimation. It seems her boyfriend – he's a struggling photographer or something in Paris – well, he got drunk one night, came home and buggered her. Can you imagine? It must have been agony. Anyway, you'll never guess what she did. She only waited until he was asleep, got out her vibrator and rammed it up his bum.'

Madeleine's shrieks of laughter brought frowns to the other faces in the room and one old lady actually told her to shush. 'You're not serious,' she gasped, wiping the tears from her eyes. 'Are they still together?'

Shamir, who had been observing her friend's hysterical mirth with cool amusement, said: 'Apparently they are. Maybe he liked it.' She smiled. 'Anyway, back to the cosmetics. What does Paul think?'

'He's delighted for me. Well, he will be once I tell him.'

'You haven't told him yet!' Shamir was amazed.

'I haven't had much of a chance. The day I came back from Ireland, where I was doing those shots for *Penthouse*, he went off up north researching. He only got back last night.'

'And don't tell me you had better things to do than talk about make-up?'

'Last night we did, yes. This morning was a bit different, though.' The light had dimmed in Madeleine's eyes, and as she lowered her head Shamir noticed that her lips had started to tremble.

'What is it?' she asked, an expression of mild interest crossing her flawless face. 'You haven't had a row, have you?'

Madeleine tried to laugh it off. 'A bit.'

'What about?'

'Oh, nothing really. But . . .'

'But what?' Shamir said impatiently.

'No, it doesn't matter. No doubt we'll make it up tonight. What about you? Are you still seeing your rock star?'

Shamir shrugged. 'God knows. He's still in Los Angeles, but he's staying at my house there so he'd better not be screwing anyone in my bed.'

'What about that guy you met when we were at Annabel's? Have you heard from him?'

'Morning, noon and night. He's got a title, I found out.'

'What, you mean, like a book?'

Shamir choked on her tea. 'Yes, the most boring one you can think of. Still, he should be good for a few weekend parties at that country house of his. I'll keep you posted, we can all go.'

'Fantastic. And if they're anything like the one we went to in . . . where was it?'

'Cocking.'

Madeleine giggled. 'That's it. How could I forget? Well, if they're anything like that one then we'll all be back in the Sunday newspapers. Wasn't it a scream? Paul loved it.'

'*Paul* loved it! So did everyone else. Where did you learn to strip like that?'

'Oh, here and there. But the best bit was when we all went out driving in the nude. Do you remember that man and woman at the bus stop?' She screamed with laughter.

Shamir smiled. 'If the traffic lights hadn't turned green when they did, I reckon the old boy would have died of a heart attack. And did you see Tony Rudley-North in the car behind? He only waved his willie at the old dear.'

'That's right! I'd forgotten that,' Madeleine gulped. 'Well at least he was safe when it came to the pictures in the Sunday papers. I mean they can't show a man's thing, can they? Who told the press we were there, anyway?'

'God knows. But they were lurking in the bushes outside all weekend with their zoom lenses.' Shamir narrowed her eyes. It was Madeleine they'd been after, of course.

'Oh, look at the time,' Madeleine groaned, glancing at her watch. 'I'd better get going or I'll be late for Deidre, which will mean I'll be late getting home – and with the mood Paul's in at the moment I don't think that's a very good idea. We're cooking dinner tonight for his editor and his wife. Paul's doing the main course – I've got to do the starter. Oh please God, let him be in a better mood when I get home. You don't mind me not giving you a lift, do you?'

'Not at all.' Then, as Madeleine put on her coat and picked up her shopping, Shamir added, 'Give me a call later, if you can. Let me know how it goes.'

Madeleine smiled, and when Shamir gave her a cool kiss on the cheek, she responded with an especially warm hug.

Madeleine's movements were jerky and self-conscious. As she spoke her words tumbled over each other, and neither her heart nor her hands were quite steady. 'So anyway,' she was saying, wandering about the kitchen while Paul lolled in a chair, watching her, 'Deidre thinks it could be launched sometime in the next few weeks. You see, it's already in production and they were just starting their search for the right face. They like mine, so we'll be signing the deal any day now.' As she sliced into an avocado she waited for him to comment. He didn't, so she went on, 'She also said something about me having my own designer collection. She's been talking to this fashion designer, and I've got to go and meet her the day after tomorrow. Deidre's pretty certain that the meeting's just a formality, though; the girl – Phillipa, I think her name was – was really keen when Deidre first talked to her. If it goes on like this, Deidre said, the next few months could be amazing. She reckons I'll be in every newspaper and magazine going, and on the telly too. Not only in commercials, but on chat shows and things like that. And she said she wants to do the same in the States, so it'll probably mean going to America quite soon. I told her I'd have to ask you if it was all right.'

Paul picked up his glass from the table next to him and took a sip of wine. 'And how much is all this amazingness going to cost?' he asked.

It was the question Madeleine had been dreading. Even she had balked at the amount Deidre had asked for. But it was vital, Deidre said, for the 'promulgation' – whatever that meant – of her plans, and the rewards to be reaped were even greater than Madeleine had dreamed of: international fame, and a style and image all her own.

'Well?' Paul prompted.

Madeleine braced herself, and with her back still turned she tripped the answer out as lightly as if she were telling him what she was making for dinner. 'No more than a hundred thousand. Investment now, dividends later,' she added, quoting Deidre. 'Do you think I should put the prawns in the microwave to defrost them?'

He waited until she had no choice but to turn and look at him. When she finally did, he smiled. Then, as her eyes filled with tears, he got up and went to put his arms round her.

Women were the strangest creatures. It seemed that the worse you treated them, the more they loved you. Before he'd left the house that morning they'd had a blazing row and he had hit her. Now, here she was at the other end of the day, nervous and contrite, ready to do anything to make it up with him. He was relieved to see that he hadn't left a mark on her face, it might have given rise to unwelcome speculation when their guests arrived later.

'I'm sorry about this morning,' she said, her voice muffled by his collar.

'No, I'm the one who should be sorry.' He held her tighter.

'But you had a big day ahead of you, I shouldn't have needled you the way I did.'

He kissed her gently on the forehead. 'And I shouldn't have been so jealous about you spending the day with Shamir.'

Suddenly she was kissing him frantically. 'I love you, Paul. More than anything else in the world. I don't want any friends, all I want is you.'

'You deserve better, but you've got me. For richer or for poorer.'

Madeleine drew back and looked searchingly into his eyes, unsure whether he had just made a proposal.

'A hundred thousand pounds.' He shook his head, laughing. Deidre would very likely end up taking Madeleine for every penny she was worth. He knew he could stop it, but he wouldn't – if anything, it fitted in rather neatly with his own plans.

'You're not angry?' she asked uncertainly.

'Not a bit. It's your money, my darling, you must do as you want with it. And if that's what makes you happy, it makes me happy too.' He kissed the tip of her nose and let her go. 'By the way,' he said, when he reached the dining-room. Madeleine looked up as he leaned in through the serving hatch. 'I love you too.' She rushed across the kitchen and gave him a lingering kiss, then after she'd demanded that he say it again, she went contentedly back to her cooking.

As he showered and changed for dinner, those last words rolled around his mind – he even said them aloud once or twice. The most curious thing was that there was every chance he might mean them. Lately, her affection had got to him in a way that surprised him. It was as if the Russian doll was slowly coming to life, and beneath the first shell he had detected a vulnerability he had so far thought her incapable of. It made her shallowness seem less abrasive and her vanity more acceptable. But whatever his feelings for her might be, or become, he had no intention of allowing them to deflect him in the slightest degree from the achievements of his objectives.

She hadn't asked him yet how his day had gone. After their scene that morning, he guessed she was afraid to. That was good. It meant she would be prepared to do almost anything to avoid another confrontation – which should make the task in hand somewhat easier. In fact his day had been bloody awful, and he was now convinced that he and Harry Freemantle were never going to see eye to eye. But whatever Harry said, Paul was adamant that not only was his book going to be published, it was going to be published *as he wanted it*. The only solution to this dilemma, as far as he could see, was to execute the plan which had been forming in his mind ever since the day he and Madeleine had lunched with Philip Hoves at Julie's Wine Bar. His initial idea had been to get Madeleine to buy Harry Freemantle's co-operation. He had been fascinated to find out how much it would cost, and to what extent Freemantle's greed could be exploited. However, since then another solution had presented itself, one that was far more nefarious and therefore far more appealing.

When he went back into the Smallbone kitchen, which he had had installed while Madeleine was somewhere in Ireland spreading her legs and pouting her lips for the camera, she was pouring dressing – from a bottle – over the prawns she had spooned into avocado halves. He winced; but now wasn't the time to tell her that one *never* served avocado and prawns as an hors d'oeuvre these days.

'Everything under control?' he asked.

'I think so. I don't know which wine to serve, though.'

He sat down. 'Leave the wine to me. Now, we've got an hour before Harry and his wife arrive, so off with your clothes.'

As she was still wearing her polo neck and jeans, it was a matter of seconds before she had complied.

'Turn round,' he said.

She revolved slowly until she was facing him again. He pulled her forward and kissed her navel. Her skin was so smooth it was almost like caressing a baby, and her hair, when he touched it, was so sleek and soft it ran through his fingers like spun gold. Despite her height and the strength of her bone-structure there was, even in her slightest movement, a femininity that made him feel as powerful as a god. It was only when she opened her mouth to speak, and the broad tones of a West Country accent spewed out like frogs, that the alluring image crumbled.

'God, I hardly know what's happening to me when I look at you,' he murmured, pulling her to her knees so he could kiss her. 'Why am I spending so much time trying to impress a boring old publisher with my boring old book?'

'Was today all right?' she asked tentatively.

He shook his head. 'He's not listening to a thing I say. He wants it his way or not at all. I'm not going to win this, Maddy.'

She didn't know what to say, so she combed her fingers through his hair and smiled sympathetically.

'Look at you,' he whispered, as he blew gently on her nipples. 'If he knew what I had in you, he'd think differently about me.' He raised his eyes to her face and felt a driving surge of desire at the sultriness of her full mouth and the slant of her eyes. 'Do you love me, Maddy? I mean really love me?'

She ran her tongue over her lips, leaving them moist and slightly parted. 'You know I do,' she breathed.

'Enough to sleep with Harry Freemantle?'

The lazy, seductive look retreated from her eyes, leaving them unsure and bewildered. She looked at him for several moments before she finally pulled away, shaking her head. 'But you've always said you'd kill any man . . .'

'This is different, Maddy. I'm asking you to do it because I love you so much that I've come to share all your dreams – the ones you have for us. I want to be successful with you, be up there at your side, but I'm not going to make it without your help.'

'Why can't I offer him money?'

'Because he's got enough.'

She stood up and he waited, wondering what was going through her mind. Silently she put on her clothes, and when at last she turned to face him her eyes were suffused with pain. 'If you really loved me, you wouldn't ask me to – don't look at me like that, I can't do it, Paul. I won't.'

His smile was resigned as he slowly nodded his head and got up from the chair. She watched him, as if in a stupor, while he opened the oven door, checked the roast duckling, then walked past her and out of the kitchen. After a minute or two she followed him upstairs to the bedroom.

'What are you doing?' she asked from the doorway.

'Calling Marian.'

The blood drained from her face. 'What for?'

He replaced the receiver and sat down on the edge of the bed. 'Come here,' he said.

She walked over to him, expecting him to reach for her hands, but he didn't touch her.

'You think asking you to go to bed with Harry Freemantle is the worst thing I could do to you, don't you?' he said. 'Well, it isn't. The worst thing I could do would be to tell Marian what you have done to her. And I think, after all Marian did for me, that I owe it to her to tell her. You see, I realise now that she is someone who has more decency and more compassion in her little finger than you have in the whole of your body. What's more, she loves you more than you could ever deserve. You know that, and that's why you're so riddled with guilt that it keeps you awake at nights. Well, it does me, too. And now I know that I'm never going to be published the way I want to be, I'm going back to her, because I'd rather be a failure with her than with you.'

Madeleine's eyes were wide with shock. 'You can't,' she breathed. 'You don't mean that. You've got to understand, Paul, it's as if you were asking me to be a prostitute.'

'No, all I'm asking is that you use your talents for me. That's what being in love is – sharing all that you have.'

She looked at him, too stunned to answer.

'You said you loved me, that you'd do anything for me. And now I've been forced into putting you to the test . . .' He shrugged and smiled. 'It's not even as if you were a virgin. Think about all the men you slept with before me.'

'You bastard!' she gasped.

'But it's true. And now I know that you are incapable of doing anything for anyone, even someone you claim to love.'

'No!' She was frantically shaking her head, and fear and confusion had turned her face to an ugly purple. 'No. It's because I love you that I can't do it. You understand that, you must.'

He got up. When he reached the door she threw herself after him, but he pushed her away. 'Paul!' she cried, grabbing at his sleeve. 'Paul! Listen to me! Please!' Again he shrugged her off, but as she fell against the banister he gripped her shoulders and turned her so that she was looking into his face. There were tears on his cheeks, and she tried to embrace him. 'What is it? Why are you crying? I don't understand!' she sobbed.

'Stop it, Madeleine,' he snarled. 'Just stop! You're making me hurt you. You're making me torment you when we both know I love you so much that if it was for any other reason than this I'd rather kill myself than ask you to sleep with another man. But what else can I do? I can't change the book, so if you refuse me this I'll end up losing you anyway – you won't be able to take me as a failure, Madeleine!' He threw her away from him and buried his face in his hands.

'No! You won't lose me. You won't be a failure. I'll do whatever you want. Just don't go. Please, say you'll stay.' She managed to prise his hands from his face and pulled his head onto her shoulder. 'It was just the shock of you saying it, that's all. It'll be all right, Paul. If you think it'll work, we'll give it a try. I'll do it. I'll do it for you.'

'Oh God, Madeleine. If only you knew how it's tearing me apart just to think of it. But . . .'

'Don't! Please don't say that.'

He looked into her face, then suddenly grabbed her and kissed her savagely on the mouth. 'I love you,' he raged. 'I love you. Hold me, don't let me go.'

'No, I won't let you go. I love you. Look, let me show you.' She started to fumble with his trousers but he clasped his hands over hers and stopped her.

'Oh God!' His voice was strangled, and he turned his face to the ceiling. 'I want you so much I can't control myself. Look at me. Look at what I'm doing to us. It's because I want you, I want you every minute of the day. Yes, touch me, Madeleine, feel me. Tell me what you're going to do to him. We'll make it a game, we'll make it so that it doesn't seem true, maybe that way I can stand it. Oh God, tell me you won't fall in love with him. Tell me I'm not going to lose you.'

'It'll be all right,' she sobbed. 'I love you. I could never love anyone else. Just tell me what I have to do, what I have to say to him. Is it blackmail? Is that what we're going to do?'

He closed his eyes as she lifted his penis from his jeans.

'Don't say that,' he groaned. 'It's such an ugly word on your lips.'

'But it's what we'll have to do, Paul, in the end. Don't you see?'

He fell against her, burying his face in her neck. 'But how?'

'We can rig up a video camera – I've seen it done in films. I don't have to go all the way, just so long as it looks as if he's having sex with me. If I can degrade him in some way, even, he'd do anything to stop his wife seeing it, wouldn't he?'

'Yes, I suppose he would.' Then taking her face between his hands, he buried his tongue deep inside her mouth. When he let her go, he looked into her eyes and said, 'We'll do it your way, Madeleine. Whatever you want, just tell me and I'll do it.'

By the time Harry Freemantle and his wife arrived at the mews house Madeleine had managed to calm Paul down sufficiently for him to be able to go and finish dinner preparations in the kitchen. Occasionally he came back upstairs to watch her and kiss her while she gelled and back-combed her hair into what she called her come-to-bed style. He selected a black leather mini, low-heeled pumps and a semi-transparent top from her wardrobe, then when she'd checked herself from all angles in the mirror, he followed her down to the dining-room and helped her set the table.

Now that she was over the initial shock, the challenge of using her sexuality in the way Paul wanted was beginning to appeal to her. She had never met Harry, but as long as he wasn't some hideous ogre – and Paul assured her that he wasn't – then all that concerned her was to prove to Paul how much she loved him – and to stop him from going back to Marian. To prevent that she would do anything, and if 'anything' meant going to bed with Harry

Freemantle, that was what she would do – not only expertly but willingly. Not for one minute did she consider the possibility of failure because, as Paul pointed out after they'd made love at the top of the stairs, sex was the one thing she excelled at. And when it came to a kinky imagination, he added, she was second to none. To prove him right, she had racked her brains and come up with the idea of getting Harry to tie her to the bed before they had sex; then it would look like rape.

When the doorbell rang at a quarter past eight Paul gave her a quick hug, then waiting a moment while she checked her make-up, he took her hand and led her down the hall to greet their guests. As he opened the door Madeleine braced herself for the sight of a short, balding, red-faced, middle-aged boor, but she very nearly gasped when she saw the suave, darkly handsome features of the actual Harry Freemantle. Her nerves evaporated on the instant and she treated him to one of her most provocative smiles, knowing that this wasn't going to be difficult at all.

'Harry, let me introduce you to Madeleine,' Paul said, and as she took the hand Harry held out, she gently scratched her fingernails across his palm and projected her bewitching smile into the very depths of his black eyes.

'I thought Paul had told me everything about you,' she said huskily. 'But he never mentioned you were so good-looking.'

A smile shot to Harry's lips, and gently but firmly releasing his hand, he said, 'Then I had the advantage over you, because I knew exactly how beautiful you were. May I introduce you to my wife, Julia?'

Madeleine smiled at the other woman, and would have turned away again but for the look in Julia's eyes. It was so openly friendly that Madeleine found herself responding to it by saying, 'It's really nice to meet you. I hope the dinner's going to be all right for you. It should be, Paul's cooked it. I just did the starter.'

'I'm sure it'll be wonderful,' Julia answered in a deep, plummy voice.

Once they were in the sitting-room with their drinks, Paul hovered for a while to see what Madeleine would do, and when she sat back on the sofa opposite Harry and crossed her long legs in a way that offered an enticing view of fishnet-clad thigh, he excused himself and went off to the kitchen. He had decided to give Madeleine a completely free rein for the evening. He would do nothing to correct either her language or her table manners, and if she offended Julia, which was highly likely, so be it. All that mattered was that she got through to Harry Freemantle.

Her avocado and prawns was already on the table, so he quickly prepared a dressing for the salad, tossed it, then went back to the sitting-room to tell them dinner was served. They walked through to the dining-room, Madeleine's face wearing an expression of dazed bewilderment as Julia told her about her job on the *Financial Times*.

'Sounds really interesting,' she said, sitting herself down at the round table and indicating to Harry that he should sit on her right. 'It's all about money that paper, isn't it?'

Julia, not knowing where she was to sit, looked at Paul, who immediately pulled back a chair for her. 'And business. And news,' she answered, as she smiled her thanks.

'I don't read it,' Madeleine said. 'Paul gets it, though, don't you, Paul? I'm useless where money's concerned, he has to handle everything – including me.' She giggled, and gave Harry an eye-fluttering shrug. 'Do you handle everything in your house, Harry?' she asked, after a pause.

'Not everything, no. In fact, if it weren't for Julia I expect everything would fall to pieces in a matter of days.' He looked at his wife and Madeleine's smile froze.

'Oh, you're not one of those wives who are good at everything, are you?' she cried, reaching out to squeeze Julia's hand. 'You'll have to give me some hints. For one thing, I can't cook. Paul's brilliant at it. Well, he's brilliant at everything really, aren't you, my love?' She looked across the table at him, hoping to outshine the look of intimacy Harry and Julia had shared a moment before.

'As I told you earlier,' Paul answered, 'there is certainly one thing you excel at.'

Madeleine gave a shriek of laughter. 'Don't ask what he's talking about,' she told Harry, 'or he might tell you.'

There was an awkward silence while Julia threw a helpless look towards her husband and Paul reclined in his chair, watching Madeleine.

Madeleine looked at her guests, wondering why they didn't start eating. Then it hit her. People like them probably said grace before meals, so they were waiting for her, as the hostess, to do it.

Immediately she clasped her hands together and closed her eyes. Paul couldn't hide his amazement, and almost exploded with laughter as she started to mumble, 'For what we are about to receive may the Lord make us truly thankful. Amen.' She looked up and smiled. 'Shall we start, then?'

'Yes, yes of course,' Julia answered, utterly bemused.

Paul waited, and at last, after glancing back and forth several times between Julia and Harry, Madeleine tentatively picked up a spoon.

'You say you made the starter?' Julia said, as she followed suit. 'Did you make the dressing as well?'

'Oh God, no,' Madeleine answered. 'It's from a bottle.'

Julia laughed. 'No one I know would ever have admitted to that,' she explained, when Madeleine gave her a curious look, 'but strictly between you and me they all use bottled dressing, every last one of them.'

'Tastes just as good, doesn't it?' Madeleine said, warming to Julia.

'Oh, absolutely.'

'The serviettes!' Madeleine cried suddenly, and leaping up from the table she ran out of the room.

Paul looked at his editor, longing to know what was going through his mind.

'Have you always written, Paul?' Julia asked him, taking a sip of wine.

'Always wanted to, but I didn't get round to doing anything about it until a year or so ago.'

'I imagine it's terribly time-consuming.'

'I was thinking after you left the office earlier,' Harry put in, 'that if we were to put our heads together and . . .'

'Couldn't find them anywhere,' Madeleine said, coming back into the room, 'so I brought some kitchen roll instead. Will that do you?' And tearing off four pieces, she handed them round the table.

'I think we're about to get into a heavy editorial session,' Julia warned her.

'What?' Madeleine looked at Paul.

Paul chuckled. 'Not at all,' he said. Knowing that Harry's mind was soon going to be changed for him, he saw little point in discussing their differences of opinion over the book any further. Not that he expected Madeleine to pull it off that night; there wouldn't be any point since they didn't have a camera yet. Nevertheless, editorial debates were very definitely redundant until such time as Madeleine had done her best – or worst, depending on which way you looked at it.

Wading into the silence, Madeleine said, 'Avocados are really fattening, you know.'

'So I believe,' Julia smiled. 'But you don't need to worry about your figure, you're so wonderfully tall and slim.'

'I have to be a bit careful,' Madeleine confessed, deciding she really did like this woman, 'especially with my kind of work. One dimple of cellulite and that's it!'

'Do you take any exercise?' Harry asked.

Madeleine turned and swept her eyes across his face

with a smile of such indolent sexual hunger that his jaw ground to a halt and his spoon clanged against the dish in front of him. 'Depends what you mean by exercise,' she purred. Then her eyes shot to Paul as he muttered something about checking the duck and darted from the room.

'Do – do you read at all, Madeleine?' Harry stammered as she brushed her foot against his shin.

'I never get the time,' she murmured. 'Always too busy taking exercise.' And she suddenly screeched with laughter.

Julia laughed too, but more at her husband's discomfort than at Madeleine's little joke. 'Don't you read anything? Not even the magazines you appear in?' she asked.

'What, the rude ones, you mean? Yeah, I read them sometimes, but not the others. They're always going on about cancer or babies or diets or all that feminist stuff. Can't be doing with all that, can you?'

'Not really,' Julia agreed. 'But *Harpers & Queen* usually has a few good articles, I . . .'

'I'm on the cover of that one next month,' Madeleine interrupted. 'I've got this fantastic hat on, you wait 'til you see it. It's all lace and fruit with a veil that finishes about here.' She indicated a spot just above her eyes.

'Sounds wonderful,' Julia enthused. 'I adore hats. I just wish there were more occasions to wear them, don't you? Have you ever been to Ascot?'

'No, but I think we're going this year. My agent's got a box or something, there's a whole crowd of us going. You know, models from the agency, photographers, important clients. Tell you what, why don't you come too?'

Julia looked at Harry. 'That would be splendid,' she said, 'I'm sure we'd love to, wouldn't we, darling?'

Harry nodded, and as Madeleine's foot moved further up his leg he looked longingly at the door, hoping for Paul's return. Julia kept up a flow of friendly feminine chit-chat while Madeleine's foot slid closer and closer to its target – Harry was on the point of excusing himself when at last Paul came back into the room.

'OK, I'll just clear this away,' he said, 'and then I'll bring in the duck. How are you all doing for wine?' He was looking at Madeleine's glass and saw with satisfaction that it was empty again. 'If you take out the dishes, darling, I'll see to the wine.' Taking the bottle from the cooler, he started to pour.

'How do you think I'm doing?' Madeleine asked him as he followed her into the kitchen.

'You're perfect,' he said, moving behind her and putting his arms round her.

'He seems a bit dedicated to his wife, though, don't you think?'

'Which only goes to prove that you're getting through to him.'

'How do you work that one out?'

'He's putting on a show for her benefit. It wouldn't surprise me one bit if he was on the phone to you first thing in the morning.' He gave her breasts a quick squeeze, then turned to take the vegetable dishes out of the oven.

'Ugh! What are those pea pods?' Madeleine said as he removed the lids.

'They're mange touts, my darling, you'll love them. Now go back in there and keep our guests amused.'

The conversation over the main course was mainly about books and writers, and as Madeleine had only managed to struggle her way through one or two Barbara Cartlands, she was completely at a loss when they started to exchange views on Anita Brookner and some French writer whose name she couldn't even pronounce. To keep herself amused, she managed to twist her leg round so that she could tickle Harry's groin with her toes. The first time she did it he choked on one of his pea pods and had to leave the room, but the second and third times he merely continued his conversation with Paul as though there was nothing at all happening under the table. Indeed, as far as Madeleine could tell, very little was happening. There was no parting of the legs to give her foot easier access, and no tell-tale bulge either. Then she realised what the problem was, and threw Julia a look of deep compassion. Poor Harry, he obviously only had a little one.

'I'll get the afters,' she said, when Paul finally put down his knife and fork. 'It's fruit salad. You wouldn't like to help me clear the table, would you, Harry?'

'Er, yes, of course,' he said, getting to his feet and this time avoiding Julia's eyes.

'Paul's such a good cook, isn't he?' she said as she stacked the plates on the draining board and directed Harry to put the vegetable dishes on the side.

'Excellent,' he mumbled.

'Don't go yet,' she said, when he made for the door.

He turned back with an awkward smile and a faint colour deepening his ski-holiday tan.

'I was wondering what you thought of my top?' she said, pulling it tight over her breasts. 'It drives Paul wild.'

'Yes, yes, I can imagine,' he stammered.

'If you like, I'll show you the pictures of me in *Men Only* later.'

'That would be very nice,' he said, taking a step back as she started to saunter towards him.

'Of course, you might be very lucky and get to see the real thing,' she told him. 'But not tonight, of course.'

'No, no. Not tonight.'

His hand was shaking as she lifted it and placed it over her left breast. 'Does that feel good?' she asked, her mouth very close to his.

'Er, yes, very nice, but I think I'd better go and fetch what there is left of the duck. Excuse me.' And he fled.

Shrugging her shoulders, and realising there was little point in taking things any further while his wife was around, Madeleine picked up the bowl of fruit salad and went after him.

When they'd finished their dessert Paul suggested they have brandy and coffee in the sitting-room, and while Madeleine was in the kitchen preparing the coffee, Julia wandered in. 'Can I help?' she said.

Madeleine looked round, surprised. 'No, no,' she said, 'everything's under control, as they say.' She wished she didn't like Julia so much, it was making things difficult. Still, the whole point was that Julia would never know, so she didn't have to feel too guilty about it.

'This is a wonderful kitchen,' Julia said. 'In fact, the whole house is wonderful. Do you think I could have a look round?'

'Of course. Let me take this coffee through and I'll take you upstairs, show you the bedrooms. We only use one, of course, there's not much in the others. And I'll take you out onto the roof garden. You can see all over London from there.'

In the sitting-room Paul and Harry had resumed their literary conversation and barely heard when Madeleine told them she was going to give Julia a guided tour. It was only when he got up to pour more brandy and happened to glance at the clock that Paul realised over half an hour had gone by, and there was still no sign of them returning.

Harry had returned to the subject of Guy de Maupassant and was at present engaged in a lengthy eulogy of the short story 'Clair de Lune'. Paul handed him another brandy and sat down to listen, but his eyes kept wandering to the door. Julia had had enough time to view every house in the street by now.

Eventually he excused himself and went to search them out. He hunted the bedrooms, the roof garden, the kitchen, the dining-room and finally found them in his study. Madeleine was sitting on his desk, Julia on the chair in front of her. Their abrupt silence as he walked in sapped the geniality from his smile, and to his astonishment he found himself apologising. 'Sorry to interrupt, but could I have a word, Maddy?'

Madeleine gave Julia a quick look, then followed him into the hall. 'What's going on in there?' he hissed, once she had closed the door.

'Just girl-talk, you know. We'll join you in a minute.'

'Well, hurry up. And when you do, walk around a bit – let him get a good look at your legs. Are you wearing any underwear?'

Madeleine nodded.

The door opened and Julia came out. 'I was wondering if I might have another drink,' she said, holding up her empty glass.

Madeleine took it. The two women's eyes met for an instant, then Julia went back into the study.

'I'll get the drink,' Paul said. 'You get rid of the underwear.'

When he returned with Julia's drink he was relieved to find Madeleine wasn't there, which could only mean that she was doing as he asked. Julia thanked him politely for the brandy, made several admiring remarks about his collection of books, then sat quietly waiting for him to speak. More than a little confused, he told her Madeleine wouldn't be long, then muttering something about topping up Harry's glass, he went back to the sitting-room.

'As long as I live,' he told Harry, 'I'll never understand how it is a woman can make a man feel so ridiculous by simply saying nothing.'

Harry looked up. 'What are they doing?'

'God knows. They're in my study. Girl-talk, I was informed.'

'I'm sure they'll be in in a minute,' Harry smiled, but his face had paled, and as he leaned forward to pick up his drink Paul couldn't help noticing the twitch at the corner of his mouth.

Another half an hour went by and again Paul got to his feet. Not only was he angry with Madeleine, but Harry's discomfort was becoming positively embarrassing.

This time he listened at the door before going in, but the heavy wood muted their voices, and though he knew it was Julia doing most of the talking he couldn't make out what she was saying. In the end, without knocking, he pushed open the door and walked in. He wasn't sure what he expected to find, apart from the two of them sitting as he'd found them before – and they were, except that now Madeleine was wearing a dress he'd forbidden her to wear, even about the house. It was white and flowery, belted at the waist, and covered everything from neck to knee.

She looked up as he came in, flicked back her hair and smiled.

Quickly swallowing his amazement, Paul forced a chuckle into his voice as he said, 'It must be one hell of a conversation you two are having. You've been in here hours.'

'Classical history,' Julia informed him before Madeleine could speak. 'I've been telling Madeleine all about what went on in the Greek *gymnasia*.'

He looked from one to the other and could see that Madeleine didn't have the faintest idea what Julia was talking about.

'Anyway, I think that's probably enough for one night, don't you?' Julia said, getting to her feet. 'Let's go and liven up the male side of the party.'

Harry's nervousness abated slightly when Julia came back into the room, and he complimented Madeleine extravagantly on her dress. 'Everything all right?' he said, as Julia sat down beside him.

'Yes, yes. Everything's fine,' she answered. 'Nothing to worry about.'

Paul found that an extremely odd remark, and watched the two of them closely as they finished their brandies.

There had been a sub-text in that small exchange, he was sure of it, but for the life of him he couldn't imagine what it might be. Eventually Harry said it was time they were going, and while Madeleine and Julia kissed one another on both cheeks, Paul walked to the door with Harry.

'Think about the suggestions I made earlier,' Harry said, once again his affable, though somewhat stiff self. 'I want to publish you, Paul, very much – but the book's too long and too obscure the way it is.'

'Yes, I'll think about it,' Paul promised, then as Julia came out of the sitting-room he gave her a polite kiss, and he and Madeleine stood at the door waving them off in their old Bentley.

'What the hell was going on?' he demanded as he followed Madeleine back into the sitting-room. 'And why are you wearing that bloody awful dress?'

Madeleine shrugged. 'It seemed more suitable for a history lesson.'

'Don't get smart with me. I thought . . .'

Madeleine was shaking her head and laughing. 'You thought wrong, Paul. There was no point me doing anything to try and seduce Harry. You see, I have it on the best authority that you're more his type than I am.'

'What!'

'He's gay.'

'But he's married.'

Again Madeleine shrugged. 'Married or not, he's gay.'

For a long moment there was silence, then suddenly Paul threw back his head and roared with laughter. 'That's what you two have been talking about all night?'

Madeleine nodded. 'Mostly.'

'Of course,' he said, drawing out the words with dawning realisation. 'Now I see the connection with the Greek *gymnasia*. What did she say?'

Madeleine was still obviously baffled by the Greek business but didn't bother to ask about it. 'Basically, she said that I was wasting my time trying to get her husband into bed.' She tilted her head to one side and pursed her lips thoughtfully. 'It's quite sad really, you know, because she's desperately in love with Harry, and I can't say I blame her – he's gorgeous. She didn't know about the way he is until after they got married; they keep up appearances for the sake of the family name and the children. He's very discreet, apparently, and never tells her who he's seeing, or when.'

Paul was watching her suspiciously. 'No one comes out with highly guarded secrets just like that,' he said. 'How do you know she's telling the truth?'

'I don't, for sure. But I can tell you one thing, *I* didn't give him an erection. Anyway, why should she lie?'

He shook his head. 'To throw you off the scent perhaps. But it's a bit excessive, going to those lengths. She could have just confronted you with it, and told you to back off.'

'Well, she didn't. And as I said, I don't think she's lying. She made me swear I wouldn't tell anyone. You know, she might be posh and all that, but I think she quite liked me. She said we ought to have lunch together some time next week.'

'Are you going to?'

She shrugged. 'Doubt it. I've got a really busy time coming up. Unless you want me to, of course.'

'Not particularly.'

She started to pick up glasses and cups and pile them onto the coffee tray. 'What are you looking like that for?' she demanded. 'He's queer, isn't he? That must give you some ammunition.'

'Ammunition, yes,' he answered thoughtfully. 'But what we need now is the gun to fire it with.'

Madeleine screwed up her face. 'What?'

'Proof,' he explained.

– 12 –

London hadn't been so hot since 1976. In the hope of even a breath of air Marian had the doors and windows open, but all that came in was the din and grime of Soho's passing traffic; and with only a paltry electric fan to keep the cloying humidity at bay she was finding it increasingly difficult to get on with her work.

In the corner the word processor was sluggishly printing out endless lists; the legal ramifications of the film, suggested production personnel, publicity proposals, actors for audition, a cash flow projection, and countless other details Marian was too hot and bothered to care about. Turning from her typewriter, she reached for yet another tissue and wiped the perspiration from her face, then glared at the telephone, willing it to ring. Since they'd arrived back from America two weeks ago, reality had returned with a vengeance and she was once again suffering a crushing sense of loneliness. To make matters worse, Bronwen had gone off to Wales and Matthew had reverted to his former arrogant self. The realisation that her moods were governed by his sat ill with Marian, especially when she had tried so hard to change things between them; and in New York, or so she'd thought, she had succeeded. She had even begun to get an inkling of why other people liked him so much, because on the rare occasions when he had bothered to flex his charm, she had found him almost irresistible. Since they'd got back he had been exeptionally busy, she knew that – but it did not excuse the way he had walked in through the door with Stephanie half an hour ago, passed straight by her office and continued on up the stairs. It wouldn't have hurt him to pop his head round the door and at least say hello. Stephanie did. And she had bothered to tell Marian about the interview they'd just done on TV-AM. But politeness was obviously too much to expect of Matthew Cornwall now that they were back in London.

It had been a different story during the latter part of their stay in America. She had spent two whole days in her hotel room, making rough drafts of some scenes for the script, and when Bronwen showed them to Matthew he'd had all the time in the world for her then, and had even spoken up in her defence to Deborah Foreman.

'Don't you see,' he'd explained to Deborah, 'because Marian has no real knowledge of either New York or the kind of life we're portraying, her imagination is giving the whole thing an almost surreal quality – magical, fantastical, and at the same time profoundly sinister too. It's what we need. It puts guts into the story that simply weren't there before.'

Perhaps not the most tactful thing to say, so it was hardly surprising that Deborah Foreman had remained resolutely unimpressed by Marian's efforts; but behind her back Matthew had winked at Marian, and after that Marian couldn't have cared less what Deborah Foreman thought.

Sighing, she picked up a pen and began toying with her football pools coupon. She wouldn't mind so much about Matthew if his unpredictability didn't make her think of Paul. Not that Paul was ever temperamental like Matthew, but the way he had so abruptly absconded with Madeleine had been such a shock to her that, ever since, any erratic or confusing behaviour made her nervous and withdrawn. She would never have admitted it to anyone – except Bronwen during a weak moment in New York – but there were still times when the hurt caught her unawares and sucked her back into a chasm of loneliness that was every bit as desperate as it had been in those early days when she first discovered Paul had gone.

Bronwen had told her that it was asking too much of herself to expect she should be over it all in such a short time, but nevertheless, she was determined to conquer it. It was just that being back in London, and being so often on her own again, made it particularly difficult. She wondered if having a friend to pour her heart out to would help, but there wasn't anyone, so there was no point in thinking about it. Just as there was no point in buying magazines or newspapers any more, because Madeleine was always in them. Sometimes she felt as though Madeleine were dead, and that the pictures that smiled up at her from the glossy pages were ghosts coming back to haunt her. Two weeks ago, driving back to London from the airport with Stephanie, they had passed a bill-board with Madeleine's evocative face plastered all over it, and Marian had made up her mind then to stop wondering what her cousin was doing at any given moment of the day, and to start hating her. But it simply wasn't in her nature to hate someone, so that had lasted no more than twenty-four hours.

'Ugh!' she snorted, throwing her pen across the desk. 'You're so bloody feeble, you can't even get together a good, healthy dose of hatred. Why do you always have to go pussy-footing round people, trying to make them like you? What bloody difference does it make whether they do or not? Tell them all to go to hell, why don't you?'

The buzzer sounded on her desk, startling her, and she prodded the button angrily.

'Marian, can you bring up the budgets I asked you to type out yesterday, please?' Stephanie's voice asked.

'No!' Marion snapped, and jabbing the button again, she turned back to her typewriter.

Within seconds she heard footsteps on the stairs, then Stephanie saying uncertainly, 'Marian?'

Marian continued typing, faster and faster, trying to keep up with her heart-beat.

'Marian?' Stephanie said again. 'Is something the matter?'

'No, I'm fine,' Marian answered in clipped tones.

'Oh well, that's all right then. I'll just take the budgets if I may. Are they here? In the top drawer?'

Marian spun round in her chair and stormed over to the filing cabinet. 'No! They're where they . . .'

'Aaagh! Don't hit me!' Stephanie yelped, snatching her hands away as Marian yanked open the second drawer.

For several seconds Marian glared at her, then suddenly her mouth started to twitch and her head dropped forward as her shoulders began to shake.

Tentatively, Stephanie lifted her curtain of hair and peered into her face. 'Are you laughing?' she said, her own voice bubbling with mirth.

When Marian looked up her eyes were swimming with tears, and she fell against the filing cabinets, holding her sides and gasping with laughter. 'Hit you?' she cried. 'As if I would!'

'Well, you sounded pretty angry,' Stephanie laughed. 'I didn't know what to expect. What's got into you?'

'I don't know,' Marian choked. 'I think I'm becoming hysterical.' She was suddenly whooping with laughter again, and the fact that Stephanie joined in only made matters worse.

'Stop it!' she pleaded. 'Stephanie, don't!'

'I can't help it!' Stephanie gasped. 'It's you, you're making me laugh!'

'What on earth's going on in here?' Matthew asked, looking from one to the other as they tried to pull themselves together.

One look at his bemused face was enough to send Marian into another paroxysm, and the more she laughed, the more Stephanie laughed.

'Go away before I hit you,' Marian managed to squeal,

and Stephanie collapsed against the desk, pointing at his shocked face.

'You're both insane,' he grinned, and shaking his head, he went to sit on Marian's chair and watch while they rolled hysterically about the office.

That was how Kathleen found them when she walked in five minutes later.

She stood planted in the doorway, hands on hips, glaring at Stephanie. Marian was the first to see her, and found the frown on her face so hilarious that the stitch in her side gave an agonising leap and she howled with pain.

'There's someone at the door,' she wailed.

Stephanie lifted her head and turned towards the door, wiping the tears from her eyes. The instant she saw Kathleen, the blood drained from her face. Matthew rotated in his chair – and he too looked suddenly pale.

Keeping her lips pressed firmly together in an effort to stifle her hiccoughs, Marian looked again at the large, intimidating woman in the doorway – then flinched as she sneered at Stephanie.

'Yes, I thought I'd wipe the smile from your face,' she spat.

Marian's mouth dropped open, and she turned to look at Stephanie. Then a great, heaving hiccough bolted through the silence, and Stephanie exploded into laughter.

'Don't you fucking laugh at me, you bitch!' and to Marian's utter amazement, the woman launched herself towards Stephanie and would have hit her had Matthew not stepped between them and grabbed the woman's striking arm.

'For God's sake, Kathleen!' he hissed, twisting the arm behind her back and pulling her away from Stephanie.

'Don't you for-God's-sake me, you bastard!' she bellowed in a strident cockney voice. 'I've had just about . . .'

'Shut up!' he snapped. He jerked his head back as she

tried to slap his face, then winced as she trod heavily on his foot and wrenched her arm free.

'Don't you tell me to shut up,' she seethed. 'It's about time I had my say. All the years I was married to you and now you treat me like this. What kind of man are you? You're a bastard! A fucking bastard! Can't even . . .'

'Kathleen!' Stephanie shouted.

Kathleen spun round, her eyes blazing with hatred – and Marian giggled.

'If you don't mind, you're in my office and you're trespassing.' Stephanie bit out the words angrily, but Kathleen was undaunted.

'Trespassing!' she sneered. 'And just what the fuck do you think you're doing, you little whore! You're screwing my husband, that's what you're doing. And I don't suppose you thought for one minute what it would do to my family!'

'Whatever's happened to your family is of your own doing,' Stephanie answered. 'If you didn't go round making such a damned ridiculous spectacle of yourself . . .'

'Spectacle of myself!' Kathleen screeched. 'Is it making a spectacle of myself to want my children's father to at least speak to them? Is it . . .'

'He does speak to them. He . . .'

'To Bobby, yes! He's turned him against me, hasn't he?' She rounded on Matthew. 'What have you been saying to him? Why won't he come home to visit me? You've seen him, haven't you? Oh don't deny it, I know you have . . .'

'I'm not denying it,' Matthew said through gritted teeth. 'I . . .'

'See! See! He's admitting it. He's turning my own son against me. What do you want next, Matthew? Samantha? Do you want to take her away from me as well? Leave me with nothing? Is that what you're trying to do?'

'It's you who are poisoning Samantha's mind against

her father,' Stephanie shouted. 'And if you ask me, your son can probably see for himself what a harridan of a mother you are!'

'Stephanie! Leave it!' Matthew barked.

'You fucking bitch!' Kathleen shrieked. 'How dare you speak to me like that. Well, go on, do it some more! Show him what you're really like. I'll bet it's you putting him up to all this. Stopping my money, turning him against his own daughter.'

'Don't be ridiculous, Kathleen! Nobody's turned me against Samantha. Now, can we go somewhere a little more private to discuss this, please. Just you and I.'

'Oh no! It's her I came to see and it's her I'm going to have,' and she hurled herself across the room and grabbed Stephanie by the hair. Matthew was after her like a shot, and as the three of them struggled, Kathleen yelling obscenities, Stephanie screaming with pain and Matthew shouting for them to break it up, Marian finally managed to get a grip on herself and ran to the phone.

'Stop it!' she yelled, as she put the receiver to her ear. '*I said stop it!*' To her utter amazement, they all turned to look at her.

Pulling herself together quickly, she snapped, 'Stephanie, Frank Hastings is on the line for you, I'll put it through to your office.' She pushed another button on the switchboard, then when she saw Stephanie was still gawking at her, she said, 'Can you go and take the call, please? He says it's urgent and he's on the line from America. Hello? Yes, Ryder and Evans here. Oh hello, Woody. Yes, OK I'll tell him. Thank you.' She put the phone down and turned to Matthew. 'Is your car parked in Brewer Street?'

'Yes.'

'Then I'd get round there quick if I were you, it's about to be towed away.'

'Shit!' Matthew dashed his fingers through his dishevelled hair and looked at Kathleen. Then suddenly remembering that Woody was still on holiday, he turned back to Marian.

'Hurry up, Matthew!' she snapped. Then walking round the desk, she held her hand out to Kathleen. 'Mrs Cornwall?' she said. 'My name's Marian. I'm sorry nobody introduced us earlier.'

Matthew watched her, astonishment in every line of his face. This was a Marian he'd never seen before, but understanding completely what she was up to, he tried to stop her.

'Look, Marian,' he began, 'this is extremely . . .'

'Extremely unfortunate if you have to go down to Park Lane and reclaim your car,' she interrupted, looking at her watch. 'Especially when you've got a meeting at twelve thirty in Streatham.'

'Streatham?'

'Yes, Streatham. Now hurry up.'

'Marian . . .'

'Matthew! Do you have to stand there arguing?'

He looked at her, stunned, then threw up his hands and left.

When Marian turned back to Kathleen she was startled to find her smiling, quite pleasantly. And then she burst out laughing. 'Nice one,' she said. 'Did you see his face when you said Streatham? He didn't have a clue what you were talking about.'

Marian looked at her uncertainly.

Kathleen grinned. 'Don't worry, I saw straight through your little trick.' Then, shaking her head, 'Always takes a kid to make you see what a fool you're making of yourself.'

Marian grinned back. 'Well, you were a bit,' she said. 'If you don't mind me saying so.'

'More than a bit,' Kathleen smiled, and glancing around the office she asked, 'Well, what now?'

'Fancy a coffee?'

She nodded. 'I'd love one.' And suddenly she looked so weary that Marian gave her arm an impulsive squeeze.

'Let's go to the café down the road,' she suggested. 'I could do with getting out of here myself.'

'And Stephanie's still upstairs,' Kathleen added for her.

Marian smiled, and picking up her handbag, she followed Kathleen out into the sweltering heat of the day.

'God, I feel exhausted,' Kathleen muttered as they sat down at a window table in the cluttered café.

'Hardly surprising, expending all that energy on a day like this,' Marian said. 'I thought for one horrible minute you were going to mash Stephanie to a pulp.'

'I'd like to, believe me,' Kathleen sighed, and as she combed her fingers through her short dark hair, Marian thought how attractive she was when she wasn't scowling.

'Hardly the answer, though, is it?' she ventured.

Kathleen looked at her for a long time, resting her chin on her hands. There was a hint of amusement in her eyes. 'How old are you?' she asked finally.

'Just twenty-three,' Marian answered. 'Two coffees please,' she told the waiter as he approached.

Kathleen smiled. 'You seem older. And that wasn't supposed to be rude, I suppose it's just that I've never seen anyone handle Matthew like that before. You don't stand for much argument once you get going, do you?'

'To be honest,' Marian confessed, 'I've never made a stand like that before. In fact, I'm pretty certain it was only shock that made Matthew do as I told him. If he'd bitten back, I mean *really* bitten back, I haven't the faintest idea what I'd have done.'

Kathleen chuckled, then sat back as the waiter put their coffees on the table. 'I didn't mean to go off the handle like that, you know,' she said when he'd gone. 'No, that's a lie, I did. I was bloody livid.'

'I got the impression you were a little upset,' Marian said with a wry grin.

'It was seeing them together on the telly this morning that did it. You just don't know how it feels.'

'I think I've got a pretty good idea,' Marian answered quietly.

'Mind you, I could just about have stood that, but when Bobby rang up to say he'd seen it too, and called that bitch a cracker, well, that was the final straw.'

Marian compressed her lips into a thin, tight line. 'Not very tactful, no,' she said, thinking how like his father he sounded.

She watched as Kathleen stirred two sugars into her coffee, and tried to imagine Matthew married to someone like her. It seemed incredible, and not only because she'd got used to seeing him with Stephanie. Kathleen didn't seem his type at all. She was so housewifely – and coarse. 'You've been split up about six months now, haven't you?' she asked, in a gentle voice which only she knew was designed to try and take the edge off her own uncharitable thoughts.

'Eight,' Kathleen answered. 'Well, that's how long ago he left home. But things were pretty bad – no, fucking awful – between us for years, I just refused to see it. He never wanted to marry me in the first place, but I was pregnant with Bobby and he did the decent thing. I did it on purpose, you know. Got pregnant, I mean. I knew it was the only way I was going to keep him.'

Marian swallowed a mouthful of coffee. 'If you don't mind me saying so,' she spoke up, after a pause, 'I wouldn't have thought that doing what you did just now would . . . Well, I don't know Matthew that well, but . . .' She shrugged.

'I know what you're trying to say, and you're right. He hates scenes, so throwing one sure as hell won't get him back. But where that woman's concerned I just can't help myself.'

'You still want him back? Even though . . .' Again Marian stopped.

'He doesn't love me?' Kathleen supplied.

'That's not what I was going to say,' Marian assured her quickly.

'Wasn't it? Well, it's true, he doesn't. And as for wanting him back, that's the funny thing, I don't really. Not any more. Well, I do, but I know it's a lost cause. We were never suited, me and Matthew, he was much too sophisticated for the likes of me. It was just that I knew he was going places and I wanted a slice of the action. And now I've had it, well, it's not really for me. I don't fit in. I can live with that, but what I can't stand is him being with that little tart. She's the bitch who broke up our marriage in the first place.'

Marian looked her straight in the eye, and Kathleen laughed.

'You're a smart one for twenty-three,' she said. 'All right, he wouldn't have been having an affair in the first place if things had been right at home.'

'But it's only natural to look for someone else to blame,' Marian said. 'We all do it.'

'Do we? Who do you blame when things go wrong in your life?'

'Myself, unfortunately. Then I collapse in a pathetic, miserable heap, and feel so sorry for myself I make myself sick.'

'But you don't go round making a public spectacle of yourself?'

'I haven't got the courage.' And they both laughed.

Picking up her cup and holding it in both hands, Kathleen studied Marian's face with her penetrating blue eyes. 'You know,' she said, after a while, 'I always imagined Matthew ending up with someone like you, really. Older, of course, but calm and decisive and . . . well, strong, I suppose.'

'Strong? Me?' Marian exclaimed.

'Yes, you,' Kathleen smiled, and reaching across the table she tweaked Marian's nose.

'I know you won't want to hear this,' Marian said, 'but Stephanie's pretty strong.'

'I expect she is,' Kathleen sighed. 'But I've got a bee in my bonnet about her, and I don't suppose it'll ever go away.'

'Not even if you were to meet someone else?'

'Not even then. And I know, because I have. But don't tell Matthew, will you?'

'Why? I mean, of course I won't. But why don't you want him to know?'

'Frankly, I enjoy making him suffer. And he can handle it, so don't look so worried. There's very little in this world Matthew can't handle.'

'What about Samantha? Stephanie tells me he gets quite cut up about her.'

'Yes,' Kathleen said, nodding her head slowly. 'I'll bet he does. But it's nothing to do with me, I swear it. Well, she knows I don't go much on Stephanie, but I've never done anything deliberate to turn her against Matthew. If anything, I try to make her see him, but she won't. She says she doesn't want anything to do with him, and then refuses to talk about it. I suppose she'll come round in the end. I hope so, for her sake; after all, he is her father and they used to be really close.'

Marian stared down at her cup, shocked by the sudden surge of emotion that had locked in her throat.

'Like another?' Kathleen offered.

Marian swallowed hard and looked up. 'Yes. Yes, please,' she smiled.

'Everything all right, is it?' Kathleen asked. 'You've gone a bit pale.'

'No, I'm fine,' Marian answered, taking a deep breath. 'I expect it's everything that's happened. I'm a bit like Matthew when it comes to scenes, I guess.'

'Sorry.' Kathleen squeezed her hand, then waved to the waiter. 'So what do you do in Stephanie's little set-up, then, apart from getting her out of scraps?'

'I'm her secretary. And Bronwen's her partner.'

'Nice, is it? Do you like working for them?'

'Truthfully, I don't know where I'd be without them.'

'And what about Matthew?'

Marian shook her head, confused. 'What about Matthew?'

'Well, do you get along with him?'

'Sometimes,' she answered, suddenly feeling as though the heat was stifling her. 'But to be frank, he frightens me a bit.'

Kathleen threw back her head and gave a shout of laughter. 'You don't want to let Matthew Cornwall frighten you, Marian. He's nothing more than a great big softy at heart. He just gets carried away with his work and forgets to be polite occasionally – I should know, I lived with it long enough. But you'd have to look a long way before you found a man more genuine, more kind and, dare I say it, more romantic, than my husband when he wants to be. Don't tell him I told you that. But if you ask me, you're safer the way it is, because if he did decide to turn on the charm, those eyes of his would have your knees turning to jelly. There are more broken hearts in Matthew's career than there are films, and don't tell him I said that, either. In fact he probably doesn't even know about half of them.'

'How can he not know?'

'Because I made sure he didn't. I can see the signs a mile off, and I used to have a quiet word with them before they went to work on him.' She shrugged. 'I don't know why I bothered half the time, it's not as if he's an easy catch, he never was. In fact his only real affair was with Stephanie, and even then he came back to me. Well, to Samantha, really. But I knew then it would only be a matter of time. He never stopped loving Stephanie, even though he didn't see her, that's why I can't forgive her. He never loved me like that.'

'But in the beginning . . .'

'I told you, I trapped him. And let that be a lesson to you, Marian. By doing something like that you might win yourself a husband, but you'll never win the man.'

'And the man you're seeing now? Do you love him?'

'In a way, yes. But there are very few men around to match up to Matthew. He's got something, I don't know what it is, but . . .' She looked out of the window and Marian's heart turned over at the sadness in her face. 'This might sound odd, coming from me, but behind that fierce exterior is one of the few decent men in this world. He's someone you can trust, someone you can turn to in a crisis.' She paused, and for a moment Marian thought she was going to cry. But then, with a small toss of her head, she seemed to pull herself together. 'Don't fall for him, Marian,' she said, turning back. 'Please, promise me you won't fall for him. He'll only hurt you in the end.'

'Me?' Marian spluttered, a burning heat rushing to her face. 'Why do you say that? I mean, he's old enough . . . Well, he's . . . He's . . .'

'Oh God,' Kathleen groaned. 'You don't even know it, do you?'

'Know what?'

'I told you, I can spot it a mile off.'

Stephanie and Matthew were waiting in the downstairs office when Marian returned.

'Where have you been?' Stephanie cried, leaping up from her chair. 'Where's Kathleen?' She put an arm round Marian's shoulder. 'What did she say? God, I've been so worried about you. She didn't get violent again, did she? Oh Marian, you little nutcase, you shouldn't have done that. Not that we're not grateful, of course, but . . .'

'Stephanie,' Matthew interrupted. 'Why don't you let Marian speak?' He turned to Marian, and Marian felt a slow paralysis creeping over her tongue as she remembered what Kathleen had said. 'Well?' he prompted gently.

Pulling herself upright, Marian unhooked her bag from her shoulder and went to sit down. 'Kathleen and I have been for a coffee,' she said. 'We talked for a while, and that's all there is to tell.'

'But what did you talk about?' Stephanie urged.

'Oh, this and that. The weather, you know.' She was acutely aware of Matthew's eyes on her and wished he would go away.

'Marian!' Stephanie exclaimed. 'She must have said something about what happened.'

To Marian's relief, the phone rang, and when she answered it Bronwen's voice came over the line, clear and bubbling and asking for Stephanie.

Stephanie was about to take the receiver when Matthew said, 'Take it upstairs.'

'Pardon?' Stephanie said. Then, as he nodded towards the door, 'Oh, yes. Yes, put it through to my office, will you, Marian?'

When she'd gone, Matthew rested an elbow on the top of the filing cabinet and silently waited for Marian to look at him.

'Oh, the printer's finished,' Marian said, getting up from her chair.

As she passed him, Matthew caught her hand and turned her round. 'Thank you,' he said, his dark eyes smiling with sincerity.

Marian shrugged and looked at the floor.

'And I apologise.'

She looked up. 'What for?'

'Leaving you to deal with it.'

'As I remember,' she said, grinning and blushing, 'I didn't give you much choice.'

He laughed. 'Nevertheless, Kathleen's my wife and it shouldn't have been left to you to sort out the mess.'

'I didn't see it quite like that.'

'Shall I ask how you saw it?'

'Better not.' Her heart was thumping so hard that she was sure he must be able to hear it. Her fingers started to shake but he didn't let go of her hand.

'Was she very upset? I mean, when you talked to her.'

'Not really. She'd calmed down by then.'

'Where is she now?'

'Gone home.'

He nodded, and for a moment he seemed to withdraw into himself. When his eyes returned to hers she saw they were smiling. 'You're quite a surprise,' he said.

'A surprise?'

'First you threaten to hit me, then you order me out of the office, then you take my hysterical wife in hand. And that's after you've shown us all the best way to write a feature film. I'd call that a surprise. In fact, I could go further and tell you that I'm just beginning to realise you're a very special person who's been hiding her light under a bushel, but it would only make you blush.'

The air was locked in her lungs, and as a fire burned across her cheeks she felt as though she would drown in the wonderful lambency of his eyes.

'What goes on behind those shy grey eyes of yours, Marian?' he asked quietly. 'What are you going to do next?'

Neither of them heard Stephanie's footsteps on the stairs, nor were they aware of her walking into the office until she said, 'Sorry, am I interruping something?'

A bolt of guilt-laden horror shot through Marian and

she tried to snatch her hand from Matthew's. But his grip tightened as he turned to face Stephanie.

'Bronwen's coming back to London tomorrow,' she said cheerfully, and Marian almost collapsed with relief when she threw out her arms and walked towards her. 'Sorry about badgering you just now,' she said, giving Marian a hug. 'Are you all right? Is there anything I can get you?'

'Actually,' Marian answered, feeling suddenly dizzy as Stephanie pulled away and Matthew let go of her hand, 'just as you came in, Matthew was wondering what I was going to do next.' She turned to Matthew. 'I'm going to ask you to make me a cup of tea,' she said grinning.

His eyes flew open, then in a voice simmering with laughter he said, 'Don't push your luck,' and stuffing his hands in his pockets, he walked out of the office.

'*I'll* make you one,' Stephanie said. 'And then I'll tell you the good news Bronwen's just asked me to pass on to you.'

As Stephanie swept off to the kitchen, Marian turned to the word processor and began leafing through the documents it had finished printing what now felt like a lifetime ago. She was still smiling at Matthew's remark, and each time she repeated it to herself she felt a heady surge of euphoria. Although she had been shocked by Kathleen's warning, she had assured her that this time she had read the signs wrong: she was simply overawed by Matthew, nothing more, and now that the awe was fading she was finding that she genuinely liked him. It was for Stephanie's sake that she cared about being friends with him, because Stephanie had said often enough that she wished that was the case. Well now it looked as if it was going to be. She laughed aloud. Considering that it had started with her so down in the dumps, the day was turning out surprisingly well. Of course, there was always tonight, when she'd have to go home and spend yet another evening alone – but that thought was too depressing for the mood she was in now.

'Here we are,' Stephanie said, plonking a mug down on Marian's desk. 'Mm, that's wonderful,' she murmured, as a welcome breeze from the fan lifted her hair. She picked up a wad of crumpled paper from Marian's desk. 'What's this?' she asked.

Marian turned. 'Oh no,' she groaned, 'I've been rumbled. It's the football pools.'

'I never had you down for a closet gambler,' Stephanie grinned.

'I do them every week. Habit, I suppose. Part of a dream Madeleine and I used to have.'

Stephanie put the coupons down and turned to perch on the edge of the desk. 'Any news of her whereabouts yet?'

'No.'

'But I thought the man at *The Sun* was going to pass your message on?'

'Whether he did or not, she hasn't called, so no, I still don't know where she's living.'

'It shouldn't be too difficult to find out, if you'd like me to help.'

Marian shook her head. 'No. No thanks.'

'Do you miss her?' Stephanie asked, watching Marian as she picked up her cup and sat down.

'Yes.'

'Then why not let me help?'

'Because I know Madeleine. She'll never let it show, but deep down she'll be riddled with guilt about what's happened, and she'll have mistaken the guilt for hate. I won't be able to reason with her while she's like that, so I've decided it's better if I give her some time to sort herself out.'

'Jesus, you're a saint, Marian. And Paul?'

Marian shrugged. 'It still hurts, but I keep reminding

myself of the deceit. It doesn't always help, and there are still moments, when it's *really* bad, when I long to go back to the way we were – even though I know now that it was all based on lies. I just hope to God he doesn't do anything like that to Madeleine. She'd go to pieces – not that I didn't, but it'll be different for Maddy. She's so insecure. I used to be taken in by her bravado, I used to think that nothing could touch Madeleine, but since this has happened I've thought about her a lot – obviously – and now I can see things much clearer. It's all to do with her parents going off when she was so young; it's as if, ever since, she's been trying to find all the love and appreciation they denied her. Naturally, my parents tried to give it to her, and they loved her every bit as much as they did me, but it's not the same. To her it probably looked as though I had everything, and when Paul came along, well, that was the final straw. In her heart she believes I stole him from her, not the other way round – and in a way I suppose she's right. I knew how much she wanted him, but . . .' She shrugged and smiled. 'Well, it's history now, and my only real regret is that I didn't stop to consider how she must have been feeling all the time I was with him.'

'You care for her very much, don't you?'

'Yes. But I always knew that one day we would go our separate ways. I never dreamt it would be like this, of course. I thought we would still be in touch, you know, visiting each other as often as possible, her turning up in her chauffeur-driven limo and carrying me off into the afternoon, while a classful of pupils looked out of the window, boggle-eyed at the idea that dowdy old Miss Deacon was related to the famous Madeleine Deacon.'

'I didn't know you had an ambition to teach, Marian?'

'I *don't!*' she laughed. 'I just had that picture in my mind's eye: the famous actress or model, and the frumpy schoolmistress. I even used to imagine Madeleine having hoards of babies and dumping them on the old spinster aunt while she went jetting off round the world. Great future I was planning for myself, don't you think?'

'Just thank God I came along when I did,' Stephanie laughed, 'or the world at large might never have known anything about your amazing wit and intellect, not to mention the very real beauty of your smile.'

Marian stuck out her tongue.

'Well, whoever is lucky enough to win your heart in the future will have me to thank,' Stephanie declared proudly, 'and when the time comes, I shall tell him so.'

'You do that. Meanwhile, let me remind you that half the fantasy is already coming true. Maddy's in just about every publication you pick up these days. It wouldn't surprise me to turn on the TV any time now and hear her announcing some major Hollywood deal.'

'Just as long as you don't get out your knitting needles yet, because I need you here. However, Bronwen has other ideas.'

'Oh?'

'You and she are off to Italy the week after next. Or you will be, once you've booked the tickets. That's what she was calling me about, to check that I could spare you. Why are you frowning? I thought you'd be thrilled.'

'I am. Well, I ought to be. I suppose it's just all this talk about Madeleine and Paul. We went to Rome together, you see, the three of us.'

Stephanie reached out to brush her hand across Marian's hair. 'Sorry, I'd forgotten. Well, this is Florence, so it shouldn't be too bad.'

Feeling it was too petty to say that Florence was almost as bad because Paul used to go there with his parents, Marian put on a bright smile and said, 'It'll be great. And if you were coming too, it would be absolutely fantastic.'

'You say all the right things,' Stephanie laughed. 'Now I'd better go upstairs and have a look at the newspaper cuttings we've got on Olivia in Italy, and try to pin Matthew down to thinking about it too. He's dubbing at De Lane Lea this afternoon, isn't he? I'd better ring him there. Damn it, he's dubbing all day tomorrow as well, and over the weekend. Still, we've got all next week.'

'No, you haven't,' Marian said, opening the diary. 'He's shooting another commercial on Wednesday, Thursday and Friday – Monday's a bank holiday.'

Stephanie sighed. 'He's doing something with his son that day. And if he's shooting Wednesday, Thursday and Friday that'll mean he's editing next weekend. I know he's always in demand, but I wish he didn't say yes to everything. Well, we'll have to squeeze it in somewhere before he goes. Now, what time is it in New York? I think I'll give Deborah Foreman a call.'

When she had gone, Marian leaned her elbows on the desk and looked out of the window. As her mind wandered back over the events of the past few hours, a warm feeling of happiness spread through her. She was liking her new life, in fact she was liking it a lot. Then she laughed as her imagination ballooned into a vision of a future that had her writing films for Madeleine to star in, Stephanie and Bronwen to produce and Matthew to direct.

– 13 –

Deidre and Sergio forged a path through the steady flow of students, winding their way along the drab corridors of the Accademia. Occasionally Sergio stopped to speak to one of the students, and each time he did so Deidre's tension increased. She wasn't sure why she was so agitated, but it was the same feeling she'd had five years ago when the whole thing had first blown up, and just as she had then, she was looking to Sergio to put her mind at rest.

'Of course I am pleased to see you, *cara*,' he said as he pushed open a door and stood back for her to go through. 'It is only that I am surprised to see you here.'

'I had to talk to you,' she answered. 'There's something I have to tell you.' She followed him down a narrow, crowded flight of stairs and again they were in a bustling corridor.

'And what is that?' he said.

She waited while he indulged in another rapid exchange with a student. 'It's about Olivia Hastings,' she said, when he turned back to her. 'You remember, the American girl.'

He nodded thoughtfully. '*Sì*, I remember.' To her surprise, he started to walk on.

'Somebody's making a film about her,' she told him.

'I know.'

'You know?'

He stopped, then smiled when he saw her incredulous eyes. '*Sì*. A woman by the name of Bronwen Evans, she called me and we make an arrangement to meet. Soon. She want to ask me what I know about Olivia when she was here in *Firenze*.'

For a moment Deidre was non-plussed, then, as he started down the corridor again, she slipped her hand into his. 'You've agreed to see her?'

'But of course. Why should I not?'

Deidre didn't have an answer to that. 'I just thought . . .' she mumbled, 'after . . . well, when Olivia disappeared the police questioned you for so long. I remember how upset you were by it . . .' She felt suddenly ridiculous, as if she were creating a drama out of nothing.

He chuckled softly, and still walking, lifted a hand to her hair. 'You come all this way to tell me about this film when you could have telephoned. But I am glad you are here.'

When they reached the end of the corridor he stopped at an open door. Inside, students were unpacking their overalls and setting out their materials.

'Sergio,' she said.

He turned to her, and his eyes seemed to touch her like a caress. 'Wait for me at the apartment,' he murmured. 'I will come soon.'

He went into the classroom then, and as he closed the door Deidre turned away and slowly started to make her way outside. She didn't know why she was making such a fuss, except that she had never forgotten his anguish when Olivia first disappeared. She had been in Florence with him at the time, but he had sent her back to England when the police started their investigation, saying he didn't want her involved. She had never questioned his decision, any more than she had ever *seriously* considered the possibility that he might have had something to do with the disappearance. But every now and again a horrible, sinking doubt would assail her, and then only being with Sergio could assuage her fears.

As she walked out into the brilliant sunshine her unease was already beginning to wane. The police enquiries had been unpleasant for Sergio because he cared for Olivia, as he did all his students – it was no more than that. And then she smiled quietly to herself as she recalled the evening Olivia had appeared at the door of his studio.

'I've come to apologise,' she had said in her twangy American voice, and Deidre had noticed how, for once, Olivia's eyes didn't have that look of crazed depravity that she had always found so particularly chilling in a girl so young.

'Oh?' Sergio had been standing just inside the room with his arm about Deidre's shoulders.

Olivia had shrugged and lifted a hand to sweep her blonde hair from her face. The hand was shaking uncontrollably, and Deidre's heart had gone out to her in the fruitless and frustrated sympathy one had for drug addicts.

'I can't make love with you, Sergio,' she had declared. 'I want to, but I can't. You are a great man, I worship you, and I feel humility and longing when I am near you. But I can't do it.'

That was all she had said before slipping on her peculiar sunglasses, turning on her heel and tripping lightly back down the stairs. Sergio and Deidre had looked at one another in astonishment, until the street door slammed below and they burst out laughing.

It was not a rare occurrence for students to proclaim their love for Sergio, and Deidre knew she would probably have forgotten all about Olivia had she not disappeared shortly after that night. Some American student had driven her into the mountains late one evening and dropped her at a village called Paesetto di Pittore. He hadn't gone into the village with her, he claimed, but had driven on to Pisa where he had taken a plane to Amsterdam the following day. Once the police caught up with him they had questioned him for weeks, but had let him go in the end through lack of evidence. Still, five years later, nobody knew what had happened to Olivia.

By the time she let herself into the apartment, which she found in its usual state of disorder, Deidre's thoughts had turned to Madeleine. For the past month Phillipa Jolley, a dress designer Deidre had been at university with, had had a team working round the clock to get together an exclusive collection for Madeleine. Now it was ready, and the following day Madeleine would be showing it in Paris. Deidre wanted to check that there were no last-minute hitches, so she picked up the phone to call her secretary. Anne reassured her that everything was going according to plan, then went on to tell her about the proofs she had received from a session Madeleine had done the week before for the new cosmetic range. It was probably because she was talking about Madeleine that Deidre didn't at first find anything odd in the fact that she was staring at a photograph of her, propped up on Sergio's desk. But by the time she put the phone down, she was curious to know what it was doing there. She recognised the picture, it was one of the shots Dario had taken when Madeleine first came to them. What on earth was it doing here in Sergio's studio?

'I ask Dario to send it,' Sergio laughed, when she asked him later. 'When you talk about her to me the last time you were here, you were so happy about her and so mystified that I want to see her for myself. Of course, I see her all the time now. She is in the Italian papers too, you know.'

'And magazines,' Deidre told him, touched by his interest in her work. 'Getting Madeleine to the top is proving even easier than I thought.' She picked up the photograph and smiled. 'She *is* very beautiful, don't you think?'

'*Sì*, very beautiful. And I think you become fond of her, no?'

Deidre nodded. 'Perhaps.'

'The child I would not permit you to have?' he probed gently, and when she looked up into his face he kissed her tenderly on the mouth. 'Do you hate me for it, *cara*?'

'Sometimes,' she admitted. 'But you gave me the choice. I could have had children with another man, but I wanted you.'

'And now you have Madeleine.' They were both still looking down at the photograph.

'For a while, yes,' she answered. 'But one day Paul will take her away from me.' She stole a quick glance at his face to see if the mention of Paul had induced a reaction, but he was still smiling at the picture.

'Tell me why you say that,' he said.

She smiled and shrugged. 'I don't know, really. I suppose it's just that they seem so devoted to one another.

I'm glad of that because it means she'll be happy when she gives it all up, but I shall miss her.'

'You think she will give it up?'

'If he wanted her to, she would.'

'But I thought she wanted to become famous.'

'She does, and she already is famous – quite. But she's not as vain as she used to be, though she is still pretty appalling sometimes. But there's a vulnerability in her that has rather got to me. She's so easily exploited – I know I'm the exploiter, but I ease my conscience by telling myself I'm only doing what she wants me to do. And she's so happy when she's with Paul that you get the impression that nothing else matters really – to either of them. They're not always terribly comfortable to be with; they give you the feeling you're intruding – at least, Paul does.'

'He must love her very much if he is so possessive.'

Deidre put her head on one side and thought about that for a moment. 'Yes, I think he does. And possessive is the right word. It's as if he owns her, controls her even.'

'It is sometimes like that when two people are very much in love, no?' His hand moved over hers, and taking the photograph, he turned her to face him. '*Bacia mi, cara,*' he murmured.

She lifted her mouth, and as he pulled her roughly into his arms she could feel the hardness of his lean body pressing against her. 'Oh, Sergio,' she moaned, and he pushed his tongue deep into her mouth.

'I love you,' he said later, as they lay on his bed, sweat still glistening on their skin.

'Do you?' she asked, twisting herself round to look at him.

He took one of her small breasts in his hand and toyed lazily with the nipple. 'Yes,' he whispered, gazing into her eyes.

'Do you love me enough to want to shut out the rest of the world, the way Paul does with Madeleine?'

'That is what we do, is it not, my love?'

'In a way, yes. But you don't share everything with me.'

'I give you all I can.'

'But why won't you let me see your work?'

His hand fell back to the bed and he turned his face away from her. 'Why do you ask when you know the answer?' he said, a note of irritation in his voice. 'My work at the *bottega* must remain a secret until it is ready. A secret from all the world – and that must mean you too.'

'But what about the men and women who work with you? They . . .'

'Stop!' He jerked himself from the bed and stared down at her, and she could see he was angry. 'I will not talk of this any longer. You have me here and now. I tell you I love you, that must be enough.'

'But what is it you're trying to hide?' she pleaded.

'It is only you who say I hide things.'

'But you *are* hiding things. Why does your work have to be so secret, even from me? Don't you trust me?'

'It is not a matter of trust, Deidre. It is a matter of protect . . .' He stopped, suddenly, and she knew instantly that he was going to lie. 'Protecting you from those who are eager to know about the work. And protecting me from them too,' he finished.

Deidre sat up, feeling the doubt begin to pound through her brain. 'But I don't understand. Why . . ?'

'I explain this to you before,' he snapped, as he put on his black towelling robe. 'No one must go to the *bottega*, no one must know of it or where is it until I say so.'

'But can't you see how much it hurts me to know that you don't trust . . .'

'No!' His voice cut across her and his eyes were blazing with fury. Then he snatched open a drawer in the chest behind him and took out a packet of cigarettes. She watched as he struck a match, then inhaled deeply. His hand was trembling and his dark, unshaven face was alive with agitation. Suddenly she was afraid. Afraid because he had never reacted like this before about the *bottega*, and afraid because she could feel her darkest suspicions breaking loose in her mind and words of accusation erupting horribly and uncontrollably from her lips.

'You took her there, didn't you?' she blurted out. 'You took Olivia to the *bottega*?'

He looked at her, appalled. 'Why do you say such things? There is nothing to . . .'

'You took her there, didn't you?' she persisted, confused yet unable to stem the mounting tide of foreboding. 'You took her there when you wouldn't take me. Why?'

'Deidre, stop!'

'For God's sake, don't you know how much I love you? Don't you understand how important it is to me that you should trust me?'

'What are you talking about?'

'I am talking about Olivia. I'm talking about that night . . .'

'Why do you ask me about her now? She is gone, she is . . .'

'Gone? Gone where, Sergio?' And when he only stared at her, she answered for him. 'You took her to the *bottega* and she's never been seen again. Isn't that the truth?' Her mind was in torment, and all she wanted was that he should deny it.

'You don't know what you are saying. You are crazy.'

'No, I don't know what I'm saying, but I can't forget the night you sat here and wept like a child. It was the night she disappeared. And I can't forget the way you sent me back to England, but not before you'd made me tell the police you spent the whole night here with me. But you didn't, Sergio, so where were you?'

'I told you, I was at the *bottega*.'

'And Olivia? Was she there too?'

'No!'

'Then where is she?'

'I don't know,' he yelled. 'Nobody knows.'

She closed her eyes, trying to push away the doubt and make herself believe him. 'Why did you cry that night?' she whispered into the piercing silence. She heard him move across the room, and when she looked up he was standing at the window. 'Why did you cry, Sergio?'

'I cannot remember. It is a long time ago.'

'Was it because of Olivia? Because of something that had happened to her?'

He walked back to the chest and ground out his cigarette. He didn't turn round, but put his hands on either side of the chest and lowered his head. Her heart was pounding with dread. The silence simmered round her and at last she slumped back against the pillows and covered her face with her hands.

It was a long time before he went to her, but when he did he sat down carefully, putting his arms round her and resting her head on his shoulder. 'You want to know why I cry that night,' he said, stroking her hair. 'I cry for many things, but they are past now. They are over and you must not torment yourself like this.'

'But if I knew what they were. If I knew . . .'

'Ssh, *cara*, it is not important now.' He held her closer, and pulling a sheet over her shoulders, he kissed the top of her head.

'Why do I love you so much, Sergio?' she whispered.

As he answered she heard the smile in his voice. 'Today you ask me so many questions I cannot answer.'

'But there is one that you can. Will you, if I ask it?'

'Yes.'

She took a deep breath, bracing herself for the answer that every nerve in her body was screaming to reject. 'Was Olivia ever at the *bottega*?' she asked.

There was no tremor in his voice, no faltering of the

hand that smoothed her hair, and no hesitation as he calmly but firmly denied it.

She looked up, and when she saw the tenderness in his eyes, the remaining vestiges of her fear were swallowed into a tide of love and relief.

Side by side, with their glorious hair wound into unicorn rods on the tops of their heads, and their make-up glittering silver and gold about their eyes, Shamir and Madeleine glided down the catwalk. Both wore the shimmering, tight-fitting evening dresses from Phillipa Jolley's collection. All round them flash-bulbs were popping, film was spooling and pencils were scratching over notepads. It was the end of the show, and it had been the designer's idea that Shamir should join Madeleine for the finale. The contrast she offered to Madeleine's provocative violet eyes, ivory-gold skin and pearl-white hair was breathtaking in itself, but it was the looks that passed between the two of them, as they strutted and sashayed in time to the music, that were setting everyone alight. Even Deidre, who had flown in early that afternoon after spending the morning making up with Sergio, was transfixed by the mystery that seemed to lie behind that electric communication of eyes.

Watching from his seat in the front row, Paul understood that communication perfectly. He had seen the two of them parading in front of mirrors, had been the sole audience as they rehearsed the precise gestures and movements that would convey various shades of sexual nuance; he had listened to them discussing the power they had; and he knew that it was their utter belief in themselves as untouchable, superior beings that created the air of enigma surrounding them.

Now, as Shamir pirouetted in front of him and threw back her head, his eyes slid over her slender body and he felt a bolt of livid anger jar through him. The night before he had overheard her telling Madeleine that she was insane to put up with his moods. What Shamir thought didn't matter an iota to him, but he did mind that Madeleine was telling people about the way he behaved. He had said nothing at the time, it was late and she had a big day ahead of her, but now that the show was over he was going to take her to task.

Waiting only until the applause died down, he got up from his seat and pressed a path through the swarming, rhapsodic mass of people to the dressing-room.

When he got there, he saw that Madeleine was surrounded by Shamir, Deidre, Roy, Phillipa, dressers and countless others he didn't recognise. Phillipa was filling everyone's glass from a magnum of champagne and flushing with delight as they sang her praises.

'Paul!' Madeleine cried when she saw him. 'Come and get some champers.'

He walked over to the crowd, who parted to let him through, asking him if he wasn't proud of Madeleine and didn't he think she'd been superb? But as he took Madeleine's arm and dragged her through rack after rack of dresses to a distant corner of the room, their voices dried on their lips.

'What are you doing?' she grumbled, kicking off her high-heels before she fell over.

'I want you to get changed and come back to the George V, now!'

'What? But we're celebrating. Didn't you see the way . . .'

'Now!' he repeated, through clenched teeth.

'But I can't just leave.'

'I want you back there,' he hissed, and for the benefit of those who were peering through the rails he pressed his mouth against hers.

When he let her go, Madeleine giggled. 'Yes, sir,' she saluted. 'Give me five minutes.'

He wandered outside to wait in the fresh air, only to be bombarded by photographers and journalists.

'When's she coming out?' one of them cried.

'What did you think of the show, Paul?'

'How does it feel to be married to a sex bomb like Madeleine Deacon?'

'We're not married,' Paul snapped.

'When's the big day?'

'Will Phillipa Jolley design the dress?'

Paul threw up his hands – the picture made the front page of a newspaper in Britain the following day with the headline, *Will she marry me or won't she?*

Inside, Madeleine was slipping hurriedly into her jeans and telling Shamir not to make such a fuss.

'But he storms in here like some Neanderthal man and orders you out,' Shamir protested. 'I'm surprised he didn't drag you off by the hair. It's *your* big day as well as Phillipa's, you're supposed to be celebrating.'

'I'm about to,' Madeleine grinned. 'But I'm afraid the rest of you aren't invited.'

'Tell him to wait, for Christ's sake. What is he, some kind of animal that he has to have you straightaway?'

'That's right. All animal,' Madeleine laughed as she picked up her holdall. 'And I'll let you into a secret – when Paul wants me the way he does right now, I couldn't care less if he dragged me out by the pubes.'

'Will we see you later, at La Tour d'Argent?' Shamir called after her.

'I expect so,' Madeleine called back, 'but don't hold your breath.'

As she burst out into the street, she shrieked as a plethora of white flash-bulbs exploded in her face.

'Come on,' Paul cried, grabbing her arm. 'There's a taxi waiting over here.'

They were pushed and jostled, and Madeleine's shirt was torn in the rush, but finally they managed to reach the car, which sped off in the direction of the Champs Elysées.

'You like me to lose?' the driver enquired eagerly.

'No point,' Paul answered, 'they know where we're staying.'

The driver's face fell, but nevertheless he kept his foot jammed on the accelerator and in less than ten minutes they were back at the George V, just in time to avoid the press.

'Look at my shirt,' Madeleine complained as they were going up in the lift, 'the sleeve's practically off.'

Paul took it in his hand, and to the amazement of the other people in the lift, he gave it a quick tug and completely severed it from the shoulder.

Madeleine's eyes narrowed, and with a salacious smile she murmured, 'I dare you to do that with the rest of it.'

Taking a lapel in each hand, Paul ripped open the shirt, exposing her breasts to stupefied eyes. Madeleine smiled at them happily, then as the doors opened to their floor, he dealt her a stinging blow across the face and walked out of the lift.

'Paul!' she cried, grabbing her holdall and clutching the front of her shirt as she ran after him. 'Paul, wait. What is it? What have I done?'

He said nothing until they were inside their suite, when he took the holdall from her, dropped it on the floor and flung her onto the sofa. 'You talked to Shamir about me?' he seethed.

She blinked, and shook her head in confusion. 'Shamir? What's she got to do with anything?'

'Everything!' he yelled. 'You discussed me with her, and I won't tolerate it.'

'You were listening last night, weren't you? When you were supposed to be asleep in the other room?'

'Yes, I was listening.'

'But I only told her . . .'

'I know what you told her.'

'But she's my friend. Friends tell one another things like that.'

'When are you going to grow up, Madeleine? She's out with journalists the whole time. If she mentioned to one of them that you'd complained about me being moody and temperamental, it would be all over the papers the next day.'

'Well, what difference does that make?'

'All the difference in the world. They'll start printing stories about the break-up of our relationship and the next thing you know, the pressure will be so intolerable that we'll be going our separate ways. Is that what you want?'

'No,' she said sulkily.

'Then think about what you're saying and who you're saying it to.'

'You can talk,' she spat. 'You just hit me in front of a lift full of people. What if that gets in the papers?'

'We can deny it. Nobody in that lift knows us, and it's their word against ours. Whereas anything Shamir says would inevitably have come from you and you alone. You're always together, you're known to be friends, and she wouldn't welsh on you unless it were true.'

'You're jealous of Shamir,' she accused him.

'Of course I am. It's hard for me, coming to terms with the fact that you need someone else in your life besides me. So give me a break, will you?'

He turned away, burying his face in his hands, and she got to her feet.

'I don't need anyone but you,' she said in a small voice. 'I told you that before.'

'Then stop seeing so much of her,' he raged.

'All right. All right, I will. But we've got that session for the *Fairplay* centrefold the day after tomorrow, I'll have to see her then.'

He turned to look at her, and when he saw her pale,

worried frown and the tatters of her shirt hanging from her shoulders, the anger and revenge drained from him, and shaking his head he held out his arms. 'Oh, my darling,' he sighed, as she went to him, her hands stuffed stubbornly in her pockets. 'I'm such a bastard to you.'

'Yes, you are,' she agreed.

He kissed her tenderly, then said, 'Promise me you won't confide any more of my grim little secrets to Shamir?'

'I promise.'

'You know why I'm jealous of her, don't you? I mean, the real reason?'

She shook her head.

'Because I don't want you going to the top with her, I want it to be with me.'

'Oh, so do I,' she cried, throwing her arms round him. 'And we will, I know we will, because I've had an idea about Harry Freemantle.' She stepped back and looked into his face.

'Oh?' he said, weighing her breasts in his hands.

'Well, I was thinking, he's pretty good-looking, Harry, isn't he? I mean, no self-respecting queer would turn him down, would they? So I thought, if I paid one of the boys from Deidre's agency to do it with him, in our bed, then we could rig up a camera and hey presto, we've got him.'

'Mm, not bad,' he said, leading her back to the sofa and pulling her onto his lap. 'But how do we get them into our bed?'

'That's the easy bit. I'll give the boy the keys to our house while we're away in New York next week, and he can take Harry back there. The difficult bit is introducing him to Harry and getting Harry to fancy him. But you know what male models are like. As long as Harry's not into a bit of rough, it should be plain sailing.'

'About New York,' he said, fingering her nipples and

brushing his lips over her neck as she started to purr. 'I can't come.'

'Oh Paul!'

'I've got too much work to do, and you'll be so busy I'd hardly see you anyway. But while you're there I could engineer this meeting between the model and Harry, and if need be, go and spend a night in a hotel while they do the business.' He circled her lips with his tongue. 'Did I ever tell you what a brilliantly devious mind you've got?' he murmured.

'Did I ever tell you how much I love you doing that?' she answered, as he blew gently in her ear.

'About Shamir,' he said, as he started to unzip her jeans. 'I'm sorry.'

'So am I.'

'Are we seeing her later?'

'Mm.'

'Then I'll make an effort to be especially nice to her.'

'Not as nice as you're being to me now, though?'

'Oh no, not that nice.'

Her eyes fluttered open, and as she gazed into his face he saw the stirrings of that now famous look, and knew that if they did make it to dinner that night they would be very, very, late.

Deidre was sitting in a dark corner of the studio with Roy Welland, watching the set-decorators and photographer's assistants at work. So far there had been no sign of Madeleine and Shamir, though she guessed they were upstairs being dressed and made-up. To say Deidre was shocked when Shamir had called up to say she'd like to do the *Fairplay* session with Madeleine, would be an understatement. Never, in the three years Shamir had been with Deidre, had she ever shown any inclination for this kind of exposure. Not that she would be revealing anything more than a beautiful face herself, it was just astounding that she should want to appear in a publication of that kind at all. However it was an indication of how close the two girls had become, and it pleased Deidre a lot since Madeleine seemed to have no one in the world besides Paul. Except that there was a cousin somewhere who had tried to make contact through *The Sun* newspaper a while ago.

'Oh *her*,' Madeleine had sneered when Deidre told her. 'She's after Paul, not me. She was always trying to break us up, that's mainly the reason we left Bristol. If she calls again, tell her to get lost.'

Not wanting to become embroiled in some kind of family feud, Deidre had thrown the phone number away, but she was saddened by Madeleine's response, and that was why she had been so heartened when the friendship between Madeleine and Shamir seemed to blossom – quite apart from their indisputable success as a professional duo. Madeleine needed a friend, all girls did at that age, regardless of whether or not they were in love, and Deidre felt there had been a marked improvement in Madeleine since she'd known Shamir.

The impact they had made in Paris was still being felt throughout the fashion world, and Deidre guessed that the same would happen in the glamour world once this particular edition of *Fairplay* hit the stands. It was a shame Madeleine didn't want so much joint publicity after this, but she had told Deidre that she wanted to share her limelight more with Paul than Shamir, and as Madeleine was paying, Deidre had quite naturally agreed.

A young secretary in a short, tight black skirt handed Deidre a cup of coffee, and as Deidre watched her walk away she frowned at the distant memory of her own mini-skirt days. Then hearing Roy chuckle beside her, she threw him a look before asking him what he had lined up for them in New York.

A few minutes later the door opened and Madeleine and

Shamir walked into the studio. Behind them were dressers, make-up artistes, a team of editors from *Fairplay*, and an elderly man with a handle-bar moustache wearing starched Edwardian clothes. Madeleine's costume was covered by a robe several sizes too big, but Shamir looked positively imperious in her ankle-length black satin skirt, white chiffon blouse and grey satin jacket with panniered hem. Her hair, rolled back from her face, was hidden beneath a glorious feathered hat. Taking the role of the gentleman's half-caste wife who had returned with him to England after he had been injured in battle 'somewhere in India' – so Deidre read from the notes in front of her – Shamir could have stepped right out of 1910. Madeleine's part was that of the miscreant maid who had been caught trying to steal her mistress's sapphire and ruby necklace, thus availing her mistress of a long-awaited opportunity to inflict humiliation and punishment on a white woman. That was how the story would begin, told in more detail by one of *Fairplay*'s sub-editors, and from there the photographs would take over.

Neither Shamir nor Madeleine had noticed Deidre and Roy sitting in the shadows at the back of the room; so, unobserved, Deidre watched as Madeleine talked, giggled, and eyed up the men like a schoolgirl. Then Madeleine spotted Deidre and ran across the studio to throw her arms round her agent. She babbled on with excited chatter about what they would be doing in New York, how she had been practically mobbed in Oxford Street the day before, and the 'fab pics' in one of the morning papers that must have been taken weeks ago. Deidre smiled and laughed and urged her to calm down. But she needn't have worried, because when the photographer came into the studio some ten minutes later and Madeleine was called to the set, her manner immediately reflected Shamir's, which was one of serene confidence and professionalism.

'That girl's really getting to me,' she sighed to Roy. 'She's such an innocent she makes me feel a hundred years old, and I actually like her for it.'

'Nothing to do with the fact that she's making you rich?' he queried.

'Cynic,' she bit back.

'Which reminds me, the fund is running low and we've got an expensive few months coming up.'

'I know,' Deidre answered. 'The glossies wanted an arm and a leg to put her on their front covers for August at such short notice – anyway, she should be on all editions now, New York, Rome, Paris and London. Last-minute – or should I say, instant – publicity doesn't come cheap, as well you know. And I'm not only talking about bribery, I'm talking about the practicalities of turn-around.'

'Out of interest, are you paying her anything at all? A wage, as it were?'

'No. All her fees go straight into the fund. But it goes without saying that all the money is spent on her or to benefit her. But do you know, she hasn't even asked me about money.'

Roy shrugged and reached into his top pocket for his diary. 'She seems to have so much, she doesn't need to,' he said. 'Want to go over things now, while we're here?'

'Why not?' Deidre took her diary from her bag. 'Tell me what's coming up when we get back from New York.'

'Right. The day you come back there's a party at Silverstone, following the Grand Prix. I think she should go to that, she can always get over her jet lag the day after, and Dario's keen to photograph her with the sporting fraternity. We've missed Twickenham and the FA Cup Final, but Lords is just around the corner, we'll get her lined up with the players.'

'OK,' Deidre said, writing it in her diary.

'Now, on the English social calendar there's Royal Ascot the week after next, then polo at Windsor, then Henley.'

'All arranged,' Deidre said. 'We'll be going with Charles Anstey-Smythe's party, so we'll have all the right passes etcetera. As far as I know Paul's coming too, though he can't make New York. By the way, Madeleine tells me things could be looking up for him on the publishing front.'

'Good. Ask her for a bit more loot and we'll see what we can do about getting him to the top of the best-sellers.'

'She's already offered it.'

'That's my girl. They'll be quite the golden couple if he succeeds.'

'Now,' Deidre went on, 'there's a royal film première coming up' – she flicked over a couple of pages – 'ah, here it is. Can you speak to Dario about the photographers?'

'No problem.'

'The BBC are interested in making a documentary about her and her rise to fame. Can we fit that in sometime in August, they want to know?'

Roy pondered that a moment. 'It'll be difficult, she's pretty busy, but we'll see if we can't squeeze it in somewhere.' He made a note of it, then slapped his forehead as he suddenly remembered something. 'Pirelli. They want Madeleine and Shamir for their next calendar. Just the two of them. South of France, middle of September.'

Deidre chuckled. 'Just wait until I tell Madeleine, she'll be cock-a-hoop. Nothing she likes more than taking her clothes off.'

'No,' Roy said, drawing out the word and nodding towards the other side of the room where the *Fairplay* session was by now in full swing; and with their diary meeting more or less complete, he and Deidre sat back to watch.

Madeleine's hair fell in wisps about her face, and her chambermaid costume was hanging from her shoulders, revealing her left breast. She clung to a bedpost, gazing imploringly up at the man, who was looking to his wife for further instruction. Shamir, sitting at a jewel-laden dressing-table, watched the proceedings with an expression of pure contempt. The photographer and the editorial staff of *Fairplay* were milling about the set, arranging detail no one would ever notice, and giving instructions to the three models.

As Madeleine's clothes were taken from her body and draped about the set, so the tension in the studio increased. Her sexuality was so potent that even the women in the room were reacting to it, and whether playing for the camera or not, Madeleine was constantly aware of the effect she was having. Between shots Deidre and Roy watched as she searched out one man at a time, fixing him with half-closed, penetrating eyes and filling the air between them with the kind of promise guaranteed to set his pulses throbbing.

'Shit, she's even getting to me,' Roy muttered, as Madeleine circled her lips with her tongue and gazed into the eyes of an electrician. By now she wore only white frilly drawers and stockings that were at that moment being wrinkled round her knees. A make-up artist was coating her breasts in baby oil, and when she'd finished Madeleine tweaked the nipples so that they stood out as red and firm as the rubies on Shamir's fingers.

When she was ready, Shamir's 'husband' slipped his hand in under the elastic of the white drawers and Gerry, the photographer, reeled off his shots. Then *Fairplay*'s editor stepped in and talked quietly with Madeleine. Gerry joined them, and a few minutes later called out for everyone to take ten.

The set-designer and his team stripped the bed, littered it with jewellery from the dressing-table and put up a screen.

The screen was there only to protect Madeleine's modesty as she removed her final garment. Deidre had to choke back the laughter when someone told her this –

Madeleine didn't know the meaning of the word. Still, she was intrigued; Madeleine was obviously up to something.

When it happened, it took even Deidre's breath away.

It was almost lunchtime by now, and with only the final sequence to shoot Madeleine was aware that she was losing everyone's attention. She wasn't unduly worried, because within seconds of Gerry giving the word there wouldn't be one person in the room whose eyes weren't concentrated just where she wanted them to be.

As someone yelled for quiet, Madeleine removed the frilly drawers and handed them to a dresser. The make-up girl applied a few finishing touches, then nodded to Gerry. Gerry gave the answering signal and Madeleine stepped out from behind the screen.

There was an audible gasp. Roy's lips parted in what sounded like a whimper and even Deidre shifted in her chair. Madeleine's expression was one of mortal shame; her hands hung loosely at her sides and her breasts jutted proudly toward the camera. But just as she had known it would be, every eye in the room was focused on the join of her legs. There, she was as smooth and exposed as the day she was born.

When she was sure of everyone's full attention, Madeleine turned to Gerry. His face gave nothing away, but his hand shook slightly as he guided her to the bed and led her down amongst the jewellery. After the first shots had been taken, his assistants moved the camera to the foot of the bed, the lighting was reset and Madeleine parted her legs for Gerry to drape a ruby and sapphire necklace between them.

'That's a wrap!' someone shouted ten minutes later. Two secretaries came in with bottles of wine and glasses on a tray, and the editor of *Fairplay* poured. Madeleine was surrounded by men, throwing back her head and revelling in their admiration and lust. She made no attempt to cover herself, and every now and again turned to catch her reflection in the mirror.

Deidre was caught up with more people from *Fairplay* but kept an eye on Madeleine, mildly shocked that, now her impact had been made, she didn't get dressed. Then she noticed several glances being directed towards the door, and when, ten minutes later, Paul walked in, Deidre understood.

The room was still in semi-darkness, with only one or two studio lights left on. Paul remained at the door, hands in pockets, watching with amusement as Madeleine paraded about the set, not yet having seen him. When she did see him, Deidre felt her skin burn. The sheer concupiscence that leapt between them was like nothing she had ever witnessed before. Everyone in the room felt it; voices thinned into silence and the hush that engulfed them started to simmer with expectancy.

Madeleine handed her glass to Shamir, then reaching up, she pulled the clip from her hair and let it tumble round her shoulders. All the while she was looking at Paul, and he at her.

At last she started to walk towards him, and Deidre's breath locked inside her as Madeleine's incomparable body moved from the shadows into dusty blue-grey shafts of sunlight. The orange glow of a studio lamp lit her from behind, and in that strange pattern of light she looked almost ethereal. No one moved, not a sound was heard above the gentle pad of her bare feet. Her breasts careened gently with her movements, her skin shimmered, and all Deidre could think was, If only Sergio could see her now.

As she drew closer Paul's hands moved from his pockets, his lips parted, and as Madeleine came to a stop in front of him he took her in his arms. His mouth covered hers, and as Deidre saw their tongues entwine she felt a tidal wave of pure eroticism spread through her loins. Like everyone else she was transfixed, and watched shamelessly as Paul's long fingers splayed across Madeleine's back, then started to move slowly down to her buttocks. Then he stopped. Madeleine laughed, and the immobilising air in the room evaporated.

There was a sudden surge of activity and Paul and Madeleine were swallowed into the crowd. Occasionally Deidre caught a glimpse of them whispering to one another and laughing as though there was no one else present. Paul's arm was round her shoulders, and every now and again he put his glass to her mouth for her to sip his wine. Deidre wondered if anyone else felt the sense of intrusion she was feeling, but if they did they weren't showing it.

Gradually the party started to break up, and while Paul remained in the studio talking to Roy and the editor of *Fairplay*, Deidre, Madeleine and Shamir went upstairs to the dressing-rooms. Madeleine was in a hurry now, and didn't want to keep Paul waiting, so Deidre had time only to remind her not to be late for their flight the day after tomorrow − and then to be surprised when Madeleine enquired about the movements of one of the male models over the next week or so. It was the second time Madeleine had asked, so as they walked down the stairs together Deidre casually enquired why.

'Oh, it's just that a friend of Paul's has got his eye on him,' Madeleine answered. 'I said I'd try and fix them up. But anyway, he's definitely in London next week?'

'He is,' Deidre confirmed.

'Then I'll give Paul his number, see if he can get the two of them together while I'm away.'

'I never had you down as a cupid for gays, Madeleine,' Deidre laughed. 'Now don't forget, the flight's at . . .'

'Eleven o'clock in the morning. I have to be there at nine thirty. The flight number's . . .'

'All right, all right,' Deidre interrupted. 'Just make sure you're there.'

'I will be,' Madeleine assured her, then handing her

holdall to Paul, who was waiting at the door, she gave Deidre a quick peck on either cheek and followed him into the car park.

As they drove off in Paul's Range Rover, on their way home to change before going on to Glyndebourne, Deidre stood in the car park with Roy and waved. She felt inexplicably sad, and wanted more than anything to speak to Sergio. Seeing Paul and Madeleine together, and so much in love, had heightened her need for him. Then she smiled, and waiting until they were out of sight, opened her handbag and dropped Madeleine's cheque inside.

Paul was sitting in his study at the back of the mews house, looking at the framed photograph of Madeleine that hung on the wall opposite his desk. Her face was now being heralded as 'The Look' of the year, and everywhere he went he saw her; on billboards, in magazines, on TV and in newspapers. The cosmetics campaign, now entering its third week, was already an unprecedented success. Phillipa Jolley's dress collection was being copied by every high street chain, and the photographs Dario's team had taken in Paris hung in every other shop window from Land's End to John O'Groats. And now there was to be a perfume named after her, she'd informed him the night before, but she'd know more about that when she got back to England.

She would be away for several more days yet, and though she called every night with news of the 'influential people' she was meeting, the 'fabuloso restaurants and nightclubs' she was being taken to and all the shopping she'd done for him, he was missing her badly. He loved to hear her voice and imagine she was there in the room with him, struggling with her grammar and insisting that he put her right. He loved, too, the way she described the places she'd been to as 'fab' or 'brilliant' or 'supremo', and most of all he loved the way she ended each call by saying 'Miss you with all my body, love you with all my heart.' Such simple words, yet they touched him in a way no poetic eloquence ever could.

The longer he stared at Madeleine's picture, the more he found himself becoming perturbed – and then angry. It had a power over him that he was finding impossible to resist. It was as though he had taken the Russian doll to pieces, and while putting it back together, had somehow locked himself deep inside one of the layers. He could no longer look at Madeleine objectively because he was trapped inside her, and though he had no desire to escape, he knew he must – before he filled the empty shells so full of love that his longing to write became stifled by it.

Before she left she'd given him the telephone number of a male model, and each time she called she asked if he'd arranged things yet. He hadn't, though the camera was there, he had installed it the day before; the will to do it was strong in him, too, stimulated by her and her ambition for them both; and the numbers were sitting on his desk, waiting to be dialled. But he just couldn't bring himself to pick up the phone.

Morality played no part in his reluctance. What delayed him was that he suspected there might be something supremely, excitingly exploitable in what he was about to do – and if only he weren't so in love with Madeleine, he might be able to see what it was.

– 14 –

It was eleven o'clock at night and Marian had just left Bronwen at her pied-à-terre in Sidney Street, where they'd had a take-away dinner while talking over an itinerary for Florence. When she left, Bronwen hadn't been too happy about the idea of her walking home alone, even though

Stephanie's flat was only ten minutes away, but Marian had insisted. It was such a lovely night, she'd said, and the cool air would make a welcome change after the intense heat of the day.

As she strolled down the Fulham Road she let all thoughts of Olivia Hastings and Florence ebb to the back of her mind, and concentrated on the weekend ahead. While she was looking forward to seeing her mother, she knew that the visit wasn't going to be easy, for she had finally come to accept that she could no longer go on pretending about Madeleine. The rift would hurt her mother deeply, which was why Marian had fought shy of telling her about it for so long. But now that Madeleine's fame was increasing at such an incredible rate, it was proving impossible to continue shielding Celia from the truth. Marian smiled sadly. How bewildering it must all seem to Celia, tucked away down there in Devon with not the first idea what her two girls were really up to in London. Though Marian was sure her mother must have guessed by now that something was amiss – Celia might be naive and simple-hearted, but she wasn't stupid. The problem, really, was that once Celia knew her girls had fallen out to such a degree that they no longer saw or spoke to one another, she would be bound to want to contact Madeleine, and Marian couldn't bear the idea of Celia putting herself in a position where Madeleine could hurt her.

Suddenly a car horn blasted through the tranquil night, breaking her reverie, and realising she'd been dawdling, Marian hooked her bag higher on her shoulder and quickened her step. It wasn't until she was outside the Brompton Hospital that she became aware of someone walking behind her. The close proximity made her uncomfortable, and she slowed down to let the person pass. But though the footsteps drew closer there was no attempt to overtake her. At first she tried to shrug it off –

there were several people about, the traffic was still flowing, and it was a clear night. Nevertheless she stepped up her pace again, and for a moment thought that whoever it was had turned off into the mews she'd just passed. But as she reached the corner of Old Church Street, and had to stop before crossing the road, a man came alongside her at the kerb. She kept her eyes fixed straight ahead, telling herself he was probably quite harmless, just taking a stroll home like her; but her hands were clenched tightly in her pockets and her nails dug painfully into the palms. A couple passed behind them and Marian struggled with the impulse to follow them, but then the lights changed and she started to cross the road.

To her horror, the man kept abreast of her, and as they reached the other side he laid a hand on her arm. Her eyes flew to his face, but it was hidden by shadows, and as his grip tightened on her arm she opened her mouth to scream.

'No,' he hissed. 'Please don't be frightened. I'm not gonna hurt you. All I ask is that you follow me. There's a café down the road here where we can talk. It's about Olivia.'

Marian stared at him, her eyes achingly wide, her mouth slack and her heart thudding like a hammer. She tried to move but found she couldn't – it was as if she had suddenly been hypnotised. The American voice, Olivia's name, and the extraordinary drama of his approach, had pushed her into that bizarre, dreamlike-state she had been in in New York. It was as if she was once again an actress playing a role, and she blinked as the man moved on ahead of her – as if she was trying to remember what was expected of her. Dumbly, she started to follow, and tried to recall whether she'd seen that red shirt or those jeans anywhere before. From the quick glimpse she'd had of him, the man's face looked thin and his hair sparse. She didn't know him, she was certain of it. But he seemed to know her.

As he reached the traffic lights at the cinema he had to wait again to cross the road, and Marian caught up. In the distance was the sound of a police siren, and as it got louder and louder until it screamed past, she was slowly shaken back to a sense of reality. She had already guessed that he intended them to go into Parson's, so she decided that once he was inside the door she would make a run for it – round the corner, into Callow Street and home. Stealthily she peered up into his face. He was looking up at the rooftops, his face expressionless. She looked away again and across the road to the bright lights of the cinema where people were beginning to file out. She was quite safe now.

'Your name's Marian Deacon. You live in Callow Street with your boss Stephanie Ryder,' he muttered. 'She's not there tonight.'

Her head spun round, but he was still nonchalantly gazing into space, and she wondered if she had been hearing things. Then it hit her. He had just let her know that he knew where she lived. If she ran away, he would follow.

A minute later he was holding the door open for her to go into Parson's.

They were shown to a table for two at the back of the crowded restaurant, and the man ordered two coffees and two bowls of chilli.

'I've already eaten,' Marian told him.

He smiled. 'Sure, but we can't just have coffee. The name's Art Douglas, by the way.'

'Oh.'

He licked his lips, then pulled a strangely thoughtful face. 'Are you still afraid?' he asked.

'Not with all these people around,' she lied.

'Sure, that's cool.'

'You – you mentioned Olivia,' she stammered, after a lengthy pause.

'That's right.'

'Do you mean Olivia Hastings, the girl we're making a film about?' she asked stupidly.

'That's the girl.'

'Well, what about her?' she said, when he didn't go on.

He leaned forward to rest his elbows on the table. 'I thought a long time about you after Jodi told me,' he said.

'You mean, you're the man she . . .'

'Sure. I'm the man who really knows what went on back then, before Olivia went away. That's what you . . .'

'But I told Jodi I didn't want to know,' Marian interrupted. 'We've been instructed by Olivia's father not to . . .'

'I know what Frank's told you,' he said. 'But he's wrong. It's gotta come out, sooner or later.' He sat back as two bowls of chilli were placed on the table, but neither of them made any attempt to eat.

'Who are you?' Marian asked, as he delved in his pocket and pulled out a packet of cigarettes. 'I mean, who are you really?'

He laughed. 'Me, I'm the guy you guessed at, Marian. I'm the guy the editor told. I was a journalist working for that paper way back then. When they killed Eddie I got out. Fast. But five years have gone by and Olivia ain't come home – and I don't reckon she's ever coming home.'

'You think she's dead?'

At first he didn't answer, and Marian watched as he lit a cigarette and blew out a cloud of smoke. None of this is real, she was telling herself, it's just some kind of elaborate joke and any minute now he'll let me in on it. She tried to imagine telling someone about him, but knew they would never believe her. Why should they, she didn't believe it herself.

'I don't know about that,' he said finally. 'All I know is,

she *can't* come back. Not after what she did. And now I feel the way Jodi feels – people have got to know. They have a right to know what scum there is in their city, and how high up that scum goes. And the only way we can tell 'em is through your movie.'

'But I've already told you, we can't do anything. Frank Hastings has said . . .' She broke off as he waved his arm dismissively.

'You gotta persuade Frank. You gotta tell him, you know, make him understand that the only way to get his daughter back is to blow the scam and get shot of those bastards.'

'What bastards?' She couldn't believe she was going along with this. She sounded as if she was playing a part in a cheap Western. And if everyone around her had suddenly picked up a gun and started a shoot-out, she doubted she'd have blinked an eyelid.

'The bastards that are scumming up our city,' he answered. 'The bastards that corrupted a young kid like Olivia and made her do what she did. You know about the drugs, Frank told you. She was so hooked she'd have done anything to get 'em. Crack, coke, heroin, you name it, she took it. It'll kill her.' He thought about that for a moment, then added, 'Maybe it already has. But she sure was alive the last time I saw her.'

He took a long draw from the cigarette and Marian's eyes widened as a thought suddenly occurred to her. 'Just a minute,' she said, 'are you the "A" of the note Mr Hastings received?'

He shook his head, and exhaled through his nose. 'Nah. Not me,' and he smiled as her face fell. 'Last time I saw Olivia she was in New York. People saw her alive after that, in Italy. Like the kid who drove her out to the Tuscan village that night. He was the last one to see her alive. Least, the last one we know of. But he's innocent, he knows nothing. We none of us know anything about Italy.

What I'm gonna tell you about is New York and that bastard Rubin Meyer.'

'The man who owns the art gallery where Olivia . . .'

'That's the guy. He knows more than he's telling, but Frank says no. Frank's questioned the guy himself, he's convinced he knows nothing about Italy, but I'm not. It was Meyer's idea to send Olivia there to study under that guy at the Accademia.'

'Sergio Rambaldi.'

'That's him. And she ain't been seen since. But that's not for me to sort out, that's one for Frank. But I keep telling him the only way you're gonna find out where she is is by exposing what went on in that apartment over Meyer's gallery.' He ground his cigarette into the ashtray, then leaning forward again he looked into her face, and his own was twisted and snarling. 'Kids, Marian. Young kids. No more than twelve or thirteen years old, some of 'em. And who was there waiting for 'em when Olivia brought 'em in? The filth of our city, that's who. It was a club, a club formed by Meyer. You know what they did? Gang rape is what it's called, gang rape and murder. Black kids, white kids, yellow kids, boys and girls. If they lived, and the crime was reported, no one was ever found. If they died, well, all I can say is, lucky them, 'cos the ones who did live will never have normal lives now. And Olivia Hastings rounded 'em up and brought 'em in. Everyone knew who she was, all the kids loved her. They trusted her. And while she sat in a corner shooting heroin, grown men were shoving their cocks up little boys' asses.'

Marian winced and turned away.

'I'm sorry, Marian, but it's not a nice tale.'

'But why?' she asked. 'Why did she do it?'

''Cos Frank found out about the drugs and cut off her allowance. He got her money frozen in the bank so she couldn't touch it. That's why.'

'Oh my God,' she murmured. 'It's so horrible.'

'My editor was the guy who threatened to blow it. He was invited to join the club. He didn't know what it was at first, but when he went along to Olivia's apartment and got offered a ten-year-old girl, he got out fast. He went straight to Frank and that's when the heat really started, and when Meyer told him about this friend of his in Italy. Frank got Olivia out, and then . . .'

'But surely you could have reported all this to the police?'

'Uh-uh,' he said, shaking his head. 'There were cops in the club, and we're talking high-up here, Marian. I mean, real high-up. Any lesser cop try to get his teeth into that one and . . .' He slid a finger across his throat.

'But there must have been some way to stop it.'

'There mighta been if Olivia hadn't disappeared. Frank's a real powerful man, he was already searching out the cancer, collecting evidence so's he could report it high up somewhere, higher'n the scum can reach, and he would have done it, but then Olivia upped and disappeared and now he swears one of 'em has her and he's afraid to do anything in case they kill her.' He stopped, and Marian flinched as his face suddenly turned ugly. 'She's his daughter, he wants to protect her,' he snarled, 'I can't blame him for that. But there are mothers out there grieving over kids who don't even know what happened to 'em. There are kids out there who can't even walk any more, can't even talk. And kids who are still in danger. And you and your movie are the only ones who can help.'

'But I don't see how,' Marian protested. 'I mean, if they – this club – were to find out what we were doing, from what you're saying all our lives would be in danger.'

'If you can persuade Frank to do it, he'll give you the protection.'

'But if he thinks they're holding Olivia, how on earth are we supposed to persuade him?'

'Olivia's in Italy. As God is my witness, she is in Italy.

Those jerks back home don't have her, though they'd sure like to.'

'But how can you know that for sure?'

"Cos they're looking for her too. Frank says they're shamming but I don't believe it. I'm telling you, alive or dead, Olivia Hastings is in Italy, but none of those bastards in New York knows where. With the possible exception of Meyer.'

'If he does know, aren't Frank's fears justified?'

'Sure. It's a gamble. A gamble with his daughter's life. But think about all those kids, Marian, then ask yourself: if she is still alive, does she deserve to be after what she's done?'

'That's not a question I can *ever* answer,' she declared passionately. 'I have no right to say who deserves to live or die. No one has, except God.'

'You'd change your mind if you met some of the kids, I'm telling you.' He started to get up from the table. 'Think about it, Marian, and when you've thought about it, talk to Frank. I'm flying back to the States in the morning. If you want to contact me, do it through Jodi. But you got what you need for your movie, you don't need any more than that. Do it how you want, Marian, but for God's sake, do it.'

Marian watched him weave his way through the restaurant, stop at the cash desk, then walk out onto the Fulham Road. There was a stultifying block in her mind and she could not think beyond it.

Eventually she got up and walked round the corner to Stephanie's flat. She let herself in, still so numbed by what she'd been told, and the extraordinary way in which she'd been told it, that her actions seemed automatic, mindless, like a robot's.

You've got to think about this, she was telling herself as she padded about her tiny bedroom. You can't pretend it hasn't happened. You can't keep telling yourself America is another world. It was here. Art Douglas came to find you.

She drew the curtains together, then as she turned back into the room she muttered aloud, 'Oh God, why did I go to see Jodi that day? Why didn't I tell Bronwen I'd been? Why did I lie to Matthew? I'll have to tell them now.' She walked over to the bed and pulled back the covers. Then suddenly, as she sat down, it was as if something exploded in her brain. She swung round as the thought, with all its appalling implications, swept over her; then the sweat on her forehead turned to tiny beads of ice, her nerve-ends screamed against her skin, and her heart was shuddering in great bounding spasms. She couldn't tell them. She couldn't tell anyone. If she did, she would put their lives in danger. Which meant that, now she knew, her own life . . .

She stared at herself in the mirror. Her eyes were twin pools of terror, dwarfing her other features, and her skin was pallid. It couldn't be true, things like this didn't happen to people like her. It was a dream, a nightmare, and any minute now she would wake up and find herself at home with her mother in Devon. She blinked, trying to lift the curtain of sleep – but there was no curtain of sleep, no nightmare, this was reality. She jerked to her feet as though to escape the clamourings of her imagination, and at that instant a key grated in the lock of the front door.

'Marian! Marian! Are you asleep?'

Marian tore open her bedroom door and almost fell into the hall as her knees buckled with relief. 'Oh, Stephanie!' she gasped. 'Thank God it's you.'

'Why, you weren't expecting someone else, were you?' she teased as she switched on the light and closed the door. Then, as she turned round and saw Marian's face, she cried, 'Marian, what is it? Are you all right? You look as though you've seen a ghost.'

'No, I'm fine. I just ... It was only ... I thought someone was following me earlier, after I left Bronwen's.'

'They weren't, were they?' Stephanie asked, still concerned.

Marian shook her head. 'No, I just got a bit spooked, that's all. But what are you doing here? I thought you were at Matthew's.'

Stephanie pulled a face, then dropping her bag on a table, she sighed, 'I was. But we've had a row and I walked out.'

'You walked out on Matthew?' And it seemed to Marian that the world had suddenly started to spin. 'What did you row about?' she asked. When Stephanie only looked at her, she mumbled, 'I'm sorry, it's none of my business.'

'I asked him to let me move in with him, properly, so that his wife would *have* to accept that we were together now, and he said no. So I walked out.'

'Just like that?'

'No. We shouted at one another, I slapped his face and he accused me of being another Kathleen.'

'Oh.' Marian looked round the hall, not quite sure what to say next, and acutely aware that the shattered pieces of her nightmare were slowly re-forming into a vision she couldn't bring herself to face.

'He hasn't called, I take it?' Stephanie asked.

Marian shook her head, then watched helplessly as Stephanie seemed to crumple.

'I'm sorry, Marian,' she said, fumbling in her pocket for a tissue. 'You must think I'm an absolute idiot. I am, where he's concerned, I can't help it. Excuse me.' And she stumbled into her bedroom.

A few minutes later Marian knocked gingerly on the door, and when there was no answer she pushed it open and peeped in. Stephanie was sitting at the dressing table, her face buried in her hands.

'Come in,' she sniffed, lifting her face and looking at

Marian's reflection in the mirror. 'What's that you've got?'
she asked.

Marian held up a bottle in one hand and a tin in the
other. 'At moments like this,' she said, 'Madeleine and I
always used to break open the wine or make some cocoa.'

'Oh, Marian,' Stephanie sobbed, 'what would I do
without you?'

'Make your own cocoa?' Marian suggested. 'No, it
wasn't very funny, was it?' she said, when Stephanie
closed her eyes and swallowed hard on a fresh rising of
tears.

'Marian,' Stephanie whispered, as she started to leave
the room. Marian turned back. 'Are you broad-shouldered
as well as kind?'

Marian looked at her curiously.

'I'd like to talk,' Stephanie explained.

'I'll open the wine,' Marian smiled.

From the moment Concorde touched down in the blister-
ing heat at Heathrow, Madeleine was whirled off her feet.
Roy took a taxi into London while Anne, Deidre's secretary, whisked Deidre and Madeleine off to a studio in
Fulham. Phillipa Jolley was waiting to fit Madeleine for
yet more new clothes, and while they were there Roy
turned up with a peculiar little Frenchman who sniffed
her, scratched her, and took samples of her sweat and her
hair. Then four executives from the cosmetics company
arrived with plans for a brand new, more exclusive range,
and while Phillipa pinned, snipped and measured they
started to probe Madeleine's pores, pull at her cheeks and
finger her neck, all the time discussing colours and shades,
skin texture and age, day creams and eye lotions. This
went on until Deidre looked over the dress Phillipa had
just squeezed her into, and announced they were off to a
party to celebrate the climax of the British Grand Prix.

Although she was revelling in the attention, uppermost

in Madeleine's mind was Paul. There had been no time to call him since she'd arrived back, and she was longing to see him. But the party was important, Deidre told her, mainly because Dario had gone to a lot of trouble to organise the photographers. That didn't seem like a particularly good reason to Madeleine, but she refrained from saying so as Deidre would only point out that people were working round the clock to ensure she attained the kind of fame she wanted.

Sitting in the back of Deidre's Daimler as they sped along the M1 towards Silverstone, Madeleine took out her compact and studied her reflection. Helen Daniels – the stylist who worked with Phillipa – had done a fab hair and make-up job, considering the time she'd had to do it in. She wasn't too sure about the dress, though. It was a sort of sky-blue, with diamanté things all over it. Well, that bit of it was all right, it was the high neck she didn't go too much on, and the straight cut that finished just above the knee – and not just because of the heat.

Seeing her look, Deidre said: 'It's right for where you're going. No flaunting the rude bits tonight – every other woman there will be doing that, and the last thing we want is for you to be one of the crowd, eh?'

Madeleine couldn't argue with that, so she passed the rest of the journey going through the proofs of the *Fairplay* session that Anne had brought along. They weren't half-bad, and she could hardly wait for Shamir and Paul to see them. It had been a good gimmick, that, to shave off all her pubic hair, though it was driving her mad now that it was growing back.

The Grand Prix party, hosted jointly by Marlboro and McLaren, was being held in a giant marquee at the edge of the track. Seconds after Anne pulled the car to a halt, Roy came out of the marquee with the British racing team, followed by an army of photographers. Deidre stood to one side, watching Madeleine and marvelling at the way nothing seemed to faze her. She laughed and joked with the press, and sympathised with their disappointment that she was revealing no cleavage. She was as familiar with them as if she'd known them all her life – it was no wonder, Deidre reflected, that she was so popular with them.

'Is that all we're going to see of you, Maddy?' a photographer from the *Daily News* called out.

''Fraid so,' she laughed, 'but there's always the legs,' and everyone cheered as she hitched up her dress, fell back into the arms of one of the drivers and nestled a foot in the lap of another.

'This way, Maddy,' someone called out.

'Over here,' shouted another.

'Let the drivers put their hands on your legs. That's it.'

'Smile, Maddy.'

'How about giving us the look?'

'How about sitting on one of the cars?'

Madeleine looked at Deidre, and when Deidre nodded she allowed the photographers to lead her over to the pits. The British drivers followed, and as she sat astride the cylindrical bonnet, her lovely hair glinting like silver in the brilliant sunshine, they climbed on behind her, laughing as she threw out her arms and let herself fall against them.

'Faaantastic!'

'Into the lens, Maddy.'

'Give us that famous pout.'

'Beeeautiful!'

'Lick the lips. That's it.'

'Go for it, Maddy!'

Laughing, Madeleine threw herself forward and spread her hands across the bonnet. Then her eyes narrowed, and gazing to a point just beyond the lenses she assumed a look of pure ecstasy – as if she were making love to the car.

'Disgusting,' Deidre teased, as the session finally started to break up. 'Roy's gone back to the marquee so let's go and see if we can find him.'

Straightening her clothes and running her fingers through her hair, Madeleine followed Deidre across the grass. She looked about her, at the empty stands and rambling acres of countryside beyond, and had a sudden disturbing sense of isolation. It had happened to her when she was in New York too, when she'd wondered what she was doing there with so many people who were little more than strangers. In a few short months her life had changed so completely that at times it almost frightened her. It was difficult to associate herself with the strip-o-gram girl in Bristol now, or to believe that she had ever been that little girl who grew up in Devon – and was always up to no good. She wondered what Marian was doing, and if she had gone back to Devon to live with her mother. Her eyes moved restlessly across the distant horizon and she was suddenly overwhelmed by a longing to see them.

'You can't go into a party with a face like that,' Deidre told her. 'What's the matter?'

'Nothing,' Madeleine answered, 'just a bit tired after New York and everything, I suppose.'

Smoothing the hair back from her face, Deidre gave her an affectionate smile. 'Well, you can have a nice long lie-in tomorrow, so come on, cheer up.'

Madeleine shrugged, then lifting her eyes to Deidre's, she treated her to one of her more mischievous grins, before taking her arm and informing her that she was like an old mother hen.

Inside the marquee more photographers were buzzing around, and scantily-clad blondes draped themselves over Enrico Tarallo, who had that day taken Ferrari to their third win of the season. Madeleine sipped her champagne and watched the brainless bimbos with their fluffy blonde hair, piano teeth and sun-wizened tits. Tarallo seemed embarrassed, as if he wished he was anywhere in the world but in the clutches of these glory-seeking women, and Madeleine smiled to herself – given half a chance, she'd have him eating out of her hand. But Charles Anstey-Smythe, Deidre's newspaper editor friend, was busily introducing her to his glitzy aristocratic set, and Dario was there, camera at the ready, to capture the moment. Madeleine smiled disdainfully at the other models, who started whispering and snickering behind their hands as they realised she was once again stealing the limelight.

'Aren't I going to have my picture taken with Enrico whatever-his-name-is?' she whispered to Roy as he emerged from the depths of the party.

'We were just talking about that,' he answered, struggling with a champagne cork, 'and we thought not. The British boys didn't do so well today, and it'll look better if you're seen to be supporting them, rather than deserting to the winning side like everyone else. Get your popularity stakes up, you know what I mean?' The cork suddenly popped and Madeleine shrieked as a fountain of champagne gushed from the bottle. Then she was grabbed from behind and someone whispered in her ear:

'Come and dance, you sexy creature.'

It was no one she recognised, but it didn't stop her kicking off her shoes and twisting and gyrating in time to the music. Roy kept passing her more glasses of champagne, and as the band played on, so the circle of men around her started to thicken. The champagne was going to her head and she was tempted to do a striptease, but Paul had said he didn't like her doing it unless he was with her. So she made do with rubbing herself against whoever she was dancing with, then backing away, laughing, when hands started to roam too close to their targets.

As the evening wore on and Dario and his team slipped away with their cameras, Madeleine's energy began to wane. Noticing this, Deidre led her to a chair and sat her down with a glass of lemonade.

'Enjoying yourself?' she asked.

'Fantastic,' Madeleine slurred. 'But I wish Paul and Shamir were here too. Where *is* Shamir?'

'At her house in Los Angeles.'

'Really? When did she go there? She didn't mention it to me.'

'As a matter of fact, she did, while you were getting dressed after the *Fairplay* session, but you were so preoccupied you didn't hear. Anyway, you've got her number there, haven't you?'

Madeleine nodded. 'Somewhere. How long's she there for?'

'A few weeks. She's working out there.'

Somebody came up to Deidre then, and started talking about mutual friends of theirs; yawning, Madeleine looked round the room to see what everyone else was doing.

She was gratified to find that most of the men were still looking at her, even though they were dancing with other women. She spotted Enrico Tarallo sitting in a far corner with a real plain-Jane, so she fixed him with her eyes, willing him to look her way, but she didn't have much success because he seemed engrossed in whatever the woman was saying.

'It's his wife,' Deidre informed her.

Madeleine's eyes rounded with surprise and she turned back for another look.

'You're asking yourself the question the whole world asked when he married her,' Deidre chuckled. 'But it seems he's been in love with her since they were children.'

'But she's so ugly!'

Deidre's face darkened. 'That's a cruel remark to make about anyone, Madeleine,' she said, 'and I don't want to hear anything like it again. Especially not in public.'

Feeling suitably chastened, Madeleine mumbled an

apology, but then ruined it by saying, 'I bet *I* could change his mind about her.'

Deidre sighed. 'Try exercising some modesty, Madeleine. And at the same time forget Tarallo. Better women than you have tried and not one of them succeeded – and I don't want you making a fool of yourself. What you're looking at in the corner over there is true love, so don't go tampering. Besides, what about Paul?'

Madeleine's face fell. She really wished he was with her. It's all very well being in a place like this, she thought, but it'd be a heck of a lot better if Paul was here too. She reckoned it was that sort of thing Enrico was thinking. All very nice, winning and that, and being the star of the party, but being with someone you love is much nicer.

She danced some more, and screamed with laughter at the most inane compliments, but her eyes never moved far from the Tarallos; and when they eventually got up to leave, sneaking away quietly, she looked round for Deidre. 'Can we go now?' she said, when she found her.

Deidre smiled and squeezed her hand. 'Missing Paul?'

Madeleine nodded. 'I haven't seen him for nearly two weeks.'

'I know. I'll just go and tell Roy we're leaving, I expect he'll want to stay on. Then once I've found Anne I'll get her to bring the car round. You wait here – and don't drink any more.'

Madeleine grinned, and Deidre tweaked her nose. 'What am I going to do with you?' she laughed, and shaking her head, she disappeared into the crowd.

On the way back in the car Deidre sat quietly watching Madeleine as she stripped off her clothes and decked herself out in the fishnet body-stocking, suspenders and other accessories she'd bought in New York. What she took off she stuffed into a bag, then sat back in her erotic splendour to wait for the journey's end.

By the time Anne pulled up outside the mews house in

Holland Park, it was past one in the morning. Anne helped Madeleine to the door with her luggage, and Deidre tried not to be shocked that Madeleine hadn't bothered to cover herself up while she was in the street. They kissed one another goodnight, and Madeleine was still standing at the door waving when Anne and Deidre turned out of the mews.

Once inside, Madeleine's only stop en route to the bedroom was the bathroom. There she looked herself over in the mirror, daubed perfume between her breasts and her inner thighs, then pulling her nipples through the holes of her body-stocking, she licked her lips before turning off the light and creeping quietly up the stairs.

The bedroom door was ajar and she could hear the steady rhythm of his breathing. She could have sneaked in beside him and woken him in a way that always aroused him, but then he wouldn't see the way she looked. So, resting one foot on the dressing table stool, giving a final check to her suspenders and hitching the body-stocking higher on her hips, she threw back her head and flicked the switch, flooding the room with light.

She heard a movement in the bed as Paul turned over and blinked open his eyes. She waited, so aroused now that she couldn't even smile at what she was doing. The bed creaked gently as he left it, and though he didn't touch her she could almost feel his hands on her body.

'Madeleine.' His voice was quiet.

She lifted her head. He was standing beside her, completely naked, and she smiled right into his eyes. He didn't return the smile, but turned to look at the bed. Frowning, she followed his eyes – then shock turned her blood to ice. Not even a sheet covered the nudity of the sleeping figure. Her eyes flew back to Paul's, but he looked away. Then slowly he walked back to the bed and gently shook Harry Freemantle awake.

– 15 –

Hearing footsteps in the hall outside, Marian looked up from her desk, wondering if Stephanie had come back for something; but it was Matthew, and when she saw him, his black hair curling round his collar and his strong chin sporting at least a day's growth of beard, her heart twisted in a way that only plunged her deeper into melancholy.

He glanced up from the newspaper he was reading, and when he saw her looking at him, he frowned. 'Why the long face?' he asked.

She attempted a smile. 'Oh, no reason. I was just thinking.'

'About what?'

'Nothing in particular.' And she turned away. Even if she knew what was really going on in her mind he was the last person she'd be able to tell. She wondered, from his relaxed manner, if the row he'd had with Stephanie had actually mattered to him, but that was none of her business, so she picked up a handful of letters and stuffed them into a drawer. Then she realised that she hadn't meant to do that, and took them out again.

Matthew strolled across the office and came to stand in front of her. 'I won't bite,' he smiled, and again Marian's heart responded with a painful lurch. It was the first time she'd seen him since the day Kathleen had come into the office, and since then she had done her utmost to persuade herself that she was not falling for him. She'd thought she had succeeded, but now, seeing him stand there with his dark head on one side, his hands stuffed into the pockets of his jeans, and those wonderfully compelling eyes looking down at her, she knew she hadn't.

Again she tried to smile, but realising that her eyes were

about to fill with tears, she excused herself and disappeared into the kitchen.

But even away from his scrutiny it was no better; her mind felt as though it might burst with the confusion of her thoughts. For days, now, she had been increasingly oppressed by the weight of all that was happening to her. First there was her mother, who, just as she had expected, insisted that she make contact with Madeleine; Marian had now been back in London for three days following her weekend in Devon, and had yet to do anything about it. Then there was Stephanie, who had poured her heart out the night she'd walked out on Matthew, and was still suffering because, though he had called on several occasions, she had refused to speak to him – for reasons of pride, Marian supposed. And then there were her own feelings for Matthew, feelings that she now knew had been stealing up on her for weeks. Only Paul had ever aroused her in this way before, though somehow with Matthew it felt different. Perhaps it was because her feelings were in no way reciprocated – or perhaps it was the way he sometimes looked so intently into her eyes – but whatever it was, there was an aura about him . . . Several times, she had found herself fantasising about him in a way that made her skin prickle with shame. Shame because of her disloyalty to Stephanie, and shame because she could imagine how horrified Matthew would be if he knew. Then, of course, there was the strange encounter with Art Douglas. But that she wouldn't think about, she would just pretend it hadn't happened, then maybe it would go away.

She filled the kettle and stood gazing at it, waiting for it to boil. Her thoughts were striking out in so many directions that when Matthew spoke to her, she almost leapt from her skin.

'Sorry,' he said, putting a hand out to steady her. 'I didn't mean to startle you.'

'No, no, I'm fine,' she said. 'I was miles away. What were you saying?'

'Only that I wouldn't mind a coffee if you're making one.'

'Of course.'

He let her go and went to perch on the high stool in the corner. She was achingly aware of his closeness in the cramped space of the kitchen, and didn't know whether she longed for him to go or stay.

'We haven't seen you for a while,' she remarked, taking another cup from the cupboard. 'How did the commercial go last week?'

'Slowly. I'd forgotten how much I'd come to rely on Woody, but don't tell him, it'll go to his head.'

'He's back from holiday now. He called in here yesterday.'

'Did he? How was he?'

'Brown. Smoking. Restless.'

'Sounds like Woody.'

They lapsed into silence and Marian spooned coffee into the cups, then turned to the kettle, willing it to boil. She knew he was watching her, and knew too that his eyes were gently mocking – the way they always were when someone showed signs of discomfort.

'So,' he said finally, 'where's Stephanie?'

'Gone to lunch with Hazel Ridley.'

'Where?'

'I don't know.'

'And even if you did, you wouldn't tell me. But tell me this, is she ever intending to speak to me again?'

Keeping her eyes on the kettle, Marian shrugged. 'You'll have to ask Stephanie that.' She took the milk from the fridge and started a hopeless struggle with the carton.

'Which I would if she'd answer my calls,' he said, taking the carton, opening it, then handing it back to her. 'It can't go on like this, you know. Apart from anything else, it might prove a little difficult trying to shoot a movie with the producer and director not on speaking terms.'

'I'm sure you'll find a way,' she smiled.

His eyebrows rose at that, and then he laughed. 'I don't suppose my daughter called this morning, did she?'

Marian shook her head. 'Were you expecting her to?'

'Not expecting, hoping. I saw her yesterday at the house and thought I had persuaded her to have dinner with me tonight. She said she'd ring and let me know.' He sighed. 'I guess she's decided against it.'

At last the kettle boiled and Marian filled the two cups. As she handed one to him, his fingers brushed against hers and he looked surprised at the colour that seeped into her cheeks.

'You think I'm a bastard for the way I've treated Stephanie, don't you?' he said.

'Does it really matter what I think?'

He grinned, then took a mouthful of coffee. 'Did she tell you what we rowed about? Yes, of course she did. But if she hadn't walked out, or would deign to return my calls, then I could explain to her why I don't want her to move in with me.'

Knowing he was about to tell her, Marian's heart started to beat faster. Of course, it would be nothing to do with her, it was preposterous even to think it, but nevertheless she couldn't look at him as he continued.

'It's Samantha,' he said. 'She hasn't got over me leaving Kathleen yet, and I don't want to complicate matters further by moving Stephanie in. At least, not until Sam's settled down.'

Marian looked down at her coffee, the nauseating grip of envy clenching her stomach – though whether the envy was directed at Samantha or Stephanie she didn't know.

'There is something the matter,' he said, putting his fingers under her chin and forcing her to look at him. 'What is it?'

She turned her head away, unable to meet the concern in his eyes. 'Oh, it's nothing.'

'It looks more than nothing to me. No one's upset you, have they?'

'No, no. It's just my mother, she wants me to contact Madeleine and I'm not sure how to go about it, or what I'll say when I do.'

He smiled. 'Well, what you say is up to you, but as for finding her, maybe I could help.'

'I don't know,' she sighed. 'It's very kind of you, but . . .'

'But what? Is it Paul? Is he the problem?'

'No! No,' she assured him.

'Then what?'

The truth at that moment was so utterly absurd that even she could hardly believe the way she was thinking. But she was afraid that if Madeleine were to meet Matthew and somehow find out how she felt about him, she would try to steal him from her. And that was the most ridiculous part of it – he wasn't even hers to steal. 'I'm just afraid she'll say or do something to upset my mother.' She looked at him and smiled brightly, then put her cup down. 'But that's for me to worry about.'

'You can't go around protecting people all your life, Marian. They have to fight their own battles, you know. Even your mother. And what about you?'

'What about me?'

'Well, who's protecting you?'

'From what?'

'Me.'

Her heart thundered to a stop and she stared at him with wide, incredulous eyes.

He laughed. 'Oh, don't worry, I know you've got me down for the prize bastard of all time. But I guess Stephanie protects you from me – just as you're protecting her. What kind of monster am I, I ask myself.'

Her head was spinning, and her shoulders heaved as she tried to steady her breathing. 'A selfish one,' she blurted out.

He gave a shout of laughter, then said, 'You're absolutely right. A bloody selfish one. But not so selfish that I won't help you find your cousin. What on earth are you laughing at?'

'I don't know,' she answered. 'You, I suppose.'

He gave her the ironic look she'd so often seen him give Stephanie, then said, 'You should laugh more often, Marian. It suits you. In fact,' he went on, looking her up and down, 'you're looking extremely good today. Is that a new outfit?'

'No,' she answered. 'I bought it ages ago for my first date with . . . With Paul.'

'So does that mean you're off on a date tonight?'

'Yes, it does, actually. I'm going out to dinner.'

'Oh? Anyone I know?'

'Yes. Woody.'

The smiled suddenly froze on his face. 'You're going out with Woody tonight?' he repeated, as if to make sure he'd heard her correctly.

'Yes,' she answered, rather baffled by his response.

His cup suddenly hit the draining-board and he got to his feet. 'No!' he said, shaking his head.

'I beg your pardon?'

'You heard me. You are not to go out with Woody.'

'Yes, I did hear you, but I fail to see what business it is of yours.'

'I'm making it my business, and I'm telling you you're not to have anything to do with him outside this office. You know his reputation. You've only got to look at your own cousin to know . . .'

'How dare you!'

'I dare. He's only after one thing, and he'll make damned sure he gets it. You're not going, and that's final.'

'It's nothing to do with you,' she cried. 'He happens to have invited me out because I was feeling low, and I resent . . .'

'You can resent all you like, but I'm not having him put his hands all over you as if you were one of the tarts he picks up at Stringfellow's. Haven't you been hurt enough?'

'What?' And she gasped as he suddenly took her by the shoulders.

'Do you want it to happen again? Because I'm telling you, if you go out with Woody, it will.'

'What difference does it make to you?' she demanded, too shocked to think clearly about what she was saying.

'Not a bit,' he snapped, then let her go abruptly.

'Then why are you interfering in my life?'

'Because I've known Woody a long time. I know what he's like and I don't want to see you become one of his victims. He's married. Did you know that?'

She shook her head.

'No, I didn't think so. He also has three children, I don't suppose you knew that either?'

'No,' she admitted. 'But it's not that kind of date.'

'As far as Woody's concerned, there is only *that* kind of date. Now call him wherever he is, and tell him you can't make it.'

'I will not,' she said mutinously. 'And stop ordering me around.'

'Well, someone has to. Jesus, you haven't got a clue how many sharks there are out there, have you? If you want to cheer yourself up by going out to dinner, then you can come out with me.'

'I'm going out with Woody,' she said, hardly able to believe her ears.

For a long time they glared at one another, then shaking his head, he turned and walked out of the door.

The instant he'd gone Marian wanted to go after him, but instead she burst out laughing. She had no idea what that had all been about, but she was certain it was about more than her going out with Woody. And he'd actually invited her out himself – to cheer her up! – when he was scowling at her in a way that less than a month ago would have had her shaking in her shoes. Oh, Matthew Cornwall, she sighed to herself, and she had a sudden longing for him to put his arms round her and tell her everything would be all right.

Ten minutes later Stephanie returned with Hazel Ridley, who was going to be the production manager on *Disappearance*. As they walked in Marian gave them a beaming smile. 'Nice lunch?' she enquired.

'Not bad,' Stephanie answered, 'but obviously not as good as yours.'

Marian laughed, then turned to Hazel whom she hadn't actually met yet – but Hazel was casting a gloomy eye about the office.

'Oh God, Steph,' she groaned. 'Wonderful as it is to be working with you again, I don't know if I can take this ghastly office! I mean, *really*.'

Stephanie winked at Marian, then folding her arms, she leaned against the door while Hazel poked around and scattered complaints in a voice that was almost unbearably shrill. 'It's so pokey,' she said, 'I mean, how are we all going to fit in here once we get under way?'

'It's all just as it used to be,' Stephanie said, 'except for our new secretary. Marian, meet Hazel Ridley. You two are going to be sharing this ghastly office.'

'Hello, Hazel,' Marian said. 'It's really nice to meet you. Stephanie's told me all about you.'

Hazel, an ex-debutante from the crown of her impeccable short hair to the tips of her perfectly shod feet, treated Marian to a withering look. 'This *is* going to be fun,' she said, after a pause that embarrassed both Marian and Stephanie. 'I'm afraid I shall have to shove all your stuff back into your corner,' she told Marian. 'Well, I mean, you do seem to have spread out a bit, don't you? I'll set myself up over by the window, can't bear not having enough light. Now, how about you making a nice cup of tea, Maz, and Steph and I can carry on with our little chat.'

Stephanie threw 'Maz' an apologetic look as she left the office, but Marian merely shrugged and went off to do Hazel's bidding.

When she came back some five minutes later, it was to find Hazel sitting in her chair, feet on the desk, telling Stephanie about some 'unspeakably appalling' occurrence in the royal enclosure at Ascot that year. She carried on speaking as Marian put her tea in front of her, and didn't even pause to say thank you. '. . . Anyway,' she was saying, 'the ghastly girl told me to fuck awf. Can you imagine? And it was *she* who had sat on *my* hat. I wouldn't have minded, except that I found out later – as we all did – that she wasn't wearing any underwear. I tell you, Steph, it quite turned my stomach. I shall never be able to wear the hat again and it cost me an absolute fortune.' As Stephanie laughed, she smiled grudgingly, then picked up her cup. One mouthful of tea was enough. 'Oh! Yuk!' she gulped. Then turning to Marian, 'This isn't Earl Grey. I asked for Earl Grey.'

Marian looked at Stephanie. 'As a matter of fact, you didn't,' Stephanie said. 'But we'll get some.' Again she threw an apologetic look at Marian.

Fractionally appeased, Hazel went on. 'Apart from that, the day was quite a hoot really. Oh, and guess who else I saw there? Roland "I direct movies" Kirk. He simply couldn't believe it when I told him you'd got Matthew Cornwall to direct your film, he's absolutely livid, darling. I mean, green isn't the word. It was as much as he could do to be polite to the Queen Ma – but then he won an absolute packet on one of the old girl's trotters, so that cheered him up a bit.'

'How is Roland?' Stephanie laughed.

'Oh, yawnsville as ever. But, enough about all that. What I want to know is, where's the delicious Matthew? Didn't I hear somewhere that you and he had a thing going once, before your glory days?'

Marian saw the warmth seep from Stephanie's smile as she answered. 'At the moment I've no idea where he is, but I'm sure he'll turn up when it suits him.' She was longing to ask Marian if he'd called again, but that could wait until later.

'He's not still with that gruesomely ghastly wife of his, is he?' Hazel shuddered. 'I don't think I could . . .'

'No, he's not with her now,' Stephanie interrupted, and Hazel's expression turned to one of pure rapture.

'So the field's clear? Oh, this is going to be bliss. I've had my eye on him for simply ages. Who wouldn't, with a body like that?'

Stephanie looked at Marian, then mumbling something about having to return phone calls, she excused herself and went upstairs to her office. Hazel got up and walked round the desk. 'The first thing we've got to get in here is another fan,' she told Marian, using her handkerchief to wipe the sweat from her neck. 'Never going to stand a chance of pulling old Matthew if I look like this, am I? Get him on the phone for me, will you? I think I'll have a chat with him now, no point in wasting time, is there.'

'He's not at the end of a phone at the moment,' Marian answered stiffly.

Hazel lifted her head and glared down the length of her perfect nose. 'I'm given to understand you've never worked on a film before,' she said, 'so perhaps I should point out that in this business it helps if everyone knows their place. I only say this so that we know where we stand from the beginning. Do we have that clear?' And she gave Marian the most condescending smile Marian had ever seen.

Her face was crimson as she nodded.

'Now, if you can let me have a copy of all you've got on Olivia Hastings,' Hazel continued, 'I'll be on my way.'

Marian handed over a file. 'I've got more here that needs typing,' she said. 'Would you like me to send it to you when it's ready?'

'No, I'll collect it.' Hazel zipped up her shoulder bag. 'Sorry if I sounded a bit harsh, Maz, but most of us have worked damned hard to get where we are; you've come up the easy way because Stephanie has a kind heart. Don't abuse it. Now, just one other thing; Matthew's telephone number, please.'

Marian jotted it down on a piece of paper and handed it over, saying: 'I'll have the office sorted out by the next time you come in. And, of course, some Earl Grey tea. If there's anything else you can think of that you might want, just let me know.'

Hazel waved the piece of paper. 'Good girl. I can see we're going to get along just fine. Have to get things straight early on, don't you think? Saves any unpleasantness later. Ciao for now – if Matthew calls, tell him I'll be in touch very soon.' And she breezed out of the office.

Marian watched her pass the window, then once she was out of sight, she closed the newspaper Matthew had left on her desk and grinned. That's what you think, she muttered, then chuckling to herself, she went upstairs to see Stephanie.

A yellowy warm glow from the lamp-post outside fell across the tangled sheets lying in a heap on the floor. Every now and again, as a car passed, the beam from its headlights lit up the room, and for those few short seconds the shadows across their bodies disappeared. The room was quiet, but only moments ago, as they'd reached the zenith of their passion, Stephanie had thrashed wildly beneath him, almost screaming with the power of her climax. Now, with his hands locked behind her head, Matthew raised himself on his elbows and looked down into her face. Her hair was dishevelled and her cheeks flushed with colour. His eyes darkened and he lowered his head to kiss her lingeringly on the mouth, moving his hips gently back and forth and feeling her orgasm slowly subside around him.

'Oh God, Matthew,' she groaned.

He pushed his tongue deep into her mouth and she responded by sliding her hands down over his buttocks.

'Jesus Christ,' he muttered, as he felt himself growing hard again. Her eyes held his, and as her legs circled his waist she ran her hands over his shoulders, then wound her fingers through his hair. 'I can feel you,' she murmured, 'I can feel all of you deep inside me.'

'I've missed you,' he breathed, pushing in and out of her with long, lazy strokes.

'I love you. Oh, Matthew, keep doing that. Don't stop, don't ever stop.'

He pushed his hands against the bed, raising himself until he was only just inside her. Then, when her eyes fluttered open, he slammed into her, hard.

'Oh, Matthew,' she cried.

He did it again – and again, watching her face, and holding himself back until she was ready for more.

'Now,' she moaned, 'do it now,' and as every muscle in his body started to tense he wrapped her in his arms and hammered into her until they were both gasping for breath.

'Oh yes,' she cried, 'Yes. Yes. Yes.' And as the final seed of his climax shuddered from his body, his mouth found hers and he kissed her with such savagery that he could taste her blood on his lips.

'I'm sorry,' he whispered, but she put her arms round his neck and pulled him down to kiss her again.

'I didn't know that was possible,' she murmured. 'I mean, a man coming twice like that.'

He laughed, and pulling gently away from her, rolled onto his back. 'Depends who he's with,' he said, not without irony, and lifted an arm for her to nestle in the crook of his shoulder.

They lay quietly for a while, each with his own thoughts, while Beethoven's third concerto wafted gently up to them from the flat downstairs. Eventually Stephanie got up and went to get the wine they'd left on the table in the sitting-room. He watched her go, entranced by the grace with which she moved. With her small breasts, long, slender legs and tiny waist, she could have been a ballerina.

When she came back into the room he had an arm across his eyes, but lifted it as she said, 'You're very quiet.'

'Mm. Just thinking.'

'What about?'

He smiled. 'As a matter of fact, Marian.'

Stephanie sat on the edge of the bed and combed her fingers through the hair on his chest. 'She told me about your conversation at lunchtime, if that's what you mean.'

He chuckled. 'What did she say exactly – I mean, that made you call me?'

'That,' she said, squashing his nose with her finger, 'is between Marian and me.' She handed him a glass of wine, then lay back in his arms. 'You know, you should have told me about Samantha, I would have understood.'

'I would have told you, if you'd stopped to listen.'

She giggled. 'Did it hurt much when I slapped you?'

'Yes.'

'I'm sorry.'

'So you should be.'

She turned to kiss his arm. 'Well, thanks to Marian everything's all right now.'

'You know, I can't fathom that girl at all,' he said. 'She used to be so unassertive it practically drove me out of my mind, but now it's as if she's gone through some kind of metamorphosis. Take Kathleen, for instance. God only knows what Marian said to her that day, but she's been a different woman since.'

'Are you complaining?'

'Not in the least. I'm just curious to know what Marian said to bring about such a transformation.'

'Mm,' Stephanie said thoughtfully. 'My guess is that Marian didn't say anything at all. She's more of a listener. But there are ways and ways of listening, and whichever way is the right one, she's got it.'

'You know, there are times when she gives me the impression that she's wiser than all of us put together. She made me feel a proper fool today. I take it she told you how I over-reacted about Woody?'

'Yes,' Stephanie chuckled, 'she did.'

'And even after that she still persuaded you into returning my call?'

'Why shouldn't she?'

He shrugged. 'Well, I was a bit heavy-handed with her, and there's no doubt she considers you to be better off without me.' He paused to take a sip of wine. 'She's quite a girl, really, don't you think?'

'Do you want me to say I told you so?'

'If you must.' And they laughed.

'Poor Marian,' Stephanie sighed a little while later. 'No sooner does she make friends with you than along comes Hazel Ridley. A couple of months ago she'd have gone to pieces over what happened with Hazel this afternoon, but not now, the wily old thing. When Hazel demanded your number Marian gave her the number of some dating agency – and don't ask me how she came to have it to hand, because I didn't enquire.'

He was laughing. 'So old Haze is back on the warpath, is she? I'd better warn Woody. The last time he had a run-in with her, he thought he was going back to her place for beans on toast. He emerged three days later looking thirty years older, and all we could get out of him for the next week was "never again". Has he ever told you what he calls her?'

Stephanie shook her head.

'Hazel "cracks your nuts" Ridley.'

She burst out laughing. 'Trust Woody. Anyway, whatever she does to the male anatomy she's damned good at her job, and that's all that concerns me. To quote her, she's opened more doors than Jackie Onassis has cheque books, and when it comes to organising and administering a budget she makes the rest of us look like amateurs. So I'm afraid Woody will have to look out for himself. It's Marian I'm worried about. I don't want Hazel driving her off. She's already proving quite a gem, and if she carries on like this she'll become indispensible.'

He yawned, and reached over her to put his glass on the bedside table. 'I wonder how she got on with Woody tonight?'

'Where were they going?'

'I didn't ask, but if I know Woody, somewhere with heavy seduction potential.' He kissed the top of her head and started to stroke the hair from her face. 'Why don't you give her a call, make sure she's got back all right?'

'I can't do that.'

'Why not?'

'Because it's none of our business. And besides, she's twenty-three years old, she can look after herself.'

'Do you think so?' He said it in a way that implied he clearly didn't. 'Knowing Woody, he's probably managed to worm his way into the flat, so she might appreciate a call to help fend him off.'

'She'll cope.' She lifted a hand and trailed it lazily over his chest. 'Do you think we ought to be getting on with some work? Bronwen's already put off the trip to Italy by a week because you and I haven't got together about things.'

'Sure, if you like. But it's late, and I'm free in the morning if you are.'

Stephanie shrugged. 'OK, we'll do it then. Like some more wine?'

He nodded, and lifted his arm for her to sit up. She refilled their glasses, then went to the mirror to brush her hair.

'I still think you should call Marian,' he said as he watched her. 'Make sure Woody's behaved himself.'

'For heaven's sake, Matthew, anyone would think you were jealous.'

'Jealous? What kind of accusation's that?'

'It *wasn't* an accusation. It was merely a word to try and make you see how ridiculous you're being.'

A look of anger flashed across his face as he said, 'You wouldn't call me ridiculous if I was showing this kind of concern for you. So perhaps it's you who are jealous.'

For a moment Stephanie looked stunned. 'I don't believe I'm hearing this.'

'Then why won't you ring her?'

'OK, I will,' she snapped, and slamming down the hairbrush, she spun round and stalked across the room. Then, feeling unaccountably uncomfortable with her nudity, she slipped on his robe and went into the sitting-room to make the call.

The phone rang for some time, but eventually Marian answered.

'Marian, it's Stephanie. Are you OK?'

'Yes, I'm OK, are you?' Marian yawned.

'I'm fine. Did I wake you?'

'It doesn't matter. Everything's all right, is it?'

'Yes, yes. Everything's fine this end. How about you? Did you have a nice evening?'

'Yes, it was OK.'

'Where did you go?'

'To the pasta bar at the end of the road here.'

'Really?' Stephanie smiled. The pasta bar was hardly a venue for seduction. 'And Woody? He's gone home now, has he?'

'Oh yes, he went ages ago.'

'Did he come in for coffee?'

'Just a quick cup.'

'And he didn't try anything ... well, anything untoward?'

'No,' Marian answered, drawing out the word.

Stephanie turned round as Matthew walked into the room.

'Ask her what they talked about?' he said.

Stephanie immediately covered the mouthpiece. 'I can't do that,' she hissed. 'It's none of our business.'

'Hello? Steph? Are you still there?'

'Yes, I'm here. So you're all right?'

'I'm just great. And tell Matthew we spent the whole evening talking about *him*.'

Stephanie chuckled at the humour in Marian's voice. 'I'll tell him,' she said. 'Sorry to have woken you.'

'Not to worry. See you tomorrow.' The line went dead.

'Satisfied?' Stephanie said, turning back to Matthew who, still naked, was leaning against the door frame. Her eyes were sparkling with amusement. 'She told me to tell you they spent all evening talking about you.'

He gave a shout of laughter, and as she got up from the chair he pulled her into his arms and rested her head on his shoulder.

'I don't know why you put up with me,' he said, still smiling, 'but I'm damned glad you do.'

'I put up with you, Matthew, because I love you.'

He cupped her face with his hands and gazed into her eyes. 'Do you?' he whispered.

She nodded. 'Very much.' And as he lowered his mouth

to hers she peeled the robe from her shoulders and let it slip to the floor.

'There's something standing between us,' she said, a few minutes later. Her voice was bubbling with mirth, but his expression remained dark and intense.

'I know,' he said huskily, and lifting her into his arms he carried her back into the bedroom.

– 16 –

Madeleine stood among the conservatory plants, gazing out onto the roof garden. There had never been a time in her life when she had stopped to think about what she was doing, or the consequences her actions might have for others. All she had known was her own beauty, her own needs, her own desires. But in the past two weeks her dreams had been distorted by a monstrous image of herself, as she now began to consider all she had done to those who loved her. She was certain that what had happened now was a punishment, and as she struggled to understand, to make some sense out of the devastation, her longing for Marian had become so intense that she had gone as far as to pick up the phone and dial the number in Devon. But at the last minute her courage had deserted her, and instead she had turned to her work for the release she so desperately craved. At every function, photograph session or press interview she attended, she parted her glossy lips, narrowed her eyes and looked sensuously into the camera; she laughed and flirted, drank champagne, and displayed her long legs for all to admire. There was never a minute in the day when she wasn't being pampered, photographed or beautified. Stylists, hairdressers, designers – everyone was at work on her; and like a puppet she reacted to every pull of the string. But no matter how hard she worked, how much she drank, or how late into the night she danced, there was no getting away from Paul, from what he had done or the way it was tearing her apart inside.

They'd slept in separate rooms since the night Harry Freemantle had climbed from her bed, put on his clothes and left the house. Once he'd gone Paul had tried to make her listen, had insisted he could explain, but she had locked herself in the bathroom and refused to come out until he swore he would never touch her again. But being repelled by what he had done, and hating him for having done it, had not stopped her loving him. Nor did it stem the swell of dread that swept through her each time that horrible, mocking voice inside her head told her that if he truly was a homosexual, there was *nothing* she could do to keep him. She had tried so hard not to think about it, had kept herself so busy that when she came home at night all she wanted was to sleep. Her only hope lay in the fact that he was always there; but she couldn't speak to him, she couldn't even look at him.

In the end she had become so desperate to speak to someone that she had called Shamir in Los Angeles. It hadn't helped, because Shamir had only told her to do all the things she knew she ought to do, but was afraid to.

'Throw him out!' Shamir said vehemently. 'Throw him out and change the locks.'

'But he says there was a reason . . .' Madeleine objected, sounding pathetic even to her own ears.

'What reason can there be, except that he's a faggot. Get rid of him, Maddy.'

'But I still love him, Shamir.'

'You'll get over it. Look, he treats you badly enough as it is, and this has *got* to be the final straw. I don't know why you've put up with him this long, I know I wouldn't have. And I don't trust him, Maddy. He'll do it again, or something equally vile, you mark my words.'

Madeleine sighed. 'Oh, I just don't know what to do.'

'Do as I tell you and throw him out.'

'I'll think about it.'

That was three days ago, but despite what she'd told Shamir she hadn't thought about it, she had pushed it away from her and carried on working. But now, as she gazed out at the garden, the shutters of her mind were again sliding open and she knew that somehow she was going to have to make herself face it.

Hearing him move about in his study downstairs, she opened the door and walked out into the garden. The heat was like a solid mass beating down from the sky, and all around her the rooftops of Holland Park rippled in the shimmery haze. She wandered over to the hammock, sat down and started to rock gently. After a while she closed her eyes, hoping that sleep would come, but just like the solution to her problems, it eluded her, and instead her mind churned up images of Harry lying in her bed, and Paul's hand touching his shoulder to waken him. The gesture had seemed so intimate, as if Paul really cared for him. Then, when Harry opened his eyes and saw her standing there, he had turned immediately to Paul, and the look that passed between them had made her feel like an intruder.

'Get dressed,' Paul had told him, and while Harry picked up his clothes and started to put them on, not looking at Madeleine once, Paul had stood beside the bed, doing nothing to cover his own nudity. For her part Madeleine had simply stared at them, rooted in shock and feeling strangely detached from herself, as if she were an invisible being who had stumbled upon two people she didn't even know. Then somewhere deep inside her, revulsion and denial had started to heave, surging upwards from her gut, past her lungs and into her throat until it had vomited forth on a scream of pure torment and confusion. Paul swung round and made to grab her, but she had backed away, snarling and clawing like a wild animal. As she ran down the stairs she heard him coming after her, but then Harry called out and Paul had gone back. A few minutes later she had heard the front door close. She'd wondered then, as she did now, whether Paul had dressed to see Harry off, and whether they had kissed as they parted.

She opened her eyes, unable to bear the persecution of her imagination. In front of her, on the table, a magazine lay open, so she picked it up and started to flick over the pages. She could concentrate on nothing, but nevertheless she didn't hear the conservatory door open, nor did she know he was in the garden until his shadow fell over her.

She turned away, and the magazine slipped from her lap to the floor. For a long time neither of them spoke, only the sounds of distant traffic stole the Sunday afternoon silence, then a lawn mower, then a dog barking. Despite everything, her body ached for him to hold her, to protect her from the torment of what was happening to them. If only it had killed her love, but it seemed only to have intensified it.

Realising that she was holding her breath, she closed her eyes, then let it out slowly.

'Maddy, we have to talk.'

She shook her head. 'No.'

His shadow moved and then she felt him sit beside her. She stood up and walked towards the conservatory, but before she could open the door he was in front of her, blocking the way.

'Listen to me, please, Maddy. Let me explain.'

She turned her head, fixing unfocused eyes on a bay tree he had brought home once to surprise her.

'You can't keep avoiding me. We have to face this, Maddy – together.'

'I can't,' she breathed. 'I've tried, but I can't.'

'Let me help you.'

Her expression was closed to him, but he searched her face, trying to find a way inside the shells of the Russian doll that were now so firmly closed to him.

'It was a man,' she whispered. 'You went to bed with a man.'

'I know.'

She looked at him, imploringly. 'Then where does that leave me?'

'It doesn't *leave* you anywhere. You're still here. We both are.'

Tears, like two crystal beads, ran down her cheeks. Using his thumbs he wiped them away, then crushed her against him. She didn't respond, but neither did she try to break free.

'Come on,' he said, and with his arms still round her he gently led her across the garden and sat her in the deep wicker chair next to the hammock. Then kneeling in front of her, he took her hands between his. 'You know why I did it,' he began. 'You know . . .'

She snatched her hands away. 'No, Paul, I don't know. Any normal man, a man who likes women, couldn't have done that.'

Resting his elbow on the chair-arm, he pushed his head into the heel of his hand. 'I couldn't help myself, Maddy,' he groaned. 'I couldn't see any other way.'

'But I gave you a name. All you had to do was call him, he could have done it.'

He shook his head. 'It wouldn't have worked, Maddy. I thought about it and thought about it until it almost drove me out of my mind, but in the end I knew I couldn't open you up to blackmail.'

'What do you mean? How would it have . . ?'

'The boy would have been suspicious. He would have wanted to know why we were so keen for him to go to bed with Harry. Then he might have threatened to expose what we were doing. At the very best, it would have come out that we were paying men to sleep together. At worst, if he'd got to find out the whole truth, all three of us – you, me and Harry – would have been ruined.' He paused, giving her a moment to digest this. 'So do you see now why I had to do it myself?' he added softly.

He watched her eyes as uncertainty deepened the anguish, yet from their clouded, doubt-filled depths he could see a tiny glimmer of devotion beginning to surface. He waited, watching for the moment when her indecision reached its peak; then just a few seconds more until the light of love began to eclipse the cloud of misgiving; then he whispered, 'And I needed to do it, Maddy.'

Immediately the light was extinguished. '*Needed!*' she cried. 'You need . . .'

'Stop! Listen to me. I had to do it. For us, for my book, and for the next book I write. I needed, yes *needed*, the experience. I've tried to imagine two men in bed together, but I couldn't. That's why, when you told me about Harry, I laughed. I laughed because it was the solution to everything.'

'And what about me?'

'It was never meant to change anything between us. If Harry and I hadn't fallen asleep that night, you'd have known nothing about it. Christ, Maddy, I love you, do you think I'd . . .'

'Who did it to who?' she snapped.

'*What?*'

'I said, who did it? Who was the man?'

'Oh God, Madeleine, does it matter?'

'Yes.'

His mind was racing. What was she thinking? Why did it matter? Then it hit him. She wanted to know if he had been aroused enough to achieve penetration. 'He was the man,' he answered quietly.

Her head fell back against the seat, her lips were open,

her eyes closed. 'Did you have an erection? While he was doing it, were you excited?'

'Maddy, for God's sake!'

Her head snapped up. 'Does his prick turn you on?'

'Shut up!' He grabbed her hair and pulled her face down to his. 'You're asking things that don't matter.'

'Oh, they matter!' she spat. 'I need to know, Paul, and you're going to tell me. Do you get hard thinking about him? Let me feel. *Let me feel!*' she yelled. He slapped her hands away and she rocked back in the chair. 'What next, Paul? You on top of me and him on top of you? Is that what you're after – for the book! Or doesn't anything I have interest you now?'

Suddenly his hands were under her dress. She screamed as she slid to the floor and tried to kick him away. The hem of her dress had snagged on the chair, leaving her naked from the waist down. He grabbed her shoulders and pushed them to the ground, then taking her knees, he forced her legs apart.

His breathing was heavy and sweat poured down his face. He stared down at her, his fingers digging painfully into her thighs. Then he tore open his jeans.

As he started towards her, their eyes met. And when his face was over hers she braced herself for the pain of what he was about to do.

'Oh no,' he sneered. 'I'm not going to rape you. You've seen it, you know it's there for you. Now, you tell me you want it.'

She lowered her eyes to his mouth, then gasped as he took her dress between his hands and ripped it from her body.

'Do you want it?' he yelled. 'Look! It's here, it's hard for you.'

Her breath panted through open lips, her hands twitched at her sides and there was an ache in her loins more acute than she had ever known before.

'Tell me, Madeleine. Tell me you want me, or . . .'

'*I want you!*' And her legs locked about his waist, pulling him from his knees. He entered her brutally, but her scream was stifled by his tongue.

She tore at his hair as he pushed his arms under her, hooking his hands round her shoulders. 'Is this good enough for you?' he snarled. 'Is this what you want?' He was ramming into her so hard that she cried out with every stroke. 'This is what I thought about when I was with him. Yes, my prick was hard, like it is now. All I wanted was you, your legs around me, your tongue in my mouth, your hands on my balls. I wanted to fuck you, Madeleine, like this. Tell me you love me, you bitch. Tell me you forgive me.'

'I love you!' she cried. 'Oh God, Paul, I love you!' He slipped a hand between them and pushed his thumb into the soft flesh. And then it was upon her, wave after wave of exquisite pain pumping viciously through her loins, whooshing through her veins and propelling her into the throes of frenzy.

'OH MY GOD!' she screamed, and as she arched herself towards him he grabbed her hips, holding her up to him, pushing, stabbing, every muscle on fire as the juice flowed from his body in spurt after spurt of burning, devastating, beautiful gratification. 'It's for you, Madeleine!' he roared. 'This is for you!'

Finally, as the strength ebbed from his body, he slumped over her, heaving great shuddering breaths as sweat poured from his skin. Her arms were thrown wide, across the ground, but her face was turned to his and he could feel her breath on his neck. After a while he rolled onto his back and they lay side by side on the baking tiles, for a long time too exhausted to utter anything beyond a moan or a sigh.

Madeleine was the first to speak. 'So,' she said, turning

her head to look at him, and narrowing her eyes against the brilliant sun, 'did you get the video?'

His jaw tightened and he kept his eyes closed – a small physical reaction to relief – and victory. When he faced her his expression held only love, and he smiled at the smear of dry earth on her cheek. He nodded.

'When will you show him?'

'He's coming here tomorrow night. If you'll allow it.'

She tensed, and her breasts swung gently against her rib cage as she sat up. 'I'll do it,' she said finally.

'Do what?' he asked, smoothing a hand over the breast closest to him.

She pushed it away. 'I'll tell him about the video. There's no need to show him; after all, he knows what you did together.'

'Why?'

'Because we're going to do this my way. You owe me that.'

The corner of his mouth flickered into a smile. This sudden display of mettle impressed him and he was intrigued to see what she would do with it, especially as he had now proved to himself, by doing what he had with Harry, that he could control his love for her. 'I'm in your hands,' he said. 'I'll do whatever you say.'

The following evening, when Harry arrived, Madeleine was dressed in a pale silk blouse and matching knee-length skirt; her hair was in a low plait and her face, though pale, was devoid of expression. As she opened the door she registered his shock by the mere flicker of an eyebrow, then stood back to let him in.

He followed her into the sitting-room where Paul was standing with his hands resting on the mantlepiece, staring down at the empty hearth.

Madeleine stepped to one side and waited. At last Paul turned, and as the two men faced each other it was Harry's face she watched. It had been clear from the moment he arrived that he hadn't expected to find her at home, and Madeleine couldn't stop herself wondering how they would have greeted one another had she not been there.

'Would you like to kiss him?' she said to Harry.

Harry's eyes shot to hers.

'For Christ's sake, Madeleine . . .' Paul groaned.

'I'll have a glass of wine, thank you,' she said, walking across the room and settling herself into a corner of the sofa. 'Harry, what would you like?'

Harry looked at Paul, then running a hand nervously through his hair, he said: 'Look, I think I'd better leave. I don't . . .'

'Oh no, you can't leave,' Madeleine protested. 'Not yet, anyway. Sit down. Paul will get you a drink.'

As Harry walked to the opposite sofa he glanced at Paul, waiting for some signal that would tell him how they should play this, but Paul was spooning ice into tumblers and didn't look up. Since the night Madeleine had caught them together they had made love twice more at Harry's pied-à-terre in Pimlico. He wondered if she knew about that. He wondered, too, how Paul could stand living with someone like her, someone who degraded herself the way she did.

He smiled awkwardly and complimented her on the fashion spread that had been in the *Daily Mail* that day. Her response was a glance from the corner of her eyes, which surprised him – Paul had said that one thing she couldn't resist was flattery. Suddenly his defences were up. She was going to hurt him, he knew it; there was a dangerous air in the room which he hadn't noticed before. His eyes darted warily between Madeleine and Paul.

As Paul handed Madeleine a drink she ran her fingers through the dark hair of his forearm and he stooped to kiss the top of her head. When he stood up again, she looked at Harry. Until now Harry had always managed to keep his homosexuality under control, express it in a way that wouldn't affect the rest of his life, but seeing Paul respond to this woman ignited feelings in him he was finding it difficult to repress. He recognised the symptoms of love, he'd had them before – but never so quickly and never so profoundly as with Paul. He had even considered what it would be like to live with Paul, openly, but of course that was impossible, and the hopelessness of his situation weighed heavily on him.

As Paul passed him a drink their fingers touched, and Harry flinched as though he had been burned. He looked no higher than the legs that were in front him, he was frozen by the sudden power of his need.

Paul went back to the fireplace. The excitement he felt was unbelievable; for the moment he was unable to drink or even to speak, his tension was so great. He had no idea what Madeleine was going to do or say, nor how Harry would react. The only thing he was sure of was that they were both in love with him.

Folding one leg over the other, Madeleine raised her glass. 'Here's to you, Harry. I know you weren't expecting to see me, but this *is* my house and Paul is *my* man.'

Paul winced, and again Harry ran his fingers nervously through his hair.

'I'll do anything to keep him,' she went on, 'and anything to further his career, as you're about to find out. It's not your fault you're queer, I suppose you've got feelings too, but you're barking up the wrong tree with Paul. The only thing he is after is to get his book published the way he wants, and I told him that going to bed with you would do it. It took me a long time to persuade him, but now he's done it I'm going to make damned sure he gets what he wants out of it.'

Harry looked to the floor, mentally hunching himself against the possibility of further blows, but she waited until he looked at her again before continuing. 'Something you may not know about Paul is the fascination he has for watching himself make love,' she said. 'You see the videos there, by the TV? They're mostly of us – there's even one of us fucking while we're watching ourselves fucking on the screen.'

Paul's surprise and curiosity glittered in his eyes. She was lying, and he wasn't yet following her train of thought.

'The video there, on top of the TV,' she pointed, 'is of you two. I've got a copy, so you can have that one to keep. I'd take it if I were you, because it's all you're going to have of him after tonight. Except on the professional front, that is. You see, I am going to be famous, very famous, and I want Paul to be famous as well. He needs your help for that, so I'm going to blackmail you.'

Jesus Christ! Paul choked and had to turn away before either of them realised he was laughing.

Only Madeleine saw the deep sadness that seeped into Harry's eyes as he put his glass down and wiped a hand across his face, and despite everything her heart went out to him.

When he looked up again, it was at Paul, and slowly he shook his head. 'There was no need to do it like this.' His voice was barely above a whisper.

'He's not,' Madeleine interrupted. 'I am. He had no idea what I was going to say to you tonight. He didn't even know I had a copy of the video. He's only here now because I wanted him to be. I wanted him to see what I am prepared to do for him.'

Again Harry looked at Paul, but Paul only shrugged and turned away.

'An unedited publication,' Madeleine said. 'That's what Paul wants – to begin with. After that, well, you can't tell me there aren't ways of making sure books get into the best-seller lists, so I want you to do that too. There'll be more, you may even need some money, which I'll give you.' She stopped as Harry stood up and walked over to Paul.

'Why?' he said, his black eyes searching the handsome, impassive face. 'Surely you must know that . . .'

'Get away from him!' Madeleine snapped, and in one quick move she had crossed the room and picked up the video. 'It's nothing to do with him. All he wants is his book published, I told you that. Here, take it. Wank over it if you like, but every time you come, think about how much it's costing you.'

Ignoring the video, Harry looked clear into her eyes, and his distaste was evident. 'The cheapness of that remark I will ignore, but the fact that you think you love him, I won't. Because you don't have the first idea of what it's like to be in love with someone other than yourself. Paul will have his book published, but not because of you, or what you say you're prepared to do for him – because you're doing it for no one but yourself. Oh, I know he doesn't return my feelings, but he will, in time. Which is something it's going to be a damned sight harder for you live with than it is for me.'

'Don't kid yourself, Harry.'

'You're just a child. You know nothing about life. Let me tell you, it's not easy being homosexual, as Paul is finding out. I'm going to help him.'

Madeleine laughed. 'You'd better get in tune with the fact that it's me he wants, Harry. It's me who can give him everything, like I do now. And don't think he'll be sleeping with you again, because *you're* the only queer in this room.'

As she turned to the door she missed the quick look Paul shot Harry. Harry understood, and saying no more, he picked up his keys. When they got outside he hesitated. 'You're hurting inside, Madeleine, I know that. So am I. Out of kindness I suggest . . .'

'Just fuck off, will you?' And thrusting the video at him, she slammed the door in his face.

When she returned to the sitting-room Paul was on the sofa nursing his drink, with his legs crossed and one arm stretched across the back. She stood looking across the room at him.

Paul spoke first. 'I know what you're going to say; you want me to understand what you've done for me. Well, I do. Whether you've succeeded I don't know, but it was your intention to make him hate you and continue to love me. Am I right?' She didn't answer, so he went on. 'Yes, I'm impressed with the way you've thought things out, and shocked by the way you delivered your threat. No, I don't think there'll be any problem working with him, I don't think he'll blame me for any of this. You're a genius . . . I see, still nothing to say. OK, I've got it. You want me to swear I'll never have anything to do with him in that way again. I swear.'

'Now tell me you're a fucking liar. Tell me what a fucking bastard you are.'

'Why should I do that?'

'Because he's a decent man who's worth more than a dozen of you, and you made me humiliate him. You stood there and let him shrivel and never said a word. And it was you who fucked him, in every sense of the word.'

Paul smiled. 'So you watched the video.'

'I didn't have to. I'm a woman, for Christ's sake. I recognised that look on his face. It was the look of someone who's been used, who's body has been invaded and abused. But yes, I watched the video, and now you're going to pay for those lies. I'm not going to leave you because I love you and I can't help it. But you're going to pay, Paul O'Connell. My God, are you going to pay.'

His delight was now evident and he took a sip of his drink before saying: 'I'm waiting.'

She left the room and ran up the stairs. Several minutes

later he heard her come down again, then go into the bathroom. He heard the rattle of pots, then she came back into the room. When he saw what she was carrying he stood up, delight giving way to uncertainty.

'Take off your clothes,' she commanded.

Slowly, keeping his eyes on her, he did as she said.

'Now, turn round and put your hands on the fender,' she said.

His eyes widened. He knew now what was coming, and he was afraid of the pain, but at the same time he would do nothing to stop her. When he was in position she opened the jar of vaseline. It was cool on his skin, and he closed his eyes as the blood started to surge through his penis. Then, hearing the gentle whirr of the vibrator, he braced himself; and as it touched him, started to edge into him, his fingers bit hard into the fender. Then her arm jerked and a high-pitched cry escaped through his teeth. She did it again and again, ordering him to scream, to feel the pain, to beg her to stop. But he did neither, and as her hand closed around his erection the semen started to pump from him and he fell to his knees. She spun him round to face her, then gasped at the look in his eyes. They were blood-shot and swollen, awash with tears, and dazed with an agonising, blinding ecstasy.

– 17 –

Marian and Bronwen were sitting at a small table outside a café at the corner of the Ponte Vecchio, fanning themselves with menus and sipping iced lemonade. Above them, peeping in patches through the Gothic, Renaissance and Baroque towers, the sky was the most beautiful shade of blue imaginable, with not a cloud in sight. As Marian looked up she thought how tranquil it seemed up there, compared with the mayhem created by the street artists, traders and tourists who seethed all around them. She and Bronwen had arrived in Florence the day before, after a rushed meeting at Heathrow with Stephanie and Matthew, whose flight to New York was called just an hour before theirs. Knowing that she had played a part in their reconciliation depressed Marian, but she had hidden it well, and had even managed a cheerful laugh when Matthew took her to one side and told her she shouldn't believe a word Woody said about him.

Overhearing, Stephanie had laughingly put her arm through Marian's. 'You see, he's so conceited he actually believes you meant it when you said you and Woody spent the evening talking about him.'

'But we did,' Marian said truthfully, though her eyes were alive with humour.

'Of course they did,' Matthew chipped in. 'I mean, what else is there to talk about?'

'I could hit him,' Stephanie said, seriously.

'You already have,' Matthew reminded her.

At that point a voice announced the final call for their flight to New York, and Bronwen returned from the telephone.

'A few last minute details,' she said to Stephanie, and the two of them started to walk towards passport control, leaving Marian and Matthew to follow.

'I'm intrigued by this urgent summons,' he told her, 'but I for one will be glad to meet Frank Hastings.'

'Stephanie mentioned something about him wanting to pull the film forward.'

'I know. Which we could if we had something to shoot in Italy. So it's over to you, oh wise one. Dig up what you can, but remember, no wandering from the beaten track.'

Her dismay at his words must have shown, because he gave her a quick hug; then he made a joke about being tearful at goodbyes, before prising Stephanie away from Bronwen and marching her through the barriers.

Now, as she glanced at her watch and calculated what time it would be in New York, Marian smiled sadly to herself. She knew it was foolish to torment herself like this, but Matthew and Stephanie would still be in bed, probably wrapped in each other's arms, maybe even making love, and a raw despondency crept over her at the complication of her feelings. Her dread of Florence was now nothing to do with Paul, it had only to do with Matthew, and that made no sense at all, except that he wasn't with her, would never be with her, and Florence – despite the heat and the unbearable tourists – was even more romantic than she'd imagined.

'If Sergio Rambaldi doesn't arrive in the next five minutes, I'm going to have my picture done by one of those portrait chappies over there, so that when I melt into a little pool you'll be able to remember what I looked like,' Bronwen complained.

'Do you think he'll turn up?' Marian asked, as she watched a party of school children file past.

Bronwen shrugged. 'Right now I'm so hot I couldn't care less. Why did he have to suggest we meet here? Couldn't he have picked somewhere that was at least in the shade?'

Marian moved her chair round to let a Japanese couple pass, then gasped as one of their cameras got caught in her straw hat. 'Well, that's good-bye to *my* dignity,' she remarked wryly, after they'd apologised, picked up her hat then gawked at the way her hair was plastered in tiny clips to her head.

'Put it on again before anyone sees,' Bronwen laughed, then watching the ebb and flow of tourists as they crossed the bridge, she pulled a face. 'They must be mad, coming here at this time of year. Look at them, they're all sog and dust, and the smell of those drains is making me ill.'

'I know what you mean,' Marian said, as a particularly foul stench wafted past on a solitary breeze. Though she liked the city herself, she could see now why Paul had described it as being steeped in its own past; despite the crowds and the roaring traffic, the ancient buildings had an air of detachment from what was going on around them, as if they were yawning sleepily and closing their shutters to the mild irritation of twentieth-century life.

'Do you know if Matthew's ever been to Florence?' Marian asked casually.

'I've no idea, *cariad*, but heaven help us if he were to come here filming at this time of year. Can you imagine poor Woody trying to stop the traffic?' She chuckled at the very absurdity of it. 'And knowing Matthew, he'd make him. Mind you, knowing Woody, he'd probably succeed.'

'They go back a long way, those two, don't they? Woody was telling me all about it the night I went out with him.'

'I think so, yes. They were certainly working together when Stephanie first knew Matthew. What do you think of Woody? No romance blossoming there between you two, is there?'

'No. Apart from anything else, he's married. And even if he weren't, I don't think I'm quite his type.'

'No offence, *cariad*, but I think you're right. He likes the ones who carry their brains a bit lower than their heads, if you get my meaning.'

Marian chuckled. 'So that they'll be on a level with his, you mean?'

Bronwen burst out laughing. 'You've obviously got Woody well and truly sussed. But you wait 'til we start shooting, then you'll see some real sharks. Woody's quite mild by comparison, according to Stephanie. But he's good at his job, which is all she's concerned about, and apparently he calms down quite a bit once the filming gets under way.'

'I wonder what Matthew's like when he's shooting?'

'Unbearable, probably. Most directors are.'

'Why?'

'Tension.'

'Signora Evans?'

Both Marian and Bronwen looked up, squinting through their sunglasses, and Marian almost gulped when she saw the face of the man standing over them.

'Er, Signor Rambaldi?' Bronwen stammered, equally overcome by his magnificent looks. Stumbling to her feet, she held out her hand. 'I am very pleased to meet you. This is my secretary, Marian Deacon, I hope you don't mind if she sits in on the interview.'

'Not in the least.' And as he smiled Marian felt as though she were sinking in the compelling depths of his black eyes. 'It is very hot here, no?' he said, turning back to Bronwen, whose pale skin had already turned to an angry pink. 'Maybe you would like to come to my studio, there it is a little cooler, I hope.'

Bronwen snatched up her bag. 'What a wonderful idea,' she said, delving into her purse for the several thousand lire needed to tip their waiter.

'It is not far from here,' he told them, and as he glanced at Marian she was again affected by his overwhelming charisma.

'I wouldn't care if it was as far away as Venice,' Bronwen said. 'Anything to get out of this sun.'

Laughing, he stood aside to let them out from the table, then guided them through the crowds in the direction of the Palazzo Torrigiani.

In less than ten minutes they were in his studio, gazing wide-eyed at his remarkable paintings and drawings of details taken from fifteenth-century paintings.

'Did you do all these?' Marian asked, looking up from an easel that was supporting a charcoal sketch of Andrea del Sarto's *Charity*.

'Some,' he answered, opening the window and pushing back the shutters. 'Some were done by my students.'

Marian and Bronwen exchanged looks, but as he turned round Marian moved on to study a Leonardo Madonna.

'Are any of them Olivia's work?' Bronwen asked nonchalantly.

He laughed and shook his head. 'No. Once I have her work here, but now I have removed it.'

'Oh?'

As he answered he sat on the window ledge, then waved his arm in a gesture that told them to make themselves comfortable on what little furniture there was. 'You understand, in the five years since Olivia was here I have many students. I cannot hang all their work, so I change things around each few months.'

'Of course.' Bronwen slipped her bag from her shoulder and settled on the arm of the voluminous chair that Marian had chosen. Marian had intended to perch on the edge of it, but had found herself sinking further and further to the ground so that now her head was on a level with Bronwen's legs. She had never felt quite so absurd, especially since she was still wearing her hat.

'Can I get you something to drink?' Sergio offered. 'I have fresh mango juice if you would like it.'

'Sounds delicious,' Bronwen answered. Incapable of stopping herself, she watched him as he walked out to the kitchen. 'Have you ever seen such a gorgeous man?' she whispered, turning to Marian. Then her eyebrows arched in astonishment. 'Heavens above, *cariad*, what on earth are you doing down there?'

'I think the springs have gone,' Marian answered, 'you wouldn't like to give me a hand out, would you, while he's not looking?'

Trying to smother her laughter, Bronwen took Marian's hands and hauled her out of the chair. 'Sit on the other arm,' she told her, 'and listen carefully from now on, because I'm feeling decidedly awful and he's our only real contact here in Florence.'

'Will do,' Marian nodded, as she balanced on the arm of the chair.

When Sergio came back with the drinks he gave Marian a look of surprise, then smiled mournfully. 'I am sorry. The chair, she is broken. Are you comfortable there?'

'Oh yes, very,' Marian assured him, then thanked him for the mango juice.

'So you would like me to tell you what I know about Olivia,' he said, resuming his position at the window. Both Marian and Bronwen were thinking the same thing – that with the light behind him it was impossible to see his face. And both wondered if that was his intention. 'Where would you like me to begin?'

'Why not start with what she was like as a student?' Bronwen suggested. 'I mean, was she a good artist?'

'She was not outstanding, no. Though I think in America they thought so.'

'Was she disciplined?'

'On occasions. Sometimes her mind – her mind was not always with what she was doing.'

'Would that be because she was taking drugs, or because she was maybe not as devoted to art as she made out?'

'A little of both, I think. But no, it would have been the drugs. It was very sad, she took heroin, you know.'

Bronwen nodded. 'Can you tell us something about her class life? Who her friends were, where she went in the evenings – that sort of thing?'

'The class life you will be welcome to see for yourself if you care to visit the Accademia,' he answered. 'As for her friends, she had many. They were mostly American, I believe. I can find in the records who they were, maybe they can help you to know where they go in the evenings.'

'That's very kind,' Bronwen smiled, 'it'll be very helpful.' She put a hand to her mouth to stifle a yawn. 'I'm sorry,' she apologised, 'it's the heat. We'll be visiting the village where the American boy dropped her off while we're here,' she went on. 'Do you know it at all?'

'Paesetto di Pittore? Not well, I am afraid.'

'So you haven't got any idea why Olivia went there?'

Sergio shrugged, and Marian turned to Bronwen. It was quite unlike Bronwen to put answers into the mouths of her interviewees, especially negative ones.

Bronwen took a gulp of air and continued. 'Can you paint us a picture of Olivia – in words, I mean; what she was like when she was in Florence, how she looked, how she behaved.'

'Ah ha,' he laughed, 'I am not so good with the words, but I will try. She was very, how you say, statuesque? Yes, that is the word. Tall and upright, and her eyes often had the appearance of being alert, but that was the drugs. When she was coming down, as they say, then her eyes were . . . they were not so good to look at. She had blonde hair, very fine, and her face was very beautiful. Though sometimes not so beautiful, but again that was the drugs. But when she took the drugs, afterwards she was filled with life and energy. All the students wanted to be her friend. She was a little crazy and they like that.'

'Crazy? How do you mean?' Bronwen's voice was thin, and when Marian turned to look at her she saw that she had turned a peculiar colour.

'I mean crazy, like students are sometimes. She would do extraordinary things to her paintings, sometimes blasphemous things.'

'Blasphemous? In what way?'

'I would not like to tell you. After all, I am a Catholic and it was a profanity that I think is now best forgotten.'

'I understand,' Bronwen answered, then suddenly she lurched forward, clutching her stomach. 'I'm sorry,' she gasped, 'but can I use your bathroom, I'm feeling a little . . .'

'But of course.' Sergio was immediately on his feet, and taking her by the shoulders, he guided her into an adjoining room.

'Thank you, thank you,' she heard Bronwen mumbling, then a door slammed and Sergio came back into the studio.

'It is probably the heat,' he told Marian. 'She should be sensible, like you, and wear a hat.'

Marian smiled, then gazed awkwardly about the room. She wasn't sure if this was some ploy of Bronwen's, but she really had looked strange, and if she was ill, then perhaps she had better continue the interview alone. She asked Sergio if he had any objections.

'Not at all,' he answered, moving back to the window.

'The blasphemous paintings,' Marian reminded him. 'Why do you think she did it?'

'Again the drugs.' He paused. 'But that is too simple an answer. It was as if she wanted to paint something from her soul – to exorcise it, you understand?'

Marian nodded.

'I believe she was disturbed in some way. I cannot say how, but that is my opinion.'

'Disturbed by something that had happened in New York, perhaps?'

'Maybe. Yes, I think so.'

Marian knew that if Art Douglas's suspicions were right, and Sergio Rambaldi did know something about what had happened in New York, then she was approaching dangerous territory, so she smiled stupidly and said, 'I wonder what it was. Perhaps she had a boyfriend over there and wanted to get back to him.'

'It could have been that.'

Marian shook her head. 'No, that wouldn't account for the blasphemy in her paintings, would it?'

'It might, if he had broken her heart. Maybe she was

feeling God had deserted her. A lot of people feel such anger when a lover lets them down.'

Marian's eyes grew large with feigned excitement. 'Perhaps that's it. It would make an interesting turn for the film, wouldn't it?'

'I'm sure it would,' Sergio laughed. 'And with all the boyfriends she had here in Florence, maybe she was, how you say, on the rebound.'

'She had a lot of boyfriends here, you say?'

'Oh, very many. As I say, she was very beautiful. And exciting.'

'I wonder where she is now,' Marian mused. When he didn't answer she made a pretence of pulling herself back to the present. 'Are there any incidents you can think of that might make for a good scene for the film?'

As Sergio searched his memory Marian wished she could see his face, but the sun was dazzling her eyes, making it impossible. But as he answered she could hear the laughter in his voice, and she listened intently as he told her about the night Olivia had come to his studio and told him she could not make love with him.

'Had you asked her if she would?' she enquired, then blushed as she realised the impertinence of the question. She started to apologise, but he interrupted.

'As a matter of fact, I had,' he admitted. 'You see, I too was a little in love with Olivia. She had a very magnetic personality. Maybe that is another scene for your film, the time that I ask her to come to me. It happened in the Casa Buonarotti, while we were making sketches from Michelangelo's *Battle of the Lapiths and Centaurs*. She was watching my hand as it moved over the paper, then she touched it and held it. Then she tell me that she is in love with me. I tell her that students often think that way about their tutor, but she insist that for her it is different. I am a man, you understand, it is not always easy to resist a woman, especially a woman like Olivia. I say to her that I would like to make love to her, and then we continue to sketch. It was two days after that she came to this apartment and said she could not do it. The lady who is like my wife was here, but she is used to students behaving like that with me. It is immodest of me to say so, but it does happen often.'

Immodest or not, Marian was thinking, it's hardly surprising. 'Does the lady, your wife, know that you asked Olivia?'

'No.'

'Then wouldn't it make things a little awkward for you if we were to put that in the film?'

'Of course. But we will say that it is fiction to enrich the film, no?'

Marian's face broke into a smile as she nodded. 'When you next saw Olivia, was it . . . ?'

'I did not see her again,' he interrupted. 'Very soon after, I think one or two days, she disappeared.'

'Oh, I see,' Marian said pensively. Then, 'Did you know that her father received a note telling him Olivia *was* alive?'

'Yes. I read it in the newspaper.'

'It was signed by someone with the initial A. Did you know any of her boyfriends? Did any of them have the initial A?'

Again Sergio laughed. 'It is a difficult question because many men have the initial A. Maybe when you go through the records of that year you can check to see.'

They both turned as the door opened and Bronwen came in, looking pale and drained. 'I do apologise,' she said to Sergio, 'it must be the heat.'

'I am sure,' he smiled. 'Can I get you something?'

'No, no, I'm feeling much better now. If you just carry on, I'll join in where I can.'

Sergio turned back to Marian. 'We were speaking of

Olivia's boyfriends,' he said, 'and the initial A. Have you considered that the A may stand for a woman's name?'

As that had never occurred to her, Marian looked at Bronwen. 'It is something we have discussed,' Bronwen answered, 'but the handwriting has been analysed by experts and all concerned believe it to be a man's.'

Sergio nodded. 'But maybe you should not rule out the possibility it is a woman.'

Though Marian still couldn't see his face, she knew his eyes were fixed on Bronwen, and for no accountable reason she had the feeling that he was trying to lead her along the wrong track.

'We are none of us keen to rule out anything,' she told him, 'but the note is something we won't be putting into the film. It is too vague.'

'I see.' He looked at his watch. 'I have soon to be back at the Accademia, so unless there is something else you would like to ask me . . .'

'Only about when Olivia first arrived in Florence,' Bronwen interrupted. She looked at Marian. 'Unless you have already covered that?'

Marian shook her head.

'Did she come alone?' Bronwen asked, turning back to Sergio.

'As far as I know.'

'Did she seem happy to be here?'

'All I can say is that when she came to me, after the summer term already begins, she was very famous in America and I think she did not really want to be here.'

'Because of her fame, you mean?'

'I would say so.'

'I wonder why she came, then?' Bronwen said, giving Marian a bemused look. Then suddenly her face paled again, and she clenched her bottom lip between her teeth.

'All I know is that she applied, late, but in the usual

way. I confess before she came I had not heard of her, but now, of course, everyone in Italy has heard of her.'

'But I thought Rubin Meyer had told you about her?' Marian blurted out. Immediately her mouth snapped shut, and she couldn't believe she had said it.

Sergio smiled. 'Rubin Meyer? I do not know Rubin Meyer. Does he say that he knows me?'

'No, no,' Marian assured him. 'But I expect a man in his position must have heard of you. I just thought that he might have recommended Olivia to you – I mean, you to Olivia.' She was thrashing wildly about in her mind. Did the others know that it had been Meyer's suggestion that Olivia should go to Florence, or was it something Art Douglas had told her? Whichever it was, Sergio had denied knowing Rubin Meyer, just as Rubin Meyer, when they'd interviewed him, had claimed not to know Sergio. That was it, he had said that he didn't *know* Sergio, but that naturally he had heard of him by reputation, and that was why he had recommended to Frank Hastings that Olivia should study under him for a time. So the others did know. However, Art Douglas had said that he was certain these two men were in some way involved in what had happened to Olivia – if they were not the very perpetrators of it.

She knew she was in grave danger of betraying both herself and Art Douglas, and as she had made a pact with herself not even to think about it, she threw out her hands and laughed. 'I've got things a bit muddled. Forgive me, I was thinking of something else.' She groaned inwardly as she realised she was only making things worse.

But as Sergio got to his feet she saw from his relaxed expression that he was in no way perturbed by what she had said, and she gave an audible sigh of relief. She watched him as he put a hand on Bronwen's shoulder and his face broke into a smile of sympathy. 'You should go back to your hotel,' he said kindly.

'Yes,' Bronwen mumbled, 'yes, I think you're right.

Thank you very much for seeing us. You've been a great help.' She looked to Marian for confirmation and Marian nodded.

As he walked them to the door, Sergio said, 'I have your name, it is Bronwen Evans.' Then turning to Marian he said, 'But I am afraid I have forgotten yours.'

Marian looked up into his face. He was smiling urbanely, and as the smile washed over her it brought a spot of colour to each cheek.

'Marian Deacon,' she told him.

He nodded. 'It was a pleasure to meet you, Marian. . .'

'I don't believe it,' Bronwen gasped when they were out on the street. 'A man like that, and I have to go and chuck up in his bathroom. But I do feel terrible, *cariad*, I really do.'

'Yes, you look pretty dreadful,' Marian informed her. 'Come on, let's get you out of this heat as quickly as we can.'

But their progress was slow as Bronwen was continuously engulfed by dizziness. 'You'll have to type all this up on your own tonight, Marian, do you mind?' She howled as she was gripped by another wave of pain. 'What was all that about Rubin Meyer?'

'Oh, nothing,' Marian said as she took Bronwen's arm and walked her a little further down the street. 'I just got confused, that was all.'

'I think I'm in love with that man,' Bronwen gasped. 'What do you reckon he thinks of me?'

'Depends what a mess you made of his bathroom.'

'Oh, don't make me laugh,' Bronwen groaned. . .

From the window of his studio Sergio watched them until they disappeared round the corner. Then he walked into the bedroom and picked up the phone.

He didn't have long to wait before the connection was made and a sing-song voice came over the line saying, 'Meyer's Gallery.'

'Put me onto Rubin Meyer,' he said.

'I'm afraid he's out right now. Can I take a message?'

Sergio thought for a moment, then said, 'Tell him to contact the *bottega*.'

'I'm sorry, sir, can you spell that, please.'

'The *bottega*,' Sergio repeated, and hung up.

Frank Hastings' office was situated in the south wing of the penthouse suite at 55 Water Street, downtown Manhattan. His company occupied floors fifty-five to fifty-nine. They'd moved to this address three years ago from the corner of Wall Street and Broadway – the financial district of New York had well and truly broken its boundaries.

Frank was standing at the vast window, looking down at the ceaseless flow of traffic that swarmed over the Brooklyn and Manhattan bridges. He was a tall man, well-built, with a shock of grey hair that glinted silver in the sunlight. Beneath his dark, heavy brows the expression in his brown eyes was normally a captivating combination of shrewdness and humour, though at that moment he was frowning. He ran a finger down the length of his regal nose, and his wide mouth was a compressed line of concentration. After a while he followed the progress of a chopper as it swooped out of the Downtown Heliport until it disappeared from view behind the tower blocks of Brooklyn Heights; then he inhaled deeply, slid his hands into his trouser pockets and turned back into the room.

Sitting round the mahogany mini-conference table that jutted from the rear of his desk were Stephanie, Matthew, Deborah Foreman and Grace Hastings, his wife. He looked at them all, one at a time, then strolled back to his desk.

'I understand your reservations about bringing the movie forward,' he said, resting his large hands on the back of his chair. 'I understand all you've said about weather, light, short days and what that'll mean in terms of cost' – his eyes returned to Matthew – 'but you got Bronwen and Marian out there in Italy now, and it's not gonna take them long to sort out what you're gonna shoot there, 'cos Olivia wasn't there more than four weeks. And I want to get this movie on the road.'

Stephanie looked at Matthew as he answered. 'You're probably right about Italy,' he said, 'and I've got no objections to shooting in late autumn; I just wanted you to be aware of what it could entail – not only in terms of cost, but weather too.' He shrugged. 'However, at the end of the day, it amounts to the same thing. Bad weather costs money.'

Frank nodded.

Matthew went on, 'And it also means that Deborah here will still be writing the end of the screenplay while we're shooting the beginning of it in Manhattan.'

'That's fine by me,' Deborah chipped in, and Matthew tried not to wince at the sycophancy in her voice. Deborah had a certain reputation as an investigative journalist, but nothing she had come up with – either in her book, or for the screenplay – had so far impressed him. Her writing was lazy, repetitive and very often included straight lifts from the newspapers of the time. He guessed that in her day she might well have been a force to be reckoned with, but now she was little more than a tired old hack whom Frank Hastings had taken on because her fading glory made her malleable. She was a large woman, probably in her early fifties, though the thick powder on her cheeks, black-pencilled lines round her eyes and syrupy coating of tangerine lipstick gave her the look of a gruesome thirty-year-old caught up in a sixties time-warp.

Matthew turned back to Frank. 'Of course,' he continued, 'plenty of films have been shot this way before – I mean, without the script being complete – but what I want you to realise is that there could be developments in Italy that might entail a re-shoot in Manhattan.'

'How do you mean?' Grace asked.

'I don't know until Deborah has written the Italian scenes, but what I'm thinking is that if she fictionalises something to take place in Florence, or the Tuscan village, that should have its roots in Manhattan, we might not know in time.'

'Know what?' Deborah asked sourly.

'What you're going to write,' Stephanie explained patiently.

'Well, how can I know until we've spoken to Bronwen?'

'You can't. But what Matthew and I are trying to point out is that scenes can't be scheduled until you have written them. Now, what we have for Bennington stands, so do most of the New York scenes – those we can schedule; but if we're shooting in Manhattan while you're writing the Italian scenes, and you come up with something that affects New York, we won't be able to put it into the schedule.'

'Why?'

'Because once the schedule has been drawn up, actors will be contracted according to that schedule, as will locations, camera equipment, special effects – the list is endless. Therefore we won't be able to change it without incurring enormous costs. So unless you can come up with a working script for Italy within the next three to four weeks . . .'

'That's impossible,' Deborah interjected heatedly.

'Precisely.' Stephanie turned to Frank. 'The bottom line is that there should be something in the budget to facilitate a return to New York, should it be necessary. If there is, then Matthew and I are right with you on pulling the film forward.'

Frank chuckled. 'Thank you, Stephanie.' He looked at Grace, and though neither of them spoke, both Stephanie and Matthew could sense the almost tangible bond that held them in mental and physical togetherness. 'Yeah, sure, it figures.' Frank nodded, and pulled out his chair to sit down. 'When are you speaking to Bronwen?'

'Later, I hope,' Stephanie answered. 'I called her yesterday, but it must have been around ten o'clock at night in Florence and she wasn't very coherent – she seems to have got herself a bad case of heat-stroke. I did manage to get out of her that they'd interviewed Sergio Rambaldi yesterday afternoon, and got some pretty useful stuff, but apparently Marian has the details, and when I tried her room there was no answer.' She looked at her watch. 'I'll try again when this meeting's over, and naturally, if she's come up with some draft scenes – which, knowing Marian, she will have – I'll get her to call Deborah straightaway.'

Frank rested his chin on a bunched fist and again looked at his wife. She gave an almost imperceptible nod and he said: 'OK, I've got no objection to the cost in principle, but I'd like to take a look at the figures before I give the go-ahead.'

'Of course,' Stephanie answered, and unzipping her attaché case she took out the rough breakdown she and Bronwen had cobbled together since Frank had mooted the suggestion that the film be brought forward. She handed it to him, and watched as his keen eyes perused it, but they gave nothing away. In her lap her hands were clenching and unclenching; she knew that what it amounted to was little short of a further million dollars. She glanced at Matthew, but his mind didn't seem to be on what was happening in the room. He was sitting with an arm hooked over the back of his chair, his long legs stretched out in front of him, while he tapped a pen thoughtfully against his chin. But when he caught her eye he winked, and Stephanie pursed her lips as she realised that his nonchalant air was a deliberate ruse to tease her.

When Frank had finished he pushed the budget across the table to Grace.

'OK,' he said, 'if that's what it costs, then that's what it costs. But if I paid my boys even twice what you're paying yourself, Stephanie, they'd be out of here faster than you can say God Save the Queen. Now all I wanna know is when to free up the capital?'

Again Stephanie delved into her case, and this time she handed him a calendar breakdown of estimated financial commitments.

'Very impressive,' he said, as she passed it over. 'Shrewd anticipation breeds healthy results.'

Matthew grinned as Stephanie preened herself at the compliment, and noticing, she dealt him a swift kick on the shin.

'I'll have my accountants look this over,' Frank told her, then after exchanging yet another look with his wife, he said, 'I want you to talk with my lawyers about the film, Stephanie. You and Deborah. We don't want any libel suits, or anything that might cause embarrassment. I know you've heeded my request not to dig too deep on this, and I appreciate it. I also appreciate you not asking me to explain. Now, I've instructed the attorneys to be here at three thirty, so why don't we take a break until they arrive. Matthew, my wife would like to talk to you, in private, if you don't mind.'

'Not at all,' Matthew answered, unable to hide his surprise.

'Just a minute, before you go,' Deborah said stiffly. She looked at Frank. 'Rubin Meyer.'

Frank sighed. 'Yeah, sure.' And his lips tightened as Deborah Foreman folded her arms and sat back in her chair with a supercilious look on her face.

Frank turned to Stephanie. 'The scenes with Meyer, did Marian write them?'

'More or less,' Stephanie answered.

His eyes met Grace's. 'Yep, I thought so.'

'Why? Is there something wrong with them?' Stephanie asked, baffled.

'No, they're all great. The guy's as jittery as she's written him, and just like the script suggests, he's been feeding narcotics to art students in this town since the mid-seventies. Which reminds me,' he said, as he made a note on the pad in front of him, 'that's something else we'll have to bring up with the lawyers. I notice Marian's already changed Meyer's name, but it's not enough. We'll work on that. No, the real point is the final scene with Olivia and Meyer in New York. There are undertones of an ulterior motive for telling her to go to Italy. I want it changed.'

It was on the tip of Stephanie's tongue to ask why, but she knew that Frank's answer would be evasive.

'Deborah's already drafted an alternative scene,' he went on, 'which she'll show you. There's nothing portentous in it and that's the way I want it to be.'

Stephanie nodded. 'OK.'

Frank smiled. 'Now is there anything else before we break up?'

'Nightclubs,' Matthew said. 'We'll be engaging a location manager as soon as we get back to London, but my feeling is that he's going to have some trouble getting permission to film if we're going to say that drugs were taken in the club. Can you help?'

'Sure. I'll have my secretary get onto it right away. I guess there'll be no problem with Bennington?'

Matthew shook his head. 'Not according to Bronwen.'

'Good. And I've got a couple of downtown art galleries in mind that you might like to take a look at while you're in town.'

Matthew smiled, and it was clear to everyone in the room that the two men both liked and admired one another. 'Just lead me to 'em,' Matthew said, affecting Frank's New York accent.

Frank's amusement was evident as he said, 'I think you're gonna like 'em, Matthew.'

'So all we're needing now is a workable script for Italy.'
Matthew thought it odd that it was Deborah who had
reiterated the obvious, especially as she made it sound like
someone else's responsibility. Still, considering what she'd
been coming up with, it probably was.

'Shame Marian didn't come over with you,' Frank said,
as he capped his pen and poked it into his inside pocket.
'Grace and I would like to meet her. Sounds like a bright
kid, judging by her latest ideas.'

'She is,' Matthew answered, wondering if the snub to
Deborah was deliberate.

'Now, you all coming out to the house for dinner
tonight?' Frank said, getting to his feet. 'I'll have my
chauffeur pick you up at your hotel around seven, that do
you?'

They all stood up, and catching Stephanie's eye, Grace
smiled. 'When it comes to mundane matters like eating,
you can always rely on a man to overlook what's important,' she said. 'Is anyone a vegetarian?'

Stephanie laughed. 'No vegetarians.'

'Except me,' Deborah added.

'And there was I thinking she was a cannibal,' Matthew
breathed in Stephanie's ear – and from the smile that
flitted across her face, it was evident that Grace had heard
too.

'See you tonight, then, Matthew,' Frank said, walking
Stephanie and Deborah to the door.

'Looking forward to it,' Matthew responded. 'It'll give
me a chance to do a recce on the place.'

He was still smiling as he turned back to Grace, and she
waved a hand for him to sit down again. She was a woman
whose manner held all the poise and serenity her name
suggested, and when Matthew was first introduced to her
he had been hard put to it to hide his surprise. Though
her hair – which she wore in a knot at the back of her neck
– was greying, and fine lines fanned the corners of her blue

eyes, her delicate face was an uncanny replica of Olivia's, though of course older – and devoid of malevolence. He'd watched her over the past two hours, how she held her position at Frank's side with sensitivity and subtlety, and he knew intuitively that although it was unlikely that she was responsible for Frank's success, she was almost certainly at the core of his strength. Not, he imagined, because she was in any way manipulative or cunning – she probably knew little about the day to day running of the Hastings' empire – but because she truly loved her husband and he her.

Grace waited for him to sit down, then folded her hands on the table in front of her, and as she spoke her blue eyes were watching him carefully. 'I want to talk to you, Matthew , to ask you if you've ever heard of a man by the name of Art Douglas?'

Matthew frowned as he searched his memory. 'I don't think so. Who is he?'

'He's a reporter, here in New York. *Used* to be a reporter, would be more correct.'

'Should I know him?'

'No, but now I know you don't, it makes this conversation all the more necessary.'

Mystified, Matthew waited for her to continue.

'Art Douglas knows what happened to Olivia before she went missing.' Grace paused, and her eyes dropped to her hands. 'You have heard about the newspaper editor who died in a car smash?'

'Yes.'

'Art Douglas believes that it wasn't an accident' – and as she lifted her head she looked straight into his eyes. 'He believes that certain people here in Manhattan killed his editor.'

Though she hadn't emphasised any of her words, hadn't altered the tone of her voice nor changed her expression, there was suddenly an air in the room that

– 373 –

Matthew found unsettling. He held her gaze, but when she didn't continue he ventured, 'Something to do with Olivia?'

Grace nodded. 'Eddie Kalinowski – the editor – knew things about the people Olivia was involved with. He told Art, and consequently Art considers his own life to be in danger. After the car smash he went into hiding – went to ground, as they call it. Frank has regular contact with him, but respects Art's wish to remain hidden; after all, if Art is right about the accident, he has cause to think his life is in jeopardy. I'm telling you this, because that's what it could mean to know what Olivia was mixed up in. So if you don't wish to know, please say so now.' Her expression was deadly serious and Matthew felt a cold chill run down his spine.

'Is there a reason why I should know?' he asked.

She nodded. 'You should know because Marian knows.'

Matthew couldn't have looked more shocked if she'd hit him.

'Marian knows,' he breathed. 'How?'

'Art Douglas told her.'

'He what? When?' He dashed his fingers through his hair, then suddenly leapt to his feet and started to pace the room.

'If you just hang on, I'll tell you. As far as Art is aware, he and Frank don't agree on what might have happened to Olivia. Art believes that Olivia is in Italy, and that there was a conspiracy between Rubin Meyer and Sergio Rambaldi to keep her there.' She paused. 'In fact, that's exactly what Frank thinks too, and that is why he doesn't want that scene in the film, because if Rubin Meyer does know where Olivia is, he's the last person Frank wants to upset. The reason Frank hasn't confided his suspicions to Art is because he's afraid Art might do something stupid, like confront Meyer.'

'But why did Douglas tell Marian? Jesus Christ, Marian of all people. She's only a kid.'

'He told her because she'd been to see Jodi Rosenberg, an old friend of Olivia's, and Jodi and Art are both of the opinion that Frank should be persuaded into accusing Meyer through the movie. As Marian had expressed more interest in the cover-up than anyone else, Jodi and Art assumed her to be the person to tell, in the hope that she would join them in persuading Frank.'

'How do you know all this?'

'Because Art's conscience was troubling him after he told Marian, so he confessed to Frank what he had done – for Marian's protection.' She pronounced the last three words with ominous deliberation. 'If she were to let something slip to the wrong person, then . . . Well, who knows what might happen to her.'

'Oh God,' Matthew groaned. 'Why hasn't she told anyone about this?'

'Both Art and Jodi swore her to secrecy. The only person she was to speak to was Frank. It is a dangerous thing to know, but . . .'

'But what about Jodi? If she knows, why isn't she in hiding?'

'She employs a team of bodyguards to watch over her twenty-four hours a day. Art doesn't have that kind of money.'

Matthew slumped back in his chair and dropped his head in his hands. 'Neither does Marian.'

'Which is why I'm telling you.'

He nodded. 'Shit!' he muttered, as he remembered the scene he'd had with Marian after she'd been to see Jodi. He looked at Grace. 'She did it for me, you know.' And when Grace looked perplexed, he waved a hand dismissively. 'She had some notion in her head that I thought she didn't count for anything, so she went to see Jodi in the hope of getting to the bottom of things, to try and make me change my mind about her.'

'I see.' Grace smiled inwardly as she realised that she probably understood a great deal more from that than he did. 'Well, now it's only for me to tell you what Olivia was doing. Of course, you don't have to know . . .'

'No, no, I do,' he interrupted. 'She can't carry this on her own.'

'Sure, but it could put you in a position of . . .'

'Don't let's worry about that.'

'OK. But obviously, once I've told you it should go no further. It can't possibly go into the movie, and we don't want to put anyone else at risk.'

'Of course not.'

'I don't even know if Marian is at risk, but there's no point in taking chances.'

He nodded, then he noticed that her expression was changing, and as he listened in growing horror and disgust to what she was telling him, a look of such suffering came over her face that he told her to stop. But she shook her head and went on, pouring out the loathsome exploits of the paedophile club and her daughter's part in it, as if she were going through some kind of ritualistic exorcism. Images of his own children at that age sprang to Matthew's mind, and he clenched his teeth against the revulsion and violence he felt not only towards the men who were committing the rapes, but towards Olivia Hastings too. He knew that even if he lived to be a hundred, he would never understand why a girl with parents like Frank and Grace, a girl who had the world at her feet, had ever needed to take the drugs that drove her to commit such atrocities.

By the time she finished, Grace's face was ashen and her eyes were filled with tears. 'Frank does everything he can to help the families of the children who died,' she said, 'anonymously, of course. And he's set up a charity for abused children, to make sure that the victims who have been maimed by what happened are helped. But I don't think he'll ever forgive himself. He believes that if he hadn't frozen Olivia's money at the bank, she'd never have got into it. But it was my idea to do that, to try and stop her taking the drugs, so if anyone's to blame it's me.'

As Matthew looked at her he felt such overriding compassion that he had to swallow hard on the lump in his throat. What could this woman ever have done to deserve such torment? 'The sins of the children,' he whispered, and Grace's answering smile was so tragic it tore right through his heart.

'Our concern now is for Marian,' she said, 'which is why Frank asked me to tell you.'

'Yes, of course.'

'What will you do?'

'I don't know yet, but one thing's certain – she won't be able to come filming with us in New York. But how am I going to explain that to Stephanie?'

'I think you should bring her,' Grace told him. 'She will be safer here, with you and Frank's people watching over her, than she would in London, alone. The same goes for Italy. Keep her with you, make sure she's surrounded by people the whole time. We could be over-reacting, but we can't take the risk. Of course, no one but Frank, Art Douglas, Jodi and ourselves, knows that she has any idea what went on ... What's the matter? Did I say something ...'

Matthew was shaking his head, and a look of foreboding had come over his face. 'She's in Italy now,' he said. 'She saw Rambaldi yesterday, and she wasn't in her room when Stephanie called last night. If she's let something slip to him ...' He leapt to his feet. 'Can I use the phone?'

'Of course.' Grace too was on her feet. 'Use the grey one, it's a direct line.'

Matthew snatched up the receiver, then remembering

he didn't have the number of the *pensione* where Bronwen and Marian were staying, he slammed it down again. 'I'll have to get the number from Stephanie.'

Grace immediately picked up another phone and pressed a button. 'Is Frank still with the attorneys, Lydia?' she enquired, and when she had got the answer she rang off. 'Stephanie left ten minutes ago, to go back to the hotel.'

Matthew looked at his watch. 'She won't be there yet. Look, I think I'd better jump in a cab and get back there myself. Maybe Marian's left a message.'

'Sure. I'll call the front desk and have them hail you one while you're on your way down.'

After he'd told the driver his destination Matthew sank back in the seat, trying to think himself into a state of calm as the traffic thickened round them, making the journey agonizingly slow. 'Marian, Marian,' he muttered, gazing blindly out at the heat-soaked streets, 'why did you do it?' But he knew the answer, and his eyes closed as a dreadful premonition swelled through his gut.

After their meeting with Sergio Rambaldi two days ago, Marian had finally managed to get Bronwen back to the *pensione* where they were staying, near the Pitti Palace, and had put her to bed. Afterwards she had carried her typewriter up to the roof garden to work in the fresh air, careful to position herself in a sheltered corner under the shade of a rose-covered pergola. She had spent the first hour gazing out over the crazy pattern of Florentine rooftops, watching the lizards as they scuttled in and out of the warped sienna tiles, and letting her eyes wander from Brunelleschi's splendid dome to the long, thin towers of the Bargello and Signoria, then on to the slumbering mountains far in the distance. All the while she was mulling over in her mind exactly how she was going to commit the afternoon's findings to paper, but for a long time not even so much as a sentence would fuse itself together.

Her stumbling block had nothing to do with what Sergio Rambaldi had said – that she had quite clearly in her mind. What was causing her the problem was Sergio Rambaldi himself. How was she even going to begin to describe a man like that when he had such magnetism, such presence, such . . .? Again the words escaped her, but if she didn't get it right, how on earth was Matthew ever going to cast someone who could even remotely match up to him? But did such a man exist? She strongly doubted that there could be two men in the world like Sergio Rambaldi; but then, for no apparent reason, Paul drifted into her mind. Yes, in some ways they were similar, she decided, but Paul was blond, and not only that, he wasn't an actor, so that was of no use at all.

Finally, as a welcome breeze drifted across the garden, she turned to her typewriter, and once she began to type she found the words flowing from her fingertips, and became so immersed in what she was doing that daylight faded into dusk, residents wandered up for pre-dinner drinks and a waiter placed a lamp on the table beside her – but she didn't notice a thing. It was past midnight by the time she packed up and went downstairs to her room. She dropped off her typewriter, then looked in to check on Bronwen before she attempted to persuade a sandwich out of the kitchen – if indeed there was anyone still there at this hour.

'Did you speak to Stephanie?' Bronwen asked when she saw Marian's straw hat peeping round the door.

'No,' Marian answered, coming further into the moonlit room. 'I've been up on the roof. How are you feeling?'

'To tell you the truth, *cariad*, I wouldn't mind too much if I died right now. Are you OK?'

'Yes, I'm fine. Look, why don't you let me get you a doctor?'

'No, no. There's nothing he can do, I've had this before. But there is something you can do.'

'What's that?' Marian asked, perching on the edge of the bed.

'First of all, you can close my window, I don't think I can stand the noise any longer. What are they all doing out there at this time of night, it sounds like Piccadilly Circus in the rush hour. Anyway, tomorrow, if I'm not any better, I'd like you to walk round Florence and photograph anything and everything for Matthew. Oh yes, and those records Sergio talked about, maybe you'd . . .' Her voice was fading, and from the look on her face Marian could see that the effort was too much for her.

'I've got a better idea,' Marian said, walking over to the window. 'Why don't you go back to sleep now, and if you're feeling up to it in the morning, I think we should go out to the mountains and carry on our research there. It'll be cooler, and a lot quieter, and we can always come back to Florence when you're feeling more like yourself.'

'Did I ever tell you you were brilliant?' Bronwen whispered. 'Mountain air, it sounds like heaven.'

So the following morning Marian organised a taxi to pick them up and drive them the eighty or so kilometres to Paesetto di Pittore. As it was then the middle of the night in New York, and as neither of them knew where – if anywhere – they would find to stay in Pittore, Marian hadn't called Stephanie back.

As they sped along the main autostrada towards Lucca, Bronwen sat hunched in a corner of the back seat, shivering, perspiring, and cursing the sudden change in the weather. They had woken that morning to a grey, overcast day that had quickly produced a series of thunderstorms.

'What's the matter with this country?' Bronwen grumbled. 'First of all it frazzles me to a chip, then the next thing I know it's pissing all over me. I want to go home.'

Knowing that she probably didn't mean it, Marian smiled and turned to watch the passing scenery, trying to imagine what the undulating hills, olive groves and vineyards would look like on a bright day.

The steady beat of the rain and the monotonous rhythm of the car engine eventually lulled both her and Bronwen to sleep, and by the time Marian woke they were approaching the outskirts of Lucca. Realising that if this weather kept up they were going to need protective clothing, Marian instructed the driver to turn into the town so that she could buy wellington boots and umbrellas. As the car stopped in the Piazza Napoleone, Bronwen stirred. Quickly Marian told her what she was doing and Bronwen somehow summoned the energy to tease her for her indomitable common sense.

'You go to Pittore, *sì*?' the driver asked, as they drove out of Lucca and rejoined the autostrada.

'*Sì*,' Marian answered, running the full extent of her Italian.

The driver nodded, and it seemed only minutes later that he turned the car sharply off the road, and with much grinding of gears and roaring of the accelerator they started to climb a steep, forbiddingly narrow hill. Marian wished he would slow down a little; the rain was sweeping down in torrents, making it difficult to see, and the hairpin bends they seemed to fly past had nothing round them to prevent the car skidding over the edge and plunging into the vineyards below.

'Pittore, *sì*?' the driver said again.

'*Sì*,' Marian confirmed.

'You know Pittore?'

'No.' Marian looked at Bronwen, but she was asleep.

'You rest there? Tonight?'

'If we get there,' Marian gasped, as he took his hands off the wheel and made one of those gestures peculiar to the Italians. 'Do you know if there is a hotel there?' She spoke precisely and loudly so that he could understand.

'*Sì, sì*. There is *piccolo albergo*. In the café.'

'Oh, well, that's a relief,' Marian said, assuming *albergo* meant 'inn'.

'You no want to stay at the *albergo*,' he said a few minutes later.

Thinking it was a question, Marian said, 'Yes, we do want to stay there. If there is room.'

'No. You no stay at *albergo*. You stay in Camaiore,' he waved an arm, 'the town, over there.'

'Why?' Marian said, confused.

'Because Pittore is no good in the night.'

'I'm sorry?'

'In the night there are, how you say, the screams. You hear her scream.'

'Who?'

'The girl.'

'What girl?'

'The American girl. In the night, she scream.'

Marian's mouth was open and she stared at the driver in the mirror. 'You mean, she is there, in Pittore?'

'*Sì*. She is there. She scream in the night.'

'But if she's there, if you can hear her screaming, why doesn't somebody help her?'

He answered in Italian; then in English he added, 'Maybe she is dead.'

'But if you can hear her screaming . . .'

'It is the ghost, no?'

'Oh my God,' Marian muttered as an icy chill slithered down her spine. Then she remembered how the Italians loved to dramatise, and decided that the story had very probably been invented by superstitious and over-imaginative tourists who had been to the village since Olivia disappeared.

'You like me take you to Camaiore?' the driver offered.

'No, no. Paesetto di Pittore, please,' Marian told him – then only just managed to swallow a scream herself as the car swerved dangerously to avoid a motor-cyclist coming in the opposite direction. Bronwen woke up then, and Marian recounted what the driver had just told her.

'Well, I hope he *is* making it up, *cariad*,' Bronwen said, looking gloomily out of the window, "cos this place looks spooky enough without screaming in the night. Just look at those clouds coming in over the mountains. Do you think that's Pittore over there, in amongst the trees?'

'*Sì*, Pittore,' the driver confirmed.

'Thank God, because if I don't get to a loo pretty soon there's going to be a dreadful accident.'

A few minutes later they drove into the village. It was bigger than Marian had imagined it would be, but nevertheless there were probably no more than thirty cottages scattered over the hillside – most of them nestling amongst the trees on either side of the narrow main street. She frowned, thinking that there was something odd about the place, and then she realised what it was. There wasn't a soul in sight. And as they inched their way along the cobbled road she gazed at the closed shutters with a feeling that the entire population was watching them from between the slats. Quickly she pulled herself together, and when the car came to a halt beside the deserted café, which was at the far end of the street, she opened the door and got out. 'I'll just run in and check they've got rooms,' she said to Bronwen. 'Wait here. I won't be long.'

She ran up to the door of the café, shielding herself from the rain with her new umbrella, but the door was locked. She turned back to the car, throwing out her hands as if to say, No good, but she saw that Bronwen was pointing towards the side of the café. Quickly she ran round the corner and onto a wide terrace that jutted out over the mountain, and there she found another door which, thankfully, was open.

Inside, at the opposite end of the café's sparsely furnished main room, an old woman was sitting beside a great stone fireplace, a string of rosary beads in her lap and a black woollen shawl round her shoulders. Hearing the door open, she looked up, and when she saw Marian, her crinkled, nut-brown face broke into a smile of welcome.

'*Buon giorno, signora,*' she rasped, heaving herself to her feet. '*Desidera bere qualche cosa?*'

Laughing, Marian waved her hands and shook her head. 'I'm afraid I don't speak Italian,' she explained.

The woman stopped dead. 'You are American?' And Marian very nearly took a step back at the venom in her voice.

'No, no, English,' Marian told her.

'Ah, *sì*, Eengleesh.' The old woman relaxed and was smiling again as she said, 'You like coffee?'

'Actually, I was hoping you might have some vacancies. Some rooms. In the hotel – *albergo.*'

'*Sì*, I have room. How many?'

'Two. Two rooms, that is.'

The woman nodded. 'How long you stay?'

Marian shrugged. 'Four days perhaps.'

'Four days, this is good. My name is Signora Giacomi. I call my husband, he help carry the *bagagli.*'

Marian thanked her and went back to the car. 'We're in,' she told Bronwen, and dug into her purse to pay the driver several hundred thousand lire. As he drove away he muttered something under his breath, and though Marian didn't catch what it was, she guessed he was put out because he hadn't succeeded in frightening her.

Signora Giacomi took one look at Bronwen and marched her straight across the café and up the stairs to an oppressively beamed garret at the back of the house. It smelt of mothballs, but everything was scrupulously clean, and there was even a jar of wild flowers on the small table beside the bed. 'You are sick, no? I take care, but first you rest,' she told Bronwen, then turning to Marian, 'You have the room the other side.' Leading the way, she took Marian into the next door room which was a mirror image of Bronwen's.

'Thank you,' Marian said, smiling at the old woman and liking her instinctively.

'You come to have meal with my family in one hour, *sì*? We have the tripe, a good dish here, but not in your country I think.'

Marian laughed. 'No, not in my country. But I've never had it, so yes, I'll join you. Thank you. I'm not sure about Bronwen, though.'

'I make something special for your friend, make her well soon, and I have the cream to soothe the skin,' and chuckling happily, she went out of the room.

Marian flopped down on the bed, and lay quietly listening to the rain outside. The wind seemed to have picked up too, but she guessed that was because they were so high up. She must have dozed off then, because the next thing she knew there was a tap on her door and Signora Giacomi was calling out that her meal was ready.

When she got downstairs she was surprised to see Bronwen. She was huddled into a blanket by a fire that hadn't been lit when they first arrived, and sipping from a bowl of hot soup.

'How are you feeling?' Marian asked.

'Better now we're out of Florence. You should taste some of this, Marian, I don't know what it is, but it's delicious.'

'This is only for the sick one,' Signora Giacomi informed them as she bustled into the room, carrying a tray of piping hot tripe. 'Here is for you,' she told Marian, and as she set the tray down on the table her husband came in, followed by a young man with a thin, dour face, dressed in shabby clothes as though he had just come in from the vineyards, and a woman who looked rather smarter.

Signora Giacomi introduced them as her son and daughter-in-law who lived in the village.

The meal passed pleasantly, the tripe was delicious, Marian told the Signora – and she meant it. From her place in the corner Bronwen joined in the conversation – much to Marian's relief, for Bronwen's Italian was good and, apart from the old woman, none of the Giacomi family spoke English. It was odd, Marian thought, that neither she nor Bronwen mentioned Olivia, especially since there had been no pre-arranged pact not to do so, but she told herself that it was a sensitive subject and not one to be broached so soon after their arrival.

When lunch was over, Bronwen returned to her room and Marian went off in search of a phone, but all she could find was a battered old contraption in a booth that opened off the café. She sighed wearily; it looked as though it hadn't been used since the war. Signora Giacomi saw her looking and laughed. 'You like to make telephone call?' she said.

Knowing she was about to ask the impossible, Marian made a grimace of apology. 'I need to call America,' she said, and immediately wished she hadn't because the Signora's face became suddenly hostile.

'America?' she repeated. 'But you say you are Eengleesh.'

'Yes, I am,' Marian assured her, 'but . . .' She searched her mind for ways to explain, but they all seemed hopelessly complicated. In the end she said that her sister was in New York on business and that she had promised to call to let her know when she was returning to England.

Apparently satisfied with the explanation, Signora Giacomi resumed her cheerful manner, and with a beckoning finger told Marian to follow.

She took Marian into a cosy sitting-room at the rear of the café which Marian assumed to be the family's private quarters. 'You like to make call in your room?' the old woman offered.

'Yes, if I can,' Marian answered doubtfully, and then she watched in amazement as the Signora unplugged a modern telephone, carried it upstairs and plugged it into a socket beneath Marian's window.

Marian laughed at her own stupidity. The village might be ancient, the couple old, but nevertheless both *were* approaching the end of the nineteen eighties along with the rest of the world, so why shouldn't they have modern technology? It was just that it seemed so out of place here.

After the Signora had gone she sat in the window seat, curling her legs under her, and picked up the receiver – Stephanie and Matthew were probably just getting up, so she should catch them now. After she had dialled the number she rubbed a circle into the steamy window and gazed out at the mountains, not for a moment expecting to make the connection. There was little to see; thick clouds were now swirling about the village and floating in wisps through the dense foliage that lined the steeply sloping banks of the valley. The village seemed to be even higher up than she had realised, which would account for the sudden drop in temperature. Then, to her astonishment, a voice came over the line announcing the Dorset Hotel. Impressed and amused, Marian gave the number of Stephanie's room, but the phone rang and rang until the operator intercepted and asked if she could take a message. Marian read out the number on the dial, then spelt Paesetto di Pittore, and hung up, wondering if it would be as easy to call into the village as it was to call out. Well, it doesn't really matter, she told herself, I can always ring them again later. Then she dashed the tears angrily from her eyes, wondering what in heaven's name she was crying about – yet knowing the answer, too.

She rested her head on the hard stone wall behind her

and closed her eyes. 'I just wanted to hear his voice,' she whispered aloud.

'Whose voice, *cariad*?'

As she jumped, the phone fell from her lap and clattered to the floor.

'Oh, no one's,' she answered quickly, stooping to retrieve the phone. 'I was just . . . I was just . . .' She couldn't think of anything to say and knew she was in grave danger of bursting into tears.

'It's OK, I understand,' Bronwen smiled. 'Like I told you before, it sometimes takes a long time to get over a broken heart, and being in a place like this makes you just *yearn* for the one you love, doesn't it?'

'Yes,' Marian said, on a laugh. Obviously Bronwen thought she'd been talking about Paul. 'Anyway, what are you doing out of bed?'

'I just came in to see if you'd managed to speak to Stephanie or Matthew yet?'

'No, not yet. But I'll keep trying.'

'Good girl.' She sat down on Marian's bed and wrapped her arms round one of the corner-posts. 'Have you mentioned anything to the Giacomis about Olivia yet?' she asked.

Marian shook her head. 'No. To be honest, I don't think it would be a good idea.'

'That's what my instincts are saying.'

'I made the mistake of mentioning America just now, and the old woman looked at me as if I were the devil incarnate.'

'Did she? Well, I suppose they must be pretty fed up with people coming round asking questions about Olivia, it must have been going on for years.'

They both thought about that for a while, then Bronwen said, 'What are you going to do for the rest of the day?'

Marian turned to look out of the window again. 'Not a lot I can do, really, with the weather like this. I've typed up everything from yesterday, I suppose I could go over it again, but I'm still reading the last book in Dorothy Dunnett's *Lymond* saga, so I might as well curl up with that.'

'Lucky you,' Bronwen said, as she got to her feet. 'Francis Crawford did things to me no other character in literature ever has. Just wait until you get to the end.' She sighed rapturously. 'I think I might read it again one of these days.'

Laughing, Marian said, 'He reminds me of Matthew in a way.'

'Does he?' Bronwen said, turning round in surprise. 'What, you mean invincible, like?'

'Yes, I suppose so.'

'Well, if Matthew Cornwall is anything like Francis Crawford, all I can say is, our Stephanie is one lucky woman.' Chuckling quietly, she picked up a sheaf of notes from the chest by the door. 'This yesterday's stuff?'

'Yes.'

'Can I take it, give it a read-over?'

'Of course,' Marian answered, surprised, though pleased that she had asked. That was the best part of working for Stephanie and Bronwen, neither of them treated her as though she was a secretary. If anything, they treated her as an equal; both encouraged her to become as involved as they were in the film, and listened to her ideas with the kind of appreciation that made her want to do all the more. Which was why, during the lonely evenings in Chelsea, she had spent her time watching films on the video to get an idea of how they were made. She had watched everything Matthew had done, so many times that she now recognised his style and understood why he was so successful. So it was for him that she was throwing her heart so profoundly into the research, as well as for Stephanie and Bronwen; she wanted him to respect her – which was, she knew, the most she could ever hope for from him. . .

It was well past midnight when she suddenly sat bolt upright in her bed. Sweat was pouring from her skin, and her heart was booming violently against her ribs. She could see nothing, all around her was total blackness, and in a panic she groped for the lamp. But the light that flooded the room did nothing to quell the furore of pounding blood that charged through her veins. The screams. She had heard them, whining, echoing, shrilling through the hills. As if paralysed, she sat listening to the wind outside, to the rain against the windows, straining her ears . . . And then it was there, piercing through the night, a blood-curdling, panic-stricken cry that seemed to surge out of the mountains, tear through the sky, then coil round the house like a lashing whip.

She shot from the bed and ran out to the landing. Everything was in darkness, the whole house was still. She looked at Bronwen's door, and seeing that it was ajar she pushed it open. The bed was empty.

'Oh no,' she sobbed, and in that moment she knew the true meaning of terror.

Then, hearing voices below, she swung round. She listened, trying to make out what they were saying, but she could only hear the muted tones of Signor Giacomi. A door opened, and instinctively she shrank back into the shadows. But then, as she heard Bronwen's voice saying 'Grazie, grazie', she rushed to the top of the stairs.

'Bronwen!' she cried.

'Marian?' Bronwen looked up. 'What are you doing out of bed, cariad? It's almost two in the morning.' As she came further up the stairs, her face creased with concern. 'Are you all right? You look as though you've seen a ghost.'

'I have,' Marian gasped. 'At least, I heard one.'

'What?' Turning back to Signor Giacomi, who was

staring up at Marian with wide, curious eyes, she gabbled something in Italian, then ran the rest of the way up the stairs. 'Come into my room,' she said, and taking Marian's arm she ushered her over to the bed and sat her down. 'Here, have a sip of this, I don't know what it is but Mr Giacomi swears by it.'

'No, no,' Marian said, pushing it away. 'Oh God, Bronwen, it was awful.'

'What was?'

'The scream. I heard it, just now. Didn't you?'

Bronwen shook her head. 'No, I didn't hear anything except the wind.'

'But you must have heard it, it was terrible.'

'No, I'm sorry, *cariad*, but . . .' She laughed. 'It's that blasted taxi driver, putting the spooks up you. You had a nightmare, that was all. Honestly, you frightened me for a minute out there, I thought the place was haunted.'

'It is,' Marian insisted. 'Either that, or Olivia really is out there, screaming.'

'No, no,' Bronwen soothed. 'You had a nightmare. It's not surprising on a night like this. I had a bit of one myself, that's why I went downstairs to get a drink. Here, have some.'

This time Marian took the mug, and as she sipped the warm spicy brew she felt herself beginning to relax. 'A nightmare,' she grinned sheepishly. 'But, oh Bronwen, it sounded so real.'

'They usually do,' Bronwen told her, taking the mug back. 'Now, this might seem a bit unorthodox, and heaven knows what the Giacomis will think, but would you like to sleep in here with me for the rest of the night?'

'I wouldn't mind,' Marian confessed.

'Neither would I, so come on, in you jump.' And she pulled back the sheets for Marian to get in.

The next morning Marian felt extremely foolish when she woke to find herself in Bronwen's bed and remembered how she'd come to be there, and she silently cursed the taxi driver for planting the screams in her mind.

'Signor Giacomi has offered to drive me into Camaiore this morning,' Bronwen informed her over breakfast. 'I'll see if I can pick up a hire car there, it's a bit isolated out here so I think we need one. Besides, I think we'd better start looking round for an alternative village to shoot in, I can't see them letting us film here, somehow, can you?'

Marian shook her head.

'And just to cap it all, it's suddenly the time of the month for me, so I'll have to find a chemist and apparently there's not one here in the village. I wonder how on earth they manage. Do you want to come with me?'

'I'll go for you,' Marian answered. 'I mean, do you think you should be up and about? It's still raining out there. And I can drive, though I haven't done for ages, but the roads aren't too busy. Besides, the general rule here seems to be, put your foot down and pretend you're the only one on the road. I think I could manage that.'

Bronwen laughed. 'The Italian highway code, now there's a mystery that makes even our own pale to insignificance. But a bit of rain won't hurt me, it's not as if I've had the flu. Mind you, it felt like it, and worse. No, I'll go myself, *cariad*. I can do a bit of asking around about you-know-who as well while I'm there.'

'OK,' Marian said, helping herself to more of the delicious hot chocolate Signora Giacomi had just put on the table. 'I think I'll take a walk round the village, see what I can come up with here – if anything.'

'Right you are, and if you hear any screams it'll be me, flying over the edge of the road.'

Two hours later Marian was wandering back through the main street of Paesetto di Pittore. Her wellington boots were covered in mud and grass from the mountain path she'd strolled along, and her flimsy jacket was buttoned and zipped to keep out the wet. It was mid-morning and the rain had just stopped, but from the look of the clouds it would be a brief interlude.

Again there were no signs of life, and as she looked around she wondered where everyone could be. No one had come to the café the night before, and apart from the Giacomi family she had seen no one. It was as if the village were uninhabited. But then a door opened further down the street, and a portly man waddled out and got into a battered old Fiat. Marian pressed herself against the high wall as he drove past, a ready smile on her face, but he didn't even glance in her direction. She shrugged. Probably hates tourists, she told herself.

A light drizzle started up again then, and she strolled on until she reached a gap in the wall where she turned in. It was an alternative route to the café that would lead her part way down the mountain, circle round, then up onto the terrace; so, taking care on the treacherous stone steps, she made her way down them, peeking surreptitiously into the windows of the cottages whose battered doors opened onto the steps. She was toying with the idea of knocking on one of them when suddenly she slipped and sat down hard on a jagged stone. Fortunately she managed to hang on to the wooden rail that lined the steep path, and this stopped her falling any further, but she was bruised and winded, so she gave herself a few moments to regain her breath. As she sat there, massaging the ankle that had twisted, she noticed that the clouds were once again thickening menacingly overhead, and then a low rumble reverberated through the eerie silence of the village. 'Where is everyone?' She said it aloud in the hope that her own voice would break the ungodly spell that seemed to have invaded the air. But her only answer was the wind, moaning through the trees. 'I don't like this place,' she murmured. 'Nightmare or no nightmare, it gives me the creeps.'

Then suddenly every nerve in her body spiked and her

blood turned as cold as the rain. Something had moved in the bushes, only feet away. She sat very still, listening, then her heartbeat jarred as she heard it again. She turned slowly, on the point of screaming – then, as a chicken broke free of the bramble, fluttering its wings and clucking irritably, she all but choked on her relief. Then pulling herself up she limped on down the steps.

Fat drops of rain dripped from the bamboo canopy over the café's terrace. The tables looked strangely as though they had been recently abandoned, but she knew no one had been there. She walked over to the door, but when she turned the handle she found it was locked. She was about to knock when she heard voices coming from inside. They were raised in anger, and she recognised them to be the voices of Signora Giacomi's son and daughter-in-law.

Naturally they spoke in Italian, so she couldn't understand what they were saying, but nevertheless she felt uneasy at eavesdropping, and was about to turn away when she heard one of them shriek Olivia's name. Instantly she was alert, and a sixth sense told her that the argument was not only to do with Olivia, but with her and Bronwen too. Even knowing that it was futile, she pressed her ear to a crack in the door, but several minutes went by during which neither of them said anything she understood. Then, suddenly, she knew that someone was standing behind her. Every muscle in her body tensed, froze, as an icy chill gripped her. She could hear the quiet breathing, so close it could be no more than a foot away. Slowly she started to turn, but before she had a chance to scream a hand closed over her mouth. She sprang back, hitting her head on the wall, and as she looked up at the face looming over her, her eyes dilated with terror and her knees buckled under her.

'I am sorry,' Sergio said, 'it was not my intention to frighten you.'

'No, no, I understand,' Marian mumbled.

They were sitting inside the café now, and Signora Giacomi was fussing around them with wine and *prosciutto*, and from the way she was behaving anyone would think she was in the presence of a deity.

Sergio smiled at her, said something in Italian, and she backed out of the room, bowing and muttering, '*Sì, signore. Sì, sì.*' Then turning back to Marian, he asked, 'Are you all right now?'

'I'm fine, thank you. You startled me, that was all.'

He laughed. 'More than the snake, you mean?'

Marian shuddered with revulsion as she remembered seeing the tail end of it slither into the undergrowth. 'I didn't even know it was there,' she said. 'Oh God, what if it had touched me?' She shuddered again.

'They are unpleasant creatures, no?' Sergio said, as he poured wine into two glasses. 'But there are a lot of them here in the mountains. They are mostly harmless, though.'

'I don't care,' Marian said, 'I hate them. I don't even like worms.'

'Worms? Ah, *il verme*.' He laughed.

Grudgingly, Marian smiled, then looking at him curiously, she picked up her wine. 'If it's not an impertinent question, what are you doing here?'

'I come to see you,' he answered. 'I have little to do at the Accademia today, so I call your hotel to see if you would like to look at the records. Then I find you have come to Pittore, so I think, maybe I can help some more, so I come here too.'

He was lying. She didn't know how she knew that, she just did. And he'd been lying when he said he didn't know the village well, for Signora Giacomi obviously knew exactly who he was. 'Help?' she said. 'You mean, you have more to tell us?'

'I can think of nothing specific, but if you would like to

tell me what you have discovered so far, maybe it will prompt my memory.'

'As a matter of fact, you're the only person we've spoken to about Olivia since we've been in Italy. We'll be going back to Florence in a few days, and hopefully talking to more people there, but as you are our only source of information so far . . .'

'I see.' He nodded thoughtfully, and helped himself to salami. 'And New York?' he said. 'You have completed your research there?'

'More or less,' she said, instinctively cautious.

Signor Giacomi came into the room then, but as he was behind her she was surprised when Sergio looked past her and spoke rapidly in Italian. *'Perchè non mi hà fatto sapere che aveva degli ospiti?'*

'Ho provato, signore, ma lei non ha mai risposto al telefono.'

'Gli altri ci sono?'

'Sì, signore, sono già nella bottega.'

Marian looked over her shoulder at Signor Giacomi and wondered what Sergio had just said to him to make him look so edgy.

'I am telling Signor Giacomi that I am disappointed for you that the weather is not good,' Sergio explained.

'Oh, I see.' Marian smiled and turned back to the old man, but he was no longer there.

'You were telling me about New York,' Sergio reminded her, and as his curious eyes seemed to melt into hers, Marian wrested herself from the gaze and looked down at her wine. 'The script is written for this part of their film already?' he prompted.

'Yes. We're just waiting for final approval from Mr Hastings.'

'This is very good, no? So soon you will begin to make the film?'

'Maybe. I'm not sure really.'

'Is something the matter? Are you unwell?'

'No, no,' Marian assured him. 'I think I'm still a bit shaken by what happened outside.'

'Ah. Again, I am sorry.'

The urge to look at him was almost overpowering, but she knew that she must avoid his eyes. There was something strange about them, hypnotic, and she was afraid that once they held her she would lose control of what she was saying. Then, to her overwhelming relief, the door opened and Bronwen came in.

'Ah, Signora Evans,' Sergio said, and smiling, he got to his feet.

'Signor Rambaldi?' Her astonishment was so obvious that it made Marian laugh.

'You are feeling a little better now?' he said. 'Come, sit down and drink some wine with us.'

As Bronwen sank into the chair he held out for her, she shot a look at Marian, but with Sergio standing over them there was nothing Marian could say.

Having heard the door open, Signora Giacomi came into the café and took another glass for Bronwen from a shelf behind the counter. By the time she went out again Bronwen had regained her composure. She said to Marian, 'I think I've found a village, just over the brow of the hill. We'll take a drive over there later.' Then turning to Sergio, her jolly expression was suddenly transformed into one of unmistakable lust and she proceeded to flirt outrageously.

Deciding that it would be politic to leave them to it, Marian excused herself, saying she wanted to ring her mother. Signora Giacomi gave her the telephone, which she carried up to her room to make the call in private.

'Mum, it's me, Marian,' she said when she heard her mother's gentle West Country tones at the other end of the line.

'Oh, Marian!' Celia cried, sounding surprised. 'I thought you were in Italy.'

'I am.'

'But you sound like you're in the next room. How are you, lovely?'

'I'm all right, Mum. The weather's not too good, though, but we'll battle on. I'm really calling to see how you got on with Madeleine. Did you write to her in the end?'

'Yes, I did. I sent it to that address what you gave me, the one for her agent, wasn't it?'

'That's right. Have you heard anything?'

'No.' And Celia's voice sounded so flat that Marian wished she was there to hug her.

'Never mind, Mum. I'm sure you will. Maybe she's out of the country and hasn't got it yet.'

'Yes, you might be right.'

There was a pause, and Marian said, 'Are you all right, Mum? There's nothing else, is there?'

'Well, yes, there is, I'm afraid. You see, Mrs Cooper came up the other day and she brought this saucy magazine with her, one of her husband's, she said it was, and there's these pictures of our Madeleine in it – well, Marian, I shouldn't like for you to see them, not really.'

'Oh Mum, I'm sorry. But Mrs Cooper shouldn't have shown you.'

'Yes she should. After all, our Madeleine is my responsibility and now I don't know what she's up to. There's her face always there on the telly, with the make-up and stuff, and she looks so beautiful I feels right proud of her, I do. But then when I saw those pictures . . .'

'Mum? Are you crying, Mum?'

'No, no.' But Marian knew she was, and suddenly her own eyes were full.

'Look, I shall be in Italy for another week or so, but I'll come down and see you as soon as I get back. Have you got something to take your mind off things in the meantime?'

''Course I have. I'm going down the Legion tonight

with Mr Butcher, you know, the man who comes round for the football pools. I still do them for you, Marian, so I might make you rich one day.'

Marian laughed, but because of the lump in her throat it sounded more like a sob. 'There's not a new romance blossoming, is there?' she teased.

'Oh no,' Celia cried. 'He just said he was a bit lonely like, now his wife's passed on, and did I fancy a drink down the Legion one night. So I said yes.'

'And why not!' Marian declared. 'No getting drunk, mind you?'

Celia chuckled. 'Drunk! Listen to you, our Marian. When have you ever seen me drunk?'

'There's always a first time. Anyway, I'd better ring off now, but try not to worry, Mum, and if anything happens, ring me. I'll give you the number here, and I'll call you again when I get back to Florence.'

'All right, then. I've got a pen here, so I'm ready.'

Marian gave her the number, then said, 'Bye now, and try not to worry too much about Madeleine, I'm sure she's all right really.'

'Yes, I 'spect so. Cheerio then, my lovely, enjoy yourself over there, and keep yourself warm.'

'I will,' Marian answered, and she rang off quickly before her mother could realise that she was crying. 'Oh Mum,' she sighed, as she wandered over to the bed, 'why does loving you so much make me want to cry?' And laughing at herself, she took a tissue from the box beside her bed and sat down to blow her nose.

For a while she toyed with the idea of rejoining Bronwen and Sergio, then decided that Bronwen might not appreciate an intrusion. But though Bronwen was undoubtedly enjoying Sergio's company, Marian realized that his unexpected appearance in the village was making her distinctly uneasy. His enquiries about New York had seemed innocuous enough, but she was half-afraid that his visit might have something to do with what she had said about Rubin Meyer. But that was nonsense, she'd hardly said anything – at least, nothing coherent enough to draw any conclusions from.

She leaned back against the pillows and stared blindly at the foot of the bed. Art Douglas, Rubin Meyer, Sergio Rambaldi, Olivia Hastings. What was it all really about? She knew about the children in New York, but something had happened after that, and now she was as convinced as Art Douglas that Sergio Rambaldi knew what it was. But how had she managed to become so deeply embroiled in it? Why did she feel that events were moving beyond her control? She wondered about Pittore, why there were so few people around, why Sergio had said he didn't know the village when she was certain he did. She wondered if she really had heard screams the night before, or if, as Bronwen said, they were part of a nightmare. She remembered then what her mother had said about Madeleine. 'Our Madeleine is my responsibility and now I don't know what she's up to.' What would Celia say if she knew what she, Marian, was involved in? She would worry herself to an early grave, was the answer – and the thought of her mother dying brought the tears back to her eyes. She was such a wonderful mother, so trusting, so innocent and so warm.

Suddenly the phone rang, and having forgotten it was there, Marian's heart nearly leapt from her body. 'God, I'm a bag of nerves since I've been here,' she mumbled to herself as she looked at it. Then remembering it was the only one in the house, she supposed she ought to answer it – though with no Italian she wasn't going to be of much use to anyone.

She got up from the bed to lift the receiver, then sat back in the window seat. 'Hello, Paesetto di Pittore *albergo*,' she announced, hoping that was the right thing to say.

'Marian? Is that you?'

'Matthew!' And again her heart lurched, but this time it was from pure joy. 'You got my message? What time is it there?'

'Ten in the morning. Look . . .'

'You must have been up early. I called . . .'

'We spent the night at the Hastings' house, Stephanie's gone off to another meeting with their lawyers and I've just got back. Now listen, Marian, I need to speak to you.'

'Yes,' she said. 'Do I need a pen and paper?'

'No, I just want you to listen. Are you alone at the moment, or is Bronwen with you?'

She swallowed, wondering what on earth he was going to say. 'Yes, I'm alone, Bronwen's . . .'

'Good. Marian, Grace has told me about Olivia – I mean, everything about Olivia – and she's also told me about Art Douglas.'

'Oh, I see,' Marian said, and her mind was suddenly spinning. 'I would have told you, Matthew . . . I wanted to . . . I just . . .'

'It doesn't matter, my darling, just as long as you're all right. When we couldn't get in touch with you I was afraid you might have said something to Rambaldi. You didn't, did you? Marian? Are you still there?'

'Yes, I'm here,' she breathed. 'I'm sorry. What did you say?'

'I said, did you say anything to Rambaldi about Rubin Meyer?'

'Well, yes, I did, but I made a bit of a hash of it and I don't think he took much notice. He's here at the moment, downstairs talking to Bronwen.'

'He's there, in Pittore? Why?'

'I'm not sure, really. He said he wanted to help with the research.'

'Did he?' There was a pause, but she knew he was still there because she could hear him breathing. Finally he said, 'Now look, I don't want to alarm you, Marian, we're none of us certain about anything as far as Meyer and Rambaldi are concerned, but I want you to make certain that wherever you go, Bronwen is with you. Have you got that?'

'Yes.'

'And if anything untoward happens you're to ring me straightaway. OK?'

'OK.'

'Now tell me what's been happening over there.'

In a state of utter jubilation, Marian told him all about Pittore, starting with the taxi driver who had brought them there, and going on to the screams in the night and how she had ended up sleeping with Bronwen, then to the chicken in the undergrowth, and Sergio, and the snake on the terrace – remembering to spice it all up with gruesome details of the weather. 'I promise you, Matthew, I don't think my heart can stand any more shocks,' she finished, but he was still laughing and she doubted if he'd heard.

'Sounds one hell of a place,' he said.

'Hell being the operative word. It's really creepy. I honestly won't be sorry to leave.'

'Well, we'll be back there for the film, but you'll have me to look after you then, so no more snakes or chickens. I'm not too sure about the screams in the night, though; with a film crew around there'll probably be plenty of them. You've gone quiet again, are you still there?'

'Yes, I'm here,' she answered, relieved that he couldn't see her face. 'I'm not sure we'll be able to shoot in this village; they seem to despise Americans.'

'Yes, that could be a problem. Is Bronwen working on it?'

'Yes, in fact she may already have found an alternative village. It's just round the brow of the mountain from here.'

'Good. When are you going back to Florence?'

'I'm not sure yet, maybe in a couple of days. Shall I call you before we go?'

'If you want to. Now don't worry about any of this, you'll be all right just as long as you remember not to mention Rubin Meyer. Come to that, tell Bronwen not to, either, and if she asks why, say it's an instruction from Frank.'

'OK.'

'Take care of yourself now, I want to see you back in London pretty soon, we'll get together then and talk.'

'OK. Matthew?' But the line had already gone dead, and she wasn't sure what she'd intended to say anyway.

She looked out of the window, and laughed as the sun suddenly broke through the clouds and perched haughtily on the mountains – it was as if it was trying to outshine her. But it would take more than the sun to out-dazzle the way she was feeling at that moment. He had called her 'darling', he had said he would be here to look after her. She had heard his voice, had listened to him breathing, and she'd made him laugh. You're as bad as Signora Giacomi, she told herself, behaving as though Matthew's some kind of god. Well, at the very least he was her protector, but the funny thing was, now she'd spoken to him she wasn't afraid any more.

Smiling, she got to her feet, then unplugged the telephone and carried it downstairs. She shouldn't be thinking this way, she knew she shouldn't, but his voice had sounded so intimate over the phone, as if he really cared about her, and impossible as it seemed, and disloyal to Stephanie as it was, she truly believed that maybe there was a chance he was beginning to feel something for her. Just to think of it sent a thrill shooting through her body – and in its wake a longing to feel his strength embrace her, not only mentally but physically.

With a beaming smile she handed Signora Giacomi the telephone, then wandered into the café to find Bronwen.

She was alone, studying a map spread out on the table in front of her.

'What with you and the sun, I think I'd better dig out my sunglasses,' she remarked when she saw Marian's face. 'I take it your mother's heard from Madeleine?'

'No,' Marian laughed. 'No, I was just talking to Matthew. Where's Sergio?'

'Had some business to do locally, he said, but he's offered to take us to dinner when we get back to Florence. By the way, very obliging of you going off like that, *cariad*, leaving me to do my worst.'

'Never let it be said that I don't know when I'm not wanted,' Marian said chirpily. 'And you a married woman. Whatever next?'

'I'll let you know,' Bronwen grinned. 'Now, what did Matthew say was happening in New York?'

'I don't believe it, Matthew,' Stephanie said as she walked ahead of him into their room at the Dorset Hotel. 'You say you spoke to Marian, but she didn't tell you what they managed to get from Rambaldi?'

'No.'

'But *why* didn't she?'

'I confess, I forgot to ask.' He closed the door, and when he turned back it was to find her standing beside the bed, staring at him with bewildered eyes. 'Then what *did* you talk about?' she asked.

He shrugged. 'Chickens, snakes, and things that go bump in the night.'

Irritation flashed through her eyes as he grinned. 'Oh, very amusing,' she said curtly.

'Yes, it was, actually.'

'Matthew! I'm trying very hard to remain patient here. Now what did Marian tell you about Rambaldi?'

'That he was downstairs talking to Bronwen.'

'And nothing about the afternoon they spent with him?'

'Nothing.'

She watched as he walked over to the phone and dialled the number for messages, then waited while he scribbled them down.

'There's one here for you,' he told her.

She ignored it. 'Matthew, what is going on? Only two days ago you couldn't wait to speak to Marian, and now you have, you tell me you talked about snakes and bumps and God knows what.' She peered at him suspiciously. 'Is there something you're not telling me?'

'I told you I loved you last night,' he teased.

She stamped her foot. 'Matthew! For heaven's sake, I'm the producer of this film, so stop playing games with me and treating me as if I'm still you're PA. And you haven't told me yet what Grace Hastings wanted to talk to you about, either.'

He strolled over to an armchair and sat down. 'Olivia, what else?' he said.

'I don't know what else. You tell me.'

'Characterisation.'

'Is that it? Characterisation?'

He shrugged. 'I'll go into more detail if you like, but right now I think you should return that call. It was Eleanora Braey's agent, and after all, as the producer of this film you should be pandering to our star.'

'Don't mock me, Matthew,' she snapped, but realising she was getting nowhere, she stalked across the room and snatched up the phone.

Making himself comfortable, Matthew picked up the remote control and started to flick through the profusion of TV channels. He wasn't particularly happy about having to lie to Stephanie, but he couldn't tell her the truth, so evasion, he'd decided, was the only route open to him. But it had been damned stupid of him, forgetting to ask Marian what she'd got out of Rambaldi, and he couldn't think now why he hadn't. But he hadn't, and as they'd find out what Rambaldi had said soon enough, there was no point in dwelling on it.

He was just getting involved in Oprah Winfrey's 'Good News' show and chuckling as some man turned down his girlfriend's proposal of marriage in front of twenty million viewers, when Stephanie cried: 'But the contract's ready for her to sign! We start shooting in September. No, I know you didn't know that, but we had an option, right? For Christ's sake, she's playing the part of Olivia, we can't re-cast just like that.' There was a long pause, then Stephanie said: 'I see. Well, of course I'm very happy for her' – which, it was clear from her tone, she wasn't. 'OK. Yes, thank you, goodbye.'

She slammed down the receiver, then thumped her fist on the table. 'Damn! Damn and fucking damn!'

'Something wrong?' Matthew asked, not taking his eyes from the screen.

'Eleanora Braey is pregnant! Five bloody months pregnant!'

'Oh.'

She swung round. 'Oh? Is that all you can say? Our star goes down the pan and you say oh.' She tapped her foot, her pale skin darkening with anger. 'I'll sue,' she declared.

'Fine.'

'Matthew, this is serious. Where are we going to get someone else at this short notice?'

'We've got two months. We'll find someone in that time.'

'Like who?'

'Off the top of my head, I don't know.'

'Oh, great! She was your choice, you could at least express some disappointment.'

'I am disappointed, but five months is very pregnant and there's not a lot we can do about it. Except find ourselves another star.'

'Oh well, if it's so easy I'll leave it all to you.'

'Good. Now, come and sit down. Better still, get room service to bring us up a couple of gin and tonics.'

'Matthew!' Her hands were pressed either side of her head as if she was trying to hold in the frustration. 'I can't stand this any longer. What's got into you? Doesn't anything I say get through to you?'

'All of it. Especially when you're shouting.'

'I'm shouting because I feel as if I'm going out of my mind. I tell you we've lost our star and you don't bat an eyelid. Grace Hastings asks for a private meeting with you and you won't tell me what was said. And then you talk to Marian on the phone and don't find out what's happening in Italy. What is it with you? Or should I say, what is it with you and Marian? You get back here after that meeting with Grace and the first thing you ask is, has Marian called? Not Bronwen, but Marian – and not a word about what you and Grace have talked about. Then you proceed to ring Italy, every hour on the hour, getting increasingly agitated when you can't get an answer – and you never once asked for Bronwen's room, only Marian's. Then, when you finally speak to Marian, you talk utter gibberish – at least, that's what you tell me – but over lunch this afternoon you cheerfully inform Frank Hastings that she is your great white hope for the script, with, I might add, a total disregard for Deborah Foreman's sensibilities. And that's not all, is it? What about the night you made me call Marian after she'd been out with Woody? You wouldn't let it drop until I did. So just what is going on, Matthew? Are you falling for her or something?'

'Come and watch this,' he said, 'it's hilarious. That woman has just informed her boyfriend she's . . .'

'Matthew!' she screeched. 'Please listen to me. Perhaps I'm sounding hysterical, perhaps I'm paranoid, but you can hardly blame me when you remember what's happened to us in the past. And now, with all this business with Marian, I'm terrified it's going to happen again. Please, Matthew, tell me it won't.'

'It won't. Oh, and by the way, now we've seen the Hastings' house I've had a great idea for the opening sequence. It involves a helicopter, two cranes and two crews. How does that grab you?'

Stephanie closed her eyes. It was useless, utterly and completely useless. She looked at him again, but he was still watching TV, so she turned on her heel and walked into the bathroom.

Ten minutes later he strolled in after her, carrying a gin and tonic in each hand. 'Feeling a bit calmer now, are we?' he said, pulling back the shower curtain.

'Don't patronise me, especially when I haven't got any clothes on.'

'Sorry.'

He put her drink on the washbasin and perched on the edge of the lavatory. 'Do you really feel so insecure? I mean, about me?' he asked as she stepped out of the shower.

'No, I was making it up.'

He nodded and handed her a towel.

'For God's sake, Matthew, don't you ever see yourself the way other people do?'

'No, I can't say I do. To be perfectly honest, I'm not too sure how to go about it.'

'Stop making me laugh, I'm furious with you and you know it.'

'Yep, I guess you are.'

'Well, don't you think I've got good reason to be? I mean, first there's Kathleen, then there's Samantha, now there's Marian. Do I figure anywhere in the picture?'

'Sure. You're the producer.'

'God help me, Matthew, I'm going to take a swing at you in a minute. Pass me that body cream behind you and then start psyching yourself up to tell me what the hell's going on inside your head.'

He picked up the body cream, but instead of handing it to her he held onto it.

'What now?'

'I'm psyching myself up, remember? Stop interrupting. Ah, that's it, I think I'm ready now to tell you what's in my mind. Yes, yes, I definitely am. Stephanie, will you marry me?'

She stared at him, her mouth half-open, her hand frozen in mid-air. He looked back, his eyes full of irony and the corner of his mouth drawn in a smile. Then he stood up and went to turn the shower on again. She watched him, but said nothing as he removed his clothes; then he picked her up, put her back under the water and got in with her. He looked round for the soap, then he rubbed it between his hands and started to lather her shoulders.

'Would you like to say that again?' she whispered, the blood rushing through her veins with the same vigour as the water that cascaded over her face.

'What's that?'

She stood aside, so that she was no longer under the water. 'What you said just now.'

'Oh, that. I said, will you marry me?' He looked into her face, but she still seemed to be in a state of shock.

'Why now?' she breathed. 'I mean, what happened?'

'You.'

'Me?'

'I want you to believe that I love you. That Kathleen, Samantha, Marian, none of them figure in the picture, only you.'

She gulped as he pulled her back into the shower, but the soap slipped from his fingers, and as he bent to retrieve it she caught him by the hair and pulled him back up again. 'I love you,' she said.

He grinned. 'You know, I had an idea you might.'

'And despite the fact that I hate you, I'll marry you.'
'Then why not stop talking and kiss me, woman.'

They decided that for the time being they would keep their engagement secret, mainly because of Samantha, but also because there was still the worry of Kathleen – although she had been keeping a low profile of late, if she were to discover their plans then, given the way she felt about Stephanie, she would probably do something to delay the divorce proceedings which she herself had put in motion. However, it didn't stop Matthew taking Stephanie into Tiffany to buy a ring, which she wore on her left hand when they were alone together, on her right when they were in company. While they were in Tiffany Matthew also bought a trinket for Marian – to thank her for the way she'd handled Kathleen, he explained when Stephanie protested.

The rest of the week in New York was taken up with lawyers, location-finding, deals and casting. Now that the role of Olivia was again open, Judith, the casting director Stephanie had hired just before they left London, flew over to handle the bombardment of young hopefuls. Frank, true to his word, set about fixing the nightclubs they wanted, and he and Stephanie, together with an army of lawyers, went through contracts, clauses and disclaimers until she began to feel as though the whole of life was one big loophole.

Bronwen called from Florence and at last Stephanie found out what Marian had learned from Sergio Rambaldi. 'And just wait until you see the scenes she's written as a result,' Bronwen enthused, 'they're out of this world. We're going to have to do something about her when we get back to London. I mean, she should be paid for all this work, and credited.'

'I quite agree,' Stephanie told her. 'Where is she now?'
'In her room, getting changed. Sergio's taking us to

dinner tonight. She didn't want to come because she knows I fancy him like crazy, but I can't leave her in on her own, not on such a beautiful night as it is here. Besides, apparently Matthew's told her she's got to glue herself to my side.'

'Matthew told her that? Why?

'Because he thinks I'm a loose woman, to quote Marian.'

Stephanie burst out laughing. 'Well, he's not far wrong, is he? Enjoy your dinner, and see you in London next week.'

When Stephanie teasingly tackled Matthew about his instructions to Marian, he snapped at her and told her to stop bothering him about the girl. He'd been on a short fuse ever since they had seriously discussed the opening sequence of the film. Stephanie had given a categoric no to Matthew's idea; it involved enormous expenditure, and as far as she could see the shot did nothing to tell the story, it was merely a vehicle for opening credits. She liked straightforward credits, white on a black background.

Not a day passed that wasn't spiced by a bitter row on the subject. He accused her of having a parochial mind typical of someone from television, and she hit back by reminding him that she held the purse-strings so she called the shots – an unfortunate choice of phrase that sent him slamming out of the room before he became violent.

'If you wanted the helicopter and cranes for an action sequence, it might be different,' she told him the next time the matter was raised. 'What if they don't have the cranes in New York? We'll have to get them shipped out from California, and just imagine what that will cost! Plus the extra camera crew. No, Matthew. You heard what Frank said, the budget won't be increased, and I've got to make sure the money's used where it's absolutely necessary.'

They were in the art-deco bar of the Dorset Hotel, so Matthew refrained from raising his voice as the place was jammed with media people. 'Am I going to have to justify every shot of this fucking film?' he hissed. 'Is that what you want? Or are you just after my balls?'

Stephanie's implacable stare began to crack. She kept up the struggle as long as she could, but ended up exploding into laughter.

The irony of what he'd said didn't escape him, but though he let the matter rest for the time being, he wasn't going to give up that easily.

'By the way,' she said as they rode the elevator up to their room, 'why *did* you tell Marian to glue herself to Bronwen's side?'

'Stephanie,' he sighed, 'just let it drop about Marian, will you? It's late, I'm tired, and I don't want another row tonight.'

'Row? But why should it cause a row?'

'Because that's what happens every time you mention Marian's name.'

Stephanie's next words died on her lips as she realised that this was true – and it was her fault. Even though he'd asked her to marry him, she was still unable to disentangle herself from the web of unreasonable jealousy and insecurity she'd wound herself into.

Later, as they got into bed, she settled into the crook of his arm and started to curl her fingers through the hair on his chest. 'I'm very fond of Marian, you know,' she told him in a quiet voice.

'Yes, I know.'

She looked up at his face and he bent his head to kiss her. 'And I'm sorry,' she said afterwards.

'What for?'

'Because she called this morning and left a message for you to ring her, and I didn't pass it on.'

He threw her aside. 'She called me this morning and you're only telling me now?'

She flinched as his arm shot past her, reaching for his watch. 'Matthew, for God's sake, why are you so angry?'

'I'm angry because of your damned jealousy,' he said through clenched teeth, and throwing back the covers, he got out of bed.

'Where are you going?'

'Down to reception to ring her,' he answered as he pulled on his jeans.

'But why can't you do it from here?'

'I just can't. Now leave it at that, will you?' And before she could say anything else, he slammed out of the door.

– 18 –

It was about four in the afternoon when Paul, carrying a brown paper parcel, left Harry Freemantle's pied-à-terre in Pimlico. Already the evening rush hour was starting to build up, and the dust and grime of overheated London streets was thick in the air. As he turned into Ebury Street he saluted a couple of Chelsea Pensioners, then tossing his parcel into the air, he started to whistle. Everything was going so perfectly according to plan, he could have kicked his heels together with the joy of it. His first book had already been to the printers, and his second, now that Madeleine and Harry had given him the experiences, responses and emotions his characters required, was spilling from his mind with such intoxicating fluency that it hurt to tear himself away. But this afternoon's assignation had been necessary, and as a result he had good reason to believe that his publication date was no more than six weeks away. In England, that was. In the States it would happen the following month. Funny that, how quickly they could turn things around, given the right incentive.

Reflecting on the past hour, and all that had passed

between him and Harry, Paul grimaced – not at himself for doing something that only a month ago would have been totally repugnant to him, but at Harry. The man was so malleable in his hands that he found it almost distasteful. A man in his position should have dignity, Paul felt. But then he shrugged; there was never any telling what depths a man might plunge to in the name of love.

Take what he himself had allowed Madeleine to do to him, for instance. That had been pretty demeaning – though he still wasn't sure what she had got out of it. As for him, well, it had totally blown his mind. Not that he particularly wanted to repeat the experience, but subjecting himself to her anger, and giving her free licence to do as she pleased with his body, had completely smashed the boundaries of eroticism – *that* he might repeat. The funny thing was, Madeleine had changed since that night. She had become withdrawn and less certain of herself, she no longer socialised quite so much, and had actually turned down three centrefold offers. On the other hand, the new perfume was about to be launched, and that she was looking forward to.

As far as their relationship was concerned, she seemed to love him even more than she had before, and had become so dependant on him emotionally that it seemed the empty Russian doll at last had a heart and a conscience which, like her mind, were his to command. She was dependant on him financially now, too, but she didn't know that. As for him, he was still baffled by the way she had taken him captive. Her coarse, countrified voice and – until lately – inordinate vanity; her near obsessive love for him and her zealous drive to get them both to the top, had closed in around his heart to such a degree that to be without her now was inconceivable. Just to picture her face set off all kinds of reactions within him; and despite what he had done to prove to himself that he was still in control of his feelings for her, could still hurt her if he chose, he was sometimes afraid that he loved her too much. But why, when he loved her, did he actually *want* to hurt her? That was a question he'd asked himself a thousand times, and the answer he gave was that it proved he was able, at will, to detach himself from all emotion – even his own. For him, emotion must be merely something to experience before exploiting it on the page. Nevertheless, to experience the emotion was vital, he felt; he truly believed that he could not write about something that he had not actually known for himself.

Though he'd taken a shower before leaving the flat he could still smell Harry on his clothes as he got into his car. He waited for the fuse of desire to ignite, but it didn't happen, and laughing quietly he dropped his parcel onto the seat next to him and started the engine.

It would all be over with Harry soon, once his book was out. Naturally, rejection would make Harry more compliant than ever, but there would be no more afternoon trysts, no more rough male hands exploring his body. In his mind's eye he caught a glimpse of Harry's penis, erect yet vulnerable, and his hand moved to his own – well, maybe it wasn't all quite over with Harry yet.

When he drove into the mews the car valet service was waiting for him, so after unlocking the front door he tossed over his keys, then took the parcel from the car. As he walked into the house he inhaled the fresh, tangy smell that told him the cleaning lady had been there earlier, squirting substances from her ozone-friendly bottles.

He was on his way through to the kitchen when, hearing voices in the sitting-room he stopped, and opening the door, saw Madeleine sitting in front of the TV. On the screen were highlights of Enrico Tarallo's fourth Grand Prix win of the season, but it was evident from the way she was sitting – her head resting on her hand and her face, puckered with anguish, tilted towards the ceiling – that she wasn't paying attention. Immediately his heart leapt to his throat, then a wave of anger tautened his muscles. Somehow she had found out about Harry, and that she should have discovered now, when the relationship was all but over, was too damned unfortunate for words.

He walked further into the room, looking at her curiously, and when he spoke guilt gave a stilted edge to his laugh. 'When I left you this morning you were on your way to Morocco,' he said, hardly hearing himself above the pulses drumming in his ears.

Her eyes didn't move, so putting the parcel down he went to turn off the TV. The room plunged into silence. 'What are you doing here?' he asked. 'I thought you'd be lying on a beach by now, soaking up the sun through Ambre Solaire. I've got the right commercial, haven't I?' he added, when she made no response.

She sighed. 'Trouble with the air traffic controllers. We're going tomorrow.'

'Oh, I see.' He sat down on the edge of the coffee table in front of her, and rested his elbows on his knees. 'So why the long face?'

She shrugged. Then after a while she pulled a hand from her pocket, producing the letter she'd received from her aunt. When he saw it he had to check himself rapidly as relief bubbled in his throat like laughter. He took the letter, then tossing it onto the table he moved across to the sofa and slipped an arm round her shoulders.

'I thought we'd gone over all this,' he said gently.

'I know. But I can't help it. Please don't be angry with me.'

'Sssh, I'm not angry. I understand, my darling.' He knew she loved it when he called her darling, and to confirm this she nestled herself closer to him. 'But what did you expect? Of course she's upset. She doesn't know where you are, or who you're with, she doesn't know anything except what she reads in the papers. And she knows that I was once involved with Marian, so obviously she's not happy about us being together, especially as you've never contacted Marian to explain.'

'But how can I explain when we took all that money? I know I don't have to tell her, but she'll sense something, I know what Marian's like. Anyway, it's not that I'm worried about. Well, it is, but apart from that, it's what my Auntie Celia said about everything else. She's really upset.'

'Maddy, just because she doesn't approve of your modelling doesn't mean it's wrong, it only means that she's an old woman who's never been any further than the end of the road, so you can't expect her to understand. It would be kinder to ignore the letter than go home and start up all the arguments you know you'll have. You don't want that, do you?'

He felt her shake her head. Then she whispered: 'Where have you been?'

A quick vision of Harry's face flashed into his mind's eye. 'Later,' he said. 'You're what's important right now.'

'Am I? Do I really matter to you, Paul?' she asked, lifting her head to look at him.

'If only you knew how much.'

She sighed, and resting her head on his shoulder again, she laced her fingers into his. 'I wish I did. It's just that sometimes you seem . . . I don't know, I can't describe it. I know you do things because of your writing and all that, but it's difficult for me to understand. Oh Paul, I feel so lonely sometimes.'

Putting his fingers under her chin, he lifted her face and kissed her. 'I'll always be here for you,' he murmured, using his thumb to wipe the tears from under her eyes.

For a long time she looked at him, studying the contours of his full mouth, the smooth line of his nose, the black brows and lashes, the intense eyes, and then the shock of white blond hair that lent such a contrast to his colouring.

He watched her, sensing that she was on the point of saying something, but then, shaking her head, she turned away.

For a while now, even before she'd received the letter from her aunt, she had been longing to ask him, but fear of his answer stifled the words. Even now, as she tried again to find the courage, her heart churned. But in the end, in a voice that was barely audible, she made herself say it. 'Paul?'

'Yes?'

'Would you marry me?'

He gave her a quick squeeze. 'Yes. If that's what you want.'

She closed her eyes, unsure whether the last few words had been played out only in her imagination. 'When?' she breathed.

'When I think the time is right. You're too busy now. So am I. We've got so much going for us already, if we do everything at once, what will there be left?'

She looked up. 'But you do want to marry me?'

He chuckled. 'Oh yes, I want to marry you.' And pulling her across his lap, he laid her back against the cushions. 'That's what's been on your mind these past few weeks, isn't it? Why you haven't really been yourself. You've been wondering whether I would marry you.'

She nodded.

'Why? Did you think I would say no?'

'I don't know. I never really know anything with you.'

'Would it help if I told you I love you more than I've ever loved anyone in my life? Or that I love you more than anyone else will ever love you?'

'Yes, it helps.' At last she smiled.

'So no more talk about your aunt? You're going to stay here with me, just the two of us?'

She nodded, and after he'd kissed her she turned to the coffee table. 'What's the parcel you brought in?'

'My page proofs. Want to have a look?'

Not having the first idea what page proofs were, Madeleine was surprised when he pulled them out. 'Is that your book?' she gasped.

'It most certainly is.'

'Can I read it?'

He laughed. 'Not yet. It'll be full of printer's errors which I have to check over, and it'll be easier for you to read in book form.' He knew she'd never get through it even then, but it didn't matter. 'Now who can that be?' he said, as the phone started to ring.

'It might be Shamir.' And suddenly animated, she leapt to her feet. But it wasn't Shamir – it was British Telecom testing the lines.

'Where is Shamir?' he asked when she sat down again.

'Still in Los Angeles. It feels like ages since I last saw her. I really miss her.'

He put down his page proofs and went to pour them both a drink. 'I know what's happening to you,' he said. 'All this publicity, constant demands upon you, press following you everywhere – it's enough to make anyone jittery. And it's all happened so quickly that it's beginning to frighten you. And because you're frightened you're clinging onto everything and everyone you know.' He smiled. 'You remind me of a butterfly trying to get back inside its chrysalis. But there's nothing there for you now, Maddy. It's all here, right ahead of you. So take that letter and throw it away.'

She picked it up and turned it over in her hands. Just to look at her aunt's handwriting brought a lump to her throat. 'I wonder what Marian's doing now,' she said sadly.

'Does it matter what Marian's doing? Isn't what we're doing more important?'

She took the Martini he held out to her. 'Yes, of course it is,' she sighed.

'Then why are you thinking about Marian?'

'I suppose because we used to be so close, and I get worried sometimes that no one likes me any more. I mean, I know I'm not the same as everyone else, I'm not clever or anything, but I'm not stupid either, it's just that I can't talk as well as other people. You know, the ones we mix with. Oh, I know I've been having lessons and all that, but I can't always think of the right words and I'm afraid people are going to laugh at me. I just wish everyone was like Marian. Or Shamir – she never picks me up on anything I say wrong, she doesn't seem to notice even. Nor do you.'

'That's because both Shamir and I love you.'

The telephone rang again and he got up to answer it. It was Deidre confirming the time of Madeleine's flight the next morning.

She waited until he sat down again, then taking his hand, she said, 'Paul, if we do get married . . .'

'Not if, when.'

'When we get married, can I invite them? Marian and Auntie Celia?'

'I don't think that's a good idea, Maddy, for lots of reasons. Besides, if you're going to be my wife I don't want to share you with anyone.'

She smiled. 'I love it when you're possessive with me. It makes me believe that I really am special to you.'

'Shall I tell you what you are to me?'

She nodded.

'A whore.'

Her head jerked up. He was laughing, but still she looked uncertain. 'That's a horrible thing to say.'

'But if you take off your clothes I'll show you it's not such a horrible thing to be.'

She tutted and rolled her eyes as she realised he was teasing, but inside, the sudden rush of alarm was still pumping viciously at her heart. She wondered if she would ever get used to his rash cruelty. He only did it to test her, gauge her responses and add them to his book; he'd explained it all after that mess with Harry. But still she lived in dread of what he might do next. In truth, it was why she sometimes longed for her aunt and Marian. It wasn't that she really wanted anything of her old life, she only wanted to feel secure in her new one.

The next morning Paul drove her to the airport himself. It was the most difficult parting they'd had yet. He didn't want her to go, and after the night before, when he'd made love to her with more tenderness than he'd ever shown before, she was beginning to realise that fame and fortune meant nothing compared to being with him.

It was Deidre who finally prised them apart, and as Paul stood at the window watching Madeleine walk out to the plane, waving and blowing kisses, she wondered why it was he seemed to love Madeleine so much when they had so little in common.

'If I could explain it,' he said, when she asked, 'I'd have the answer to a question man has been asking since the beginning of time. All we know, Deidre, is that love has no logic. Can I give you a lift back to London?'

When she didn't answer he turned to look at her. He was surprised to find her normally inscrutable face suffused with an emotion he couldn't quite identify. Then he realised it was pain. He made a move towards her, but suddenly she had herself back in control.

'Take no notice of me,' she said, blinking the even more surprising tears from her eyes. 'But you're right, it doesn't have any logic.' What she didn't add was that the very illogicality of it was tearing her apart inside.

As they were driving through Hammersmith on their way to Deidre's office in Knightsbridge, Paul said casually: 'When's Shamir back?'

'The day after tomorrow.'

'If you'll give me her flight details I'll pick her up.' He laughed. 'The things I do to please Madeleine.'

Deidre smiled. 'I'm very fond of her myself, you know.'

'I thought you were.'

A few minutes later she said, 'If the times of the flights coincide, perhaps you could give me a lift to the airport when you go to meet Shamir?'

'Of course.' He sounded surprised. 'Are you going anywhere nice?'

She turned to look out of the window, wondering how she could answer that. In the end she said, 'I'm going to see someone who will give me more pleasure than anyone else in the world – and probably more pain.'

Sergio was sitting up in bed reading the English newspaper he'd strolled out to buy for Bronwen early that morning. While he was gone she'd cooked breakfast, and after they'd eaten he had made love to her again. Now she had returned to her hotel, leaving her newspaper behind, a newspaper that contained what he knew to be an old photograph of Madeleine – and Paul O'Connell. His expression, as he looked at Paul's face, was impenetrable, but he studied it for a long time before finally the telephone broke his concentration.

'*Pronto*,' he snapped, snatching the receiver from the cradle.

'Sergio? You called me.'

'Rubin, my friend, I called you some days ago. Where have you been?'

'Out of town. On business.'

'We missed you at the *bottega*.'

'I'm sorry, the message didn't get through to me in time. How is it going? How is she?'

Sergio put down the newspaper and leaned his head against the wall behind him. 'Aah,' he sighed, his voice saturated with pleasure, 'she is very good. She is magnificent, and in less than a few weeks she will be ready. You were unwise to miss our last meeting, Rubin.' He allowed a few seconds to pass while Meyer swore under his breath, then on a more controlled note he said, 'But I wish to speak to you on another matter. You know about the film?'

'Sure. Everyone's talking about it.'

'In New York, maybe. Not here. At least, not yet. You have been interviewed by the people from the film, I believe?'

'Yes.'

'Did you tell them of your association with me?'

'Are you insane? Why would I have done that?'

'Then what did you say to them of me?'

'Only that I had heard of you, as anyone in the art world would have. That I had recommended to Hastings that he should send Olivia to study under you.'

'And you are sure this was all you said?'

'Positive. Why?'

'Because the young girl, she gives me reason to believe that she knows more than she should.'

'You mean the mousey kid who came here with the Welsh woman?'

'Her name is Marian Deacon. I cannot be sure, but I believe she has a suspicion about the connection between us.'

'But how can she have?'

'That, my friend, is your concern, not mine. I tell you because you should tread with care from now on. I also tell you because I want nothing to happen to her.'

'But if she knows, or even suspects, then the *bottega* could be blown before . . .'

'Rubin. I do not want her harmed because I have discovered that she is the cousin of Madeleine Deacon.'

There was a sharp emission of breath at the other end of the line, followed by a long, pregnant silence. Then

Meyer said: 'But once you've, we've, got Madeleine, if there's even so much as a whisper of either of our names this Marian kid'll be bound to shoot her mouth off.'

'Not necessarily. I understand there is a rift between them.'

'But family quarrels get made up.'

'Then we shall have to hope that this one does not. However, if it does, you understand that Marian Deacon will become my concern and I will act accordingly. Do you follow me?'

There was a groan at the other end before Meyer said, 'We gotta get her out of the way, Sergio.'

'No! If she suspects the connection between us, someone must have told her. Therefore, if she disappears now the person who told her will know why she has disappeared and will also know where to start looking for her. The net will close, as you Americans say, and in it will be two fish, Marian and Olivia. But the net must close when I say so, and in it must be *Madeleine* and Olivia. Now do you follow me?'

'Sure, I got it. In the meantime, do you want me to put someone on this Marian's tail?'

'Do as you wish, just don't harm her. I am already beginning to think that when it comes time for Madeleine, this Marian might be very useful to us.'

'In what way?'

Sergio laughed. 'I will let you know, my friend. And now it is *addio*, or I will be late at the *bottega*. Today, it will be only Olivia and me.'

Half an hour later Sergio strolled out of the apartment building and got into his car. As he drove away down the Via dei Bardi and turned onto the Ponte alle Grazie, he didn't notice the tiny blue Seat that had started to follow him.

Deidre's hands were clenched tightly on the wheel, her eyes fixed rigidly on the black car ahead. For years she had fought to stop herself doing this, had urged herself to trust him, but now she had to know. The day before, while he was at the Accademia, she had searched his apartment, and after finding what she had found, she had taken herself off to a *pensione* and spent the entire night trying to persuade herself that there was nothing ominous in it, that she should go home and forget all about it. But she knew that she had come too far now, and for the sake of her own sanity she must find a way either to confirm or deny her dreadful suspicions. Whatever she discovered, it would make no difference to the way she felt about him, that would never change; she just needed to know where he went when he got into his car, because the only time he ever used it was when he was going to the *bottega*.

She followed him through the suburbs of Florence, always keeping her distance, then out onto the autostrada towards Lucca. Inside she was crying, begging him to stop, to turn round or to take a road that would not lead him to Paesetto di Pittore. But an hour and a half later, just after they'd passed Lucca, he swung his car onto the steep, winding road that would eventually lead him to the village where Olivia had been taken the night she disappeared. The road led nowhere else, there could be no mistake – and with her heart constricting with sadness, love and trepidation, Deidre turned her car round and drove back to Florence.

– 19 –

'You had me scared half out my mind,' Matthew chuckled, as he handed Marian the glass of mineral water she'd asked for, then sat down next to her on the sofa. 'It was just as well you were there when I rang or God only knows what I'd have done. Called in the CIA, no doubt. Anyway, apart from a few awkward moments with Stephanie later, there was no harm done.'

Marian's smile was shamefaced. She hadn't meant to cause him alarm, she hadn't even meant to ring, really, it was just that she had wanted to hear his voice, so she'd telephoned with the excuse of telling him that Bronwen was going to spend the night with Sergio, and did he, Matthew, think that Bronwen would be safe?

'By the way,' he said, 'does Bronwen know you've told me about her and Sergio?'

'No. And please don't let on that you know or she'll never trust me again.'

Matthew laughed, and saluting her with his gin and tonic said, 'My lips are sealed.'

They were sitting in the front bar of the Groucho Club, and as it was just after six o'clock, it was already beginning to fill up with the media and publishing people who frequented it. Marian looked around at the lively faces, listening to the gushings of 'darling', and 'precious', and 'wonderful', and smiled as she pictured Hazel, their production manager, in this setting; she'd be as thoroughly at home here as the winged armchairs and overstuffed sofas.

'Getting on any better with Hazel now, are you?' Matthew asked, as if reading her thoughts.

Marian grimaced. 'We're getting there. She completely reorganised the office while we were away, I expect you noticed. I wouldn't mind, except that I can't find a thing. And now that she's moved her secretary in as well, and Woody's arrived with his paraphernalia, we're like sardines in a paper factory down there. Still, it's all go now that we're off to New York in a few weeks, and I rather like the company, to be honest – even if Hazel does keep grumbling about my hair, or my lack of style, or whatever else she feels like complaining about.'

'Tell her to mind her own business. You look perfectly all right to me, and not everyone has to deck themselves up like a Christmas tree or go about frightening people in their widow's weeds, as Stephanie calls them.'

'Well, as long you think I'm all right, that's all that matters, isn't it,' Marian teased, then almost melted at the ironic look that came over his face.

'Enough about old Haze,' he said, 'I want to talk to you about this Art Douglas business, young lady.'

'Don't call me young lady like that,' she retorted, 'it makes me feel as if I'm in kindergarten. Besides, there's no more to tell if Grace has told you everything.'

'OK, but I don't want you going anywhere or doing anything alone. If Douglas can come to London to find you, so can others.'

'Why should they do that? I haven't told anyone what I know, and I don't intend to. Besides, *they*, whoever they are – unless we're talking about Rubin Meyer and Sergio Rambaldi – don't know that I know, do they?'

'Let's hope not.' He took a sip of his drink, then looked at her quizzically. 'Doesn't any of this frighten you, just a little?'

'Not now. Not since you told me that you know too. I feel quite safe in your hands, Matthew.'

He laughed. 'Don't, whatever you do, let Stephanie hear you say that. Anyway, whether you're frightened or not I don't want you taking any chances, so I've spoken to Bronwen and asked her to stay at Stephanie's flat with you until we go to New York.'

'You've what? Didn't she think that was a bit odd?'

'Yes. But I told her you were lonely, and that it made little difference to her whether she was in Stephanie's flat or her husband's pied-à-terre, seeing as he's not in town at the moment, so you two could keep one another company.'

'I'd have thought she was sick of me by now. We've just spent over two weeks in each other's company, twenty-four hours a day.'

'You do yourself an injustice. She quite liked the idea, actually. She's moving in over the weekend while you're away.'

Marian looked at her watch, but she still had plenty of time to get to Paddington for her train.

'I've read the scenes you drafted for Italy,' he told her. 'They're exceptional. You've got quite a talent, you know, Marian, you should think about using it more profitably. I think Stephanie's going to have a word with you about that.'

'Oh?'

'I'll let her tell you.'

'Matthew,' she said, after a pause, 'do you think Olivia's still alive?'

He compressed his lips together thoughtfully. 'I don't know,' he answered finally. 'Sometimes I think she is, other times I don't. What about you?'

'I think she is.'

'Why? Not because of the screams you heard in Tuscany, surely?'

'No, I'm pretty certain that was a nightmare now.'

'Then why do you think she's alive?'

'Well, nobody's ever found a body. I mean, surely one would have turned up after all this time if she were dead. So I think she's alive.'

'And don't tell me, it's your intention to find out,' he said, arching his brows humorously.

'Oh no. I'm not so conceited as to think I can succeed where everyone else has failed. But I will admit that it's driving me nuts trying to work out what's happened to her, isn't it you?'

'Yes, it is.' He put down his drink, and taking her hand, he turned her to face him. 'But I hope you mean it when you say you're not going to try and find out. I know that sitting here in London, America and Italy seem a whole world away, but please don't underestimate the crimes –

or indeed the people – Olivia was involved with. I'm sure you feel as strongly as I do about what happened to the children, anyone would, so the men who committed those atrocities will stop at nothing to hide their identities. If you dig too deep then whatever's happened to Olivia could well happen to you. Remember, it's because she knew what they were doing that she was sent to Italy, and no one's ever seen her since. And fond of you as I am, Marian, I don't want to be making a film about you.'

He was looking so deeply into her eyes, and his hand was holding hers so tightly, that by the time he'd finished her face was suffused with colour and her pulses were racing. She gazed into his face, for the moment unable to utter a word as the pretence of light-heartedness which had so far carried her through this meeting was eclipsed by the truth of what she felt for him.

'Well, hello.'

Both Matthew and Marian looked up, and Marian's heart foundered as she saw Stephanie and Bronwen standing over them.

'Not interrupting anything, are we?' Stephanie said, sweeping her eyes from Marian's crimson face to their joined hands.

'Not at all,' Matthew smiled, getting to his feet. 'As a matter of fact, we were just talking about Olivia.'

'Really?' Stephanie said archly, and neither Marian nor Matthew missed the knowing look that passed between her and Bronwen.

'Yes, really,' he said. 'Now, what would you two like to drink?'

Ignoring Matthew, Stephanie said, 'I thought you were catching the six o'clock train to Devon, Marian.'

Marian's eyes flicked nervously to Matthew. 'I was only . . .'

'I asked her to come and have a drink with me so she

could fill me in in more detail on what happened over in Italy,' Matthew finished for her.

Again Stephanie looked at Bronwen, but Bronwen, not wanting to get involved, was studying the cocktail menu.

Then Matthew put an arm round Stephanie and whispered something in her ear. Stephanie burst out laughing, and dropping her bag on the floor, she gave him a quick kiss before sitting down on the sofa facing Marian. Certain that whatever he'd said had been about her, Marian was mortified and reached quickly for her bag, mumbling that she had to leave now.

'No you don't,' Matthew told her. 'Your train's not until a quarter to nine so you'll have another drink. And you, Bron? What'll you have?'

'I'll have a Kir Royale,' she said, obviously relieved that the awkward moment had passed.

'Me too,' Stephanie said, then turning to Marian, she smiled. 'Have you called your mother to tell her you'll be late?'

Marian nodded. 'I used the phone out there, in reception.'

'Good. When are you coming back?'

'On Sunday night,' Marian assured her. 'I'll be at work on Monday.'

'That's what I like to hear, don't you, Bron? Dedication – and loyalty.'

The was no mistaking the sarcasm in Stephanie's voice, and Marian looked down at her hands, not knowing what to do or say.

Bronwen sat down next to her. 'Have you heard?' she said. 'I'm going to be your flat-mate?'

'Yes,' Marian smiled, 'Matthew told me.' Immediately she wished she could take back the last three words.

Then, to Marian's relief, someone Stephanie and Bronwen both knew came over to talk to them, and by the time he went away Matthew was back with the drinks.

Over the next hour Marian hardly spoke at all, while Stephanie and Matthew resumed their argument about the helicopter and cranes for the opening sequence, with Bronwen playing devil's advocate. The outcome was, as ever, a stalemate, and Bronwen declared that they should discuss the more pressing matter of who was to play the part of Olivia.

When eight o'clock finally came round Marian waited for a lull in the conversation, then announced that she would have to leave.

'How are you getting to Paddington, *cariad*?'

'I'm taking her,' Matthew answered.

Marian looked at him in astonishment. He hadn't said so before.

'You haven't got your car here,' Stephanie informed him acidly.

'I know. I'm taking her in a taxi.'

'But she's perfectly capable of getting a taxi on her own, aren't you, Marian?'

'Yes,' Marian answered with alacrity.

'I'm sure she is, but I'm taking her. Will you still be here when I get back, or shall I meet you at the flat?'

'Please, Matthew,' Marian said, 'I can get a taxi on my own, honestly. Thank you.' But looking at Stephanie's face, she knew she'd only succeeded in making matters worse.

'I've got a terrific idea,' Stephanie said. 'Why don't you go to Devon with Marian, Matthew. That way you'll be absolutely certain she's got there in one piece, won't you?'

'And I've got an even better idea,' he said. 'Why don't you come in the taxi with us to Paddington, and then we can take it on home, together?'

'No, thank you,' Stephanie replied. 'I'm having a drink with Bronwen. Goodnight.'

Rolling his eyes and letting out a deep sigh, Matthew turned to Marian and jerked his head towards the door.

'You needn't come with me,' Marian told him as he flagged down a taxi. 'I can make it to Paddington on my own, I promise you.'

'Nevertheless, I'm coming.'

'But why? No one's following me as far as I'm aware, and it's just causing friction between you and Stephanie.'

'Let me worry about Stephanie,' he said as he pushed her inside the taxi. 'Paddington Station,' he told the driver, then getting in himself, he sat back in the seat beside her.

'Really, Matthew,' she protested, 'you needn't worry so much about me. I can look after myself. After all, if you didn't know anything about it . . .'

'But I do know, and I do worry, so let's leave it at that, shall we?'

'How can I leave it at that when Stephanie thinks . . .' She gulped, and turned quickly away.

'When Stephanie thinks what? That we're having an affair?'

She shrugged. 'I'm sure she doesn't think that. I mean, that would be preposterous.'

'Would it?' he said, then laughed as she spun round in her seat and looked at him with disbelieving eyes.

The rest of the journey was spent in silence, and when they arrived at the station Marian expected him to let her out, then ask the driver to turn round and take him back to the Groucho. But he didn't, he got out with her, paid the fare, then carried her case onto the platform.

'You're overdoing this, you know,' she told him. 'I mean, what happens at the other end? I shall be on my own then.'

'Isn't your mother meeting you from the station?'

'Well, yes, she is. Though she doesn't usually.'

'Well, if she is, then you won't be alone, will you? Now here you are, sit in this carriage here, it's quite full so you should be all right.' He helped her on, then found her a seat next to the window and put her case in the storage space above. 'Now I'd better be getting back to make my peace with Stephanie. Have a good time, and don't speak to any strange men.'

'I won't,' Marian promised, laughing.

By the time the train pulled out of the station, five minutes later, he had vanished into the crowds and was probably, she surmised, already in a taxi on his way back to Stephanie. She wondered if Stephanie would be waiting when he got there, and though part of her hoped she wouldn't be, another part remembered Stephanie's remark about loyalty, and she felt herself burn with shame. She, more than anyone else – with the possible exception of Bronwen – knew how insecure Stephanie was when it came to Matthew, and now it was she, the very person in whom Stephanie had trusted and confided, who was scheming to take him away from her.

But although she didn't like herself too well for the way she felt about Matthew, it actually wasn't true to say that she was scheming to take him from Stephanie. She would never do that to Stephanie, nor to anyone, not after she had had it done to her and knew exactly how it felt. Besides, even if she were scheming, it was utter nonsense to think she had even an iota of a chance of succeeding; Matthew was so much older than her, and he was obviously very much in love with Stephanie – even if Stephanie did refuse to believe it. Now she must spend the rest of her journey trying to make herself accept the truth. And the truth was, that no matter how concerned Matthew was for her, or how fond of her he claimed to be, he would never, *never*, seriously consider giving up Stephanie for someone like her. Someone who seemed to have forgotten, these past few weeks, what a thoroughly unattractive and unconfident person she really was.

Sergio was waiting for Deirdre in her office. She'd known he was there the instant she saw her secretary's face – no one but Sergio Rambaldi could ruffle Anne's imperturable calm. As she opened the door she saw him sitting at her desk, flicking through a magazine, but when he saw her he put it down and stood up. Straightaway she felt the sensitive force of his mind; it was as though he were reaching out for her misery, telling her that he was there now, so she must release it and let it go to him. She tried to speak but her voice was engulfed by emotion, and as she walked into his embrace, he smiled, and taking her face in his hands, he pressed his lips gently to hers. Then, as he gazed at her with his magnificent eyes, she felt her weakness turning slowly to strength.

She wanted to speak, to tell him all that was in her mind, but knew that she would be unable to until he let her go. But when he did so, she found herself moving back to him, drawn by the sheer power of his presence. It was a long time since he had affected her so profoundly, and she was reminded of the early days between them when she'd have given him her life if he had asked it. Perhaps she had given him her life . . .

He spoke quietly, in his soft, hypnotic voice. 'I came as soon as I could, *cara*. Now you must tell me all you have learned.'

In a tremulous whisper she told him how she had searched his apartment, then followed him to the hill that led to Paesetto di Pittore.

'I see.' He smiled. 'But tell me, *cara*, in your heart you always knew?'

She nodded. 'About Olivia, yes. But not about . . .'

He put his fingers over her lips. 'And yet you have never betrayed me. I am undeserving of your love.'

'Will you tell me now,' she said, 'what happened?'

He shook his head. 'It is difficult, my love. But when it is over I will tell you. I will tell you before Olivia returns to the world.'

'Then she is alive?'

The question seemed to haunt him and his eyes had a faraway, almost ethereal look as he stared past her. '*Sì, è ancora viva.*' Then, as if he had relinquished his thoughts to a passing cloud, he turned back to her. 'You have come to love Madeleine, no?'

She nodded; and as he smiled, sadly, the dread that had been with her ever since she'd searched his apartment suddenly tore at her heart. She turned away, moving to her desk and resting her hands on the edge. 'You're going to take her, aren't you?' she whispered. 'That's why you have all those pictures of her. I knew when I saw them, but . . . Sergio, please tell me it's not true. Please tell me you're not going to take her.'

She waited for a long time, feeling the silence creep between them like the spectre of doom. In the end she turned to look at him, her eyes imploring him to deny it, but he said nothing.

'Why? Why Madeleine? Oh Sergio, don't take her away from me, I beg you. Please, don't take her away.'

'I must, *cara.*'

'Then tell me why. Please, Sergio,' she begged, 'please tell me why.'

As he walked towards her, her eyes moved over the immaculate beauty of his face. 'There are many reasons, reasons I cannot explain now.'

'If there are many, tell me one.'

'You have made her famous.'

She shook her head, bewildered. 'But that doesn't make any sense.'

'It will. I promise you, one day it will.'

'And what about Madeleine? Where will she be then?'

'She will be with Olivia and together they will return to the world.'

'Sergio, it sounds so horrible. What does it mean, they will return to the world?'

'It means that you will see her again.'

'When?'

He lifted a hand to stroke her hair. 'You are a brave woman, my darling,' he whispered. 'I have stolen your heart and know what this has cost you, but my gratitude and love are all yours. I need you now, I need you to help me and to trust me.'

'Oh Sergio.' Her voice trembled, but the potent touch of his fingers steadied her. 'If I knew what was going to happen to her, if I knew . . .'

'Sssh! It would not help to know. Please, just trust me, *cara*.'

Though he was barely touching her, she felt as if he was pulling her to him, wrapping himself around her, swallowing her into the depths of his love. And though not a muscle in her body moved, she felt herself join with him, and knew that he was so much a part of her now, it was as if her personality had merged into his. 'Hold me,' she gasped. 'Hold me, please.'

When Marian arrived back at Stephanie's flat on Sunday night, Bronwen was sitting out on the balcony, checking through the script and basking in the evening sun.

'Ah, *cariad*,' she said as she saw Marian walking across the sitting-room towards her. 'Come and have a glass of wine with me. Good weekend, was it?'

Marian dropped her bag on the sofa. 'Don't ask,' she sighed. Then, smiling, 'Actually, it wasn't so bad. I played a game of bingo and won twenty pounds.'

Bronwen laughed and Marian wandered outside to sit down, picking up the pages Bronwen had already been over with her blue pencil. The air was still and fragrant, and in the distance church bells chimed.

'This is nice, isn't it?' Bronwen said after a while. 'Just you and me. Gives us a chance to have a little chat – without any interruptions.'

'Interruptions?' Marian repeated. 'You make it sound as though you've got something particular to say.'

Bronwen smiled awkwardly, then took a mouthful of wine. She was already beginning to regret agreeing to this, but she'd promised Stephanie. Besides, Stephanie was right, Marian was making such a chump of herself over Matthew that it was the only decent thing to do. She looked across the table at Marian, and the cheerful smile she received made her heart sink. This wasn't going to be easy. 'How was your mother?' she said.

A frown briefly crossed Marian's face. 'As a matter of fact, she wasn't too well. She said she'd had a cold recently, but she was taking some sort of pills and I've never, in all my life, known her to resort to medication for anything as simple as a cold. And then, when we went to visit my father's grave this morning, she had a dizzy spell. She won't admit it, but I think she's fretting over Madeleine. She's still hoping she'll answer her letter.'

'Do you think she will?'

'I hope so.'

'Do you still miss your cousin?'

Marian nodded. 'Yes. Both Mum and I do. The house was always so lively when she was around, I think we both feel a bit lost without her. Still, as Mum says, as long as we've got one another and Madeleine's happy, there's nothing for us to worry about. I read in the paper that she's going to a party tomorrow night at the The Roof Gardens. Paul's book is coming out the day after. I've read it, actually – well, most of it. It's quite good. All about a young boy growing up.'

Bronwen smiled, and as she gazed at Marian's small, pale face she wondered how, in this world of egotists and self-seekers, Marian's selflessness and simplicity had remained so refreshingly and enviably intact. And not for the first time, Bronwen felt a surge of affection for her. There was something special about Marian. Maybe it was her modesty, maybe her intellect, or perhaps it was her extraordinary gift for making people, no matter who they were, feel important. 'Do you still care for Paul?' she asked gently.

'No,' Marian laughed. 'Well, not in the way I used to. Funny, really. I thought at the time that I'd never get over it, but I have.'

Bronwen hesitated before continuing. 'Would that be because of Matthew, *cariad*?'

In an instant Marian's face was so painfully red that Bronwen felt herself beginning to blush too. 'It is, isn't it?' she said. 'That's what I want to talk to you about, pet.'

Marian looked away.

Bronwen had been rehearsing what to say all afternoon, but now the moment had arrived it was proving almost impossible to say it. 'Matthew's . . . Matthew's a lot older than you,' she stumbled. 'Of course, you know that, that's not what I'm trying to say. What I'm trying to say is that we have all been captivated by that roguish charm of his, even me.' Her laugh sounded hollow even to her own ears. 'It's those eyes of his, isn't it? They look right into you.' She attempted another laugh. 'He's a rotten old tease, really. The trouble is, people – well, some women – fall for it. And because you're so young . . . The thing is, Marian, Stephanie and Matthew go back a long way. They've suffered a lot for, and because of, each other. They've a great deal to repair, and it's not always easy for them, but you have to believe me, Marian, when I tell you that in the end they will straighten themselves out. Matthew will make certain of it. You see, he's very much in love with Stephanie. He's been in love with her ever since he's known her. Oh, *cariad*, I didn't say that to hurt you, I just wanted to try and make you understand.'

'Before I make an even bigger fool of myself?' Marian said.

'No. Before you do or say something you might regret.'

'Which means the same thing.'

'Oh, Marian. It's not so bad as . . .'

'It's all right, Bronwen, I understand what you're trying to say and I know that this is probably as embarrassing for you as it is for me, but . . . Tell me, was it Matthew who asked you to speak to me, or was it Stephanie?'

When Bronwen only looked at her, Marian felt a despondency that was even worse than the torment she had put herself through over the weekend, when she had told herself, vehemently, that Matthew would never return her feelings. And now she could see what had happened on Friday evening when he'd returned to the Groucho. Knowing the way she felt about him, both he and Stephanie had asked Bronwen to intervene before the situation became intolerable for them all.

'I think I'll go and take a bath,' she said, and as she stood up Bronwen had to swallow hard at the look of misery and humiliation in her grey eyes.

'Wait,' she said. 'Don't go yet. I've seen this coming for some time, and it's not your fault, *cariad*. Matthew is to blame, really. He shouldn't . . .'

'No, please don't blame him,' Marian interrupted. 'It's my fault – all of it is my fault. If I hadn't gone . . .' She stopped abruptly and her eyes flew to Bronwen's face.

'Hadn't gone where, *cariad*?'

'Nothing,' Marian mumbled. 'It doesn't matter.'

Bronwen reached out for her hand. 'If there's something on your mind, pet, you know you can tell me, don't you? It won't go any further, I promise.'

'I know it wouldn't,' Marian smiled. 'But there's nothing on my mind, truthfully.'

Bronwen smiled. 'OK, go and take your bath and I'll make us a nice salad for our supper, how does that sound?'

'Lovely,' Marian answered, swallowing the lump in her throat. Then, as she was about to go back inside, she suddenly turned and gave Bronwen a hug.

'Oh, be off with you now, *cariad*, or you'll have me crying here.' But as Marian turned away she caught her hand and held it between her own. 'I know it hurts, Marian, I know it hurts a lot, but remember I'm here and if you want to talk . . .'

Marian nodded. 'Thank you.' And before the tears spilled from her eyes, she went off to the bathroom.

The following morning Marian went into the office dreading having to face either Stephanie or Matthew. However, to her relief neither of them was there when she first arrived, so she put the kettle on and set about opening the mail.

When Stephanie came in ten minutes later, without Matthew, she ran straight upstairs to her office. The fact that she had ignored her made Marian feel even worse than she did already, and she would have gone upstairs to talk to her had Woody not come rushing in at that moment, followed by Adrian, the location manager.

'Got that rough schedule printed out yet?' he asked Marian.

'Good morning,' Marian said. 'Yes, it's over there on the printer.'

'Good morning,' Woody grinned, then snatching up the schedule, he turned to Adrian.

At that point Hazel came in with Freddy, the designer.

'It's here,' Woody told them, using his middle finger to push his metal-rimmed glasses further up the bridge of his nose, 'Now, let's get Stephanie and we'll go through it. Is she in yet, Marian? Can you give her a call, then?'

Marian picked up the phone and buzzed through. 'Be right down,' Stephanie answered, and almost instantly Marian heard her footsteps on the stairs.

'OK,' Stephanie said as she walked into the office, looking, Marian thought, exceptionally elegant in her pale-grey-and-white-striped dress. 'Hit me with it, you lot. By the way, I've already told Matthew and he's agreed in principle, so let's see what you've come up with.'

'We haven't come up with much yet,' Woody confessed. 'I mean, this schedule is for America and Italy only, obviously. But as I told you on the phone yesterday, Adrian's drawing a blank wherever he goes in New York with regard to the nightclubs, not even Frank Hastings can persuade them – drugs, they don't like 'em, don't want to be associated with them. So Hazel here came up with the brilliant idea of cheating on the locations and cutting the budget in one go.'

'I'm all ears,' Stephanie said.

'Right, well, it's quite simple really,' Woody went on. 'Freddy and his army of able-bodied layabouts can dress the exterior of clubs in New York, changing the names and so on, and then we can shoot the interiors here in London.'

'When?'

'That's why I wanted to look at the schedule. But we've got a couple of weeks between the American and Italian shoots, so there doesn't seem to be any reason why we can't do the nightclub stuff then. They don't even have to be night shoots – well, that depends on Matthew, really, but . . .' He shrugged. 'What do you say?'

'I say, if it's going to save me money, brilliant. But talk to Matthew before you go ahead and arrange anything. He's working at home this morning. Morning, Josey,' she added, as the production secretary walked in.

'What's this?' Josey cried. 'I know I'm late, but there's no need to send out a posse, Steph.'

'You are indeed late,' Hazel remarked, looking at her watch. 'When I called you yesterday I asked you to be here for nine.'

'Yes, but you forgot to inform British Rail, didn't you?' Josey quipped. 'Anyway, what's all the fuss?'

'I'll explain on the way over to Matthew's,' Woody told her. 'Can you fit five in your car, Adrian?'

'Don't worry about me,' Hazel interrupted, 'I'll stay here. Just take Josey, and she can fill me in on the details later. Unless you'd like to come round for dinner tonight and tell me yourself?'

'Well, actually, I'm ... busy tonight,' Woody said, backing away from her.

Sitting at her desk in the corner, Marian watched Stephanie as she turned to walk out, and seeing that she was laughing, she tried to catch her eye. But Stephanie didn't even glance in her direction as she picked up a pile of audio cassettes and went back upstairs to her office.

Two hours later, Hazel was resting her chin in her hands, staring across the office at Marian who was reading over some letters she had just typed for Bronwen. Marian was aware of Hazel's eyes, but was deliberately avoiding them. The fact that Stephanie had snubbed her twice already that morning was causing her a great deal of distress, and if Hazel was about to start picking on her, she was afraid she might disgrace herself by breaking down altogether. She'd thought she had changed over these past few months, that her erstwhile retiring and timid nature had left her for good, but since her conversation with Bronwen the night before she had felt it stealing up on her again in all its odiousness. Just a trip to the newsagent's an hour ago had brought tears to her eyes, and though she was fairly certain Hazel hadn't noticed, she had given her a peculiar look when she'd come back into the office with nothing.

In the end Hazel broke the silence. 'You really are the most appalling creature to look at sometimes, Maz,' she said. 'No, I'm sorry, but you are.'

Marian seemed to shrink behind her hair and her fingers curled the edges of the paper she was holding.

'I mean, really,' Hazel went on, 'it's too much to expect

me to sit here day in, day out . . . Are you crying? Oh, for heaven's sake, Maz, you're going to give me a guilty conscience. Just when I'd made up my mind to be nice to you.'

'There's no need,' Marian whispered. 'I've always looked like this. And anyway, I'm not crying.'

Hazel swivelled in her chair and stood up, hands resting on her hips. 'You were blubbing earlier, weren't you? When you came back from the newsagent.'

'Hazel, there's something I'd like to discuss with you . . . upstairs, if you don't mind.' Until she spoke neither of them had seen Stephanie standing in the doorway. As they turned, hope for a friendly word, or even a smile, flared in Marian's chest, but Stephanie merely dropped the audio cassettes onto her desk, asking her to return them to the composer, then glanced at Hazel and waited to follow her out.

When they'd gone Marian folded her head in her arms and let the tears run. This was all so awful, and she didn't know what to do about it. She couldn't help feeling as she did about Matthew – if anything, she'd give the world *not* to, especially as she knew she couldn't continue to work for Stephanie when Stephanie now so obviously despised her. But to leave Bronwen would be such a terrible wrench, almost as bad as not seeing Matthew again. How had things become so complicated, when only a few months ago she'd been living happily in Bristol with two of the people she loved most in the world? Now, to cap everything else, Madeleine and Paul were in the newspaper again this morning, laughing into one another's eyes as they left The Roof Gardens in Kensington. The caption referred to them as 'the golden couple' and declared that Paul was be 'one of the great literary talents of the decade, who has just been signed up by Freemantle's for an unspecified sum'.

Marian had no idea why this particular article had

upset her so much; after all, they were in the newspapers almost every day, she should be used to seeing them by now. Perhaps it was because it seemed as if everyone had someone, except her. She winced at her nauseating indulgence of self-pity and took the newspaper from her handbag. It was crumpled, but she spread it out and looked at her cousin's lovely face. She wondered if Madeleine ever thought about her, ever missed her. She probably had lots of glamorous friends by now, and was too busy even to remember how close they had once been. Marian wished she could forget, too, but no matter what happened, who she met or how far she travelled, life somehow didn't seem complete without Madeleine.

The door opened and Hazel walked back into the office. Quickly Marian stuffed the newspaper into her bag and turned to her typewriter. There were still tears on her cheeks, but she didn't dare pull out a tissue in case Hazel noticed.

'You can stop whatever it is you're pretending to do on that typewriter,' Hazel said, 'you're coming with me.'

'But I've got to type all this up for Stephanie.' Marian's red-rimmed eyes were uncertain as she looked up.

'Ugh,' Hazel groaned. 'You look like an accident in a jam factory. Go and blow your nose, put some powder on those blotches, and forget the typing. Well, go on,' she said, when Marian continued to stare at her.

'I haven't got any powder,' Marian sniffed.

'Then we know where our first stop is, don't we? Go on, take mine for now.'

When, a few minutes later, Marian came back from the ladies' with Hazel's powder in small crusts on her cheeks, Hazel was waiting outside in a taxi and Stephanie was in the office.

'It's all right,' she said, when she saw Marian's look of dismay, 'Hazel's told me she's taking you off for the day, and I've approved it.' She sighed and put a hand on

Marian's arm. 'I'm sorry about last Friday. I behaved abominably and I owe you an apology. No, no,' she said, as Marian started to speak, 'I don't want to hear another word. Take the day off, see if Hazel can cheer you up a little.' And taking Marian by the shoulders, she steered her out into the street.

'Oxford Street, Selfridge's end,' Hazel barked at the taxi driver, and hauling a bewildered Marian inside, she closed the door.

'I am going to make a new woman of you, Marian Deacon,' she declared as they hit the first snarl of lunch-time traffic.

Marian's misgiving pushed her eyes wide. But even if she had wanted to protest, Hazel allowed her no time: not only for the rest of the day, but over the following week too, when make-up counters, dress shops, beauty salons and hairdressers' were the only resting places between endless tube and taxi journeys. When her bank account ran dry, Stephanie put more in, and Marian's face was prodded, pinched and scrubbed, her hair pulled, cut and highlighted, and her body squeezed into shapely dresses she insisted she'd never have the courage to wear. Stephanie merely laughed every time she tried to apologise for not being at her desk, and Bronwen twirled her about in enthusiasm for her new look. Baffled as she was by what was happening to her, Marian couldn't stop herself watching for Matthew's reaction. But he said nothing – didn't even seem to notice as he raced up the stairs to Stephanie's office, then out again. Worst of all was that everyone seemed to realise she was waiting for his verdict, and took great delight in teasing her about her crush – which made her feel almost sick with self-consciousness each time she looked in the mirror and saw the elfin face peering back at her through her own grey eyes, which now seemed larger and somehow more defined. Her skin looked healthier, her mouth less narrow, and her hair – well, she could hardly believe how sophisticated it looked.

'Turn around, let me see how utterly brilliant I am,' Hazel said two weeks later. They had just returned from yet another shopping spree and Marian was wearing a pale blue skirt with matching top; her short silvery hair was cut over her ears, shaped into the back of her neck and swept back from her forehead; and her red dangling earrings matched her beads, bangle, belt and shoes. As far as she could remember, she'd never worn red in her life. 'I'd hardly recognise you for that dowdy little creature sitting across the office a week ago,' Hazel said, tweaking at a stray strand of hair. 'You've still got some weight to lose, though, honeypop.' She poked at Marian's thighs. 'Cellulite, ghastly stuff! Still, we'll soon put paid to that. Now here you are, all dressed up with nowhere to go, I'll bet. Well, seeing as you're so frightfully presentable now, I'm going to take you to Kettner's with me. Like champagne, do you? No, don't tell me, you've never had it. You'll break that earring if you keep twisting it.'

They turned round as Matthew rushed in and up the stairs to Stephanie's office. Hazel rolled her eyes as they heard Stephanie shriek, and Marian's earring snapped in her fingers.

The next day she was sitting alone in the office, staring with mild disgust at a tub of cottage cheese, when footsteps on the stairs took her attention to the door and Hazel, followed by Stephanie and Bronwen, came in for her bag.

'Hi, Cinders,' Stephanie grinned. It was a name they'd all taken to calling her recently. 'We're off to lunch. If Frank Hastings calls we'll be at the Gay Hussar.'

'OK,' Marian answered.

'Good girl. See you later.' Stephanie turned, then burst out laughing at something Marian couldn't see. Then Matthew appeared with Freddy, the designer and Adrian, the location manager. 'Get a move on, you lot,' Stephanie said. 'And stop making me laugh, we've no right to be happy when everything's falling about our ears.'

As they bundled down the hall and out into the stifling heat, Bronwen waved through the window at Marian, and dolefully Marian turned back to her cottage cheese. She grimaced. It was truly the most revolting stuff.

'Charming.'

She looked up to see Matthew standing at the door, and immediately her pulses started to race.

'Aren't you joining us?' he said.

Not wanting to admit she hadn't been invited, Marian said: 'Hazel's put me on a strict diet.'

He smiled, and perching on the edge of her desk, he gazed into her eyes with such lambency in his own that she almost regretted the loss of her long hair to hide behind. 'Well, if you don't mind me saying so, you're looking good on it.' He pulled a face, and checking over his shoulder to make sure that no one was listening, he whispered: 'Not so sure about the lipstick, though.'

Marian burst out laughing. 'Neither am I,' she declared, and pulling a tissue from the box in front of her, she wiped it off.

'Come on,' he said, laughing, 'throw that muck away and treat yourself to a proper lunch.'

'I'm not brave enough to face Hazel,' she admitted. 'Besides, I've got to wait in in case Frank Hastings calls.'

He nodded, then stood up. 'Everything all right, is it? No more strange assignations on the Fulham Road?'

'Nothing like that. But there is something . . . I was going to tell you before, but I could be imagining it.'

'What's that?'

'I keep getting the feeling that someone's watching me.'

His expression was immediately serious. 'What makes you say that?'

She shrugged. 'It's just a feeling I get every now and again. I expect it's nerves.'

'Well, we don't want to take any chances, so you'd better lock up and come to lunch with us.'

She shook her head. 'It's all right, Josey and Woody are on their way back. In fact, there they are now, getting out of a taxi, so I'll be fine. Anyway, as I said, I'm pretty sure I'm imagining it.'

He still seemed uncertain. 'I'd feel happier if you were with me.'

'Honestly, Matthew, I'll be fine.'

He looked at her for a moment or two, then said, 'Look, I'm having a drink with my daughter tonight – if she turns up – why don't you come? You're about the same age, you might get along together.'

Dumb pleasure swirled through Marian's chest. 'Hazel's booked me into an aerobics class,' she mumbled. Then, decidedly more cheerful: 'But I can always cancel it.'

'You do that. I'll pick you up here around six.'

'Are you ready yet?' Stephanie shouted.

'Almost there,' Matthew called back. 'Have you got the photographs Judith gave me yesterday?'

'Yes,' Stephanie said, with exaggerated patience.

'Did you call Bronwen back? She rang while you were in the shower.'

'Yes, I called Bronwen back.'

'Where are my keys?'

'Out here on the table.'

'Then I'm ready to go,' he grinned, as he came out of the bedroom. His hair was still damp from the shower, and seeing his teeth gleam as white as his shirt, Stephanie thought how unspeakably handsome he was. She ran her eyes over the hard muscles of his forearms and felt a surge of desire.

'I thought there was a taxi waiting,' he murmured, as she lifted her mouth for a kiss.

'There is.'

'Then pull yourself together, woman, and get down those stairs.'

Laughing, Stephanie swept a pile of documents into her briefcase, snapped it shut, then waited out in the hall while he locked up.

Sitting in the taxi on the way to the Savoy, she took out a handful of photographs. These were of some of the actors and actresses they were about to audition. Matthew had chosen them, passed their names on to Judith, the casting director, and now he was going to test them out with some dialogue scenes from the script.

As he looked over Stephanie's shoulder at the assortment of faces, he rubbed his hands with glee. 'The power,' he grinned, 'their lives in my hands.'

'You're sick,' Stephanie said lightly. 'I quite like this guy for the Rubin Meyer character.'

'Do you? If we're going by looks, I prefer this one.'

But instead of looking at the picture, Stephanie was looking at the way the dark hair curled round his watch-strap and over the backs of his large but slender hands. 'God, you really turn me on, do you know that?' she murmured, turning her eyes to his.

'So you were feeling as randy as you looked just now,' he grinned, and his eyes narrowed as she pressed her hand against his thigh. 'I'd be careful if I were you,' he warned.

'Why?'

'Because the driver's watching you in the mirror.'

'Don't be silly, he can't see anything.'

'But,' he said, removing her hand, 'this is hardly the time or the place.'

A flood of colour suffused Stephanie's cheeks, and she turned away, angry and embarrassed. A few minutes ticked by, during which she struggled to keep a rein on her tongue, but in the end, unable to stop herself, she hissed, 'Tell me, Matthew, do you find Marian so easy to resist?'

'I'll ignore that remark,' he said. 'It was unworthy of you.'

'Myself, I'd say it was pretty unworthy of you, staying out until past midnight with her last night. Where were you all that time? You say your daughter didn't turn up, so what was it, a cosy little dinner for two?'

'Stephanie, leave it, before you say something you'll regret.'

'Yes, I suppose I would regret it if you were trying to hide something. Are you?'

'No.'

'So she's still virgin, is she?'

'What! Steph nie, you're in grave danger of pushing me too far over this I thought we'd had it out about Marian. I thought . . .'

'No, Matthew, we didn't have it out. All we decided, all *you* decided, was that she had a crush on you. What we never got to the bottom of is what your feelings are for her.'

'For God's sake, she's only a . . .'

'Yes? She's only a what? A kid? She doesn't look much like one these days though, does she? In fact she looks rather good, rather desirable, wouldn't you say? Obviously more desirable than me.'

'God, talk about hell hath no fury,' he muttered. 'If you must know, I took her to an Italian restaurant in Covent Garden. We ate a meal, we talked . . .'

'What did you talk about?'

He shook his head. 'I'm not getting into this, Stephanie. Now, either we discuss the casting session coming up, or we continue this journey in silence, the choice is yours.'

It was obvious from the way she turned back to the window that she had chosen silence, and he sat back in the seat, staring straight ahead and feeling the good humour with which he had begun the day dissolve into discontent.

Judith was waiting in the foyer of the Savoy, and led them upstairs to a third-floor room. The session went off much as expected, one or two possibles and a dozen nos.

Still feeling irritable, Matthew snapped at Judith to get her act together over the re-casting of Olivia, then said he was going to meet Bob Fairley, the lighting cameraman, for a drink – if that was all right with Stephanie.

'Perfectly,' she answered, the pinched corners of her mouth indicating how nettled she still felt – although she knew she was in the wrong.

'Good, then I'll see you at the office some time this afternoon.'

'Don't rush,' she said.

He shot her a look of pure exasperation, then turned and walked out.

When Stephanie returned to her office, still seething with fury – as much at herself as at Matthew – she found Marian sorting through a pile of paperwork on her desk. 'What are you doing?' she snapped.

Marian spun round, obviously startled. 'I was looking for the contracts Hazel gave you to sign yesterday. She needs them to take to the lawyers this afternoon.'

'Can't she come and find them herself?'

'She would have, but I offered, as I know your desk a little better than she does.'

Stephanie slung her briefcase on a chair, then looking at her watch, she said, 'Shouldn't you be at lunch?'

'I'm still dieting,' Marian answered, feeling the incongruity of her smile as Stephanie glared at her, her eyes filled with contempt, her mouth a thin hard line.

Marian shifted uncomfortably under the gaze, but understanding only too well what it was about, she decided that there was no point in running away from it, she must say something. 'After Bronwen talked to me the Sunday before last,' she began, 'I could see straightaway what a fool I'd been making of myself, and I wanted to speak to you then, but everything seemed to sort itself out so I decided there was no point. And then, when everyone started teasing me about the crush I had on Matthew, including you, though it made me feel even more foolish, I was glad because it meant that you and I were friends again. But now I can see that you're upset again, and obviously I know why. But there isn't any need to be, Stephanie. Matthew invited me to dinner because he thought it would be nice for me to meet his daughter, someone more or less my own age. Samantha didn't turn up, so as we were already in the restaurant we had something to eat. I talked most of the evening, bleating on ad nauseum about my mother, because she hasn't been well lately and I've been worried about her. Matthew was kind enough to listen, but I feel embarrassed about it now, and even worse because you're feeling the way you are when there's no need to.'

Marian paused, then grinned disarmingly. 'I could treat you to some of my amateur psychology here, but I don't think you'd appreciate it, and besides, I don't have any wine or cocoa handy. Anyway, it's none of my business how you . . . Well,' she shrugged, 'I just want you to know that I understand why you're angry with me, and to know that if you no longer want me to work for you, that it will make me very unhappy but I shall understand.' As she finished, she felt suddenly dizzy, though whether with the relief of getting it off her chest, or with trepidation, she didn't know.

Stephanie regarded her closely, her face still solemn. 'I'll tell you what, Marian,' she said at last, 'I wouldn't blame Matthew if he was in love with you. Now come here and give me a hug and tell me what a stupid, jealous, nasty old bag I am.'

'You're a stupid, jealous, nasty old bag,' Marian said, walking into her embrace, 'but I love you to bits.'

'And me you,' Stephanie laughed.

'I bet,' Marian said, as she was walking out of the door, 'that you and Matthew had a row this morning.'

Stephanie nodded.

'Where is he now?'

'Drinking somewhere with Bob Fairley. He'll be in later.'

'Then why don't I cancel your appointments for the afternoon and send him home so that you can make things up?'

Stephanie seemed hesitant. 'I don't think he'll come. Not after what I said this morning.'

'You leave him to me,' Marian said, and grinning broadly to cover what she was feeling inside, she walked off down the stairs.

– 20 –

Madeleine giggled. Deidre, her dark auburn hair tucked behind her ears, leaned back in her chair and watched her, an indulgent smile hovering about her mouth. Inside, her emotions were in turmoil, but she was sufficiently in control of herself not to let them show.

'This great love of yours is beginning to make me feel old,' she smiled, when Madeleine finally put the phone down and threw out her arms in an expression of joy. 'How did he take it?'

'He already knew,' Madeleine answered, flopping down on Deidre's leather sofa and putting her feet up. 'He wondered if you'd like to come out to dinner with us tonight, to celebrate?'

'Love to. Is Harry Freemantle invited?'

Madeleine pulled a face. 'Yes.'

Deidre wondered if it was worth getting to the bottom of Madeleine's dislike for Paul's editor, but decided that if she wanted to tell her, she would. The fact that Paul's book had entered the best-seller lists in its first week was the reason for Madeleine's elation, though it shouldn't have come as a surprise, exactly – it had cost her a great deal of money.

'So what do you think?' Madeleine said, holding out her hand for the umpteenth time so that Deidre could get a good look at the ring.

'I think two things,' Deidre answered. 'First, no matter what the size, a diamond can never be vulgar – though yours comes close, madam. Secondly, it's good to see you. Morocco obviously agreed with you.'

'Loved it. Paul bought me this ring with his advance. It cost him the whole amount. It's an engagement ring, you know?'

'I did gather that,' Deidre answered dryly. 'Congratulations. As you say, we'll celebrate tonight. Now, how would you like to open up your diary so we can get down to business?'

While Madeleine leafed through her new leather-bound Mulberry – something else Paul had bought her – Deidre buzzed through to Anne. A few minutes later Anne brought in the newspaper and magazine cuttings for the past week, and left them for Madeleine to peruse.

Self-admiration came so easily to Madeleine that Deidre might have been appalled if she hadn't been used to it. Besides, she liked Madeleine better when she was being narcissistic, at least it meant that everything was back to normal. Obviously Paul's proposal of marriage was just the tonic she'd needed – there hadn't been a single mention of her aunt and cousin since, no refusal of work, and the haunted, almost frightened expression had gone from her eyes. If anything, she was looking more striking than ever.

Deidre immediately despised herself for the feeling of relief this gave her; but there was no getting away from the fact that, when Sergio gave her the word, she would find her task much easier to carry out if she felt that Madeleine had known happiness. She wouldn't be able to bring herself to do it, she thought, if the rift with Paul had continued. She wondered if it would please Sergio when she told him that Paul and Madeleine were now engaged; he had told her that she must report every development in their relationship to him, and everything she knew or found out about Paul. His request confirmed to Deidre that she had been right all those months ago when she suspected that Sergio knew Paul – but exactly how he knew him, or what their relationship was, he had refused to say.

'Right,' she said, picking up the booker's cards in front of her, 'you've got everything up until tomorrow, haven't you? Good. The next day. In the morning they want you on the 'This Morning' programme up at Granada TV. They'll be asking you about the new perfume, so someone will be there to give you the necessary details. From there Roy will take you into Manchester where you'll meet up with Paul. He's doing book-signings at Waterstone's and, let me see, Smith's and . . . well, Anne's got a list of the bookshops. The BBC local news will have their cameras there, I expect Granada will, too. Roy is writing a little speech for you in case you're asked to say something. In the afternoon Paul is on the radio in Leeds while you're going off to open a new beauty salon. They're holding a raffle, I believe, and it's being fixed for you to win a prize, don't forget it goes to charity – Roy's got the name of a couple of local ones. From there both you and Paul go to Birmingham for more book-signings and personal appearances. Local TV news and again newspapers will be there. At ten tomorrow night there's something happening at Stringfellow's. Anne's got the tickets. She'll pick you both up from Euston station, drive you home to get ready, then on to the club. Don't insult Peter Stringfellow again – at least, tell Paul not to. He's a nice chap and can do you a lot of good.'

'Now, on to Friday. An eight o'clock morning flight to Glasgow for you both. There you part company. Paul's publicist has his schedule, Roy will have yours. It's mainly fashion stuff. *Café-Society* and *Tatler* will have photographers going round with you, Roy will probably have a few more lined up, too. Obviously Phillipa will be with you, so will Helen and her team to sort out your make-up and hair. You'll catch up with Paul in Edinburgh where you'll both be on a local chat show. Overnight in Edinburgh, then the big fashion shoot on the Orkneys for the following two days. I've spoken to Harry Freemantle and the publicity people at Freemantle's, and they're quite happy for Paul to go with you. Phillipa's arranged to borrow some men's clothes from the Armani collection, so Paul will also be involved in the shoot – if he wants to be. Again, TV cameras will be there, this time from 'The Clothes Show' and a new programme TVS will be launching next month. How are you doing so far?'

'I think I've got all that. Does Paul know about everything?'

'Harry should be talking to him this afternoon. When you come back from the Orkneys, you'll have a day to pack and then you're both off to Los Angeles. I think the Johnny Carson Show is recorded rather than live, but I'll check that out before you go. Then you've got an audition for a major movie – no, it's not the starring role. I've booked you into the Beverly Hills Hotel for the night, but Shamir has invited you to stay with her. Yes, OK, I'll cancel the Beverly Hills. Right, you're then flying to New York where Paul's publishers and their publicity people will take over. Is that enough to be going on with?'

Madeleine's pleasure was more than touching. 'Can I take all these cuttings home to show Paul?' she asked.

'Of course.' Deidre stood up, pushing her hands into the deep pockets of her black cotton dress. 'Now, off you go, I'll see you tonight. Where are we going, by the way?'

'I'll get Paul to ring and let you know.'

'You'd better, if we want Roy to send along some photographers.'

Madeleine hooked her bag over her shoulder. It was the same subtle shade of orange as her shoes, belt and the suede panels in her cream-coloured dress.

'Tailored clothes become you, Maddy,' Deidre remarked.

'Just wait until you see my outfit for tonight,' Madeleine gushed as they walked out into Anne's office. 'It's white with sequins and things. Skin-tight, I won't be able to wear a thing underneath. Well, I couldn't anyway, because the top's completely see-through and there are great chunks cut out of the hips right round to here.' Her hands rested on either side of her pubis. 'It's something else,' she sighed.

'Sounds delightful,' Deidre murmured, then she kissed her on either cheek, and waited until Madeleine was in the lift before turning to Anne. 'Is Dario around?'

'No. He went off on a shoot at the weekend – I mean, a gun shoot – and hasn't come back yet.'

'Abysmally hung-over, knowing him. If he does manage to drag himself in at some point, have him come in to see me, will you?'

'Will do. By the way, I still haven't managed to get an answer from Sergio's apartment.'

'OK. But keep trying.'

Back in her office, Deidre closed her eyes and leaned against the door. It was several days now since Sergio had been here, but she was still reeling from the shock of discovering that Dario, the photographer who had been her partner for seven years, was a member of the *bottega*. Sergio had told her so that she wouldn't feel so alone in what she was doing. But having Dario to support her made little difference; since she'd agreed to help by taking Madeleine to Italy, she had barely slept or eaten. She tried so hard not to think about it, there was still some time before he needed her, Sergio had told her – but not knowing what was going to happen to Madeleine once she got to Italy was tearing her apart inside. And having to face Madeleine day after day, and pretend that everything was normal, only increased her anguish. But she knew she would do it, not only because those few days he'd spent in London had sharpened her love for him in a way that made it almost too painful to bear, but because he had asked her to marry him and go to live with him in Florence. It was what she had always wanted.

'They're still arguing about those damned cranes,' Hazel grumbled as she walked into the office. 'It's simply beyond me how they do it. Lovers by night, adversaries by day. Something Freudian there, must be.'

The office was crowded and noisy, so no one paid her much attention. Besides, Stephanie and Matthew's difference of opinion over the film's opening sequence had long since lost its joke-value.

Bronwen was standing over Marian as she typed, and Woody was bobbing up and down from his seat, rearranging the schedule cards he had pinned all over the wall. Franz, the Swiss make-up artist, and Belinda, the costume designer, were at Hazel's desk, leafing through the budget she had presented them with, while Josey, the production secretary, screamed down the telephone at someone in the passport office.

'Do ve know who's playing Olivia yet?' Franz asked.

'No,' Hazel answered.

'Vell, I have to bloody know.'

'What cast *have* we got?' Belinda asked.

'Judith will give you the details,' Hazel answered, taking Belinda's hand and pulling her out of her chair. 'She'll be in later. Matthew wants to see you both before you start shopping.'

'If he can spare the time,' Woody put in. 'I don't know why Stephanie can't just give in to him. He'll win in the end, he always does.'

'Matter of pride, darling,' Hazel answered. 'Franz, get your sweaty feet off my desk and for God's sake put your shoes on.'

'Fucking moron!' Josey spat as she slammed down the receiver. 'I'll have to go down there. Marian, can you book me a cab?'

'Hail one,' Bronwen said, 'she's busy.'

At that point Matthew thundered down the stairs and marched out into the street.

'Looks like we're back at stalemate,' Woody said, watching him go.

'Well, they've got two weeks to sort it.' Hazel batted Franz's feet from her desk and picked up the phone. 'Any news from Adrian, anyone?'

'He's on his way. Production meeting at six?'

'Six thirty,' Hazel answered. 'Stephanie and Matthew can't make it before. Final auditions for Olivia' – she turned to Franz – 'you'll be pleased to know.'

'Dollink, ve all vant a star. Vill she be English?'

'Don't be a prat,' Woody butted in. 'An unknown American. Judith picked up three of them from the airport yesterday.'

'Why is it always like this in the final couple of weeks' prep?' Josey complained. 'I'm so panicked I can't sleep at night.'

Marian's fingers moved rapidly across the keyboard but she was neither listening to what anyone was saying, nor paying attention to what she was typing. Her mind, as always these days, was on Matthew. Every time someone spoke to her about him she thought she could detect pity or amusement – and Stephanie's kindness only drove her humiliation deeper. Since she had had her talk with Stephanie she had told herself that from now on she must with never be alone with him again. It had taken a great deal of courage to do what she had, especially when Matthew returned to the office and she set about persuading him to go home. In fact, he hadn't taken much persuading, and after he'd gone Bronwen's words rang clear in her mind: ' . . .but they will straighten themselves out. Matthew will make certain of it.' It was that, more than anything else Bronwen had said, that convinced her of the strength of Matthew's love for Stephanie, and the ridiculousness of her own behaviour. But even knowing that, she hadn't been able to stop herself dwelling on the things he had said when they'd had dinner together, like: 'We'll work something out, don't worry. It'll just take time.' Much as she wanted to believe he was talking about them, in her heart she knew he was talking about his daughter. Yet he had taken up her hand and given it a squeeze as he said it . . .

She wound the letter out of the typewriter and handed it to Bronwen.

'Thanks,' Bronwen said. 'I'll sign it, then if you can get it in the post tonight . . . Josey, before you go, did you take the script to be photocopied?'

'Yes,' Josey answered impatiently. 'I'm picking it up at six. If I'm back.'

'I'll do it,' Marian offered.

'No you won't,' Bronwen broke in. 'I need you later to go over the draft scenes Deborah Foreman faxed us this morning. Woody, can you pick it up?'

'I'm the first assistant director, not a slave,' he stated.

'Thanks, Woody. Josey will be forever in your debt.' And Bronwen swept from the office.

Later in the day, as everyone started to pour in for the meeting, Bronwen waited for Marian to pack up. The downstairs office and stairway were teeming with people, everyone from the gaffer spark to production buyers to stunt arrangers. Bronwen and Marian pushed a path through them, then just as they were going out of the door, they came face to face with Stephanie and Matthew.

'And where might you two be going?' Matthew asked.

'The Groucho Club.' Bronwen answered. 'Any luck with Olivia?'

Matthew was smiling. 'Perfect. Girl called Christina Hancock.'

'At least they've agreed on something,' Bronwen muttered as they walked on.

'Marian!'

Marian turned round, then watched as Matthew spoke rapidly to Stephanie before stepping back into the street. 'Wait for me at the Groucho, I'll join you when the meeting's over. Stephanie's going to see her mother so I'm at a loose end.'

Marian cast a quick look at Bronwen, but she was walking on down the street. 'I'm afraid I can't,' she said, with a slight toss of her head. 'Bronwen and I are only going for a quick drink, then we're going home to look at the script.'

'Oh.' He seemed disappointed. 'Oh well, maybe some other time.' He started to move off, then having second thoughts, he turned back. 'Do you still think you're being followed?'

'No,' Marian answered. She did, but there was little point in telling him when she was fairly sure it was paranoia on her part.

'Good,' he said. Then, peering into her face: 'Everything's all right, is it? You aren't still worrying about your mother?'

'No, I'm fine, please don't fuss over me.'

He looked as astonished as she felt at this, and her immediate instinct was to apologise, but gritting her teeth, she forced herself to remain silent.

'I'm sorry,' he said, 'I suppose I have been overdoing it a bit.' Then, when she didn't answer, 'Am I forgiven?'

'Yes,' she said stiffly. 'I'd better go now, Bronwen's waiting,' and before he could say anything else, she turned and walked off down the street, her heart and her cheeks burning with misery.

After that she did her utmost to avoid him, and this was made easier when he suddenly declared that he would be working from home until they went to New York. Though he rang in several times a day, and always asked how she was, Marian never returned the compliment. She didn't enjoy being rude to him, but told herself it was the only way – for Stephanie's sake as well as her own.

Then, five days before they were due to fly out, he called Josey to ask her to go and sit in on a scheduling meeting between him, Bob Fairley, Woody, Freddy, and make-up and costume. Hazel took the call because Josey was at the carnet office, filling in last-minute details, and from there would be going on to the American Embassy to pick up visas for the actors who had recently been cast. Hazel needed the finalised schedule with such urgency that she and Woody had been yelling at each other all week about it, so now that Josey wasn't there to go to Matthew's meeting and bring the schedule back with her, she could have screamed. Marian happened to walk back into the office at that moment.

'Call yourself a cab, honeypop,' Hazel ordered. 'Get over to Matthew's and don't leave until you've got that shooting schedule.'

Marian didn't get the opportunity to protest, for Hazel picked up a handful of files and swept up the stairs to Stephanie's office.

When Marian arrived at the flat in Chiswick, Belinda,

the costume designer, let her in. Immediately she was ushered into the kitchen and told to make coffee. When it was done Woody helped her give it out, then sat on the floor again beside Matthew who was going through the first week's shoot, scene by scene. He hadn't acknowledged Marian's arrival, nor did he look up as she passed him a cup.

There was nowhere to sit, so she went back into the kitchen where, seeing his things lying about, she got caught up in a fantasy of what it would be like if she lived there with him. She knew she was torturing herself, but couldn't stop. Nothing else seemed to live in her mind now, except him; even the mystery of what had happened to Olivia, and how they had both become embroiled in it, seemed no more than a distant dream. At first, when he had rung her in Italy to tell her he knew about Art Douglas and Olivia, she had harboured a hope that it would bring them together. In a way it had, for a time, but now, because of Stephanie, it was driving them apart. The constant ache she felt for him was like nothing she had ever known, even with Paul. She tried to reason with herself, telling herself that it was because her feelings were unrequited, because she was on the rebound, but nothing seemed to help. Sometimes, at night, when she knew he would be holding Stephanie in his arms, she wanted to scream with the pain of her jealousy. She wanted to forget everything Bronwen had said: above all, she wanted to forget how she had asked Bronwen if it was Matthew who had asked her to speak to her – and how Bronwen had remained eloquently silent. She wanted to run to him and . . . And what? Beg him to tell her he loved her? It was like asking for the stars, and already, in her mind's eye, she could see his embarrassment and feel the fire of humiliation curl through her limbs as he backed away.

Then, hearing his voice in the other room, she suddenly knew that she couldn't go to New York, that she couldn't take any more. She had to get away from him and try to end this torment. She'd speak to Bronwen, Bronwen would understand.

It was almost an hour after she'd gone into the kitchen that Woody finally yelled out for her. When she went into the room, the others were leaving, and Woody was holding out a wad of handwritten notes. 'This is what you've been waiting for,' he said. 'Glad I'm not in your shoes, giving this to Josey. She'll be up all night.'

Marian took the notes, and mumbling a thank-you, she started to follow Woody out of the door.

'How are you getting back to the office?' Matthew asked. It was the first time he'd spoken to her.

Of course she didn't have an answer. It hadn't even occurred to her to book a return taxi.

He smiled, then called out to Woody: 'Get onto the special effects people about that scene. Have them call me here if there's any problem.'

When Woody had gone, Marian was left standing in the centre of the room, surrounded by the debris of coffee cups and overflowing ashtrays.

'Serves me right for holding a production meeting in my own home,' Matthew laughed.

'If it's all right, I'll use your phone to ring for a taxi. Then I'll help you clear up, if you like,' she offered, carefully avoiding his eyes.

'Thanks. But don't bother about the taxi, I'll drive you over there myself. What happened to Josey?'

She explained about the carnet office and the Embassy. 'So I came instead,' she finished, shrugging and looking out of the window.

'But you didn't want to?'

'No! Yes, I mean . . .'

He took the notes from her hands and led her to the sofa. 'You've been avoiding me for days,' he said, sitting her down. 'No, don't deny it. Now, what's going on? What have I done this time?' —

'Nothing. You haven't . . .' Her voice was coming with no breath, but she was afraid to let go.

'You're shaking. Something's happened, hasn't it? Come on, you must tell me.'

Suddenly she leapt to her feet. 'Nothing's happened, at least, nothing that you're thinking. I'd better call for a taxi – Josey and Hazel will be waiting for the schedule.'

He stood up slowly, watching her as she used the phone. Afterwards, he helped her carry the cups to the kitchen, but though neither of them spoke she was acutely aware of his eyes on her.

When the doorbell rang she quickly gathered up her handbag and the notes, but when she turned she went right into his arms.

It was too late. She wouldn't be able to get away now before breaking down. But still she fought it, breathing deeply to try and keep herself under control.

'Oh, Marian, Marian,' he murmured as he stroked her hair. 'What am I going to do about you?'

Her answer came in a sudden rush. 'It doesn't matter,' she gasped. 'I won't embarrass you any more. I won't be coming to New York. I'm sorry, Matthew, I didn't mean to embarrass you.'

'Embarrass me?' he said, pulling her away from his shoulder. 'How on earth have you embarrassed me?'

'Please, don't make me say it.' Her face was strained but still she managed not to cry.

'Say what, for heaven's sake? And what's all this nonsense about not going to New York?'

'I can't!' she cried. 'Not after . . . Not when you know . . .'

He pulled her back into his arms and squeezed her. 'Not when I know what, mm?'

When she didn't answer, he let her go and walked over to the entryphone to tell the driver to wait.

'Sit down,' he said when he came back.

She did as he told her, but couldn't look at him as he knelt in front of her and took her hands in his. He had a fair idea of what it was all about, and though he didn't want to do anything to exacerbate her distress, he knew they had to talk.

'Come to New York,' he said. 'Please.'

'But . . .'

'I want you to.'

'But I feel such a fool. Everyone's laughing at me.'

'Who's laughing at you?'

'Everyone. No one. Oh, I don't know. Oh God, this is all so awful, I feel such an idiot, especially after you asked Bronwen to . . .'

'Asked Bronwen to what?'

She shook her head.

'I think you'd better tell me, Marian.'

So, haltingly, with her cheeks glowing her humiliation, she told him.

When she'd finished he sighed deeply, then got to his feet. 'I didn't ask Bronwen to do that,' he said. He looked down at her, feeling anger at Stephanie who he knew was behind it, and an overwhelming compassion for Marian because of the way she had suffered as a result. But it was more than compassion. He didn't understand what he felt for Marian, he had never tried to analyse it, not even when Stephanie had challenged him about it; but whatever his feelings were, he knew now, as he gazed down at Marian, that Stephanie had cause to feel jealous.

He took Marian's hands and pulled her to her feet. 'Look, maybe you'd better go now,' he said. 'I need some time to think. But I want you to promise me one thing?'

She nodded dumbly.

'Don't leave. Come with us to New York. Finish the

film, at least. Perhaps by that time we'll have a better idea of what we're . . .' He stopped, shaken by what he'd been about to say. 'A better idea of what has happened to Olivia,' he finished, smiling.

Swallowing hard, Marian nodded, then suddenly she was laughing. 'I must be driving you mad,' she said. 'I always seem to have a problem, and you're always the one to sort it out. First Art Douglas, then getting Madeleine's agent's address, then listening to me bleat on about my mother, and now this . . . Well, I will come to New York, and I promise you I won't do or say anything to embarrass you. I understand the way you feel about Stephanie, I love her too. And so I should, after all she's done for me.'

'You're quite a girl, Marian,' he smiled. 'But don't forget the problems of mine that you've sorted out. Now we share one, which just at this moment seems a million miles away, I know. But Rubin Meyer and Sergio Rambaldi do exist, as do the men Olivia kept company with in New York. And as for Stephanie, you're right, I do love her and I always will. Please remember that.'

He had no idea how brutal his words were because he had no way of knowing how deep her feelings ran. Had he been looking at her, perhaps he might have seen the flash of pain in her eyes, but he was staring into the distance, his gaze for once brooding and withdrawn.

As she walked to the door he said: 'I think it would be better if you didn't tell Bronwen that we've spoken. In fact, don't mention anything to anyone. I'll deal with this myself, and you're not to worry about a thing. It'll all be all right.'

As Roy Welland let himself in through the front door of Shamir's Beverly Hills home he was listening for the sounds of the TV, but the house was in silence, and as the sun was in the dying throes of its struggle with the smog, it was in semi-darkness too. He walked across the white-tiled hall and pushed open the door of the sitting-room. On the floor were discarded newspapers and half-finished drinks. Then, hearing voices, he went over to the window, and pulling back a lace curtain, he saw Shamir and Paul in the pool.

'Hey!' he called, knocking on the window. 'It's almost over.'

'What?' Shamir called back. 'Speak up, I can't hear you.'

Leaving the sitting-room, Roy walked through the conservatory and out to the edge of the kidney-shaped pool. 'I said, it's nearly over,' he repeated. 'Why aren't you watching?'

'Oh my God!' Shamir gasped. 'I forgot all about it. Quick, go inside and turn on the TV, Paul!'

'Yes, I heard,' Paul said, heaving himself out of the water, and he smirked as he noticed the peculiar look Roy gave him before turning back into the house. The look, he knew, was not because he had forgotten that he and Madeleine were on the Johnny Carson Show in an interview they had recorded the day before, but because he was stark naked. And so, if Roy had looked a little more carefully, was Shamir.

As Shamir walked into the sitting-room, the final credits were rolling.

'You've missed it,' Roy said, looking up. 'Just as well I remembered to set the video tape before I took Madeleine to the audition or she'd wonder what the hell you'd two had been up to, forgetting the Johnny Carson Show.'

'I know what you think, Roy,' Shamir said, walking over to the bar and pouring herself a drink, 'but you're wrong. Skinny-dipping is quite normal in these parts, everyone does it – even you.'

'Yes, but not with someone else's man.'

'I should hope not,' Paul grinned, as he walked into the

room, a towel wrapped round his waist. 'I'll have one of whatever you're having,' he told Shamir, and picking up a newspaper, he flopped down on the billowing cushions of the sofa. 'Did we miss the interview?' he said, glancing at Roy.

'Yes.'

As Paul turned back to the paper, Roy was still watching him. Deidre had asked him to keep an eye on Paul and Madeleine, wanting to make sure, she told him, that their relationship was well and truly clear of the rocks. Her request hadn't surprised him, for everyone in the agency knew how fond she had become of Madeleine, but he wondered how she would take it if he told her about Paul and Shamir swimming together in the nude. She'd probably just laugh and accuse him of being a prude – which was exactly what Madeleine did later when the limousine service delivered her back to the house and Paul told her how he and Shamir had shocked Roy by taking a swim in the all-together.

'Oh Roy,' Madeleine laughed, throwing her arms round him, 'you're such an old fuddy-duddy sometimes. You were swimming with me yesterday while Paul was upstairs asleep and Shamir was down town shopping, and unless my eyes were deceiving me you're quite a man. So what's the difference?'

'None, I suppose,' Roy admitted with a reluctant grin. 'And don't call me an old fuddy-duddy.'

'Just a fuddy-duddy, eh?' Shamir said.

'Less of your cheek, madam. Now, how about telling us what happened at the audition, Maddy?'

'Not a lot really,' she answered, sinking into the sofa next to Paul and relaxing against the arm he held out for her. 'Thanks,' she said, as Shamir passed her a cocktail. 'They just said they'd be in touch with my agent.'

'But did you have to act? Or read anything?' Paul asked.

'Yeah, they gave me a scene from the script and I read that.'

'What's it about?'

'I don't know, really. My part's not very big – if I get it. Something to do with this bloke who goes around picking up women in bars – or at least, the part I read was.'

'You're one of the women?'

She nodded. 'Though I get to go to bed with the guy, which is more than some of them do. And you'll never guess who the guy is? Robert de Niro. So naturally, I said I didn't mind taking off my clothes for the camera. I mean, who would if it's with Robert de Niro?'

'You wouldn't mind, whoever it was,' Shamir commented.

'Oooh, you can be so cutting sometimes,' Madeleine laughed. 'Anyway, did you watch the interview?'

'No, we recorded it so that we could watch it with you,' Paul answered, before anyone else had a chance to.

Madeleine pressed her head back against his shoulder, and looking up into his face, she waggled her tongue between her lips.

Laughing, he covered her mouth with his own and gave her a long, lingering kiss.

'If you don't mind us,' Shamir remarked, throwing a cushion at them. 'Are we going to watch this interview or aren't we?'

'No, we can watch it any time,' Madeleine answered. 'Right now I'm for a shower and something to eat. Shall we all go out tonight?'

'Why not?' Roy said. 'As the rest of us are flying to New York tomorrow, let's take Shamir out on the town. Come on, Shamir, where do you want to go? The world's your oyster in a twenty-mile radius.'

'So kind,' Shamir smiled sweetly. 'When I've come up with the most expensive place I can think of, I'll let you know.' She linked arms with Madeleine and the two of them went giggling off towards the stairs.

'So, Royston,' Paul said when they'd gone, 'I still can't tempt you into becoming a murder victim?'

'Not today, no,' Roy answered blithely.

'I've got to kill someone, or how am I going to experience what it's like being on trial for murder?'

This was a conversation that had started between them on the plane from London, and one which they had gone back to several times during the past forty-eight hours because they both found it highly entertaining.

'Why do you have to experience it? Can't you go to a prison and ask someone who's done it?'

'Nah,' Paul said, shaking his head, 'it's not the same, is it? I need to write it from the gut.'

'What about the actual act of killing? Who's going to do that?'

'It's not important, not the way I'm writing it. The guy's in a kind of trance, he doesn't know what he's doing, and he only regains his senses when he's in the courtroom.'

'I see. Well, sorry, mate, but I'm all out of the need to die right now.'

'If I can't persuade you, I'll have to think of someone else. At the moment my editor's top of the list. The publishing house couldn't turn it down, could they, if one of their own was despatched by a writer?'

'Do you think he'd be agreeable?'

'I could get Harry to agree to almost anything these days, but being murdered might prove difficult. However, he can always come back to life once the trial's over. I don't want to end up spending the next twenty years in prison.'

'Oh, so you only want someone to *play* dead?'

'Yes, but for real. The authorities have to think they're dead, otherwise it won't work.'

'But you'll need a body.'

'Yes,' Paul said, drawing the word out thoughtfully, 'I haven't quite managed to overcome that slight hitch yet, but I'm working on it.'

– 21 –

'OK, Woody, let's have a look at this schedule.' Stephanie stood over his desk, a hand planted on either side of her slim hips and a wry smile raising the corners of her mouth. 'No, the second week,' she said, when he tried to push the first week's to the top of the pile. She glanced over at Marian and winked. Hazel was turned to the window, pretending to be on the phone, and Josey was snickering behind her hand. 'It's all right, Woody, I know what you've done,' Stephanie said. 'I just want you to convince me that it's going to work.'

Accepting that he'd been caught out, and indeed knowing he would be sooner or later, Woody pulled out the second week's schedule for America. Stephanie studied it for several minutes, then handed it back.

'How long have you worked with Matthew?' she asked.

Woody shrugged. 'Ten years?'

'And you're telling me he'll get that opening crane shot in a morning.'

'We'll have to because of trying to match it. The helicopter stuff we can do any time. I've got it down for the next day because it'll probably take all day.'

Stephanie was shaking her head. 'Sorry, that crane shot can't be done in a morning, I'm not buying it.'

At that point Matthew walked in. 'Buying being the operative word,' he said. 'I take it she's found out.'

'She has,' Stephanie confirmed. 'And you don't impress me by sneaking it into the schedule like this, though I should have expected as much. So I'll sanction it, but you'd better make damned sure it works.' She paused. 'And one other thing. *Don't*, under any circumstances, put an actor in it. The shot's complicated enough without having to contend with motivation or whatever other rubbish they want to discuss. The clock will be ticking in dollars that morning, Matthew, remember that, won't you?' She smiled sweetly, then disappeared up the stairs.

'Does anyone have a good word to say about actors?' Marian asked Josey.

'If they do I haven't met them,' Josey answered, then throwing her arms wide, she embraced Matthew. 'You wily old fox, you. Of course, you know the shot's jinxed now, don't you?'

'One more comment like that and you're fired,' Matthew said, unwinding himself. He rubbed his hands together. 'Well, Hazel, get onto Chapman's in Hollywood and confirm our provisional booking.'

'What provisional booking?'

'The one Bob Fairley made for the cranes. Well, get on with it, woman, we need them in New York in ten days time. And while you're at it, let Bob know, will you, and confirm the helicopter too. Now Woody, I think you deserve a drink, my friend. Come on, Marian, get that umbrella of yours, we're off to celebrate.'

'Some of us have work to do,' Josey commented.

'Which is why I didn't invite you,' Matthew retorted.

Marian adored him when he was in this mood, and abandoning not only Stephanie's and Bronwen's last-minute correspondence but her own resolution to avoid him as much as possible, she rushed out to the kitchen for her umbrella.

It was the first time she'd seen him since the afternoon at his flat. Afterwards she had gone over all he'd said a thousand times – but never for a minute allowing herself to dwell on what he'd said about Stephanie. As for the rest, it was so ambiguous that it was difficult to draw any definite conclusions, but a sixth sense told her that, though it might take time, things really might have a chance of working out for them. She wouldn't allow herself to think further than that, mainly because of what it would mean for Stephanie, but there were occasions when she could do nothing to control the hope that sprung mischievously into her mind, painting glorious pictures of the future and telling her that all she had to do was trust Matthew to come up with a solution that would make everyone happy.

'Now, Woody,' Matthew said, as he set down a tray of drinks on the table in front of them, 'make up your mind before we go who you're going to screw, and stick with her; I don't want any make-up girls snivelling into their tea because you're giving them a hard time – in or out of the sack.'

Marian's mouth dropped open, but as she turned to look at Woody, she started to laugh.

'He thinks he's such a wag,' Woody remarked. 'As a matter of fact, I'm celibate these days.'

'That sounds a bit harsh on your already long-suffering wife,' Matthew said, sitting down next to Marian. 'Or maybe she likes it.'

'It doesn't include her. What I meant to say was, I'm faithful.'

'What he meant to say,' Matthew told Marian, 'is that she's caught him out again. Am I right?' he added, looking at Woody.

'Nail on the head.'

'On the subject of wives,' Matthew said, laughing as he turned back to Marian, 'Kathleen asked me to send you her love, and said something about seeing things coming and was she right?'

Marian swallowed her laughter and looked at him shyly, wondering whether he knew what Kathleen meant. 'Tell her she was right,' she said, 'but I'll cope.'

'Women,' Woody grunted. 'Not only do they talk in

riddles, they expect you to pass them on. What was all that about?'

'Search me,' Matthew shrugged, 'but over the years I've learned not to ask. Now, how many assistants have you got yourself when we're in New York?'

'Four. One's flying out with us, the others are hired locally. That should keep the natives happy, anyway.'

'What about Bennington?'

'Same.'

'Bit excessive, four for Bennington, it's mainly interiors.'

'That's because *you're* a bit excessive, guvnor,' Woody told him. 'Besides, we've got thousands of extras when we're at Bennington.'

'Don't exaggerate.'

'OK, hundreds. Have you ever been on a shoot before, Marian?'

'No, never.'

'Then this will be an experience, I can tell you. While Matthew here sits back and gives orders, you'll see the rest of us running around like headless chickens, and then at lunchtime he'll ask us what we've been doing all morning. This question, I might add, will very likely be delivered from the window of his own personal winnebago.'

'Winnebago?' Marian said curiously.

'Caravan.'

'When have I ever had a winnebago?' Matthew demanded.

'You've got one this time, Hazel's booked it.'

'Well, you can just tell her to unbook it, I don't like all that pretentious stuff and you know it. Besides, with you and Rory what's-his-name, the camera operator, running loose on the set, it'll only end up being used as a knocking shop.'

'Would we defile your holy territory?'

'You do it on your own doorstep so I can't see my winnebago going unmolested.'

Marian burst out laughing at the pained expression on Woody's face.

'Don't encourage him,' Woody sulked.

'Just listen to who's talking.' They all looked up as Stephanie shook out her umbrella beside them and nodded when Bronwen asked her if she'd like a shandy. 'You were the one who encouraged him to schedule that sequence,' Stephanie said, looking accusingly at Woody as she sat down between him and Matthew. 'I should have remembered what you two are like when you get together.' She rolled her eyes. 'I didn't really stand a chance, did I?'

'Not really,' Woody told her cheerfully, removing his glasses and giving them a wipe with a lens cloth. 'But some of us have to learn the hard way.'

'About what?' Bronwen asked, handing Stephanie a drink.

'Matthew, and his inimitable talent for getting his own way . . .'

The light-hearted banter continued, and Marian listened, thrilling to the way so much of it was directed at Matthew. When the rest of the production team arrived they instantly picked up the frivolous mood and began ribbing and ridiculing one another, though always with an eye on Matthew to see if he was listening. Only those very close to Matthew had the nerve to tease him, Marian noticed, but it seemed as if everyone's purpose was to make him laugh.

Franz, the make-up supervisor, was undoubtedly the victor. He and Hazel had been at each other from the minute they walked in, though Marian hadn't caught much of what they'd said until now. But following Matthew's eyes, she started to eavesdrop on the conversation that was going on behind her.

'. . . and I don't vant vun of those bloody make-up

caravans with the low chairs again,' Franz was saying. 'It gives me the fucking back-ache, having to bend over all day.'

'I don't know why,' Hazel retorted, 'you bend over all night without any problems.'

Matthew roared with laughter, but Franz was not to be outdone, and after shooting Matthew a quick look, he said studying his fingernails: 'At least there's alvays somevun behind me vhen I'm bending over in the night, vhich is more than I can say for you, dollink.'

Matthew choked on his beer and Marian laughed so hard that tears started to stream down her face.

'Oh God, Hazel and Franz aren't at it again, are they?' Stephanie groaned. 'What are they saying now?'

It was some time before Matthew could repeat it, and when he did everyone collapsed into laughter.

'OK, my round,' Woody declared, getting to his feet.

'No, I'll get them,' Stephanie said, 'but you can come to the bar and give me a hand.'

Once they'd sorted out what everyone wanted and gone off to the bar, Matthew turned to Marian. 'Are you all right?' he said quietly.

'Of course,' she answered. 'Shouldn't I be?'

He grinned. 'Bit of a motley lot, aren't they, but I think you're going to enjoy New York.'

'I'm sure I am,' she said enthusiastically.

Matthew watched her as she picked up her drink, but when her eyes met his he looked away.

Three days later, on a rainy Saturday morning, thirty-two members of production and crew boarded the British Airways flight to New York – the rest of the unit would be flying out the following day. Shooting would begin on Tuesday at Bennington, where Olivia Hastings had been a student. Marian was so excited that she didn't sleep for one minute of the seven-hour flight. She sat between Matthew and Woody, who started telling her horror stories about what usually happens to novices on a film set. Stephanie, Bronwen and Hazel were at the back of the plane, smoking, and the others were dotted about the aircraft, either sleeping or drinking.

Halfway across the Atlantic, Woody's head dropped onto Marian's shoulder and he drifted into a noisy slumber.

'God, he's disgusting,' Matthew grinned as Woody gave a particularly loud snort. 'Push him off.'

'He's all right,' Marian laughed.

Matthew turned back to look out of the window, then a few minutes later his hand moved across and covered hers. 'You're not nervous, are you?' he said, turning to her. 'I mean, about going to New York now that Art Douglas has told you about Olivia?'

'No, I'm not nervous,' Marian answered, amazed that her voice could sound so calm when her insides were churning so disturbingly.

He wondered if he should tell her that someone was following her, but he decided not to – it would only alarm her, and there was a chance he could be wrong. But he didn't think so; the man who was sitting four rows behind them now had been standing at the bar of the pub they'd had a drink in a few days ago. He'd also seen someone very like him walk past the office yesterday, though the man was so nondescript, with his wavy brown hair and bland face, that it was difficult to be sure. 'Good,' he smiled, giving her hand a squeeze. We're probably making too much of all this, but nevertheless, don't go taking any risks, will you?'

'Like what?'

'Like going to see Jodi again – and then not telling me about it.' Except that if she did, he would know. Frank Hastings' people were going to keep an eye on her during their time in New York.

The moment Marian would never forget was six and a

half hours after take-off, when the plane tilted and the captain came over the PA system to tell those who hadn't already noticed that the Manhattan skyline was to their left. The last time she had come to New York the weather had been so grey and overcast that she had been unable to make out even the very tops of the highest buildings, but now, there it was – a city of skyscrapers, projecting through the shimmering heat haze like rockets on a launch pad. She'd seen it so many times in movies, on TV, in books, but there was nothing like seeing it for real. Her chest swelled with excitement and she was certain that somehow, in some way, New York would be the turning-point for her and Matthew.

After passport control, baggage collection and customs, they emerged from Kennedy airport into a blanket of wet heat. It clung to their nostrils and trickled over their skin in clammy beads of sweat. Thankfully, the stretch limousines waiting to drive them into the city were air-conditioned, and when they arrived at the Dorset Hotel Marian took great delight in the reception she got from Tony, the doorman, who had been there the last time she was in New York with Bronwen.

'Well, my oh my,' he said in his Southern drawl as he looked her up and down, 'is that really you? I'd never have recognised you. Don't you look just the gal.'

'Young lady,' Hazel corrected him, as she passed by with Bob Fairley, the lighting cameraman.

'Sure, that'n'all,' Tony grinned. 'Pleasure to see you again, Miss . . .'

'Marian,' she reminded him.

'Sure. And where's Miss Bronwen, she's a-coming with y'all?'

'She's in the car behind,' Marian answered, and after digging into her purse for a generous tip, she followed one of the liveried bellhops upstairs to her room.

On the fourteenth floor a two-bedroomed, two-bathroomed suite had been taken over for production offices, there was even a galley kitchen just inside the door. Marian found Josey already there when she went exploring, organising removal men who were carrying in desks, chairs, shelving units and typewriters.

'There's a photocopier in there,' Josey said, pointing to one of the bedrooms. 'Couldn't run off a couple of dozen of these, could you?'

Marian took the sheet of paper she held out and saw that it was a list of everyone's room number. Her eyes raced down the page, and when she found what she was looking for her heart lifted.

'We thought it might be a bit off, the producer and director shacking up together,' Stephanie explained, when Marian handed her a list and asked if everything was all right.

'But why?'

'Lots of reasons, really. If anyone wanted to talk to one of us confidentially, say, they might not feel so inclined to come if they thought they might be interrupting something. And Matthew's going to need all the sleep he can get; so am I, come to that; besides, there'll be enough shenanigans going on with the rest of the crew without me behaving like the madam in a travelling brothel.'

'Doesn't Matthew mind?'

'I don't think so, he didn't really say much when I told him. Ah, Josey,' she said, as the door opened and Josey came back into the production office, 'Hazel was looking for you just now, she wants you to go down to the art gallery location with her.'

'But I've got tons to do here,' Josey protested.

'I'm only passing on the message,' Stephanie said.

'I suppose I'd better go and find her, then.' And muttering under her breath, Josey went back out again.

'Well,' Stephanie sighed as she looked around at the

chaos in the room. Then, laughing, she threw an arm round Marian's shoulders and gave her a hug. 'We're really going to have our work cut out, you and I. We'll have to be at least five steps ahead of the shoot at all times, racing about town pacifying lawyers, getting last-minute deals struck every time Matthew changes his mind – which he will, at least a dozen times a day – and making regular visits to the set to make sure they're on schedule. Think you can cope? 'Cos I'll let you into a secret, I've hardly slept a wink this past week, worrying whether or not I can.'

'You don't mean that?'

'I do. Still, don't let's think about it now, let's just concentrate on enjoying the time we've got left to us.'

'Anyone would think you were on death row,' Marian laughed.

'You're not far wrong there. Anyway, to take my mind off things, I'd like to take you to the Village tonight for dinner. Just the two of us. Bronwen's having a meeting with Deborah Foreman, and Matthew's got costume and make-up parades in here at six, then he's taking Christina Hancock out to the Hastings'. They'll be talking over the ins and outs of Olivia's personality so I'm going to leave them to it. Much to Matthew's relief, I might add. So, if you're willing and able, go and take a shower and put on your glad rags – we're off to Il Mulino, one of my favourite Italian restaurants.'

'You as well,' Marian smiled. 'Bronwen took me there last time I was in New York. But I'd love to go again,' she added quickly when Stephanie's face fell.

At seven o'clock, when Marian wandered downstairs to the lobby to meet Stephanie, she was wearing a loose white shirt tucked into the wide belt of a figure-hugging mustard skirt which finished just above the knee, and matching shoes. It was the first time she'd worn the skirt because it hadn't really fitted her when she bought it, but now she had lost weight, and as she had noticed when she looked in the mirror, the mustard skirt contrived to make her look even slimmer. Her silvery hair was brushed and shining, and the only make up she wore was mascara. In fact, she was feeling rather pleased with the way she looked until the elevator doors opened and Stephanie walked out with Matthew.

It was bad enough that Stephanie had such elegance and style, and towered above Marian's five feet five inches in a way that, despite her new slimline figure, made her feel frumpish; but tonight Stephanie's red hair was woven into a French plait, and the glimmer of her gold earrings and subtle lip gloss was matched by the light in her tawny eyes. She looked beautiful in every sense of the word. But Marian felt decidedly better when Matthew treated her to a long, appreciative wolf-whistle, and she laughed with delight when he swept her into his arms and gave first her, then Stephanie, an exaggeratedly passionate good-bye kiss.

As the yellow taxi drove them down-town, Marian craned her neck to look up at the obelisk-like buildings, waiting for the bizarre suspension of reality that had overtaken her the last time she was in New York. Everywhere she looked, glaring neon signs blinked and flashed, while on the ground steam swirled from the drains. The colour, the hustle and bustle, the sounds, the chaos of life, were all the same, but for some reason she wasn't responding to it as she had before. She didn't know whether this was because the city no longer held the same magic for her – or because the sense of unreality was with her constantly now and she hadn't realised it.

The driver dropped them at the restaurant and, once inside, they were shown straight to their table. 'Right,' Stephanie said, after the waiter had taken their orders, 'let's get down to some serious gossip. Things have been so hectic these past few weeks, I've hardly seen you. So, tell me everything, sparing no detail.'

'Well, *cariad*,' Marian began, giving a wonderful rendition of Bronwen's Welsh accent, 'did you know that Bronwen's been trying for days to call Sergio Rambaldi?'

'Yes, I did,' Stephanie laughed. 'She wants a repeat performance with him when we go to Italy, I believe.'

'If you ask me, darling,' Marian said, sounding exactly like Hazel, 'I think she's *frightfully* brave. I mean, the guy might be good-looking but, quite frankly, he gives me the spooks. No, I'm sorry, he does. I feel as if he's looking right into me with those eyes of his. Just wait 'til you meet him, darling, you'll see exactly what I mean.'

'Oh, are you English?' a voice behind them called out suddenly.

Marian and Stephanie turned round to see a lumpy, middle-aged American woman sitting at a nearby table with her husband, and beaming all over her face at them. 'Can you talk a bit more,' she said, 'I just love that accent.'

'Oh my god,' Marian muttered.

'Over to you,' Stephanie said, grinning widely.

'Actually,' Marian began, 'I don't really speak like that, you see, I was mimicking a . . .'

'Will you just listen to that voice!' the woman said.

Thankfully their food arrived then, so the woman left them alone.

'I didn't think that happened for real,' Marian hissed under her breath.

'Me neither,' Stephanie said, still laughing. 'We'll have to tell Bronwen, she'll find it hysterical. Now what's that you've having there?'

'Tuna fish and beans.'

'You're not still trying to lose weight?'

'Have you ever had Hazel as a dietician?'

'No,' Stephanie chuckled, 'but I can imagine. You really do look terrific on it, though.'

'Why, thank you,' Marian grinned, and sat back as the waiter refilled their glasses.

Like any Italian restaurant, Il Mulino was crowded and noisy, with greenery and empty chianti bottles decorating the walls. As Marian looked about she suddenly felt that someone was watching her – not in the curious way some Americans had of ogling foreigners as though they were playful aliens, but in the way she had felt it before, back in London. She shivered – but then told herself that Matthew's mention of Art Douglas on the plane must have made her jittery.

'Did you mean what you said earlier?' she asked, turning back to Stephanie and picking up her fork. 'About not sleeping?'

Stephanie pulled a face. 'Don't remind me. A nervous producer's all we need, isn't it? But I don't mind telling you, Marian, it feels like I'm about to launch myself off the edge of a precipice with no wings.'

'You amaze me. You seem so perfectly in control.'

'That is thanks to Matthew. Between you, me and the gatepost, if it weren't for him I think I'd have gone to pieces by now.'

'But why?'

Stephanie took a deep breath and picked up her glass of wine. 'This is my first major film. Everything else I've done has been for TV, with a budget only a fraction the size of this one and shot either on videotape or sixteen millimetre film. This, as you know, is being done on thirty-five millimetre, which makes a hell of a difference – not only the look of it, but the cost. Matthew's used to thirty-five mill, of course. Thankfully we're not plagued with a horde of executive producers and studio heads interfering and changing things – including producers – every five minutes, the way they do on most films. Nevertheless, this is my proving ground, and if I flunk this one . . .' She left the sentence unfinished.

'I can't see that happening,' Marian said, swallowing a mouthful of tuna. 'I can't see *you* letting it, for one thing, never mind Matthew.'

Stephanie smiled. 'You know all the right things to say, don't you? But the truth is, I don't think I could do it without him. He's carrying the brunt of everything right now, which is the main reason why we're not sharing a room. I can't go on burdening him with my blasted nerves, he's got his own job to do.'

'My guess is,' Marian said, 'that once the shooting starts and you're right in the thick of it, you'll forget all about your nerves and just get on with it.'

'I hope you're right,' Stephanie laughed. Then holding her glass out to Marian, she said, 'Here's to *Disappearance*.'

They drank the toast, and when they'd finished their meal the waiter brought two espressos.

'You seem to be over that crush you had on Matthew now,' Stephanie said, resting her elbows on the table and holding her cup between her hands.

Though Marian managed a smile, she couldn't meet Stephanie's eyes.

Returning the smile, Stephanie said: 'God, when I think back to all the crushes I had on older men. Silly, really, isn't it. Still, in this case it was Matthew's fault entirely, he shouldn't go around behaving the way he does. The trouble is, I'm not sure he knows what effect he's having. But there's no harm done, is there?'

Marian's mouth had become dry and a horrible drumming was starting up in her chest. Somehow she managed to force another smile. 'None at all.'

'Good. That's what I want to hear. Now I can let you to my little secret. I've been dying to tell someone, but Bronwen's so engrossed in that Sergio fellow, my mother's somewhere in the Bahamas, and Hazel couldn't keep a secret if her life depended on it. Anyway, Matthew's asked me to marry him.'

It was strange how the room seemed suddenly to dip away from her and everything appeared to be happening at the end of a long tunnel. Mentally Marian shook herself, as if trying to free herself from a dream. The words were there, but somehow they hadn't quite reached her. She looked into Stephanie's face; then, as she heard herself mumble something about fantastic news, the reality of what Stephanie had said came thundering towards her in a great ball of screaming, panic-filled denial. This couldn't happen. This wasn't right. Somehow Stephanie had got it wrong. She tried to move but her hands were paralysed, her legs weighted like lead.

'Of course, we've got to wait for his divorce to come through,' Stephanie was saying. 'God knows how long that's going to take. That's why it's still a secret. If Kathleen finds out she'll do everything she can to delay it.' Her frown lifted, and reaching for Marian's hand, she gave it a squeeze. 'You know how much I've always wanted this, how I was so terrified I'd lose him again. I still don't think I'm quite over that yet, but . . . God, I must have bored you to tears with it by now. But I feel so incomplete without him, Marian. He says he feels the same without me, but can you imagine Matthew anything but completely together?' She laughed, and Marian watched as Stephanie's love enveloped her as clearly as if Matthew were there, taking her in his arms.

Somehow she got through what was left of the evening, but she knew it was only pride – which had solidified into a kind of numbness – holding her together. Once she was inside her hotel room, her breath started to choke in her throat and she could feel her resolve beginning to splinter. But no, she told herself, you musn't let go. You can't, or there will be no way of surviving this.

There was a red light on her phone. She called down for the message, then literally fell to her knees as she replaced the receiver. Matthew had called from the Hastings'. He'd be back around midnight and he wanted her to wait up.

Trust him, she reminded herself. He knew what he was doing, and now he was coming to explain.

Her half-unpacked suitcase was lying open on the bed. It was a quarter to twelve now, he could arrive at any minute. Frantically she rummaged through her clothes until she found the pale blue satin nightgown she'd bought in a moment of extravagance. She draped it over the bed, then made a quick trip to the bathroom to check on the way she looked. Her face was pinched, haunted, but there was nothing she could do about it, the shock of Stephanie's news had been too great.

By the time he knocked, at twenty past midnight, she had run the gamut of every possible reason he might have for asking her to wait up. But no matter how hard she tried to convince herself that it was something to do with Olivia, or how many obstacles she tried to put in the way of her hope, it wouldn't go away. It was going to work out for them, it just had to.

When she let him in, she almost gasped – she had never seen him so handsome. He was wearing a black suit, his tie was undone and the top button of his white shirt was open. Dressed like that, he seemed so remote from the Matthew she knew that she felt herself being sucked into a world of absurdity, and from the shadowy margins of her mind there seemed to come a doom-laden warning that she was in danger of making herself ridiculous. He wouldn't be able to miss her paltry attempt at seduction, with the lights turned down low and a subtle hint of perfume in the air, and already she was on fire with embarrassment.

'Secret trysts at midnight, what would everyone say?' he joked, as she closed the door.

She tried to laugh, but he was standing so close, and the

smell of him sent the blood rushing so fast through her veins that it came out as a sob.

He smiled, and slipping an arm round her shoulders he led her over to the bed and sat down.

'I hope I haven't alarmed you,' he said.

'No, no,' she assured him.

'Good, but I do have some news. It's nothing to do with Olivia or Art Douglas, but I wanted to tell you before you went to bed.'

'What's that?' she said, breathlessly.

'You'd better prepare yourself for a bit of a shock. It seems that apart from the bank and several other businesses Frank heads, he's also the chairman of a company called Seeberg and Wright. They're a publishing house, and next week they're launching Paul O'Connell's book. Paul and Madeleine were there, at dinner tonight.

'I wanted to tell you now,' he went on, 'before you picked up a newspaper or switched on the TV and saw them. Forewarned, and all that. It's the most bloody coincidence, I know, but we can't do a thing about it. Anyway, New York's a big town, it's unlikely you'll run into them. She recognised me, of course, from Bristol, but I didn't mention anything about you, I thought it was something you'd prefer to handle yourself.'

It was the one thing that hadn't even entered her head, and as she listened to him she had been too stunned to interrupt. Now she wanted only to scream. To yell at him that she didn't give a damn about her cousin any more, or Paul. To beg him to explain why he'd asked Stephanie to marry him, when . . . When what? She turned to look at him, and when she saw the way his dark eyes were so filled with concern for her, she was suddenly engulfed by the hopelessness of her situation. Wrenching herself away, she threw herself against the pillows, crying, 'No! No, no.'

Matthew closed the door quietly behind him, and as he walked to the lift his face was grim. So she *was* still in love with O'Connell, and it was no more than a rebound crush she'd felt for him. But the relief he'd expected to feel didn't come, and as he closed the door to his room he tried to remind himself that she was just a kid. 'You feel sorry for her, want to comfort her because she's lonely,' he told himself. 'It's nothing more than that.'

'How many more times do I have to tell you, Harry,' Paul sighed irritably. 'It's over between us. I don't even know what you're doing here in New York.'

'I'm here as your publisher, and because I thought you wanted me to be here.' Harry's face was taut, and his hand trembled as he picked up the cup of coffee that had just been put in front of him.

Paul looked around the shadowy enclaves of the Twenty-One Club to make sure no one could hear. It was lunchtime, and, mercifully, not crowded. 'I said nothing to indicate I wanted you here. Shit, if Madeleine were to find out . . .' He pushed his hand through his hair in exasperation. A thought suddenly occurred to him and he looked at his editor with undisguised loathing. 'You're not considering turning up at the party tomorrow night, are you?'

'I was. But contrary to what you think, I haven't come all this way to cause a scene. I'm here because what we have between us is real, and you know it.'

Paul thumped his hand on the table, rattling the cups in their saucers. 'For the last time, Harry, I am not a homosexual. I am a writer doing his research. It's done, I don't *need* to do it again.'

'You may not need to, but you and I both know you want to.'

Paul stared sightlessly up at the curious collection of planes, baseballs, soup tins and tankards that hung from the club's oak-beamed ceiling. He didn't want to lose Harry's friendship – apart from anything else, his next book wasn't far off completion – but the man was a parasite. 'OK,' he said eventually, what will it take to convince you?'

Harry's face relaxed. 'I'm staying at the Freemantle apartment on the Upper East Side, Sixty-Fourth and Third.' He took a pen from his inside pocket and jotted down the address. 'Spend an afternoon there with me, and if nothing happens between us . . . Well, then I could be convinced.'

Paul took the slip of paper, looked at it, then ripped it into shreds. 'I can remember the address,' he said bitterly. 'I'll call you when I can make it.'

The two cranes inched slowly through the trees, crunching a path over dried leaves and pine-cones. The drive's sweeping crescent was fringed by weeping hemlocks, beech and horse chestnuts, and hidden behind their dense foliage were billowing acres of park and woodland. At the end of the quarter-mile approach, the road curved past the Gothic revival mansion and snaked off into the woods beyond.

Matthew stood in front of the colonnaded porch with Frank Hastings. They were looking up at a narrow arched window on the second floor and discussing how much wisteria would have to be chopped away. Behind them, Woody was shouting instructions into a walkie-talkie while at the same time windmilling directions to the crane drivers. His assistants rushed about with call sheets, teas and coffees, while props men unloaded their vehicles and electricians unravelled miles of cable. The make-up and wardrobe caravans were parked in the stable complex, adjacent to the house, along with the winnebagos and catering trucks.

Marian stood under a cluster of sugar maples, feeling a little overwhelmed by all the activity. It was the first time she'd visited the set, for during the first week Stephanie had flown out to Bennington alone, leaving her to take care of things back at the Dorset. Now the crew had returned to New York, and they had all left Manhattan at six that morning to drive to the Hastings' home in Westchester, where they would begin shooting around nine.

Franz and Belinda were wandering about with their assistants, as the artistes weren't called for costume and make-up until midday. In fact Franz and Belinda wouldn't have been there themselves if it hadn't been the day of the much-talked-about-crane shot. They strolled over to join Marian who, never having seen a chipmunk before, was gazing round-eyed as two of them scampered through the trees. Franz gave her a critical up-and-down, then, leaning on her shoulder, turned to watch the cranes as they moved slowly into place.

'Vill you just look at that Hazel,' he hissed, a minute or two later. 'Vhy she doesn't just put her tits in Bob Fairley's hands I'll never know. I svear she's doing it on purpose to annoy you, Belinda, dolling. After all, everyvun's noticed how your tongue starts hanging out vhen he's around.'

Belinda threw him a sour look and Marian giggled. She dreaded being at the receiving end of Franz's vicious tongue herself, but in this instance, he was hardly exaggerating – Hazel was rubbing herself against the lighting cameraman as if they were actually engaged in the sexual act.

'Ah, there's Rory,' Franz sighed, as the blond camera operator, wearing only shorts and a vest, carried one of the 35mm cameras across the forecourt and into the house. 'Dolling, my cock's gone hard just looking at him,' he drooled. 'He had Christina Hancock, our star, vhen ve vere in Bennington, but don't tell anyvun. Oh God, save me, here comes Beat-me-up Beanie.'

'Shut up, Franz, she'll hear you,' Belinda snapped.

Marian watched the continuity girl as she parked her

picnic chair behind the camera van and took out her script. Ben, the focus puller, carrying a lens case in one hand and a cup of tea in the other, fell straight over her as he rounded the vehicle, and Franz and Belinda hooted with laughter as Beanie's script scattered across the gravel. A couple of riggers ran over to rescue the lens case, leaving Ben to mop the tea from his face while Beanie swore at him. Marian turned to Franz.

'Why Beat-me-up Beanie?'

'Because, dolling, she's had every bastard in the Western hemisphere. Cries herself to sleep over vun of them every night. It's how she gets her kicks. She's in love vith Rory now, but then who isn't?' His pale blue eyes rolled in their sockets as Rory emerged from the house with the operator of the second camera. Bob Fairley called out to them and then Matthew joined in, waving his hands in the air as they all looked up to the sky.

As Marian watched Matthew, she tried to fight back the misery that welled into her throat. Since the night he'd come to tell her about Paul and Madeleine, she had hardly seen him, because he'd flown to Vermont with the rest of the crew on the morning they arrived. But during the few minutes she had spent in his company before he went, and again after his return, she had sensed a change in him. He seemed distant, somehow, as if he were uncomfortable in her presence; but then Stephanie had remarked on how aloof he was, too, and added that he was always like that once filming was under way. Like most directors, she told Marian, he became so engrossed in what he was doing that he ate, slept, lived and breathed it – which had a lot to do with his apparent lack of concern about his and Stephanie's separate rooms. Hearing that had gone some way to cheering Marian, but as she watched him now she was aware of the ache inside that longed for him just to glance in her direction.

'So when we do the helicopter shots tomorrow,'

Matthew was saying to Rory, 'I want you to come in as fast and as close as you can to each window of the house, then just as it looks as though you're going inside, veer off and up. It's got to look as though you're trying to find a way in. The final helicopter run should take you over the top of the house, so that we can get a good aerial view of all four wings with the courtyard in the middle, then crash-zoom down to the fountain. Got that?'

Rory nodded.

'Right, we'll go over it again in more detail tomorrow, but that's how the sequence begins. Now for today's stuff. The second camera and crew need to be on the crane inside the courtyard, starting on the fountain then swinging up, very slowly. As soon as it's clear of the house, I want them to hold rock-steady on the sky, and then you, Rory, pick up with your camera, pull back across the roof, get in as much of the parklands and river as you can, then bring it down to the second-storey windows, pan round the house to the front and track in to the bedroom window. Simple as that.' He grinned. 'It's got to look like one shot, so we have to hope that there's never a cloud in the sky. The sun's perfect. As soon as the cranes are ready I'll come up with you and show you exactly what I mean. Woody!'

Woody came rushing round from the back of the house. 'Yes, guvnor?'

'How are we doing round there?'

'Trouble getting the crane in at the moment. The one at the side of the house is in position if you want to go up and have a look.'

As the crane soared over the north wing of the house, Stephanie and Grace Hastings came out of the front door. 'It's very kind of you, but I can assure you we've no intention of shooting here any longer than three days,' Stephanie was saying. 'We're on schedule at the moment, and as far as I'm concerned, that's the way it's going to stay. But I confess this damned shot makes me nervous. I wish I hadn't made so much fuss over it now, something's bound to go wrong.'

Grace was smiling. 'I never had you down for the superstitious type, Stephanie. Anyhow, you stay as long as you like. If Frank can handle the disruption, so can I.'

'Well, come what may, we have to be at the art gallery on Friday. Ah, there are the sound boys. I want to talk to them about the nightclub, if you'll excuse me.'

As Stephanie ran across the forecourt to where the sound equipment was being loaded onto a trolley, Franz whispered in Marian's ear. 'Every man on the set's get the hots for that vun. But rumour has it our director is the vun getting the how's-yer-father there.'

Marian's face was stony. 'Really?' she said, and stalked off towards the house. She bumped into Woody as he came hurtling round the corner, and asked if she could do anything to help.

'Yes, just keep out of the way, darling,' he said, and lifted his walkie-talkie to speak to Matthew who was still up in the crane.

Turning round, Marian saw Grace laughing, and started to laugh herself 'I think we're all in the way,' Grace said, as Marian joined her. She held out a slim hand. 'I'm Grace Hastings.'

'Marian Deacon,' Marian said.

'Yes, I know, Matthew pointed you out to me earlier.'

Marian's cheeks turned pink and for a moment she wondered if Grace was going to say anything about Olivia and Art Douglas.

'I believe Matthew and Frank are relying on you to come up with a sound end to the movie.' Grace said.

'I hope they're not relying on *me*,' Marian answered. 'Bronwen and Deborah are working on it now, but like everyone else I'm doing my best.'

'Sure you are.' Grace covered her ears as behind her an

electrician bellowed for more cable, then she moved swiftly behind a pillar to avoid two props men carrying ladders. 'How's about I introduce you to Frank?' she said. 'He's been just dying to meet you.' As she turned, she happened to glance up at the front of the house. 'I see. Looks like he's kinda busy right now.'

Frank was hanging from an upstairs window, chopping away at the wisteria that covered it. At that instant Woody came round the corner, and seeing what Frank was up to, yelled: 'Scenes! Props!'

Grace's voice was simmering with amusement. 'Reckon he's kinda in trouble too, what do you say?'

Marian burst out laughing. She'd heard about Grace's warmth from Stephanie, and despite feeling anxious about the bother she'd caused, she had nevertheless been looking forward to meeting her. She didn't look at all as Marian had imagined: her limited experience of wealthy American women had taught her to expect loud, sequinned clothes, heavily jewelled fingers and inch-thick make-up, but Grace, from her immaculately groomed, though greying hair to the tips of her Ferragamo shoes, was every inch a lady. The pale skin of her face was as smooth as her voice, and in the faint lines around her eyes Marian read kindness and humour as well as the deep sadness she had expected.

Franz and Belinda were watching Marian and Grace as Hazel wandered up, sipping black coffee from a polystyrene cup.

'I see you've let Bob Fairley up for air,' Belinda remarked through gritted teeth.

Hazel smiled sweetly. 'I'm sure Franz can lend you a file for those claws, Belinda darling. And if you speak to me like that again I shall be forced to remind you of my position.'

'The contortions of your sex life hold no interest for me, *darling.*'

Franz was almost popping with delight. 'You girls are so catty over your bouncey-bouncey.'

'Nothing compared to you boys,' Hazel said. 'So come on, Franz, tell us who's getting the benefit of your charms these days.'

'Anyvun who vants them, darling.'

'He's after Rory,' Belinda informed her.

Hazel laughed. 'Who isn't? But of course you've had him, haven't you, Belinda? Tell me, what's he like?'

'Better than Bob Fairley.' Belinda's smile was sugary.

'Touché.'

'Try him,' Belinda continued. 'They say he'll fuck anything that moves.'

'I wonder at your success then, my sweet.'

As the crane swooped down from the sky like a great black bird, they all looked at Matthew. Belinda's and Hazel's eyes met and Hazel shook her head. 'Strictly off-limits.'

'Tell that to young Marian,' Franz tittered. 'The girl practically vets her knickers every time she sees the man.'

Hazel looked shocked. 'Marian! Franz, my precious, Marian might have a crush, but if it came right down to it she wouldn't know what a man was if he unzipped his fly and waved it at her. She's a virgin.'

'A vhat!'

'I thought they went out with the dodo,' Belinda said. She shuddered. 'Ugh! I don't know that I can bear one around me. Especially not one of her age. It's not normal.'

'It certainly isn't,' Hazel agreed. 'And she's so much more attractive these days. Still, with so many gorgeous men around . . .' Again her eyes met Belinda's.

'Are you two thinking vhat I think you're thinking?' Franz trilled.

'I rather think we are,' Hazel answered, a smile slowly curving her lips.

Grace put her hand on Marian's shoulder as the clapper

loader rushed past them. 'It's like Grand Central Station here,' she remarked. 'Shall we go inside? Maybe you'd like to see around the house?'

'I'd love to,' Marian said, ducking as an electrician swung a lamp dangerously close to her head.

Marian had always loved looking round old houses, ever since her father used to take her and Madeleine to visit the stately homes of Devon, but even they paled by comparison with the grandeur of Paulynghurst. The entrance hall was octagonal, with white marble pillars standing two feet out from the eight corners, and a beautifully carved bust on a pedestal stood against each alternate wall. In the centre was a vast black marble table, and the floor was chequered with black and white marble tiles. It was breathtaking in its simplicity, but only an introduction to the splendours that Marian was to see next.

She had little knowledge of antiques, but Grace pointed things out as they went: the Dutch bombé chest that had been passed down through her family, and the porcelain mounted cabinet – a wedding gift from the Vanderbilts. Glorious Adam fireplaces were summer homes for brass and cast-iron baskets filled with logs and vases of exotic dried flowers. The furniture was a mixture of French and English eclecticism, most of which, Grace told her, had been collected by her and Frank when they travelled in Europe. But the paintings in the drawing-rooms, study and dining-hall were all works of twentieth-century American artists.

By the time they reached the end of the second floor of the west wing, Marian had no idea of the time or what was going on outside, and didn't much care. She was completely smitten with Grace, and could have spent an entire week looking round her house if it meant being in her company.

At the top of a narrow staircase Grace opened a door

and stood back for Marian to go ahead. 'The Long Gallery,' she announced, and as she turned a switch, the room was slowly suffused with a subtle yellow glow. 'Most of the paintings on the west wall,' she said, 'are old masters. I'll take you through them if you like.' But Marian had spotted the portraits on the opposite wall and asked if they were ancestors.

Grace smiled. 'Some. Some are still alive. You see there, in the middle, is Frank. Next to him, his father.' Marian followed her down the room. 'Here am I on my eighteenth birthday. And the old rogue next to me is my father.'

Marian's eyes flitted across the next few portraits. 'No, no mothers,' Grace chuckled. 'They are both still alive and both still opposed to our marriage, even after all these years.'

'Why?'

'Frank is Jewish. My family are Irish Roman Catholics. It probably sounds archaic to your young ears, but that sort of thing still exists, believe me. Frank's father is dead, but he was our ally until the last. His wife doesn't know, but he had a Catholic love of his own once, but never stood up to his father.' Her eyes suddenly had a far-away look. 'Olivia used to love hearing about the family,' she sighed. 'She always said it was more romantic than a book. That's her, over there. She was twenty when she sat for it.'

Marian moved slowly towards the painting on the far wall. It was larger than the others, but framed in the same elaborately carved wood. The small, delicate face had Grace's pointed chin, her wide mouth and slanting eyes. As she gazed up at the portrait, Marian was aware of a strange sensation creeping over her. For the first time she was seeing Olivia as the person she had been before her life was so tragically corrupted. She was seeing her as someone who had loved and been happy, someone who had really lived – and perhaps still did. It came as such a shock to Marian that she couldn't speak. She was appalled to think that until now she had perceived Olivia as little more than a project, a make-believe character they were making a film about, when all the time she was as real to Grace as she, Marian, was to her own mother.

Feeling Grace move beside her, she murmured. 'She's so beautiful.'

Grace nodded. 'It was done before . . . Before the drugs.'

Suddenly the weight of this woman's loss seemed to move into Marian's heart. 'Grace,' she whispered, 'I know we're making the film to try and get someone to come forward, but what if . . . What will you do if . . .' She couldn't say it, but Grace had read her mind.

'That's something Frank and I discussed a great deal before we decided to go ahead with the movie. But you see, Marian, she's our only child. Probably we loved her too much, but to have lost her this way . . . We have to know, even if, at the end of it all we find that she's dead. It'll be better than living with this kind of torture.'

Marian turned back to the portrait. So little was actually known about the disappearance. Police and private detectives had searched and hypothesised for five years, but still nothing had come to light. Yet somebody must know something – someone like Rubin Meyer or Sergio Rambaldi. Marian felt herself turn cold. If they were guilty, what had they done with her? Where were they hiding her? Maybe the screams she'd heard in Paesetto di Pittore had been Olivia after all . . . She turned to Grace, wondering if she should tell her about it; but no, it would only add to her pain. Besides, Pittore had been subjected to countless searches and no one had ever found anything.

'I know that you know what she's done,' Grace spoke quietly, 'and I know that there is no excuse. All I can say is that for the last two years before she . . . vanished, she wasn't like my daughter any more. She wasn't like the child who had grown up here, who had lots of friends and boyfriends, who had a normal, happy life. She wasn't like the girl you're looking at now. That's the girl I want to find, Marian, the girl I loved. But it frightens me, and I know it frightens Frank, that if we do find her she will still be the monster that the drugs and those people made her into. But even if she is, I still want to find her. I want to persuade her to make good the wrong she has done, even if it means she has to do it from jail.'

Instinctively Marian reached out for Grace's hand. 'I'm sure you will find her,' she said.

Grace smiled and covered Marian's hand, holding it between her own. 'Would you like to see her bedroom?' she asked, but before Marian could answer she shook her head. 'No, of course you wouldn't. This is all too depressing . . .'

'I'd like to see it, really,' Marian assured her.

As they walked back through the west wing and out onto the first-floor veranda, they heard the clapper-loader yell: 'Shot 73 Take 5!' They looked over the railings, and in the courtyard below a camera emerged from behind the fountain and started to glide slowly upwards.

'*Cut!*' Woody popped up from behind a bush. 'For Christ's sake, Marian what the hell do you think you're doing. Clear shot!'

Grace and Marian exchanged sheepish looks, then vanished through the nearest door. 'I think we'll go round the other way,' Grace said, and giggling, they crept back through the house.

Olivia's bedroom was at the end of a long corridor in the south-east corner of the house. As Grace opened the door Marian felt as though she were stepping inside a fairy tale. The curtains, the drapes round the bed, the furniture, the carpet, even the walls were white. There was lace, silk, satin and damask. The only colour came from the abstract paintings which she quickly realised had been done by Olivia herself. Grace smiled as she saw the expression on

Marian's face, then walked across the room to close a wardrobe door that had fallen open. Marian was immediately aware of the clothes that hung behind the door, never worn now.

From the window she looked out over the woods that sloped down to the river. A single cruiser bobbed on the waves, and Marian found herself imagining what it must have been like for Olivia to grow up in a house like this – taking trips on the river with her father, exploring the woods and gardens.

'What's that over there?' she asked, as Grace joined her at the window. She was pointing to an ornate cast-iron dome nestling in the trees.

'The gazebo,' Grace answered. 'And over there, you see, beside the apple orchard, is the summer house. Olivia and her friends used to play there all the time when they were young. It was anything they wanted it to be, from a witch's castle to an oriental temple.' She laughed. 'Such imagination, children.'

Marian laughed too, and allowed her eyes to wander over the paintings, searching for the OH! that was to be found somewhere in every one. 'I can't imagine what this must be like for you,' she said, her voice thick with compassion. 'I wish there was something I could do or say, but . . .'

Grace smiled, and putting an arm round Marian's shoulders she drew her over to the dressing-table, where they both sat down on the ottoman. 'It's nice of you to care, Marian,' she said, 'and I want you to know that Frank and I care about you, too. We will make certain no harm comes to you, so please don't be afraid of what you know. If you are afraid, ever, please come to us and we will do all we can to help you. Have you noticed the men following you?'

Marian's eyes widened. 'You mean, there *is* someone following me?'

'Sure, they're Frank's people.'

Marian was amazed, and not a little flattered. 'What, even in London?' she said. 'I kept getting the feeling someone was watching me, but I put it down to a vivid imagination.'

Grace suddenly frowned. 'Someone was watching you in London, Marian, but it wasn't one of Frank's people. Matthew noticed him a few days before you came to the States, so he told Frank and we've had the guy checked out. He's a private investigator, working for Rubin Meyer. That's why Frank's people are following you everywhere you go now.'

'I see,' Marian said, her throat suddenly constricting with fear. 'But how does Rubin Meyer know that I know anything? I haven't even seen him since I was last here with ... But I've seen Sergio Rambaldi. I mentioned Meyer's name to him.'

Grace nodded. 'Sure, Matthew told us. We thought, like you, that you'd probably gotten away with it, but it doesn't look like it now. So that's why I say, please don't be afraid to call us any time of the day or night. But Frank thinks this guy who's been tailing you is harmless, otherwise something would have happened to you by now. Which means that Rambaldi and Meyer aren't sure whether you know or not, and the investigator is giving them a progress report on everything you do and everyone you speak to. So you mustn't try to contact Art Douglas while you're here, and it would be better to stay away from Jodi, too. OK?'

'OK,' Marian mumbled.

'What are you thinking?' Grace asked, when Marian had remained silent for some time.

Marian's eyes moved to hers and slowly her face broke into an incredulous smile. 'I don't know what I'm thinking,' she said, 'I just can't take it all in. I know I should be afraid, but it's as if I'm only getting small flashes of fear, and then ... It's like a dream, as though it's happening to someone else who isn't me, yet I know it is.'

'Probably a touch of shock,' Grace told her. 'But when it wears off, I want you just to continue your life as normal. You don't even have to worry about being with someone all the time, because Frank's people are watching you, they'll be with you wherever you go.'

'So you do think Meyer and Rambaldi are behind everything. Matthew said you did.'

'We're certain of it,' Grace answered, 'but we can't prove a thing. So we have to tread very carefully, because Olivia's body has never been found. Of course that doesn't mean that she's still alive, but it does give us hope.'

'Yes,' Marian whispered, thinking again of the screams, but she kept her silence and smiled when Grace suggested they go downstairs to find out how the filming was going.

As they walked back to the door, the wardrobe fell open again, and this time Marian went to close it while Grace wandered out into the hall. She resisted the temptation to take a peek at the clothes, afraid they would disturb her in the same way the portrait had.

Downstairs in the hall, one of the runners put his fingers to his lips and held up his hand for them to go no further. Several seconds later Woody was heard yelling, 'Cut!' and the runner waved them on.

Outside, the crane was swinging Rory back across the roof. Everyone was looking up at him, then broke into cheers and spontaneous applause as he raised a thumb.

'It's in the can!' Woody shouted, trying to make himself heard above the din. 'And that's lunch. Back at two thirty.'

Arm in arm with Bob Fairley, Stephanie walked round the side of the house, then catching sight of Marian and Grace, she ran over to them, her face covered in smiles. 'Seventeen takes,' she cried, 'but it's done. The video assist went down at the last minute, but I'd seen enough by then. He's right, damn him! It's going to look spectacular, and he's managed to get it in the can before lunch. Why did I underestimate him when I know he's a genius?' Laughing, she hooked her arms through Marian's and Grace's and led them off to the stable complex.

The three of them were sitting in one of the air-conditioned winnebagos, picking suspiciously at their location lunches and talking about the scenes Deborah Fore-man had added to the ones Marian had written for Italy, when the door suddenly flew open and Matthew walked in. Without saying a word he grabbed Stephanie by the arm and dragged her outside.

'What are you doing? What's happening?' she protested as he proceeded to drag her round to the back of the house, much to the astonishment, and amusement, of those still ambling off the set.

His answer was to march her down the bank into the woods, and when they reached the clearing in front of the gazebo he stopped and swung her round to face him. His eyes were bright, but he was frowning.

'Matthew?' she said tentatively, then she shrieked as he suddenly swept her into his arms and spun her round. 'Matthew,' she laughed, 'stop it, someone might see.'

He carried her into the gazebo and set her down in front of him. Then lifting her face in his hands, he began touching her lips gently with his own. But as the passion between them rose, he pushed her away.

She watched him as he walked to the edge of the gazebo and leaned against it. He looked back at her, standing against the background of flowers, surrounded by a blaze of colour. 'I want you,' he said. His voice was gruff and he closed his eyes as another rush of desire spread through his loins.

Stephanie moved slowly towards him, then putting her arms around his neck she pushed herself against his erection. He groaned, and taking her roughly in his arms he found her mouth and pushed his tongue deep inside.

'I want you now,' he growled.

Her laugh was unsteady. 'To think I could have forgotten the effect these arty shots of yours can have on you.'

He gave her a wry grin, but his eyes were still simmering.

Knowing that she was on the verge of losing control, and knowing too that this was neither the time nor the place, she took his hand and started to lead him back to the woods.

'Steph?' he said, as they were about to climb the bank. 'Sleep with me tonight.'

She turned round, surprised by the sombre note in his voice.

'All this sleeping apart nonsense,' he said. 'It's getting me down. I miss you.'

She smiled and reached up to stroke the dark hair that curled over his collar. 'Just you try and keep me away,' she whispered.

– 22 –

Morale was running high. They were ahead of schedule, with the celebrated crane shot already in the can; Bronwen and Deborah Foreman had managed to produce some excellent scenes for Italy to go with Marian's; and it was looking as if they might come in on, if not under, budget.

Stephanie was sitting in the production office on the fourteenth floor of the Dorset Hotel. She was alone – at least until breakfast was over. She grimaced at last night's empty beer cans which summoned up images of the unsubtle seductions that had probably taken place. As far as she knew, Hazel was still getting it together with Bob

Fairley, while Rory and Woody were systematically working their way through the entire female population of the unit. Franz was doing the same with the men – though she imagined Franz's success fell far short of Woody's and Rory's. Still, whatever they were up to was no concern of hers; as long as they dragged themselves out of bed on time in the mornings, they could do as they liked in the evenings.

She jerked herself from her chair and went to open the French windows. The unmistakable New York morning chorus rose to a crescendo and she wandered out onto the terrace, hoping the noise and the heat would drown her restlessness. Michael Douglas's film, *Black Rain*, had premièred the night before, and Matthew had escorted Marian. Frank and Grace Hastings had invited them. Stephanie wasn't sure whether Marian was Grace's choice or Matthew's, but it hardly mattered. No, that wasn't true – it did matter. Marian and Matthew, it was like a recurring nightmare, and although he had asked her to marry him, and despite those few moments in the gazebo the day before, and the fact that she had slept with him last night, she was still unable to rise above her jealousy. She knew only too well how damaging it was to their relationship, but it seemed there was nothing she could do to control it. It seemed so ridiculous to be tortured with jealousy over a girl almost half her age – but she had only to look around her to see how many men wrecked the lives of those who loved them by setting up home with a younger woman. Yet it all seemed so improbable with Marian. She gave a dry laugh. Once it might have been, but not any more. There was no denying he felt something for the girl – the question was, what?

She looked at her watch. The crew would be leaving in ten minutes and she wanted to speak to Matthew before he went.

Downstairs in the restaurant, from the table she shared

with Hazel and Josey, Marian was keeping an eye on Matthew. He and Bob Fairley were listening intently to Christina Hancock, who was waving her arms about and distorting her beautiful features in a series of frowns and manic laughter. They were obviously discussing Olivia's character, and Marian knew that no one, but no one, interrupted the director when he was talking to an artiste. But she really wanted to speak to him before he left for location.

After lunch the day before, she and Stephanie had come back to the Dorset, then Stephanie had gone off to a meeting with Frank's lawyers, leaving Marian alone in the production office to think over her conversation with Grace. But instead of thinking about that, she had found her mind wandering back to Olivia's portrait, and gradually ideas for the end of the film had begun to formulate. Then, when Grace rang at five o'clock to invite her to the film première and she discovered she was to spend the evening with Matthew, she had looked upon it as a gift of fate. But a movie, particularly one as loud and violent as *Black Rain*, was not the ideal background against which to tell him her ideas, so she had hoped they might have a drink together when they got back to the hotel. But as they walked into the lobby, Stephanie was waiting for them, and the look she'd given her had told Marian she would be wise to go straight off to bed.

Eventually Christina Hancock got up to leave and Marian went over to Matthew and asked if she could have a word.

'Sure, sit down,' he said, and she was relieved to notice that he didn't seem quite as withdrawn as he had of late. In fact, his piercing eyes were softened by a tenderness that flooded her cheeks with colour, and smiling, he brushed the back of his fingers over the rosy stain. 'What is it?' he smiled.

She glanced at Bob, and Matthew nodded to the lighting

cameraman, a polite dismissal. But she had time only to tell him she'd come up with an idea before Woody interrupted. She tried to look interested as they talked about dead areas and other things she didn't understand, but as time ticked on she knew she wouldn't get the chance to tell him anything before he left.

'After rushes tonight,' he said, as they walked out of the dining-room. Stephanie was walking towards them, and he waved out to her. Then turning briefly back to Marian, he said: 'I'll come and find you in your room.' He smiled, and though his eyes had their normal teasing light, he had spoken quietly, making the rendezvous sound almost intimate.

It was more than she could have hoped for, and the rest of the day, spent mainly at the Dorset, seemed to drag endlessly while she waited for seven o'clock to come round.

But at seven thirty he still hadn't come. Trying not to be hurt, Marian wandered upstairs to the conference suite where rushes were screened. The door opened as she approached, and Bob Fairley came out with Stephanie. Seeing Marian in the corridor, Stephanie looked quickly over her shoulder, then closed the door.

'If I were you, I'd make myself scarce,' she whispered.

'But I was looking for Matthew,' Marian protested. She had nothing to hide, after all, it was *Disappearance* she wanted to talk to him about.

'Do as I say,' Stephanie snapped. 'If Matthew sees you . . .' She broke off as the door opened and Matthew came out.

Marian brightened, but the words dried in her throat as she caught the expression on his face.

'Get her out of my sight,' he spat at Stephanie – and when no one moved, he yelled it.

Quickly Stephanie took Marian's arm and whisked her back down the corridor. Marian was shaking. 'What is it? What have I done?' Stephanie's fingers were digging painfully into the bare flesh of her arm and she tried to break free.

'You've fucked up the shot, that's what you've done,' Stephanie hissed.

'Me?' Marian's bewilderment was, for a second, greater than her shock. 'What shot?'

The lift doors opened and Stephanie pushed her inside. 'Is there any other shot?' she said. 'The crane shot – you're in it. At the very end, as the camera tracks into the bedroom window, you're reflected in the mirror, fiddling about with some cupboard. What the hell were you doing there?'

Marian felt herself turn cold. She remembered going back to close the wardrobe door, remembered what she was thinking at the time, but she'd had no idea . . .

Stephanie left her outside her room, told her not to move from it, and went back upstairs to find Matthew.

Marian waited, a drum of apprehension beating hard in her heart. She wished she was someone else, or somewhere else, anything rather than see that look in Matthew's eyes again. After all the arguments about the opening sequence, the cost of it, the scheduling of it, the complexity of it, then his euphoria when it had worked . . . She remembered Josey's remark about the shot being jinxed, and buried her face in her hands. She would probably be fired now, sent back to England in disgrace. She hated herself so much that nothing was too horrible to contemplate.

When someone knocked on the door an hour later, she was tempted not to answer. In the end, sickened by her own cowardice, she dragged herself from the bed. It was Josey.

'You've really blown it,' said the production secretary, as she put a plate of sandwiches on the bedside table. 'Stephanie asked me to bring these up, thought it better you didn't venture down for dinner.'

Marian's misery was painted all over her face. So

everyone knew. They were all talking about her, and despised her.

'Do you think I'll get the sack?' she asked, in a small voice.

Josey shrugged. 'Who knows? But if I were you, whatever happens, I'd keep out of Matthew's way for a while.'

'What will they do about the shot?'

'Bob got onto the labs just now and asked them to print all the other takes. Hazel's going over the schedule with Woody to see if there's any possibility of a re-shoot.'

'A re-shoot!'

'Well, what did you expect? It's no good with you in it, is it? Jesus, Marian, whatever came over you? Everyone knew where the shot was going to end up, so why the hell were you in there?'

Marian only looked at her. Eventually she said, 'Nothing you say can make me feel any worse than I already do, Josey.'

'No, I guess not. Well, I've got tomorrow's call sheet to finish, so I'll leave you to your sandwiches.'

As the evening wore on and the shadows in the room merged into darkness, Marian sat on the edge of her bed, sinking deeper and deeper into a tide of despair. By the time midnight came round she knew no one was going to come, and no one would ring. She was filled with self-loathing at the way her hopes had continued to foment, even after Stephanie had told her her secret. How could she have made herself so ridiculous? How could she have entertained the idea, even for a minute, that Matthew would return her feelings when, despite everything that had happened over the past months, despite the way she had changed not only in appearance but in character, she was still the same nonentity she had always been.

She sat staring at the phone, willing herself to pick it up. If only she could speak to him, try to explain, but the anger in his voice when he told Stephanie to get her out of his sight, stole over her courage and turned it into weakness.

But no! She wouldn't allow this to destroy everything. She wouldn't allow herself to be ruled by self-pity, ever again. Snatching up the phone, she dialled his room number. She had to speak to him, try and apologise at the very least. But when the ringing stopped it was Stephanie's voice that answered.

She hung up, feeling as though everything inside her was breaking into tiny pieces. She felt so far from home, so alienated from those around her that she couldn't understand how she had even come to be here. She didn't belong, she never had.

She picked up the phone again and started to dial. Looking at her watch, she caught a glimpse of her mother in her mind's eye, washing up her few dishes after tea. She didn't know what she was going to say to her, she just needed to hear her voice. Finally the connection was made, and thousands of miles away, in Devon, the phone rang – and rang, but no one answered.

She slept fitfully. Dismay and humiliation continually slithered into her dreams, wrenching her back to wakefulness, so that in the end she switched on the light and dragged out her suitcase. She would tell Stephanie that she was going back to England, so that Stephanie wouldn't have to go through the awkward business of sacking her. But before she did that, she was going to face them all, show everyone – and herself – that she had nothing to be ashamed of; that she was going away not because she wanted to, but because she understood that she had to.

When her ashen face appeared in the breakfast room the following morning, a horrible silence punctured the morning buzz. Bronwen immediately rose from her chair, and the crew members watched as she took Marian by the arm and led her back to her table.

Bronwen asked the waiter to bring more coffee, then turned to Marian. 'Bad night, *cariad*?'

When Marian nodded, Bronwen took up her hand and squeezed it. 'It's only a film, pet. Not the end of the world.'

'I know, but it feels like it. Where's Matthew?'

'Never mind Matthew. He's a big boy, he'll get over it.' She looked up, and following her eyes, Marian saw Stephanie heading towards them. As she sat down, she glanced at Marian. 'I'd have come to see you last night,' she said, 'but it was late before things settled down. Coffee please,' she told the waiter, 'and toast.'

'Stephanie . . .' Marian began.

Stephanie shook her head. 'I know what you're going to say, but if I were you I'd save it for Matthew.'

'Is he still angry?'

Stephanie nodded. 'I'm afraid so. It looks as if there's another take we can use, but he's not too keen on it. We've been up half the night fighting. He refuses to understand that apart from the fact that the cranes are on their way back to California, we can't afford the time to go and do it again.'

Marian looked down at her cup. There was nothing she could say.

When Matthew came in a few minutes later, he sat at their table. His face was still thunderous and he didn't even acknowledge Marian. She was acutely aware that every eye in the room was focused on them.

She took a deep breath. 'Matthew,' she began, haltingly.

He relinquished his study of the breakfast menu and looked up, but she only shook her head, unable to go on.

The waiter took his order, then leaning his elbows on the table, Matthew fixed her with implacable eyes. 'You're sorry, I suppose. Well not as sorry as I am. I don't want details of how it happened, I just don't want you anywhere near the set again, is that clear?'

Marian's face began to twitch with unshed tears, then suddenly Bronwen was on her feet. 'Come on, Marian, come and help me pack.'

Gratefully Marian got up. She kept her eyes fixed on Bronwen's back as they walked out of the room, knowing that everyone was watching her and, wondering what Matthew had said.

'Why have you packed?' she asked Bronwen, as they walked into her room.

'I've done all I can here for the time being, so I'm going home to spend a few days with my old man. I'm actually missing him,' she chuckled.

'That'll be nice,' Marian said. 'Maybe I can book myself on the same plane.'

'What for? You're not due to leave for another ten days.'

'I think it would be better all round if I went home,' Marian said.

'No!' Bronwen's tone was vehement. 'You made a mistake, yes, but you're not the Marian I know if you go running away from it. It was an accident, we all know that . . .'

'Matthew doesn't seem to think so.'

'That's because he's being irrational. No one gets themselves in shot purposely, he knows that, and he'll realise it soon enough.'

Marian stared at her, her white skin patched with nervous blotches, and Bronwen's face softened.

'Oh, *cariad*, don't think I don't understand, I do. The pain hasn't gone away yet, has it? You still care for him.'

Marian looked down at her hands and Bronwen hugged her. 'You'll survive, pet. You mark my words, in a few days you'll be laughing about this.'

'I won't if Stephanie sacks me.'

'If Stephanie sacks you, I'll have something to say about it. But she won't, I doubt it's even crossed her mind.'

'I'll bet it's crossed Matthew's.'

Bronwen laughed. 'I won't lie to you, I'll bet it has, too. But he won't do it. Apart from anything else . . .' She stopped, and Marian looked into her face.

'What?' she whispered.

Bronwen shook her head. 'Nothing. Well, I was going to say that apart from anything else, he's much too fond of you, but I didn't want you to take it the wrong way.'

'Don't worry, after the way he looked at me last night I'm quite aware of what Matthew thinks of me. Just as I'm quite aware of the way I've been reading much more into the things he's said, and the situations we've been in, than I should have done. God knows, I've tried to stop myself, but it's so difficult, Bronwen. I hate myself for it, especially after all Stephanie's done for me. It seems so disloyal, so bloody treacherous.'

Bronwen smiled. 'You're only human, pet,' she said, 'just like the rest of us – including Matthew. I think I told you once before,' she went on gently, 'that Matthew hurt Stephanie very much once; she wanted him at a time when he wasn't ready to leave his wife, you see. Now he has, but they've still got a lot to work through and they're both making mistakes all the time, Stephanie with her jealousy and Matthew with the way he's been behaving towards you. But try not to hold it against him, *cariad*, try and see it for what it is.'

'But I don't know what it is. At least, I didn't, but after last night . . .'

'The only thing that matters about last night is that it has brought this to a head for you. And now you're going to find the courage to deal with it, just like you've made Stephanie do in the past. As for Matthew, well, you're so much younger than he is and he's flattered that you should be interested in him. Any man would be, Marian, you're very special, you know.'

For a moment or two Marian held her breath, wanting to stop the tears that were threatening to choke her voice.

'You know,' she said, 'on the plane over, just as we were coming in to land, I thought, I really got a feeling, that New York was going to be the turning-point for me and Matthew. Well, it looks as if I was right, but I didn't expect it to be like this.'

'Oh Marian,' Bronwen sighed, folding her into her arms, 'I wish it hadn't been like this, too. And I wish I wasn't leaving today. You could so do with a friend right now.'

Half an hour later Marian wandered up to the production office. She knew now that it had been a mistake to pour her whole life into her work the way she had been doing ever since she left Bristol. She loved her job, and if Stephanie wasn't going to sack her, she would stay; but she needed a release, not only from the work, but from the people she worked with, something that would take her mind off Matthew and help her to forget the way she felt about him – and something to stave off the horrible feeling of loneliness that was beginning to creep up on her.

Wearing only a towel, Paul strolled from the bedroom of their luxury suite at the New York Plaza into the sitting-room. Room service were clearing away the remains of lunch and a few journalists were still hanging around talking to Madeleine. He moved to the mirror, combing his damp hair, but it was Madeleine's reflection he was watching.

He was wondering what Deidre would have to say about the way Madeleine had flown in the face of the world's conservationists by buying herself the white sable coat she had worn throughout lunch. He'd sat quietly on the sofa, watching her while she picked at a salad and fluttered her lustrous eyes at the press, knowing that she wore nothing underneath it. Now, so did everyone else. The last photograph they'd posed for was for American *Playboy*, with her coat open and his hand on her breast.

The exposure they were receiving at the moment was ostensibly to do with the publication of his book. Their relationship had nothing to do with that, of course, but everyone wanted to see him and Madeleine together, just as they had when his book came out in England. He had no qualms about going along with this – the publicity it generated would almost certainly launch him into the best-seller lists. That morning they had done an interview on Fox 5 TV, and later they were attending a party to celebrate the publication of his book in America. And after today's lunch, the following morning was guaranteed to see their pictures in – if not on the cover of – every newspaper in New York.

It amused Paul that it took so little to incite the public's interest – two beautiful faces, a flaunting of sexuality and public proclamations of love seemed to be all it took. Achievements obviously counted for nothing, because between them they had achieved very little – at least, very little of value: a look of extraordinary concupiscence that sold any number of luxury products, and a novel which in his heart Paul knew to be far short of brilliant. But reviewers could be bought, and they had been; though it was mainly due to Madeleine's skilful handling of the press – something she quite guilelessly excelled at – that they had not fallen prey to the poisonous pens of scandal, envy and conjecture. That would come, sooner or later, Paul was convinced of it. It was the same the world over – build a pedestal for your subject, sit him upon it and crown him with glory, then, just when he's least expecting it, pull the pedestal away and make his fall as ignominious as possible. It made no difference whether the scandal was fact or fabrication, it sold newspapers and it was the one thing for which the public had a bottomless appetite. So their turn would come, and when it did Paul would be intrigued to see just how it happened.

At last Madeleine closed the door behind Jay Blackwell

from *People* magazine and turned back into the room. She put a hand up on either side of the high collar of her coat, and as she snuggled deeper into the sumptuous fur Paul could see how aroused she was. He glanced at his watch. Three o'clock – he'd told Harry he'd be there at three thirty, but what did it matter if he was late? The only reason he was going was to try and persuade Harry to become the 'murder' victim for his current book – and he felt certain Harry would refuse. If he did, he would fire him; there were plenty of publishers after him now.

He turned from the mirror and, crooking a finger, beckoned Madeleine towards him. She came slowly, moving like a cat until she stood in front of him, when he removed his towel and she curled her long fingers round his erection. As she started to purr, he leaned back, resting his elbows on the overmantle and watching her face. Her eyes were closed, her succulent lips moist and ripe, and as she rubbed herself against him that famous look started to spread across her features. His chest tightened as he was engulfed by his feelings; he loved her so much now, he was no longer able to stop the tide of it. At times he hated her for it – even beat her – but the crushing weight of contrition that followed was becoming too heavy to bear. He knew he would have to concede defeat sooner or later, and acknowledge what she truly meant to him. It would bring an end to his writing, it would bring an end to everything beyond her.

Suddenly the phone rang. He reached out for the receiver then let it fall back in the cradle as, with a salacious smile, Madeleine dropped to her knees. The ecstasy of her mouth around him was excruciating. His head fell back and the rigidity started to seep from his knees. Then, taking her face between his hands, he pulled her back to her feet and kissed her. She led him to the sofa where she shrugged off her coat and pushed him back into the plush cushions. Then, sitting astride him, she positioned herself for the penetration and looked deep into his eyes.

'Oh God,' he groaned, and placing a hand on either side of her hips, he jerked himself into her.

They moved from the sofa to the floor and from there to the bed, their lust for one another almost insatiable, until finally, as the shuddering spasms of climax subsided to a gentle pulse, he rolled off her and lay staring at the ceiling, too exhausted to speak. After a time her hand moved over his thigh, and lifting the arm that was across his eyes, he turned to look at her. Her hair was in chaos and her skin glistening with sweat. Smiling, he raised himself on one elbow and leaned over to kiss her.

'You don't know what you do to me,' he murmured.

'Oh, I think I do,' she said, on a low laugh.

'I don't want to leave you.'

'But you have to go and see Harry if you want to persuade him to help you with your book.'

'I know.' He kissed her again. 'You don't mind that he's followed me here to New York?'

'Why should I?'

'I just thought, after . . . after what I did . . .'

'Ssh, it's all in the past, and as long as you don't feel the urge to do it again, what have I got to be worried about?'

'Absolutely nothing,' he told her. 'You know how much I love you, I can't even tolerate the idea of sleeping with anyone else, least of all Harry.'

'Well, that's all that matters. Mm, keep doing that,' she murmured as he started to roll a nipple gently between his fingers.

'Tell me you love me, Maddy.'

'I love you,' she whispered, and he lowered his mouth to hers for a long, lingering kiss.

As he dressed, she lay on the bed watching him, knowing that she was happier than she had ever been. They were so close, so much a part of one another now,

that she couldn't imagine living without him. She knew he
felt the same way, which was why he came almost
everywhere with her these days; even his writing seemed
less important to him than it had.

'Are you sure you want to come to France straight after
New York?' she said, as he tucked his shirt in his jeans. 'I
mean, you haven't had much time to do any writing
lately.'

'I'll write there,' he said, buttoning up his fly, 'while
you and Shamir are out posing for the cameras. Unless
you don't want me to come, of course.'

'Don't be silly, of course I want you to come. I hate
being away from you, even for a minute, you know that.'

He smiled. 'Then how are you going to cope this
afternoon?'

'I'll manage,' she laughed. 'I might get some sleep
before the party tonight.'

'You do that. Now, are you going to see me off?'

She pulled herself up from the bed and walked to the
door with him. She was still naked, and as he pulled her
into his arms he ran his hands down her back, cupping
her buttocks to draw her closer. But he kissed her lightly,
then pulled the door open. 'Tomorrow we'll spend the day
together,' he said. 'No publicity, no parties, just you and
me.'

'You're on. Oh, by the way, will you bring me a copy of
Vanity Fair, Shamir's on the cover.' She was looking
straight at him, pretending not to be aware of the two
porters who were walking past, and he shook his head,
laughing. That was something about her he would never
change, her exhibitionism; he found it almost as erotic as
she did.

When he reached the lift he looked back, and she blew
him a kiss. 'Don't forget *Vanity Fair,*' she called.

'I won't,' he answered, knowing that when he called
Shamir from Harry's, she would remind him anyway.

Once the lift doors had closed, Madeleine ran back into the room and over to the window. A few minutes later Paul emerged from the hotel and strode across Fifth Avenue, heading towards the Upper East Side. He had already turned the corner, but she was still looking after him, when the telephone rang again. This time she answered the call.

Half an hour later Madeleine was fully dressed. She wore a torn pair of jeans and a white basque top, and her hair was scraped back in a pony tail. Her hand trembled slightly as she finished applying her lipstick, but when the knock came on the door her features were drawn into an expression of indifference, and she didn't even bother to turn round as she called 'Come in.'

For several seconds there was silence. Then Marian said: 'Hello, Maddy.'

The sound of her cousin's voice, the gentleness and the apprehension in it, turned her insides to liquid.

'How are you?' Marian said.

'Oh, I'm fine, fine,' Madeleine stumbled. She picked up a pen and made a pretence of copying something from a magazine. 'What brings you to New York?'

Marian told her, and as Madeleine listened, astonishment dilated her curiosity so that she started to turn. Then she received her second shock of the day. 'My God, who's been to work on you?' she said, interrupting Marian and gazing disbelievingly at the new cropped hair, tailored khaki dress and slim-line figure.

Marian gave a self-conscious shrug. 'Hazel. She's our production manager.'

Madeleine pulled a face, then walked across the room and sat down in an armchair. Crossing her long legs, she surveyed her cousin, unsure of herself but not wanting it to show. But when her eyes returned to Marian's, she looked away quickly. 'Sit down if you like.' She hadn't meant to sound so offhand, it just came out like that.

Marian perched on the edge of the sofa and put her bag on the glass coffee table. After a while Madeleine looked at her again. Marian smiled, and suddenly all Madeleine wanted to do was throw her arms round her and tell her how much she had missed her – but she heard herself saying: 'Go on, you were telling me about this film.'

As Marian continued, Madeleine was only half-listening. Marian's call had come as such a shock that she was still reeling from the discovery that she was in New York, but now, seeing her and hearing what she was doing – as well as trying to come to terms with the way she looked – was too much to take in. She wondered what Paul would do if he were to walk in now, and it occurred to her that instead of being angry, he might welcome Marian. He might even fancy her now she was all dolled up and nearly thin. Unwittingly, she threw Marian a nasty look – and with the sad realisation that it had been a mistake to come, Marian stopped speaking. There was an awkward pause while they both struggled with their feelings, and outside a siren whooped through the silence, followed by the roar of a helicopter flying low over the city. Suddenly Madeleine was on her feet.

'You said on the phone there was something you wanted to talk to me about.'

Marian hadn't really figured out what she was going to say. She had simply felt that it was time she and Madeleine talked, tried to deal with the rift that had developed between them, and tried to overcome it. But how to begin when Madeleine was so hostile? 'I've fallen in love,' she said, surprising herself.

Madeleine's eyebrows were raised. 'Really? Who with?'

'His name's Matthew Cornwall. The director. You remember, he was staying in the flat downstairs when we were in Bristol.'

'Matthew Cornwall!' Madeleine didn't know if she was up to another shock. 'I saw him the other night at a dinner party. He didn't say anything about you.'

Marian took a breath. 'No, I know.'

'Anyway, he's a bit old for you, isn't he?'

Marian blushed. 'It doesn't matter, really. He doesn't feel the same way about me.'

'Hardly surprising, a man like that!'

'It's not, really, is it, but you didn't have to say so.'

Madeleine shrugged. 'Have you slept with him?'

'No.'

'Of course you haven't. Oh, don't worry, Paul's told me all about your chaste little nights together in Bristol. When are you going to wake up to the fact that a virgin never gets the man, let alone hangs onto him?'

'That is something we've never agreed on.'

'Well, you didn't manage to hang onto Paul, did you?'

'No, Madeleine, I didn't.' Marian's voice was full of meaning and Madeleine felt as though she was shrinking before those steely grey eyes. Then suddenly Marian's face softened. 'I didn't come here to talk about that,' she said. 'I came to talk about you.'

'What about me?' Madeleine demanded belligerently.

'What you've been doing. How you are. Anything you want to tell me.'

'Have you seen me in the papers and everything? I'm quite famous now, you know.'

Marian nodded and smiled. 'Yes. So's Paul.'

Madeleine flinched.

'I always thought you would be successful, you two,' Marian chuckled, 'but I never imagined it would be together.' It was the wrong thing to say, she knew it instantly, but it was too late and Madeleine's face was already flushed with anger.

'If you're here on some sort of revenge trip, Marian, you

can forget it,' she spat. 'Paul's not interested in you now, he never . . .'

'No! No. I'm not here for revenge, Maddy. I only wanted . . .'

'Yes? What do you want? To steal him away from me, like I . . .'

'Like you stole him from me, is that what you were going to say, Maddy? Well, the answer's no. I've been over Paul for some time. As I told you, there's someone else now, even though it's not going to work out.'

'Surely you didn't come here to talk about that.' Madeleine could hardly believe what she was saying. In her heart there were so many other words fighting to be spoken, but they were trapped in a welter of guilt. And she was afraid. Afraid that Marian would suddenly announce that she knew about the money, afraid that Marian was going to expose her for the fraud she was.

Marian's heart was aching. She could see that the barrier that had arisen between them was now insurmountable, but she had to try. 'I've missed you, Maddy,' she said. 'I've thought about you every day, and I have to confess I often wondered why you left me like that. It would have been difficult, but I would have understood about Paul, you know.'

'Spare me the noble act!' Madeleine scoffed, and even as she said it, a scream of denial which never reached her lips was wrenched from her heart. She hadn't meant to say that, it was guilt that had spoken. What she really wanted to do was beg Marian to forgive her, tell her how much she had missed her too.

'I wasn't trying to be noble,' Marian answered. 'I was only trying to say that I'm happy for you.'

'Oh God!' Madeleine's distaste curled her lip.

Marian picked up her bag. 'I'm sorry,' she said, standing up. 'It's obvious that anything I say is going to annoy you, so I'd better go.'

'For Christ's sake!' Madeleine screamed. 'Can't you lose your temper for once? Can't you stand up to me? No, you never could stand up to anyone, could you. And there you go, running away again. You might have a new image, Marian, but deep down you're the same snivelling little coward you've always been.'

Marian looked at her cousin's face with the deepest sadness she had ever felt. 'You're wrong, Maddy,' she said, 'it took a great deal of courage for me to come here today. And deep down, whether I'm a coward or not, I love you, that's why I'm not going to lose my temper. Of course I can stand up to you, but there's no point when you feel the way you do.'

'Why don't you just fuck off?'

Marian's face was taut but she was determined to remain calm. 'That always was your answer when you knew you were in the wrong,' she said. 'I'd hoped you might have changed, but you haven't. I don't mind so much for myself, but what I'll never understand, Maddy, is why you had to hurt my mother too when you know how much she loves you. What's happened to you? You've got no conscience, no integrity.'

'I don't have to explain myself to you, just because you come swanning in here all dolled up to the nines, acting like someone who knows everything. And just you remember, Marian Deacon, that you were the one who stole Paul from me in the first place. I only took what was mine.'

Marian sighed deeply. 'Did you, Madeleine? Did you really?'

'What's that supposed to mean?' Madeleine snapped, suddenly nervous.

'Nothing,' Marian answered, shaking her head, 'nothing at all.' Hooking her bag over her shoulder, she started to walk to the door.

'Marian . . .'

'Yes?' she said, turning round.

Madeleine stared at her, willing herself to say just one word that was in her heart, but in the end all that came out was, 'Don't come back.'

'I didn't intend to,' Marian answered. 'You and I have nothing to say to each other any more, Madeleine, I can see that now, and I was a fool to come. But I know you, Maddy, I know you better than anyone ever will, and that's why I'm so, so, sorry it has to be like this. Take care of yourself.'

As she closed the door behind her she heard something smash inside the room, but she carried on walking. For the moment she was numb, but she knew that later it would hurt. It would hurt more than she could bear, but she would face it.

When she pushed through the revolving doors of the Dorset she saw that the crew had returned. Their gear was piled in reception and Rory was checking film cans with the clapper loader. She smiled as she walked past and Rory whistled, the way he did at all the women. She threw another smile over her shoulder and stepped into the lift.

You see, she told herself, it's not so difficult to be strong. Keep cheerful, make sure no one knows what's going on inside, and after a while you might forget it yourself. The fact that she wouldn't be allowed on the set again was better than being fired, so there was even a bright side to that. Matthew's face rushed to her mind but she pushed it away – it did no good to dwell on things that hurt.

In her room she found a message from Hazel – would she like to go out for dinner with some of the crew? That little touch of kindness put a chink in her armour, but no more than that. She had a fleeting yearning for Bronwen, but put it out of her mind and went to take a shower.

Later, as she was leaving the hotel with the others, she was laughing at one of Franz's caustic remarks when she saw Matthew and Stephanie walking into a restaurant opposite. He had his arm round her – and Marian's breath was sucked into a great well of loneliness. She would miss the closeness she had shared with him, but it was over and she must move on. Then she laughed again as Franz took her arm and they walked off down the street.

'. . . So you see,' she was saying to Rory an hour later, blinking to try and keep him in focus, 'there weren't seven sages at all, there were twenty-two. Yes, I'll have another one of those champagne things,' she said to Hazel. 'Anyway, I wrote about them in my thesis, but I can't remember a damned thing I put, now.' She screamed with laughter, and everyone applauded. 'What the hell has it got to do with the price of eggs, anyway,' she added, and again she whooped with laughter.

'I hear you've written most of the script,' Rory said, closing his fingers round hers.

'Oh no,' Marian said, waving a hand dismissively, 'I only wrote a bit of it. Well, more than a bit, actually; in fact, quite a bit.' She giggled. 'I've even come up with an idea for the end, but I'm not going to tell anyone now.'

'I think you should be credited as the writer,' Rory told her.

'We all do,' Hazel added.

'Rory, you're really good-looking, do you know that,' Marian said, leaning across the table towards him. 'Don't you think he's good-looking, Hazel?'

'Absolutely divine, darling,' Hazel answered.

Marian picked up her glass and took a generous mouthful of champagne cocktail. 'Where's Woody?' she said, 'I want to speak to Woody.'

'Won't I do?' Rory murmured.

'No, it has to be Woody. No, it doesn't, I can tell you. I didn't mean to be in that shot, and Matthew shouldn't have shouted at me like that. If Rubin Meyer gets me now, he'll be sorry.'

'What's she talking about?' Rory muttered to Hazel.

Hazel shrugged. 'Search me. A few too many of these,' she said, tapping a finger against her glass.

'So, Marian, tell us,' Franz piped up, 'do you fancy our Rory?'

'No, I fancy you,' Marian slurred, then burst out laughing. 'Does Rory know that you fancy him, Franz?' she asked.

'The whole world knows I fancy him,' Franz answered, giving Rory a lewd wink. 'But I think he fancies you, Marian.'

'Do you?' Marian said, turning to Rory in amazement.

'Oh, very definitely,' Rory answered. 'I've had my eye on you ever since I first met you.'

'Did you hear that, Hazel? Rory fancies me.'

'I know he does, darling.'

'Shall we go dancing?' Marian said suddenly. 'I vant to dance with you, Franz. Dance with you, Franz – it rhymes,' and throwing out her arms, she started to sing it.

'Come on,' Belinda said, 'let's get her out of here. We'll take her to the Limelight Club. Go and call a cab, Franz.'

Linking arms with Hazel and Rory, Marian tripped into the Limelight Club, still singing. The building was a converted church, and Marian spent some time trying very hard to focus on the stained-glass windows. Then she spotted the organ and wanted to go up to the gantry and play it, but Rory and Franz swept her onto the crowded dance-floor. Hazel and Belinda plied her with more drinks, and she couldn't remember ever having had such a good time.

'Bronwen was right,' she told Hazel as they were leaving the China Club in the early hours of the morning. 'She said we'll all laugh over this one day. Matthew shouldn't have been so cross with me. I'll tell him when we get back to the hotel. I love Bronwen, don't you?'

'We all love Bronwen,' Hazel laughed, 'and you're repeating yourself, darling. Now come on, get into this taxi with Rory, and the rest of us will follow in the next one.'

'We can get more in this one,' Marian said helpfully.

'I know, but I think Rory wants to kiss you good night,' Hazel whispered.

'Does he?' Marian turned to look at Rory who was already sitting in the taxi.

'Yes, now go along,' Hazel said, giving her a gentle push, but Marian had had so much to drink by that time that she fell sprawling into Rory's lap.

'I think I'm going to fall asleep,' she told him, once he had straightened out her dress and sat her comfortably in the seat.

'Here,' he said, lifting an arm, 'rest your head on my shoulder.'

With a sigh Marian closed her eyes and nestled against him. Five seconds later she was sitting bolt upright. 'Everything's spinning,' she told him.

Rory chuckled. 'I thought it might be. Just look out of the window and concentrate on nothing. Here, hold my hand, it might help.'

'I think you're wonderful, Rory,' she sighed, looking out at the passing streets. 'I think New York's wonderful too.'

Rory laughed, and ran his fingers through her hair. 'You're pretty OK yourself, you know. Now don't speak any more until we get back to the hotel.'

'Yes, sir,' she said obediently.

Tony, the doorman, was on duty when they arrived back at the Dorset and laughingly helped Marian to climb from the taxi as Rory paid.

'There y'all go,' he said, steering Marian past the revolving doors and in through a side door.

'I think you're wonderful, Tony,' she giggled, then falling happily into Rory's arms, she allowed him to lead her to the lift.

'Everyone's in love with you,' she informed him, as he

took her key and unlocked her door. 'Oh, this is my room,' she said, as he picked her up and dropped her gently on the bed.

He turned on the bedside light, and as she blinked she looked at him and said cheerfully, 'I'm a virgin.'

'I know,' he answered, as he sat on the bed next to her. 'But it's curable.'

Marian exploded with laughter. 'Curable,' she repeated. Then she gasped as his hand slipped under her skirt, and pulling her face round to his, he pushed his tongue deep into her mouth. She was aware of him opening the buttons of her dress and the way he pulled her forward to slide it down over her arms, but she did nothing to stop him because he was still kissing her and she liked the way it felt. Then he laid her back against the pillows, and giving the dress a quick but gentle tug, he draped it over the chair beside him. Vaguely she remembered him standing up, then pulling back the sheets and lifting her between them, but after that she knew nothing until she woke the following morning.

The bedside light was still on and rays of sunlight streamed through the window, cutting into her eyes like blades. Groaning, she turned her face back into the pillow. A few minutes later she tried to get up, but the room dipped away from her as her stomach rose and she threw up all over the floor.

'Oh, what's happening to me?' she mumbled. 'Mum, where are you? I think I'm going to die.'

As she drifted back towards oblivion, the door suddenly crashed open and Franz rushed in. Picking up her dressing-gown, he threw it at her and told her to get up.

'I can't,' she slurred.

'Get up!' he shouted, 'all hell's breaking loose downstairs. Matthew overheard Rory telling us . . .'

'Telling you what?' Marian asked, her eyes closed and

her lips barely moving. 'Franz?' she said, prising open an eye, but thankfully he was gone.

But again the blissful escape eluded her as someone shook her shoulder and called her name. She dragged her eyelids apart and tried to focus on the face.

'Marian! Marian! It's Stephanie, can you hear me?'

'Mm,' Marian mumbled.

'Oh my God. Josey, see if you can find the unit nurse and get the maid up here to clean up.'

Marian passed out then, but Stephanie waited with her until the nurse arrived.

'Sleep,' the nurse declared. 'The only guaranteed cure for a hangover.'

'I was more worried about alcohol poisoning,' Stephanie informed her. 'She's not used to drink.'

The nurse shook her head. 'Unlikely. Besides, she seems to have vomited up most of it. I'll keep an eye on her for the rest of the day, but there's no cause for alarm.'

'That's what you think,' Stephanie muttered, and casting an exasperated, though sympathetic look at the sleeping figure, she left the room.

At the end of the day Matthew stormed into the production office with Bob Fairley and ordered everyone out. He waited only until the door closed behind the runner before rounding on Bob. 'I respect your position as crew chief,' he said, 'but if you won't do it, I will. She's a kid, for Christ's sake. What does he think he's playing at?'

'Matthew, calm down. Try to see this rationally.'

'There's nothing rational about getting a child drunk and then taking advantage of her.'

'She's not a child! She's twenty-three, old enough to take care of herself.'

Matthew thumped his hand on the desk. 'That is patently not the case! And last night proves it. Jesus

Christ, I heard him boasting about it myself. I want him off this shoot.'

Bob blew out a cloud of cigar smoke and strolled over to the desk. When he was face to face with Matthew he said: 'We've known one another for a lot of years, you and I, so how about some straight talking? You're getting yourself involved in something that we both know you wouldn't normally give a second thought to. So what's really going on here?'

Matthew was the first to surrender the stare and sank back into the seat behind him, rubbing a hand over his face. 'I don't know, Bob,' he sighed. 'I just don't know. I guess it's the way I behaved over that bloody shot. I feel so damned responsible.' His head snapped up. 'But that bastard bragged about what he'd done. The man's a menace where women are concerned. He's got the pick of the bloody unit, so why Marian?'

'Why not Marian, Matthew?'

Matthew's face was stony. 'What are you trying to say, Bob?'

'I think you know. However your feelings are your own affair, Rory is mine. What happened last night was a set-up, and Rory wasn't the only one involved. Are you going to fire Hazel, too?'

Suddenly Matthew's fury returned. 'She doesn't have the equipment to commit rape! Go away!' he shouted as someone knocked on the door.

'Pardon me for interrupting,' Rory said, pushing the door open, 'but I'd like to talk to you, Matthew.'

For a moment Matthew glared at him, then turning to Bob he said, 'Would you mind asking them to wait rushes tonight, this might take some time.'

'OK,' Bob answered, and with a solemn look at his operator, he left the room.

'Well,' Matthew said, getting up from the chair and

walking round the desk, 'what have you got to say for yourself?'

Beneath the tan Rory's face was pallid, and as he combed his fingers nervously through his hair his eyes moved uncomfortably about the room. 'I just wanted to tell you that it wasn't . . . that it didn't . . . That I didn't sleep with her. What you overheard me saying at breakfast . . . Well, I was lying.'

'Oh no,' Matthew said, shaking his head, 'no, I'm not buying that.' His mouth curled with distaste. 'Christ, what kind of a man are you? Can't you at least face up to what you've done, take what . . .'

'I would take whatever was coming to me, if it was justified,' Rory interrupted, 'but in this instance it's not. I didn't sleep with her, she's still a virgin.'

Matthew sank back against the desk, relief sapping the strength from his legs. But as he spoke there was still a trace of anger in his voice. 'Then why did you tell everyone you did?'

'You're not going to believe this, but it was to get them off her back. They had it fixed in their heads that someone should . . . well, you know . . . and they asked me. At first I thought they were kidding. Then I realised they were serious, and that if I said no, they'd only get someone else to do it. So I pretended to go along with it.'

'You expect me to believe that?'

'Yes. Christ, Matthew, do you think I have to resort to sleeping with drunken virgins to get my kicks?'

'It was you who got her drunk in the first place,' Matthew snapped.

'I know. I'm sorry about that, but it was the only way I could see of getting her so that she didn't know what was happening to her, so that she might wonder . . . Oh God, it's no use, I have to be honest and say that I wanted to. I really wanted to. She's bloody attractive, and she was broken up about what happened with that shot, anyone could see . . . Well, I know it might sound ridiculous but I started to feel protective towards her, and then she was lying there on the bed and . . . Well, maybe I would have if she hadn't passed out. But she did, so I put her into bed and left her. Then I told the others I'd done it, so that they would leave her alone. I swear to you, that's what happened. But I still think the others should believe that I did sleep with her, otherwise it'll only happen again and the next guy might not be quite so . . .' he shrugged self-consciously '. . . quite so honourable.'

At that moment the phone rang and, still watching Rory, Matthew snatched it up. As he listened his face turned white. 'Does she know?' he said. He waited, then leaping to his feet he cried: 'I'll meet you there. We'll continue this later,' he told Rory, and rushed out of the room.

By the time he reached the eighth floor, Stephanie had already arrived. 'It seems they've been trying to trace her for a couple of days,' she told him as he got out of the lift. 'The call just came through.'

'Where is she now?'

'In her room. I thought I ought to tell you before I go to see her. I . . .'

'I'll tell her.'

Stephanie was taken aback by his vehemence, but started to protest. Matthew caught her by the shoulders and forced her to look at him. 'I said, I'll tell her.'

'I see,' she said quietly. 'She means that much to you, does she?'

His hands tightened their grip and she shrank away from his look. 'Marian's mother is dead and you ask me a question like that,' he hissed. Then, releasing her, he turned and walked on down the corridor. Stephanie watched him go, her face devoid of colour and a dreadful premonition swelling in the recesses of her mind.

*

He held her in his arms, rocking her gently as quiet sobs shook her body. The room was in darkness now, but he made no attempt to turn on the light. She would be leaving in the morning, again alone – why did she always seem so alone? He wanted to go with her, but of course that was impossible. All he could do was hold her, try to let her know how sorry he was – for everything.

Eventually she lifted her head from his shoulder and looked at him with eyes that were full of pain and bewilderment. 'Maddy,' she said. 'I'd better ring Maddy.'

'I'll do it.' He picked up the phone and asked to be connected to the Plaza. While he waited she took the receiver from his hand.

'Let me tell her,' she said.

'Are you sure?'

She nodded, then hearing a voice at the other end she said: 'Paul, it's Marian. Can I speak to Madeleine, please?'

'I don't know how you've got the nerve to call here,' Paul spat. 'Don't you think you've done enough damage? I don't know what you said to her yesterday, but I'm going to make damned sure you don't get the chance to do it again.'

'Paul. Please, it's my mother . . .' But the line went dead.

'It's all right,' Matthew said, taking the phone from her, 'I'll deal with it,' and after he'd replaced the receiver he wrapped her in his arms again, and sitting back against the pillows, he held her, stroking her hair and her face and trying to soothe the exhaustion and suffering from her limbs.

She slept for a while, and when she woke and found him still there, she smiled. He smiled back.

'How are you feeling now?' he whispered.

'I don't really know. As if I'm in a nightmare, I think. But you being here . . .' She swallowed. 'I'm sorry, Matthew. I'm sorry about the shot. I didn't . . .'

'Ssh,' he said, pulling her back into his arms. 'It doesn't matter. And I'm the one who should be sorry.'

He heard her laugh and pushed her gently away to look at her. As she gazed back at him, her eyes overflowing with tears, his hand spread through her hair and he felt a tightening in his chest that was almost painful.

'Oh, Marian,' he murmured, looking from her eyes to her mouth. Then pulling her towards him, he covered her lips with his own, and easing her gently back against the pillows, he lay over her, kissing her, holding her and comforting her.

The following morning Marian made a solitary figure in the Concorde lounge of Kennedy airport. Matthew had come with her in the taxi, but now he was gone, leaving her as if in a crevice between despair and happiness. Every now and again tears sprang painfully to her eyes. Matthew . . . But she couldn't think about him, she could only think about her mother. She knew now that when she had called two nights ago, Celia had been dying and no one knew.

Lifting her head, she gazed out of the window, her eyes turned to the sky. For a long time she watched the clouds, drifting, changing shape, so gentle, so soft, while in her heart there was a maelstrom of grief. Oh Mum, she whispered, if you can hear me, I love you. Please God, tell my mother that I love her. Please take care of her. Then, as a crushing wave of sadness swept through her, she closed her eyes and silently cried, Please God, don't let this be true; please let her be there when I get home.

Finally a voice came over the tannoy announcing her flight, and she lowered her head. So much had happened in these past few days and she had tried so hard to face everything, to prove to herself that she could be strong, but now it was impossible to go on. In her heart she cried out for someone to lean on, someone to care, someone to be with her now – but there was no one, and she was racked by such loneliness and sorrow that for a moment she couldn't move. She took a deep breath, willing herself to withstand this; then, feeling a hand on her arm, she looked up, ready to tell the stewardess that she was coming. But a look of confusion came over her face when she saw the kind and compassionate eyes that were smiling down at her.

'Come along,' Grace said softly, 'I'm coming with you.'

– 23 –

Tired rays of a late summer sun fractured the shadows of the meandering, dark alleys. Burnt sienna buildings, cracked and crumbling, rose in towering curves over the cobbles, their shutters closed and plants trailing from their wrought-iron balconies. The ground was parched, drains seeped a pungent aroma into the soggy air, and the muted cries of children at play laced the afternoon stillness.

As he walked, Sergio pushed his hands into his pockets and allowed his weary eyes to lose focus. *Firenze*. The great city of the Renaissance. Horses, traders, the swirl of worsted skirts, the clink of florins, the stench of the gutter; the filth, the opulence, the poverty – he could feel it all. A coach thundering past, a beggar clutching at his legs, and in the distance the Medici trumpets muted by the sounds of rejoicing as Il Magnifico passed by. Then the crackle and hiss of Savonarola's bonfires, followed by the triumphant cries of his executioners. A voice seemed to echo through the tragic din, persistently calling his name, until the plangent sounds of the quattrocento faded and the voice rang clear. Looking up, Sergio saw one of his students leaning from a window and waving to him. He waved back, and as he moistened his lips the bitter taste of marble dust coated his tongue; his fingers still bore the indent of the chisel.

Smiling at his entrapment between past and present, Sergio stopped and let the euphoria wash over him. He was a part of Florence, just as it was a part of him. Every face, every stone, every masterpiece spoke to his soul, nourishing his ambition until it became a crying hunger for recognition – a recognition that would belong not only to him, but to his cherished city. He could no more deny this hunger than he could the life-giving needs of his body. When it was all over, people would say that he was insane; it would be their only way of rationalising what he had done. It saddened him to think that they would never know the ecstasy, as well as the torment, of his mind, but maybe one day, when the shock had lessened, they would begin to understand.

Years ago, when he was a young man of twenty, he had thought he might be a reincarnation of the great man himself. But as he grew older he realised that though neither his dedication nor his suffering was any less than Michelangelo's, his art, though achieved with the tools and through the mind of the great genius, must take a different path. It was time now, in the twentieth century, to celebrate woman.

He moved on, a sudden lightness in his heart. His route led him through the elongated courtyard of the Uffizi. Ahead were the *pietra serena* arches, beyond them the Arno. When he reached the embankment he stopped at a news-stand to buy the evening paper.

He wasn't surprised to find the story relegated to the second page – it had broken the day before, and now the whole world knew the secret tragedy of the Tarallos. Rosaria Tarallo, wife of Enrico Tarallo and mother of his sons, was dying of cancer. Enrico had returned to Italy, saying he would no longer drive the great Ferrari machine.

Sergio walked on, but now his pace was slow, and in his

heart the shadow of grief darkened. It had been a long time since he had allowed himself to think about the Tarallo family, but now the memories of his childhood came flooding back. He could see Rosaria as a child – always, even then, she was with Enrico, she had been devoted to him. And he, Sergio, had loved her too, but as a sister. She had listened to him, shared his dreams and never mocked. With everyone else she had been shy and afraid, but Enrico had protected her, shielding her from the cruelty of her own mother, just as Sylvestra, Enrico's grandmother, had protected the young Sergio from the cruelty of his. But he had seen his mother so rarely that Sylvestra had come to take her place. Sylvestra, the grand lady who lived in the palazzo had treated him, the urchin who played in the dirt and dust of the village, like a son. As Enrico had treated him like a brother. The Tarallos had become his family, he had been there when Enrico's father died, he had shared their lives and loved them. But in the end he had betrayed them.

He stopped, and putting a hand on the wall to steady himself, he tried to push the memory of Arsenio's beautiful face from his mind. Arsenio, the beloved younger brother of Enrico and cherished grandson of Sylvestra. Arsenio, the boy who had come to worship him, who had begged him to take him into the *bottega*.

He walked on, unable now to stop the memories flowing back to him. The tragedy, the heartache, the suffering he had caused to the family that had been like his own.

He let himself into his apartment. The air was stale, but he didn't open the windows and throw back the shutters. Instead he removed his clothes and stood under the shower. It all seemed such a long time ago, but there were times when his skin crawled at the memory of the blood. And yet one day, when their work was at an end, the whole world would reel at the magnitude and method of his accomplishment. His place in history would be assured, but he was paying the price.

The following morning Rosaria's death was announced on the radio news. Now Sergio knew, he would soon feel the full wrath of the magnificent Sylvestra and the depth of her hatred. But now more than ever he must not forget his life's work – nor his need for revenge on Paul O'Connell, the man who had caused him, and thus the Tarallos, so much pain. Thoughtfully, he picked up the phone to call Dario in London.

Deidre strolled out of the villa at La Turbie and onto the terrace. Clusters of geraniums and trailing lobelias sprouted from baskets that hung overhead, reaching out to the climbing rose that had been trained artfully over the balustrade. Beyond the terrace and on either side of the honeysuckle-covered steps was a rock garden, and from the steps a weathered stone path led through the grass and under a pergola, where it divided to circle the swimming pool. From an upstairs window the view down over Monte Carlo, the sea and the Italian coast in the distance, was uninterrupted and spectacular.

The villa belonged to a friend who was on business in the Far East until the end of the month. Deidre, at Madeleine's expense, had taken it for the week of the Pirelli shoot, which was now almost at an end. That night they were joining a group of models and photographers who were on the Riviera as the guests of the Société des Bains de Mer, for dinner at the Hotel de Paris. The following evening Deidre was organising a small party at the villa to celebrate the end of the session – and Madeleine's twenty-first birthday.

As she ambled down the steps Deidre inhaled the flowery fragrance and slipped on her sunglasses to shield her eyes from the brilliant sun. At the edge of the pool she sat down to watch Paul as his powerful arms carved a path through the translucent water. Genevieve, a local woman who took care of the villa, brought out a pitcher of iced lemonade and two glasses. Deidre thanked her, and a few minutes later she heard the front door slam. Genevieve had gone home.

Paul whistled as Deidre removed her sarong and stretched her legs out on the lounger. She held up a glass of lemonade, but he shook his head and plunged back into the water.

After a while her thoughts drifted to the telephone call she had received from Sergio the week before. But for that, she might not have been in the South of France at all, but things had changed, he'd told her – he wanted Madeleine soon, though he wouldn't say when, or tell her what had happened to cause the agitation in his voice. Since the call she'd had many sleepless nights; she would do everything he wanted, she was sure of that, but already her troubled conscience was causing her real distress.

Over the past few weeks she had become wary of Paul, wondering why he'd never told Madeleine the truth about himself – his wealth, his connections, his heritage. Why had he shaken it off, she wondered, and how much longer could he keep it hidden? She wanted to ask him the reason for his deceit, but Sergio had warned her not to. There was a connection between those two men that she was beginning to find sinister even though she did not know the nature of it; and that Madeleine was caught between them only added to her feelings of foreboding and guilt. Shamir's sporadic coolness, and the rift in Madeleine's family, bothered her too. Somehow it seemed to push Madeleine into an isolation that only she recognised. That was the real reason why she was in France: she wanted to be near Madeleine. She was anxious about Madeleine, too, because she was sure that something important had happened in New York, though neither Paul nor Madeleine would admit it. Whatever it was, it seemed to have brought the two of them closer together, and for that at least Deidre was grateful.

Suddenly her hand tightened on the glass she was holding. She hated salving her conscience like this. As long as someone loved Madeleine, was that what she was telling herself? A token of happiness before she, Deidre, and Sergio destroyed everything? Because if Madeleine were to disappear, in the same way as Olivia and for as long as Olivia, everything *would* be destroyed. Deidre closed her eyes, trying to block out the haunting, apocalyptic visions that had started to torment her night and day. Could she really allow Madeleine to pay the price of her own happiness? Could she really sacrifice her like that? The answer was that she could, she had waited too long to let her dreams go now. Five years Olivia had been at the *bottega*, five years; would Sergio release her once he had Madeleine? But no, he had said that they would come back to the world together. So she *would* come back, she would know love and life again. Did that make it better? Yes, dammit, it did. And if Paul were to be honest, she really could believe he loved Madeleine, and that would make it all so much easier . . . She jerked herself to her feet. Who was she trying to fool? Nothing would make it easier. Nothing!

'Aren't you coming in?' Paul called out as she walked away.

Without turning round Deidre raised a hand and told him the sun had given her a headache.

Escaping into the cool shadows of the dining-room she heard girlish laughter and turned back. Shamir and Madeleine were coming in through the battered wooden gate at the side wall. She watched as they sauntered through the long grass, then lazily stripped off their clothes at the pool's edge. Behind them was the orchard, rich and colourful with unplucked fruit, and the sea sparkling blue on the horizon; as Madeleine turned her golden head,

Deidre's heart turned over at her resemblance to the Graces in Botticelli's *Allegory of Spring*. Was that why Sergio wanted her? Had he seen the resemblance too?

An hour later, after she'd called the office and tried unsuccessfully to reach Sergio, Deidre wandered back onto the terrace. There was no sign of the others, so she decided to go upstairs to see if she could sleep off her headache before they went for dinner . . .

Paul was lying in the grass between Madeleine and Shamir, all three of them naked, all three asleep. They were hidden from view by the loose stone wall that bulged from the rock garden, and oblivious to the beginnings of a glorious sunset that smouldered on the horizon.

At last Madeleine stirred, woken by the cool evening air. She sat up, then touching Paul's cheek, said she was going inside to take a bath. He opened his eyes and pulled her down for a kiss. 'Are you all right?' he asked.

She nodded.

'Love you,' he whispered.

She climbed drowsily to her feet and he watched as she rounded the honeysuckle and meandered up the steps to the terrace. He waited a minute or two, then hearing the door swing closed behind her, turned his head to Shamir. Her black hair was spread like a fire-burned bush on the grass round her head, her eyes were closed, her wide, full lips slightly parted. In the pink wash of the setting sun her skin glowed like dying embers.

Raising himself on one elbow, Paul stretched out a hand and smoothed it over her flat belly. Her eyelids flickered, telling him she was awake, and he smiled as he eased his fingers into the black hair at the join of her legs. She lifted a knee, then let it fall to one side, and he probed the moist flesh, circling and stroking, then lowered his mouth to her hardening nipples.

Her hand found his penis, imprisoning it in a firm but gentle grip, and he allowed her to massage him for a while, bringing him to the aching fullness of erection. Then he pushed her hand away and moved over her, holding himself above her with his hands planted on either side of her. Slowly, as her long legs encircled his waist, he lowered himself onto her. She gave a soft murmur as their bodies joined, then her eyes opened and she stared up at him. He waited for the slow smile, then gently pulled back and pushed into her again. His mouth covered hers and he probed the depths with his tongue while rotating his hips the way she liked it.

The roof of The Grill at the top of the Hotel de Paris was already open when they arrived. The sky was black, the stars pin-points of glittering light and the smell of fresh fish grilling on the wood fire mingled with the heavy scent of perfumed bodies. Madeleine's party was the last to arrive, the others were already seated at the table for twelve which stood alongside the huge windows that overlooked the Riviera. But for once the magnificent view was not drawing attention. From the other side of the room the buzz around their table was evident, but it wasn't until they sat down that Madeleine discovered the reason for it – Enrico Tarallo was sitting alone at a table several feet away.

'They say his wife's death hit him hard,' one of the girls told her. 'Apparently he's been on his yacht for days, refusing to speak to anyone.'

'I feel really sorry for him,' said another. 'He looks so sad. I wonder where his children are?'

'With the grandmother, no doubt. Apparently she's one of the richest women in Italy and he stands to inherit the lot.'

'Did you ever see his wife?' Shamir asked of no one in particular. 'Quite unspeakably plain.'

'And quite unspeakably rich, at least, her family are. Wonder if that was why he married her? They go in for that sort of thing in Italy, don't they? You know, arranged marriages. Bet he's dying for a bit of glamour now he's got rid of the wife, how do you fancy my chances?' It was Sophie, one of Deidre's more recent signings, who had spoken, and Deidre eyed her with marked distaste. 'Well,' Sophie said sulkily, 'what else is he doing in a place like this?'

'Minding his own business,' one of the photographers answered pointedly.

But the conversation didn't end there, and it quickly became evident that Sophie had only spoken what every other girl was thinking.

Madeleine was unusually quiet, but Paul noticed the way she kept glancing in Tarallo's direction. He was seated between Shamir and Deidre, who was at the head of the table, and Madeleine was opposite him, beside Sophie. There had never been any love lost between the two girls, and he wondered if Madeleine was attempting to flirt with Tarallo just to annoy Sophie. Except that she wasn't flirting, it was as if she was trying to relay compassion to the man – which both surprised and annoyed him. He began studying the driver himself, sizing him up as a possible rival, but it was hard to take the idea seriously. Though Enrico was sitting down, it was obvious that his height would miss Madeleine's by at least an inch, and his hair was receding, and his physique, while not exactly puny, could hardly be described as muscular, either. Nevertheless Madeleine's interest was manifest and when Shamir's hand slipped across his thigh Paul brushed it off irritably.

Enrico himself was fully aware of the attention he was generating, particularly from Madeleine, the only one in the party he recognised, apart from Paul. He neither reciprocated nor encouraged her glances, he merely gazed straight through her, but inside him was a fury that burned like a furnace. He loathed the empty-headed superficiality of women like Madeleine Deacon. Such beauty was ugly when flaunted the way she flaunted hers, and he was enraged at the affront she offered when she crossed her legs and revealed a side-split in her dress that ran right up to her waist. Her lack of underwear disgusted him. Did she think to excite him when she, like the rest of the world, must know that his wife had been dead for less than two weeks? Suddenly he could stand no more and called for the waiter.

Madeleine heard him cancel his dinner, then watched as he got up from the table.

'Do you think grief has got the better of his appetite?' said one of the models at the other end of the table.

'No, he's angry,' Madeleine answered quietly. 'We're treating him like an animal in a zoo.'

'Speak for yourself,' Sophie sneered.

Madeleine started, realising only then that she was more guilty than any of them – and the look of malevolence Enrico directed at her as he left the restaurant turned her face pink with embarrassment.

She lowered her head, and sensing that she was about to cry, Paul got up from his chair and led her from the restaurant to an alcove beside the lifts.

'What is it?' he whispered, putting his hands on her shoulders.

'I don't know,' she answered, trying to swallow the tears. 'I just felt so sorry for him. He looked so lonely sitting there, and so sad.'

'That's why you're crying?'

There was a catch in her breath as she inhaled deeply. 'I don't know. No, not really. It's Marian, but I know you don't want to talk about it, so . . .'

'Maddy, we've talked about little else since she came to the Plaza, that's the only reason I don't want to discuss it again. And do you, really, in your heart?'

'No, I suppose not. It doesn't get me anywhere.'

'Of course it doesn't, because it's in the past. All that matters now is us.'

'I know. But seeing Enrico Tarallo like that, I know it sounds silly, but it reminded me of her. I was all right before I saw her, I didn't really think about her any more.'

'You'll get over it, darling, and I'm here.' He hooked his fingers under her chin and tilted her face up to his. 'You do want me to be, don't you?'

She smiled. 'Of course I do.'

'I was beginning to think you were setting your sights on Tarallo.'

'Oh Paul, as if I could even look at another man.'

'You managed it with Tarallo.'

'But that was different. I told you, I felt sorry for him. You're not angry, are you?' she said, looking curiously into his face.

'No,' he sighed. 'Yes, dammit, I am. I'm angry because I get so bloody jealous where you're concerned.'

'I like it when you're jealous,' she laughed, 'it makes me feel secure.'

He smiled and looked searchingly into her eyes. 'Kiss?' he whispered.

She nodded, and putting her arms round his neck, she raised her mouth to his.

'Ready to go in again?' he murmured, as he pulled away.

'I think so.' And slipping her hand into his, she allowed him to lead her back to the restaurant. 'Paul?' she said, as they were going through the door. Do you know Enrico Tarallo?'

She felt the grip tighten on her fingers as he turned round. 'No,' he said, truthfully, 'but I do know someone who does.'

When Enrico got back to his room he lay down on the bed, already regretting the look he had given the girl. It was not her fault, he should not condemn her for something she could not help. She had probably meant no harm, but the display of her legs and the searching of her eyes had seemed to mock him. Yet, he had known that morning, as he stood on the deck of the *Rosaria*, with the great citadel of Monaco in the distance like a mirage in the haze, that it was wrong for him to come to such a place. But he had come, and now his anger increased the tension inside him.

After the funeral he had left his home and taken his pain to the sea. There he had yelled at the injustice of so young a death, his words petering out in the vast space, his loss swelling so that he felt it might strangle him. He had grieved in a way that no man would want witnessed, lacerating himself with memories, doing all he could to deepen the pain – but it was already so great that he could not increase the punishment further. There were so many things he could have done, should have done, so much he still had to say, but would never be able to now.

It was a long time before he drew himself up from the bed. His heart was like a weapon, discharging pain through his body and he wondered if it would ever end.

High-spirited laughter and female shrieks took him to the window and he saw the Deacon girl and her party leaving the hotel. He was suddenly glad of his earlier virulence and hoped he had wounded her. She deserved it, for being alive and meaning nothing.

As he turned back into the room Rosaria's face was watching him from the frame beside his bed. She seemed to be laughing, as though amused by his belligerence. Grudgingly, he smiled too. He was becoming engrossed in things that didn't matter.

When the operator connected him with his home in Tuscany he was told that Sylvestra and his sons were already on their way to Sardinia, so he telephoned the *Rosaria*'s crew and arranged for them to fly into Nice the next day. The morning after they would sail to Sardinia where he would put an end to this bitter lamentation and take up his life with those he loved.

Those he loved. The jaws of guilt yawned, presenting him with a picture of Arsenio. The slick, jet hair he combed behind his ears, the wide brown eyes, pronounced Florentine nose and laughing mouth. That was how he had been once – but not any longer. For hadn't his looks forsaken him, along with his family? Enrico swung round, as if to answer the accusing voice. He loved Arsenio above all men. What he'd done was for his brother's own good. But his excuses, as always, seemed to lack conviction and he knew that the day was drawing close when he must face what both he and Arsenio had done, and – with Rosaria no longer there to protect him – what Sergio Rambaldi had done too.

It was Madeleine's birthday. That morning, over a champagne breakfast on the villa's terrace, she had received cards and gifts from Deidre and Shamir, and when she'd arrived at the harbour – the location for that day's shoot – the Pirelli executives and the photographer had presented her with a collection of exotic underwear accompanied by a particularly obscene cactus.

'Very funny,' she said, pinching Shamir, who was laughing so hard she'd started to choke; but it had set the mood for the day, and by the time she returned to the villa she was exhausted from laughing so much.

Now she was upstairs in her room, dressing for the dinner Deidre was giving in her honour. But as she perched on the edge of the bed and started to coat her tanned legs with oil from 'The Look' range, she wasn't thinking about the celebrations, or the surprise Paul had in store for her, she was thinking about Enrico Tarallo. She had seen him again that afternoon, standing on the deck of his boat, and when she'd seen the name of the boat her heart had gone out to him, just as it had the night before. She'd had the impulse then to go over and invite him to the party tonight, but as she started to move from the set she suddenly remembered not only the look he had thrown at her, but the way Paul had responded to her interest in him. It was a shame, she was thinking to herself now, because there was something about him that made her want to get to know him.

As she stretched out her legs and hitched her flesh-toned body-stocking higher on her hips, Paul watched her, one hand resting on the ceiling beam over his head, the other holding a drink. Together with the delicious aroma from the kitchens and the haunting music of Gluck's *Dance of the Blessed Spirits,* night insects floated in through the open window, flinging themselves against the brass candle lamps on either side of the bed. The delicate glow fell in a nimbus around Madeleine's blonde head and touched her skin with coppery light. She looked lovely.

'I love you,' he said.

Unaware that he'd been watching her, Madeleine started, then smiled at the way he looked, his crisp white shirt tucked into the black trousers of his dinner suit, his bow tie hanging loosely around the collar, waiting to be knotted. She stood up and went to put her arms round him, and he slid a hand down her back, drawing her closer as he moulded his lips gently over hers.

When he pulled away he still held her, looking deep into her eyes. 'Aren't you going to tell me you love me?' he said.

'I love you,' she breathed, and he laughed.

He knew she'd seen Enrico, and Shamir had told him how pensively she had gazed at him. But he wasn't unduly worried. The man had made his feelings plain in that one inimical glare the night before, and Madeleine's assurances that she did not find him attractive had been satisfyingly vehement when he had challenged her over it again as they were getting into bed.

She rested her head on his shoulder, not wanting him to see the tears that had come into her eyes. Even if she'd been able to put her feelings into words, she would have kept them to herself, for they would only make him angry. Besides, it seemed ridiculous, when she had so much, to be longing for Marian. But fame and fortune were not turning out to be all she'd expected. It was as if she was just a face and a body; no one was interested in what she thought or felt about anything. Her whole life was spread across newspapers, magazines and TV, but no one knew the fear she felt every day that something would happen to destroy it all – that Paul would leave her, when he was all she had. He was the only person who knew what she had done, how callously she had treated her family, yet still he wanted her. But for how long? Until his book was finished? She couldn't bear to think about it, because he was the only person who could make her feel safe, who gave her a sense of identity and value when everyone else, she was certain, sneered at her behind their hands. If he left her she knew that she would not be able to survive, because after what she had done to Marian, she had nowhere to go and no one to turn to. The terror of that realisation seemed suddenly to drain the energy from her body, and she tightened her embrace as if to stop herself from falling.

Taking her hand, Paul led her over to the bed. She thought he was going to make love to her, but he sat her down, then turned her to face him. 'I want to talk to you, Maddy,' he said.

The seriousness of his expression started the fear churning inside her. Was he going to tell her now that it was over? Was he going to say he had made a mistake and didn't love her after all? But he had told her only moments ago that he loved her, so why was she thinking like this? 'What about?' she asked in a small voice.

'About trust,' he answered. 'I want you to trust me. No, no. I know you're going to say you do, but you don't. And you've good reason not to trust me when I treat you the way I do, and especially when there are things about me you don't know.'

Her head was on one side, her eyes curious, and the wobbly smile that tried to cover her confusion moved him deeply. She was like a child with a cruel parent – no matter what he did, she still loved him.

He stood up and wandered over to the window. The night was black and soon it would be time for them to go down to dinner. But he had to tell her now. He'd worked it all out, rehearsed it, even. He wanted her trust, it was imperative. Not only for what he was going to do, but for what was to come after. He tensed as love drove through his body like a physical force, twisting his abnormality and exposing it for the abomination it was. He felt suddenly nauseous, and didn't know if he could go through with it; he was aware that his detachment had been eroded by love, making the paradox of his conflicting needs increasingly difficult to govern. But then he inhaled deeply of the tangy Mediterranean air, and putting his hands in his pockets, he turned round and sat on the window ledge. 'Your money has gone, Maddy,' he told her. 'There is nothing left.'

She blinked, but she was still smiling, as though waiting for the punchline to a joke.

'In fact,' he went on, 'the three-quarters of a million pounds ran out some time ago.'

Her smile started to dissolve. He knew she was waiting for him to laugh, but he fixed her eyes with his and willed her to believe him.

'Do you mean we're in debt?' She laughed, uneasily.

He smiled and shook his head. 'No, my darling, it just

means that we're living on my money now. Which,' he added, 'isn't money I've earned from the book.'

Again he waited while she struggled to understand.

'Then where . . .?' she began.

'I'm a wealthy man, Madeleine. I always have been. My estate, as it stands, is worth in excess of ten million pounds, my personal fortune around five. The reason why I didn't tell you before was because I wanted to observe you, to see how you would use the money we stole from Marian and how low you would stoop to attain success – for us both. It's an unpleasant thing to hear, I know, and I'm not proud of what I've done, but unless I'm completely honest with you I can't expect you to trust me. I've treated you badly, and though you know why I do it, that doesn't make it any easier for you.

'But it's going to stop, Maddy. No more lies, no more trickery. I love you, and I never want to hurt you again, but you should know that I no longer intend to pay Deidre for your career, which I have been doing ever since your money ran out. It's my belief that, if you want to, you can make it on your own merits now.'

Uhe was staring at him and he could see it was all too much for her to take in.

Nevertheless, he went on: 'The house is now in my name, so are the cars. Your account at Coutts has been cancelled.'

'You mean, I'm broke?'

He laughed. 'In a manner of speaking, I suppose you are. But I'm not, and that's all that matters, isn't it?'

She shook her head, bewildered. 'Yes. Yes, I suppose it is.'

He walked over to the bed and took her in his arms. 'Is it so bad to be dependent on me?' he smiled.

For a long time she said nothing, and he watched her, trying to read her face. Eventually she said, 'I think I understand. You told me I was broke, then straightaway told me you were rich. That means you didn't want me to panic, even for one second, or to think I had nothing.'

'That's right,' he said, stroking her hair and feeling no surprise at her inability to deal with anything but the practicality of the situation. The strong feelings that underlay his manipulation of her, the complexity of his deceit, were beyond her powers of comprehension.

She looked up at him, and her face was suddenly imbued with feeling as she took his hands and held them up to her mouth. 'Paul, I love you so much, I wish I could put it into words.'

He smiled. 'Don't even try, my darling. All that matters is the love itself.'

Her hands looked so fragile in his, and his one desire was to crush them. He tore his eyes away, choking back the unholy yearning to impair, to destroy, then relaxed as love washed over him again.

'And you love me, even though all I've got left is my body and my looks?' she said.

'Which is more than enough. And although you don't have a single sou to your name tonight, or any means of getting any money, we'll soon put that to rights. In the meantime, you're at my disposal, woman.'

She giggled. 'But I might make you pay for what you've got on your mind right now. After all, I need the money.'

'These,' he said, taking her breasts, 'have already cost me several thousand apiece, so I think I'm owed at least one tumble on the house, don't you?'

She pondered this a moment, then said: 'Have I really spent that much money?'

He nodded. 'Almost two million.'

'How?'

He knew he could disguise the exaggeration by blinding her with figures, though the truth was that she had overspent on the lottery money by the amount of the house and the cars, which was something in the region of half a million. But that could wait. As could the news of her aunt's death. He had cheated and lied as well as loved and cherished, until finally everything had started to fall into place. He had reached the final chapter, both metaphorically and literally; the book he was bringing to completion now would be his last. After that he would devote his life to loving her, with no more chicanery, no more heartache or brutality.

He laughed. 'I think Deidre could answer that question better than I can. But she's helped you achieve everything you wanted – all I'm asking is that you should forget Marian, and everything that went before, and want only me now.'

'I want you,' she murmured, after a while.

'And trust me?'

'Yes,' she said, as she closed her eyes. 'I trust you.'

The night air was alive with the sibilant sound of cicadas, and in the distance could be heard the gentle sough of the waves as they splashed onto the rocks before being sucked away by the undertow. From the next room came the hum of conversation, and here in the dining room the romantic strains of Rachmaninov filled the air. Each place on the long oak dining-table was set with red folded napkins; silver cutlery and crystal glasses reflected the flickering candlelight, and outside on the terrace coloured lamps swayed in the breeze. Deidre surveyed the room critically before nodding to Genevieve that she could show the party of twenty guests through from the sitting-room.

Once Madeleine was seated, at the head of the table, photographers took out their cameras and she and Paul smiled into one another's eyes. At Sergio's request Deidre had paid colossal sums to ensure that the birthday celebration, small though it was, would hit every gossip column, if not front page, the world over. Madeleine's publicity must continue, he had said, right up to the last.

There was a great deal of laughter as the shots were taken – the photographers and journalists had been chosen specially by Madeleine and Paul – and once they were done, notebooks and cameras were stowed away and Geneviève's brothers, François and Pierre, poured the wine, while Geneviève and her friend served the pâté de foie gras followed by fresh sea bass, then beef in a burgundy sauce made to Geneviève's own special recipe. The conversation swelled in volume as everyone tried to better the last anecdote, and raucous laughter accompanied lewd remarks and outrageous attacks on friends and acquaintances. Deidre noticed how Shamir's eyes glittered, and was intrigued by her erratic bursts of laughter – it was so unlike her usual behaviour. She was seated between John Roddy, French correspondent for the *New York Times*, and Dario, the photographer they all knew so well. It wasn't the first time Deidre had wondered about Shamir and John Roddy, and when she caught Madeleine's eye they exchanged a smile at the prospect of a blossoming romance.

Before dessert was served, Deidre signalled to Dario, who several minutes later slipped out of the room to follow her into the hall. She watched him as he strolled towards her, a small, thin man with a smooth face and immense brown eyes. She had known him for seven years, but ever since she had discovered he was a member of Sergio's *bottega* he had felt to her like a stranger.

'Did you speak to Sergio?' she asked, as he drew close.

'The *bottega* met last night,' he answered. 'I spoke to him after.'

'Well, what did he say?' she asked, trying but failing to hide her irritation.

As Dario's eyes moved over her face she thought she detected a glimmer of disdain. 'He wants her soon, Deidre. Sooner than you think.'

Deidre's face paled. 'When?'

'In three weeks.'

She gasped. 'He told me everything had changed, that a complication had arisen . . . but so soon . . . What is it, Dario? Tell me, please.'

Dario had long suspected that Deidre knew nothing about Sergio's connection with the Tarallo family, and this confirmed it. He shrugged. 'You know I cannot tell you, Deidre. It is the way Sergio wants it.'

She nodded, swallowing hard on the harsh feeling of exclusion, but she knew better than to try and push Dario. She looked at him again and was suddenly overwhelmed by the need to ask about Olivia. He was a member of the *bottega*, he could give her the answers. She just wanted to know whether Olivia was still alive. But as his implacable Italian face softened with regret she realised he had read her mind.

'I can tell you nothing,' he said, shaking his head. 'But you have my promise that one day you will see them again. Now you must make the plans for Madeleine to be in Italy within three weeks. Can you do it?' There was no menace in his voice, the need for threats did not arise. She loved Sergio, perhaps beyond life itself, she would do nothing to jeopardise their future together. However, should she at any time appear to be failing in her promise, then he, Dario, would kill her. Sergio had given that instruction the night before; she knew too much, he had said, and they could not risk losing everything now.

'Yes, I can do it,' Deidre answered. She would not show her fear, for behind those dark, inscrutable eyes of his she had read the darker intention. 'Now come along,' she smiled, threading her arm through his, 'time for the birthday cake.'

It was evident when they walked back into the dining-room that, despite the guests who had had more than enough to drink – or maybe because of them – everyone was having a wonderful time. Deidre was pleased for

Madeleine, and smiled as she glanced up at her. Madeleine had whispered earlier that Paul had already told her what her surprise was, but she refused to say more because Paul wanted to make the announcement himself. Certain that they had set a wedding date, Deidre could already see the confetti fluttering about Madeleine's face, but she would allow herself no feelings on the matter as she clapped her hands for everyone to follow her out to the terrace.

François was already there, filling champagne glasses, and as soon as everyone was gathered, Geneviève and her friend, followed by two local lads blowing a trumpet and banging a drum, came out of the kitchen carrying a birthday cake ablaze with candles and sparklers. They all sang 'Happy Birthday', then Deidre rapped a table for silence and Paul stepped forward to a chorus of ribald remarks.

He laughed as he waited for everyone to settle, then raising his glass, he looked from one face to the next and said: 'As you are all no doubt aware by now, I have a surprise for Madeleine. She thinks she already knows what it is, but in fact, she doesn't. So, if you are ready, ladies and gentlemen – Madeleine, I'd like you to be the first to congratulate us. I have asked Shamir to be my wife and she has accepted.'

As shock froze every smile on the terrace, so all eyes moved to Madeleine. But Madeleine, too stunned to move, was staring at Paul as, still smiling, he held a hand out towards Shamir. The silence stretched beyond endurance until suddenly Madeleine's glass slipped through her fingers and smashed on the tiled floor. Only then did she move, and so quickly that no one could stop her. Her silvery dress fluttered in the darkness as she ran across the garden and plunged into the black shadows of the orchard. From the other side of the terrace Deidre started after her, fighting through the cluster of bodies to get to the steps.

But by the time she reached the old wooden gate in the side wall and rushed out into the narrow mountain road beyond, Madeleine had vanished.

— 24 —

Enrico paused, watching the coast melt like wax into the pink, early morning haze. Surf-topped waves lapped lazily against the hull of the *Rosaria,* and he inhaled deeply before opening the cabin door and going inside.

The bitter aroma of coffee was sweetened by a delicate scent of soap, and he smiled at the scrubbed face that turned to look at him. Madeleine tried to smile back, but his kindness pushed tears into her eyes.

'I thought you would sleep,' he said, taking the coffee pot from her and filling the cups she had set out. She watched as he stirred milk into the dark liquid, then put his head back through the door, calling out for the crew to come and get their coffee. 'Come,' he said, turning back to her, and he led the way into the saloon. The cushions were still dented where she had been sitting, curled into a ball, as if cowering away from the world. Her dress was hanging from a cupboard door, glittering silver and gold in the dusty columns of sunlight that shone through the portholes. He was grateful that she had chosen to put on his robe rather than Rosaria's.

He still wasn't sure whether he was doing the right thing in taking her with him, but since he had found her, in the early morning darkness, sitting on the forward deck in all her evening finery, he had been unable to tell her to go. She'd seemed almost frightened when he stepped on board, and had backed away as if she thought he would strike her. There was a confusion at first as he spoke in Italian, then French, until he remembered that of course she was English. He'd asked for an explanation, sounding harsher than he intended, and her eyes had widened, giving her the look of a persecuted animal. Then suddenly she had lunged forward, trying to push past him, but he had grabbed her, and asked again why she was there.

His English was good, but sobs shook her voice, making it difficult for him to understand. In the end he gave up and took her inside, where he poured her a brandy. It was some time before her breathing steadied, and while he waited he remembered how she had inflamed his anger two nights before. Since then he'd all but forgotten her, but now her distress began to feel like an intrusion.

Eventually, when she made no effort to try again with an explanation, he stood up. 'I think you must go now,' he said, and started to walk to the door.

'No! No, please.'

He swung round, half expecting, from her desperate tone, to find her on her knees, but she was still sitting, holding her empty glass, shivering and looking so vulnerable that he could not help but feel he must take some responsibility for her.

'But I must sail soon,' he said, fighting it.

She lowered her head and started to mumble.

'I cannot hear. You must speak up.'

'Can you take me with you?' She lifted her face. 'Please! I can't go back. I can't . . .'

He looked at her, trying to feel the anger he had managed to inject into his voice. It eluded him, while her helplessness cut a direct route to his sense of chivalry. 'Tell me why you cannot go back.'

She nodded, and took a deep breath; and at once words began to tumble incoherently from her mouth. Afraid she might become hysterical again, he stopped her, and with the patient tenderness he normally reserved for his sons, he took her over each stage of the night before until he had a full picture of what had taken place. When she finished her face was taut and white, as if she were only then grasping the full horrific truth of what had happened. He refused to allow himself any feeling on the matter, nor did he ask why she had chosen to come to his boat; he figured he already had the answer to that. Everyone knew that Enrico Tarallo had lost his wife, and this English *bellezza* had thought to find one broken-heart understanding of another. The transparency of her motive irked him, but still he found himself agreeing to take her with him. What he would do with her once they arrived in Sardinia, he didn't yet know, but as his grandmother would be waiting with the boys, there was no question of her staying with him.

Now, as they drank their coffee, he said: 'You should call your friend, Deidre, let her know you are safe. We can use the radio.'

'Not yet,' Madeleine answered. 'Maybe later, when we get to Porto Cervo.'

He nodded. 'As you wish.'

They sat quietly then, cradled by the *Rosaria* on the gentle rise and dip of the waves. The rhythm was soothing and Madeleine rested her head against the side of the boat. Enrico thought she would sleep, but when he looked at her again there were tears on her cheeks. He surprised himself by reaching for her hand, and when she turned to look at him he pulled her head onto his shoulder. Then she slept.

Later, she found him sitting up on deck. The two crew members were at the helm, and quietly she crept past them and settled herself next to Enrico.

He looked round. 'Feeling better?'

'I think so.'

Her eyes roamed over his tanned legs, which were covered in a mass of black hair. His sinewy shoulders were not broad, but their firmness reminded her that he was a sportsman, and his beaky nose added strength to a face that was almost handsome when he smiled. Turning away, she gazed into the vast, wide open space and followed the sparkling lines of sunlight along the water. It was so peaceful.

'It is beautiful, no?' Enrico said.

Madeleine nodded, then swallowed hard against a sudden surge of emotion.

He smiled. 'It is a good place to bring sadness because nature is at her kindest when the sea is calm, the sun is warm and the sky is blue. She tells you there is no need to feel trapped by your sadness, because it is no more than one raindrop in the ocean. Here you may see your life as but one strike of a clock in the great passage of time.' He lay back and closed his eyes. They had been Rosaria's words the day they had sailed together and she had told him she was going to die.

Madeleine said, 'I'm sorry.'

'You are sorry? Why?' His eyes remained closed and she turned back to watch the waves.

She wanted to say that she was sorry about his wife, but she was afraid to, so instead she said, 'I'm sorry for foisting myself on you like this.'

He smiled. 'Maybe it is good that you did. Where else would you have gone?'

She knew he was teasing, but the question bit into her anguish like a vice and she flinched against the physical surge of pain. 'I don't know,' she answered quietly. 'I haven't got any money, I left with nothing, but I haven't got any money anyway – not now.'

'But you are famous. Your face is seen everywhere, surely you must . . .'

'No, I've spent it all. There's nothing left.'

'So you are destitute?' There was an irony in his voice that made her smile despite the way she was feeling.

'Yes,' she said. 'Destitute. No money, no friends, no family.'

'This is very sad,' he said, opening an eye to look at her, but her face was turned away, and sensing that she no longer wanted to speak, he said no more.

Some time later Madeleine turned to look at him again. 'Somebody told me about your grandmother and your sons. It must be nice to have a family. Do you love them?'

Surprised by the question, he laughed. 'But of course.' Then, when she didn't go on, he opened his eyes. 'And you, Madeleine? Do you love your family? Or do you really have no one?'

'I've got an aunt and a cousin, Marian. She was more like a sister, really. But I've done terrible things to them, especially to my cousin. I wish I had the courage to do something about it, but I'm afraid it's too late, that she'll never be able to forgive me.'

He raised his hand, as if her words were tangible things he could push away. She couldn't know, of course, but her voice was like that of the accuser that had followed him everywhere since Rosaria had died. But the accusing voice had been there before, muted yet persistent, and he had ignored it because Rosaria had loved Sergio, and despite what had happened to Arsenio, she had wanted to protect him. Abruptly he stood up and walked to the other side of the boat, with Madeleine's words echoing in his conscience. *'I've done terrible things . . . I wish I had the courage to do something about it, but I'm afraid it's too late.'*

It was now five years since he had sent his brother to the asylum, and hardly a day had passed when he hadn't heard a voice demanding to know what had given him the right to act as Arsenio's judge and jury. He could tell himself that it had been for Arsenio's own protection, but he knew that it was the name Arsenio spluttered and screamed in his madness that had made him send him away. So that still only the Tarallo family knew of Sergio's *bottega*, and only they knew that whatever had happened there that night – the night Olivia Hastings disappeared – had caused Arsenio's insanity.

Since that time, Sylvestra had banished Sergio from their home, though she was still protecting him for she had never told the police what she knew. Though what she knew fell far short of the full truth. Neither of them, Enrico, nor Sylvestra, knew what had really happened on that fateful night. If he could find out, he might be able to destroy this devil of guilt that lived within him and bring Arsenio home. But only Sergio had the answers, and he knew that Sergio would never tell.

Easing himself slowly back to the present, Enrico looked around to find Madeleine. Whatever she had done to her cousin, it could not be as terrible as the way he had sat in judgement on Arsenio, drawing conclusions from circumstances of which he knew nothing. In consequence, he had labelled his brother a murderer, had expelled him from the love of his family and reduced him to a shell of a man, all for the sake of protecting Sergio Rambaldi.

He found Madeleine in the galley, mixing eggs in a bowl. She was wearing one of his shirts now, the way Rosaria used to, and because she looked so much more beautiful than his wife, it offended him.

Madeleine looked up from what she was doing, then laughed nervously at the harsh expression on his face. 'I never was much of a cook,' she said, 'but I suppose we ought to eat.'

He nodded, and seeing his bitterness intensify, she looked away. A few minutes later, with the omelettes rising in the pan, she turned back to him and smiled. He was watching her closely, but his eyes held no answering smile.

She spoke hesitantly, unsure if this was the right thing to say, but she had nothing else to offer. 'Paul always said that if he was feeling down or angry, it helped him to make love. Perhaps . . . I know how unhappy you are, so maybe

it would comfort you if we . . . I feel I owe you something
. . .' She gasped as his face turned ugly with contempt.

'This is my wife's boat,' he snarled. 'You shame both
me and her by even suggesting such a thing.'

'I'm sorry. I'm sorry, Enrico. Don't be angry, please. I
only thought . . .'

'Take your hands off me!' he spat. 'Take that shirt off,
put your own dress on and stay down here until we reach
Porto Cervo. I do not want to see you.' He slammed out
of the galley and went back on deck, knowing that his
anger and disgust were with himself – he despised the way
his body could so easily have betrayed his heart.

Sensing his mood, the crew kept their distance as Enrico
stood on the forward deck, holding onto the guard rails
and refusing to hear or see anything beyond the sough of
the waves and the strident cry of the gulls. The sun slid
slowly through its arc, uninterrupted by cloud, and his
guilt was as uncompromising as the heat, burning him
from the inside with more vengeance than the sun on his
skin's surface. He knew nothing about the girl apart from
what he'd read, but his own experience of the press told
him how unreliable that was. But she had behaved like all
the English girls he'd met, offering herself to him because
he was famous. Yet she was famous herself. She need not
have done it, except to be kind to him. Maybe it was the
only language she knew and he had spurned her as cruelly
as the man she loved.

By the time he went below again, the *Rosaria* was
accompanied by her own dark shadow, billowing on the
sea. He stood in the doorway looking at Madeleine,
knowing he must say something, but inside he was so tense
that his words were strangled. She looked so young and
timid, sitting on the edge of the bunk and wearing her
dress just as he had told her to. If they could see her now,
he thought. People knew so little about what went on
behind the public face of women like her.

'I'm sorry.' His voice was a harsh whisper. 'You have your own sadness and I should thank you for trying to help mine.' She bowed her head, shielding her face with her hair, and he walked across to her and sat down.

'You really loved your wife, didn't you?' she said.

'Yes.'

'I saw her once. After you'd won the race at Silverstone. It seems such a long time ago now. I thought then that you loved her. Was she ill then?'

'Yes.'

'Did you know she was going to die?'

'Yes.'

Madeleine lifted her head, and seeing the anguish in his face she covered her own with her hands. 'I'm sorry,' she cried. 'I'm so sorry. I hate myself. I know I'm worth nothing, but I didn't mean to make you angry or ashamed.' She threw herself onto his chest and clasped her arms round his neck.

He hadn't wanted to cry. He had sworn to himself that after the savagery of his grief in those solitary days at sea, he wouldn't again. But he couldn't help himself.

Feeling his shoulders begin to shake, Madeleine sat up. He turned away, but she took his head and leaning back, she cushioned him in her arms, smoothing her hand over his hair. She remembered Marian once telling her that sometimes it took great strength for a man to cry; she hadn't understood at the time, but now she did. If only Marian were here, to tell her what to do.

She clung to Enrico, the tears for herself spent, though she wept again now for him. She had never felt this kind of tenderness with Paul, but looking down at Enrico's dark head, she couldn't stop herself wishing it was Paul's blond one she held. The selfish thought stabbed at her with a quick pain, but Paul had no vulnerability, no need of her the way Enrico did now. As if in a daze, she kissed the top of Enrico's head – and for a brief moment she felt like

Marian. She was doing what her cousin would have done, and for the first time she understood Marian's kindness and humility. She understood what a rich person Marian was to know such feelings, and she understood too how Marian must have felt when she stole Paul away. Marian had lost everything then, and now, so had she.

Eventually Enrico lifted his head. He expected to feel shame, but when he saw the compassion in Madeleine's eyes he laughed and rubbed the tears from his face. 'Maybe I shall open the whisky and for a while we will be sad together, no?' he said.

Madeleine nodded, and when their glasses were on the table she relaxed against him and they sat quietly.

'Your cousin,' Enrico said, after a while. 'I think, whatever you have done it cannot be so terrible that she will not forgive you.' He knew he was speaking for himself too, but he continued, 'At a time like this you need your family, Madeleine. It is only your family who can forgive and love without condition. Does she know, your Marian, what it is you have done?'

'Partly, yes. I think she might have forgiven me that already. But you see, I lied to her, I cheated and stole from her, and I was really cruel when she came to see me in New York. The strange thing was that I didn't mean to be, but I felt so guilty that I couldn't stop myself. I've been thinking about her ever since, and I know now that I've never really been happy ever since I did what I did. But you see, I wanted Paul so much I'd have done anything to get him away from her.' Her voice caught in her throat but she went on, 'He's tried to destroy me. I've got no home now, no money, no friends, no family, I've got nothing. But I still want him, can you believe that?'

He smiled. 'Yes, I can believe that. Love doesn't go away so easily.'

She sighed. 'You're so lucky, Enrico, that Rosaria loved you.'

'Yes, for that I was very lucky.'

'Why is love so important?'

He chuckled. 'I do not know, *cara*. But I do know that without it we are nothing. And there are so many different kinds of love, but being *in* love is the greatest and the saddest of them all. Now you have achieved your fame, and I have become the great racing driver, maybe we can look at love and appreciate its greatness, because we know that success is pale beside it and fame has not protected us from its sadness. It is a lesson I think we both had to learn, and now we must do right by our families because it is from them we must draw our strength to continue.'

Madeleine turned in his arms to look at him. 'You sound like Marian,' she said. 'Sometimes she would say things like that.'

He laughed. 'Then Marian must be a very wise person, just like me, no?'

Madeleine laughed too. 'I wish I could see her right now. I don't even know where she is, she might still be in New York, but do you know what? As soon as I get back to England I'm going to find her. My aunt will know where she is, and then the three of us will sit down together and I shall confess everything I've done.'

'And they will forgive you, because in your heart you love them. But now, unless we plan to sail right past Porto Cervo I think I had better, how do you say, get my act together.'

Later, each dressed in a pair of Enrico's shorts and shirts, they strode along the busy jetty at Porto Cervo to hunt out the noisiest café where, over succulent pizzas and glasses of chilled Frascati, they laughed and talked quite oblivious to the crowded tables around them – and for those few precious moments they allowed themselves to forget. Enrico told her about racing, and Madeleine could almost feel the thrill of speed and danger as he described the moments of sheer terror that were so soon followed by an unsurpassable exhilaration, and she teased his modesty when it came to telling her about his victories. Then he asked her about modelling, and feigned shock when she told him how often she removed her clothes for the camera.

'You don't really think it's so terrible, do you?' she asked, uncertainly.

'Oh, *sì*, it is very terrible,' he told her. 'It is very, very, terrible.' His face was grim, but as he peered at her from the corner of his eye, he laughed at her look of dismay. 'You are a beautiful woman, Madeleine, I am certain you have given much pleasure by showing to the world such a magnificent body. And you, do you like to do it?'

'Yes,' she answered, but she was frowning.

'You seem to have doubts. Maybe you do not want to do it any more?'

'I don't know. It all seems as if it doesn't matter now.'

'Did it matter once?'

She shrugged. 'I think so. I know it was all I ever wanted to do.'

'Then you have achieved an ambition, that is good. But there will always be others, so I wonder what you will do next?'

She looked across the table at him and her eyes were sparkling with mischief. 'Become a racing driver?' she suggested.

He burst out laughing and reached across the table to tweak her nose. Neither of them saw the photographer sneak up, nor the one that followed him. They were blissfully unaware of having attracted any attention at all, until the first flash-bulb popped.

Enrico's horror at being discovered in such a situation, and so soon after his wife's death, was total, but he only made matters worse by leaping from his chair and knocking the photographer to the ground. Suddenly the night was lit up as if by fireworks, as the press fought to capture this remarkable and unexpected scoop on film. Madeleine tried to push her way to Enrico, but someone grabbed her arm and started pulling her through the crowd. She screamed and struggled to break free, but her assailant shouted for her to get out fast. And before she knew what was happening, a hand was over her mouth and she was being bundled into the back of a car.

'Bloody hell!' Stephanie exclaimed. 'I don't believe it.' She handed the newspaper to Hazel and sat down. 'The damned cousin's gone missing now.'

It was their first day back in the office since filming had finished in New York. They were beginning again the following day in London.

Hazel didn't bother to read the article, she'd already seen it.

Stephanie looked at her watch. 'I suppose Matthew'll be here any minute. I just can't wait to see what sort of Sir Galahad stroke he pulls this time.'

Hazel perched herself on the edge of the desk. 'Steph,' she began haltingly, 'he's already gone to Devon. He went last night.'

Stephanie looked suddenly haggard and slumped forward, burying her head in her arms. 'I should have known. Oh, Haze, what's happening? Why is he doing this?'

Hazel put a hand on her shoulder. 'I don't know, Steph. It just doesn't add up. She's young enough to be his daughter and that simply isn't Matthew's style. He's still in love with you, I'm certain of it, but he seems obsessed with the girl.'

'What shall I do? Tell me, for God's sake, before I go out of my mind.'

Hazel gave a long sigh and shook her head. 'I wish I knew. But you can't give up, Steph. I don't know how you fight it, but you can't have come this far to lose him now. Did you talk about any of this after she'd left New York?'

Stephanie sat up, rubbing her hands over her tired face.

'Not really. If I broached the subject he just reminded me that I was the one he'd asked to marry him, and said that nothing had changed as far as he was concerned.'

'Did you ask him right out what his feelings were for Marian?'

'Only once. He flew off the handle and told me to grow up. You know, it was as if he had a guilty conscience. It's that I can't forget. What's he got to feel guilty about if he isn't in love with her?'

Hazel knew she was clutching at straws, but she had to try. 'Maybe you were imagining it. You know what it's like when you're so madly in love with someone, you read all kinds of things into situations that mean nothing.'

Stephanie smiled. 'Haze, we both know that there is something to be read into this one. But what, for heaven's sake? Is he bringing her back to London with him, did he say?'

Hazel nodded. 'Later today. Are you going to give her her job back?'

'What else can I do? If I don't he'll accuse me of victimising her because of my jealousy. He'd be right, of course, but I can't help it, I'd do anything to get her out of our lives.'

'But that isn't the solution, I know.'

Stephanie looked up into Hazel's solemn face. 'When did he speak to you, Haze? I mean, about going to Devon. And why didn't he call me?'

'Last night. I don't know why he didn't call you, he just asked me to pass the message on. Were you in?'

Stephanie nodded. 'But we rowed on the way from the airport. About his damned daughter, would you believe? He's still refusing to let me meet her.'

The intercom buzzed and Stephanie flicked the switch. It was Josey, downstairs.

'Is Hazel with you, Steph?'

'Yeah, go ahead.'

'Adrian's just rung in. There's some problem with blocking the traffic in the Gloucester Road tomorrow.'

'OK,' Hazel answered. 'I'll be right down.' She stood up and walked slowly to the door.

'Haze,' Stephanie said. 'Why do you suppose he didn't sack Rory in the end?'

'I guess events just went beyond it, you know, with her mother dying and everything. I know the two of them talked, but Rory never let on what was said.'

'Do you think Marian and Rory might fall for one another?'

Hazel shrugged. 'Who knows.'

Stephanie closed her eyes. 'I'm going to pray every day that they will, because if I lose him this time I think I'll go under.'

Since he'd arrived the night before, Marian had been longing for him to hold her the way he had in New York, but he hadn't. They'd sat up the whole night, talking, mainly about her mother and Madeleine. Matthew had told her about his family too. Neither of them mentioned Stephanie, but Marian felt her presence as if she were there with them, in that little room that used to be cluttered with the bric-à-brac and trinkets her mother had collected over the years.

Grace had organised everything when they arrived. She had even contacted the council about putting her mother's things into storage until Marian decided what to do with them. The house was being taken over by a young couple and their little boy the following week, but that was something Marian couldn't bring herself to think about.

After Grace had flown back to New York, leaving Frank's men to watch over her, Marian had roamed about the house, steeping herself in memories of her childhood and wondering why Madeleine didn't come. But now

Madeleine had gone missing – Paul had jilted her publicly and she had run away.

'If only she had come to me,' she sighed. 'She needs me now. Just as much as I need her.'

Matthew smiled and ruffled her hair. 'You've always got me,' he laughed, but he turned away as her eyes asked him the question he couldn't answer – have I?

'I'll take you to Christie's,' he said, as they were locking up the house. 'You can spend the money you saved up to repay your mother on a painting. Then you'll always have something to remember her by. How does that sound? Have you ever been to an auction?'

She shook her head.

'Neither have I, so it'll be a first for us both.'

Four hours later, as they drove into London, Matthew stopped at a news-stand in Earls Court. Again Madeleine's picture was across the front page, but this time it showed her in a brawl she and Enrico Tarallo had become involved in in Sardinia.

'Well, at least we know where she is,' Marian said.

'I'm afraid not,' Matthew answered. 'Read that bit there.'

Marian read it. Then suddenly she started to giggle. When Matthew looked startled, she laughed again – and again, until she was laughing so hard that tears streamed down her face. 'She always said she wanted adventure,' she gasped. 'Well, she's really got it this time. Kidnapped by someone in a big black limousine. I'm sorry, I know it's not funny but I can't help it. Do you think it's serious?'

'God only knows,' he answered, and then he laughed too.

Wearing the loose yellow skirt and white gypsy blouse that had mysteriously appeared on her bed that morning, Madeleine was sitting in a nook of the hillside that sloped down from the Tarallo family's villa in Sardinia to their private beach below. As she gazed sightlessly from the golden cupped flowers around her, moving her eyes slowly across the rich turquoise waves to where the sea and sky blended in a hazy, colourless horizon, the sun's warmth on her skin was like a comforting embrace and she smiled listlessly as she thought about the events of the past twelve hours.

After she had been dragged out of the restaurant in Porto Cervo, then bundled into the limousine, her assailant had kept her head covered as they sped round the semi-circular harbour road until they reached the dark labyrinth of back-streets. Then the car had stopped; Enrico, together with another man, had leapt in, and they had roared off into the night.

There was a great deal of shouting, all in Italian, and Madeleine had stared uncomprehendingly at Enrico, terror rendering her speechless. When finally he turned to look at her and saw her stricken face, he laughed. 'There is no need to be afraid, *cara*,' he said softly. 'It is only my grandmother, come to take us home.'

At that moment Madeleine heard a deep, croaky voice and gaped into the dark corner of the car that it had come from. Then, as if someone had lifted a veil, a white face emerged from the shadows of the seat opposite.

Enrico took Madeleine's hand. 'Madeleine,' he said. 'Please meet Sylvestra Tarallo, my grandmother. She has her spies everywhere, and they were watching from outside when the fight started. Sylvestra, this is . . .'

'I know who she is,' Sylvestra rasped. Her English was heavily accented, her breathing laboured. She spoke rapidly to Enrico, using her mother-tongue, then turned again to Madeleine. 'I tell him you bring disgrace on my family. I see your pictures, you are no good.'

'Sylvestra!' Enrico continued in Italian and Madeleine shrank back in her seat.

When they reached the villa, Madeleine and Enrico

followed Sylvestra's frail figure up the steps and into the magnificent grey marble hall. Two servants were waiting; Sylvestra gave them instructions, then turned to Madeleine. 'They make a room for you. You follow Orsola, she show you. You have luggage, no?'

Madeleine shook her head and Sylvestra made an impatient sound as she tucked her arm through Enrico's. Looking back over his shoulder, Enrico winked, then nodded for Madeleine to go after Orsola, who was waiting on the balcony at the top of the stairs.

She was woken the next morning by children playing outside, but after the reception she had received from Sylvestra the night before, she didn't dare to leave her room. She had found the clothes neatly folded across the foot of the bed, and as neither her dress nor Enrico's shorts and shirt were anywhere to be seen, she assumed that the skirt and blouse had been left for her to wear. Eventually Enrico came in, followed by a maid carrying a large breakfast tray which she set up on the terrace outside the room. When she'd gone, Enrico spread out the morning newspapers, all of which had the previous night's brawl on the cover, and made her laugh as he translated the dramatic story of her kidnap.

'Kidnapped,' she said gleefully as she broke the crust of a hard roll. 'If this is what it's like being kidnapped, I don't know why people make such a fuss about it.'

Giving her a sardonic look, he said, 'Nevertheless we must put matters straight. I will speak to the press and hope that they do not turn the story into one of elopement.'

'It gets more romantic all the time,' she laughed, then suddenly she thought of Paul and her face fell.

'You are letting the ghosts haunt you, and Lara our cook will not be pleased if you do not drink her tea. She made it especially for you because you are English.'

Madeleine smiled. 'Then even though I never normally drink tea, this morning I will, just for Lara.'

After breakfast he took her downstairs and out into the garden. 'You take a walk, maybe down to the beach, and I will come to find you later,' he said, as she gazed appreciatively at the carefully pruned trees, neat flower-beds and sprawling lawns.

'You can't come with me now?' she said, for some reason afraid that he was going to go away and leave her there.

'I must speak with Sylvestra,' he explained, then pulling a face, he added, 'and to the press.'

Now she looked up as a shadow fell across her, and seeing him standing there beside her, she moved over to make room for him to sit down.

'I quite like being kidnapped by you,' she said, lifting her face to the sun and shaking out her hair.

He rolled his eyes, but smiled as he said: 'If you say that again I shall be forced to send out a ransom note.'

'How much do you think I'm worth?'

'In lire or sterling?'

She shrugged. 'I don't have any money, so it doesn't really matter, does it? Did you speak to Sylvestra?'

He nodded gravely. 'She is a formidable woman, my grandmother. You are afraid of her, no?'

Madeleine nodded, then shuddered at the memory of her first meeting with the old lady.

'She would like to speak with you,' he said, then laughed at the look that came over her face. 'There is no need to be afraid. I have explained everything and she would like to apologise for her, how you say, brusqueness?'

Madeleine would have liked to call it something else, but refrained from doing so and gave him a winsome smile instead.

'Oh, by the way,' he went on, still chuckling at her reaction, 'I have issued a statement to the newspapers, informing them that you have not been abducted. Does that disappoint you, *cara*?' he asked, when she lowered her head.

She nodded. 'I know it's silly, but I wanted Paul to worry about me.'

'I think, if I am any judge of a man, he will be much more worried to learn that you are in the clutches of the infamous Enrico Tarallo.'

'Infamous?'

'I tease. Oh, come, no more of the sad face. Maybe it is better this way. If he can wound you so, and in public, then he cannot be such a good man. Nor Shamir such a good friend.' He sighed. 'But that does not make the love or the hurt go away, I know.'

Madeleine lay back in the grass and gazed up at the sky. Shamir and Paul – their betrayal and deceit were stalking her like the preying phantoms of a nightmare, yet somehow, while she lay here with Enrico, it was as if they were afraid to touch her. But in the night the nightmare had smothered her, denying her the release of sleep and forcing her to remember and accept what had happened. In those dark, lonely hours she had thought about Paul, recalling the way he had asked her to trust him, the way he had promised there would be no more trickery, while all the time he had known what he was going to do. Had he ripped her heart from her body and wrung it with his bare hands, he could not have hurt her more, and the final twist of the knife had come when she realised that he had known that, and that was why he had done it. And yet, if he were to walk over the brow of the hill now and hold out his arms, she knew she would run to him.

She turned her head to look at Enrico and smiled at the far-away look in his eyes as he stared out to sea. This island was so peaceful and Enrico was so kind, she wanted to stay here forever.

'I wish I didn't have to go,' she said.

'But what would your public do without you?' he teased.

She didn't know why that made her want to cry, but her vision was blurred as she whispered: 'Don't. Please don't say that.'

He smiled. 'Beautiful, sad Madeleine. The girl who has captivated the world by revealing her charms.' He was quoting from the morning paper. 'May I say what I think?' he added.

She nodded.

'I think it is difficult for a child to lose its parents, and that maybe the recognition you seek comes from that. Everyone needs approval and admiration and love. You have envied Marian because she had it from her mother and father. You were what you English call, the poor cousin. So you have shown the world all your beauty, hoping from them you will gain what you seek. But you will not find it out there, *cara*. You will find it where it has always been, with your cousin and your aunt – the family you have tried not to love.'

She turned her head in the grass and watched a butterfly as it flitted between the flowers. Tried not to love. Had she really tried not to love them? Was he right, had she done it all out of envy and a childhood need for approval and admiration? She longed to be able to answer those questions, but she realised now that she knew too little about herself, too little about what really happened deep down inside her. Then suddenly she remembered what Marian had said that day at the Plaza. 'I know you better than anyone ever will, and that is why I am so, so sorry it has to be like this.' Had Marian been trying to say what Enrico had just said? Did she really understand her so well? Madeleine swallowed hard on the lump in her throat, and closed her eyes, as if to block out the painful memory of that day in New York. She couldn't think about Marian now, the need for her was too great.

'I've been thinking,' she said, after a while. 'About Paul. He might have done this for his book. He used to shock me sometimes, to see how I would react. Then he wrote about it.'

When she looked up she saw that Enrico's thick brows were drawn in a frown. 'But like this?' he said. 'It is too horrible, *cara*.' He smiled. 'But if what you say is true, and you still love him, then you will forgive him. But I think it will be hard.'

Madeleine gave no answer. She didn't know how she felt any more, about anything, and she didn't want to think about it, either. All she knew was that somehow, this man, who was little more than a stranger, had struck a chord somewhere deep inside her and she didn't want to leave him.

'Now,' Enrico said, jumping to his feet, then helping Madeleine to hers, 'what have you done with those sons of mine? I promised them a trip in the *Rosaria*.'

'They went back into the house,' she answered. 'I don't think they liked me much.'

'Ah, *cara*,' he sighed, 'you must try to understand more. They are only children and their mother is so soon dead. They think you have come to steal me away. Now I will put their minds at rest, and you shall go to Sylvestra.' He laughed as she pulled a face, then draping an arm round her shoulders he walked with her through the gardens and back to the villa.

During the afternoon Enrico's mother arrived with her two daughters and their husbands. Sylvestra had told Madeleine to wait upstairs until she sent word; the family had come to demand an explanation for what had happened. As she waited in her room, listening to the raised voices and the doors slamming downstairs, Madeleine was filled with such trepidation that even Sylvestra's apology and the kindness which had followed were not enough to quell her nerves. She felt so far from home, so lonely and so utterly helpless that by the time Enrico came to fetch her, her agitation was so great that for a moment it alarmed him.

'Ssh,' he whispered, taking her ashen face between his hands. 'It is all right. Sylvestra and I, we are on your side. My mother, she does not always understand, but she will do you no harm.'

'Do I have to meet her?'

'But of course, what will she think if you do not? She will think that you are a coward, no?'

'I am,' Madeleine said, then despite herself, she laughed, because now that he was here nothing seemed quite so bad.

'We are dining early this evening,' he told her, as she quickly ran a brush through her hair, 'so that the boys can see their grandmother before they go to bed. There will be all of us at the table, and you will not feel so conspicuous.'

Madeleine gave him a dubious look, and grinning broadly, he took her hand and led her downstairs.

Throughout the meal the atmosphere was strained – it was clear that neither Sylvestra nor Enrico had said anything to pacify his mother's strong disapproval of Madeleine's presence in their home. She was an awesome, angry-looking woman, who with her thin, almost pinched face and ochre hair bore no resemblance to Enrico whatever, and the little conversation she forced herself to direct Madeleine's way was delivered with such hostility that Enrico invariably found himself answering on Madeleine's behalf. His sisters were at the other end of the table, and though they appeared engrossed in Enrico's and their own children, Madeleine could sense that their resentment of her was as great as their mother's.

'I'm glad that's over,' she sighed, as Enrico walked her up to bed. 'God, they really hated me.'

'They showed bad manners and an unforgivable lack of sensitivity,' he snapped, 'and if you were not leaving tomorrow I would order them from the house tonight.'

'Leaving tomorrow,' Madeleine repeated, and the sudden stab of desperation was so acute that as they stopped outside her room, she turned to him with imploring eyes and whispered, 'Do I have to?'

Enrico opened the door for her to go in. 'I'm afraid you must,' he answered.

Madeleine walked over to the window to close the shutters. He watched her, silhouetted in the moonlight, as she hesitated to shut out the night, and as his heart was filled with pity, so his arms ached to hold her.

She spun round as she heard the door close, disappointed that he had not even said goodnight, but when she saw him standing there in the half light, his face hidden in shadow, her heart turned over.

'Come,' he said, holding out his arms, and she went to him. 'Tonight,' he whispered into her hair, 'I will hold you close. I cannot make love, you understand, but maybe the comfort of my arms will help you.'

'Yes,' she breathed, 'oh yes, please.'

'Come then, we will ask Orsola for something you can wear. Maybe one of my sisters has a bed-gown.'

'But I don't usually sleep with anything . . .'

He put his fingers over her lips. 'Tonight you must, as I am a mere human, Madeleine, and you are very beautiful.'

He left the room then, and a few minutes later Orsola came in with a blue silk nightdress which, when Madeleine put it on, made her giggle at the way it covered her from chin to toe, yet somehow contrived to look more sexy than forbidding. But knowing that this wouldn't please Enrico, she slipped between the sheets to cover herself before he came.

'I must hope that my sons do not wake and go to my room to find me,' he said as he got into bed wearing a pair of black cotton pyjamas. 'I think if they do that even Sylvestra would not understand.'

'I'm causing you so many problems,' Madeleine said, as he slipped an arm beneath her shoulders.

'And before the night is finished you will probably cause me some more,' he joked.

'I'll try not to,' she murmured as he pulled her against him, and she yawned sleepily as she nestled into his embrace.

'Close your eyes,' he whispered, 'and think about only nice things. You will have a lot to face tomorrow, so tonight it is imperative that you sleep well. If you like, I will tell you the story I sometimes tell my sons when they are afraid in the night and cannot sleep.'

'That would be nice, but I wouldn't understand Italian.'

'It is no matter, some of it I will tell in English and some in my own language, and soon you will be so bored you will be snoring in my ear.'

She smiled, and as he started to tell her the story she closed her eyes to listen to his deep, melodic voice, but it wasn't long before the steady rhythm of her breathing told him she was fast asleep, exhausted by the traumas of the past two days.

When she woke in the morning the bed beside her was empty and she ran her fingers over the hollow in the pillow where Enrico's head had lain. It was the first time in her life that she had slept with a man without making love, and she was baffled by the way she was feeling. It was as if she and Enrico had shared something very special, something that far exceeded the closeness of sex. She wondered where he was now, if he had stayed the whole night, and she realised that probably he hadn't – because of the little boys who might have needed to hear the story too.

Eventually she got out of bed and went to let in the morning sunshine, but as she looked out at the pale, distant sea she could feel the weight of dread starting to drag at her as if it would take all the strength from her body. What would she do when she got to England? Where would she go? There would be no one to meet her, no one to take the burden of her misery as Enrico had last night; she would be alone, with no money, no home and nobody. A lump rose in her throat and she closed her eyes. 'I can't go,' she whispered. 'I can't face it.'

'Yes you can.'

She turned and saw Enrico standing in the doorway. He was wearing black trousers and a loose white shirt with the sleeves pulled back over his arms, and on his face was a look both tender and determined.

She gave him a resigned smile. 'I know I have to,' she said quietly, 'but I'm afraid.'

'There is no need to be. I have made the arrangements for you. I will take you to the airport at Olbia, and from there you will fly to *Roma* to make the connection for London.'

'I haven't got a passport. I left it in France.'

'I know, but I have had a courier bring it for you from your agent, so it is all arranged.'

Her heart sank as this last obstacle to her departure was removed. 'Thank you,' she murmured. She tried to smile. 'I don't know what I'd have done without you, Enrico. You're so kind, and I'm going to cry because I don't want to leave you.'

'Aah,' he chuckled, 'you touch my heart with your tears, but to remain here is not good, *cara*, because it is running away, and whatever you run away from will always come to find you.'

She bit her lips to stop them trembling. 'Will I see you again?' she asked.

He shook his head. 'I think not. But I am glad to have known you, Madeleine, and to have loved you just a little. Now you must get dressed and come downstairs to meet the courier who will travel with you to London. And to say good-bye to Sylvestra, yes? I will wait for you in the garden, you will take breakfast with me there. Orsola will bring you the clothes to wear for travelling.'

'Are they Rosaria's?' she asked.

He nodded. '*Si.*'

'Don't you mind?'

'No, *cara*. Rosaria would want you to have them.'

As she dressed, Madeleine choked back her tears and tried to wrest her mind from the emptiness that lay ahead. She knew Deidre would be pleased to see her, but it didn't help because she no longer had the desire to continue modelling. All she wanted, deep down in her heart, was for none of this to have happened, to be back in Bristol with Marian, before they'd met Paul, before her jealousy, narcissism and greed had destroyed everything. Again she fought to suppress her tears as the simplicity of her old life made everything that had come after seem worthless and trite. She knew she had got no more than she deserved – public humiliation and rejection. And now there would be no safety net to catch her in her fall from glory, because she had removed it the day she stole the money from Marian and walked out of their home with the man Marian loved.

By the time she went downstairs, though her face was strained she was still in control, she had not broken down and she wouldn't. It didn't matter to her whether she was strong, but she knew it mattered to Enrico, so until he took her to the airport, until the moment when the plane took off and she had seen him for the last time, she would hold on.

As she passed the small parlour Sylvestra called out to her, and when she walked in, the old lady stood up and embraced her.

'*Mia bambina,*' she said in her husky voice. 'It is goodbye today. You give a little happiness to my Enrico at this difficult time, for that I thank you.'

Madeleine couldn't answer, her heart was too full.

Sylvestra smiled, crinkling the weather-beaten skin of her face so that her eyes almost disappeared. Then turning to the huge black oak chest beside her, she picked up an envelope. 'Here,' she said, handing it to Madeleine. 'I go now with my daughter to take her away from the villa. This is *lira e sterlina*, maybe it will help a little. Be happy, child.' And before Madeleine could speak, she turned her round and pushed her towards the door. 'Enrico wait for you,' she said, 'go now to him.'

As she walked, every muscle in her body was tensed with the effort of trying to hold on. She had done nothing to deserve such kindness, yet this family . . . She swallowed very hard and took a deep breath. She wasn't going to give in.

But then, as she walked into the garden and saw Enrico standing beside the table talking to the courier, her whole body was suddenly flooded with emotion and her hands flew to her face.

'Oh no!' she sobbed.

At the sound of her voice Enrico and the courier turned. Both were smiling and both watched her as, with tears streaming from her eyes, she ran into Marian's arms.

'I thought you'd never want to see me again after the way I treated you at the Plaza,' Madeleine said, tucking her blonde hair behind her ear and staring down at the grass.

Marian chuckled. 'I have to confess I didn't much, then.'

Madeleine turned to look at her. They were sitting in the hollow where she and Enrico had sat the day before, and Marian was fingering the soft petals of a scarlet pimpernel she had plucked. 'I'm sorry,' Madeleine said. 'I'm sorry for that, I'm sorry for everything.'

'I know,' Marian said, 'and so am I.' She was gazing out to sea, watching the yachts bob on the waves. 'Who'd have thought it,' she said, a laugh in her voice, 'that you and I would end up here, sitting on a hillside in Sardinia. It feels a very long way from Bristol, doesn't it?'

'Yes.'

'In fact, if feels like many years since Bristol, yet it's only eight months. How could so much have happened in so short a time?' She turned to Madeleine and reached for her hand. 'You've been more successful than either of us ever dreamed, and I've . . . well, I'm not quite sure what I've achieved – at least, I don't know how to put it into words without sounding indecently pleased with myself – but whatever our accomplishments, I've missed you, Maddy.'

'I've missed you too. More than I would allow myself to realise. Thank you for coming.'

'I'm just so glad Enrico called me. I only wish you'd come to me when it happened.' She looked into Madeleine's face. 'Poor Maddy,' she said, lifting a hand to stroke her hair, 'it must have been terrible.'

'It doesn't feel so bad now that you're here.'

Marian smiled. 'Good.' Then after a lengthy pause, during which Madeleine stared down at the ground, lost in her thoughts and looking more vulnerable than Marian had ever seen her, she said, 'He wants you back, you know.'

Madeleine's eyes flew open. 'You've seen him?'

'No, I saw Deidre, to get your passport, she told me.'

'But what about Shamir? He said they were . . .' She stopped, unable to bring herself to finish the sentence.

'Shamir is in Los Angeles. Apparently she and Paul had a terrible fight the night it happened. Deidre says Shamir knew nothing about it, that it was as much of a surprise to her as it was to you.'

Madeleine looked away. 'So he did do it for his book,' she murmured.

'I don't know. All I know is what Deidre told me – and that I have the keys to your house in Holland Park. Paul wants you to go back there, but he won't come himself unless you say you want him.'

'It's his house now,' Madeleine said, the remoteness still in her eyes. 'He bought it from me.'

'Well, it would seem that he's giving it back to you, at least for the time being. Do you want it?'

Madeleine shrugged. 'I haven't got anywhere else to go, so why not? Unless . . . Where do you live, Marian? Can I come and live with you?'

Marian laughed. 'My circumstances are, how shall I put it, difficult and becoming more temporary by the day, otherwise our being together again is the thing I'd like best of all.'

'But we can be,' Madeleine said, suddenly brightening, 'you can come to live with me in Holland Park, if Paul's going to let me have the house. It's got three bedrooms, so there's plenty of room. Oh, say you will. Please, Marian!'

'But what about Paul? As I said, he wants you back.'

Sighing, Madeleine rested her elbows on her knees and buried her face in her hands.

'Do you still love him?' Marian asked, after a while.

'I don't know. Yes, yes, I still love him, but . . . Oh Marian, I don't know what to do. Please come and stay with me.'

'OK, if that's what you want, I'd love to.' She laughed. 'It'll certainly ease my situation, anyway. But I'm not so sure about yours. He'll want an answer, Maddy.'

'I know.' She lifted her head and looked down over the hillside. 'But that's in the future. All I want to think about now is us.' She turned to look at Marian, and sensing that she wanted to say more, Marian smiled her encouragement.

'There's something I have to tell you, Marian,' she began hesitantly. 'Something that you might not be able to forgive me for, and if you can't, I won't blame you. No, no, don't say anything, please just hear me out. It's something I did when I left Bristol, when Paul and I left Bristol. I didn't only steal him from you, I stole something else as well.'

'Really?' Marian said, her voice submerged in laughter. 'I didn't think I had anything else to steal. We were pretty destitute, as I remember.'

Madeleine nodded. 'Yes, we were. But then . . . You remember the lottery ticket, the one I shouted at you for buying in Broadmead . . .?' She stopped. For the moment her courage had failed her.

Marian's mouth fell open. 'You're not trying to tell me I won?'

'I am,' Madeleine answered, then before Marian could reach any false conclusions she went on hurriedly, 'but because you'd filled the ticket out in the name of Miss M. Deacon, the cheque was made out in that name, so . . . so I took it.'

'How much was it?' Marian asked excitedly. 'God, I can't believe it, I actually won something at long last. So come on, did I get first, second or third prize?'

'First. It was three-quarters of a million pounds.'

Madeleine steeled herself, waiting for the reproaches, the anger, the contempt, but when none of it came she turned to look at Marian and saw that she was too shocked to speak. 'It's worse than that, I'm afraid,' she said quietly, 'because I've spent it all. There's nothing left.'

Still Marian was silent, though her grey eyes were blinking as if she were trying to take it in. Eventually she said, 'You've spent it all? Three-quarters of a million pounds? How long did it take you?'

'According to Paul, about five months.'

'What! As long as that? You could spend that much in five minutes when we were planning it! What took you so long?'

Madeleine looked at her, shaking her head in bewilderment. 'Aren't you angry?' she said.

'Angry? Why should I be? Of course, I might have been if I'd known about it when I was left in Bristol to sort out all the bills, but that's done, you've got your success, I've got mine, what's there to be angry about? It won't bring it back, will it? And after all, it's only money.' She grinned. 'I bet I could have spent it quicker, though!'

'Marian?' Madeleine said, looking into her cousin's smiling face.

'Mm?'

'Can I hug you?'

'Oh, Maddy!' Marian laughed, 'of course you can, darling, come here.' And pulling Madeleine into her arms, she wrapped her in the tightest embrace she could give. 'Oh, it's so good to be with you,' she said. 'Three-quarters of a million pounds! Madeleine Deacon, what am I going to do with you?'

'Anything you like,' Madeleine laughed, 'I deserve it.'

Eventually, when they let one another go, Madeleine said, 'The day you came to the Plaza you mentioned Matthew Cornwall. I'm sorry for the way I reacted, Marian, it was cruel, unforgivable. Tell me how things are between you now. Has he fallen in love with you too?'

Marian sighed deeply. 'I don't know, Maddy. I honestly don't know.'

'Would you like to tell me about it?'

'Not now. Later, when we get home.' Her face suddenly lit up, and looking at Madeleine from the corner of her eye, she said, 'You can make us some cocoa and we'll sit up half the night while I tell you.'

'You're on,' Madeleine laughed. 'But let's make it wine, shall we? No, champagne, to celebrate us being together again.'

'Very extravagant,' Marian quipped, 'and I'm going to hold you to that – champagne it is.'

'Then tomorrow afternoon – our hangovers will be too bad in the morning – shall we go home and see Auntie

Celia? I've got a lot of . . . Marian, what's the matter? I know, she doesn't want to see me, does she?' Tears stung Madeleine's eyes and she took a deep breath to steady herself. 'I don't blame her, after what I've done. She wrote me a letter, you know, asking me to go home and see her, and I ignored it. But please, Marian, will you talk to her, try and persuade her to see me?'

'Oh, Maddy, Maddy, Maddy,' Marian said, tears coming to her own eyes. 'You don't know, do you?'

'Know what?' Madeleine said, a stab of fear suddenly piercing her heart.

Marian reached out for her hands and held them tightly. 'Try and be brave, Maddy, try not to let this . . .'

'What, Marian? What is it?'

'Mum died, Maddy. She had a heart-attack two weeks ago. I'm sorry, I thought you knew.'

'No!' Madeleine cried. 'NOOO! She can't be dead, Marian. Please tell me it's not true.'

'I'm sorry, darling.' Marian could barely speak.

'NO! NO! AUNTIE CELIA!' Madeleine's agony echoed round the hills, but when Marian tried to take her in her arms she fought her off, screaming for her aunt and begging Marian to say she was lying.

Suddenly Enrico was there. 'What is it?' he cried, helping Marian to hold Madeleine down.

'It's my mother,' Marian sobbed, 'Maddy didn't know.'

'Know what?'

'That she'd died.'

'Oh my God,' he breathed. 'Come on, we'd better get her back to the house. I'll call the doctor, see if he can give her something to calm her.'

As they half-carried, half-walked her up the hill Madeleine was still screaming, trying to wrench herself away from them, saying she wanted to die, that there was nothing left now, that it was her fault her aunt had died and she didn't deserve to live. 'It's too late, Enrico!' she cried. 'I can't tell her. I can't speak to her now. She's gone. Auntie Celia! Please come back!'

The enormity of her grief was difficult for Marian to cope with, for she had had so little time to get over her mother's death herself, but as she struggled to try and contain Madeleine she felt Enrico's hand close over hers, as if he was telling her that he understood, and as their eyes met, Marian smiled her gratitude for his concern.

Madeleine's hysteria had already lessened by the time the doctor arrived, but nevertheless he gave her a tranquillising injection, telling Enrico that she should rest and that he would come back again the following morning.

'I think, if so much else had not happened to her so recently, maybe she would not have taken this so hard,' Enrico said, as he and Marian walked down the stairs together, leaving Madeleine in the room that only two hours before she had so reluctantly vacated. 'But it has been a difficult time for her.'

'Yes,' Marian said, still too shaken to say more.

'It is early in the day, I know,' Enrico said, as they crossed the hall, 'but I think I shall have a little brandy. And you?'

'That would be nice, thank you,' Marian said. 'And thank you for everything you've done.'

He waved a hand as if to say it was nothing, and led her into the drawing-room. 'I am very sorry to hear about your mother,' he said. 'When did it happen?'

'Just over two weeks ago. It was a heart-attack.'

'It must have been a very difficult time for you,' he said, handing her a small balloon glass and gesturing for her to sit down.

'It wasn't easy, I loved her very much, so did Madeleine' – she laughed without mirth – 'as you have seen. But I had someone to help me, someone who came over from New York with me, and then a . . . a friend came down to Devon to take me back to London.'

'You work in London? Ah, here is my grandmother returned,' he said, before she could answer. 'Sylvestra, Marian and Madeleine are still here, I am afraid Madeleine has had a shock.'

'A shock?' Sylvestra repeated. 'But the girl has already had one. Surely not another?'

'I am afraid so,' Enrico answered, and Marian was touched by the way he explained what had happened in English so that she would not feel excluded.

'But this is terrible,' Sylvestra declared, sitting down on the sofa next to Marian and taking her hand. 'To have lost your mother, you poor child. But how did Madeleine not know?'

'I don't know,' Marian answered. 'Matthew – he's the director on the film we're making – Matthew rang her after I'd left New York, but she wasn't there so he spoke to Paul. Now it would seem that for some reason Paul didn't tell Madeleine.'

Sylvestra's face was suddenly filled with distaste. 'This is Paul O'Connell that we speak of, is it not?'

'Yes.' And Marian frowned as Sylvestra started to mutter under her breath in Italian.

'What's the matter? What is it?' Marian said, looking from Sylvestra to Enrico. She saw that Enrico's face had turned white. 'What's she saying?' Marian cried. 'Please, Sylvestra, what is it?'

Sylvestra got up, and when she put her hand on Enrico's arm Marian saw that it was shaking. 'It is a wicked thing he has done to keep this from Madeleine,' Sylvestra croaked. 'You must take care of her, Marian, you must be there for her . . .'

'Sylvestra, I think you've said enough,' Enrico interrupted. He had fully understood what his grandmother had told him, and the shock was still so great that he had no idea yet what should be done about it, except that he saw no reason to alarm Marian when she had already suffered enough for one day.

In the end he decided to let Marian and Madeleine return to England in ignorance – it was a mistake for which they were all to pay a bitter price.

– 25 –

Sergio was in his study at the Accademia. Outside in the corridors the pandemonium of students returning after the summer break rose to an almost intolerable pitch, and as he paced up and down his room his hands were clasped over his ears in an effort to block out the din and keep in his temper. With each footstep he swore violently under his breath, and each time he turned he threw a virulent look at the newspapers strewn across his desk.

At last the phone rang, and in his haste to snatch it up he sent a miniature bust crashing to the floor. '*Pronto!*' he snapped, kicking the marble fragments under the desk.

'You sound angry,' Deidre told him.

'Why have you taken so long to call?'

'I spoke to you last night, Sergio, there wasn't much point in ringing you again until I had some news.'

'And have you?'

'Yes. She arrived back in England about an hour ago.'

'Where is she now?'

'At home, with her cousin.'

'Her cousin? Do you mean Marian Deacon?'

'Yes,' Deidre answered, sounding surprised. 'She flew out to Sardinia to bring Madeleine home.'

'What! Why did you not tell me this before?'

'I didn't think it was important. All you wanted was that Madeleine should be got away from Tarallo. Besides, I didn't know you even knew about Marian.'

'Of course I know about Marian,' he spat, 'do you think I am an idiot? How long was she there?'

'Just one night. Why? Why does it matter?'

'Did she speak with Sylvestra?'

'I don't know,' Deidre answered, quite bewildered by this sudden turn in the conversation, 'I didn't ask her. I was more concerned about Madeleine.'

'Then you must find out if she has told Sylvestra what she is doing.'

'Why? What is she doing?'

'She is working on the film about the life of Olivia.'

There was a long silence at the other end which only increased Sergio's rage. 'Deidre, are you still there?' he shouted.

'What does Sylvestra Tarallo have to do with it?' Deidre asked finally. 'Come to that, why were you so keen that Madeleine should be got away from Enrico? What are these people to you, Sergio?'

'They are people I care about, Deidre, people I do not want to become involved. They have suffered a great deal . . .'

'Suffered? What do you mean, suffered?'

He thought quickly. 'Tarallo has lost his wife, you must have read it in the papers.'

'Yes, I have,' she said, 'but there's more to it than that, Sergio, I can tell by your voice.'

'Do not ask any more questions. Just make certain that Madeleine and Marian are kept away from the Tarallo family. Have you spoken with Paul?'

'Last night. He's waiting to hear from me so that I can let him know when she gets back. But he'll probably have heard it on the radio by now.'

'What does he plan to do?'

'Come back to London when she does, I believe. He wants to see her, in fact he's asked me to . . .'

'You must make certain that he does. Speak with

Madeleine, tell her she must see him. Then speak with Marian, ask her if . . .' He stopped, realising that if Sylvestra had told Marian about the *bottega*, it was already too late.

'Ask her what?' Deidre prompted.

'Ask her nothing. Do not speak to her of her visit, it is not important.'

'But only a moment ago . . .'

'It is not important, I tell you. Now, you are to see to it that Madeleine has no further contact with Tarallo, that she is reunited with Paul as soon as possible.'

'And if she doesn't want to be?'

'It will not change the fact that I want her here in two weeks, but I also want him to be with her.' Suddenly his voice softened. 'Try your best, *cara*. I know it is difficult for you, but I love you, and after this is done we will be together, as man and wife. Now I must go, but I am sorry, my love, for the way I have shouted at you these last few days. You do so much for me, and one day you will see that it was worth it.'

'I hope so,' Deidre mumbled, and she was just on the point of ringing off when something occurred to her. 'Sergio?' she said.

'*Sì*?'

'If Marian is involved in the film about Olivia's life, well . . . have you met her?'

'Yes. She came here to Florence and spoke to me.'

'I see,' Deidre said.

'Why?'

'I just wondered how you knew her, that was all. I'll speak to you again once I've some more news of Madeleine and Paul. But you're no longer interested in Marian, is that right?'

'That is correct,' he lied, and he waited only until the line had been disconnected before dialling Rubin Meyer's number in New York.

He had a long wait while the maid went to rouse Meyer from his bed, which, as it turned out, was a good thing; it gave him time to calm down, to think things through a little more rationally than he had with Deidre. He pressed a hand to his forehead in an effort to ease the throbbing in his temples. Now that Madeleine was away from Tarallo, he would sleep easier, because whatever happened in the next few weeks, he wanted at all costs to avoid the Tarallo family being involved again. He had caused them so much pain and anguish in the past that he shrank from the idea of doing it again; his remorse for what had happened to Arsenio was greater than Sylvestra would ever know. As for Marian, if Sylvestra *had* told her about the *bottega*, then the police would almost certainly have been here by now. But he could only find out for certain from Rubin Meyer and the men he had following Marian. If she knew, and was keeping the information to herself for the sake of her film, she would be bound to do something to give herself away – and if she did, well, he would have to take her before he was ready. And if Sylvestra had informed Marian of his connection with Paul O'Connell . . . He closed his mind to the possibility, because if she had, then everything, but everything, would be at an end.

Almost immediately after Deidre had finished her call to Sergio, the phone rang again.

'I don't care who it is,' she told Anne, 'I'm not in.'

'It's Paul O'Connell,' Anne said in her usual flat voice, and knowing it was a call Deidre would take, she flicked the buttons and put him through.

Deidre waited, holding the receiver away from her ear as Paul yelled down the line. 'Why didn't you tell me she was back in the country?' he demanded. 'And why the hell didn't you tell me that Marian was with her?'

'Good afternoon, Paul,' she said mildly. 'I was about to

ring you, but you beat me to it. Yes, she's back, and yes, Marian's with her. Are you still in the north?'

'Yes. But I'm coming back to London tomorrow. Did you find out what the delay was? Why didn't she come back yesterday?'

'Apparently Marian broke the news of her aunt's death to her and she took it badly. She had to be put under sedation, so Tarallo tells me.'

'If you hadn't had the damned ridiculous idea of sending Marian out there, that wouldn't have happened. For Christ's sake, Deidre, what the hell were you thinking of, asking *her* of all people to . . .'

'Now look here,' Deidre yelled back, 'I've had just about enough of your bloody tantrums. In the first place it wasn't my idea to send Marian out there, it was Tarallo's. In the second, I was no happier with the delay than you were, but *I'm* not the one who drove her away. You have caused me more trouble than you'll ever know this past week, Paul O'Connell. I don't know what your game is, but I'd say you're sick! You say you're in love with her; well, I say you've got a funny way of showing it. And why the hell is everyone panicking about Marian?'

'What do you mean, everyone?'

She sighed, realising that she had chosen her words badly. 'Oh, I don't mean anything, I've just had a rough day that's all, so I can do without you yelling at me as though it's all my fault.'

'Have you asked Madeleine if she'll see me?' he asked, making the effort to sound a little calmer.

'No. I left it to Marian.'

'Oh, that's just great!' he fumed. 'You do know about our history, don't you, Deidre? How Marian and I had a thing going, how I practically asked her to marry me, then dumped her for Madeleine?'

'No, Paul, I didn't know, but it doesn't surprise me. After all, you've just proved what a bastard you are with

that stroke you pulled in the south of France. Shamir and
Madeleine were best friends, so what the hell did you
think you were doing?'

'I don't have to explain anything to you, Deidre. I just
want Madeleine back where she belongs, with me. And if
you're as keen as you say you are to see that happen,
you'd better get Marian out of the way.'

'Impossible! Madeleine would never hear of it. Besides,
you flatter yourself if you think Marian still cares about
you, because I have it on the best authority that she
doesn't.'

'And whose might that be?'

'Marian herself. She told me, before she left here to go
to Sardinia, that if Madeleine was still in love with you
she would do nothing to stand in the way of your getting
back together. But it doesn't stop her seeing you for the
despicable shit you are.'

'Ease up, Deidre,' he laughed. 'I had my reasons for
doing what I did, and though they weren't particularly
honourable, in time you'll see why I had to do it.'

'For your damned book, I suppose?'

'In this case, no. But I still have one stage further to go
with the book, so remember, Deidre, that I'm looking for
a "murder" victim.'

'Is that some kind of threat?' she demanded.

'Take it as you like. But I'd say Marian fitted the bill
rather nicely, wouldn't you?' He laughed. 'In the meantime, as I said, I'm returning to London tomorrow, so
until Madeleine agrees to take me back I'll need somewhere to stay. How about with you?'

'Forget it. I'll talk to Roy, you can stay with him. Have
you spoken to anyone from the press, by the way?'

'No, I'm keeping a low profile. How about you?'

'Same here.'

'Before you go, Deidre, when you spoke to Marian this
morning did she tell you anything . . . anything unusual?'

'Like what?'

'Anything about the Tarallo family, or people they know?'

Deidre was immediately wary. 'Not that I can think of. Why do you ask?'

'No reason, other than that the family intrigues me.'

'Why? They're just a family like any other, aren't they?'

'I don't know, Deidre. You tell me.'

Deidre closed her eyes and gritted her teeth. 'For God's sake!' she seethed, clenching her fist and only just managing to refrain from banging the desk. 'Why the hell is everyone talking in riddles today? Why can't you just come straight out and ask the question?'

'What question?'

At that, the last strand of her control snapped. 'That's it!' she declared. 'I can't take any more.' And before he could even so much as laugh at her confusion, she hung up.

As the taxi drew to a halt outside the film production offices in Soho, the door flew open and Marian almost fell onto the pavement she was laughing so hard.

'Quick! Quick!' she said to Matthew, who was getting out behind her. 'Look, he's down there, just getting out of a taxi. No, don't look, he'll see you.'

'Well, do I or don't I look?' Matthew laughed, as he delved into his pocket for the fare.

'Don't,' Marian said, sidling round him and glancing shiftily out of the corner of her eye, 'he's watching. Oh look, he's just ducked into a doorway.' She collapsed into laughter again. 'It's like something out of an Agatha Christie movie,' she gasped. 'He must realise we know he's there.'

'Cheers,' Matthew said, as the taxi driver handed him his change. Then turning to Marian, he said, 'I expect he does, especially as you keep laughing at him.'

'You can hardly blame me, can you?' she said. 'Oh! My painting!' But as she started to make off after the taxi, Matthew caught her arm and dragged her back.

'It's here,' he said, pointing to the brown paper parcel balanced between his legs.

'Oh, thank goodness for that,' she cried. 'I would have taken it as a very bad omen to lose the painting I bought with my mother's money.'

'But you're not too worried about him?' Matthew said, nodding his head towards the sandy-haired man who was studiously not watching them further up the street.

'Well, you have to admit, it's difficult to take him seriously when he gets himself into such a pickle trying follow me. I don't think I'll ever forget that woman's face as he hauled her out of her taxi when we left Christie's. Thanks,' she added, as he handed her the painting. 'Do you know, I think life would seem extremely dull if he went away – I've become rather attached to him in a funny sort of way.' And looking back up the street she gave Boris – as she now called him – a friendly wave.

'I despair of you,' Matthew chuckled, draping an arm round her shoulders and steering her towards the office.

'Cup of tea?' she offered, as they walked in through the door.

'I'd love one,' Josey piped up.

'Me too,' Woody added.

'I'll give you a hand,' Matthew said, laughing at the long-suffering look Marian gave them.

'Stephanie's looking for you, Matthew,' Hazel said, as they started to walk out to the kitchen, and her tone was so sharp that Marian's eyes flew to Matthew's face.

'Really?' he said, quite unruffled by Hazel's manner. 'Where is she?'

'Upstairs, where do you think?'

'In that case, once Marian and I have made the tea I'll

take her one up, OK?' And treating Hazel to an exaggerated smile, he took Marian by the shoulders and pushed her into the kitchen.

'Matthew,' Marian began as he filled the kettle.

'Don't give it another thought.'

'But you don't know what I was going to say.'

'I do, and there's no point. If Hazel has a problem about you and me going to an auction, then let her sort it.'

'I wasn't thinking so much about Hazel, as a matter of fact, I was thinking about Stephanie.'

'Were you? She's probably only looking for me to find out if I've read the stuff Bronwen gave me last night.'

'That's not what I mean, and you know it.'

'You're right, I do, but this is hardly the time or the place to discuss it, is it? Now, if you'll excuse me I'd like to get some cups out of the cupboard and you're in my way.' And taking her by the arms, he pulled her towards him.

Marian giggled as he stuck his head under her arm to bend down to the cupboard, and was just about to give him a playful push when Stephanie appeared in the doorway.

'I don't wish to interrupt anything,' she said acidly, 'but I'd like to have a word with you, please, Matthew. When you can spare the time.' And after fixing Marian with an inimical glare, she turned and walked out.

'Oh God,' Matthew groaned, getting up from the cupboard. 'Women, they're the bane of my life.'

'Mine too. Especially when they make me feel so guilty.' Marian laughed, but the tease didn't quite reach her voice and there was a sudden pounding in her ears as she realised the implications of what she'd said. 'You shouldn't have come in to help me make the teas,' she added hastily, succeeding only in compounding her discomfort.

Eyebrows raised, he looked down into her face, and her

heart skipped a beat as she saw that lazy smile come into his eyes. 'Are you objecting to my services?'

'No, but . . .'

'But nothing. We are making tea, Marian, there is nothing to feel guilty about.'

He was standing so close and was looking at her so intently that her eyes moved involuntarily to his mouth, and she felt the colour burn in her cheeks as she turned away. 'Isn't there?' she mumbled.

'What did you say?'

'Nothing. Except that I think you should go and see what she wants.'

'I guess you're right.' And chucking her under the chin, he went off upstairs.

Sighing, Marian fell back against the wall. She just didn't know what to think any more. She didn't know what he was feeling, whether there was hope, or whether she was just imagining everything. One touch, one glance, one smile, and it was as if her whole body came suddenly to life. To make matters worse, she knew that as soon as she'd left for Sardinia Stephanie had moved back into her flat – though whether it was a gesture intended to let Marian know she wouldn't be welcome back, or whether she had walked out on Matthew, Marian didn't know. All she did know was that her premonition had proved right: New York *had* been the turning point for her and Matthew; yet she had no idea in which direction they were now travelling.

It was strange how she'd found the courage to deal with so much these past few months, but now, faced with asking Matthew what he really felt about her, she was as timorous as she'd ever been.

What the hell's the matter with me? she sighed to herself as she switched off the kettle and started spooning tea into the pot. Why can't I just come right out and ask him? She pulled a face; she knew only too well why she couldn't –

she was afraid of the answer, afraid that what had passed between them that night in New York had meant nothing to him. Yet she had only to think about the way he had behaved to her since to know that that couldn't be true.

She threw up her hands in frustration. She was simply going round and round in circles.

Upstairs in Stephanie's office Bronwen, Matthew and Stephanie were sitting round Stephanie's desk going over the suggestions Bronwen and Deborah Foreman had come up with for the final sequence of the film. With Bronwen present, neither Matthew nor Stephanie had referred to the incident in the kitchen, though Bronwen was acutely aware of the hostility between them.

'Anyway,' she was saying, 'I know these ideas fall a long way short of being brilliant, but I wanted to see if they might inspire some genius in either of you.'

'Mm,' Matthew said, tapping his fingers on the desk and looking down at the scenes with an ambiguous expression. 'They're not as bad as you think, Bron, but – ' He reached into his inside pocket and pulled out several sheets of handwritten notes; then, avoiding Stephanie's eye, he went on, 'In my opinion, with some careful scripting, this *will* work. But I do stress careful scripting; it comes pretty close to being libellous.'

'In that case there's no point in us looking at it, is there?' Stephanie said.

He looked across the desk at her sour face, and as their eyes met Bronwen almost winced at the enmity that sparked between them. 'I think you should,' he said.

'Why?' Stephanie asked.

'What do you mean, why?'

'I mean, why should we look? Because the idea is good, or because the idea is Marian's?'

Bronwen started to get to her feet. 'Look, I think we'd better resume . . .'

'Sit down, Bron,' Stephanie said, and sighing heavily,

Bronwen sank back in her chair. 'Well?' Stephanie said, glaring at Matthew.

'Does it matter whose the idea is as long as it's good?' he asked.

'In this case, yes.'

'And you call yourself a producer.'

For one moment Bronwen thought Stephanie was going to hit him, but instead she folded her hands on the desk in front of her and said, 'As a matter of fact, I do. And what, besides a director, do you call yourself?'

'I'm not staying for any more of this,' Bronwen said. 'If you two have got something to say to one another, then say it, only wait until I've gone. But just for the record, I think you're both behaving extremely unprofessionally. We haven't got an end sequence worked out yet, and that's what this meeting should be about, not . . .'

'It's all right, Bronwen,' Stephanie said, 'it's my fault, and you're right, we have to get this sorted out.' She turned back to Matthew. 'So what has Marian come up with?'

'You can read it for yourself,' he said, pushing the notes across the desk.

She picked them up, and after barely more than a cursory glance said, 'A solitary car driving down the autostrada in Tuscany? Is that it?'

'Why don't you finish reading it?'

' "The car," ' she read aloud, ' "belongs to the American student. He drives Olivia down an empty autostrada at dusk, stops halfway up the hill to Paesetto di Pittore, and Olivia gets out. In the background we can just make out the village through the mist. Olivia starts to walk up the hill – camera on high shot – and as she approaches the village the credits start to roll." ' She looked at Matthew. 'I'm supposed to be impressed?'

Biting back what he would really like to say, Matthew fixed her with an obdurate glare and remained silent.

'Why is it libellous?' she asked uninterestedly.

'That part of it isn't. It's the montage of shots that comes before, which you haven't bothered to read. It involves close-ups of the characters we most strongly suspect.'

'That's impossible,' Stephanie stated. 'We can't do that, I wouldn't allow it and neither would the lawyers.'

'They might if we found a way round it.'

'There isn't a way round it. Libel is libel.'

'And you're not even going to try, are you?'

'Well, I am,' Bronwen said. 'It's the best ending there is, because it's the real one, and so far not one of us has had the guts to admit that we're frightened to death of doing something like this because of what Frank Hastings might say. What else have we got to end with? A whole bunch of half-baked theories that wouldn't lend themselves to a soap opera, let alone a feature film. Thank God someone's come to their senses at last and had the courage to do this, even if it is libellous. And I think that if we temper the approach, and combine some of Marian's notes with what Deborah and I have come up with, we're there. The only other solution is for us to find out what really did happen, and that's not very likely, is it?'

'She's right, and you know it,' Matthew said, looking at Stephanie who was staring down at her hands. He hated himself for doing this to her, and he wished it wasn't Marian who had written the sequence; he knew Stephanie couldn't take much more. But what the hell more could he do to reassure her? He'd told her he loved her, he'd asked her to marry him, he'd all but pleaded with her not to move her things back to her own flat, but none of it seemed to convince her that his feelings towards her hadn't changed. And they hadn't, he was certain of it. But what he couldn't get to the bottom of were his feelings for Marian. After that night in New York things had changed between them, he couldn't deny it; but how could he talk about that to Stephanie when he didn't even understand it himself?

At last Stephanie lifted her head, and looking from one to the other of them, said, 'OK, moderate it, check it with Frank Hastings, and if he approves, so will I.'

Matthew refrained from breathing a sigh of relief, then bracing himself for her reaction to what he was about to say, he looked straight into Stephanie's eyes. 'It won't be easy to persuade Frank, of course, but I think Marian should be the one to do it.'

'Why?' Stephanie demanded angrily, the strain she was under beginning to show.

'I can't explain why, I just think she should.'

'What the hell's going on here?' she spat. 'Bronwen is the co-producer and editor of this screenplay, not Marian, or are you planning some sort of take-over?'

'Don't be ridiculous!'

'Then Bronwen will talk to Frank.' And she snatched up the phone as it rang.

Matthew turned to Bronwen. 'What do you think?' he said.

'If I told you what's really going through my mind, Matthew, I don't think you'd like it much. Anyway, I have to be going.'

'It's for you,' Stephanie said, thrusting the receiver at Matthew. 'Come along, Bron, I'll walk you downstairs.'

'Who was that on the phone?' Bronwen asked as she and Stephanie walked out into the street.

Stephanie shrugged. 'Sounded like his son. Bron, I'm sorry about all that just now, it must have embarrassed the hell out of you.'

'Don't worry about me,' Bronwen answered, placing a comforting hand on Stephanie's arm. 'Just sort things out with him.'

'When I get the time.'

'Make it, or you're going to drive yourself insane. I'll

never know why you moved yourself back to your own flat.'

'I'll tell you why. We weren't having sex any longer, that's why. Now, doesn't that tell you something?'

'Me, no. But obviously it does you. Look, Steph,' she said, giving her a quick hug, 'I'm sorry but I have to run, I've promised to have tea with my aging aunt at five o'clock. I'll come over to the flat later, if you like, and we can discuss this idea of Matthew's that Marian should speak to Frank.'

'But in principle what do you think of it?' Stephanie asked.

'I think he might be right. Don't ask me why, but I get the feeling she's got some influence – if that's the right word – with Frank, or if not with him then with Grace. Anyway, we'll talk about it later. In the meantime, keep your chin up, *cariad*.'

'I will,' Stephanie smiled, and as Bronwen ran off down the street she wandered back inside.

She was about to go upstairs to her office when her eye was caught by the brown paper parcel propped against Marian's desk, and turning back, she put her head in through the door. 'You got it, then? The painting?'

Marian looked up. 'Oh, yes,' she said, her discomfort more than evident.

'Can I see it?'

'Of course.' Getting to her feet, Marian walked round her desk, glancing nervously towards Hazel and Josey – but they were both studiously engrossed in their own business.

'Did you actually bid yourself?' Stephanie asked, as Marian started to unwrap the parcel. 'I've never been to an auction myself. I keep saying I will but I never get round to it. Was it fun?'

'It was OK,' Marian answered, pulling the painting from the protective padding and handing it to Stephanie.

'Here it is. It might not be quite your taste, but Mum always loved flowers so I thought . . .'

'Oh, it's beautiful, Marian,' Stephanie cried. 'Have you seen it, Hazel?'

Hazel looked up. 'Yes, isn't it divine?' she said, then turned back to what she was doing.

At that moment the phone rang, and as Marian leaned across the desk to answer it, she noticed Hazel glance up again and saw the strange, almost malicious smile that came over her face as she caught Stephanie's eye.

'Hello, Ryder and Evans,' Marian said into the receiver, but she was barely listening to the voice at the other end because she was watching Stephanie and Hazel, certain that they were going to do something to damage the painting. Then she realised that it was Madeleine speaking to her, pleading with her to go home, and because of the panic in Madeleine's voice Marian turned her back on the room and whispered down the line, 'It's all right, I'll be there in half an hour.' And before Madeleine could say anything else, she rang off.

When she turned back, Stephanie was still admiring the painting and telling Hazel what wonderful taste Marian had. There was no sarcasm in her tone, but the remark hung so heavily in the air that Marian wanted to snatch the painting away and tell her to mind her own business. Then Stephanie asked who was going to hang it for her.

'I'm sure Maddy and I can manage between us,' Marian answered shakily. Inside her there was a fomenting rage which she knew came from guilt, making her want to yell at Stephanie, strike her, even – anything to make Stephanie lash out with the hatred she must be feeling. They all knew that she, Marian, was to blame for the way things were between Stephanie and Matthew, yet no one, not even Matthew, would talk about it.

'Would it be all right if I left now?' she said, taking the

painting from Stephanie. 'I'll come in early tomorrow to make up for it, but I . . . something's come up at home.'

'Of course it would be all right,' Stephanie said, starting to help her with the wrapping. 'Nothing's wrong, I hope?'

'No, no,' Marian answered. 'It's . . . Ever since Madeleine found out that my mother was dead, she's been in a pretty bad way, and now Paul's just rung her and she's agreed to see him.'

Stephanie picked up the phone. 'I'll call you a taxi,' she said. 'You don't want that painting getting crushed on the tube, do you?'

'There's really no need,' Marian insisted. 'I'll hail one.' And taking her coat from the stand, she started to leave the office.

'Aren't you going to say good-bye to Matthew?' Stephanie enquired.

Marian tensed. 'No, he's still on the phone,' she said, without turning round. Then, with a muttered good-bye to Josey and Hazel, she left.

Stephanie's and Hazel's eyes met, and without relinquishing the gaze Hazel asked Josey to leave the room.

'I don't know how you do it,' Hazel said, when they were alone.

Stephanie's smile was sardonic. 'Neither do I, but what else can I do? So he did take her to the auction. I don't know why I'm surprised, he said he was going to. The day after a night shoot, as well. What won't he do for her, I ask myself?'

Hazel turned quickly as Matthew walked in. 'Off now,' he said. 'Shall I see you later?'

Stephanie looked up. 'No, sorry. I've got a lot to finish off here, then I promised to call in on the accountants.'

Matthew turned to Hazel. 'Stood up again,' he joked, but his anger was obvious. 'See you in the morning, Haze. Seven o'clock call?'

Hazel nodded, and watched him walk out into the

street. 'Why did you do that?' she said, turning back to Stephanie.

Stephanie shook her head. 'What's the point in seeing him? He won't give me any answers, he can't even meet my eyes when I ask him a question.'

'But you can't *keep* running away from him.'

'I can and I will, until he's sorted himself out and made up his mind what he wants.' She paused. 'Do you think Marian's trying to find out where she stands, too? Maybe she already knows.'

'For heaven's sake, darling, she doesn't even come into the picture.'

'Are you blind, Hazel?'

'No, and nor am I so riddled with jealousy that I can't see what's staring me in the face. You're driving him away, behaving like this, Stephanie. Instead of talking to him about it and trying to sort it out, you're just making matters worse by pushing him straight into Marian's arms.'

'He doesn't need pushing, Hazel,' Stephanie snapped, and before Hazel could answer, she walked out of the office.

– 26 –

When the knock on the door came, Madeleine dropped the glass she was holding and her hands flew to her face. 'It's him!' she cried, and leaping to her feet, she ran to the middle of the room.

'It's all right,' Marian said, stooping to pick up the glass which fortunately hadn't broken, 'just keep calm and remember you don't have to do anything you don't want to.'

'But what am I going to say?'

'I should have thought it was more a question of what he was going to say,' Marian answered, and taking Madeleine's hands between hers, she added, 'Are you sure you want me to let him in?'

Madeleine's eyes were wide with a confusion that bordered on hysteria. She wore no make-up, her lips were pale and her skin taut and colourless. For days they had discussed what she should do if Paul called, and Marian had thought they'd agreed that she wouldn't see him for at least a month. She needed some time to think, and to re-settle after all that had happened. But Marian realised now that she should have known better; just the hours Madeleine had spent poring over the photographs and cuttings of herself and Paul should have told her that Madeleine was pining for him.

'Well?' Marian prompted.

Madeleine nodded her head. 'Yes. Yes, I'll have to see him now, I said I would.'

'OK. Now, you wait here and I'll go and let him in. Do you want me to stay in the room with you while you talk?'

Madeleine's agitation was so great that Marian smiled and gave her a quick hug. 'Don't worry,' she said, 'we'll sort something out.' And letting Madeleine go, she walked out to the front door.

She had wondered, over the past hour, how she would feel when she saw Paul again, remembering all he had once meant to her, how deeply she had felt his betrayal; but so much had happened to her since that she felt as if it was a stranger who had loved him then, not her at all. However, she knew that when she opened the door she would be sure to feel something; a final pang, maybe; regret; pleasure, even. Contempt never entered her head.

He smiled at her, and she remembered only too well the effect that smile used to have on her, but, God, it felt like such a long time ago – another world. Now here she was, standing on the threshold of a luxurious house in one of

London's smartest districts, a house Paul had bought from Madeleine because he was, and always had been, a wealthy man. Suddenly the smile offended her and she didn't bother to return it.

'Hello, Marian,' he said, raising an eyebrow at her disdain. 'How are you?'

'I'm very well, thank you,' she answered, standing back for him to come in.

'You've changed,' he said. 'I wouldn't have realised it was you if I hadn't known you were here. Your hair suits you like that, you look . . .'

'Madeleine's in here,' she interrupted, and passing him, she walked ahead into the sitting-room. Shrugging, though mildly put out by her apparent indifference, he followed.

Madeleine was still standing in the centre of the room, and as Paul walked in, her violet eyes – the eyes he had come to love so much – darkened with pain. He saw immediately that she had lost weight, and her beautiful face seemed almost gaunt. Marian went to stand beside her, as if to protect her, and for one blinding instant he wanted to kill her. But then his eyes returned to Madeleine's and he saw that behind the fear and mistrust there was a hunger; it was as if she was fighting to hold herself back from him. Since she'd agreed to see him he had considered a thousand different ways of how he would begin, but now, seeing her so torn apart he merely held out his arms and whispered, 'My darling. Oh, my darling.'

As Madeleine moved towards him, Marian lifted a hand to stop her, but before she had a chance to touch her Madeleine threw herself onto Paul's chest and clung to him like a child.

'You don't know how sorry I am,' he murmured. 'I've missed you so much. Deidre told me about your aunt. Oh, Maddy, I don't know what to say.'

His eyes were closed, but Marian waited, willing him to look at her. Even if she weren't prepared to say so in front of Madeleine, she wanted him to know that she knew he was lying. Matthew had told him about Celia's death the day after she'd left New York.

But as he took Madeleine's face between his hands, he didn't look at Marian. 'Can we talk?' he said, kissing her gently on the forehead.

Madeleine turned to Marian. 'It's all right,' she said. 'I'll be all right.'

Again Marian looked at Paul, but he was gazing at Madeleine.

As she walked up the stairs to her room, Marian's footsteps were slow, and there was no denying that the suddenness of their reunion and the power Paul seemed to have over Madeleine had shaken her. It confused her even more that, despite what he had done, despite the lies he had told, she was now in no doubt that he loved Madeleine. In fact, the power of his love was so strong that the moment he set eyes on Madeleine, even she, Marian, had felt it. It was like a living thing that fused them together, making them, in some peculiar way, into the same person. It was the first time Marian had seen them together, and she realised now that there was a great deal more to their love than she'd believed and for some reason, it made her feel uneasy. She hesitated, listening for their voices, wondering what he was saying to her, but then, annoyed with herself for trying to eavesdrop, she ran on up the stairs. When she reached the top she heard the sitting-room door close, and she shivered: she had the uncanny feeling that Paul had been watching her . . .

Turning back from the door, Paul took Madeleine's hands and led her to the sofa. He sat down with her, his arms around her, and started to smooth the hair back from her face. 'You know it was for the book, don't you?' he whispered.

'Well, I . . . Well . . . Oh Paul, I wanted it to be, I kept telling myself it was, but I just didn't know.'

Suddenly his head dropped back and he shut his eyes tightly as if he were in pain. 'Oh God!' he groaned. 'I can't tell you what all this has done to me too, Maddy. I knew I loved you before, but now . . . Oh Maddy, hold me, for God's sake, hold me. Tell me you forgive me, tell me that nothing's changed between us.'

She lifted her arms and brought his head down to her shoulder, and as the tears ran down her face she thought of Enrico, and how she had held him the same way. She'd thought about Paul then, wanting to share the same closeness with him, and now he was here, vulnerable at last, and she loved him so much she wanted to go on holding him forever. 'I forgive you,' she said, kissing his face. 'I'd forgive you anything, Paul. I still love you. I missed you so much.'

'Did you? Did you truthfully?'

'Every minute of every day I thought about you.'

'Then why?' he cried, grabbing her roughly by the shoulders. 'Why did you go to him? I've been going out of my mind, thinking of all the things you might be doing together.' He clasped her to him. 'But I deserved it, didn't I? After what I did to you.'

'Don't think about it,' she said. 'It's over now. We're together again and that's all that matters.'

'Oh, my darling,' he said, pulling her hands to his mouth and kissing them. 'I've got so much to make up to you. You're so beautiful, so innocent, and I exploited you in ways you don't understand; ways I don't even understand myself. It'll never happen again, Madeleine. Never! I know now that you're all I want in my life. You're everything to me, more than everything, you're my whole life.'

'Then why did you do it? I know it was for the book, but . . .'

'It's so difficult to explain, my darling, and I hoped I would never have to, but you see Shamir . . .'

- 613 -

At the mention of her friend's name Madeleine blanched, but as she turned away he pulled her back to look at him. 'You have to let me tell you, Maddy, you have to know what she's really like. I know it will be painful, but you must face it.'

He allowed her a few moments to collect herself, holding her against him and kissing her hair. 'Are you ready?' he asked gently, when her hand finally reached out for his.

'Yes,' she whispered.

'OK. Well, she came to me first when you were in Morocco, doing the sun tan commercial. She said she was in love with me and that I was wasting my time with you. Naturally, I told her to get out. She went, but then she came back again the following day. It was pitiful to see her, to see the way she begged me, on her hands and knees, to make love to her, but even though I pitied her, I despised her. In the end I picked her up and threw her bodily into the street, telling her that if she pulled a stunt like that again, I'd let you know just what sort of a best friend you had.

'That was it for several weeks. She flew back to Los Angeles and we didn't see her again until we went there ourselves. There was nothing she could do with you under the same roof, thank God, but the day you went for your audition, the day Roy found us in the pool together . . . Well, she'd told me she was going shopping, so, left to entertain myself, I decided to take a swim. I'd only been in the pool a few minutes when she walked out of the house, holding a knife. She said if I didn't make love to her she'd . . . well, she'd do certain things to my anatomy. I thought she was kidding me at first, but then she dived into the pool and started to swim after me. Even then I thought it was some kind of game. It was only when she held the knife to my throat and ordered me to kiss her that I realised she was serious – that she really would use the knife if I didn't do as she said. So I kissed her, pulling her

– 614 –

under the water at the same time, until I managed to break free and swim to the other end of the pool. It was then, thank God, that Roy came back, otherwise God only knows what sort of mess I'd be in now.

'I toyed with the idea of telling you at the time, but it all seemed so far-fetched that I could hardly believe it had happened myself. But I couldn't stop thinking about it, and I knew that, bizarre and horrible though it was, I would have to write about it. The only problem was, there was no conclusion, and having the perverse mind of a writer, I wanted one that was as sensational and lurid as possible. Naturally it occurred to me that I should make her the victim of the "murder" I need for the end of the book, but that wouldn't have solved the problem of how to end the particular sequence she was actually involved in. I lay awake night after night, trying to think of how to do it, but all the time it kept coming back to the same thing – I had to live out the fiction of you discovering. It had to become a reality, and . . . well . . . the rest you know.'

Madeleine shivered. 'I had no idea all that was going on . . . What a bitch, and she called herself my best friend. But you should have told me, you could still have done what you did in the south of France, I would have acted it all for you . . .' She stopped as he started to shake his head.

'Yes, you could have,' he said, 'and God knows, I wish I had told you now, but at the time I was hell-bent on making it authentic. I'd thought it all through, and I'd already written what had happened up to the point of my speech on the terrace . . . I'd even written the conversation we'd had before dinner. Can you see now, Maddy, why I was asking you to trust me? I knew what I was going to do, and I was trying as hard as I could, without actually saying the words, to warn you. I thought I'd succeeded, but . . .' he gave a dry laugh '. . . I know now that I'd failed, miserably. Oh God, if only we could go back to that night, I'd never have done it if I'd known what was going to happen afterwards.'

'Do you mean the fight you had with Shamir?'

'Good God, no. That was nothing. I mean this, us sitting here, trying to repair the damage I've done. But God help me, I wanted to kill Shamir that night. She flew at me like a wild cat, accusing me of wanting to destroy her friendship with you, saying that I'd always been jealous of it, and . . . oh, I don't know, I can hardly remember now what she did say, but what incensed me was the way she made me out to be the villain of the piece when all the time she was the one who drove me to it.'

'So you didn't ever make love to her?'

He shook his head. 'No.' He looked at her. 'And what about you?' he said. 'Did you and Enrico . . .?'

Madeleine smiled. 'No. But we did spend a night together. He just held me and comforted me and told me a story, would you believe? It was really nice.'

'But he didn't make love to you?'

'He couldn't,' she answered. 'His wife had only just died, he was still too unhappy. Do you know, next to you he's the most wonderful man in the world.'

Abruptly he let her go and sat forward, burying his face in his hands. 'Does that mean you would have let him? If his wife hadn't . . .'

'No! No!' She was quick to lie, afraid his jealousy would mar their reunion. 'I couldn't make love with another man, you know that, Paul.'

'Do I?' he said, reaching for her hand. 'Maddy, I love you so much I can't believe a man could hold you and not want you.'

'But that's what happened.'

'Do you swear it?'

'Yes, I swear it,' she said.

'And you're not in love with him?'

'How can I be? I'm in love with you.'

'But the press, they were hinting at a romance between you.'

'You know what the press are like. They'll twist anything to make it into a sensation or a scandal.'

His eyes shot to hers, hard and serious for a moment. Then he smiled. 'Yes, of course,' he said, and scooping her back into his arms, he kissed her.

It was a quarter to seven in the morning. Stephanie was alone in the downstairs office, looking at Woody's rough schedule for Italy, but she was finding it difficult to concentrate. She'd had little sleep the night before, but that wasn't unusual, she'd hardly slept at all these past few weeks. She just couldn't understand how swiftly and radically the situation with Matthew and Marian had changed; her jealousy of Marian before they went to New York was nothing compared to the way she felt now. Things were so bad, in fact, that she feared she was in danger of letting her emotions get in the way of her professional decisions, which was something she simply couldn't afford to let happen. Because, if Matthew really was going to leave her for Marian, her career would be the only thing left to her. She closed her eyes as a wave of desperation seemed to reach into every corner of her body. Please, she prayed silently, just let me get to the end of this film. Don't let him tell me it's over yet, I couldn't handle it, not seeing him every day when there's still such a long way to go. Afterwards – afterwards I will deal with it. And then, as if it were calling her a liar, her heart discharged a flood of pain through her chest that very nearly took her breath away. Oh Matthew, she cried silently, what is happening to us? Why have we come so far only for this to happen?

Mentally, she shook herself, and forced her eyes back to the schedule in front of her, but she smiled sadly as she saw Matthew's handwriting at the bottom of the page. Abruptly she put the schedule down and turned away.

Hazel's mirror was propped up on the bookshelf beside her desk, and in the grey early-morning light, Stephanie looked at herself. 'God, I'm even beginning to look my age,' she said, smoothing her fingers over the lines round her eyes.

'I wouldn't agree with that.'

She spun round and her heart lurched savagely as she saw Matthew standing at the door. 'I didn't hear you come in,' she said, trying to ignore the chaotic pulsing of blood through her veins.

'Too busy talking to yourself,' he grinned.

Unable to bear his smile, she looked at her watch. 'Shouldn't you be on location?'

He nodded. 'They're still setting up,' he answered, walking across the office towards her. 'I called you this morning but you must have left. I thought you might be on the set when I got there, but when you weren't I guessed I might find you here.'

He was standing so close that she could smell the cool air he had brought in with him, and she put her hands in her pockets because the urge to touch him was so strong. 'Is there something you want to discuss?' she said nonchalantly.

'You know there is.'

She started to turn away, but he stopped her and pulled her back to face him. 'What is it, Stephanie? Why are you running away from me?'

'You have to ask?' Her voice was husky and he could see how close she was to tears.

He let her go. 'No,' he answered wearily. 'I don't have to ask. What I have to do is explain. The trouble is, where to begin? How to put it into words.'

She closed her eyes, steeling herself. He's going to tell me now . . . He's going to say . . .

'Oh no!' he groaned.

She looked up, then following the direction of his eyes, she saw Marian crossing the street. I've got to get out of here, she panicked. I can't see the two of them together, not right now.

'Stephanie!' he cried, as she ran past him. He caught her at the door, just as Marian was coming through.

'I'm sorry,' Marian mumbled when she saw them standing together at the foot of the stairs. 'Uh, I said I'd come in early today, but I can . . .' She started to turn back.

'It's all right,' Matthew said. 'Stephanie and I were just . . . Stephanie!' But she had wrenched herself from his grip and was running up the stairs. Helplessly, he watched her go, then swore under his breath as the door slammed behind her.

'I'm sorry,' Marian said again. 'If I'd known . . . I mean, I wasn't expecting to find anyone here.'

'Don't apologise,' he said. 'It's not your fault, it's mine. I'd better go after her.'

'No!'

Startled by the emphatic note in Marian's voice, he turned back.

'No,' she said, more calmly. 'I'll talk to her. You've tried before, and got nowhere. Now it's my turn. I know I can't tell her what we know about Olivia, but that's what's causing all this. She doesn't know what on earth is going on, why we stop talking whenever she comes into the room, why you come almost everywhere with me . . .'

'So how are you going to explain it?'

'I don't know, but let's just hope I make a better job of it than you.'

'You're quite a lady, Marian Deacon.' He had started to smile, but then his face became serious, and drawing her from the narrow passageway into the office, he said,

'You don't have to do this, you know. We both know the way you . . . the way . . .'

'Do you mean, the way I feel about you? Well, Stephanie's always known that, but as long as you don't return the feelings there's nothing to feel guilty about, is there?'

Letting her hand go, Matthew pushed his fingers through his hair and turned away. 'You know that's not true.'

'Do I? I don't know what to think, Matthew.'

He turned to look at her. 'Neither do I,' he said quietly. 'All I know is that I'm going through hell right now, and it's as much because of you as because of Stephanie, so there's plenty to feel guilty about. But it can't be sorted out until this film is over. We're all too tired and too damned confused.

Then, to her amazement, he cupped his hands round her face, pulled her mouth to his and kissed her gently. 'I've been wanting to do that ever since New York,' he said, 'but I shouldn't have done it, and now . . .' he pushed her away '. . . I'm going to the set because this morning I don't seem to have much control over myself and God knows I want to do it again.' And before she could stop him he had walked out of the door.

It was hard for her to register exactly what she was feeling as she walked up the stairs to Stephanie's office. Part of her was so ecstatically happy that she wanted to rush out and do something rash, like sing in the street or dance on a bus, but another part of her felt as though she was the only one of the three of them in control, the only one who could make decisions, say what had to be said. It was strange to harbour such opposite feelings, and she couldn't even begin to make sense of it.

She tapped softly on Stephanie's door, and when Stephanie didn't answer she was tempted to go away. But her resolve was firm; she turned the handle and pushed the door open.

Stephanie was standing at the window, gazing sightlessly out at the buildings opposite. Her arms were folded, and though Marian didn't think she'd been crying, her face reflected the pain she was suffering.

'Stephanie,' she said. 'I'd like to talk to you.'

'Would you?' Stephanie said, still looking out of the window.

Marian came further into the room and closed the door behind her. 'I think we should talk, don't you?'

Slowly Stephanie turned to face her. 'And what should we talk about, Marian?'

Marian tensed, not wanting to say the name even though she knew she couldn't avoid it. 'Matthew.'

Immediately Stephanie bristled. 'What about him?'

Marian sighed. 'Stephanie, this isn't easy for me either, but . . .'

'Then why the hell did you come up here?' she spat, planting her hands on the edge of the desk. 'I didn't ask you to. As far as I'm concerned . . .'

'As far as you're concerned there's something going on between me and Matthew. But Stephanie, I want you to know that he still loves you, that he's going through hell . . .'

'How dare you come into my office talking about him as though you know him better than I do. "He still loves you",' she mimicked. 'Just what do you hope to gain by telling me that?'

'Nothing at all. I just wanted you to know that he does, and that despite what you think, I've done nothing to try and change that. Though, as you know, I'm . . . I have very strong feelings for him myself.'

'I don't believe what I'm hearing,' Stephanie cried, throwing a hand to her head. 'You are half his age! You are barely older than his own daughter, and knowing the way I feel about him you have the nerve to come in here and tell me that you have very strong feelings for him. Get out, Marian. Get out before I do something we might both regret.'

'Stephanie, you've got to stop running away from this. Apart from anything else, Matthew needs you. You have to help him sort this out.'

'Sort what out? The way he feels about you?'

'Yes, if you want to put it that way.'

'And you're asking for my help? You really are amazing.'

'Don't you think it will help you in the end as well? Help all of us? We none of us can carry on as we are.'

'You're damned right we can't. So perhaps you'd like to start by telling me what it is about you that Matthew finds so damned precious? Why he can't keep away from you? Why he's so defensive every time I mention your name? I think I know the answer, but I'd like to hear it from you, Marian. Have you got the guts?'

'Yes, I have. However, I can't tell you and neither can he. And the reason we can't is for your own good.'

'You patronising little bitch.'

'No, it's not patronising, it's to do with a particular trust which has been placed in us both by Frank and Grace Hastings. But this much I will tell you; I know what Olivia did in New York and so does Matthew.'

Stephanie had already drawn breath to speak, but at that her head snapped up and she stared at Marian, speechless.

'We know,' Marian went on, 'and we – at least, I – could be in danger because of it. And if you want to be rid of me you can walk out into the street and tell the man who will probably be standing outside the newsagent's, that Marian Deacon *does* know what happened and has a damned good idea who was involved in Olivia's disappearance.'

Stephanie slumped into her chair, shaking her head in astonishment, but her eyes never moved from Marian's. 'How do you know?' she said.

'It's a long story, but I do, and so Frank and Grace Hastings decided to tell Matthew because they didn't want me to be the only one on the film who knew. They felt Matthew could watch over me while we were in London – Frank's people did it when we were in New York, and in fact they're also in London now, but they check in with Matthew to find out when he can't be with me. If he can't be, they are.'

'So that's why Matthew wants you to talk to Frank about the end of the film,' Stephanie muttered, almost to herself. 'You know who and what you're talking about.'

'Exactly.'

Marian was silent then, allowing Stephanie some time to take it all in. She had no idea whether she'd done the right thing in telling Stephanie even this much – but of course Olivia Hastings and her crimes in New York were only a factor in the problem. The real nettle was still waiting to be grasped.

'Thank you for telling me that,' Stephanie said tersely, 'it explains a lot. But it still doesn't solve anything, does it?'

'No,' Marian answered, 'it doesn't. Nor does it make it any easier for us to work together, which is why, if it's what you want, I am prepared to resign.'

'Oh no,' Stephanie said with a bitter laugh, 'don't think I'm falling for that one. I'd like nothing more than to see you out of our lives, Marian; it's pretty unpleasant harbouring a viper in the bosom; but if I accept your resignation, Matthew will say I pushed you into it. No, what I'm going to do is promote you. You're going to be credited as the story editor of this film, and you're going to have a joint credit with Deborah Foreman as the writer

of the screenplay. Now, how below-the-belt does that feel?
Doesn't do much to ease the guilt, I'll bet.'

'You're right, it doesn't. But I'm quite happy being a
secretary, thank you.'

'Perhaps you are, and that's just what you're going to
continue to be, but you'll have the damned credits whether
you like them or not.'

'If you've made up your mind, there's nothing I can
say. After all, you're the producer.'

'Yes, I am, aren't I? The same producer who hired you,
Marian, who took you out of that garret in Bristol and
gave you a life when you had nothing. Do you hear me,
nothing! And this is how you repay me. I don't know how
you found out about Olivia, Marian, but I do know that
you're more devious, more conniving and more disloyal
than anyone I've ever met in my life. Jesus, you're even
more poisonous than his wife, who, just by happy chance,
happens to like you because you sat there and listened to
her pour out her problems. That's a nice little ingratiating
technique of yours, isn't it, listening to people pour out
their problems. You want me to fight you for Matthew,
don't you? Well, you can forget it! If he wants you he can
damned well have you, because I have no intention of
fighting a fucking teenager for a man who has asked me to
marry him, and whom I intend to marry. Do you hear
me?'

'Yes.'

'Then get out.'

Marian walked to the door, but as she was leaving she
turned back. 'Stephanie,' she said, 'whatever conclusions
we've reached here this morning – and I'm not sure yet if
we've decided anything – don't let's either of us forget that
the person who will make the final decision is Matthew.'
And closing the door behind her she walked slowly down
the stairs, leaving Stephanie sitting at her desk with her
head in her hands.

*

Deidre pushed her way through the crowd, edging towards the back of the room. Make-up artistes, stylists and dressers flanked the walls, watching as photographers angled their cameras and adjusted the lights. Madeleine and Paul were sitting together on the sofa, whispering to one another and laughing. Their closeness was unmistakable, and made Deidre feel like an intruder, which was ridiculous, given the relentless attention they were receiving from the press. It had been Madeleine's idea to hold the conference at home, and Deidre had to agree it wasn't a bad one. The domestic setting was so much in contrast with the glitz and glamour they were normally associated with that it gave them an attractive air of wholesomeness. Deidre murmured a quick hello to a journalist from the *Daily Mirror*, then sweeping her unruly hair over her shoulders, she sat back on the windowsill to watch the public reunion of the world's golden couple.

The initial idea of a press conference had been Paul's, mainly because he wanted to refute any suggestion that either of them might still be involved with Shamir or Enrico, and Deidre had jumped at the chance of one last flourish of publicity before she took Madeleine to Italy. But, as she watched them now, her spirits plummeted – she still had no idea how she was going to do it, and she didn't want to be the one to do it, either. Sergio had been almost violent with her when they'd discussed it that morning. If only Paul would suggest a holiday, then she could recommend Tuscany and his would be the burden of responsibility for taking her there – which was utter nonsense: hers would be the crime of procurement, or kidnapping, if that was what it amounted to in the end. And even supposing Paul agreed to take Madeleine to Tuscany how would she get him to move quickly enough? Time was running out. Sergio wanted Madeleine next week.

'Are you feeling all right?'

Deidre looked up. It was Phillipa Jolley, Madeleine's dress designer. 'Just a bit of a headache,' she smiled. 'Nothing serious.'

'What do you think of the dress?' Phillipa asked.

'I'll let you know when I see it,' Deidre chuckled, as she attempted to peer through the throng of journalists who were homing in on the couple now that the photographers had finished.

Paul was relaxed, sitting with an ankle resting on his knee and one arm along the back of the sofa. Deidre was touched to see how he was giving Madeleine centre stage; she was perched on the edge of her seat, eager to let everyone know that they were still in love. After she had put the phone down on him, the day Madeleine had returned from Sardinia, he had called back to apologise for making her angry, and after seeing him with Madeleine the night before and being reminded of how much they meant to one another, Deidre had understood and sympathised with the desperation he must have been feeling at the time.

'The dress is beautiful,' she whispered to Phillipa as the crowd parted for a moment. 'You've surpassed yourself, again.'

'I know. I simply don't know how I do it,' Phillipa grinned.

The fashion editor for *Café Society* was at that moment asking Madeleine about the dress, and everyone took notes as Madeleine reeled off the details Phillipa had given her, smoothing her hands over the soft blue wool that clung to every curve of her body.

'And your perfume?' someone asked. 'Is that doing well?' Then there were questions about 'The Look' cosmetic range, and other campaigns yet to be launched, all of which Madeleine handled with her usual panache, making everyone laugh by throwing out outrageously flirtatious looks, and delivering a great many more *double entendres* than she was actually aware of. It was amazing, Deidre thought as she watched Madeleine's glowing face and listened to her excited laughter, what an effect Paul had on her. But that was what it was like, being in love, she mused; the sun shines no matter what the weather. Then Roger Harper from *The Sun* took the initiative and steered the interview in the direction everyone wanted to take. Deidre listened intently.

'Now that you're back together,' he said, 'will you be taking up your old lives? Will you be gracing page three of my newspaper again, Madeleine, and the centrefolds of girlie magazines? Will Paul continue to write?'

'Of course Paul will continue to write, won't you darling?' Madeleine said, turning to him. He nodded and caressed her cheek with his fingers as she gave him a look of pure devotion. 'As for me,' she went on, turning back to Harper, 'that's up to Paul. We've been talking about retiring quietly to the country, you know?'

There was a flurry of hands across paper at that, and a bombardment of questions. Then Judith Wratten from the *Daily Express* asked: 'Does this mean you'll be getting married?'

'Yes,' Paul answered, and as he reached for Madeleine's hand his eyes moved to Edward Bingham of the *Daily Echo* who was sitting on the fender.

Bingham straightened up. 'So we can all safely say that there is no longer a romance between you and Enrico Tarallo, Madeleine?'

'There never was,' she answered.

'You mean to say that you spent, what was it, at least three days with him at his villa in Sardinia, and nothing happened between you?' He laughed. 'Either the man's considering holy orders, or you must be losing your charms, Maddy. Come on, tell us, which is it?'

Madeleine's answering laugh was uncertain. She turned to Paul who smiled encouragingly – just be honest, he had told her earlier, that way there can be no mistakes and no come-backs.

'Neither,' she said. 'As you know Enrico's wife has just died. He didn't want to . . . Well, he couldn't . . .'

'How did it feel to be rejected?' Bingham leapt in.

'I wasn't,' she answered, heatedly.

'But you just said he didn't want to. Does that mean you asked him?'

'No, I didn't. Well, yes, I did, but it wasn't quite . . .'

'So you didn't sleep together?'

As a matter of fact, we did, but we didn't make love. Actually, he told me a story because I couldn't get to sleep.'

'Wouldn't you have preferred it if he'd made love to you, Maddy?'

Paul immediately sat forward. 'I think we're getting a little personal here,' he said. 'Both Madeleine and I deny any intimate relationship with Shamir and Enrico, I think that's what you came to hear. However, if there's anything else you'd like to ask, such as when and where we plan to get married, please feel free.'

The press stayed for a further half an hour until, satisfied with their stories, they started to pack up. Edward Bingham tucked his notebook into an inside pocket and strolled across the room towards Madeleine. 'I'm happy for you, Maddy,' he said, shooting a glance at Paul as he shook her warmly by the hand. 'At long last you're getting everything you've always wanted – that man of yours is one hell of a lucky guy. And may I say you're looking more radiant than ever. Not pregnant, are you, by any chance?'

'Definitely not,' Madeleine laughed.

He shrugged. 'No harm in trying. You know me, always looking for a scoop. Anyway, pregnant or not, you look stunning.'

'Thank you,' Madeleine said, and as she slipped an arm

through Paul's he kissed the top of her head, so that she didn't see Bingham's brief nod or Paul's answering smile.

They strolled out into the mews to wave everyone off, and as the last car pulled away Madeleine caught sight of Marian coming down the street. Abruptly she let go of Paul and ran up to Marian, flinging her arms round her. 'Paul and I have just announced to the press that we're getting married,' she cried. 'Isn't it fantastic? You will be the bridesmaid, won't you? She must, mustn't she?' she added to Paul as he ambled up.

'We both insist,' he answered, giving Marian a curious look.

'It would be an honour,' she said, but she was unable to smile and she turned away, not knowing whether it was because of her mistrust of Paul or her jealousy of their happiness.

'What's the matter with her?' Paul said, as they watched Marian walk into the house.

'It'll be about Matthew,' Madeleine whispered. 'I'd better go and see if she's all right.'

She found Marian upstairs, sitting on the edge of her bed and staring angrily into space.

'I know he says he's going through hell,' Marian cried, when she saw Madeleine standing at the door, 'but what does he think it's doing to me – and Stephanie? She hates me so much now, she can barely look at me. I know he's bang in the middle of directing a film – but if only he'd put us out of our misery, make up his mind who he wants.'

Madeleine walked over to the bed and sat down. 'Have you seen him today?'

'Yes, I popped out to location just after lunch but he was talking to the actors. No time for me. That's why I'm in such a bad mood, I suppose.'

'What did you expect? Him to sweep you into his arms and kiss you right there in front of all those people?'

Marian turned to look at her. 'Well, it would do for

starters.' And Madeleine laughed as with a long, weary groan, Marian lay back on the bed. 'This is hell, Maddy. I know he said he cares for me, but not knowing how much and having someone like Stephanie as a rival – God, I can't bear it. Do you know, I had the damned nerve yesterday to walk in on Stephanie and practically challenge her to a fight over Matthew. No wonder she told me to get out, I'd have hit me if I were her. Mind you, I'm pretty glad she didn't, she's bigger than me.'

'And older. She'll be all crinkly soon.'

Marian burst out laughing. 'If you look at it like that, then he's older than her, so . . .'

'You'll be buying him a zimmer frame on your tenth wedding anniversary,' Madeleine giggled.

'Oh, don't say things like that,' Marian gasped, 'you don't know what it does to my stomach. And how can you sit there talking about wedding anniversaries when he hasn't even told me he loves me. Do you think he does, Maddy?'

'Of course he does, it's impossible not to love you.'

'You're biased.'

'I know, but I'm right. And just think, you're off to Italy next week . . .'

'Oh no!' Marian wailed, 'I don't want to think about it, I don't even know if I want to go.'

Madeleine hugged her. 'Of course you do. It's so romantic there, I'll bet you anything you like that everything sorts itself out and you come back an extremely happy woman.'

'I hope you're right,' Marian sighed. Then taking Madeleine's hand she said, 'It's so good to have you back, Maddy, to have someone to talk to. I wish you could meet him – properly, I mean. He's so . . . He's so . . .'

'Well, come on, spit it out,' Madeleine giggled. 'Say something really wicked.'

'He's so sexy!' Marian exploded.

'Oh *wick*-ed!' Madeleine laughed, as they rolled over on the bed together. 'What about his muscular thighs, his powerful arms, his smouldering eyes, his throbbing . . .'

'Get out of here!' Marian cried.

'Go on, I'll bet you think about it all the time.'

'I try not to, and don't make me, because he's got an uncanny knack of reading my mind sometimes. Besides,' she added, suddenly gloomy again, 'it's about more than sex, isn't it? It's about being together, working on the script the way we do, watching him laugh when I say something that's not even particularly witty. It's about knowing that he's thinking about me, that he's . . .'

'In love with you?'

'Yes.'

'He is, Marian, I know it. And just you wait until this film's over, everything will be sorted out and . . .'

'And either Stephanie or I will have a broken heart.'

'It'll be Stephanie.'

Marian pulled a face. 'That's the problem, I don't want it to be me, but I don't want it to be her, either. Oh, what a mess! Anyway, enough about that. What's all this about you and Paul getting married? When did he propose?'

'This afternoon,' Madeleine answered, suddenly animated. 'I could hardly believe it. He just announced it to the press. Oh, it was so romantic. He's so wonderful, Marian.'

'Don't tell me, muscular thighs, smouldering eyes . . . No! No!' she cried, as Madeleine started to hit her with a pillow.

'Come on,' Madeleine said, 'let's go and see what he's doing.' And pulling Marian up from the bed, she led her off down the stairs.

The following morning Marian was the first to rise. By the time she'd showered and dressed the newspapers had arrived, so she carried them into the kitchen to read while the kettle boiled. The *Daily Echo* was the third paper in the pile, and when Marian saw the banner headline, she snatched it up, scowling.

SEX SYMBOL SPURNED! it said. Then, as she quickly devoured the story below, her blood turned to ice. Surely Madeleine hadn't said all that about Enrico? He had been so kind to her, and Madeleine was so fond of him. Why would she want to hurt him like this? Then, hearing someone on the stairs, she shoved the paper into her bag and busied herself with the teapot.

'Great!' Madeleine cried, tossing back her tangled mass of hair. 'The papers! Have you read them yet?'

'Only glanced through,' Marian answered.

The tea was made and they were on their second cup by the time Madeleine, having read aloud from all the other papers, looked up from across the table and said: 'There's no *Echo*. Damn that newsagent, I was really looking forward to Edward Bingham's piece. He was so nice to me yesterday – but only after he'd tried to trip me up, mind you. Oh well, I'll just have to go out and get an *Echo* later.'

Paul came in then, and Madeleine pulled him down beside her and started leafing through the papers again.

'No *Echo*?' he said casually, a few minutes later. Marian realised she was only delaying the inevitable, so, digging into her bag, she pulled the paper out and handed it over.

Madeleine's face turned white as she read the headline.

'What the . . .' Paul snatched the paper from her and read the story aloud. '"Sex kitten Madeleine Deacon turned sourpuss yesterday when she revealed that Grand Prix winner, Enrico Tarallo, was unable to make love to her. Tarallo's loss has gained him the compassion of the world, but slighted Madeleine has not taken her snub lightly. 'He didn't want to,' she told this reporter yesterday, then went on to sneer, 'He couldn't, so instead he told me a story.' Her acid attack on the bereaved Tarallo begs the question, What kind of viper has this nation been harbouring in its bosom since her meteoric rise to fame? Miffed Madeleine went on to say . . ."'

'Stop!' Madeleine cried. 'No more. I don't want to hear it. Oh Paul, what am I going to do? I never said any of it; at least, not like that. Where are you going?'

'To ring that bastard Bingham and ask him what the hell he's playing at.'

Marian and Madeleine followed him into the sitting-room, and held one another's hands while Paul dialled the number and waited to be put through.

'Bingham?' he spat. 'Paul O'Connell here. Yes, I have seen the garbage you printed in your fucking rag this morning, and I don't know what your game is, but I think you should know we're going to sue you and your paper for . . . The quotes might be correct, but they were not delivered in the spirit in which you've written them, and you know it. And what about Tarallo? Do you think he needs this sort of publicity when his wife's hardly cold in her grave? Jesus Christ, next thing you'll be saying the poor guy wears his dead wife's underwear to bed . . . Well, you're sick enough. You'll be hearing from my solicitor.' He banged the phone down.

Marian stared at him in horror. She turned to Madeleine, but her horror only increased: Madeleine couldn't see it, she didn't understand what he was doing.

'That told him,' Madeleine said. 'Will we really sue?'

'You bet your life we will,' Paul snapped.

Marian snatched up her bag. 'I've got to go,' she said, 'I'm already late.'

By the time she reached Deidre's office she was shaking. She was shown straight in, and found Deidre on the phone delivering a tirade similar to Paul's. 'I expect you're here about this,' she said, ending her call with a flourish and slapping her hand down on the offending newspaper.

'Yes, and to ask for your help,' Marian answered.

'My help? What for?'

'I'm afraid for Madeleine, but I don't know what to do about it. Paul set this up. Don't ask me how or why, he just did. You know the way she feels about him; even if I spoke to her, she wouldn't listen to me. That's why I've come to you.'

Deidre looked at her, smiling. 'Marian, I don't claim to understand Paul and Madeleine's relationship, I never have, but I know it's something very special – and this he wouldn't have done, not after everything else that's just happened.'

'I'm telling you Deidre, he did.'

'Why?'

'I don't know. Maybe it was simple jealousy over Enrico, but I think it's more.'

Deidre shook her head. 'You know what the press are like, Marian, they build someone up just so they can knock them down again. It's a fact of life in this country. Besides, I was there myself yesterday – the quotes are accurate, and how on earth could Paul have foreseen what Madeleine would say?'

'I don't know, but he managed it. He's got a strange sort of power over her, Deidre. I don't know what it is, but it frightens me. I'm going to Italy next Monday, and I don't want her left in the house alone with him.'

'What! Marian, I really do think you're taking this too far. I know you . . .'

Marian interrupted. 'I'd like you to make some excuse – decorators, plumbers, anything – and ask if you can go and stay with them. Please don't laugh at me Deidre, I'm perfectly serious.'

'I'm sorry,' Deidre said, falling back into her chair. 'I'm not laughing at you, Marian, I'm laughing at myself, and how stupid I've been.' She waved her arm. 'Sit down,' she said. 'Let's discuss this sensibly.'

She waited until Marian was comfortable and Anne had brought in some fresh coffee, then said: 'You're off to Italy, you say? Yes, you're working on this film about Olivia Hastings, aren't you? Madeleine told me. Now supposing, just supposing, I believed everything you've told me about Paul, well, I can't see what good me going to stay with them will do, can you? You'd still be worried to death about her. Don't you think it's a far better idea to take her with you?'

'I can't do that,' Marian answered. 'The producer would never allow it.'

'I don't see that it's up to the producer. After all, anyone can go to Italy, they don't have to have the permission of your producer, do they?'

'I suppose they don't. But we're staying in a village, miles from anywhere. Accommodation is already short.'

'Madeleine could always share with you, couldn't she? Then she'd be right where you want her, under your wing.'

'But what about Paul? They've sworn a pact never to be parted again. But that doesn't matter,' she went on, answering her own question, 'I've got a cottage to myself. Only one bedroom, but there's sure to be a sofa or something downstairs, I could always sleep on that and they can have the bed.'

'There you are, then. And who knows, your producer might even find a part for Madeleine in the film? After all, she's quite an audience puller, your cousin.'

'Yes, she is, isn't she?' Marian said. 'And we've yet to cast the part of Geraldine – a student who was in Florence studying at the same time as Olivia. Mind you,' she added thoughtfully, 'I can't see the producer going for it, but I'll speak to the director, see what he says.'

'Good. Let me know how you get on, won't you? But whether you succeed with the director or not, Marian, I still think you should take Madeleine with you – for your own sake if not for hers.'

*

Shooting was due to finish at eight o'clock that night, and though Marian racked her brains for an excuse to go out to the set, it seemed as if both Bronwen and Hazel were determined to keep her at her desk. Bronwen was flying to Italy the following day – hoping, Marian guessed, to steal a little time with Sergio before everyone else arrived. Though Bronwen was still friendly towards her, she sensed a certain restraint and it saddened her, knowing that Bronwen's loyalty to Stephanie was at the root of it.

She waited at her desk until nine thirty, hanging around while Josey typed up the call sheets and Woody's assistants telephoned the artistes, but in the end she had to accept that Matthew had gone straight home – Stephanie wasn't around either, which depressed her even more. But as she went out into the street they were walking towards her with Judith, the casting director, and then she remembered that, of course, they had been to a late casting session. Her fingers crossed in her pockets – please don't let them have got anyone for the part of Geraldine yet.

'Matthew,' she said, as they came up. 'Could I have a word with you, please?' She knew Stephanie was looking at her, but she wouldn't allow herself to look back.

'Sure,' Matthew answered, looking as awkward as she'd expected. Judith walked on into the office, and without a word Stephanie followed.

'I'm sorry about that,' she told him, glancing up the street to see if Boris – her shadow – was around. 'But it's fairly urgent.'

'Oh? Has something happened?' he asked, following the direction of her eyes.

'No, no. Well, nothing to do with Boris, he's still there, bless him, I wonder when he gets any sleep?' She looked up into Matthew's face and smiled tenderly when she saw how tired he looked. 'Hard day?'

'No more than usual. How about you?'

She laughed. 'Frustrating. I've been wanting to talk to you all day.'

'OK. Well, why don't we share a taxi home? We can talk on the way. I'll just pop inside and have a quick word with Woody, then I'm all yours.' And he laughed at her ironic look.

'I'll call a taxi,' she said in a dry voice.

She managed to hail one without too much trouble, and climbed into the back seat to wait. After a few minutes Stephanie and Bronwen came out of the office, and Marian despised herself for the way she shrank back into the shadows. Whether or not Stephanie saw her Marian couldn't be sure, but Bronwen certainly did, and treated her to a cold stare before linking arms with Stephanie and walking on up the street.

'Now, what's the mystery?' Matthew said, getting into the taxi beside her. 'Holland Park, then on to Chiswick,' he told the driver.

Marian told him about the newspaper story, repeating it exactly as it had appeared, then added her suspicions about Paul. 'So you see, I'm not too keen to leave Madeleine on her own with him,' she finished.

'But she's been alone with him all these months, surely . . .'

'I know, but I just get the feeling, now, that something's not quite right. I don't trust him, Matthew.'

'So what are you going to do about it?'

'Well, I know it's probably a crazy idea, but Madeleine might be right for the part of Geraldine, and then we could take her to Italy with us.'

Matthew burst out laughing. 'In the first place, we've already cast Geraldine, tonight, and in the second, you know Stephanie would never swallow it, no matter how small the part.'

Marian grimaced. 'Yes, I suppose you're right. But I've got to take her to Italy with me, Matthew.'

'Providing she pays for herself and doesn't get in the way, there's nothing anyone can do to stop you.'

'Will you tell Stephanie for me?'

'Coward,' he teased. 'Sure, I'll tell her, but only if you can convince me about all this nonsense regarding Paul.'

Marian pulled an envelope from her pocket and handed it to him. 'Open it tomorrow, after you've read the *Echo*, and you'll see what I mean.'

When Matthew did as she asked the following morning, he had to admit she might be right. Although what she had written wasn't exactly what it said in the paper, it was near enough. '". . . the poor guy wears his dead wife's underwear to bed," said a source very close to the black-hearted beauty.' He noticed, too, at the bottom of the page, that the Tarallo family had declined to comment.

'. . . and if you come with me,' Marian was saying to Madeleine, 'you could have the chance to see Enrico, and explain.'

Madeleine's eyes were red from crying. 'I shouldn't think he'll want to see me, not after this.'

'If my judgment of Enrico is anything to go by then he probably knows anyway that it's all lies. Please come, Maddy, you ought to speak to him.'

'But what about Paul?'

'He can come, too. The village where we're filming is made up of tiny one- and two-bedroomed cottages. I've only got a single one, but you two can have the bed and I'll sleep on the sofa – if there is one! To be honest, I could do with your moral support – everyone's practically sent me to Coventry since Stephanie and I had that row.'

'OK, I'll come, but only if Paul says he will, too. You know we've sworn a pact . . .'

'Yes, I know,' Marian teased. 'So let's ask him, shall we?'

'I think it's a great idea,' Paul said, when he came out of the shower and they told him. 'We could do with a holiday, Maddy, and being around a film shoot might be fun.'

'So it's fixed!' Marian cried. 'I'll get on to the travel agents the minute I get to the office and book your flights.'

Which she did, and later, with Matthew's help, she wrote to Enrico, telling him they were coming and going on to explain what she thought was happening. The more she thought about it, the more certain she became that her suspicions about Paul were right.

Matthew read the letter one last time before handing it back to Marian, and as she sealed the envelope his face was grim. He didn't like it. If her theory was right, and Paul was doing what she suspected, then Madeleine wasn't the only one whose safety they needed to worry about.

− 27 −

The remote village of Felitto, high in the vast, undulating hills of Tuscany, amounted to no more than a tiny cluster of honeysuckle- and vine-covered cottages. In the heat of the day lizards scuttled about the red slate roofs and chickens clucked and pecked at the dry earth. It was about an hour's walk from Paesetto di Pittore, around the brow of the mountain, and a good thousand feet above Camaiore, the nearest small town. Most evenings, cloud and mist billowed in over the mountaintops, shrouding the village and making the road up to it more perilous than ever. Precious few barriers had been erected for protection against the sheer drops, and there was no room for manoeuvre should one misjudge a hairpin bend. In fact, the drive was so arduous that Stephanie found herself bribing the electricians and props men, who were staying in Camaiore, with 'danger money' in order to get them to do it each morning.

Felitto's twenty or so stone cottages, which sprawled haphazardly amongst the trees and brush on either side of the footpath – the village's main street – had long since been taken over by an English tour operator who offered seclusion and panoramic views to holidaying painters. At the heart of the valley, which fell away from the village in tiers of vineyards and olive groves, was the cluttered town of Camaiore. On clear days, the sea glittered on the horizon between mountain peaks that rose in the distance. The surrounding hillsides were thickly wooded and beautiful walks were mapped out with yellow arrows carved into the trees so that no one should get lost.

Marian's cottage, which she was sharing with Madeleine and Paul, was at the top of a set of weathered steps that zig-zagged through a steep herb garden behind the main cottages, which were used as a dining room, bar and kitchens. The cottage consisted of only two rooms. The sitting-room had bare, whitewashed walls, a stone hearth with an age-spotted mirror above, a shabby carpet and a beamed ceiling. A sofa stood beneath the window and a chair beside the fire; this was the only furniture, apart from a rickety old cane table against the wall at the foot of the stairs. The bedroom, whose bed was neither a double nor a single, but something inbetween, had not even a wardrobe, only a curtained alcove in the corner. But it was home for a while, and Marian fell in love with the cottage on sight. Bronwen and Hazel had the cottages on either side of her, and Stephanie's and Matthew's were below the tiny piazza that jutted out of the hillside in front of the bar. Further up the hill was a group of cottages being used by cast, costume and make-up; higher still, the camera crew occupied rooms in the crumbling houses on either side of the precipitous pathway that led to the swimming pool.

Manfredo and Gabriella were the old couple who looked after the village, and when the crew arrived, late on

Monday afternoon, Manfredo had a fire blazing at one end of the bar and special toddies waiting – though the sun was still shining, with the promise of a glorious sunset, it was bitterly cold.

As soon as they'd settled into their cottages, Matthew and Stephanie wandered up to the bar to join Bronwen beside the fire. The crew were already gathering at the other end of the dimly lit room, and flexing their Italian with demands for a ceaseless flow of Manfredo's potent concoction.

Bronwen moved along the sofa for Stephanie to sit down, and Matthew perched on the fender with one foot resting on the log basket. 'Frank and Grace arrived yesterday,' Bronwen informed them. 'They've taken a villa near Volterra. It's a bit cramped for them here, I think, when they're used to that great mansion in New York. By the way, Adrian couldn't book the helicopter for the aerial shots on Thursday, so we'll have to reorganise the schedule. I think he's got it for Friday.'

Matthew nodded. 'I'll talk to Woody.'

'Anyway,' Bronwen went on, 'I can tell you, there's been plenty of activity going on over at Paesetto di Pittore these past few days and there was me thinking it was a ghost town. Cars up and down the mountain at all hours of the day and night – always travelling in convoy. There's only the one road, unless you walk from here round the mountain, and I never got close enough to the village when it was hosting its visitors to see which house they went into. Conveniently, trees would come down to block the road, or locals would wander along the path and engage me in conversation. Such a knowledge of Tuscan wildlife I have now, I could write a book on it.'

'Have you seen Rambaldi at all?' Matthew asked, reluctantly raising his voice to make himself heard over the banter going on around them.

Bronwen shook her head. 'I was supposed to on Saturday, but he stood me up. I've been ringing his apartment in Florence ever since, but he's not there; either that, or he's not answering the phone. I've called the Accademia, but they say he doesn't have any lectures until next month, so I haven't got the foggiest idea where he is.'

'So you didn't manage to get what you came for then, eh, Bron?' he grinned.

'Very funny,' she said, throwing him a droll look. 'Actually, I was hoping he might be able to tell me what all the fuss was over in Pittore, but then he says he doesn't really know the village, so . . .'

'I thought you didn't believe him,' Stephanie said.

'I don't, but it wouldn't have stopped me asking. I wonder if he does know anything about what happened to Olivia?' she mused.

'If I were you, I'd be careful who you ask that question of,' Matthew told her, 'especially now we're in Italy.'

'Really?' Bronwen said, suddenly interested. 'Do you know something we don't, then, Matthew?'

Avoiding Stephanie's eyes, he shook his head. 'No. But you have to remember that whatever did happen to Olivia very likely happened somewhere round here, and if Rambaldi was lying about not knowing Pittore, well . . . Just don't ask the question too loudly.'

'Oooh!' Bronwen said, rubbing her hands gleefully, 'it's like being in a spy movie, isn't it, Steph?'

'Mm,' Stephanie answered, with a dubious look. 'Anyway, what do you say we take a look at the final sequence once more before we give it to the actors?'

'Ah yes,' Bronwen answered. 'I've already made a couple of changes, but they're written in my awful handwriting, I'm afraid. Did Marian bring her typewriter?'

'Marian's brought everything,' Stephanie said, in a tight, sarcastic voice, and she raised her eyes to meet the look Matthew shot at her. But after a second or two of hostility, they both smiled.

'Right, I'll ask her to type them tonight,' Bronwen said. 'What time do we start shooting in the morning?'

'Six o'clock,' Stephanie grimaced. 'Michelangelo here wants a sunrise.'

Matthew gave her an ironic grin and turned back to Bronwen. 'Why don't you give us a . . . Bronwen, are you listening?'

'Heavens above,' she muttered, looking towards the door. 'Isn't that . . .? Yes, it is. I see what you mean, Steph, Marian *has* brought everything, or at least, everybody.'

Matthew got to his feet and walked across the bar to greet the latest arrivals and Bronwen turned to Stephanie, who was hunched over the fire, warming her hands. 'What's going on?' she asked in a heavy whisper.

'You'll have to ask Matthew,' Stephanie answered. 'It's all beyond me, and I've given up fighting. Just as long as the film gets made and the cousin doesn't decide to flash her tits somewhere in the back of shot, that's all that matters.'

'But you didn't say they could come, did you?'

'Not exactly, but I didn't say they couldn't, either. She was very clever, Bron, she got Matthew to ask.'

'Well I never.' Bronwen stole another look across the bar. 'Are you and Marian speaking now?' she asked.

'Just about. You know, much as I hate her, I can't help but admire her for the way she had the guts to come and talk to me that day. If I'd been in her position I think I'd have gone out of my way to avoid me.'

'So would I,' Bronwen said seriously. 'Has Matthew said any more about her?'

Stephanie shook her head. 'But things seem a bit better between him and me. I don't know what's going to happen in the end, I can't even bring myself to think about it, but for the moment we've sort of called a truce.'

'It might be a wise thing to call one with Marian, too, you know.'

'Yes, I've been thinking that myself.' Then, after a pause, 'You're quite fond of her really, aren't you, Bron?'

'I am,' Bronwen admitted. 'And so were you before all this happened. I know she's changed, Steph, but she's not the devious little madam you've got her down for, you know. If anything I'll bet all this is tearing her apart just as much as it is you. She didn't mean any of it to happen, I'm sure of it. Well, why would she?'

'The devil's advocate,' Stephanie said, with a dry laugh.

'Not really. All I'm trying to say is that if we could choose who we fell in love with, the world would be a much easier place to live in.'

'Wouldn't it just?'

There was a loud shriek from the other end of the bar and Stephanie winced. 'I'll try with Marian, Bron,' she said, through gritted teeth, 'but I'm not so sure about the cousin. Does she have to scream like that?'

'That man is beautiful, isn't he?' Bronwen said, looking in the direction of the bar.

'If you're talking about Matthew, the answer's sometimes.'

Bronwen laughed. 'I was talking about Paul O'Connell, actually. But seeing them standing there, Matthew so dark and Paul so blond, it's like . . . well, it's like . . .'

'Torture,' Stephanie supplied. 'Or Happy Families. Madeleine and Paul, Marian and Matthew. Don't they look cosy? I can just see them now; all the shared holidays, the weekend visits, Christmases, birthdays, picnics . . . Sorry, Bron, I think I'm going to have to leave before I make a fool of myself.'

'It's all right, *cariad*,' Bronwen answered. 'I'll come with you . . .'

'Don't look now,' Madeleine hissed in Marian's ear, 'but she's leaving.'

Despite the glow Marian felt inside, her heart sank. 'Don't gloat, Maddy, she's probably feeling really awful.'

'Why should you worry? He's over here with you, isn't he?'

'I know, but things aren't as simple as that.'

'What are you two whispering about?' Matthew interrupted, almost shouting to make himself heard above the noise.

'You, as a matter fact,' Marian smiled.

'Now, why don't I believe you?' he said, looking down at her in a way that seemed to close them off from everyone else.

'We were, honestly,' Madeleine piped up, then flinched as Marian trod on her toe.

Matthew could hardly restrain his grin as he reluctantly pulled his eyes away from Marian's and turned back to Paul.

'I was wondering,' Paul said, as he attempted again to pay for his and Madeleine's drinks, 'if you would let me have a schedule of your filming.'

'Sure,' Matthew answered. 'I'll get Woody or one of his assistants to drop one into your cottage.'

'Thanks. It's just that I want to find myself a couple of isolated spots to write in and I don't want to run the risk of finding myself in shot. Don't think I'd be too popular if I did that, would I?'

'Not really,' Matthew laughed, pressing himself against the bar to let someone pass. 'What are you writing about, may I ask?'

'I'm trying to imagine what it feels like to be on trial for murder. I'm not too keen on doing things this way, I like to experience everything I write, but I've invited several people to become my murder victim and they've all turned me down.'

'Not very sporting of them,' Matthew commented.

'Just what I thought,' Paul laughed. "Don't suppose you'd care to volunteer, would you?'

Matthew shot a glance at Marian, then turning aside so she couldn't hear, he said, 'If things carry on as they are, I might just do that.'

'That bad, eh?' Paul said, laughing.

'Don't even ask. Anyway, I'd better go and see what Stephanie and Bronwen are up to, there are some rewrites I need to look at. See you in the morning.' And after setting his glass on the bar, he put a hand on Marian's arm. 'Goodnight,' he said.

'Oh, goodnight,' she answered, trying not to look disappointed, then suddenly her drink slopped all over them as Woody sneaked up behind her and kicked the rigidity from her knees.

'You're a pest, Woody,' she told him, as she watched Matthew, still laughing, walk out of the door.

'But a lovable one,' Woody grinned. "Now, are you going to reintroduce me to your cousin?' He gave Madeleine an outrageously appreciative look-over.

Marian rolled her eyes, then turning Madeleine away from Paul, she made the introductions – and was still making them an hour later, since everyone on the unit wanted to meet either Madeleine or Paul. Then, about ten o'clock, Bronwen put her head round the door and asked if she could do some typing before she went to bed, so to a chorus of sympathetic groans Marian went off to unpack her typewriter.

'Well, what do you think of him?' she asked Madeleine when she wandered into the cottage half an hour later.

'Gorgeous,' Madeleine answered, flopping down on the lumpy sofa.

Marian folded her arms over her typewriter. 'Isn't he?' she sighed, then sat up quickly as the table started to rock dangerously.

'And he definitely feels something for you, Marian. It's obvious. I mean, the minute we walked into the bar he abandoned Stephanie and came to join us.'

'I know, don't remind me.'

'All's fair,' Madeleine commented. 'I've talked to Paul about it, and he thinks you should tell Matthew how you feel. You know, bring it to a head.'

Marian shuddered as a tingling sensation crept over her nerve ends. 'He already knows, Maddy.'

'Are you sure? Well, I think you should tell him again, just to make sure.' She pulled herself to her feet. 'Anyway, I'm going to leave you to your typing now, and find that man of mine before – what did you call her? – Cracks-yer-nuts Hazel gets her claws into him.'

Laughing, Marian walked her to the door and watched as, by torchlight, she picked her way down the crooked steps before disappearing into the shadows. The night was damp and inky black, and though Marian could hear the distant buzz of conversation coming from the bar, much more vivid was the twitter and rustle of night creatures and the haunting moan of the wind. A cold shiver ran down her spine as she remembered the screams – the screams everyone had said were a nightmare. And they were, she told herself firmly as she closed the door. But as she turned to look across the shadowy room she felt such a sense of foreboding, such a premonition of doom, that for a moment it seemed to stifle her. Then suddenly the screams were with her again, piercing, agonised cries of terror that whipped through her head like a savage wind through the hills. And as she stood there in the silence, fear charging through her veins, she suddenly knew that the screams were hers. That they had always been hers – as if her mind were trying to forewarn her of something so terrible that her imagination could give it no form.

Then, as abruptly as it had come, the feeling passed, and pulling herself together, she walked back to her typewriter, smiling at her absurd over-reaction, she started to type. What a strange place, so beautiful by day, yet so eerie by night!

Because of the early morning calls, and so as not to incur a massive overtime bill, the crew were wrapping at four thirty in the afternoon – which, because there were no rushes, was just about an hour before they started on Manfredo's grog. The first two days had gone well, despite grumbles and protests at the late changes to the script and a near disaster with the generator, which had ploughed off the edge of the road into a tree. However, they had finally got to the plateau beneath the village where the other vehicles were parked, and Woody was forever yelling at people to watch out for the profusion of cables that ran along the footpath into the village. An old storeroom, tucked in behind the dining cottage, had been turned into a production office, and at the end of the day Marian vacated her makeshift desk in the corner to give Beanie room to type up her continuity notes.

On Wednesday evening, as the crew were stowing their gear in the laundry room beside Stephanie's cottage, Matthew was sitting on the piazza outside the bar, drinking Campari and soda and flicking through the scenes they would be shooting the next day. Rory was at the top of the lane, talking to the runner, but waved out when he saw Marian wandering down through the herb garden. Neither of them had ever spoken about the night when she had got drunk in New York, it was as if it had never happened; but Marian knew he had told Matthew the truth about it, and was as grateful to him for that as she was for the fact that he hadn't taken advantage of her. The others, of course, still thought she had lost her virginity that night, but they could think what they liked, Marian wasn't much concerned.

'Am I interrupting?' she said, as she walked up behind Matthew.

'No, no, I'm just about done,' he said, turning round. 'Why don't you get yourself a drink, come and join me?'

'No, I don't really feel like anything,' she said, sitting down on the chair he pulled up for her. 'Like the hat, by the way. Very Slav.'

'Very warm,' he said, laughing as he pulled it off and ran his fingers through his hair. 'It's damned cold up here, especially now the wind's picked up. You should get yourself a hat, you know. How are you?'

'I'm OK. And you?'

'Apart from being my usual decrepit, shattered self, pretty good.' He sighed as he stretched out his legs and rested them on the wall in front of them. 'Will you just look at that sunset,' he said, gazing hungrily at the purple, orange and yellow wash on the horizon. 'I hope to God we get them like that next week when we start the night shoots. Ah, here comes Holland Park's answer to Jack Higgins.' They watched as Paul jumped down from the bank next to the storeroom, then disappeared between the cottages. 'How are things there?' Matthew asked, turning back to Marian.

'Nothing untoward, but there is something I want to tell you.'

'Oh?'

'Boris isn't following me any more. I haven't seen him since we've been here.'

'Maybe he got the wrong flight.'

'Probably,' she chuckled. 'It's funny, though, but I feel more nervous with him not following me than I do when he is. Well, maybe I wouldn't if I hadn't done something that will probably make you angry.'

'What was that?' he said, looking at her with wary, though humorous eyes.

'Well, when Bronwen said she didn't know where Sergio

was, and then with Boris vanishing, well . . . There's no point in beating about the bush, I rang Rubin Meyer in New York. Don't worry, I didn't say who I was, but the point is, he's not there and he won't be until the end of the month. I asked where I might contact him, but all his secretary would tell me was that he was somewhere in Europe.'

'I see.' Matthew's eyes moved from Marian's face and for a long time he stared thoughtfully towards the horizon. Finally his hand closed round the glass in front of him and he turned to look at her. 'Did Bronwen tell you about all the activity going on over at Pittore?'

'She mentioned it.'

He nodded. 'Mm. I think we'd better let Frank and Grace know about Meyer, and as for you, you're not to go anywhere near the place, do you understand?'

'Don't worry, wild horses wouldn't drag me.'

There was another lengthy silence before he spoke again. 'I don't know what's going on over there at Pittore,' he said, 'it could be nothing to do with Rambaldi and Meyer, but I've got a horrible feeling it is. Now, it may be that they've decided you know nothing, and that's why Boris has disappeared, so I don't want you frightening yourself half to death over this, but just make sure you don't go out of this village alone. Now, I want to talk to you about Paul and Madeleine.'

'OK,' she said, surprised by the sudden change of subject and wondering why he was looking at her so strangely. 'Madeleine's been to see Enrico, by the way. She went this afternoon.'

'How did it go?'

'OK, I think. He knows what the press are like, he's been subjected to them often enough before. Anyway, he didn't mention anything to her about the letter we sent.'

Matthew was still looking pensive. 'Good,' he said slowly. Then, turning in his chair he leaned towards her.

'Look, I have to say this to you, and coming on top of the news about Rambaldi and Meyer, it's not going to do much to calm your nerves. But you have to be aware of this situation Marian.'

'What situation?' she said, puzzled.

'If you're right about Paul, then you must have considered what kind of position that puts you in.'

Shrugging, she said, 'I have to admit I've thought about it, but I'm family.'

'That didn't stop him before, did it?' He watched her face, waiting for this to sink in, but as she started to protest, he stopped her. 'Look, whose idea do you really think it was to take that lottery money? I don't wish to be rude, Marian, but Madeleine isn't too bright, is she? She might have said it was all her doing, but think how easy she is for a man of Paul's intelligence to manipulate. And it got you out of the way, didn't it? At least for a while. Have you ever asked yourself why he didn't tell her about your mother's death? Because he knew she'd come running to you, that's why. It was all going very nicely for him, if you think about it. You gone, your mother dead. Then he managed to get rid of Shamir. He's refused to continue paying Deidre, and he's made Madeleine financially dependent on him. Then he very cleverly orchestrated that vicious exposé of Tarallo to make it look like Madeleine's doing, certain that Tarallo would never want to see her again. Thank God he's been proved wrong, but he doesn't know it yet. And because she appears to have attacked Tarallo, the press and the public have turned against Madeleine, too. That only leaves you.'

Marian's face was pale as she looked out over the darkening valley and she thought again how sinister those hills were at night.

Matthew reached for her hand. 'I'm sorry,' he said, 'but for your own sake I had to make you see it. We could, again, be blowing this out of all proportion, but I'd never forgive myself if anything happened to you.'

'I don't know what to say,' she murmured. 'I know you're right, it makes sense. If he is eliminating people from her life, then of course he's going to want to be rid of me. But short of killing me . . .' She turned her wide grey eyes to his, and as he nodded she felt the bottom drop from her stomach.

'The book,' he said, voicing her thoughts. 'He's looking for a victim.'

'I know, but he'd have to go to prison, so it wouldn't end up just him and Madeleine then, would it?'

'I know, but I still don't trust him. He's got an extremely devious mind, Marian, as well you know, and I wouldn't consider it beyond him to work something out. Now, I'd like to meet Enrico. Tonight, if possible. Does he live far?'

She shook her head. 'Just outside a village called Galleno, about half an hour from here in the car, so Madeleine said. And you're right, we should go to talk to him because he – at least, his grandmother – knows something about Paul. I haven't got a clue what it is, she was speaking in Italian so I couldn't understand, but she did say something about me looking after Madeleine.'

'OK. You go and call Enrico and I'll meet you back here in ten minutes.'

After she had gone Matthew sat alone on the piazza, listening to the crew who were beginning to gather inside the bar; but his mind was on Paul O'Connell, Enrico Tarallo and Sergio Rambaldi – three men who, as far as he was aware, didn't know one another. Yet they all knew Marian; and for a reason he couldn't even begin to explain to himself, he was certain that wasn't the only connection between them.

'Hello.'

He looked up, and in the dwindling light saw Stephanie,

wrapped in an anorak and a paisley shawl, walking towards him. 'Hello,' he smiled. 'Good day?'

'As far as I'm concerned it's all going extremely well,' she answered as she sat down on the chair Marian had vacated. 'How about you? Are you happy with the way things are going?'

He pulled a face. 'I'd feel better if we were seeing rushes every night. Has anything been sorted out about that yet?'

'Hazel's arranged a viewing in the town hall at Camaiore on Saturday evening.'

'Good.'

'I was wondering,' she said, after a pause, 'if you might like to go out somewhere for dinner tonight. We could take one of the hire cars, maybe drive into Lucca.'

'I'm sorry, Steph,' he groaned, 'but I don't think I can.'

'It's OK,' she said, shrugging, 'I just thought it might be a nice idea, that was all. Maybe another night.'

'Tomorrow,' he said.

'We'll see.'

'Steph,' he said, as she started to get up.

She looked down at him, her hands stuffed inside her jacket and her shoulders hunched as if from the cold.

'I'm sorry,' he whispered.

'So am I,' she said, and giving him a sad smile she turned and walked into the bar.

An hour later Matthew and Marian were being shown into the dining-room of the Tuscan palazzo which was the main residence of the Tarallo family. Matching candelabras lit the table, and a vast crystal chandelier glittered over the magnificent room. At one end a fire crackled in the hearth, and at the other, immense uncurtained windows were blackened by night.

'This is very kind of you,' Marian was saying as she walked slowly across the room, keeping pace with Sylvestra who was holding onto her arm. 'We only wanted to talk, we weren't expecting dinner.'

'But I must eat,' Sylvestra answered, 'I am hungry. Besides, it is nothing very special we have tonight, the family are at the opera in Florence. It is just Enrico and me.'

'I suppose you were going to the opera as well, before we called,' Matthew muttered to Enrico.

'It is no matter, my friend,' Enrico smiled. 'It is one I have seen many times before.'

The table was set only at one end, nearest the fire, and Sylvestra smiled gratefully at Marian as she sank into one of the stately baroque chairs. 'We are four,' she said, 'so we sit each side of the table – no one at the head. Marian, you sit facing me, beside Enrico, and Matthew, you sit beside me. You will have a little wine? It is from the Tarallo vineyards.'

'Then we can't say no,' Matthew answered, his eyes dancing with amusement at the powerful, frail old woman.

'So,' Enrico said, after the antipasto had been laid out and the servants had left the room, 'you said on the phone, Marian, that there was something you would like to ask me.'

'Yes,' she said, throwing a quick glance at Matthew. 'It's about Paul O'Connell.'

Enrico's eyes met his grandmother's and after a few seconds she gave an almost imperceptible nod.

'We had guessed that it was,' Enrico said, turning back to Marian. 'What is it you would like to know?'

Again she looked at Matthew, for a moment at a loss as to how to begin.

'Basically, what you know,' Matthew answered. 'That is assuming you know more about him than his involvement in recent events.'

'We do,' Sylvestra answered. 'I have read the letter you sent to Enrico, and that is why I have agreed to speak with you. You are right to think Madeleine is in danger from him, and so too are you, Marian.'

'In what way are they in danger?' Matthew asked.

'That, I am afraid, is a question only he can answer. You see, I have no understanding of the working of such a mind as his. But this I can tell you, Paul O'Connell is *matto* – insane.'

Marian's fork clanged against her plate as she dropped it.

'I know this,' Sylvestra went on, 'because once I know his mother. She too was insane, but she was not dangerous. And now I shall tell you why Paul is dangerous, how it is that I know this.'

Marian's face was strained and pale as she stared at the old lady, but Sylvestra was looking at Enrico. It was as if there was a silent communication between them before Sylvestra turned back to Marian – and suddenly Marian was afraid.

'Paul O'Connell killed his mother and father,' Sylvestra said, fixing her with her pale, shrewd eyes.

Marian felt as though the room was spinning, and for a moment she thought she was going to pass out, then Enrico's hand closed over hers and he was holding a glass of water to her lips.

'It was during a hunt,' Sylvestra was now addressing herself to Matthew. 'The details are now vague, I am an old lady, you understand. But I do remember that everyone was to think it was Helen, Paul's mother, who had shot her husband and then herself. Everyone knew she was unwell in her mind, but I knew Helen, I had seen her only one week before she died. She would not have killed herself then, because of what she was planning to do. Paul knew what she planned, and that was why he killed her. It is my belief that his father saw him do it, and that was why Paul killed his father too. It was a scandal, but no one believed that a boy of eleven would kill his parents, so everyone believed it was Helen.'

'But what was Helen going to do?' Matthew asked, when this had had time to sink in.

'She was planning to leave them, to come here to Italy.'

'He killed her for that?'

'He is insane, you remember. His reasoning is not like yours.'

'I remember Paul telling me that his mother loved Italy,' Marian murmured, 'Florence in particular. They used to come every year.'

'Yes, they did. But Helen came more often. She had a reason to, but that reason is maybe better to die with her. Now only I know, my son Enrico, and Paul. And one other person, the person she wanted to be with. Paul loved his mother a great deal, he did not want her to go, and now he is afraid that one day someone he loves will leave him again. That is why he is doing this to Madeleine. He wants to keep her with him, away from everyone but him. He wants her to love no one else, even you, Marian.'

'So you think he's likely to kill Marian to achieve this?' Matthew asked.

'I do not know. As I say, it is difficult to understand the mind of the insane, and I do not wish to alarm you.'

'I can't see any way round this,' Marian said, looking at Matthew with wide, frightened eyes. 'Even if we told Madeleine, and even if she believed us, Paul's not going to let her go, is he?'

'No,' Sylvestra answered flatly. 'There is nothing you can do, and I cannot advise you. All I can do is tell you what I know.'

It was approaching midnight when Marian and Matthew finally left the palazzo, by which time they had talked over and over what they could do to get Madeleine away from Paul. But there was no solution; as Marian had pointed out, even if they could persuade Madeleine to leave him, there was no knowing what lengths he would go to to get her back, and God only knew what revenge he would seek on those who had interfered.

As they drove away Enrico stood at the door with Sylvestra, watching the tail lights disappear through the gates. 'Why did you not tell them everything?' he asked.

'Because it is a very tangled web, this fate that has brought them here,' Sylvestra answered, 'and I am not clear in my mind what is the right thing to do.'

'But still I think you should have told them.'

'Maybe,' she answered, 'but maybe they have no need to know everything. So many years have passed, Enrico, so many tears have been spilled and so much blood. I do not want to see it happen again. I must think, I must think what is the best thing to do to avoid it . . .'

'I wonder,' Marian was saying, as Matthew drove them through the darkened village of Galleno, 'who it was Paul's mother wanted to be with.'

Matthew was silent for a moment. 'I have a horrible feeling in my gut,' he said, 'that it has something to do with Sergio Rambaldi. I know it sounds crazy, and I know I've got nothing to found it on, but . . .'

'That's what I was thinking, too,' Marian said quietly. Then, a long time later, she turned to look at him. 'I'm frightened, Matthew,' she whispered. 'This has all gone so far beyond me now that I don't know what to do any more. I can't even begin to make any sense of it. Maybe I should take Maddy back to London, back to Bristol even, but how can I even begin to explain to her . . .? Oh, if only we could go back to the beginning, back to our little flat in Clifton, before we knew Paul. God, Matthew, how has this happened? How have we become involved in such a nightmare?'

'I don't know, my darling, but what I do know is that you've got to carry on as though Sylvestra never told you any of this. It'll be difficult, impossible almost – but for your own sake you have to try.'

'It won't be easy sleeping under the same roof as Paul now, knowing what I do.'

'And if it weren't for the fact that it would cause unwelcome speculation, not to mention insurmountable problems, I'd insist that you stayed in my cottage with me. As it is, I think you'll be all right as long as you don't tell anyone where we went tonight.'

She turned to look out of the window, then closed her eyes, not wanting to see the great black mass of the mountains as they passed.

A few minutes later he chuckled quietly.

'What are you laughing at?' she asked.

'Has it struck you yet that there's a damn sight more drama going on behind the camera than there is in front of it? And what's more, you, Marian Deacon, are the star.'

'God give me anonymity,' she muttered. Then she laughed, too, as he reached out for her hand and brought it to his lips.

The following morning Marian and Madeleine were standing at the edge of the set, watching the action. The camera was tracking slowly round the piazza as Christina Hancock, who was playing Olivia, read aloud from a letter she was writing to her father. A hush hung over the valley, even the birds were quiet for once. The air was still and every member of the crew was holding his breath. Then suddenly the sound of bells crashed into the silence, resounding through the valley and echoing from one mountain to the next.

'Cut!' Matthew walked into the middle of the set. 'Woody! Woody! Where are you?'

Woody rushed in, almost knocking Beanie from her picnic stool. 'Here, guv.'

'Get one of your damned assistants, give him a gun and tell him to go down there and shoot that bloody bell ringer.'

'Yes, guv.' Woody saluted, then yelled for Colin, the runner.

'He's not really going to give him a gun, is he?' Madeleine asked Marian, her eyes wide with alarm.

'God save me from religion, especially at eleven thirty on a Thursday morning,' Matthew muttered.

'You had the perfect opportunity last night,' Madeleine hissed as they watched him walk over to Christina. 'You could have told him then how you felt about him. For Christ's sake, he took you out to dinner, didn't he? What more do you want?'

Marian shivered and pulled her jacket tighter. 'I thought we'd agreed that he knows how I feel.'

'Marian.'

Marian turned round, and her face drained as she saw Stephanie standing behind her.

'Can I have a word, please?' Stephanie said, and without waiting for an answer she walked down the lane. Marian and Madeleine exchanged wide-eyed glances, then with her heart thudding, Marian went to catch up.

'God, I'm not that alarming, am I?' Stephanie smiled, when she saw Marian's face. 'Look, I just wanted to say that I'm sorry for the way I told you about the credits you're receiving on the film. I shouldn't have given you the news in such a hostile manner, and I wanted you to know that it's something you deserve for all the hard work you've put in, and that Bronwen and I appreciate everything you've done to make this film work. But of course, the credit isn't enough, so after discussing this with Frank we've decided we're going to pay you as a story editor, plus half the fee Deborah Foreman received. All in all, it should amount to something in the region of fifty thousand pounds. It'll be paid into your bank account as soon as we get back to London. Is that all right with you?'

Marian was too stunned to do anything more than nod.

'Good,' Stephanie smiled. 'Well, that was all.' And

shrugging, she turned back up the lane, feeling the tension beginning to ebb from her body. It hadn't been as difficult as she'd expected, and already she was glad she had done it. She had done it to prove to herself and to Matthew that, no matter what was going on in her heart, her professionalism remained intact.

'We can cover it on wild track,' the sound man was telling Matthew, as Marian walked back to Madeleine. 'Or better still, post-sync it.'

'What did she want?' Madeleine hissed.

'You'll never guess,' Marian answered. Then she put her fingers over her lips as Woody yelled for everyone to stand by for another take.

Ten minutes later the unit broke for an early lunch – it seemed the bell ringer had a job to do and he was going to do it despite any feature film. 'OK, let it go,' Woody said into his walkie-talkie, grinning sheepishly – he'd been in danger of forgetting his assistants, who were dotted around the valley playing traffic warden. Almost instantly the blast of car horns started up as vehicles that had been kept stationary further down the mountain were allowed to resume their journeys – each driver having pocketed several thousand lira in return for the favour of a forty-minute delay.

As everyone else filed down the lane to the plateau where the caterers had set up lunch, Marian and Madeleine wandered over to the wall that ran round the piazza.

'Don't knock it!' Madeleine laughed, once Marian had told her Stephanie's news. 'Fifty thousand pounds, eh? Bit like winning the pools, isn't it?'

'Not as good as a lottery, though,' Marian said dryly.

'Oh God, I fell right into that one, didn't I?'

'Head first. And I'm not going to play any games with you about how *we're* going to spend it because this is all mine.'

'You selfish old cow, you.' Madeleine lifted Marian's wrist to look at the time. 'Hey, I'd better go and take Paul his sandwiches. I won't tell you what we got up to in the woods yesterday, but I think I'll take a blanket with me today. You don't think there are any snakes in Tuscany, do you?'

'As a matter of fact there are. So, why don't you come and have some lunch down at the caterers with me?'

'I can't, I promised Paul.'

Let her go, Marian was telling herself. Don't make a fuss. She went yesterday and everything was all right, so there's no reason why it shouldn't be all right today. 'Are you seeing Enrico later?' she asked.

'We're going into Lucca to look at the sights. You know, I think it should be you keeping him company, he talked about you practically all the time I was with him yesterday, and you like buildings and all that stuff much more than me.'

Marian smiled as Madeleine stood up, then turning to see how the queue was doing at the catering truck, she frowned as a familiar figure broke out of the crowd and marched up the lane towards them. 'Maddy,' she said, 'isn't that Deidre?'

Madeleine turned round. 'Yes,' she said, mystified. 'Yes, it is.' Suddenly she whooped for joy and took off down the lane to meet her agent.

'I'm staying with some friends in Florence,' Deidre told her, once Madeleine had relinquished her stranglehold of an embrace, 'so I thought I'd come along and see how it's all going over here. I'm not in the way, am I?' she said to Marian as she ambled up.

'No. Everyone's at lunch, as you can see. In fact, I'm just off to get mine. You're more than welcome to join me if you like, or there's a bar over there if you'd prefer a drink.'

'A drink sounds like heaven,' Deidre sighed. 'Come on, Maddy, you can show me where it is.'

Marian found Matthew sitting on the steps of Christina Hancock's winnebago, eating his lunch with Frank and Grace, who were seated at a picnic table the caterers had set out for them.

'Isn't this a glorious day?' Grace said, as Marian perched on the steps beside Matthew.

'Wonderful,' Marian agreed, glancing up at the clear blue sky. 'Bit cold to be eating al fresco though, isn't it? Still, either that or the dining bus, and I suppose you've made the wiser choice.'

'That's just about what I reckoned,' Frank chuckled. Then peering at Marian from beneath his bushy eyebrows, he asked in a low voice, 'You doing all right out here, are you? I mean, Matthew's told us about – ' he glanced over his shoulder to make sure no one was in earshot, ' – you calling Meyer.'

'Oh, I'm fine,' Marian answered, wishing that just for a moment she could forget all about it.

Sensing the way Marian felt, Grace engaged her husband in lighter conversation, and when Bronwen joined them a few minutes later, Marian turned to Matthew and whispered: 'Madeleine's agent has just turned up.'

'Really?' he said, not hiding his surprise. 'Then let's hope she stays for a bit. One more person to keep an eye on Madeleine won't do us any harm, will it?'

Hazel had seen Bronwen climbing the steps to her cottage, and called her in when she knocked. 'Manfredo's grog,' she groaned, dragging herself up from the lumpy armchair. 'Trying to sleep off the hangover. They're not looking for me on the set are they? Aagh!' she cried, as she bent over to pick up her handbag. 'Remind me not to make any sudden movements.'

Bronwen smiled sympathetically and shook her head as

Hazel offered her a cigarette. 'I want to talk to you about Stephanie,' she said, coming straight to the point. 'Or, to be more precise, Marian and Matthew.'

'Ah yes,' Hazel sighed, releasing two jets of smoke from her nostrils. 'A mystery that, is it not?'

Bronwen perched on the edge of the dilapidated table in front of the window. 'Has he ever mentioned anything to you about Marian?'

Hazel shook her head.

'No, me neither – not that I'd have expected him to, really. Do you think there is something going on between them?'

'It certainly looks like it,' Hazel answered. 'But why he should rub it in Stephanie's face like this is simply beyond me. I mean, it's monstrous.' She took another puff of her cigarette. 'It's a funny old world, isn't it?' she mused. 'There's you married, me divorced and Stephanie still single, yet not one of us has the answers to a damned thing.'

'But we do know the reason Stephanie's never married,' Bronwen said.

Hazel nodded. 'And so does Matthew. You know, if I were Stephanie I'd want to claw the damned kid's eyes out.'

Bronwen sighed with exasperation. 'Oh, I don't know what to do, Hazel. Ever since she's known him she's been in love with him. In the years they were apart there was never another man. He, and their shared career, is all she's ever wanted. And I thought, this time, that it would work out. He seemed just as crazy about her, if not more so. So what's going on?'

The silence was heavy and Hazel waved an arm to clear the air of smoke. 'Do you think there's anything either of us can do? Should we talk to Matthew, confront him with it?'

Bronwen shook her head. 'It's Stephanie who has to do

that, but she won't. She's not really fighting this, and that's what worries me. You see, if he really is in love with Marian and leaves Stephanie again, I'm not sure she'll be able to get over it this time. So we can't let her give up Hazel, we just can't.'

'What!' Sergio spun round, his black eyes blazing. 'She has been to see Tarallo, you say? When?'

'Yesterday. And again this afternoon.' Deidre had already taken an involuntary step back, and now, as he came towards her, she took another.

His face was lined with fatigue, but for the moment anger had pumped adrenalin into his system. He smashed his fist against an easel, sending it flying across the room and adding to the chaos of his already disordered studio. 'She is not to go again, do you hear me? You must stop her. Do anything, but she is not to go near the Tarallo family again.'

'Why?'

'Do not ask questions,' he seethed. 'Just do as I say. It is Thursday afternoon now, you have only to stop her until tomorrow night. Is that clear?'

Deidre's head jerked into a nod. She was still backing away, out of confusion as much as fear. 'And then?' she whispered.

'That need not concern you. The arrangements have been made. You can go back to England.'

'Meaning, I have served my purpose?'

For several seconds Sergio's face remained obdurate, then slowly it relaxed and a softer light came into his eyes. 'You make me sound so callous, *cara*, and I do not mean to be. You are to be my wife soon, is that not what you wanted?'

'You know it is I just wish it didn't have to happen like this.'

Gathering her into his arms, he started to cover her face

with kisses. 'I understand your confusion, my love, but soon it will be over and you and I will marry, here in Florence, and we shall be happy and grow old together.'

'But Madeleine . . .'

'Ssh, *cara*, Madeleine does not matter, it is only you who matter. Tomorrow is for Madeleine, all the tomorrows. Today is for us.'

She knew it was useless to pursue it, and as his kisses grew steadily more passionate she melted against him. This may be the last time, she told herself; he may never hold me like this again and oh God, I don't know if I can bear it.

Later, when he had left for the *bottega*, she sat amongst the confusion of his apartment, staring into space. Her hand was resting on the telephone, which rang once or twice, but he had told her not to answer it. She didn't care who it might be, who he was trying to avoid, that wasn't in her mind at all. She was thinking only about the call she knew she had to make, because she knew now that no matter how much she loved Sergio, nor how much she longed to be his wife, she couldn't go through with it – not when she didn't know what was going to happen to Madeleine. She would lose him anyway, a sixth sense had already told her that, and the glittering excitement in his eyes after they had made love – an excitement almost manic in its intensity had confirmed it. So the fact that she was putting her life at risk by making the call hardly mattered now.

She stared down at the phone. From the way Sergio had behaved when Madeleine turned up on Sardinia, and again just now, she knew that there was only one person who had the answers to her questions, but would he tell her? With dread thumping through her chest and a leaden despair in her heart, she picked up the phone.

Five minutes later she fell back in the chair. Her hair was dishevelled and her hands shook, but the call had been made and tomorrow she would go to the Tarallo villa. Her eyes were drowned in tears which trickled slowly down her face, curving into her mouth and dripping from her chin. 'Forgive me, Sergio,' she sobbed. 'Please forgive me. I love you. I love you so much that it is breaking my heart, but I just can't let you take her away.'

– 28 –

'But it's perfect,' Matthew raged, 'just look at how sinister the place is like this.'

'It's not my fault the helicopter pilot refuses to go up,' Stephanie countered. 'I can't make him risk his life in fog, can I?'

'Have you offered to pay him more?'

'Of course I have, but he turned it down, and quite frankly I don't blame him.'

'And quite frankly, neither do I.' Along with everyone else who was standing on the hillside in the murky morning fog, they burst out laughing. 'Well, there's nothing else for it,' Matthew went on, rubbing his hands together to try and keep them warm, 'we'll have to move the unit up to the swimming pool. I want a high shot, and if that's the highest I'm going to get today, it'll just have to do.'

'It's so good of you to compromise,' Stephanie returned, then covered her ears as he yelled for Woody, and soon the crew were lugging their heavy equipment up over the treacherously steep path to the swimming pool.

Marian, huddled into her padded anorak and the woolly hat she'd borrowed from the wardrobe department, was leaning against the wall outside her cottage, watching them, when Madeleine crept up behind her and dug her in the ribs. 'Boo!' she cried, and laughed as Marian practically leapt from her skin.

'I wish you wouldn't do that,' Marian complained irritably.

'Oh honestly, you're like a bear with a sore head these days. I suppose you were hoping it was Matthew.'

'No, I know where Matthew is, thank you very much, and keep your voice down. Where's Paul?'

Madeleine shrugged. 'I don't know, gone off somewhere to write, I expect.'

'Are you seeing you-know-who again later?'

'Yep. We're going on a tour of Florence today – now won't that be interesting.'

'Maddy, I don't expect Enrico much likes sight-seeing either, especially as he's lived here all his life, but he's bothering to do it to keep you entertained, so you could at least show some appreciation.'

'All right, don't bite my head off. I'll let you into a secret, sight-seeing with Enrico is better than listening to Paul bore on about his book – he's having problems with it and he keeps going on about them. I wouldn't mind, but I don't understand what he's talking about half the time.'

'I wouldn't let him hear you say that if I were you.'

'Oh God, no. Look, if you're not working at the moment why don't we go over to the kitchens and see if Gabriella's got any hot soup.'

'It's supposed to be for the crew, Maddy.'

'Oh God, you really are in a bad mood today, aren't you?'

Marian managed a smile. 'OK, soup it is,' she said, 'but we'll take some up to the crew as well.' And taking Madeleine's arms she allowed herself to be led off down the steps, saying, 'How are you getting down to Camaiore to meet him?'

'Oh, someone will give me a lift, they're up and down all the time.'

As the kitchen door swung closed behind them, Paul walked out from the narrow alley that ran between the cottages. At first he was tempted to go after them, to drag Madeleine out and beat her with all the savagery that was quaking in his body, but something inside him was telling him that wasn't the way, and with a supreme effort he wrenched himself round and stumbled up the steps into the cottage. For several minutes he stood with his back against the door, his breath heaving in his lungs and a blinding rage pounding through his head. Tarallo, the bitch was seeing Tarallo. After everything he had done to stop it, now she was seeing him again. Did they think he was so stupid that he didn't know who they were talking about? How dare they treat him as though he were an imbecile? His fists were clenched so tightly that as he banged them against the wall, his knuckles split and blood poured down his hands. Then, as he raised his face to the ceiling, his top lip curled back over his teeth and his nostrils flared like a wild animal's. He had never known such purity in his hatred, such venom in his anger – all he had worked for, all he had sacrificed himself for, and now she was betraying him. She was slipping from his control, she was lying to him, cheating on him, laughing at him, and he felt such loathing, such uncontrollable jealousy that he wanted to kill her.

Eventually he staggered over to the stairs and dragged himself up to the bedroom. He had to think. He had to sit alone and think. He must forget the fact that even now his people were preparing his house for her, he must forget how he had planned to share his life with her, he must forget everything, and think. Concentrate on her betrayal, on the way she had ridiculed him, on her lies and deceit. He must decide what he was going to do. The anger would pass, he just had to wait and then he would know. Then it would all become clear.

By two thirty in the afternoon the fog was beginning to clear and the sun's rays striped the hillside in a fan of defiant light; as a result, filming had come to a standstill. 'Light won't match,' Matthew explained to Marian when she wandered out of the production office to find out what was going on, 'and no one can find the helicopter pilot.'

'So what are you going to do? Where's everyone going?' she asked, watching the camera assistants wheel their equipment down the lane on a trolley.

'We're going down to the autostrada to pick up some driving shots. The intrepid Hazel has managed to come up with a low-loader.'

'You coming down in my car, guv?' Woody called out as he zoomed past.

'Be right with you,' Matthew answered.

'Christina's costume for Day Twelve is still wet,' Belinda wailed, coming up behind them.

'Then put her in something else,' Matthew barked. 'Speak to Beanie, find out how her continuity is for another day.'

'I've got my own continuity notes, thank you,' Belinda retorted hotly.

'Then use them, and we'll shoot the scenes we can.'

Belinda threw him a resentful look and turned back up the steps.

'Matthew! Do we need the car with the sun roof or the one without?' the man from Action Cars called from down on the plateau.

'Speak to Woody,' Matthew shouted back, then rolling his eyes he took Marian by the arm and led her into the production office, saying, 'You'd better pick up whatever you need pretty sharpish, or knowing Woody, he'll go without us.'

'Not without you, surely.'

'I wouldn't put it past him.'

'Well, you go on, I'll follow later with someone from make-up or costume. In fact, I don't think I'll come. Those car shots always take for ever, and it'll be freezing standing on the side of the road.'

'I can't say I blame you, but we're all going down. You don't really want to stay here on your own, do you?'

'Oh, I'll be all right. Frank's people are in the bar, and besides, I might try to get some sleep.'

'Keeping you awake at night all this, is it?'

She nodded.

His face softened, and as he took a step towards her, her heart started to beat faster. 'I can't say I'm surprised,' he said in a low voice. 'Where's Madeleine?'

'With Enrico.'

'Good.' Then putting his head on one side and looking at her with mild amusement, he said, 'You don't think there might be something starting up there, do you?'

'I don't think so, she's too besotted with Paul.'

'I notice he's not writing today. Has he finished the book?'

'Not as far as I know. I thought he was in the woods somewhere, fighting it out to the bitter end.'

'He wasn't an hour ago because I saw him drive off down the hill in that little Panda they've hired.'

'Really? I wonder where he was going.'

Matthew frowned. 'He doesn't know anything about Madeleine seeing Enrico, does he?'

'Good God, no!' Marian laughed. 'We've been very careful to keep that a secret. We don't even mention his name.'

He looked pensive for a moment, then turned his eyes back to hers. 'It can't go on like this, you know.' Her eyebrows flickered, but then she smiled ruefully as she realised he was still talking about Madeleine and Paul.

'You're right, it can't,' she said, throwing him a look as she leaned across her desk to pick up a paperback.

He caught her hand and turned her back to face him. 'I know what you're thinking,' he murmured, 'but you've got enough on your mind right now without me adding to it. But we will talk, and soon.' He winced as Woody's voice blasted from a loud-hailer, calling his name. 'I think I'm wanted,' he said, with a grin. 'I'll see you later, and no wandering into the forest.'

'At least not in a red hood for the nasty big wolf to get me.'

Laughing and shaking his head, he turned and walked out of the office, leaving her with a storm of emotions hammering in her chest.

At the wheel of her hired Fiat Deidre drove slowly, looking out at the rugged countryside and bleakly wondering how much of it belonged to the Tarallos. Probably all of it, she decided, as she passed acre after acre of vineyards and olive groves; they were one of Italy's wealthiest families.

When she reached the black iron gates with the Tarallo crest, she got out of the car and pressed the bell. A few seconds later the gates swung open, and it was only as she drove through them that she noticed the camera, almost hidden behind a gargoyle on top of the red brick wall.

The drive, which was shorter than she'd expected, was covered in autumn leaves, but the gardens on either side were immaculate: stone and marble statues, fountains and waterfalls, topiaried hedges bordering the flowerbeds. There were no flowers now, but it wasn't difficult to imagine how exquisite it would all look in spring and summer. Deidre parked at the front of the palatial villa, and smiled cordially at the cheery-faced retainer who was waiting for her at the door, and who led her across the sparsely furnished hall towards a door that was already half-open. Deidre's heels clicked on the marble tiles, and from somewhere very far away in the great mansion came the sound of children playing.

The first thing she noticed about the room she was shown into were the vast windows that opened onto a terrace, and then the superb paintings that hung on every wall. Smiling to herself, she walked towards one of them – she'd always wondered whose private collection included this particular Titian. She lifted a hand to touch the frame, then seeing the alarm wires, she pulled back.

'Deidre.'

Starting at the sound of her name, she turned to see a diminutive figure swathed in black lace sitting at one end of an uncomfortable-looking sofa. Sylvestra. It had to be.

'*Buona sera, signora,*' Deidre said. '*Piacere di . . .*'

'We speak English, please,' Sylvestra interrupted. 'I want no one to hear.'

For the first time that day, a tremor of anxiety shook the resolve Deidre had so painfully built up throughout the night. 'I was expecting to see Enrico,' she said.

Sylvestra shook her head. 'It is not my grandson Enrico you wish to see, it is my grandson Arsenio, but I am afraid that is not possible.'

Deidre was confused. 'But . . .' She stopped as Sylvestra raised a bony hand.

'Enrico cannot help you, Deidre, only I can help you. Please, sit down.'

Deidre sat on the more comfortable chair at the other side of the immense marble fireplace and waited patiently until Sylvestra was ready to continue.

'In my heart I always know this day will come,' she began, and her opaque eyes were brimming with sadness. 'I know I cannot protect him forever because it is wrong. What I have done is wrong. Very, very wrong. We are all to blame, maybe me most of all.' She stopped, but understanding that, for the moment, Sylvestra was not with her, Deidre merely looked into the pale, haggard face and tried to swallow her trepidation.

Finally Sylvestra's eyes focused again, and she continued in her thin, heavily accented voice. 'In few days Enrico will bring his brother from the asylum,' she said. 'I will not know him, Enrico tells me, for he has become old. My beautiful Arsenio is old man at thirty. Sergio Rambaldi make him old man. I hate Sergio Rambaldi for what he do to my family, I hate him, yet once I love him as a son. Maybe still in my heart I love him, but he must pay, always I know that one day he must pay.'

'But what has he done?' Deidre pressed, when Sylvestra's attention seemed to drift.

Her answering laugh was more of a croak. 'You wish to know what has happened to Olivia, do you not?'

Deidre's surprise showed. When she'd spoken to Enrico the night before, she had mentioned only that she wanted to talk to him about Sergio Rambaldi and the *bottega*.

'Olivia.' Sylvestra repeated. 'Sergio, he tell me what she do in America, how she took the children to the men who wanted them, how she take the drugs they give her for doing this. She take the drugs, and the men, they take the children. Then someone find out what she does, and she must be taken away from New York before she tells what she knows. You understand, for the drugs she will do anything, she will even confess what she has done. So Rubin Meyer, he ask Sergio to take her. He ask Sergio, because he knows of the work Sergio does at the *bottega*.' She paused. 'Always Sergio wait for this, for one day a woman to come to him this way . . . He took her, but now she is not enough for him, he must have Madeleine too.'

'Why? Why Madeleine?'

'Because of Paul O'Connell, of course.'

'Paul!' Deidre cried. 'Why because of Paul?'

Sylvestra's eyes darted to hers and there was a puzzled

frown on her face. 'You do not know? Sergio did not tell you?'

'Tell me what?' Deidre was now more confused than ever.

Slowly Sylvestra's expression changed from disbelief to resignation. 'Then I shall tell you,' she said flatly. 'Paul O'Connell is Sergio's brother.'

Deidre was dumbfounded. 'Brother?' she repeated at last. 'But he can't be. Sergio is Italian.'

'They have the same mother, but not the same father. I know not who is the father of Sergio; Helen, she never told me. She give birth to Sergio when she is only a child, before she was even sixteen, and then she leave him in Galleno with the Rambaldi family. She knew them a little, but not well. They take her son because I ask them to, but I raise Sergio like he is my own son. Not until Sergio is ten years old does his mother come to see him, and then she tells him he has a brother and that she is married now, she wants him to go to live with her in England, but Sergio has come to love my family and will not leave. So she come sometimes to visit him – not so often – but when she does, she take him to Florence to see her husband and her son, Paul, but Sergio is upset by her visits and he asks her not to come again. But she does not listen, she still come though she leave her husband and son at home. Then slowly Sergio grow to love his mother. He was gifted even as a child, we all knew so, and his mother, she want to help him with his art. She tell him stories of the great Michelangelo and tell him he is genius just like him. For a while Sergio believes, because she tells him, that he is Michelangelo, the, how you say, *reincarnazione*. Then one day Helen, she says she is to leave her family in England to come and live with Sergio here in Italy, to help him with his work, and because Paul does not want her to leave, he kills her.'

'What!' Deidre gasped. 'But this is insane. It's . . .'

'Yes, Deidre, they are all insane, Paul, Sergio and their mother. Paul and Sergio, they inherit her beauty and they also inherit her mind. But in the sons the mind is a dangerous thing. And now Sergio wants to take revenge on Paul, so that is why he wants Madeleine.'

Deidre could feel herself shrinking away from this woman, telling herself that Sylvesta was the one who was insane. Yet in her heart she knew that, despite the unbelievable horror of it all, there was an undeniable truth in what the old woman was saying. She remembered the way Sergio had reacted when she first mentioned Paul's name, she remembered his insistence on knowing what Paul was doing, on making certain that Paul and Madeleine stayed together . . .

'But first,' Sylvestra said, 'I shall tell you of Olivia.'

Again Deidre felt herself pulling away. She could tell from Sylvestra's manner that the story was only going to get worse, and she didn't want to hear any more.

'Everyone, they do not know where she is,' Sylvestra said. 'They do not know if she lives . . .'

'She lives. Sergio told me. I know that she's alive.'

'No, Deidre, Olivia is dead.'

Deidre stopped breathing. She stared at the old woman, a scream of denial ripping through her body. 'But Dario . . . Dario and Sergio, they said . . . They said I would see her again.'

'You will, but not the way you think. I know this because I know what happen at the *bottega*. That is why I see you now, not Enrico. I am very guilty woman, now I tell you why. You are in love with Sergio, no?'

Deidre nodded.

'So you understand the way he, how you say, *ipnotizzare?*'

'Hypnotise,' Deidre mumbled automatically.

'*Sì*, hypnotise with his eyes and with his charm. Every-one love Sergio and want to be with him because he is genius, all Italy knows. But like I say, he is *matto*. Insane. After his mother dies, Rosaria, Enrico's wife, she try to persuade him that he is not Michelangelo, and he believes her, but still he work today how the great Michelangelo work yesterday. He do everything the same, and when he is at the *bottega* he even dress for the quattrocento. But he know there are many great artists and he want to be remembered. So, he is happy to take the daughter of very wealthy American man. Everyone know Olivia. And Madeleine he ask you to make her famous, *sì*?'

'Yes,' Deidre said, remembering the times when Sergio had insisted she do everything possible to put Madeleine in the public eye. 'But he didn't ask me to do it, I . . .'

'It is no matter, she is the one Paul O'Connell loves, and that you make her famous is better for Sergio because not only does he have his revenge on Paul, but all the world will remember him because of what he do to Olivia and Madeleine. You see, he study them the way Michelangelo study the anatomy of man.' She stopped, waiting for Deidre to grasp the magnitude of what she had just said. Then: 'Do you understand what I am saying?'

Deidre's voice was crushed by the horror of her knowledge. Yes, she understood what Sylvestra was saying.

'Michelangelo, he *sezionare*, dissect, the bodies of men. Sergio Rambaldi, he dissect the bodies of women and then he make the great sculpture.'

'No!' Deidre was shaking her head. 'No! You're lying.'

Sylvestra continued as if she hadn't spoken. 'My grandson Arsenio, Sergio is his idol, he follow him he study with him, and when Olivia comes to Italy and the people in New York wish her to die, it is the chance Sergio has waited for to work as Michelangelo worked. The night before the *bottega* meets Arsenio is to give her the drugs – too many – so many they will kill her. But Arsenio, he fall in love with her and he want to save her. The night he give her the drugs he make love with her first, and then he give her too little of the drugs. She is unconscious but she is not dead. But he is afraid to tell Sergio, so that when the *sezionare* begin they hit the, how you say, *arteria,* and her blood pump from her heart. It goes in the eyes of my grandson and it blinds him – after, it is all he can see. He was in shock for many days, and then Enrico take him to the asylum because he cry out the name of Olivia. He should not be in the asylum, but I let Enrico put him there to protect Sergio. I protect him for the sake of Rosaria, because she love Sergio, but now Rosaria is dead and Sergio must pay for what he has done. And yes, you will see Olivia again, because she lives now in the marble that Sergio creates.'

Suddenly Deidre was on her feet. Her face was grey, her eyes burning with anguish. 'Madeleine!' she cried, and ran to the windows, rattling them, trying to get out. She twisted round. 'Where is she? Tell me!'

Sylvestra too looked alarmed. 'She is with Enrico,' she answered. 'They are in *Firenze.*'

For a moment Deidre seemed to relax, and then Sylvestra understood.

'When does he want her, Deidre?'

'Tonight.'

Sylvestra shook her head. 'So soon. We must protect her and keep her with us. But there is not a way to reach Enrico. We must hope for him to bring her here before he return her to the village. You go to village and wait.'

'Yes!' Deidre gasped. 'Yes, I'll go to the village.' And sweeping her bag from the chair, she ran out of the door.

At the very moment Deidre was driving through the gates of the Tarallo villa, Paul was pulling his car to a stop outside the café in Paesetto di Pittore. As he got out, it started to rain, but he felt nothing, not the cold, nor the wind, nor the wet. His only sensations were inside, locked in a ball of fury that burned hotter and more fiercely each time it was touched by the memory of Madeleine's treachery. But despite the rage, despite the loathing and the gall, he felt pleasure – the kind of pleasure that comes when a decision has been made. Now, he had the solution to everything. He couldn't imagine, now, why it had never occurred to him before, but then the Russian doll had never needed to be punished like this before.

He walked onto the terrace of the café, frowning as his memory stirred. It had been many years, but he remembered, he would always remember – and placing his foot on the edge of a table, he kicked it against the railings, revealing the trap door which led to the cellars. Before he opened it he looked around, casting his eyes over the mass of green foliage that clothed the mountains, the sorrowful cottages, deserted as always, the locked door of the café and the rain-spattered terrace on which he stood. A gust of wind suddenly lashed at his body, and he took a step back; but then, as if the wind had galvanised him, he tore open the hatch and lowered himself onto the ladder beneath.

He had not thought to bring a torch; and as he went lower he was engulfed in impenetrable blackness. But he knew that beyond the cellar, hidden behind the endless racks of dusty bottles, there was only one passage, one route which would lead him to his brother.

It took a long time, and many bottles smashed at his feet as he groped about in the darkness, but finally he found it, and pulling back the door, he walked into the tunnel beyond. His feet slithered in the mud, and once or twice he fell against the slime-covered walls, but he pressed on, knowing that soon he would reach daylight.

As he hauled himself from the bowels of the mountain and up into the seething mass of the forest, the rain slammed into his body, pushing him back to the ground; but using the gnarled fingers of tree roots, he dragged himself to his feet and plunged deeper into the forest. He had no more than ten yards to go, and the path was already cut. It was narrow, steep and winding, and lined with vicious brambles, but running alongside was a railing which he used to stop himself falling and to pull himself finally into the sheltered basin.

The cave was an old Etruscan tomb, the mouth concealed by nature, but he threw aside the heavy branches and walked inside.

Grotesque shadows roamed the candlelit walls as men in heavy cloaks paced about a marble slab that gleamed yellowy-white in the gloom, and on the floor and ceiling were strange, warped images of Roman gods. Damp oozed from the walls, dripping grime into a gully that ran along the floor. The smell was acrid, cold and earthy, and the wind outside whistled menacingly round the desecrated tomb. But Paul saw none of this, nor was he aware that the men had stopped and turned to look at him. His eyes were held by the magnificent sculpture at the rear of the cavern, which stood in a blaze of fiery torchlight. The rippling, golden glow animated the alabaster face in a way that made its beauty at once ethereal and demonic. The marble lips seemed to speak to him, coaxing him further into the cave, and her eyes looked upon him with blind adoration. He was spellbound, his breath trapped, but the ivory stone emanated such energy that it seemed to breathe for him; it was silently whispering to him, soundlessly threatening him. In his entire life he had never seen anything so sinister or so beautiful.

'Olivia,' he breathed.

'That is right.'

The spell was broken, and as he turned to see Sergio standing beside him, a searing blade of emotion tore through his chest. Sergio, the son she had claimed to be a genius. The son she had wanted to be with, the son who had made him kill her – his own mother.

Sergio's black eyes were soft and smiling, and as Paul

studied that flawless face it was as though a soothing, icy hand was calming the fire of his rage. Slowly his eyes began to mirror his brother's look of enquiry and the corner of his mouth lifted in a questioning, disdainful smile.

'I thought you would never come again,' Sergio said.

'I was never invited.'

'You have been invited now?'

Paul lifted his eyebrows and, turning away, walked further into the cave. 'I need your help,' he said, looking across the marble slab at a man whose sharp, close-set eyes were fixed on him unblinkingly.

'I see.' Sergio nodded towards the cloaked man, and he and the other figures withdrew beneath an arch into the dark recesses of the cave. Now Paul and Sergio were alone, facing one another across the grisly cavern; two men whose beauty was almost appalling in its perfection, whose features were so alike and yet so different. They were opposite faces of a single coin, cast in the same metal, shaped by the same hand, two works of breath-taking artistry that were part of a single mould. As they looked at one another the power which radiated from Sergio's eyes was matched by the power in Paul's – as if there were a wordless battle between them. In the end it was Sergio who first relinquished the stare, but his manner suggested not defeat but victory, as if he had voluntarily withdrawn from the contest. Smiling, he folded his arms and leaned back against the wall. 'Please, sit down,' he said, indicating the slab of marble, and when Paul was seated he smiled again. 'The last time you were here, you were little more than a child. You have done well to remember the way.'

Paul inclined his head, then lifted his eyes to the face of Olivia's statue. 'I should have known,' he said, 'that she would be here. Is this what you planned for Helen, if she had come?'

'No.' Sergio's voice was flat.

'Then what did you plan for her?' Paul asked, still looking at the beautiful, evil face.

'I had no plans, I wanted only to work. She wanted to be with me for that.'

'So you did not need her. You carried on without her.'

'Of course.'

Outside, the wind screamed through the trees, and the candles round the walls flickered in the chill air that broke through the branches at the cave entrance.

Sergio said in a soft voice: 'It is in the past now. You did what you felt you must and I bear you no grudge.' When Paul said nothing, he continued: 'You say you would like to ask for my help?'

Paul scrutinised his brother through narrowed, suspicious eyes, calculating Sergio's susceptibility to shock; but of course, even if he were to feel it he would not let it show. 'I want to stand trial for murder,' Paul said, finally.

Sergio's expression remained resolutely impassive. 'So you are to confess?' he said.

'If I did, I would be imprisoned for a long time, and that I wish to avoid. No, I want you to hide someone here, let it be known that I have murdered her, then release her after the trial is over.'

'Oh? And who is this person you wish me to hide?'

'Her name is Madeleine Deacon. I see you've heard of her. I want you to hide her and to testify that you saw me murder her.'

'But if she is merely hidden there will be no body.'

'I know, but if I admit to killing her and refuse to say where the body is . . .' He shrugged.

For a long time Sergio examined the face that was turned towards him, disguising his hatred with a look of amused interest as the sweet taste of revenge rose in his throat. In the end he said, 'And when the trial is over you wish me to bring her back into the world so that you may go free? How can you be sure I will do this?'

'I can't. I'm trusting you. But remember that whatever you say in court, nothing will change the fact that I have not killed her, that she is still alive. I shall know where to tell the police to look, and I shall also be able to tell them about Olivia Hastings.'

Sergio nodded. 'Of course.' He sighed, then pushing himself away from the wall, he strolled round the slab to stand behind Paul. 'I will do it,' he said, 'but I wish you to bring her here tonight. Can you do that?'

'Yes.'

'How will you get her here?'

'I'll think of something.' He twisted his body round and peered up into his brother's shadowy face. 'You're afraid she might remember later?'

'Yes.' Sergio clicked his fingers and the man with the close-set eyes stepped into the light. Sergio spoke to him, then the man handed something to Sergio and went away again. 'These are drugs to make her sleep,' Sergio said, handing the small package to Paul. 'You will have to carry her here. My men will be waiting in the café to help you.'

Paul stood up, slipping the package into his pocket.

'Here,' Sergio said, taking a torch from the ledge behind him, 'I can see by your clothes that you came without one. Taking the torch, Paul cast a final glance at the radiant statue behind him, and left.

Sergio walked to the mouth of the cave, watching Paul as he hunched himself against the rain and made a careful journey back down the treacherous path. When he had disappeared from view, Sergio turned to the man who had come to stand beside him. 'You heard?' he said. 'It is obliging of him, no, to make things so simple for me? We will, of course, do as he asks, but you, Giovanni, are to be the one to inform the police. You will give the evidence at the trial. Tonight you must not stay at the *bottega*, you must let your neighbours see you at home, then you must let them see you go for a walk along the mountain path. Do you understand?'

'I understand.'

'Go to the police early in the morning, tell them what you have seen, and then . . .' Sergio's eyes narrowed '. . . then my brother will have his wish – and I mine.'

As he turned to Giovanni his brows were raised, as if he was waiting for his companion to answer a question, and reading his mind, Giovanni said, 'The film is being made on the *autostrada* today, Marian is at Felitto, alone. You would like for me to go there?'

Sergio smiled. 'No, Giovanni, I will go myself.'

A grey mist was rolling into the hills. It wasn't yet dark, but with the storm clouds glowering overhead and becoming thicker by the minute, it soon would be. The rain had stopped only moments ago, but it threatened to be a brief interlude, and Marian was surprised that the crew hadn't returned long before now. Unless, of course, Matthew had decided that the rain would give more atmosphere; if that was the case, they could be down on the *autostrada* for hours yet.

She put another log on the fire, then curled back in the chair to continue reading her book. But after a few minutes she put it down, defeated. There was so much going round in her mind that she had read the same page at least half a dozen times, and she still didn't know what it said.

She looked at her watch. Madeleine should have been back by now, and come to that, where was Paul? He could hardly write out there in the woods with the weather like this. But Matthew had said he'd seen him go off in the car. Maybe he'd driven into Lucca or Viareggio for something. Her mind turned back to Matthew, and she dropped her head in her hands as she started to think about him – then Stephanie, then Olivia, then Boris, then

Sergio Rambaldi and Rubin Meyer, then Madeleine and Paul . . . Round and round and round . . .

She stood up and walked across the room, then back again. She stopped at the fire, stared down at it for several minutes, then fell back in the chair, wanting to cry and yet unable to. Maybe she should join Frank's men in the bar, at least then she would have someone to talk to. But she didn't really feel like talking, she didn't feel like doing anything except curling up and pretending that when she opened her eyes, everything would be sorted out – that the mystery of Paul and Sergio would be solved, and she and Matthew would be together. She let her head loll back against the chair, then glanced at the window as the rain started again. Big fat drops, dripping from the vines that clung to the walls and forming a puddle on the ledge outside.

She started as the wind rattled the door, then closed her eyes with a half-laugh at her edginess. Maybe she should have gone with the crew, it might be cold and wet out there, but it would have been better than sitting in a mountain village driving herself crazy.

She got up again and peered anxiously out of the window. There was no one around, still no sign of the crew returning, nothing but the streaking rain and howling wind. She was about to move away when she saw someone coming up the lane. He wasn't hurrying as one might expect someone to hurry in such weather; if anything, he seemed to be enjoying the elements. Her heart leapt as, for a moment, she thought it was Matthew, but then, as she recognised the tall, lean figure, her lungs turned to two pockets of ice. She jerked herself back from the window, pressing her body against the wall, her veins flooded with fear. What was he doing here? Who was he looking for? Perhaps it was Bronwen – yes that was it, he had come to see Bronwen.

She listened for his footsteps, terror crackling over her

skin like fire. Then, as his shadow darkened the window, a whimper escaped her lips and she fell to the floor. He knocked, several times, and then, just as she thought he was going away, she heard the latch lift. Her heartbeat exploded in her ears, but as the cold air blew into the room and smoke billowed from the fire, she remained paralysed, lying on the floor in the corner behind the arm of the sofa. She screwed up her eyes and prayed to God that he wouldn't see her. She heard him walk up the stairs, his footsteps heavy on the ceiling above her. Then he came down again, and after a silence that seemed to drag on for a lifetime, she heard him walk to the door, then the door close behind him.

Relief surged through her, relaxing the tension in her limbs, but she lay where she was, her eyes still closed, her body as yet too weak to move. Why had he come? What did he want? Oh dear God, please let Matthew come back now. But she wasn't going to wait, she had to go down there, to the *autostrada* and find him. She had to get out of this village where the wind was like the mewling cry of a baby and the rain was like the drum of doom.

Opening her eyes, Marian reached her hand over the arm of the sofa; and then, as she looked up, every muscle in her body screamed with the agony of terror.

'No, oh no, no,' she whimpered as she fell back against the wall.

'But Marian, what is the matter?' Sergio said, his exquisite face creased with concern. 'Why are you so afraid? I am not going to hurt you. Please, let me help you up.' But when he held his hand out towards her, she flinched and cowered further into the corner.

'Please, leave me alone,' she wailed.

'I am not going to harm you,' he repeated. 'You must not be afraid. I only want to talk with you.' He smiled, using only his eyes. 'I need your help, Marian. Now please, come and sit by the fire, you are shaking so.'

Trying to swallow the bitter bile of panic, she somehow managed to stumble to her feet, and this time when he put a hand under her arm to help her across the room, she let him.

'What do you want?' she asked as he lowered her into the chair.

'I want you to do something for me. It is something very important that will maybe put your name in the history of my country, maybe even in your own.'

Her eyes rounded like saucers and he chuckled, a warm sonorous sound that seemed to drive out the chill in the room.

'It is a great thing to be in history, no?' he said.

'Yes,' she nodded, watching him closely and deciding it would be better to humour him.

'I am glad you think so. But still you are afraid, I can see. How can I convince you that I mean you no harm?'

Her eyes shot to the door, and he laughed.

'You would like me to go, I know. But I would like for you to come with me, Marian. I would like to take you where my work is, and to show you how it is done. I want that you should record it, so that all the world will know and understand the way Sergio Rambaldi creates his magnificent art. Only you will know, only to you will I tell the story of my life, of my family, of my art. Please say you will come, please say you will do this for me.'

'But, but I can't,' Marian stammered. 'I – I, well, I'm not qualified, I'm not a writer.'

'Ah, but you are. You write the scenes for this film, no? Bronwen, she tell me how very talented you are, that you have a great future ahead of you. That is why I ask you to do this for me. Please, it is only to ask you to come to my workshop, to listen as I tell you about my life and my methods. I have for you already the pencils and paper you will need. If you prefer I will give you a typewriter. It is up to you, Marian, you must work how best it suits you.'

She stared at him, unable to think of a word to say. She knew that in his mind he was doing her a great honour by choosing her to write his biography, that the life and work of Sergio Rambaldi was already a mystery and a wonder in Italy, and that to write such a book would change her life. But she didn't want to do it, she wanted only to get as far from him as possible. Yet she could think of nothing to excuse herself from it – except to tell him that she was mortally terrified of him.

'I am thinking that you are going to refuse me,' he said. There was no menace in his voice, only sadness, and her confusion deepened as for one earth-shattering moment she thought she might have got it all wrong about him, that he might have been speaking the truth when he said he knew nothing about what had happened to Olivia. As she gazed into his eyes, it was as if he was willing her to understand, willing her to believe him.

'Maybe, if you come to my workshop and see what I do, then if you no like it, if you feel that you do not wish to write the story, then you can leave. Just as you walk in, you can walk out again. I will not make you feel an obligation to me, I want that you do this from choice. All I ask is that you come with me now and allow me to show you some of my work. And as we drive to the workshop I can tell you about myself when I was a child. I can tell you about the Tarallo family . . .'

'You mean Enrico?'

'Sì,' he nodded, smiling encouragingly. 'I mean Enrico. He is like my brother. And Sylvestra, she is more dear to me than my own mother.'

'I didn't know you knew the Tarallos.'

'Why should you? I no longer live with them, my work is in Florence. Enrico's brother, Arsenio, he was with my workshop before he became ill. It is very tragic about Arsenio, it caused us much grief when he had to go away. But Sylvestra, she knows about my work, she understands,

– 687 –

just as Rosaria, Enrico's wife, once did. She come to the workshop often to see me. So you see there is nothing to be afraid of. I know they are your friends, too.'

'Will they be there? Now, today?'

He shrugged. 'Perhaps, but they do not come so often now. Maybe Enrico will bring Madeleine. They are in Florence together, no?'

'Yes,' Marian said, the tension starting to ebb from her body. Only Enrico could have told Sergio that he and Madeleine were going to Florence, and if the Tarallo family often went to the workshop ... But there was something not quite right, it was as if a doubt had become trapped somewhere in her mind as though a door had closed upon it before it had quite dispelled itself. If only Sergio would stop looking at her like that, she would be able to see things more clearly. She felt as though she was swaying, as if her head was filling with dreams and her dread of him was . . .

'Come,' he said, picking up her coat from the sofa. 'It is cold today, you must keep warm.'

'Your workshop,' she said, as she slid her arms into the sleeves, 'is it in Florence?'

'*Sì*,' he lied. 'And we start now by calling it the *bottega*, which is the Italian word for workshop. I should prefer for it to be called that.'

'The *bottega*,' she repeated.

'*Sì, la bottega.*' He held up her scarf, but when she made to take it from him, he laughed softly and threw it around her neck himself, pulling it up round her ears, then tucking it into her collar.

'Shall we run to the car?' he said, as he pulled open the door and they stood facing the storm.

The cold wind seemed to blow into her veins, as if waking her from a deep sleep. 'The car?' she said, confused.

'*Sì*, we cannot walk to Florence.'

'No,' she said. Then, looking up at him, she wondered what she was doing, why she felt so apart from herself. Somewhere in the deep recesses of her mind she knew she was afraid of him, yet somehow her fear no longer rang true. And Frank's men were here in the village, once she got into his car they would follow her, so she would be safe.

Smiling, Sergio took her hand. He closed the door behind them, and asked her if she was ready. Then they ran through the rain, splashing in the puddles and sliding in the mud as they dashed along the footpath to the plateau.

'It is here,' he said, pulling open the door of a red Volkswagen. 'It is not my car, I borrow it from Enrico while mine is in the garage.'

At the mention of Enrico's name, Marian felt her confidence return, and she slid into the passenger seat.

'So,' he said, as he reversed the car into the trees, 'where shall I begin with my story? Of course, when I was born.' He inched the car slowly round the hairpin bend and kept his foot on the brake as they skirted the edge of an open precipice. 'I tell you about my mother only, because I never knew my father. I do not even know his name, she never tell me, she never tell anyone.' And as he continued with the story of his childhood, his growing-up in Galleno with Enrico and Arsenio, Marian sat back in her seat, listening to his rich, melodic tones and smiling at the pictures of the hot, dusty Italian village he conjured up for her.

After a while, as they were nearing the foot of the mountain, he pulled into the side of the road to let a car pass. Marian wiped her hand across the steamy window and watched the blue Fiat as it flew past. 'That was Deidre,' she said, turning to look at him. 'Madeleine's agent.'

'She will kill herself, driving at such a speed on an

evening like this and on roads such as this,' he remarked, as he eased the car back onto the road.

'She must be looking for Madeleine,' Marian mumbled. 'I wonder what's so urgent?'

'I cannot say,' he answered smoothly.

The little blue Fiat squealed to a halt, skidding in the mud and narrowly missing Christina Hancock's winnebago. Deidre leapt out, not even bothering to close the door, and raced up the lane towards Felitto, heading straight for Marian's cottage. When she knocked there was no answer, but when she tried the door it opened, and she ran inside, screaming Madeleine's name.

She ran up the stairs, falling and yelping with pain as she banged her shin on the hard wooden steps. 'Maddy!' she yelled. 'Maddy! Where are you?' There was no reply.

She dashed outside again, the rain streaming over the unruly mass of her auburn hair and the wind rushing through her coat, billowing it like a balloon. 'Have you seen Madeleine?' she yelled as a man ran towards her.

'No,' he shouted back. 'Who are you?'

'I'm her agent. Where's Marian?'

'Isn't she in the cottage?'

'No! There's no one there.'

The man stared at her as though he didn't believe her, then suddenly he threw her to one side and ran into the cottage. Even over the howling wind she could hear him swearing, and for a moment she forgot her own panic and watched as he tore up the stairs to check the bedroom.

'Get down to the bar!' he shouted out to her.

'Why?'

'Just do as I say.' In two strides he was back down the stairs and grabbing her arm, he dragged her through the herb garden, over the flagstones and into the bar.

The warmth of the fire wrapped itself round her, but

she was too dazed to notice. 'What is it?' she cried as the man started shouting at a sleeping figure.

'Get up!' he was yelling. 'For Christ's sake, she's gone!'

'What? What!' the other man said, sitting bolt upright. 'Who's she?' he said, looking at Deidre.

'The cousin's agent.'

'What's she doing here?'

'What are you doing here?' the first man echoed, turning to Deidre.

'I'm looking for Madeleine. She's . . .' She stopped as the door crashed open and Woody all but fell in.

'Fuck me, it's bloody cold out there,' he cried. 'Tell Manfredo to get the grog ready, the unit's on its way back and we're all in dire need of it. What's going on? Why are you all staring at me?'

'Where's Matthew?' barked the man who was standing up.

'Here I am,' Matthew answered, as he came in through the door. 'Phew! Am I glad to get out of that.' Then he suddenly fell back against the wall as Deidre charged past him and out into the rain.

'What is it?' he said, his eyes darkening with alarm as he turned to look at the two men.

'She's looking for Madeleine,' one of them told him.

'Madeleine? Why? And why is she in such a panic?' But before either of them could answer, he turned and followed Deidre out of the door.

'Wait!' he shouted, as she plunged her way down the lane. 'Deidre! Come back!'

He ran after her, closing the gap between them in no time at all, but as he caught her she tore herself from his grasp and stumbled on to her car. 'For God's sake!' he yelled. 'What is it? What's happened?'

'I can't tell you, it'll take too long. But I've got to find Madeleine.'

The rain was coming down in torrents now, but she

pressed on, battling against the wind, trying to reach her car.

'You're going to tell me,' Matthew said, catching her and spinning her round again. 'What is all this? Has it got something to do with Paul?'

'Yes!' she cried, as if suddenly realising it herself. 'Yes, it's got everything to do with him. Where is he? Have you seen him?'

'No. We haven't been here this afternoon. Maybe Marian's seen him. Now, why don't you calm down and come . . .'

'Marian's not there.'

His face turned suddenly pale, and his grip on her wrists tightened so painfully that she squealed as she tried to twist herself free. 'What do you mean, Marian's not there?' he growled, closing his fingers even harder so that the blood was trapped in her veins.

'She's not there!' Deidre screamed. 'I've been there. They're looking for her, those men back at the bar.'

'Oh my God!' he cried. Then pulling her after him, he dragged her back up the lane to the village.

Madeleine was standing beside a taxi in the main street of Camaiore, trying to hang onto her pink plastic hat to stop it blowing away in the wind, while at the same time waving goodbye to Enrico as he drove off round the corner.

'Can you take me up to Felitto, *per favore?*' she called in through the window of the taxi, her voice almost drowned by the sudden crash of thunder overhead.

'*Sì, sì.* Felitto,' the driver nodded, and leaned over the seat to open the back door.

'It's all right, I'll take her.' And to Madeleine's dismay Paul's hand closed over hers, removing it from the door of the taxi.

'Hello,' she said nervously.

'Hello,' he smiled. 'Fancy bumping into you like this. I've just come down to get a newspaper. Where have you been?' he added, looking at the shopping bags she was holding.

'Into Florence,' she answered, truthfully, 'doing a bit of shopping.'

'Come on, let's get out of this rain,' he said, and taking her arm, he steered her into a café.

She didn't know if he'd seen Enrico, though from his manner it seemed unlikely, but nevertheless she was watching him cautiously as he ordered two coffees then asked the waiter where the ladies' room was.

'Why did you ask him that?' Madeleine said, once the waiter had gone. 'I don't want to go to the loo, or have you turned kinky?'

He laughed. 'I just thought you might like to go and sort yourself out a bit. You look like a scarecrow.'

'Oh, thanks very much,' she said, pulling a face at him, and playing straight into his hands she got up from the table and went off to brush her hair.

While she was gone the coffee arrived, and Paul slipped the two pills Sergio had given him into Madeleine's.

'You're looking mightily pleased with yourself,' she smiled as she slipped back into her seat, certain now that he hadn't seen Enrico.

'I ought to be,' he answered. 'I've as good as finished the book.'

'No!' she cried. 'But that's fantastic. We should be celebrating.'

'We shall,' he said, 'but not until it's absolutely complete. Come on now, drink your coffee and tell me how much you've spent in Florence this afternoon.'

'A fortune,' she giggled, picking up her cup and taking a sip. 'I've bought something for you too, but it's a secret for your birthday.'

'Aren't you going to give me a hint?'

'Nope! You'll have to wait. And I got something for Marian. It's a lighting-up Leaning Tower of Pisa. It's so naff she'll probably throw it at me, but I can't wait to see her face when I first give it to her. I'm going to pretend I like it and see what she says. You know what she's like, she'll do anything to avoid hurting someone's feelings and I know already that she'll hate it.'

He smiled, and gazed tenderly into her eyes as she prattled on about everything she'd bought, and how fantastic it was to be here even though the weather was terrible. As he watched her, he felt his insides falling apart. His Russian doll was whole at last, and in the effort of creating her he had destroyed himself. He had closed himself inside her innermost shell, wanting to be the fire that burned in her soul, but in so doing he had stifled his own. He wanted nothing now but her. He wanted her devotion, her love, her laughter, her sorrow; he wanted her life, because he needed it to continue his own.

But they would be together again one day, when all this was over, when Sergio brought her back to the world and he was set free. She would understand why he had done it, and she would love him again.

He waited until she had finished her coffee, then leaning across the table towards her, he whispered, 'You know what I would like to do now?'

'What, here, in the middle of a café?' she yawned.

He laughed. 'Not that. I'd like to go for a drive.'

'We can. Back up to Felitto.'

'No, further than that. Let's drive far, far up into the mountains and pretend we're the only people alive on this God-forsaken night.'

'OK,' she shrugged, 'if that's what you want. But don't let's be too long, I'm starving.'

'Wait here,' he said. 'I'll go and fetch the car.'

'Kiss?' she said as he passed her, but he only looked at her through narrowed, teasing eyes and told her to wait.

'I think you're nuts,' she said half an hour later, as they swung round the mountain's death-bends in the teeming rain. 'But it's quite romantic in a way, with us all cosily tucked up in our little car, safe from the storm. I just wish you'd drive a bit slower.'

He didn't answer, his eyes were fixed rigidly on the road ahead as he steeled himself against her, not wanting her to puncture his resolve.

'We should have popped back and told Marian where we were going really,' Madeleine went on. 'Still, as neither of us is there she'll guess I'm somewhere with you so she probably won't worry.'

When still Paul didn't answer, she reached over and gave his leg a squeeze. 'So you've finished the book.'

When his silence persisted, she started to become nervous. Maybe he had seen Enrico – but if he had, he would have said something by now, surely? Besides, there wasn't anything to find out. It wasn't as if she was sleeping with Enrico. But he's angry, she thought as she stole a quick look at him, I can tell.

'Have you got any idea where we are?' she joked, after a while.

'Yes.'

'Good, because I'm totally lost. Don't you think we should be heading back now? I think I'm about to fall asleep.' She leaned back against the head-rest and closed her eyes. 'God, I'm shattered,' she mumbled. 'All that shopping has worn me out.'

Paul drove on, pressing the car into the deep, cavernous shadows of the winding road. Overhead the thunder drew ever closer, and jagged flashes of light cut a swathe through the black sky and down through the black, blustering mass of trees. The violence of the storm matched the turbulence of his mind as he struggled with the vileness of his rage. He was aware only of an all-consuming need to punish her, to teach her that she must never, never ridicule him, that she must only ever love him. While she wasted and withered in the gloom of Sergio's *bottega*, he would write to her from prison and explain this to her; he would explain that he would come back for her – but only if she swore never to mock him again, if she swore to give herself to him, completely. He struggled then to fight back the flaming tentacles of his rage, he knew they were strangling his reason, destroying his detachment. But he had thought this through, he knew what was going to happen, he understood the logic of it – it all made perfect sense, and as long as he remained calm . . . A sudden bolt of thunder crashed through the heavens and he hit the brakes, plunging the car into a ditch.

As he turned off the engine the windscreen-wipers stopped, and apart from the wind and rain everything was suddenly quiet. He reached up to turn on the overhead light.

'Are you asleep?' he said.

'Mm,' Madeleine answered.

'Then wake up!' And grabbing her by the hair, he twisted her round to face him.

'What! What's happening?' she said drowsily. 'Why are you pulling my hair?'

His eyes glittered unnaturally and his teeth were bared in a savage snarl. 'I loved you,' he spat. 'You were an ignorant, vain, greedy little whore, but I was going to give you everything.'

'What? Paul, what's happening?' She could barely lift the lids of her eyes.

'Enrico Tarallo!' He hissed the name. 'You are fucking with Enrico Tarallo.'

'No, no. It's not true,' she mumbled.

'You're a liar.' He slapped her face and her head cracked against the window, but still she couldn't shake off the sluggishness that was weighting her brain.

In the rearview mirror he saw car headlights sweep

across the road, then disappear; letting her go, he reached across her and threw open the door. 'Get out,' he growled, and when she didn't move he pushed her and she rolled awkwardly into the ditch.

By the time he walked round the car, she was unconscious. Paul stared down at her, loving her and hating her, and feeling his head burst and crack with the torment of it, like the sky overhead exploding with its thunder. From here he would carry her, holding her in his arms and letting the rain beat down upon them. He would miss her, and already he could feel the ache in his body, the emptiness of his heart, the slackness of his limbs. Without her he would be nothing – but while he languished in a cell, waiting for his trial, he *wanted* to be nothing. He wanted to live only for her, for the glory they shared, and the glory they would have on the day he was set free – the day they were reunited.

The bewildering remoteness from reality Marian had felt as Sergio was driving her here had vanished. Now, as she stood at the mouth of the cave, blind terror was pinching her face, racking her body, crawling over her skin and thudding great jolts of panic through her heart. Her shoulders were heaving with the effort of steadying her breath, but as she stared at the ungodly sight of Olivia Hastings quivering in a nimbus of torchlight – so perfect, so majestic, so proud yet so obscene – the petrified weight in her stomach erupted in a bitter rush of vomit.

Sergio was standing behind her, and as she fell against the wall he nodded to someone who came forward from the shadows, took her by the shoulders and led her to the back of the cave.

'I want to leave,' she sobbed. 'Please, let me go.' But as she peered into the face of the man holding her, she knew the futility of her cries.

'What are you going to do to me?' she whispered,

turning to Sergio, knowing already that he couldn't let her go, not now that she had seen Olivia.

He smiled, sorrowfully. 'Please, Marian, do not be afraid. As I told you I do not wish to harm you. But it is necessary for you to remain here now, with me, until my work is complete – I am sure you understand.'

'But Olivia,' she mumbled, hardly aware of the saliva that was running from her mouth, 'what did you do to her? Where is she now?'

'But she is here,' Sergio said, as if surprised by the question. 'Do you not see her?'

'Oh no!' Marian sobbed, squeezing her eyes shut and trying to block out the stench of damp, mouldering earth which, mingled with the smell of candlewax, was turning her stomach over again. 'But is she alive?' she choked.

'She had to die, Marian. The people in New York wanted her to die, so they send her to me for my research.'

'Sergio,' she pleaded, 'I can't do this. I can't help you. Please let me go.'

'But I have already explained, *cara*.' He paused as a bolt of thunder boomed overhead. 'I have chosen you. You are the one to document for history what happens here at my *bottega*.'

'But it's . . .' She was about to say 'insane', but stopped herself, suddenly realising that this was the literal truth. 'You can't do this, Sergio. Someone will come to find me.'

'They will never find you, Marian.'

It sounded so like a death threat that she staggered against the man beside her, who, catching her, pushed her gently to the floor. Then she saw Rubin Meyer emerge from the shadows; but he didn't look at her as he stooped beneath an arch and disappeared into the gloom.

Sergio was still standing at the mouth of the cave; he looked more striking than Marian had ever seen him, but as he moved towards her, his large though slender frame casting grotesque shadows across the walls, his presence seemed almost demonic. His black eyes glittered in the flickering light, and the shadow of his long nose fell over his mouth so that when he smiled, it blackened his teeth. Marian recoiled, closing herself into a tight ball and crossing her fingers as if to ward off the evil he emanated.

But then he stopped, and sitting on the marble slab, he leaned towards her. 'Tonight you will witness my work,' he told her in his mesmerising voice. 'You will see with your own eyes the method I employ – the method of the great Michelangelo. This,' he went on, patting the slab he sat on, 'is the marble from which it will spring. On here she will lie, and as I begin the research and open the veins, the marble will receive her life-blood. Then we will explore her bones, her muscles, the shape of her body, and from it we shall make the sketches, the *maquettes* to carve the marble.'

Marian only stared at him. She knew now, beyond any doubt, that he was insane, and she knew too that there was nothing she could do – except pray. Lowering her head, she started to mumble the Lord's prayer. Then, to her horror, Sergio joined in, and when she looked at him his eyes were closed, and she could tell from the crease between his brows that he spoke the words in earnest. The profanity was absolute, as was her revulsion. Then her eyes shot to the mouth of the cave as the branches were swept back and a man dressed in a long black cloak, the hood almost covering his face, spoke to Sergio in Italian.

When he had finished, Sergio turned again to look at her, and his expression was tender and concerned. 'You must prepare yourself, Marian,' he said quietly. 'The woman is shortly to arrive, and it will be a great shock to you when you see her. But maybe when you see her, you will understand why it was that I chose you, for I know that you will write this from the heart.'

Marian was shaking her head, staring at him with wide, agonised eyes; she knew who the woman was going to be.

'No,' she whispered, 'no, you can't do this, Sergio. Please, you've got to get help. You can't do this, it's butchery, it's evil. Oh please, Sergio, don't kill her. I'll do anything, please . . .'

'Ssh!' he soothed. Then, as the branches at the door parted again, he turned away, and Marian's horror was compounded by the figure standing before her, rain dripping from his hair, mud spattered over his face, and in his arms the lifeless form of Madeleine.

'Paul!' she gasped. 'Paul! You can't let him do this. You love her. You . . .' But a hand closed over her mouth, cutting off her words.

'What's she doing here?' Paul said, looking from Marian to Sergio.

'She knows about Olivia,' Sergio explained.

Paul nodded, then walking to the marble, he laid Madeleine's body down. When he had arranged her hair he stooped to kiss her, placing his mouth tenderly over hers. Again Marian felt her stomach churn.

'You must go now,' Sergio told him. 'Your wishes will be carried out, you will be arrested in the morning.'

As Paul rose to his feet the two men stood facing one another, and Marian's heart stood still as she saw, for a fleeting moment, the resemblance between them. She saw also the strange power that seemed to emanate from them both – the air around them was suddenly thick with it – so that again she started to pray in a desperate attempt to ward off the evil. Her eyes remained closed as she willed herself to break free of the nightmare, for surely it could only be that this whole bizarre dream had stolen upon her in some dark hour of the night and was now refusing to let go. But when she opened her eyes again Madeleine was still lying on the slab, and Sergio was standing over her. Marian looked around for Paul, but he was no longer there. Then Sergio turned to look at her, and bent to touch her face as if to say he was sorry, but when she gazed up at him with imploring, beseeching eyes, he shook his head sadly and moved away.

It seemed to Marian as if many hours passed before he came back into the cave, and dimly she wondered what was beyond the arch behind her. She could hear nothing, even though the storm had lessened. She would have tried to run for help, but the man who had come to her when she was sick was still sitting with her. She glanced at him; he was staring sightlessly into the shadows, and when she spoke, pleading with him to let her go, he merely looked at her with round, uncomprehending eyes. She attempted to stand up, to go to Madeleine, but he pulled her back, shaking his head, and as she stumbled to the floor hot, bitter tears of rage and frustration sprang to her eyes. This *was* a nightmare, it had to be. Things like this didn't happen in real life, they belonged in the realms of fantasy. She began to sob; if this was only a fantasy, why couldn't she shake it off? Why didn't Matthew come? If only she'd gone with the unit . . . Why did Madeleine look so pale? What were they going to do to her? Her eyes flew to Olivia's face, and her breath heaved violently in her lungs.

When Sergio finally came back into the cave, he was dressed in the black cloak she had seen the others wearing, and beneath it she saw garments that were shabby and stained with white dust. She tried to speak, but the words were a dried mass in her throat. Her limbs were heavy, her eyes were aching, and her mind was slowly going numb. A few minutes later she counted seven figures moving into the cave, and she followed them with her eyes as they positioned themselves round the slab. Sergio walked to a stone ledge that was strewn with the tools of a sculptor's trade; his back was turned, so she was unable to see his face. Then there was movement round the slab, and she watched as three of the cloaked figures started to remove Madeleine's clothes while two more came to bind her hands and feet.

'I apologise,' Sergio said, 'but once the dissection begins, we cannot run the risk of you getting in the way.'

Marian was too stupefied to answer, and she put up no fight as two women, whom she had first thought were men, wound wire about her wrists and ankles; not tight enough to stop the blood, yet secure enough to cut into her skin if she tried to break free.

And then, one by one, the candles were doused, so that only the candle on the ledge beside Sergio flickered in the cold air blowing in from the hills. Marian knew she should do something, try again to persuade him to let them go, but she was paralysed, rooted in shock and fear.

Sergio began to chant in Italian, or perhaps it was Latin, moving his hands slowly over his implements as if sanctifying them. The others remained silent, all of them now standing over Madeleine's naked body. Then, as Sergio moved to the head of the slab, Marian saw the blade glint in his hand, and as he raised it high in the air above Madeleine's head there was a chorus of voices: '*Lunga vita alla donna! Lunga vita al nuovo rinascimento!*'

And then, as the knife plunged towards Madeleine's body, Marian screamed. Screamed and screamed. And suddenly the nightmare of Pittore was with her, and she understood again, as she had on her first night in Felitto, that it had been a premonition: the screams had always been hers. She carried on screaming as she saw Madeleine's blood flow onto the marble, as the silver blade was plucked from the gaping wound in her chest and moved steadily to her face, where it sank deep into the soft pink flesh of her lips.

Someone was holding her down, and the wire bit savagely into her wrists as she struggled to break free. They were speaking to her, soothing her, chiding softly in her ears, but she carried on screaming, her voice hoarse and stricken as she begged Sergio to stop.

Then there was another voice, booming through the

silence, arresting Sergio's hand, and Enrico was standing at the mouth of the cave.

'He's killed her!' Marian sobbed, and her head fell to her chest. 'It's too late, Enrico. It's too late.'

'Marian!'

She looked up, and there was Matthew, pushing past Enrico and running towards her. 'Matthew,' she cried, 'Matthew! She's dead. He's killed her.' Then, before he even had time to reach her, she passed out.

– Four Months Later –

– 29 –

Madeleine Deacon's murder was still a mystery to the world at large. The police had never released more than the bare facts of what had happened that night in the mountains, and as a result conjecture was rife. It was said that both Paul O'Connell and Sergio Rambaldi had been arrested, and that both had been charged with murder, though which of them had killed Olivia Hastings and which Madeleine Deacon, was still not clear. In the public outcry attending Madeleine's murder, the discovery of Olivia Hastings' body in a shallow grave at the back of the *bottega* had gone almost unnoticed, at least in Italy; in the States the discovery was followed by arrests and the shocking revelation of Olivia's criminal activities before she disappeared. But in Italy all anyone cared about was who exactly had killed whom up there in the hills. In the end, Inspector Vezzani, the policeman in charge of the case, issued a statement confirming that at the present time Sergio Rambaldi and Paul O'Connell were were being questioned about the murder of Madeleine Deacon, but that the police were satisfied that Paul O'Connell had played no part in the death of Olivia Hastings.

It was known that Marian Deacon had been present when Madeleine's murder took place, that she had been rushed to a hospital in Florence straight afterwards, and from there had been taken to the Tarallo villa in Tuscany where she had remained ever since. A virtual army of policemen and bodyguards now surrounded the villa to keep the press at bay, and only once had anyone managed to capture a photograph of Marian as she played with

Tarallo's sons in the villa gardens. Apart from the police, those leaving or entering the villa did so in fast-moving limousines whose tinted windows defied both the photographic lens and the human eye. For lack of anything else to write, some newspapers hinted at a romance between Enrico and Marian, but with nothing to substantiate it, the rumour quickly died.

Then one journalist got a break from Sergio Rambaldi's lawyer. Sergio Rambaldi, the lawyer declared, was not responsible for Madeleine's death; it was Paul O'Connell who had administered the lethal dose of drugs which killed her. As this was the first mention there had been of drugs, the press had a field day, and elaborated the story with a presumed love affair between Madeleine and Sergio. However, when the expected response from O'Connell's lawyer failed to materialize they started badgering the police again. Under pressure, Inspector Vezzani would say only that until such time as Marian Deacon was well enough to corroborate or deny the statements given by Rambaldi and O'Connell, he was unable to comment. The truth was that Marian, Sylvestra and Enrico had talked endlessly with the police since the night of Madeleine's murder, and that Inspector Vezzani and his superior officers now knew everything that had happened right down to the last detail; however, the Tarallo family had asked that, until such time as it became impossible to withhold the full facts of the case any longer, only the minimum of information should be given out – and after discussion, the police had agreed to comply with their request.

Sergio Rambaldi's lawyer, too, had spent a great deal of time at the Tarallo villa, questioning Sylvestra and Enrico, going over and over the details of Sergio's life and trying to find enough evidence to declare his client unfit to plead. But as soon as Sergio discovered what his lawyer was about, he had dispensed with his services – he had every intention of standing trial for the murder of Olivia Hastings.

However, Paul O'Connell had no such intention with regard to Madeleine. At first, of course, he had willingly confessed to her murder – but that was before he knew that Madeleine was actually dead, that Sergio Rambaldi had been arrested, and that Enrico Tarallo knew all there was to know about his plans for Madeleine's kidnap. In the end, after a great deal of consultation between doctors, the highest ranking police officers and the Tarallo family, both Sergio and Paul had been charged with the murder.

Now, Paul knew, his only hope of walking from San Vittore prison a free man lay with Marian. She had seen him carry Madeleine into the *bottega*, she must have witnessed all that had happened afterwards, so surely she must know that Madeleine had still been alive when the knife went into her chest. But unless Marian came forward and said so, there was only his word to say that he had felt Madeleine's breath on his cheek when he'd kissed her.

Marian was well aware of what Paul was thinking – the police kept her informed almost daily. She knew also that as soon as she said the word, the charge of murder would be dropped against him. But she wanted him to suffer, she wanted him to tear himself apart with the fear that she might never speak in his defence; she wanted him to know what it was like to be helpless, as Madeleine had been helpless the night he took her to the *bottega*.

'I understand how you feel,' Enrico said, as they strolled arm in arm through the villa gardens one morning. 'None of us wishes to see him set free, but there is always the chance that he will not be. After all, whether he killed Madeleine or not, he has still committed a crime.'

'You mean, kidnap?' Marian said.

'Yes. Or maybe even attempted murder. With Sergio, of course, there is no doubt – he will be tried for murder.'

Marian felt the chill of those words run through her

body, and as she gazed out at the undulating hills that surrounded the Tarallo villa, she felt the nightmare of that night closing in around her again. She could see Madeleine's face as she lay on the slab, so soft, so peaceful, so unaware . . . Then the knife ripping into her lovely skin, and the rich, proud colour of her blood as it poured from her chest, while the silver blade dug deep into the delicate flesh of her lips. It was horrible, so horrible that Marian still recoiled from the reality of it, desperately twisting her head this way and that to push the appalling image from her mind.

She sighed, and drew herself closer to Enrico. Overhead the sky was serene, with not a cloud in sight, and though the air was bitingly cold, the spring sunshine added a brilliance to the flowers that were just starting to bloom and a richness to the green, tangled mass of trees that spread across the distant mountains. Again she shivered; though she had roamed those hills many times since that night, had allowed Enrico to show her their beauty, she knew that if she lived to be a hundred, she would never be able to look at them without remembering. She had gone back to them deliberately, to try and force herself to accept the reality of what had happened, to stop herself shutting it out as though it were nothing more than a gruesome nightmare. To accept it, to try to understand it, was the only way she knew of coming to terms with it.

Eventually Marian turned and looked into Enrico's face, her eyes moving slowly over the smooth olive skin, the large nose, the kind, generous mouth and gentle eyes. 'I don't know how I would have coped with all this without you,' she said.

His face was suffused with sadness and guilt as he looked away. She knew he blamed himself; he believed that if he and Sylvestra had spoken earlier, none of this would have happened. She hugged his arm in an effort to return some of the comfort he had given her these past months, and as she gazed up at him, a slow, affectionate smile came into his eyes.

'The police have been very patient,' he said, as they turned to walk on, 'but they cannot continue like this much longer. Inspector Vezzani has wanted for some time that you see Paul and speak with him.'

'I know. I just wish the Inspector could tell Paul himself; that I didn't have to see him, ever again.'

'If that is what you want, then he will do so, you know that. No one is forcing you to see Paul.'

'But if I don't, it will all have been for nothing.'

They stopped at a bench that was set against the wall separating the gardens from the tiers of olive groves behind, and as she sat down, Enrico watched her, marvelling, as he had done many times before, at the truly remarkable woman she was. For all she had suffered, all the grief she had known, she had still managed to bring laughter into the lives of his sons, had touched his own heart with a warmth he had never thought to feel again, and had shown the kind of courage that might put any man to shame.

'I'll see him,' she said finally. 'I'll see him alone, if that's what he wants, but only if we do things the way Inspector Vezzani said. I want you to be in the next room, I want you to listen, and in the end I want him to know that you've been listening.'

'It will be as you wish.'

'Where will it happen?'

'At the prison.'

Marian closed her eyes and let her head fall back against his arm. 'Oh, Paul O'Connell,' she murmured, 'if only I'd known what hell you were going to bring into our lives. If only you knew the nights I've lain awake thinking about you, planning for you the vilest, most degrading death I could imagine. And now I'm going to do as you ask. Why? Why should I do it?'

'You know why, *cara*,' Enrico answered softly. 'You and I both know that you have no choice.'

She turned to look at him, a grim smile on her lips – lips that were so close to his, he very nearly gave in to the temptation to kiss her. 'Because the drugs didn't kill her,' she said, 'and because Inspector Vezzani can't hide that fact any longer.' She leaned forward then, resting her hands on either side of her knees as if to propel herself to her feet. Enrico had come to know this restlessness in her, and he put a soothing hand on the back of her neck. 'If only that was all Inspector Vezzani wanted us to reveal, this would be so much easier, Enrico. So very much easier.'

They looked up as they heard someone cough, and saw Sylvestra emerge from the blossom-covered path which led to the house. As always, her slight figure was clad in black, and her face was shrouded in a heavy veil. 'I thought to find you here,' she said, as Enrico offered her his arm and led her to the bench. 'You have spoken, you have made the decision, *sì*?'

'Yes,' Marian answered.

'Then we must call Inspector Vezzani and have him make the arrangements.' Her gnarled fingers covered Marian's and she said, 'You are very brave, child, and you must continue to be brave, for all our sakes. Then will come the time for you to continue with your life.' She paused, and despite the veil Marian could feel the warmth and compassion in her eyes. 'You understand why I say this, no?'

Marian nodded. 'Matthew.'

'*Sì*. He call again, a few moments ago. I speak with him and tell him you cannot come to the phone, but he is very worried about you, Marian. I tell him that you are all right, that we have come to love you and we are happy to take care of you, but he needs to see you. He is deeply hurt that you have turned away from him since this happen to Madeleine, but he understand why. We all understand, *cara*.'

Marian's heart was churning as she pictured Matthew's face, but somehow she managed a smile as she said, 'I'll call him, I promise. As soon as I've seen Paul, I'll ring him.'

It was just after six in the morning, the sun barely breaking the horizon, when the two cars set off on the long drive to Milan. Marian had been surprised to find the chauffeured limousine waiting for them in the villa forecourt as well as the police car – she thought Enrico was going to drive her in his own car. Then she saw Sylvestra already sitting in the back of the limousine, and giving Enrico a curious look, she got in beside her. Sylvestra hadn't said she intended to come with them, and Marian wasn't sure that she should; she rarely left the villa these days, she was old, and the ordeal of the past months had taken its toll on her perhaps more than anyone. But as the trembling fingers reached out for hers Marian smiled and lifted them to her cheek; she understood Sylvestra's need to be here – she had the right to be here.

The journey was a long one. None of them talked much, all sunk in their own thoughts. Sylvestra slept for a while, her head resting on Marian's shoulder and the black lace of her veil fluttering gently as she breathed. In the car behind them sat Inspector Vezzani and three other policemen Marian had come to know over the past four months, but only the Inspector would come into the prison with them.

At last, just after midday, the two cars turned from the road and came to a stop in front of a barrier. Enrico got out, as did Vezzani, and Marian listened as they talked to a uniformed guard. Though she understood little of what they were saying, she knew that Vezzani's superiors had contacted the prison governor about their visit. Then

Enrico got back into the car and the guard told the driver which of the sombre, grey-stone buildings they were looking for, slapping a notice on the windscreen to indicate that they not only had clearance, but were guests of the governor.

Some ten minutes later they entered the prison, and then began one of the longest journeys of Marian's life as they were led through a warren of cold, drab, sinister corridors and stairways, stopping every twenty yards for a gate to be unlocked, then locked again once they had passed through it. They saw no one, apart from prison guards and a few men in white coats whom Marian assumed to be doctors. There were none of the sounds of life being lived, nor any sign of prisoners – it was like walking through a derelict building one knew to be haunted. Marian didn't know how she was feeling inside, it was as if she had drawn apart from herself in an effort to numb the sensation of dread that had been with her ever since she had made the decision to come. She was aware of nothing now but the hand on her arm which she covered with her own, and the comforting presence of Enrico and Vezzani as they walked behind her.

Finally the guard who was escorting them, who had not uttered a word since they arrived, stopped at a blue door which he opened without using a key. Enrico and Vezzani stood aside for Sylvestra and Marian to walk in ahead of them, and Marian found herself in a small, stark room containing nothing more than a table and half a dozen metal chairs. She walked over to the window, but it was barred, and the glass was thick and frosted so that she was unable to see out. She turned round as she heard the door close, and found that the prison officer had gone. She looked at Enrico.

'Are you all right?' he asked, pulling a chair forward for her to sit down.

She took a deep breath, trying to relax the nervous

tension that had suddenly tightened her stomach. 'I think so,' she answered, smiling weakly. 'Where are you going to be?'

'Through here,' Vezzani answered, pointing to a door she hadn't noticed before. 'It is so close that we do not need the radios to hear, we shall leave the door open a little way.' He glanced at his watch, then his keen eyes moved back to Marian's. 'Now, you understand what you are to do? If we have the confession about his parents, then he will stand trial for murder; if we do not, the charge will be only one of accessory to murder – but if his lawyers are very clever there is a possibility that the accessory charge may be dropped, which means he will be set free.'

'I understand,' Marian answered. They had gone over and over this the day before. She could tell Paul as many lies as she liked, threaten and cajole as much as she needed, but in the end she was to tell him the truth – that he was not guilty of Madeleine's murder.

They all turned as the door opened and a prison officer came in. After exchanging formal greetings, he led the others through to the small room beyond, leaving Marian alone to cope with her nerves.

It seemed an eternity before the door opened again, and immediately Marian closed her eyes, willing herself to remain calm. She listened to the footsteps, to the guard telling her he would be outside; then, as the door closed again, she lifted her head and opened her eyes. He was sitting behind the table, his blond head tilted to one side and his dark eyes, as they looked back at her, seemed tired and bewildered. His handsome face was grey and haggard, and the lines round his eyes cut deep into the skin. Although the sleeves of his jacket hardly reached his wrists and the buttons strained across his chest, she could see he had lost weight, but as she looked at that powerful body it was as though the whole, horrible nightmare was with her again, and she turned away, not wanting him to see her revulsion.

'Thank you for coming,' Paul said quietly. 'I thought for a while that you weren't going to. It's so difficult to know what's going on when you're in here, even my lawyers aren't finding it easy to get straight answers from the police.'

As she turned back to look at him, her grey eyes were steely, and she knew now that she could handle this – that he would be unable to rouse any sympathy or sorrow in her because her hatred was so solid that there was no room for anything else. 'Are you expecting sympathy?' she said coldly.

'Of course not.' He looked back at her, his gaunt face torn with anguish, then taking a deep breath, he let his head fall forward. 'Oh Marian,' he groaned, 'please, don't be like that. I understand how difficult this is for you, but I didn't kill her. You know I didn't. Please say you believe me. Please say that you knew she was alive when I left.'

'But I didn't, not then. She did not regain consciousness before the knife hit her, so how could I have known?'

'But you know now?' he said, and his expression was so pathetic that for a moment her resolve wavered.

Quickly she pulled herself together, and with her hands clutched tightly round her bag she said, 'The police tell me that you've never expressed any remorse for Madeleine's death – that all you've ever sought to do is clear yourself. And yet, if you hadn't taken her there . . .'

'Marian! How can I express regret when I don't feel it? How can I tell them I'm sorry he killed her when all the time I knew he would? I wanted him to, I wanted to be rid of her. Surely you of all people understand that.'

'Understand?' she gasped, her head suddenly spinning with confusion. 'How can I understand that, when you always said you loved her?'

For a moment Paul too seemed bemused, and shook his

head as if trying to clear it. 'But I never loved her, Marian. I only ever loved you. I did it all for you . . .'

'No!' she cried, pushing herself back in her chair. 'No, you're lying!'

His eyes were filled with tenderness as he reached out for her hand, but when she ignored him he only smiled. 'I had to do it, Marian, it was the only way I could see to get her out of our lives. She pestered me when we were in Bristol, she never stopped begging me to leave you, she would never allow herself to believe that I could love you more than I did her. But I despised her. She was just an empty shell. She didn't understand your worth, she ridiculed you and taunted me with your virginity, saying I was a failure as a man. But you and I both know it wasn't like that. For us it was special, there was something beyond sex, beyond anything she could ever comprehend, and in the end the only way to show her how worthless she was was to do what I did. I got her away from you. I did it in such a way that later you would recognise her treachery, see her for what she really was . . . I was always going to come back to you, Marian, always. I will now, it's all I want in the world, to be with you again. To give you everything I have, to share my life and my love with you. That's why you've got to tell them that I didn't kill her, so that we can be together. Please, Marian, try to understand the sacrifices I have made for us. I know you still love me, I see it in your eyes every time you look at me, and God knows how it's torn me apart not being able to hold you and kiss you the way I want to. Please, Marian, don't let all this be for nothing. Even if you didn't know she was still alive when I left, you can say that she was – no one will know. Do it for us, Marian. Do it so that we can be together again.'

Throughout the entire speech Marian sat motionless in her chair, at first too stunned to interrupt, and in the end so appalled that she wanted only to get up and run as far from him as possible. He had filled her with such shame that she could not even begin to break free of it, and even now, as she gazed back at him, her face was still paralysed by the shock of all he had said.

'I love you, Marian,' he said, and his voice was imbued with such feeling that at last something inside her snapped and she spoke.

'You are a truly despicable man, Paul O'Connell. How could you think I would believe even a single word of the filthy lies that have poured from your mouth? I only realize now how truly fortunate I was to lose you when I did. You are beyond any feeling of pity I might have had for you. Some things I might just have been able to excuse: your sickening lack of integrity, the way you have tried to shift the blame for Madeleine's death onto me. But what really disgusts me, what I'll never be able to forgive, is what you've just said about Madeleine: the way you accused her of being all the things you are yourself. I will say *nothing* that will in any way contribute to your release. As far as I'm concerned, if they were to incarcerate you in the darkest, deepest bowels of hell you still wouldn't be suffering half what you deserve to suffer. You are going to stand trial for murder, Paul O'Connell, and the whole world is going to know what . . .'

'Marian, listen to me. I know this has come as a shock, I understand your anger. I'd forgotten how much you've changed, I shouldn't have broken it to you like that. Let's start again, let's go back to the beginning and forget . . .'

'I can never forget, Paul. *Never!* And you're going to pay for what you've done to Madeleine, you're going . . .'

'Revenge, Marian? Is that what you want? After all this time, are you really still so bitter?'

'This has got nothing to do with us, Paul, all that's in the past. I stopped caring a long time ago.'

'Then why did you come?'

Her mind was reeling, and as she stared at him she

knew her silence was only confirming his belief that she still loved him. Yet how could she tell him the reason why she was here? How could she say she wanted him to confess that he was a murderer?

His eyes were overflowing with emotion as he leaned towards her and said, 'Haven't you understood anything I've been saying, my darling? Do you still really believe that I cared for Madeleine? How could I, when from the first time I saw you I have only ever loved you? You must put her out of your mind now, Marian, you must forget all that has happened, or there can be no future for us. You have to let go of your bitterness because there's no need for revenge. I want *you*. I've always wanted you.'

'Stop it!' she cried. 'Don't you understand that I know what you're trying to do? Can't you see that you disgust me with your insidious lies? You're incapable of feeling, Paul, it's beyond you; you proved that the day you left me, and you've proved it over and over again with Madeleine. You're sick, Paul, you need help before you destroy any more lives.'

'Yet you're prepared to destroy ours?'

'We don't have a life to destroy, Paul. Can't you see that I despise you? I despise you for what you are, for all that you're saying, but most of all I despise you for what you've done to Madeleine. I loathe your foul deceit, the arrogance that makes you believe you're going to wriggle your way out of here and back into my life. It'll never happen, Paul, *never!* I detest the very sight of you, and I have done ever since the day I saw you walk through that door in Holland Park and back into Madeleine's life. It was as if I was seeing you for the first time that day, and I knew then that there was something about you, Paul, that was not only corrupt, but evil.'

All the time she was speaking his expression was changing, and she could see that at last she was getting through to him. Yet she had no idea what was going through his mind as he watched her, his hands bunched loosely on the table in front of him and the corner of his mouth drawn in a smile.

Finally he sat back in his chair and peered at her through arrogantly lowered lids. 'Quite a speech,' he remarked. 'Coherent, too. You are getting better. So if that really is the way you feel about me, what are you doing here? What do you want?'

Since he had first come into the room he had been in control of the situation; everything he wanted to say had been said, and he had given her no opportunity to steer him in the direction she wanted. It was almost as if he knew what she was after – though that could hardly be possible. Now she was angry with herself for having allowed him to affect her so powerfully; she had lost sight of her purpose, and for a moment, now, she was at a loss as to how to begin again.

When she looked back at him he was studying the floor, as if he had become bored with her presence, and suddenly she knew that the only way to deal with Paul was to tell him the truth. To shock him, to catch him off his guard. But he was clever, cleverer than her, and she knew it wouldn't be easy.

'I came,' she began steadily, 'because I know that you killed your mother and father.'

His head snapped up as if she had struck him, and his face turned such a deathly white that for a moment she thought he would attack her. Then suddenly he laughed, a deep, scornful snarl. 'Oh, do you?' he said. 'Just how do you know that?'

'It doesn't matter how I know, I just do.'

His eyes were watching her closely, but the ugly smile was still on his lips. She waited as he pushed the hair back from his face, then scratched his chin thoughtfully. It was some time before he spoke, and her heart was beating rapidly. In the end his smile widened, and she winced at the venom in his voice as he said, 'You silly, pathetic little bitch. I can see it all now. You've let them persuade you into coming here to try and get a confession out of me, haven't you? Well, of course, what that tells me is that I didn't kill Madeleine and everyone knows it. But you want me locked away, don't you, Marian? You want your revenge so badly that it doesn't matter whether I killed your cousin or not, you just want to see me suffer for what I did to you.'

'You did nothing to me, Paul, you did it all to Madeleine.'

'Who deserved all she got.'

'Why?'

'Don't try your amateur psychology on me, Marian, it won't wash.'

'Did you ever love her?'

'I'm incapable of feeling, remember?'

'But did you?'

'I thought I did, for a while. There's a certain satisfaction in bringing a doll to life.'

'Was the doll your mother?'

He snorted. 'Spare me, Marian. I told you, it won't wash. It'll take a brain far superior to yours, you know, to trip me up. Still, if you want to play the game, be my guest. I just hope you're a good loser.'

'I wasn't really looking upon it as a game. More as a bid for the truth.'

'Same thing. Look,' he said, leaning forward and folding his arms across the desk, 'why don't you get whoever it is who's listening in the next room to send in the grown-ups? Maybe then they'll get what they want.'

'I get the impression you'd enjoy that,' she said, skilfully disguising her surprise.

'I would. A battle of intellectual wits, why not? I feel rather insulted that they thought someone like you could do it.'

Ignoring the barb, she said, 'You'd get plenty of intellectual come-back if you confessed.'

'Ah, but then the joy of the hunt would be gone.'

'It was during a hunt that you shot them, wasn't it?'

He gave a shout of laughter. 'Very quick, Marian, very quick indeed.'

'That was almost an admission.'

'Almost, but not quite.' He laughed again. 'You're cool, Marian. I didn't think you had it in you. But I can see the sweat standing on your forehead, I can see the white knuckles, the twitch of the jaw. You're so near, Marian, aren't you – yet still so far. Because I've denied you your revenge now, your victory and your family. Madeleine's dead – she's better off dead because she'd have been nothing without me – and I can languish in a cell, happy in the knowledge that no one can have her now, no one can take her away from me. And you, Marian, can fester with your bitterness, because there's no one left for you to love.'

'Not quite no one.'

They both turned at the sound of the voice as the veiled figure entered the room. But as the slim white hands lifted the veil, Marian turned back to Paul and watched as his eyes began to bulge with hatred, disbelief and repugnance at the hideously scarred face that looked back at him.

'You see, she's got me,' Madeleine lisped.

Suddenly Paul's mouth started to twitch and his nostrils flared in grotesque, uncontrollable spasms. 'You bitch!' he hissed. 'You lying, cheating little bitch!'

Marian was on her feet, but as she turned towards Madeleine her blood suddenly ran cold as Paul screamed. He lifted his arms and wrapped them about his head, and still he screamed; his body was racked with convulsions of anger and pain, and still he screamed. Marian looked at Madeleine, but she seemed impervious to his cries; she stood quietly watching him from behind the veil she had now dropped back over her disfigured face. Then Marian noticed how she was shaking, how her poor hunched shoulders were beginning to fall, and as she reached out to catch her, Enrico was there, folding her into his arms and carrying her from the room.

For a moment the silence seemed to breathe around them, and Marian knew that Paul was remembering everything he had said, the way he had declared his love for her, Marian, the way he had scorned and ridiculed Madeleine; and as his eyes clouded with shock she realised that somewhere, so deep down inside that he barely knew it himself, he had loved Madeleine; and if that love had not been so utterly destructive, then even here and now, after all he had done, she might have felt sorry for him.

Inspector Vezzani came into the room and put his hand on her arm. 'It's over,' he said. 'Come along.'

Marian was still staring at Paul, and shaking her head she pulled her arm away. 'Paul,' she said, trying to gain his attention. She waited until at last he turned to look at her, but it was only then that she realised she had nothing left to say — Madeleine had said it all.

That night, after everyone had gone to bed, Marian crept along the landing to the room Madeleine had been using since her return to the Tarallo villa the week before. She and Enrico had driven to Switzerland to collect her from the clinic where she had been taken after her initial operation at the hospital in Florence. That operation had saved her life, though her lung had collapsed twice since, and on both occasions they had thought she would die. But finally the doctors had pronounced her out of danger and had allowed her to come to the villa for a while before they began the arduous and lengthy task of repairing the damage to her face.

'Is that you, Marian?' Madeleine whispered, as Marian pushed the door open.

'Yes,' she answered as Madeleine reached out to switch on the bedside light. 'I wondered if you were awake. How are you feeling now?'

'OK, I think. Still a bit shaky, but it was a long journey.'

'Yes, a very long journey,' Marian said, not without irony. She walked across the room and perched on the edge of the bed, tucking the sheets around Madeleine's chin. She was careful, as always, not to avoid looking at her face, even though every time she saw it she wanted to cry. 'Do you want to talk about it?' she said.

'I don't think so. Maybe one day, but not now. Inspector Vezzani said he's going to make the announcement to the press tomorrow.' She chuckled. 'It seems funny to think that everyone believed I was dead.'

'You almost were. How do you feel about being resurrected?'

Madeleine shrugged, and as she tried to smile her poor, twisted mouth seemed to pucker with pain. 'I know people couldn't go on covering for me for ever. I expect they'll all be much happier now that they can tell the truth.' She frowned, and lifting her hands from beneath the covers, she reached for Marian's.

Marian took a deep breath as she gazed down at their joined hands. 'I should have told you what he was like as soon as I suspected it. Oh God, if only I had.'

'I wouldn't have listened, I would have forced myself not to. I knew he had faults, I knew it from the start, but I refused to see them, I can't explain why. Now I don't care, just as long as he's out of our lives, that's all that matters. But I suppose, after what we did to you, we've both got what we deserve . . .'

'No, Maddy, you must never say that. You didn't deserve to end up like this, you couldn't have known then what he was really like – neither of us could. Now we just have to thank God that you've come out of it alive.'

They sat quietly then, listening to the sound of the wind

in the trees, and as the memories stirred in them both they looked at one another and smiled.

'You needn't have done that today, you know,' Marian said, as she remembered the look on Paul's face when Madeleine lifted her veil. 'I would have told him you were still alive.'

'I know, but he was so cruel to you. I wanted to shock him, I wanted him to see what Sergio had done to me.'

'Does it hurt very much?'

'Not any more. It did, until today, but now I just feel numb. No, that's not true. I feel like a different person, Marian. I feel calmer and – well, you know how I was never any good with words, but I just get the feeling that everything's going to be all right for us now. That we've come through a lot and . . . Well, I've thought about this, and I've come up with something that will make you smile, I know it will. But for us I think it's like . . .' she paused and Marian could see that she was embarrassed, but nevertheless she pressed on '. . . you know, with me taking all your money and Paul and everything, well, this is my philosophical conclusion for us . . .'

'Go on,' Marian prompted.

'It's like . . . it's like stolen beginnings but happy endings. Do you like that?'

'Oh yes,' Marian laughed, tears stinging her eyes, 'I like it very much indeed.'

It was when Marian was leaving Madeleine's room, much later, that Sylvestra's door opened and Sylvestra herself came out onto he dimly lit landing, wearing her nightgown.

'How is Madeleine?' she asked softly.

'She seems all right,' Marian answered, 'but I think she's hiding what she really feels. It must have been awful for her when she saw Paul recoil like that.'

'Sí, but she will get over it. We all get over these things

in time, and soon, very soon, she will have a lovely face once again. For now it is you who give me concern.'

'Me?' Marian said, peering through the shadows to catch a glimpse of Sylvestra's face.

'Yes, you, Marian. You have been through a great deal these past months, and it is not over for you yet. Tomorrow, I know, will be a difficult day for you. I will not ask you if you still love him, that is your own business, but I want to tell you that whatever happens, whatever you decide, you will always have a home here with us.'

'I know.' Marian choked as she gulped back the tears. 'I know, and I don't know how to begin to thank you.'

Sylvestra's thin hand was on her cheek, smoothing away the tears. 'I have said all I wanted to,' she whispered, 'and I think you understand, so now I will wish you a good night, my child, and may God go with you.'

The following afternoon Marian was sipping a capuccino and absently watching the tourists as they milled about her. She was thinking about the last time she had sat outside this café, with Bronwen – they'd been waiting for Sergio Rambaldi. Maybe it hadn't been wise of her, choosing this particular place to meet Matthew in; the memories were still too disturbing; but it had been the first place to spring to mind when she had spoken to him on the phone – and it was easy to find on the south corner of the Ponte Vecchio.

It was ten minutes later when his shadow fell over her, and as she raised her eyes, she was already steeling herself against the surge of emotion that was threatening to engulf her. But when she saw him, his dark, serious eyes, the black unruly hair, the face she had loved so much, her heart twisted so painfully that for one awful moment she thought she was going to cry.

'Hello,' Matthew said.

'Hello.' Then, as she swallowed the lump in her throat,

she somehow managed to smile. 'Thank you for coming all this way. I would have come to London, but . . .'

'I understand,' he said, sitting down and facing her across the table.

For a while she couldn't bring herself to look at him again, but just the sense of his presence was making it hard to stave off the longing to touch him. She still had no idea what he was going to say, what had been going through his mind all these months, but after she had talked to Madeleine the night before, then lain awake until the sun started to rise, she had finally come to understand what she must do. It would be the hardest thing she had ever done in her life, but in her heart she knew she must do it.

'How's Madeleine?' he asked.

'Quite well, considering. But I'm not sure we should have let her come with us yesterday. She says she's all right, but she collapsed straight after . . . It was horrible for her.'

'How did Paul take it?'

She gave a dry laugh. 'Difficult to say. He screamed when he saw her. I've never heard a man scream like that.' She closed her eyes. 'Oh Matthew, if you could have seen his face when he saw her, he looked so disgusted, so nauseated, I don't know how she stood it. It would have been bad enough for anyone, but you know how Madeleine felt about her looks. He's being flown to London some time next week, I believe, but I don't really want anyone to tell us anything about him now. I know it's a dreadful thing to say, but I wish he was dead.'

Matthew looked up as the waiter asked him what he would like, but he shook his head. 'Shall we walk?' he said, turning back to Marian.

'That would be nice.'

Matthew paid the waiter for her capuccino, then arm in arm they strolled onto the Ponte Vecchio. For once it was clear of street traders, and the shops were closed for the siesta.

'Poor Maddy,' Marian sighed, 'she keeps remembering little signs, things that he did or said. It's horrible for her.'

'Thank God for Enrico, eh?'

'Yes. Indeed.'

'Have things developed between them?'

Marian laughed. 'If anything's going to develop anywhere, it'll be with his brother, Arsenio.'

'You mean the one who . . .?'

'Yes, that's him. He came home a few weeks before Madeleine did. He goes to her room at night, she tells me, and they talk. I don't know if they ever mention the *bottega* and what happened to them there, that's between the two of them. All that matters is that they're helping one another to recover.

Matthew smiled. 'I'm glad, but I have to say that before all this happened I thought Enrico was beginning to fall for her.'

'You have to remember that it's barely six months since his wife died. I'm not sure how he's feeling now, he hides his grief well, but I can see it in his eyes sometimes – I know when he's thinking about her.'

Matthew guided her through to one of the arches, and they leaned on the wall, gazing down at the river. Despite the brilliant sun the air was crisp and cold, and few tourists had ventured forth, so for a while they had the alcove to themselves.

'Have you read in the papers about all the arrests going on in New York?' Matthew asked, changing the subject.

Marian nodded. 'It's causing quite a sensation, I believe.'

'It certainly is,' he said, following the graceful journey of a gull as it skimmed across the water, then soared into the sky. 'When I last spoke to Frank he told me that he and Grace don't want the sculpture destroyed. Has either of them mentioned it to you?'

'Grace did when she telephoned. She said she feels that destroying it would be like killing Olivia all over again – that she would have died for nothing. The experts who've been studying it have declared it a masterpiece, you know.'

'Yes, I heard. But where the hell can they exhibit something like that?'

Marian shrugged. 'A decision for the police, I suppose. After all, they own it now.'

Matthew shook his head solemnly. 'They want us to finish the film.'

'Are you going to?'

'Yes. And what about you? Will you be joining us again?'

At last she turned to face him, and her breath caught in her throat as she looked into those wondrously lambent eyes. But they weren't teasing now, they were grave and hopeful, and there was something else in them that she wasn't quite sure she understood. She smiled. 'No,' she answered, shaking her head. 'I won't be joining you.'

'I'd like you to. We all would.'

'Thank you for that.'

He looked at her profile as she turned back to watch the sunlight dance across the water. She had changed. He had noticed it the moment he saw her sitting outside the café. There was something about her, something he couldn't quite fathom. And then suddenly it hit him. The shy, diffident, ugly little duckling had become a truly beautiful swan. 'I cared, Marian,' he said softly. 'I cared a great deal. I want you to know that.'

'I do,' she said, then turned her head to look again into the face that a part of her would always love. She smiled. 'I hear you've been skiing with your daughter.'

He nodded. 'Yes.'

'I'm glad.' She paused as a couple came up beside them,

then, sensing that they were intruding, walked on again. 'That was what it was all about really, wasn't it, Matthew?' she said. 'Your daughter.'

'At first, yes.'

'You felt guilty. I was the same age, and you tried to give me the care and the love she wouldn't let you give her.'

'Something like that.'

'But it doesn't explain New York.'

'No, but things had changed by then. I . . .' He reached up to touch her face, and his dark, searching eyes looked at her with such sorrow that she felt tears spring to her own. 'I'm sorry, Marian,' he whispered. 'I'm sorry . . .'

She put her fingers over his lips. 'Please, don't say that. Please don't be sorry; I'm glad you were the first man to make love to me. I always will be.'

He took her hand and pressed it to his lips. 'You're a very special person, Marian,' he said. 'I'm going to miss you.'

'I'll miss you too. But I hope you and Stephanie will be happy together, Matthew.'

'Oh Marian,' he murmured, folding her into his arms, 'and I hope that one day you'll find the man who's worthy of you.' Then, lowering his mouth to hers, he kissed her more tenderly than he had ever kissed her before.

'So do I,' she said quietly, as she watched him walk away; and after he had disappeared into the crowd she turned back to look at the river. One year, just one short year, and her life had changed so completely that she couldn't even begin to comprehend the fate that had brought her such love and such pain, such horror and such joy. And such courage – the courage to let him go.